The
MX Book
of
New
Sherlock
Holmes
Stories

Part XLVI
Occupants of the
Canonical Realm
(1861-1889)

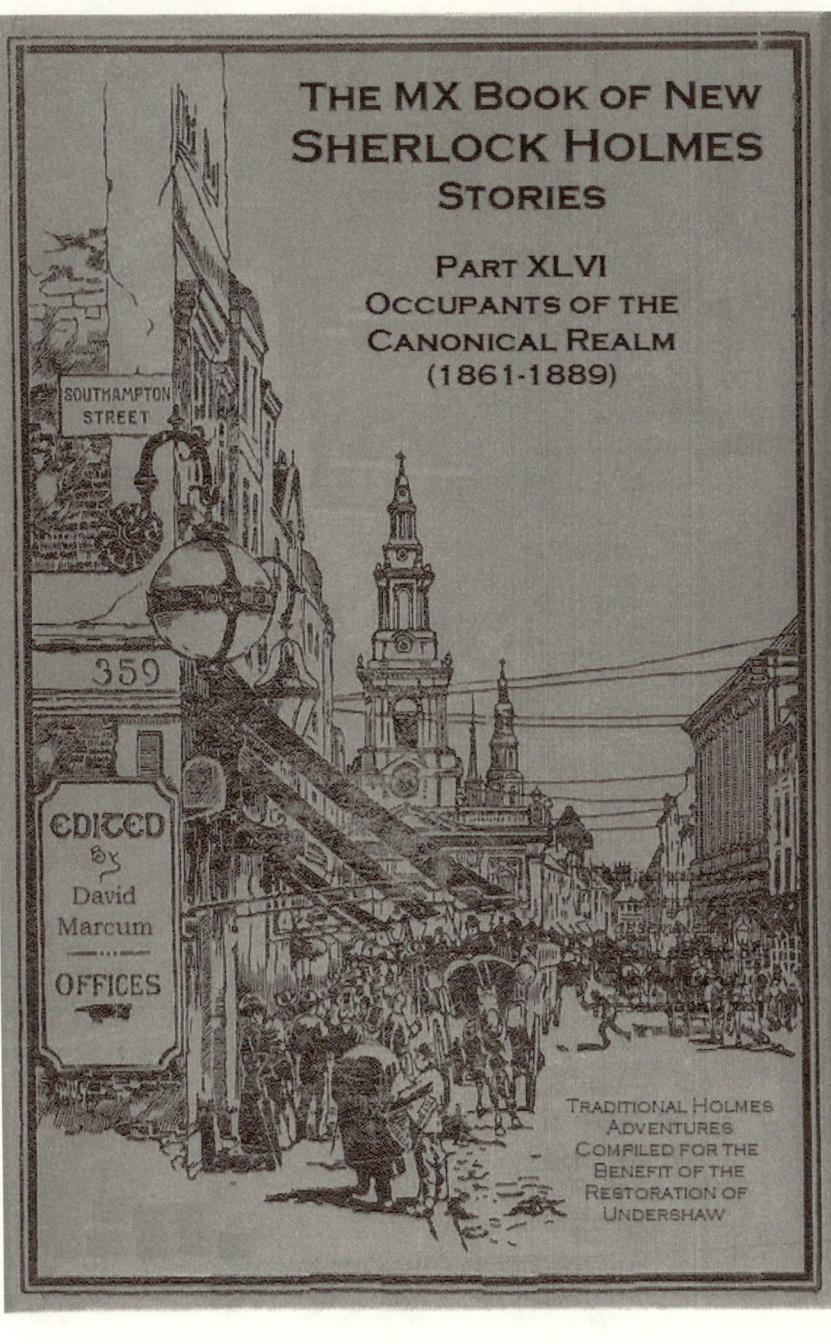

The MX Book of New Sherlock Holmes Stories

Part XLVI
Occupants of the Canonical Realm
(1861-1889)

SOUTHAMPTON STREET

359

EDITED By David Marcum

OFFICES

TRADITIONAL HOLMES ADVENTURES COMPILED FOR THE BENEFIT OF THE RESTORATION OF UNDERSHAW

ISBN Hardback 978-1-80424-559-0
ISBN Paperback 978-1-80424-560-6
AUK ePub ISBN 978-1-80424-561-3
AUK PDF ISBN 978-1-80424-562-0

Published in the UK by
MX Publishing
335 Princess Park Manor, Royal Drive,
London, N11 3GX
www.mxpublishing.co.uk

David Marcum can be reached at:
thepapersofsherlockholmes@gmail.com

Cover design by Brian Belanger
www.belangerbooks.com and *www.redbubble.com/people/zhahadun*

Internal Illustrations by Sidney Paget

CONTENTS

Forewords

Adventures

(Continued on the next page . .)

(Continued on the next page . . .)

(Continued on the next page . . .)

These additional Sherlock Holmes adventures
can be found in the previous volumes of
The MX Book of New Sherlock Holmes Stories

(Continued on the next page . . . .)

PART III: 1896-1929

PART IV – 2016 Annual

(Continued on the next page . . . .)

PART V – Christmas Adventures

(Continued on the next page . . . .)

PART VI – 2017 Annual

(Continued on the next page . . . .)

PART VII – Eliminate the Impossible: 1880-1891

PART VIII – Eliminate the Impossible: 1892-1905

(Continued on the next page . . . .)

Part IX – 2018 Annual (1879-1895)

(Continued on the next page . . . .)

(Continued on the next page . . . .)

Part XII: Some Untold Cases (1894-1902)

PART XIII: 2019 Annual (1881-1890)

(Continued on the next page . . . .)

PART XIV: 2019 Annual (1891 -1897)

(Continued on the next page . . . .)

The Poisoned Regiment – Carl Heifetz
The Case of the Persecuted Poacher – Gayle Lange Puhl
It's Time – Harry DeMaio
The Case of the Fourpenny Coffin – I.A. Watson
The Horror in King Street – Thomas A. Burns, Jr.

PART XV: 2019 Annual (1898-1917)

Foreword – Will Thomas
Foreword – Roger Johnson
Foreword – Melissa Grigsby
Foreword – Steve Emecz
Foreword – David Marcum
Two Poems – Christopher James
The Whitechapel Butcher – Mark Mower
The Incomparable Miss Incognita – Thomas Fortenberry
The Adventure of the Twofold Purpose – Robert Perret
The Adventure of the Green Gifts – Tracy J. Revels
The Turk's Head – Robert Stapleton
A Ghost in the Mirror – Peter Coe Verbica
The Mysterious Mr. Rim – Maurice Barkley
The Adventure of the Fatal Jewel-Box – Edwin A. Enstrom
Mass Murder – William Todd
The Notable Musician – Roger Riccard
The Devil's Painting – Kelvin I. Jones
The Adventure of the Silent Sister – Arthur Hall
A Skeleton's Sorry Story – Jack Grochot
An Actor and a Rare One – David Marcum
The Silver Bullet – Dick Gillman
The Adventure at Throne of Gilt – Will Murray
"The Boy Who Would Be King – Dick Gillman
The Case of the Seventeenth Monk – Tim Symonds
Alas, Poor Will – Mike Hogan
The Case of the Haunted Chateau – Leslie Charteris and Denis Green
          (Introduction by Ian Dickerson)
The Adventure of the Weeping Stone – Nick Cardillo
The Adventure of the Three Telegrams – Darryl Webber

Part XVI – Whatever Remains . . . Must Be the Truth (1881-1890)

Foreword – Kareem Abdul-Jabbar
Foreword – Roger Johnson
Foreword – Steve Emecz
Foreword – David Marcum
The Hound of the Baskervilles (Retold) (*A Poem*) – Josh Pachter
The Wylington Lake Monster – Derrick Belanger
The *Juju* Men of Richmond – Mark Sohn

(Continued on the next page . . . .)

Part XVII – Whatever Remains . . . Must Be the Truth (1891-1898)

Part XVIII – Whatever Remains . . . Must Be the Truth (1899-1925)

(Continued on the next page . . . .)

The Tollington Ghost – Roger Silverwood
You Only Live Thrice – Robert Stapleton
The Adventure of the Fair Lad – Craig Janacek
The Adventure of the Voodoo Curse – Gareth Tilley
The Cassandra of Providence Place – Paul Hiscock
The Adventure of the House Abandoned – Arthur Hall
The Winterbourne Phantom – M.J. Elliott
The Murderous Mercedes – Harry DeMaio
The Solitary Violinist – Tom Turley
The Cunning Man – Kelvin I. Jones
The Adventure of Khamaat's Curse – Tracy J. Revels
The Adventure of the Weeping Mary – Matthew White
The Unnerved Estate Agent – David Marcum
Death in The House of the Black Madonna – Nick Cardillo
The Case of the Ivy-Covered Tomb – S.F. Bennett

Part XIX: 2020 Annual (1882-1890)

Foreword – John Lescroart
Foreword – Roger Johnson
Foreword – Lizzy Butler
Foreword – Steve Emecz
Foreword – David Marcum
Holmes's Prayer (*A Poem*) – Christopher James
A Case of Paternity – Matthew White
The Raspberry Tart – Roger Riccard
The Mystery of the Elusive Bard – Kevin P. Thornton
The Man in the Maroon Suit – Chris Chan
The Scholar of Silchester Court – Nick Cardillo
The Adventure of the Changed Man – MJH. Simmonds
The Adventure of the Tea-Stained Diamonds – Craig Stephen Copland
The Indigo Impossibility – Will Murray
The Case of the Emerald Knife-Throwers – Ian Ableson
A Game of Skittles – Thomas A. Turley
The Gordon Square Discovery – David Marcum
The Tattooed Rose – Dick Gillman
The Problem at Pentonville Prison – David Friend
The Nautch Night Case – Brenda Seabrooke
The Disappearing Prisoner – Arthur Hall
The Case of the Missing Pipe – James Moffett
The Whitehaven Ransom – Robert Stapleton
The Enlightenment of Newton – Dick Gillman
The Impaled Man – Andrew Bryant
The Mystery of the Elusive Li Shen – Will Murray
The Mahmudabad Result – Andrew Bryant

(Continued on the next page . . . .)

(Continued on the next page . . . .)

Part XXII: Some More Untold Cases (1877-1887)

(Continued on the next page . . . .)

(Continued on the next page . . . .)

Part XXV: 2021 Annual (1881-1888)

(Continued on the next page . . . .)

(Continued on the next page . . . .)

Part XXVIII: More Christmas Adventures (1869-1888)

(Continued on the next page . . . .)

Part XXIX: More Christmas Adventures (1889-1896)

Part XXX: More Christmas Adventures (1897-1928)

(Continued on the next page . . . .)

The Adventure of the Chained Phantom – J.S. Rowlinson
Santa's Little Elves – Kevin Thornton
The Case of the Holly-Sprig Pudding – Naching T. Kassa
The Canterbury Manifesto – David Marcum
The Case of the Disappearing Beaune – J. Lawrence Matthews
A Price Above Rubies – Jane Rubino
The Intrigue of the Red Christmas – Shane Simmons
The Bitter Gravestones – Chris Chan
The Midnight Mass Murder – Paul Hiscock

Part XXXI: 2022 Annual (1875-1887)

Foreword – Jeffrey Hatcher
Foreword – Roger Johnson
Foreword – Steve Emecz
Foreword – Emma West
Foreword – David Marcum
The Nemesis of Sherlock Holmes (A Poem) – Kelvin I. Jones
The Unsettling Incident of the History Professor's Wife – Sean M. Wright
The Princess Alice Tragedy – John Lawrence
The Adventure of the Amorous Balloonist – I.A. Watson
The Pilkington Case – Kevin Patrick McCann
The Adventure of the Disappointed Lover – Arthur Hall
The Case of the Impressionist Painting – Tim Symonds
The Adventure of the Old Explorer – Tracy J. Revels
Dr. Watson's Dilemma – Susan Knight
The Colonial Exhibition – Hal Glatzer
The Adventure of the Drunken Teetotaler – Thomas A. Burns, Jr.
The Curse of Hollyhock House – Geri Schear
The Sethian Messiah – David Marcum
Dead Man's Hand – Robert Stapleton
The Case of the Wary Maid – Gordon Linzner
The Adventure of the Alexandrian Scroll – David MacGregor
The Case of the Woman at Margate – Terry Golledge
A Question of Innocence – DJ Tyrer
The Grosvenor Square Furniture Van – Terry Golledge
The Adventure of the Veiled Man – Tracy J. Revels
The Disappearance of Dr. Markey – Stephen Herczeg
The Case of the Irish Demonstration – Dan Rowley

Part XXXII: 2022 Annual (1888-1895)

Foreword – Jeffrey Hatcher
Foreword – Roger Johnson
Foreword – Steve Emecz

(Continued on the next page . . . .)

Part XXXIII: 2022 Annual (1896-1919)

(Continued on the next page . . . .)

(Continued on the next page . . . .)

Part XXXVI: "However Improbable . . . ." (1897-1919)

(Continued on the next page . . . .)

(Continued on the next page . . . .)

Part XXXIX: 2023 Annual (1897-1923)

Part XL: Further Untold Cases (1879-1886)

(Continued on the next page . . . .)

Part XLI: Further Untold Cases (1877-1892)

Part XLII: Further Untold Cases (1894-1922)

(Continued on the next page . . . .)

Part XLIII: 2024 Annual (1874-1888)

(Continued on the next page . . . .)

(Continued on the next page . . . .)

The following contributors appear in these companion volumes:
Part XLVII – Occupants of the Canonical Realm (1890-1898)
Part XLVIII – Occupants of the Canonical Realm (1899-1924)

The MX Book of New Sherlock Holmes Stories
Occupants of the Canonical Realm
Parts XLVI, XLVII, and XLVIII

are dedicated to

Kelvin Jones *and* David Stuart Davies

Both of these long-time Friends of the MX Anthologies
passed as these volumes were being prepared.
The world – Sherlockian and otherwise – will miss them both greatly.

R.I.P.

Editor's Foreword:
More are Still in the Works
by David Marcum

In his essay, "Who Shall Ever Forget?", * Ellery Queen related his first encounter with Sherlock Holmes. At age twelve – in 1917, since Ellery was born in 1905 – the young future Great Detective was in bed with his annual earache and, as a distraction, his grandmother brought him a copy of *The Adventures of Sherlock Holmes* The first story wasn't too inspiring for a lad of that age – "A Scandal in Bohemia", with an illustration labeled *"The gentleman in the pew handed it up to her . . ."* – but the other tales fired his imagination. He wrote that he finished the book that day, passed the night without any sleep while thinking of Holmes – *"All the Queen's horses and all the Queen's men couldn't put Ellery together again."* – and early the next morning, before the city had arisen, he bundled himself up, a wad of stained cotton protruding from his ear, and set forth to visit the public library, where he expected to find shelves upon shelves – entire rooms and wings – devoted to further adventures of Mr. Sherlock Holmes.

Alas, after waiting hours for the place to open, sitting huddled on the cold stone front steps, he discovered that such was not the case. In the entire library, he found just three previous volumes, *A Study in Scarlet*, *The Memoirs of Sherlock Holmes*, and *The Hound of the Baskervilles*. I was about that age, a couple of full generations later, when I discovered Sherlock Holmes, and I completely shared his disappointment – because even though there were a few more Holmes adventures available by then, there weren't shelves upon shelves and entire rooms and wings of them.

I was ten in 1975 when I first picked up an abridged copy of *The Adventures*, and then *The Return* – unknowingly skipping "The Final Problem" and reading "The Empty House" first, thus (*Spoiler alert!*) learning that Holmes didn't die at Reichenbach, and how he survived. (NOTE: *Always always always* read chronologically if possible.) I quickly devoured the rest of The Canon, acquiring the remaining books in the form of Berkeley paperbacks with excellent cover paintings by Guy Deel, and then I purchased the flawed Doubleday edition (with the wrong versions of "The Resident Patient" and "The Cardboard Box") – my first great Sherlockian purchase, setting me back a whole ten dollars! (My dad gave me a big months-ahead advance on my fifty-cent-per-week allowance, and then he even drove me to the bookstore that night after supper. I remember riding home with that big book perched carefully on my lap, almost afraid

1

to start reading it because it was so new and perfect. It was the first major monetary loan of my life, and very much worth it.)

As I was reading the Canonical sixty stories, I was unknowingly treading closer and closer to that Great Grimpen Mire where all new Sherlockians eventually find themselves: *I've read them all! Now what?*

Of course, I re-read the Canonical stories. And I was very grateful a few months later when my parents, ordering from a catalog of remaindered books that regularly arrived at our house, bought three Holmes-related volumes as a Christmas gift: *Holmes of the Movies* by David Stuart Davies, *The Sherlock Holmes Scrapbook* as edited by Peter Haining, and a true game-changer, *Sherlock Holmes of Baker Street* by William S. Baring-Gould.

I actually read Baring-Gould's brilliant biography before I'd finished all of the Canonical stories. I don't remember feeling that any of the narratives were spoiled by meeting them early that way. Instead, it presented Holmes from a different perspective that raised him in my mind to an even higher level. At that young age, I observed and understood that Holmes and Watson were historical figures existing in a fixed place in time. I saw them both young and old, and not presented and locked into some fixed middle age. I was exposed to the idea of *chronology*, wherein the adventures occurred at specific times, influencing and being influenced by what came before and after. And I saw that there was more to the *entire lives* of Holmes and Watson than the pitifully few sixty Canonical tales.

The Holmes Canon references approximately 140 *Untold Cases* besides the published adventures – from the famed Giant Rat of Sumatra to the oft-forgotten case where Holmes caught a coiner by the zinc and copper filings in the seam of his cuff. But even these Canonical hints of other cases weren't enough. Fortunately, I was primed and hungry for more post-Canonical adventures when I picked Nicholas Meyer's *The Seven-Per-Cent Solution* (1974) at a school Reading-is-Fundamental (RIF) event, and not long after, when I bought the next related volume, *The West End Horror* (1976). *The Seven-Per-Cent Solution* touched the flame to ignite the current modern Sherlockian Golden Age that we all enjoy now, and the fire has only burned hotter and hotter over the subsequent decades . . . but it wasn't an inferno at first.

The Seven-Per-Cent Solution showed that, for members of the starving public – Like me! – additional Watsonian manuscripts were out there in the world, waiting to be found and shared, beyond those too-few "official" titles that had crossed the First Literary Agent's desk. One simply had to put forth enough effort to excavate these adventures and publish them. They initially appeared in dribs and drabs – *Enter the Lion* (1979) by Sean Wright and Michael Hodel, for instance, and *Hellbirds* and

The Earthquake Machine by Nick Utechen and Austin Mitchelson – but at least they did appear. And I was lucky enough and diligent enough to find them, grabbing them as they were published because, even at that early age, I understood that I'd better get them and hold on to them when I could, because finding them later would be either expensive or time-consuming pesterments, or both.

The New Sherlockian Golden Age began in 1974 and has never ended, but it still took a few decades for Sherlockian adventure addicts like me to start to feel satisfied. If it was up to the traditional publishing dinosaurs to lumber into motion and recognize the need, we'd all still be waiting with great yearning disappointment. Thank heavens for MX Books, and later Belanger Books, which spun into motion from MX's initial efforts. With these two defining Sherlockian publishers now in place, so many more of Watson's discovered manuscripts can finally reach a desperately hungry public.

With the availability of so many more Holmes adventures, there is room to revisit all aspects of that world – including the other occupants of the Canonical realm. The World of Sherlock Holmes is wide and deep, and it has many Canonical individuals besides Our Heroes and the regular stalwarts like Mycrft and Mrs. Hudson, and Lestrade and Gregson. The theme of this set of MX anthologies was simple: To include a Canonical character – possibly in a large role, or sometimes just in passing. All of the contributing authors did a wonderful job, and now the game is afoot for the readers to spot some of those in some stories who are less well known.

When Ellery Queen went to the library as a boy in 1917, the entire Canon wasn't yet in existence. When I was about the same age as that, in the mid-1970's, the amount of available tales – Canonical and post-Canonical – was just about as slim. Now, thank Heavens, we finally have thousands of traditional Canonical adventures, set in the correct time period, and featuring the *True* Sherlock Holmes – not a modernized sociopathic murderer or continent-shifted tattoo-covered prostitute-paying drug addict, or a Van Helsing substitute or an anachronistic era-hopping Time Lord. I'm very proud that this latest set of MX anthologies brings us to almost 1,000 of these new True Holmes adventures – and as of this writing, more are still in the works. Stay tuned . . . .

* * * * *

"Of course, I could only stammer out my thanks."
– *The unhappy John Hector McFarlane,* "The Norwood Builder"

As always when one of these sets is finished, I want to first thank with all my heart my incredible wonderful wife of over thirty-six years,

3

Rebecca, and our amazing son and my friend, Dan. I love you both, and you are everything to me!

I can never express enough gratitude for all of the contributors who have donated their time and royalties to this ongoing project. I'm constantly amazed at the incredible stories that you send, and I'm so glad to have gotten to know so many of you through this process. It's an undeniable fact that Sherlock Holmes authors are the *best* people!

The contributors of these stories have donated their royalties for this project to support the Stepping Stones School for special needs children, located at Undershaw, one of Sir Arthur Conan Doyle's former homes. As of this writing, and as mentioned above, these MX anthologies have raised over $125,000 for the school, with no end in sight, and of even more importance, they have helped raise awareness about the school all over the world. These books are making a real difference to the school, and the participation of both contributors and purchasers is most appreciated.

I also want to particularly thank the following:

☐ *Dan Andriacco* – I first met Dan in 2011 at the third *From Gillette to Brett* conference, where he was in the Dealer's Room selling his books. I saw him again the next year at *A Gathering of Southern Sherlockians* in Chattanooga. From there, we began to correspond, and run into each other on occasion at various Sherlockian events – which attends a lot, and me quite a bit less.

Over the years, he's risen from success to success in the Sherlockian World. He's written a number of Holmes novels, and additionally the ever-growning McCabe and Cody series, which I dearly love. They are Golden Age-type mysteries, heavily influenced by Nero Wolfe and Archie Goodwin, and with all kinds of Sherlockian aspects. In addition to all the other rich deep characters in the books, the setting of Erin, Ohio is a character too. I look forward to each new volume. And after all this, Dan took over as the editor of *The Baker Street Journal*.

I've been trying to recruit him for years to contribute a story these books – and I'm still trying! – and with his foreword, I'm glad that he's now part of the MX Anthology family.

Thank you, Dan!

☐ *Roger Johnson* – I'm more grateful than I can say that I know Roger. His Sherlockian knowledge is exceptional, as is the

4

work that he does to further the cause of The Master. But even more than that, both Roger and his wonderful wife, Jean Upton, are simply the finest and best kind of people, and I'm very lucky to know both of them – and I was lucky enough to see them in June 2024, during my fourth Holmes Pilgrimage to England and Scotland. I can't thank you enough, and I can't imagine these books without you.

☐ *Steve Emecz* – When I first emailed Steve from out of the blue back in late 2012 and early 2013, I was interested in MX republishing my previously published first book. Even then, as a guy who works to accumulate *all* traditional Sherlockian pastiches, I could see that MX (under Steve's leadership) was *the* fast-rising superstar of the Sherlockian publishing world.

The publication of that first book with MX was an amazing life-changing event for me, leading to writing and then editing more books, unexpected Holmes Pilgrimages to England, and these incredible anthologies. When I had the idea for these books in early 2015, I thought that it might, with any luck, be one small volume of perhaps a dozen stories. Since then they've grown and grown, and by way of them I've been able to make some incredible Sherlockian friends and play in the Holmesian Sandbox in ways that I'd never before dreamed possible.

All through it, Steve has been one of the most positive and supportive people I've ever known, letting me explore various Sherlockian projects and opening up my own personal possibilities in ways that otherwise would have never been possible. Thank you Steve for every opportunity!

☐ *Brian Belanger* – Brian is one of the nicest and most talented of people. His gifts are amazing, and his skills improve and grow from project to project. He's amazingly great to work with, and once again I thank him for another incredible contribution.

And finally, last but certainly *not* least, thanks to **Sir Arthur Conan Doyle**: Author, doctor, adventurer, and the Founder of the Sherlockian Feast. Honored, and present in spirit.

As I always note when putting together an anthology of Holmes stories, the effort has been a labor of love. These adventures are just more tiny threads woven into the ongoing Great Holmes Tapestry, continuing to grow and grow, for there can *never* be enough stories about the man whom Watson described as *"the best and wisest . . . whom I have ever known."*

David Marcum
September 25th, 2024
The 136th Anniversary of
the first day of
The Hound of the Baskervilles

Questions, comments, or story submissions
may be addressed to David Marcum at
thepapersofsherlockholmes@gmail.com

NOTE

*   Ellery Queen's essay regarding his first meeting with Sherlock Holmes has appeared in at least three different versions. The best and most succinct is his foreword to the 1975 Ballantine edition of *The Adventures of Sherlock Holmes*. Versions also appear in *In the Queen's Parlor* (1969, as "Who Shall Ever Forget?") and also – much reduced – as "Who Shall Ever Forget?" in *The Golden Summer* (1953, by "Daniel Nathan").

Foreword
by Dan Andriacco

"*A*nd so, reader, farewell to Sherlock Holmes!*" Arthur Conan Doyle wrote in the Preface to *The Case Book of Sherlock Holmes*. The exclamation point is telling. Conan Doyle was excited to be finished at last with that annoying consulting detective.

But the world was not.

The author's efforts to shed himself of his most famous creation are well known to all Sherlockians. He wanted to stop writing about Holmes after the sixth of the *Adventures*, and then after the twelfth, and then believed that he had finally done with deed with the ominously named "The Final Problem" at the end of what became *The Memoirs*. Many of us can recite most of the opening words of that story by heart: *"It is with heavy heart that I take up my pen to write these last words in which I ever record the singular gifts by which my friend Mr. Sherlock Holmes was distinguished."*

The author was wrong, of course. One of my favorite cartoons related to Sherlock Holmes is by Jeff Decker (reprinted in the Summer 2023 *Baker Street Journal*) showing Conan Doyle at his desk, pipe in hand and a startled look on his face as a dripping Sherlock Holmes stands at the open-door yelling, *"Nice try, Doyle!"*

Two novels and thirty-two short stories would follow before the Canon was complete at sixty stories. One of the later tales, my favorite, is called "His Last Bow." But it wasn't.

Why is that man so hard to get rid of? Even the death of the canonical author couldn't stop the flow of new adventures of Sherlock Holmes. (I have been guilty of a few myself.) The reason is elementary economics: Supply meets demand. As long as there are legions of us around the world who want to go back again and again to Baker Street – which is likely to be forever – new stories will be produced.

It is not entirely about Holmes, however. The world of The Canon is also peopled with dozens of other characters worth spending more time with as well. And you will find many of these occupants of the Canonical realm within the pages of these volumes – Parts XLVI, XLVII, and XVLIII of *The MX Book of New Sherlock Holmes Stories*. Some surprises await!

Dan Andriacco
Editor – *The Baker Street Journal*
July 2024

"In the Old Rooms
in Baker Street"
by Roger Johnson

The Festival of Britain in 1951 was intended as "a tonic to the nation" in the austere years after the Second World War, and every local authority was expected to make its own contribution to the festival. The Borough of St. Marylebone chose to mount a Sherlock Holmes Exhibition, with a re-creation of Holmes and Watson's sitting room as its centrepiece, and the Abbey National Building Society offered space in its headquarters, located in what had been, until 1930, Upper Baker Street. Abbey House, completed in 1932, occupied a site that had briefly included the only house that ever legitimately bore the address *221 Baker Street*, and for nearly twenty years a member of the staff had acted as Sherlock Holmes's secretary, to answer the many letters that arrived addressed to Mr. Holmes or Dr. Watson. *

The exhibition was a great success, attracting more than fifty-thousand visitors before it closed, and during that five-month period the little group of volunteers and professionals who created it had founded *The Sherlock Holmes Society of London*. Eventually the various exhibits that had been loaned were returned to their owners, and many of those that remained, including the sitting room, were bought by Whitbread, the brewers, and installed in a handsome old public house called the *Northumberland Arms*, in Northumberland Street, near Charing Cross Station. In December 1957, it was formally opened as the *Sherlock Holmes*. The sitting room is approximately one-third of its original size, but all the important landmarks are present. Diners in the restaurant can view it through the plate glass window that replaces the fourth wall of the room. There are also viewing windows in the door and corridor alongside the room and in the patio area.

In early 1992, my wife Jean Upton was having lunch at the pub and noticed that the sitting room looked very shabby. The managers told her that they had only recently taken over, and were faced with several problems, including water damage from a washing machine that had overflowed in the room above the sitting room. Jean offered to help with cleaning and restoring the items in the sitting room, and as she clearly knew a good deal about Sherlock Holmes, her offer was gratefully accepted.

8

That was the start of our direct involvement. We discovered that some items had been damaged, and some had disappeared, so we have done our best to repair, restore, and replace. It took nearly a year to find an affordable pair of brown leather boxing gloves to replace the missing originals, but other items have proved less elusive — suitable oil lamps, a handsome mantel clock in working order, a tea service that looks very much like the one Jeremy Brett and his two Watsons used in the Granada Television series . . . The deerstalker and cape now hanging behind the door were given by the director of a television programme for which I was interviewed at the pub.

Among the many things we have added are the *Legend of the Hound of the Baskervilles* — the manuscript read aloud by Dr. Mortimer to Holmes and Watson, the plans of the Bruce-Partington submarine, Watson's commission as an army surgeon, various letters and other documents. These are items that we have made ourselves. Many years ago I bought a swordstick as a theatre prop. It now has a place in the sitting room at the pub, because it is identical to the stick carried by Jude Law in *Sherlock Holmes* and *Sherlock Holmes: A Game of Shadows*.

We do our best to make sure that the room looks as if it really exists in the late 1890's. We cannot disguise the smoke alarm on the ceiling, but we were able to provide a pinboard, with appropriate documents attached, to hide a modern electric socket on the wall beside the chemistry table.

During our three decades as curators of the sitting room, the *Sherlock Holmes* has undergone two changes of ownership, several changes of management, and at least two extensive refurbishments. It is an honour for us to maintain the long relationship between *The Sherlock Holmes Society of London* and the *Sherlock Holmes* pub. Just to be able to enter the sitting -room is exciting. To be trusted with ensuring that it always looks authentic is a great privilege and a great pleasure.

The side door of the pub opens on to Craven Passage. Look to your left at the building opposite and you'll see three formidable wooden doors, above which are attractive oriental arches and decorative blue-and-white tiles. This is all that remains of the Turkish Baths where we find Holmes and Watson at the beginning of "The Illustrious Client".

Now, bear with me, please. You may remember that Neville St. Clair – alias Hugh Boone, the Man with the Twisted Lip – lived at a house called The Cedars, near Lee in Kent. Remarkably, The Cedars is a real house: It stands on Belmont Hill in Blackheath, very close to the neighbouring town of Lee, and until his death in 1878 it was the home of one John Penn, whose widow was apparently still living there in 1907.

John Penn was an English marine engineer whose innovations in engine and propeller systems led to his company becoming the major supplier to the Royal Navy as it made the transition from sail to steam power. By the time of his death, Penn's firm had built engines for 735 ships, ranging from river ferries to battleships. He was elected a Fellow of the Royal Society in 1859, and the following year he was a founder-member of the Royal Institution of Naval Architects.

Back in Northumberland Street, next door to the *Sherlock Holmes* pub, we find – Guess what! – the Royal Institution of Naval Architects.

As Mycroft Holmes remarked at his first meeting with Dr. Watson, *"I hear of Sherlock everywhere . . . ."*

Roger Johnson, BSI, ASH
Editor: *The Sherlock Holmes Journal*
August 2024

NOTE

*   That rôle ceased in 2005, when the building society sold Abbey House and departed from Baker Street.

An Ongoing Legacy
for Sherlock Holmes
by Steve Emecz

Undershaw
Circa 1900

As we head into the autumn of 2024, we're delighted to have some more volumes of *The MX Book of New Sherlock Holmes Stories*, which continues to support the wonderful school at Undershaw. It's one of several projects we work with that you can read about on our website:

https://mxpublishing.com/pages/about-us

We continue to release dozens of new titles every year, and are entering our seventh year providing cases for the mystery subscription series *Dear Holmes*, which has now had over 50,000 aspiring detectives take part.

We look forward to another busy season with a variety of books from authors old and new.

Steve Emecz
August 2024

11

The Doyle Room at Undershaw
Partially funded through royalties from
The MX Book of New Sherlock Holmes Stories

12

A Word from Undershaw
by Emma West

Undershaw
September 9, 2016
Grand Opening of the Stepping Stones School
(Now *Undershaw*)
(Photograph courtesy of Roger Johnson)

It is always a pleasure to share the latest news from Undershaw, especially on such a momentous occasion. This year, we are not only celebrating the 20th anniversary of our school's founding, but also the 8th year of being housed in the historic and inspiring building of Undershaw, the former home of Sir Arthur Conan Doyle. Moving into this incredible space in 2016 marked the beginning of a new chapter for our school, and in 2021, we renamed the school to honour its legacy, recognising its deep connection to one of literature's most beloved creators, the mind behind Sherlock Holmes.

The journey we've taken as a school has been filled with milestones, and we have been fortunate to be supported by many, but none more so than MX Publishing. The interest, encouragement, and partnership we have received from MX Publishing has helped shape our community into what it is today. Just as Sir Arthur Conan Doyle enriched the world with his stories, MX Publishing has enriched our journey, and we are deeply grateful for their friendship and support.

As we reflect on our growth, we also celebrate being shortlisted for the prestigious "Outstanding Impact" award by the National Association of Special Schools. Out of more than four-hundred schools, being in the top three finalists is a testament to the dedication of our staff and the incredible impact of the Undershaw Diploma. Designed to develop the skills young people need to succeed in life, this diploma reflects our mission to tackle the challenging statistic that only 4.8% of adults with learning needs are in full-time employment. Through our accredited program, we are equipping students with the essential skills to ensure their futures are filled with opportunity and that they can be socially and economically engaged.

In addition to these achievements, we were honoured to receive the Gold-standard Anti-Bullying Charter Mark from Surrey County Council, a recognition that speaks volumes about the culture we nurture at Undershaw. The assessment team were impressed by the ethos of our school and the positive experiences shared by students, staff, and parents alike. We take pride in creating a school environment where every student feels valued and safe, as one student beautifully expressed: "Undershaw is like a second home."

We look ahead with excitement to what the future holds. As we continue to grow, we remain committed to the legacy of Sir Arthur Conan Doyle, using the skills of creativity, resilience, and curiosity that he embodied. And as we celebrate our twenty years of transformation and success, we extend our deepest thanks to MX Publishing for their unwavering support and their role in helping us thrive.

Undershaw is more than a school. It's a community, a home, and a place where young people are empowered to become the best versions of themselves. We are proud of all we have achieved so far and excited for the road ahead.

Until next time . . . .

Emma West
Headteacher
September 2024

"Undershaw," Hindhead, Conan Doyle's House.

Editor's *Caveats*

When these anthologies first began back in 2015, I noted that the authors were from all over the world – and thus, there would be British spelling and American spelling. As I explained then, I didn't want to take the responsibility of changing American spelling to British and vice-versa. I would undoubtedly miss something, leading to inconsistencies, or I'd change something incorrectly.

Some readers are bothered by this, made nervous and irate when encountering American spelling as written by Watson, and in stories set in England. However, here in America, the versions of The Canon that we read have long-ago has their spelling Americanized, so it isn't quite as shocking for us.

Additionally, I offer my apologies up front for any typographical errors that have slipped through. As a print-on-demand publisher, MX does not have squadrons of editors as some readers believe. The business consists of three part-time people who also have busy lives elsewhere – Steve Emecz, Sharon Emecz, and Timi Emecz – so the editing effort largely falls on the contributors. Some readers and consumers out there in the world are unhappy with this – apparently forgetting about all of those self-produced Holmes stories and volumes from decades ago (typed and Xeroxed) with awkward self-published formatting and loads of errors that are now prized as very expensive collector's items.

I'm personally mortified when errors slip through – ironically, there will probably be errors in these *caveats* – and I apologize now, but without a regiment of professional full-time editors looking over my shoulder, this is as good as it gets. Real life is more important than writing and editing – even in such a good cause as promoting the True and Traditional Canonical Holmes – and only so much time can be spent preparing these books before they're released into the wild. I hope that you can look past any errors, small or huge, and simply enjoy these stories, and appreciate the efforts of everyone involved, and the sincere desire to add to The Great Holmes Tapestry.

And in spite of any errors here, there are more Sherlock Holmes stories in the world than there were before, and that's a good thing.

David Marcum
Editor

Sherlock Holmes (1854-1957) was born in Yorkshire, England, on 6 January, 1854. In the mid-1870's, he moved to 24 Montague Street, London, where he established himself as the world's first Consulting Detective. After meeting Dr. John H. Watson in early 1881, he and Watson moved to rooms at 221b Baker Street, where his reputation as the world's greatest detective grew for several decades. He was presumed to have died battling noted criminal Professor James Moriarty on 4 May, 1891, but he returned to London on 5 April, 1894, resuming his consulting practice in Baker Street. Retiring to the Sussex coast near Beachy Head in October 1903, he continued to be associated in various private and government investigations while giving the impression of being a reclusive apiarist. He was very involved in the events encompassing World War I, and to a lesser degree those of World War II. He passed away peacefully upon the cliffs above his Sussex home on his 103rd birthday, 6 January, 1957.

Dr. John Hamish Watson (1852-1929) was born in Stranraer, Scotland on 7 August, 1852. In 1878, he took his Doctor of Medicine Degree from the University of London, and later joined the army as a surgeon. Wounded at the Battle of Maiwand in Afghanistan (27 July, 1880), he returned to London late that same year. On New Year's Day, 1881, he was introduced to Sherlock Holmes in the chemical laboratory at Barts. Agreeing to share rooms with Holmes in Baker Street, Watson became invaluable to Holmes's consulting detective practice. Watson was married and widowed three times, and from the late 1880's onward, in addition to his participation in Holmes's investigations and his medical practice, he chronicled Holmes's adventures, with the assistance of his literary agent, Sir Arthur Conan Doyle, in a series of popular narratives, most of which were first published in *The Strand* magazine. Watson's later years were spent preparing a vast number of his notes of Holmes's cases for future publication. Following a final important investigation with Holmes, Watson contracted pneumonia and passed away on 24 July, 1929.

Photos of Sherlock Holmes and Dr. John H. Watson courtesy of Roger Johnson

The
MX Book
of
New
Sherlock
Holmes
Stories

Part XLVI
Occupants of the
Canonical Realm
(1861-1889)

Sherlock Holmes
by Joseph W. Svec III

S is for Sherlock, of great renown.

   Among all detectives, he wears the crown.

H is for honors, he's earned a great many.

   His greatest success, you can choose among any.

E is for effort, when the case gets tough,

   he endlessly studies. He's got the right stuff.

R is for ready, for any strange case.

   He solves them all with style and grace.

L is for logic. Of this he's the king.

   For all time his praise they will sing.

O s'for observation. He sees quite clear.

   He'll find all the answers, both far and near.

C is for clue. He finds them all,

   seen or unseen, no matter how small.

K is for the key, to answer a riddle.

   That is when he is not playing his fiddle.

H is for hound, a mysterious dog,

   with glowing green eyes, out there in the fog.

O is for that substance for which he's well known.

   I think it is something that's best left alone.

L is for London. That's where you will find

   his Baker Street lodgings, if you're so inclined.

M is for Mycroft, his brother, you know,

   A good source for information to go.

E is for endless, his stories they write.

   If you lined them all up, t'would be quite a sight.

S is for solutions to great mysteries,

   for finding the answers that no one else sees.

Sherlock Holmes, no matter the letter,

   you will never find anyone better,

than the detective from 221b,

   He is the best. It's quite plain to see.

The Adventure of the
Two Brothers
by Tracy J. Revels

"*W*atson, have I ever told you of the first case in which the Holmes brothers solved a mysterious robbery and restored a lady's most beloved and valuable bauble?"

Such was the startling question my friend Mr. Sherlock Holmes put to me one Sunday afternoon as we visited the Jewel House at The Tower of London. As we viewed St. Edward's Crown, with its magnificent gems including the Koh-i-Noor diamond and the Black Prince's ruby, Holmes had only moments before reasserted his belief that precious stones were the Devil's pet baits, speculating on how dozens of tragedies underlaid the glittering regalia. Now he stood transfixed, and I followed his gaze to a much smaller piece of jewelry within one of the cases, a single diamond brooch surrounded by a half-dozen perfect pearls.

"No, I have never heard that tale."

He gave a nod, and together we departed the crowded chamber, making our way to Tower Green, that charming spot where many of England's most distinguished individuals, including two queens, lost their heads. We purchased lemonade from a vendor and settled onto a wooden bench, effectively disguised as ordinary summer tourists.

Then, in a soft and amused voice, Holmes told me the following story. Charmed by it, I have taken the liberty to convert the tale into literary form . . . .

It was the summer of 1861, and the young Holmes brothers were at home, on holiday from their respective schools. Mycroft, a burly lad of fourteen, planned to spend his time further applying himself to his studies, learning as much as he could about the inner workings of the Empire, preparing himself for the role in Her Majesty's Government that he would one day fill. It was a pursuit his father monitored intensely and looked upon with pride.

Master Sherlock, however, was grateful to be free of his hoary old schoolmaster, his dusty books, and the endless conjugation of Latin verbs. Sherlock was a decidedly precocious boy who valued his liberty. He absented himself from his country home by seven each morning, his pockets stuffed with biscuits and a satchel bearing his field glasses,

31

magnifying lens, and notebooks slung across one shoulder. The boy's interests were wide-ranging for a seven-year-old. He observed the work of an ant colony, dissecting its chain of command, and pondering how the tiny creatures communicated with one another. He climbed about earthen barrows, certain that he would find treasure within, if only he could locate the secret passages the ancients had so cleverly concealed. He collected bottles and pails of discarded liquids, using them to conduct crude chemical experiments, taking care to record his results, especially the odiferous and explosive ones. He wandered among the effigies of crusaders and noblemen in the village church, developing an affection for the mysteries of the past. There was even a day when he felt certain he could segregate a queen from her colony of bees – but the less said about that unfortunate incident, the better.

It should be noted that Sherlock was not a snobbish or aloof boy, for he was deeply interested in the human dramas within his village, though he usually watched them from a distance. His preferred point of observation was amid the branches of a tree in the middle of the square, a great elm which had been a seedling when Edward III reigned. From that perch, he made detailed observation of the villagers. He knew how the butcher was cheating his customers by shifting the balance of his scales, when the vicar had tippled too much of the sacramental wine, and which village Romeo was courting the shoemaker's newly wealthy widow. He watched with fascination, but without judgement. He had learned by sad experience that his deductions about human behavior were best kept to himself, and that a boy who "tattled" might also run afoul of his fellow lads' fists. His father often accused him of idleness, an opinion that Mycroft appeared to share – though in fairness, Mycroft had reached the age when a boy begins a serious contemplation of a man's estate, while Sherlock had yet to realize he too would face the misfortune of growing up.

That fateful June day, Sherlock returned home just before noon, only to find the house in an uproar – his father shouting, his mother weeping, the servants cowering, and a man in a long dark coat and a high hat barking out orders to a pair of uniformed constables. Small and lithe, Sherlock deftly avoided the chaos, climbing a drainpipe to slide through the window of his brother's room.

"Mycroft!" he cried, "What has happened?"

His sibling barely glanced up from a massive book. The youth was of ponderous girth, and moved with the studied slowness of a sloth.

"Mother's diamond brooch has been stolen."

"Brooch?"

"The pin she wears upon her evening dress when she attends the theater. The one that twinkles."

A theft of a valuable object inside their own home? Sherlock was immediately intrigued.

"How did it happen?"

"Mother says she removed the object from her locked jewel case because they are planning to go to London next weekend, to visit Aunt Henrietta."

Sherlock scowled at this information. He hoped he would be allowed to remain behind with the servants. His mother's elderly maiden sister reeked of lavender, lived in a small home with a dozen cats, and insisted upon pinching his cheek. He still carried a bruise from their Christmas visit.

"Mother sat beside the window to clean the bejeweled piece, but as she began, she heard a loud noise from downstairs. She laid the brooch upon a table and hurried to the kitchen to investigate the sound."

"And?" Sherlock asked when his brother hesitated. "What did she find?"

"A minor disagreement, between the cook and myself, over the matter of some blackberry tarts. Really, what is the point of a pastry if not to consume it, especially when it is warm and extra savory?"

"You ate all of them, didn't you?"

Mycroft scowled. "Of course not!"

"The stain on your shirt hints otherwise. As does the loosened top button of your trousers."

Mycroft waved a flipper-like hand. "That is immaterial. Once the crisis was resolved – a matter of some ten minutes at most – Mother returned to her room. The brooch was not where she had placed it. She looked all about, thinking perhaps it had fallen and she had accidentally kicked it under her bed. She had not. She commenced to shrieking, and Father, who was just returning from the village, ran up to see what was amiss. They began to question the servants, to no satisfaction. Father then sent the stable boy out to fetch the inspector and his minions." Mycroft heaved a sigh. "Inspector Smith is a fool."

"What makes you say that?"

"I heard him tell Father he suspects this is the work of the gypsies who have camped half-a-league from here. He thinks they might be seeking revenge upon our family. You surely know why, Brother."

Sherlock felt his face go red. The previous autumn, following a dispute with his father, he had run away with a band of Roma travelers. In just three days he picked up fragments of their language, developed a fondness for their spicy food and their wailing violins, and apprenticed

33

himself to the company's bear trainer. Inspector Smith and his father, however, had quickly retrieved Sherlock from his new-found friends.

"Perhaps they want you back, Sherlock. I for one would gladly hand you over."

Sherlock could not let the jibe go unmet. "And I wonder if you might have borrowed Mother's jewel to give to that young lady you moon over every Sunday at church."

"I am not mooning. I am simply being observant. Now run along and play."

Amusement was the last thing on Sherlock's mind. On tiptoe, he crossed the hallway to his mother's bedroom. He inspected the chamber thoroughly, top to bottom, crawling on his belly to check every small gap in the floorboards and lift each ornate rug. His initial theory, that the brooch might have dropped through a crack in the flooring, was quickly disproved. Another idea, that it might be caught in the cushions, or somehow snagged in the curtains, was equally dispelled. Sherlock seized a hairpin and picked the lock of the jewel case. His beloved mother was, at times, quite absent-minded. What if she had returned the brooch to its proper place and it was never missing at all? Would that not be the ultimate elimination of possibilities, and a triumph of deduction?

The brooch was not there. It had truly vanished.

Holmes sat and considered what he knew of his family's servants. Their cook was also their housekeeper, and a more unpleasant and quarrelsome woman had never lived. But she was accounted for, as she was involved in the altercation over the tarts and thus in view by the victim. Might the housekeeper have an accomplice? Her husband the butler was known to be a gambler who would bet on anything from horse races to egg-carrying contests at church treats. But he had also served the Holmes family for nearly forty years. Would he really risk his reputation and honor by thievery after so many decades without a blemish upon his record? It seemed improbable. The two young maids were new to the household, and what girl could resist such a shiny object, but surely the inspector and his men had thoroughly looked through their rooms, and the maids knew their persons might also be searched. They would be fools to take such a prize unless they had an impeccable place to conceal it. The stable boy was a rascal, and Sherlock would not put such mischief beyond him, but he was not allowed inside the house, because his boots were always covered in filth. Had he snuck inside, he would have left a vile, easily followed trail of clues behind him.

Sherlock walked to the open window and looked out. His mother's room was high, on the second floor of the house. There was no convenient drainpipe on this side, nor growth of stout ivy. The stone walls of the dwelling were smooth, presenting no hand or toeholds. He peered down. The ground was still moist and impressionable from yesterday's rain, yet there was no sign of a ladder being placed anywhere nearby.

Across the lawn, much too far for an acrobatic leap to the window, stood an oak tree and an elm tree. Between them, Sherlock looked out at gently rolling fields. In the distance, the village church steeple pointed to Heaven. Somewhere just beyond was the gypsy encampment.

Sherlock sat down and folded his arms on the windowsill. He wished he was permitted to smoke a pipe. The rich smell generated by his father's oily briar always placed him in a contemplative mood.

Voices rose from below. Sherlock slipped beneath from the window, so he could listen but not be seen by whoever had come upon the lawn. He quickly recognized the clipped tone of the inspector.

"I still think it could be one of your servants – I don't like the dark looks of the parlor maid. With her complexion, she might have a lover among the gypsies. She could have snatched up the jewel and thrown it down to him."

Impossible, Sherlock thought. There were no footprints beneath the window. And how would the maid have known his mother planned to polish her jewel at that moment? The crime was not planned in any way. It was clearly an act of impulse. Nor would their watchdog, the ever-faithful Athena, have permitted a stranger to come so close to the house without claiming the seat of his trousers as a trophy.

"What will you do?" Sherlock heard his father ask.

"I'll ask you to keep a close eye on the maid. I will return to the village and wait until nightfall. Then I will take my men over to the camp and roust those gypsies until we find some answers! Don't worry, Squire, we'll get your lady's trinket back."

"It is hardly a trinket! That piece has been in my family since the reign of Henry VIII!"

"As you say, Squire. I'd best be getting back now. Oh – I meant to ask – How fares your youngest son, the scamp we had to fetch back from the gypsies just a few months ago?"

"Sherlock is a bright lad, but a feckless one. He shows no serious interests. He lacks purpose in his studies. I fear he will never be more than a pale imitation of his brother. I had almost forgotten about that embarrassment in the autumn. You don't think he . . . ?"

"Where was he this morning?"

"I have no idea. He disappears before breakfast, wanders about the countryside instead of dutifully applying himself to his books. I shall seek him out and, if he seems guilty, a stout belt shall compel the truth from him."

Sherlock's blood ran cold. He was a suspect! Now it was even more pressing for him to find and restore his mother's brooch, to prove his innocence in the affair.

A sudden idea came to him. He turned it around in his mind, until he was convinced of its merits. He even devised a trap to test it. All he needed was some money. He emptied his pockets. He had not a farthing to his name.

Sherlock hurried back to Mycroft's room. Mycroft hoarded his allowance. Perhaps he would be generous.

"Brother, can you make me a loan?"

Mycroft turned, suspicions clouding his round face. "How much?"

"At least three shillings."

"Why do you want it?"

"To help me catch the thief of Mother's brooch."

"Don't be ridiculous." Mycroft sniffed. "I already know who the villain is."

"Then tell me," Sherlock challenged.

Mycroft stated a name. Reluctantly, his younger brother nodded.

"Our thoughts run parallel. We must act!"

"What do you propose to do?"

Sherlock laid out his plan. Mycroft hummed softly, rubbing his own chin.

"It could work." He unlocked a drawer and counted out the coins. "I can even understand why this scheme appeals to you."

"I need your help – beyond the money!" Sherlock insisted. "Father suspects me of mischief. You must distract him, so I may leave the house unnoticed."

Mycroft sighed and levered himself up from his chair. Sherlock stood at the door and listened to his brother's thunderous footsteps as he walked to their father's study. He heard Mycroft cough and make a complicated inquiry into the nature of the First Opium War. Squire Holmes began to pontificate. Sherlock hurried out.

As he passed the parlor, he heard his mother quietly weeping. He dared not stop, but his chest burned with anger at the foul creature which had hurt her by stealing her most precious possession.

Sherlock ran to the stables and ordered his pony, Dupin, to be saddled. He kicked his mount into a trot, reaching the village in under an hour. He went straight to an establishment called The Ladies Shoppe. Its large window was filled with hats, fans, and fancy boots. Miss Sarah, the girl Mycroft "observed" every Sabbath, worked within as a clerk.

"Why, Master Sherlock, what brings you here?" she laughed, noting his red face and hurried manner.

36

"I need a gift for my mother. Some type of jewelry that sparkles."

"Why, a real lady like Mrs. Holmes deserves something from the jeweler on High Street."

"I only have three shillings."

"Then you have come to the right place." The girl pulled a velvet-lined tray from beneath a counter. Gaudy objects – pendant, bracelets, combs – were scattered across it. Holmes selected a *faux* emerald stickpin and a paste diamond brooch.

"Would you like these, as gifts?" Sherlock asked the girl. "I am never sure what ladies prefer."

"Oh, I would fall in love with any gentleman who gave me one of these," Miss Sarah assured the boy as she wrapped the chosen objects.

Sherlock paid the girl, then rode home. He gave his pony's reins to the stable boy and slipped in through the kitchen. He made his way carefully up the stairs, pausing to listen for a moment. His father was droning on about how the Great Rebellion now raging in America was impacting British industry. Sherlock continued silently to his mother's bedroom, where he readied his trap. He worried the light had changed, and perhaps the experiment would work better in the morning. But he felt compelled to try, for if he did not learn the truth by nightfall, his gypsy friends would suffer.

He maintained his vigil for almost an hour before he heard a sound. He had withdrawn into the room's deep shadows, and now he sat as immoveable as a statue. As he watched, the culprit appeared and brazenly made off with the stickpin. Sherlock dashed to the window, watched the thief make his escape, and then gave a shout of triumph and ran downstairs to the study, where his father was remarking on the wickedness of someone named Jefferson Davis, while his brother was enduring the lecture stoically.

"Mycroft, come quickly! The game's aloft! I saw where he went. Come on!"

Squire Holmes nearly dropped his pipe from his lips in astonishment. Mycroft moved with surprising speed in pursuit of his excited sibling. Sherlock's cries alerted the entire household, who came running to see what this new excitement could mean. Sherlock bolted into the parlor and seized his mother's hand.

"Mummy, I've found it! Let me show you!"

"Here now!" Squire Holmes shouted as the residents assembled on the lawn beneath his lady's window. "What is all this foolishness about?"

Sherlock ignored his father. He paused only long enough to unlace his boots and strip off his stockings. Before anyone could intervene, he began to climb the oak tree.

37

"Sherlock, no!" his mother cried.

But the lad continued, going ever higher, his fingers and toes crabbing against the rough bark to propel him skyward. The tree was older than his mother's brooch. He heard warning creaks and snaps amid the branches. He knew the supports might give way, and he might fall and be injured or even killed.

Yet in his pursuit of the evildoer, the boy was not afraid.

Sherlock spotted the raven's nest. She was a monstrous old thing, with a jagged beak and greedy eyes. She leveled a hateful glare at the youth.

Sherlock shouted at her in the Roma tongue, ordering her to depart or be cursed. Ravens, it seems, speak the language of gypsy magic, for the bird took to its wings, flapping free of the oak instead of attacking the boy and pecking at his eyes. Sherlock slapped the nest. It went tumbling to the earth, spilling its treasures. Sherlock carefully made his way down behind it. By the time he reached the ground, Mycroft was cleaning the brooch of bird droppings, while the maids were clapping their hands, and the cook and butler were murmuring their approval. Squire Holmes stood slack-jawed, but his wife ran forward, embracing her youngest child.

"How did you know?" she asked, as he shyly pulled away from her happy kiss. Sherlock was so embarrassed, and yet delighted, by the display of maternal pride that he remained tongue-tied. Mycroft coughed loudly and presented their shared path of deduction.

"It seemed most improbable that anyone inside the house would steal your precious jewel, Mother, and equally impossible that any person outside the house could have done so. Therefore, the logical conclusion was that a non-human intelligence must have been involved. A bird instantly came to mind."

"I've seen it happen," Sherlock said, squirming from his mother's arms. He faced his father, eager to show off. "Crows and magpies will pick up bit of tin, even a piece of bright ribbon. So I purchased some paste jewelry from the village, and put it on Mother's windowsill to see if the thief could be lured back and would show me its hiding place. I meant to catch the villain in the act, and I did!"

"How extraordinary!" Mrs. Holmes cheered, as Mycroft, with a short bow, presented her with her newly cleaned token. "I am so proud of my boys."

Sherlock grinned at his brother, who merely shrugged as if to indicate the matter was of no great importance, and his mother's praise was immaterial to him. Sherlock wondered suddenly if Mycroft would have gone to the trouble to tell his parents about his theory. He had been right from the start – he named the very type of bird responsible – and yet he had not said as much to them before Sherlock arrived, when there was plenty of opportunity to take all the credit. Was Mycroft simply too lazy to check his own theory?

That will always be the difference between us, Sherlock decided. *Perhaps I shall never be as brilliant as Mycroft is while he sits in his chair, but I shall always be willing to do the work. I will never hesitate to climb the tree.*

"Daring, are you not proud of our children?" Mrs. Holmes coaxed her husband.

Squire Holmes put his pipe in his mouth. His heavy brows came together. The party on the lawn fell silent, waiting to hear what the master of the house would say.

"How are we to know for certain that Sherlock is not merely a highly efficient criminal who stole the jewel and now 'finds' it, in order to be commended for his cleverness? If you are expecting a *reward* for your services, Son, you shall not receive it."

Sherlock's hands curled tight. His nails bit into his wounded palms.

"The work is its own reward, Father."

Squire Holmes gave a disgusted snort. "Very well. I must go to the village and tell the inspector not to bother the gypsies. Everyone, back to your business – This adventure is at an end!"

Later that evening, as Sherlock was pulling his blanket over his shoulders, his mother entered his bedroom, carrying a candle. In the way of loving mothers everywhere, she knew exactly what was troubling her son, and why not a single word had passed his lips since the conclusion of the excitement on the lawn.

"You father loves you, Sherlock," Mrs. Holmes said, in her soft and musical voice. "He wants nothing but the best for you and Mycroft – but he is not a *clever* man. I think, at times, it frightens him to see how smart you boys are, when he is merely hard-working and diligent. He is not like you, and you shall not grow up to be like him, and that can be a difficult thing for a father to accept." She gently brushed a hand through her son's disordered hair. "Promise me you will use your remarkable gifts, for they were given to you for a purpose. Always employ them for good, never evil, and know that I will forever be proud of you."

Sherlock Holmes gave his mother his word as she kissed him goodnight. It remains a promise he has never broken.

"There was an interesting epilogue to the case," Holmes said. The crowds had thinned, the air was growing cooler. One of the famous Tower ravens sat upon a fencepost near us, considering us with pure malice in his beady eyes.

"Oh?"

"I gave Mycroft the extra bauble I had purchased for the experiment. I told him how Miss Sarah had cooed over it, and her comment that she would fall in love with any swain who presented such a thing to her. I urged my besotted brother to act upon her words. But Mycroft, as usual, was slow to rouse. He did not move precipitously, but waited until the Christmas season, two years later, to make a gift of the brooch to her."

"What happened?"

"A misfortune, for, unbeknownst to Mycroft, the girl had acquired a lover named Billy 'Breakbones' Bowden. This older lad took great offense at Mycroft's tepid attempt to make love to his lady. A brawl ensued, one in which noses, rather than bones, were broken, and Mycroft proved he was not as soft and lethargic as he seemed. However, when the bully began to get the better of things, honor demanded that Mycroft's second in the duel intervene."

Holmes gave way to a full, rich laugh. He waved a hand toward the White Tower, and the bars upon its windows. "These surroundings are inspiring. Next time we are here, Watson, I shall tell you the story of how the Holmes boys spent a night in a gaol!"

The First Problem
by Elbert Henry Smith

James Moriarty ran his fingers down the front of a human skull. He carefully studied the dimensions of the long-dead fellow as he sat back in his high lounge chair. If only he knew a little more about this man, it would go a long way toward informing him of his intellectual nature. But, with the skull being somewhat symmetrical, he gathered that he must not have been a very bright man. Nevertheless, these things did fascinate him and kept his mind busy while he was writing his treatise on the Binomial Theorem. He placed the skull on a cherry-wood end table and pulled a cigarette from a tin holder in his pocket. He lit the cigarette and slowly inhaled. His entire body seemed to relax. That is, until suddenly George Davies knocked at the hallway entrance.

Moriarty looked up, Davies was an employee of his father's ship-building business. Davies and Moriarty had struck up a peculiar acquaintanceship. Both would talk about their daily affairs when Moriarty visited his father's work – which led him to wonder why Davies had shown up here at his house, and better yet, why had the butler simply let him in? Davies was a Northerner and had a Northern kind of swagger about him. He looked at Moriarty and smiled from ear to ear.

"Mr. Moriarty," he said.

"Mr. George Davies." Moriarty stood. "For what do I have the honor of your presence this evening?"

"Sorry for the intrusion, sir. I told your butler not to disturb you if you were busy. I need to have a chat."

"It's quite all right, Davies," Moriarty gestured to the sofa. "Please come in and have a seat."

"Thank you, sir. I won't be takin' up much of your time." He handed Moriarty a letter. "Your butler said to give you this. It came for you."

"Would you like some tea?" Moriarty asked.

"No, sir. Thank you again. I've come to ask of you a favor."

Moriarty sat back down and puffed on his cigarette. He found it strange that George would come to him for a favor. They barely knew each other. He didn't even know how George knew where he lived. He rubbed his hand against the surface of the skull, and George looked at him strangely.

"Please, go on, Mr. Davies," Moriarty said.

"George. You can call me George, sir."

41

"Very well. Go on, Mr. Davies," Moriarty repeated.

"Well, you know how we like to have a chin-wag about horse racing?"

Moriarty nodded.

"I thought I had a good lead on a horse, Lucky Lady. She was a nice thoroughbred, and the odds were so good, I thought I'd put some money on it for me and the wife."

"I deduce that Lucky Lady did not pull through," Moriarty concluded. "You lost your money?"

"Yes, sir," David looked down in shame. "A whole week's wages."

Moriarty stood up and put his cigarette out. He stared at Davies, and a cloud of smoke erupted from his nostrils. Davies didn't know how to take him. Moriarty looked down at him and saw an opportunity. What was money compared to power? Power over another human being. He had been waiting for something like this to happen, but who would need the help of a young twenty-year-old right out of university? Moriarty walked over to his fireplace mantel and grabbed his checkbook.

"How much do you make a week, Mr. Davies?"

"Six-pounds-fifty, sir," Davies replied.

"Let's make it an even seven, shall we?" Moriarty wrote the check.

Davies looked surprised, and stood up to shake Moriarty's hand. "Thank you, Mr. Moriarty, sir."

"Think nothing of it, Davies. You don't even have to pay me back." He shook his hand in return.

"Sir?"

Moriarty walked him to the door. Davies was ecstatic. Little did he know that he was becoming the first pawn in one of Moriarty's games. Davies opened the door and looked back at Moriarty. Moriarty smiled and patted him on the shoulder. "There is one condition, my good man: One day, I will ask a favor of you. I do not know what or when. But when I do . . . remember this day."

Davies looked at him. "Whatever and whenever, Mr. Moriarty, I am your man." Davies walked out, and Moriarty watched him go down the busy city street. He felt his breast pocket and pulled out the letter he'd received. It was from Mary Clarke, the woman he loved. He closed the door and read the letter:

Dearest James,

Hello, my love. Oh, how I long to see you again! Father will be home tonight, giving you ample opportunity to talk with him about our future together. I know he can be difficult sometimes, but be steadfast. I have this feeling that he will say yes. So be of good cheer and dress in your finest.

Your beloved always,
Mary

Moriarty smiled as he read the letter. He looked down at his watch and realized that the time had gotten away from him. He quickly dashed into another room and started to get ready for his dinner with the Clarke family. Henry, his butler, came into the room as Moriarty browsed through his wardrobe.

"Is everything all right, sir?" Henry asked.

"Yes. It's Monday!"

"I am truly aware of the day, sir. What I don't understand is why are you so rushing around so frantically."

"It is Monday, February 16th, 1863," Moriarty replied. "The day I ask for Mary Clarke's hand in marriage."

"Oh, I see. Our James Moriarty is about to take the big plunge. How exciting, sir. Have you thought of a date for the wedding yet?"

"I thought I'd leave that up to them. The old Colonel will be paying for it, after all."

"Yes, she is a fine young woman. Very beautiful, just like her mother."

"And they are loaded, Henry. Just imagine – a great big painting of me displayed in the great halls of Clarke Estate."

Henry walked up to the closet and picked out an outfit to wear.

"Then we must choose the right suit for the occasion, sir."

Later that day, Moriarty arrived at the Clarke family home. He was intimidated by the scale of their wealth. Colonel Reginald Clarke was of the proper upper class, born into his money. Moriarty's father was a self-made man, but not on this scale. He had been worried when he fell for Mary, who had come to him for tutoring in mathematics – worried that this day would come and that he would be rejected by the Colonel. But he remained vigilant. Perhaps true love would prevail in the end. Besides, Mary hated her father with a passion. In any case, Moriarty had shown up at the Clarke doorstep with a necklace to gift Mary.

One thing he found odd was the fact that Colonel Clarke had never invited his father to one of his famous game-hunting parties. As they were always held on Moriarty's cousin Bernie's estate, it seemed like the most logical thing to happen. Perhaps the old Colonel wasn't aware of his father and his wealth. Anyway, it was time for him to focus on his big day – one that he would never forget.

He knocked on the door and the butler answered. Arthur Humphreys was an old man dressed in his finest outfit, which he cleaned meticulously each day. Humphreys pushed his glasses up on his nose and stared Moriarty up and down. "Hello," he asked. "Whom should I say is calling?"

"Moriarty. Mr. James Moriarty. I have come for dinner."

"Ah, yes. The college boy. Please, walk this way, sir."

Moriarty followed Humphreys into the lavish hallway of the estate.

They went into the parlor room, where piano music and singing came hurtling out of the door as Humphreys opened it. Inside, Moriarty could see the entire Clarke clan standing around the piano, singing "The Goslings" by Sir Fredrick Bridge. Mary turned to him and smiled while she sang. At the age of nineteen, sShe was a thing of beauty. She had long, curly, dark hair that outlined the curves of her Cheshire-cat-like face. She batted her baby-blue eyes at Moriarty, and he could feel the love from across the room. It was the kind of love a man would die for – or perhaps even kill for.

Her younger brother Russell tried to keep up with the music. He was short and squat just like his father. The poor boy lived a lonely existence behind the walls of this massive estate. No friends to play with, and only servants to taunt and tease around the house. Vivian, the mother, gave Moriarty a nod while the father, Reginald, played the piano, sitting upright like he was back in the army.

Colonel Reginald Clarke was a short, burly man with a head of thick, gray hair and a thick, black bushy beard. Clarke was a man of power, having served in the military for several years. He liked to play with the lives of others. Moriarty heard that once Clarke had shot a servant for not giving his boots a proper cleaning, but that was mere rumor.

Clarke looked at Moriarty with a slight gleam in his eye as he bellowed out the song. He gave quite a devilish grin as he sang the words. His stare would always make Moriarty nervous. He could never tell what the old man was thinking, and he didn't like it when he couldn't read a person. The song came to an end, and the butler approached the family.

"Colonel Clarke," Humphreys proclaimed, "Mr. James Moriarty is here to join you for dinner,"

"Good, good!" the Colonel bellowed. "Please come in, James. Make yourself at home."

Moriarty walked forward and ran his hands down the gift box. "I have brought a gift – for Mary." He handed it to her. She smiled and looked at her mother. Mrs. Clarke nodded back in anticipation. Mary opened the box to reveal a necklace.

"It was my mother's," Moriarty said. "My father bought it for her."

"James, it's beautiful!" Mary replied.

"Yes, James, it's quite beautiful." the Colonel said as he stood up. "Bringing my daughter such a lovely gift tonight makes me wonder about your intentions."

"Well, sir, there was a question I wanted to ask, but that could wait until after dinner."

"Nonsense, my boy. You came all this way, bringing such a touching sentiment. I think you would leave us all in suspense through the whole meal. Spit it out, my man!"

"Very well, sir. I have known Mary for quite some time now. I was her tutor in mathematics, and in that time we have grown quite fond of each other. With each tutoring session, our love for each other grew and grew. When it came time for the lessons to be over, we were both deeply saddened. It has come to the point that I can no longer be without her in my life. Sir, I am on the cusp of obtaining a seat at a reputable university. My future is bright, and I will make enough to keep Mary well taken care of – "

"Spit it out, lad," the Colonel said.

"Sir, what I am asking is, may I have Mary's hand in marriage?"

The tension in the room grew thick. The women looked at the Colonel with high hopes. Even the boy Russell was waiting with anticipation for the response. The Colonel walked over to Moriarty. He looked up at him and smiled that devilish grin again. All Moriarty could do to ease the anxiety was to gaze upon the stuffed wolf that the Colonel had killed on a hunting trip.

"No," the Colonel said.

The women broke out in tears, and Mary grabbed hold of her brother for comfort.

"Excuse me?" Moriarty was taken back.

"I said *no*!" shouted the Colonel. "You think you can just walk in here and take my money, boy? We are an upper-class family, born into this right."

"Sir, my father – " Moriarty said.

"Your father, your father! Your father is nothing more than a second-rate charlatan! Your father has flashed around his wealth like he owns all of England. His claims of wealth because he owns the Moriarty Shipyards are ridiculous. The Clarke family estate has been here for generations, and I will not let some thick-headed mathematics teacher anywhere near our fortune. Now, good day to you, sir!"

The Colonel stormed out of the room. Moriarty looked at Mary with a coldness in his heart. He walked out, and Mary ran after him. Her eyes were red and filled with tears.

"I'm sorry, Mary," Moriarty said.

"James, please don't leave me!" she cried.

He wiped a tear from her cheek. "There is nothing I can do. He has made his mind up."

"We would be free to marry if he wasn't here," she said softly, but she didn't seem to realize what she was suggesting.

Moriarty stepped back for a moment. The wheels started to turn in his mind. She was right. If the Colonel were dead, he couldn't say no. Then they could be free to live and love how they wanted. All that wealth would be his to do with as he saw fit.

"I have an idea," he said.

"What is it?" she asked.

"Not here, not now. Meet me at the Cromwell Bridge, tomorrow at lunchtime. We will talk then." She looked down at the necklace. Moriarty put his hand over hers and smiled. She looked back at him and started to cry again. Once more he wiped the tears from her eyes. Then he walked out of the house and went home.

Moriarty pulled his Purdy double-barreled rifle from his gun cabinet. He held it firmly in his grasp and aimed it across the room. He smiled. *That scoundrel thinks he can play with my life as he sees fit, he thought. Well, two can play at that game.* He remembered back to the stuffed wolf he saw in the family's parlor. Then he recalled the sadness that had fallen over the room. *No man shall ever think he has power over me.* He sat down in his cozy chair and took a few drags off a cigarette. He looked over at the skull he was studying and fell asleep.

Moriarty's butler walked into the room with a cup of tea. "Tea sir?" he asked.

"Why yes, Henry, thank you." Henry brought the tea over to him. Moriarty took a sip and looked up. "Say, Henry – you worked for my father down at the shipyards for some time. Did you know George Davies?"

Henry thought for a moment and then spoke. "The man that was here earlier today? Yes, sir, Mr. Davies is a nice man and a hard worker."

"Good, good. Do you think he is a man of his word?"

"Yes, sir. He once said that he was in the Army. Any man who served is a most honorable person. If that's all, Mr. Moriarty, I will retire for the evening."

"Yes, Henry, have a good night." Henry nodded and walked away. Moriarty sipped his tea. *Things are coming together, h*e thought.

The next day, Moriarty stood in a gloomy field, looking over the Cromwell Bridge. He waited for Mary to arrive, and threw a couple of rocks in the water in front of him. He heard her cry out to him. She looked like a beautiful white angel amid all the doom and gloom. She waved to him as she left the side of her servant, Mr. Humphreys.

Moriarty was anxious. After the argument with her father, he didn't know how she still felt about him. Perhaps she had come to agree with her father's decision. Maybe she felt it was better to side with the one who controlled the money. Maybe this was her saying goodbye to him.

"It is good to see you, Mary," Moriarty said.

"I longed to see you again, James. My father was angry until morning. He and Mother fought behind closed doors all night. The whole household was up in arms over his decision."

"I must admit, my heart was ripped from my chest. But do not fear: I have a plan that will not fail."

"What is it, James? I'm hopeful for anything at this point."

"Two days from now, your father will be taking part in a hunt on my cousin Bernie's land. I have an acquaintance who owes me a specific debt. I plan on cashing in that debt by having him . . . ." Moriarty stopped for a moment. He did not know how Mary would react to the next part of his plan. He was nervous she would not approve and leave him. But it was a choice he had to make. "I'm going to have the Colonel killed in a hunting accident. He will die doing what he loves, and we will be together forever."

Mary stopped. She didn't know how to react. Moriarty knew she hated her father for all the abuse that Colonel Clarke had done to her. Moriarty felt justified in his thinking, and hoped Mary had felt the same way.

Meanwhile, it started to rain on such a dreary Lancashire afternoon. Mary pulled out an umbrella and held it over her head. She drew close to Moriarty and took him by the hand. She drew closer and kissed him on the lips. She nodded and walked away. Moriarty knew what needed to happen next.

Back at home, Moriarty laid out a crudely drawn map of his cousin's estate. He took a puff of a cigarette and placed the human skull on top of the map as a paperweight. He drew out markings on the map as though he were planning a war. Devising in his head the best hunting areas of Bernie's land. Outside, he set a target at the same height as Clarke and practiced aiming his gun at the best distance away from him. He even rode

47

out to Bernie's place and timed himself to see how long it would take for him to get around the estate. He left nothing to chance.

Later that night, he made his way to his father's business. Moriarty Shipyards was the company that gave the Moriarty family its name. It had served the family well, and now Moriarty had thought to himself that it would serve his needs too. He stepped out onto the dock late at night, lurking in the shadows. He gazed out onto the shipyard and saw George Davies working away at sanding a new boat. Moriarty lurked in the darkness, not to be seen. He crept up quietly behind Davies.

"George Davies," he whispered.

Davies whipped around in fright. "Oh, Mr. Moriarty! You kicked up a breeze, didn't you?"

"Mr. Davies, as much as I would like to stay and have a chat, or chinwag, as you like to say, I am here on business."

"Oh. Looking to build you a boat?"

"No, Mr. Davies, I have come to collect on the debt that you owe."

Davies went back to sanding the boat. "Well, sir, I don't quite have the money for you yet."

Moriarty walked closer to Davies. "I am well aware of that. Money is not what I'm looking for. I need you to do a service for me."

Davies breathed a sigh of relief. "Thank God. I lost on another horse . . . ."

Moriarty interrupted. "Mr. Davies, please, back on to the task at hand. What I need you for is perhaps one of the greatest acts you will ever perform in your life."

"That is?" Davies asked.

"I need you to kill someone for me."

Davies dropped the sandpaper.

"Look, I may be a no-good gambler, but killing a man is a different thing!"

"I told you this day would come. You said you would do anything. Well, here it is."

Davies looked him in the eyes and he seemed to collapse, giving a soft but affirmative firm answer. Moriarty produced some money from his pockets. "I will even give you two weeks of wages in addition. You owe it to your family, George."

Davies looked at the money bag and licked his lips. That was a lot of money he could put down on a horse. He snatched the purse from Moriarty's hand. "Fine, what do I have to do?" Davies asked.

Moriarty smiled. "My cousin owns a spot of land not far from here. I want you to go to the spot on this map." He hands the map to Davies. "At nine in the morning. Colonel Reginald Clarke will be in this area of the

48

estate on a hunt. I will be there, watching from afar. At the location I marked, I will leave my Purdy double-barreled rifle for you. It is capable of two shots before needing to be reloaded. That should be enough to get the job done. It will be seen as a random hunting accident."

Davies slowly nodded. "What does this Colonel look like?" He asked. Moriarty stuck his nose up in the air with distaste. "He is a short, fat man with a great beard. He's loud, boisterous, and arrogant. Trust me – you won't miss him."

"All right, I'll be there."

"Extraordinary, Mr. Davies." Moriarty said as he backed away into the shadows. "Saturday, nine in the morning. Don't forget,"

Davies picked up the sandpaper and went back to work.

Moriarty walked down the busy street as people from all walks of life littered the sidewalks and alleyways. For the first time in his life, he felt confident. This plan was foolproof, as long as Davies showed up to follow through with his promise.

Suddenly, a man called out to him from an alleyway. Moriarty turned and slowly walked into the dark, decrepit area to get a better look at the fellow. He was dirty and old, and looked as if he hadn't eaten in weeks. He called out again.

"Sir, might you have a bit of change? I am starving, and have no money."

"I'm sorry, sir. I didn't bring my change purse with me this evening."

"Just a bit, mate. Just enough to get a piece of bread."

At that point, Moriarty started to back up. The old man produced a knife from his jacket. Moriarty looked at him and found that he was ready for a fight. The attacker moved quickly, pushing Moriarty to the ground and waving the knife.

"People like you think you're so smart! Looking down on us poor folk with your fancy clothes and pretty women. All the while, we have to fight for scraps!" The old man lifted the knife over his head. "Tonight, I'm going to be rich." As he began to thrust the knife, a punch flew out of the darkness, and the man with the knife went down to the ground.

Moriarty looked up and saw the large frame of a man. He turned around and tipped his bowler hat to Moriarty.

"Sorry about that. He's out cold." And the large man helped Moriarty up.

"Thank you for your help." Moriarty said. "What is your name?"

"Rocco. Rocco Turner. Two-time heavyweight champion."

"Of England?"

"Well, of Lancashire."

"Well, that's good enough for me. If you hadn't come along, I would have been diced to bits."

"I was on my way home from work when I heard him yelling," Rocco replied.

"Oh, do you work close by?"

"I did, I was let go today."

"Ah, please take my card. You seem like the type of man I'd like to do business with."

"'*J – James Moriarty*. All right, sir. I am always looking to make a nice bit of cash."

Moriarty nodded and walked home.

Saturday morning, Moriarty leaned against a tall tree, looking through a pair of binoculars. He saw all the rich men making their way to the fields with their hunting gear. He looked around but didn't see Colonel Clarke. He grew worried that the hunt would start soon. *Did he stay home today?* Moriarty wondered. He also looked for Davies, but there was no sign of him either. Suddenly, he heard a loud laugh, and then he saw him. Clarke was all geared up and ready to hunt. He patted another rich old man on the back and headed out to the field. To Moriarty's surprise, Clarke had brought his son Russell along. *No matter.* He thought. There were two rounds in that gun. That should suffice. But still no sign of Davies.

Colonel Clarke and Russell made their way around the estate. Moriarty watched them like a hawk. He glanced over to the spot set for Davies, but still no sign of him. He put down the binoculars and ran over to the where he'd left the gun. He quickly picked it up and aimed it at Clarke. He got him in his sights and pulled the trigger. The Colonel went down quickly. Russell, the young lad, burst into tears and yelled out for help, pointing at Moriarty, who quickly aimed the gun at Russell. The boy looked back at him and kept crying. Moriarty aimed to kill Russell, but he couldn't pull the trigger. As other hunters gathered around the dead body, Moriarty fled the scene.

A couple of days had passed, and Moriarty finished his treatise. He walked into his study with a cup of tea and a newspaper. He had decided to lay low in case someone was on to him, but all had been quiet as a mouse. He opened the newspaper and noticed the death of the Colonel was still being discussed on the front page. It said that the investigation was continuing. As he sipped on his tea, he realized that he still hadn't heard from Mary. He gave the family some time to mourn, but was starting to get worried that she hadn't even sent a letter to him. *I should have shot the boy.* He thought. *Leave no loose ends.*

He stood up and paced the floor. What could he do to quiet the lad? A threat? Shoot him as well? No, this must be something untraceable. He thought back to his school days and remembered in his science class that the core of a peach contains a tiny bit of cyanide. He remembered that it would take around fifteen to twenty cores to kill a man. Perhaps a little less could kill a child? Say – if he were to grind them up in a Bakewell tart, and sprinkle almonds, it would be untraceable! What young child would pass up on such a delicious sweet? He quickly went into the kitchen where Henry was cleaning. "Quickly, Henry, I need you to go to the market and get me some supplies. I want to bake."

"Bake, sir? I must say, this is a first for you."

Moriarty looked at him. "I want to make treats for the Clarke family. I'm going to visit them."

He walked back into the study and looked over at the skull. He stared at it for a moment, then smiled.

Later that evening, Moriarty ran around his kitchen like a madman, making sure that he measured the correct amount of ingredients to make his deadly tart. He baked the goods and then placed them in a small basket. Giving the poisoned one a small red ribbon to set it apart from the others.

The next day, Moriarty arrived at the Clarke estate, again dressed in fine clothes. He knocked on the door, and Mr. Humphreys answered the door. Humphreys looked him up and down.

"Ah, Mr. Moriarty. What brings you by this time of day?"

"I have come to give my condolences to the family."

"Thank you, sir, but they are not seeing anyone but family right now. Surely you understand."

"I do, Mr. Humphreys, but it would be for just a moment. I brought some baked goods for them, and I wish to comfort Mary."

"Oh, very well. She will be pleased to see you."

He walked Moriarty down the same familiar hall and into the parlor room. This time, there was no piano playing or singing. The mother, Vivian, was sitting on the couch, with Mary trying to console her. Russell sat alone at the piano, hunching over in deep thought. Mr. Humphreys addressed the room.

"Mr. James Moriarty is here to give his condolences, Mrs. Clarke."

Vivian Clarke wiped her tears. "Thank you, Arthur. Please come in, James."

Moriarty walked into the room. "Thank you, ma'am. Even though the Colonel and I had our disagreements, I wanted to say how sorry I am over the whole ghastly ordeal."

"Thank you for saying that, James," Mrs. Clarke said. "You have always been a good boy. I want to reconcile things with you. I think you and Mary have something to talk about."

Mary stood up and walked over to Moriarty. "Please, James – walk with me."

She took him by the hand, and they walked through a long hallway full of paintings. Moriarty looked around the hall as they walked. Each painting was a portrait of a long-dead Clarke who used to rule over the estate. They stopped in front of a painting of Colonel Clarke. Moriarty looked into Mary's eyes.

"I hadn't heard from you in a couple of days . . ." he said.

"I've been busy taking care of Mother. It looks like all went according to plan."

"Yes. Has your mother said anything?" He turned away to look at one of the paintings.

When he looked back, Mary was smiling and taking a bite of the Bakewell tart with the red ribbon. "Yes, Mother has agreed for us to be married! Isn't that wonderful?"

He was shocked. *She took the wrong tart!* "Mary, please . . . ."

"Everything has been wrapped up." She bit down once more on the tart, a larger bite this time. "My brother couldn't see the face of the killer, so there are no witnesses."

Moriarty looked on in terror as she quickly ate the rest of the tart. It would be just minutes before she would succumb to the poison. She smiled at him as he gazed upon her for one last time.

"Mary Clarke, I do love you so," he said this as he kissed her cheek, taking care to wipe the remaining crumbs from her lips and to retrieve the red ribbon.

He turned and walked down the hall, placing the basket of remaining tarts on a table some distance away. He could hear her start to choke. He didn't stop and did not turn around. He walked through the parlor and stared at the grieving widow. He felt incredible guilt for her misery. He turned from her and walked out of the house.

Mary would be found dead moments later, and the police would rule it as a heart attack.

When Moriarty arrived back home, he sat in his most familiar place, the study. He buried his head in his hands and drank a glass of whisky. Everything he had tried to do up to this point had failed him. Perhaps he wasn't meant for the criminal life. Then again, he did get away with two murders. Perhaps he should concentrate on things other than love as a reason to kill. He had loved Mary ever since the day he first started tutoring her. She had a brilliant mind – one that was too good for this world. He looked at the skull once more. He wondered how it was that she was so intelligent, yet her cranium was not overdeveloped. He took another drink and sat back in his chair once more.

Later that night, Mr. George Davies was back at work, sanding down the same boat. He heard a sudden noise coming from the darkness – a whistling noise that seemed to unnerve him.

"Mr. Moriarty?" he cried out into the darkness. Then he heard the shuffling of footsteps, and a rather large man in a bowler hat stepped out of the darkness.

"Who are you?" Davies asked.

"He is a new acquaintance of mine, Mr. Davies," Moriarty replied as he also moved from the shadows. "This is Rocco. Rocco, this is Mr. Davies."

Davies looked at Rocco again, who smiled and tipped his hat.

"Now, wait just a minute, Mr. Moriarty. I was on my way to the job. I just – "

Moriarty interrupted. "Let me stop you right there. You had one task, George: Show up and kill the old man."

"I just got caught up at home, sir. My boy needed me,"

Rocco walked closer to Davies and pulled out a knife.

"You see," Moriarty explained, "Rocco is a *good* employee. He shows up on time and does his job."

Rocco shoved the knife into Davies's gut. Davies fell to his knees and tried to gasp for air. He felt the warm blood drip through his fingers as he held the wound.

"It's hard to find dedicated workers these days, Mr. Davies," Moriarty explained. Rocco then made his way around to Davies' back and pulled his head up, forcing him to look at Moriarty.

"There are not enough good workers, and money is scarce. That is why I have to let you go, George."

"Please!" Davies proclaimed. "I can make it up to you!"

"How would you do that now that you're bleeding everywhere, Davies? I think you're reaching too far for this one."

Moriarty looked at Rocco. "Another reason that Rocco is a good employee is that he doesn't make promises he knows he can't keep. He is a man who knows his limits."

Moriarty nodded at Rocco, who slit George Davies's throat. They both watched him die slowly. Rocco then bent down and took the change purse from Davies' dead body. He held it up to show Moriarty.

"Good. You may keep it as a bonus."

53

Rocco smiled and spit on Davies' corpse. Moriarty smiled at Rocco. Rocco started to whistle as he and Moriarty walked off into the shadows.

The next day, Henry the butler walked into the study. He looked around, but Moriarty was nowhere to be seen. His cigarettes were gone, but everything else remained, including the skull. Henry hated that skull and didn't understand why Moriarty kept it. He always mumbled it was for research, but exactly what research Henry had no clue. He placed a piece of cloth over the skull and slowly backed away. Then he was startled as Moriarty suddenly approached him from behind.

"Did you need something, Henry?"

The butler turned to face him. Moriarty looked bruised and battered. Henry had never seen him in such a state.

Moriarty smiled at him. He couldn't help noticing the cut above his eye. "Sir, are you all right?"

Moriarty laughed and took off his shirt to reveal even more bruising. "Of course. No need to worry. That chap, Rocco, has been teaching me a bit of boxing."

He took the shirt and wiped his bloody eye with it. "Again, did you need something?"

"Yes, sir. A letter came in the mail for you. It's from the University of Aberdeen."

Moriarty took the letter and read it. He smiled as he looked up at Henry. "They read my treatise, and have decided to offer me a position at the university. I'll be able to focus on my work, and hopefully, I can get money for research. This will be wonderful! Imagine – you and me living in Scotland, Henry. And you will have to refer to me as Professor James Moriarty . . . ."

The *X*-Marked Boxes
by David Marcum

I had joined my friend, Mr. Sherlock Holmes, late one cold night in a Great Russell Street wool shop. The owner, Mr. MacGregor, was an old acquaintance of his from those long-ago days when Holmes had lived most meagerly in nearby Montague Street. MacGregor's problem might have been considered a small case and (at that point in his successful career) not really worthy of Holmes's time – an intruder was finding his way into the shop during the wee hours when it was closed – but Holmes was fond of the old Scotsman, telling me that the shop owner had once gifted him with a tweed scarf which had subsequently held great sentimental value.

Holmes explained that MacGregor had visited him in Baker Street earlier that day to relate that for the past several mornings, his carefully arranged stock had been shifted, ever so slightly, but still obvious to the canny owner. As owner and sole employee, he knew every inch of the store and its contents. Worse – when MacGregor had straightened the items, his hands had blistered. Holmes had visited the store later that day, and an examination of a few pieces of the displaced stock – in this case some woolen scarves that were midway down in a stack – showed something unusual: Fine organic dust that, when he touched it, also caused his own fingers to blister and itch.

Separating and removing the sabotaged scarves, Holmes took them 'round to the laboratory at Barts where, with the help of a couple of old acquaintances who had worked hard to cultivate certain specialized knowledge, and also making use of assistance from the old medical librarian, he was able to ascertain that they had been dusted with crushed pieces of mucuna pruriens, a legume native to Africa and tropical Asia. The plant's seed pods and young leaves were notorious for causing itching – as evidenced on Holmes's still-affected fingers on his right hand, the backs of which displayed small red bumps for several days.

Fortunately, MacGregor confirmed that no scarves from that stack, including those doctored with the itching plant, had been sold. As other nearby stock also showed evidence of tampering, and because the shop had been violated three nights in a row, it was hoped and assumed that the next night would evince a fourth intrusion – for if the intruder had successfully entered that many times, wouldn't he be tempted to try for another? On that assumption, Holmes invited me along to lay in wait. Eating an early meal and kissing my wife goodbye for the night, I made the short trip from Queen Anne Street to Bloomsbury and entered the shop from the front as if I were a customer, hoping that no one was watching closely enough to observe that I didn't similarly exit by closing time. Holmes was already there, hidden comfortably in a back room. MacGregor had laid in sandwiches, jugs of tea, and a bottle of whisky brought down from his last trip to Inverness – "Made with the pure waters of my homeland!" he had declared with a challenging eye. I informed him of my own northern heritage, and he gave me an approving nod. Then the old Scotsman said goodnight and closed the shop as usual, locking the front door and walking away down the now-mostly empty street. We heard his echoing footsteps recede into silence, leaving the only sounds around us coming from the daily settling of the building as it cooled.

The front of the shop, just a few doors east of the Alpha Inn and directly across from the British Museum, was moderately well-lit, and we agreed that entry by way of the main door was unlikely, as foot traffic there was thin but steady and constables made regular passes along the perimeter of the Museum. Rather, the intruder was certainly going to come in by way of the single rear door that opened from a dark mews. Holmes had already confirmed fresh scratches around the keyhole, and in order to give the illicit visitor as much freedom to act as possible, we were waiting in a side room, in a nook behind shelves holding MacGregor's stacked items. The wool smell was both comforting and overwhelming, and more than once I had to stifle a sneeze. On other occasions, I would have expected Holmes to rebuke me, at least with a judgmental glance, but he had softly sneezed several times as well, and I knew that he understood that in this case, such a reaction was unavoidable.

We talked very softly of this and that, with long comfortable silences in between in the way of old friends who have known each other for two decades. He asked after my wife and my practice, and also about a mutual friend, my neighbor in Queen Anne Street, who had recently suffered an injury and sought Holmes's help in redressing the grievance. Holmes then caught me up on a few recent cases of his own, including a recent attempt to steal a sizable trove of securities from the City and Suburban Bank near the Barbican Underground Station. "A dozen years since the thieves last tried," he said, "and they almost got away with it this time. Can you believe that the bank never filled in John Clay's tunnel running from Wilson's pawn shop?[1] At the time, the bank had discussed buying out Wilson's lease, using his shop for storage, and enlarging the tunnel between the two cellars and making it permanent, but they could never come to an agreement amongst themselves, let along get to the point of approaching poor Wilson with an offer, so the plan drifted into an eddy, *spun around quietly for a while, and sank – forgotten, except by thieves who read your story and had the idea to find and re-use the tunnel."*

That led to our discussion of the recently departed Mr. Wilson, and I recalled a time when Wilson came to me for help during that period in the early nineties when Holmes was believed to be dead. Holmes had never heard the story, and of how Jabez Wilson came to be associated with a certain noted City banker, and that helped to pass a half-hour or so. [2]

Gradually our talk drifted to MacGregor and how Holmes had first met him. I already knew that there had been a presentation of the scarf from the store's owner to the needful young man – but as was often the case, there was more – much more – to the story. Refilling our small glasses of whisky, and confirming that there was no noise to alert us that anyone was trying to enter the shop (for Holmes had set a few small indicators in the alleyway that would let us know when someone arrived), we settled back, and Holmes shared the events of that cold January of 1875, during the first winter after he'd moved to London to attempt to establish himself as a consulting detective . . . .

I'd first come up to London in the summer of '74 [*Holmes related*] to spend the remaining weeks of my long vacation from school, as my original plan – rusticating for that entire time at Donnithorpe, in Norfolk – had collapsed following that ugly and uncomfortable incident at the Trevor home. Mycroft was already living in Montague Street then – Number 24, before he moved, for just a little while, to No. 42 Chad's Street, [3] and then eventually to Pall Mall – and he made room for me, mistakenly assuming that I planned to return to school in the fall, while I actually intended to remain in the capital and pursue my new profession – as soon as I built up the courage to inform my father of my decision. It must be recalled that I was but twenty years of age, and to go against the plans and wishes of one's father . . . .

Our space at No. 24 was already cramped for one – even though Mycroft wasn't quite so large in those days – and fitting in the two of us was quite the strain – although I was willing to sleep uncomfortably upon the floor, up against one of the walls and out of the way. In any case, Mycroft was already weaving his webs within the Government and making himself indispensable from morning to dusk, and I was out for most of every day, either wandering the city or spending time across the street at the British Museum, or working on chemical experiments in the laboratory at Barts – access to which being courtesy of a friend of my father's.

As I've told you before, our landlady at No. 24 was the widow of one of my father's first cousins – and this Mrs. Holmes was certainly no Mrs.

Hudson. She'd obtained the lease on the building years before, when her husband passed – almost certainly a desperate move to escape her – and she made do by renting the top three floors to a variety of tenants. On the first floor, in the most easily accessed rooms, was a tiny old woman named Mrs. Coombes, who had a small independent income, and also a proclivity for taking in small dogs and cats, in equal balance. Should she obtain a new pup, she would balance the scale by soon finding a new kitten. She worked hard at her mania, and was altogether a good neighbor. I can't recall there ever being a noise complaint, or the slightest hint of an odor problem. On the middle floor was a young chap about my age who worked across the street in the Museum – Isaiah Beddings – and Mycroft and I were on the top floor, which was useful in those days before he moved out in keeping Mycroft's weight down, as getting up there was rather like climbing a ladder into a church belfry.

It was Isaiah Beddings' situation that drew me into the business where I met Mr. MacGregor.

Holmes paused in his tale. "But you lived in this neighborhood at one time as well, as I recall," he said, "between when you graduated medical school and joining the Army. It was always a cozy little district – we all seemed to know one another to varying degrees. Yet you and I never ran across one another – that we remember. How is it that you didn't meet MacGregor in those days?"

I shifted in my seat and took a sip of whisky. "When I graduated in '78, I had enough saved, along with a small inheritance, to rent the small practice in Southampton Street. From my lodgings and practice at No. 6, I did venture up this way on occasion to drink at the Alpha – and we've discussed before how odd it was that we didn't meet either there or at Barts, where I also spent time between patients, instead of several years later when we did *meet after I returned from Maiwand. But in truth, patients were few and far between, and instead of roaming north and west into Bloomsbury during my free time, or doing as you did between clients, working on increasing the breadth of my professional knowledge, I generally headed down toward the Strand or the theatre district to pursue less-improving paths. After a year or so of waiting hopelessly day after day – rather like Hatherley when he set himself up as a hydraulic engineer, sitting along in his office for someone to seek him out, or when Doyle filled his time between rare patients scratching out his tedious historical novels – I decided to try something else and joined the Army."*

Holmes nodded. "And it all worked out for the best."

Recalling the pains from my military experiences that still assailed me from time to time, and that never entirely went away, even after more than two decades, I could still only agree.

I had stopped into the Alpha [4] one evening, [*Holmes continued*] having just earned a few shillings for a small piece of work much like what we're doing tonight – hiding and waiting for a bad fellow to show up where he wasn't supposed to be. I had spent most of the past three days down in the crypts of St. Paul's working out a little problem for the Bishop of London. It isn't worth retelling – I know that look, Watson, but the truly interesting part of the tale is that the Bishop decided to hire me in the first place. Just twenty years old and with no professional reputation to speak of, I should have been the last person he approached for assistance, but he'd heard of me from a friend of a friend . . . In any case, having located a long-buried lock-box alongside one of the eight support piers, and also having trapped the man who had learned of it and then led us to it, I was ready to return to the surface world. What shocked me was the bone-chilling cold that had settled upon London while I was down for so long in the relatively warm cavern of the cathedral's vast cellars.

I realized when I surfaced that my birthday [5] had passed during one of the days I was hidden in the crypt, but that was of no account. I had a tidy little fee in my pocket, but with the next month's rent due, I didn't want to waste part of it upon a cab, so I chose to walk back to my lodgings. It isn't much over a mile from St. Paul's to Montague Street, even with the twists and turnings of the streets, but I painfully felt every step as I faced into the icy wind, seemingly blowing from whichever direction that I turned, holding my hat to my head, lest it be blown eastward into the darkness. I recall that the skies were clear that night, with a bright moon that in contrast made the streets and alleys and areaways seem especially dark with menace. I also had the sense that there was a hint of dampness in the wind that promised rain by morning, or – if these bitter temperatures continued – snow.

Realizing that opportunities for a warm meal upon reaching my lodgings were very limited – due to both the late hour and my landlady's sour disposition – I made the decision when I reached Great Russell Street that I would part with a few coins after all and turned toward the Alpha. Walking the short distance down the dark street, I was soon inside and settled into a table near one of the windows looking into Museum Street.

Even at that time of night, the place was still halfway full, and there was a low steady murmur of conversation all around me. I was faced with the choice of what to order, and I was jealously hoarding my funds, for the rent was nearly due. By then I was responsible for all of it, Mycroft having moved out several months before. This was less than a year after my decision to become a consulting detective, you'll recall, and in those few months, circumstances had greatly changed. After my decision to become a detective, I threw myself into studies that would benefit my new profession.

I knew all of this, of course, for I'd heard it before, but Holmes was in a narrative mood, and revealing the details of an old case – which always interested me, and wasn't too common of an occurrence – so I was more than happy to pass the quiet moments letting him tell it his own way, in an uncharacteristic and comfortably rambling fashion.

I spent my time studying at the Museum and at Barts and other hospitals. I intruded on as many police investigations as I could, even if I simply stood in the crowd and watched over shoulders as the officers shuffled about where the crime had occurred, carelessly destroying evidence like a wandering herd of moor ponies, blithely going where they would. And I realized that to truly learn what I needed, I'd also have to seek out the criminals and get them to teach me their skills – all while hoping for the occasional case that would give me both practical experience and funds for food and lodging – and the occasional excellent beer at the Alpha.

When I'd told my father that I was changing professions, he was predictably unsupportive – and literally so as well, stopping my funds entirely. The plans he had for his sons required that I become an engineer, and no variation was allowed. Mycroft was more accepting – or indifferent – and he arranged for me to retain the Montague Street rooms when he moved to Chad's Street in late '74, as his position required that he reside in better lodgings reflecting his increased responsibilities. His support then was crucial, and there were many times when his charity supplemented my income – and what he provided to me during some months, along with an occasional brotherly lecture, was all that kept me from starving or being evicted.

But January 1875 was neither the best nor the worst of my times in Montague Street, and I had some spare change, and my trip to the Alpha that night led to an interesting case.

As I waited for my sausages and potatoes and a pint of beer, I let the warmth of the room thaw me out – except for the back of my head, which was near one of the large plate windows looking out over the street. I could feel the cold radiating off the glass, and I pressed forward over the small table to get away from it. I was considering a move to a better, warmer

60

spot when I heard a low argument in the back of the pub, gradually rising over the other conversations.

I glanced that way to see Old MacGregor and Isaiah Beddings, both seated at that table in the back – you know the one, where everyone prefers to sit because it's away from both doors. They were both leaning in to speak intensely, their attempts to remain quiet negated as they tried to talk over one another, getting louder and louder. MacGregor was then in his early fifties, and much more invigorated than the man we know now. Isaiah Beddings, about my age – about twenty or so – was doing most of the talking, but when McGregor would sometimes get in the occasional word, it would make the young man respond all the more vigorously.

There was always something very naïve about Isaiah. It wasn't just his wide-eyed view of the world, an expression that looked perpetually surprised. He truly was often surprised, expressing it in a multitude of ways, even during short conversations. He was tall, several inches above my own height, with broad bony shoulders that were hunched forward, taking away several inches, and more were lost by the way he held his head forward instead of upright on his long thin neck. I knew from his uniform that he was something of an apprentice guard at the Museum, although I'd never actually seen him in the public areas during my time there. What I didn't yet know was that, at that stage of his burgeoning career with the Museum, his time was spent in the bowels of the building, crating and uncrating exhibits, and the only guarding that he did was of those unseen items which were not being displayed on the public floors of the building.

Their discussion went on for some three or four minutes and, while it didn't have the effect of shutting down the rest of the conversations in the room, it did cause many to glance that way a number of times as people paused, trying to catch a sense of what was being said – and whether they should be concerned if it escalated to violence. Finally, having apparently heard enough, Isaiah abruptly pushed his chair back and stood. It seemed as if he had another thing to say, but he instead bit his tongue – he actually tucked it between his front teeth and held it there – and turned and departed, passing just by my table as the waiter brought my food. There was nearly a disastrous accident as they almost collided, but fortunately the waiter pulled back just before he was overrun by the angry young man.

My food was placed before me, and I was in the process of sawing off the end of a perfectly browned sausage, when MacGregor also went rushing past my table, seemingly following after the young man who had just banged out the front door. But then, just past me, the older man slowed and stopped, looking ahead uncertainly as if locked in indecision. The rest of the patrons had returned to their own interests and conversations, but I

61

continued to look up at MacGregor, observing him as I chewed thoughtfully.

I knew of him in a most casual way, as I was aware of so many in that neighborhood, but I didn't *know* him. I had walked by his shop countless times over the last few months since my first arrival in London, but I'd never had any thought of stopping in, and never foresaw a reason that I ever would.

I took another bite of the sausage, and then the potatoes, swirling both in the brown onion gravy that even then the pub made so well, aware that it was already cooling too soon and that I needed to eat faster. It was then that MacGregor turned back to his table. But as he passed by me, he stopped and turned his stern gaze my way.

"Ye would be that fella that fancies himself a detective," he growled in his strong brogue.

My mouth full, I could only nod.

"Wait here," he said – As if I would abandon my sausage! – before walking to the rear, retrieving his half-empty glass from his table, and then returning to my own. "If you don't mind," he said, sitting down without a response, his back to the bar.

"Ye saw what happened," he said in a low growl.

I nodded. "An argument, apparently. But I couldn't hear what it was about."

His eyes narrowed. Clearly he'd sat down to share some of his business – but he didn't like the idea.

"Isaiah is my grandson," he said. He saw my raised eyebrow. "Oh, I know he doesn't sound Scottish, but he was raised in the South – near Oakmoor, in Staffordshire. My daughter – my only child – married a sassenach who worked there in the nearby Alton train station – the Churnet Valley line, serving Morton's copper works. He and my daughter . . . they were killed a few months ago in a railway accident in nearby Crewe." He cleared his throat. "The sassenach – that is to say, my son-in-law, Stephen – he tried to save a poor woman trapped in the wreckage who had come back to England from India not long before. My daughter was initially uninjured, and raced to help him . . . and then . . . Well, there was an explosion . . . ."

He fell silent for a moment, and I felt that it would be impolite to saw off another bite of sausage just then while he gathered his thoughts back to the Alpha on that cold January night. But then he refocused on me, and I continued with my meal.

"I don't blame my son-in-law. He was doing his duty – even if it did get them both killed. After the accident, Isaiah came down here, to London, and I found him a job in the Museum, and rooms in your building.

62

It wasn't my first choice – dealing with that shrewish woman – " Then he stopped himself. "But you're both named Holmes. The landlady isn't your mother, I hope?"

I shook my head and swallowed. Then, after taking a drink of beer, I said, "A distant relative. And shrewish is a polite way to describe her. You were speaking of Isaiah. He and I – we know each other just well enough to speak in passing, but that's all."

"He's a good boy. I'd work him in the wool shop if it would support the two of us, but it won't. The same for a place to stay – my rooms are only big enough for me, and not another full-grown man. But I found him a place in the neighborhood – right across the street from the Museum and just around the corner from me – and it doesn't get much better than that. Or so I thought – but now he's in trouble, and that's what I want to ask you about. In your capacity as a *detective*."

He said the last word with a bit of emphatic distaste, as if he were forcing himself to speak with some sort of low criminal. And in those days, I suppose that might not have been entirely wrong. I had set myself up as a "consulting detective" – what I perceived as the first of that profession – but there were already lots of government detectives and lots of private ones, and some weren't fit for the job due to lack of knowledge or experience or ability, and others were corrupt. Too many displayed all of hese aspects. I had the sense that MacGregor had dealt with some of these before, but now a situation had arisen with his grandson where he needed help – and I had been sitting right in front of him at just that moment.

"Isaiah is worried about his job, and he wants to do the right thing – but he's also worried about getting his new Museum friends into trouble, and being seen by them as untrustworthy. I told him that he has to report whatever it is that he's seen, but he became angry. He said that he wished he'd never told me about it, and that it was a mistake, and that – but you saw. He stood up and walked out and refuses to talk any more."

I had nearly finished eating by then, having hurried the latter half a bit more than I would have liked. I held up a hand. "Wait – Please tell me exactly what he said."

MacGregor nodded and raised his glass. Finishing it, he said, "Wait a moment," and rose, nodding toward my glass. I shook my head. He obtained another beer at the bar, returned to his seat, and spoke again.

"Isaiah has worked at the Museum since November, not more than a couple of months, starting just after he came to London when his parents died. I had the job lined up when he arrived, thinking that it was best for him to jump right in, and not waste time grieving. He's a smart lad, and had a year or two of university before deciding that it didn't suit him. To be honest, Mr. Holmes, he doesn't yet know what does suit him, but he had to do something. I know McGinty, who is a guard of supervisory standing, and he obtained an entry job for the lad, with an eye toward being a full guard, once he's learned all the ways of the place and paid his dues.

"One doesn't simply start in the Museum proper, you understand, dealing with the public on the first day. Instead, a new guard is trained for several years behind the scenes, becoming familiar with the workings and the hidden parts. Isaiah has already seen a lot, and all that he tells me is fascinating. I've been in my shop for over twenty-five years – down here in London, while my brother keeps track of the other end of the business in Edinburgh – and I never knew a fraction of what Isaiah shared with me. Cellars upon cellars of things that may never be exhibited. What they show to the public, young Mr. Holmes, is just a fraction of a fraction of what they actually have in storage, brought back from all over the world. Egyptian things, and Oriental, and African. Old idols and books and artworks and sculptures – the best from every land that we've touched, all right here in London, preserved and safeguarded from those natives who wouldn't appreciate or take care of it if left where it was found."

I nodded, but chose not to interrupt him by either replying that the idea of appropriating art from other nations was ethically questionable, or by stating that I was already aware of what he related about the Museum, having made my own friend among the young guards who had managed to sneak me inside and below-stairs on a few occasions.

"And Isaiah stumbled across something dishonest?" I prompted.

"He has – but I don't know what. He started to tell me about it – said there's someone there that's a wrong 'un – but then stopped. I spoke too quickly. I said that whatever it is, he has to report it. That's when the argument started, and – Well, you saw. He left."

We were silent for a few moments, and I finished my beer. One would be enough for me, but MacGregor finished his and rose for yet another – the third that I knew about, and who knew how many he'd had before I arrived? Still, he showed no signs of inebriation. Then he sat back down, took a long pull, wiped his mouth, and said, "Will you help me? Help us? Help Isaiah?"

I considered all of the unanswered questions. I really knew nothing about the situation – but that was a challenge, not a hindrance. I had the payment from my last investigation in my pocket, and the rent was covered for the month, and part of the next as well, and most of all, this seemed like an opportunity to gain further experience. Not only did I have to find the solution to Isaiah's problem, but I also had to determine what exactly the problem was. It seemed like a good chance for me to add to my so-far limited experience, as another case, no matter how large or small, would help me improve my skills

I nodded. "I'll look into it tomorrow."

MacGregor nodded. "Thank you, young Mr. Holmes. I'll be forever grateful."

Although I was tired, and it was time to return to my room, I had one stop to make – at the nearby lodgings of Foster Belkirk, the young guard who had managed to get me inside the Museum on a few different occasions for an unseen tour of its non-public treasures.

Foster was always a pleasant fellow, heavy-set with wide naïve eyes, startlingly blue, and reddish hair and cheeks. By the time I met him the previous summer, he'd already worked at the Museum for a couple of years, and had navigated his way through the apprenticeship that Isaiah Beddings had just begun. Foster was smart, having won the Fortiscue Prize several years before at the College of St. Luke's before deciding that, rather than pursuing an academic path as was laid out for him, he instead wanted to retain his amateur status and seek enlightenment elsewhere. We had that in common, as I had also turned aside from my proscribed professional training – but his father was much more supportive than mine, being simply proud that his son was happy and making his way.

Foster had married several months before I met him, and now his wife, Violet, was expecting their first child. Based on how the child was being carried, they were certain that it was a boy. When I expressed skepticism one night when invited to dinner at their humble flat, they had explained the old wives' tale that carrying low and in front means to expect a boy. "My granny is sure of it!" Violet said with sincere urgency, and I didn't want to argue with her, although I was tempted to respond that Granny certainly had a fifty-per-cent chance of being right. Still, it crossed my mind that there might be some scientific reasoning behind these claims, and that there might be some study to be undertaken someday comparing predictions as based on presentation during pregnancy versus the actual birth results. It might be of some value – but with all I already had on my plate in terms of things to learn for my new profession, I had no time to waste on that.

"Good thing, too," I interrupted. "That idea is poppy-cock."

Holmes smiled. "Watson, if you keep saying things like 'poppy-cock', you'll end up being one of those calcified relics who can't climb out of his club chair, covered with Trichinopoly ash from where you fell asleep while smoking it. Turned fifty recently, didn't you, Old Man?"

Before I could respond, he held up a hand. "Peace, Watson. Now, to continue . . . ."

I'd once had occasion to help Foster and Violet find her wedding ring – a simple bit of deduction after questioning her and realizing that she had taken it off while baking and left it behind the flour tin. Ever after, they felt that they owed me greatly, and when I explained what I needed the next morning, Foster readily agreed and, even though it was getting late, he immediately set about obtaining what I'd requested.

My vigilant landlady, Mrs. Holmes, heard me when I entered, indicating that I needed to improve silent entry as one of my burgeoning detective skills. She stood in the doorway of her parlour, castigating me as I crossed by her to reach the narrow stairway. By the time I'd fully ignored her, she was snarling and pacing like a frenzied dog while I climbed upwards to the next floor and, had she truly been a canine, I have no doubt that her ill-temper would have caused her to freeze onto my ankle and cause a ten-day injury.

I had thought of MacGregor's problem during the very short walk back to No. 24, and by the time I turned out the lights and went to sleep, I knew that my plan would be, first thing in the morning.

I was up early – as is my way when there is work to be done – and before seven o'clock, I was back at Foster Belkirk's modest rooms, where he had obtained a Museum guard's uniform for me to wear. I was to accompany him to work that day, ostensibly as a new trainee, to see what I could see. "It won't be a problem," he explained. "There are always new faces about, and some don't last very long. Besides guards for the main facility, there are other sites where objects are stored – space at the Museum is limited, you understand – and you can pretend to be one of those other guards, transferred over for a day or so. No one will give you a second glance. Pay attention, jump in and help once in a while if needed, and otherwise keep an eye on Isaiah."

Although Foster tended to gossip a bit more than he should have, I felt that I had to confide my reasons for seeking his help, and he understood that whatever was going on needed to be kept quiet. "I haven't seen anything odd myself," he said, "but then I haven't been looking. It's a fault of mine, I suppose – I assume the best. It makes the days much more pleasant, you understand."

He kept looking at me with a grin on his face until I warned him to stop. I was in disguise, having altered my features with a false nose, makeup to provide different planes to my face, and pads to change the shape of my head. I felt that it was necessary so that Isaiah wouldn't notice me. While not up to the level of disguise that I managed to achieve in later years – especially after my time touring America with the Sassanoff troupe – it would be sufficient for a day or two in the dark bowels of the Museum.

We walked from Foster's residence in Guilford Street, near the foundling hospital, and around to the big rear entrance in Montague Place, with my uniform serving as a badge of entry. No one looked twice at me and, when Foster led me to where Isaiah generally worked, he left me to it.

I won't describe the full nature of my day, but in learning to be an apprentice guard, I felt that I was instead practicing to be a uniformed stevedore. My time was mostly spent moving boxes, opening boxes, emptying boxes, refilling boxes, nailing boxes shut, moving and opening and emptying and filling and closing more boxes, and so on. It was January, but quite warm in that hidden part of the Museum, and the ill-fitting borrowed wool uniform was most unpleasant. A great deal of the day was focused on worrying about whether my disguise would give up and slide down my face at an inopportune moment, but fortunately no one seemed interested in paying me any attention at all, once I had answered a summons to present myself at this or that box and do something useful.

Over the course of the day, I constantly shifted myself around to keep Isaiah in site, and I was pleased to see that he was one of the hardest-working young men in the group. But even has he did all the things that I was doing, with much-more practiced ease, he also kept his eye repeatedly on another fellow – and thinking that this must be the "wrong 'un" that he described to his grandfather, I gradually pivoted my attention to keep him in sight as well.

The supervisors called him "Todd Allen" – always by first and last name: "Todd Allen, grab that pry bar," or "Todd Allen, load that dolly with the small black boxes." I almost began to wonder if it was a hyphenated first name – it was not – since many other of the apprentices were addressed by just one name. My false name was "Victor Trevor", the first that had come to mind, and the few times it was called, it was simply, "Trevor!"

Todd Allen was also in his early twenties, but already bald. He had a very round head and weak chin on a thin neck, and a film of short-shorn whiskers upon his face. His eyes were squinty and rat-like, and this matched his thick lips, always in a half-grin that displayed his yellowing buck teeth that looked as if they needed to be worn down some. He looked like an earless rat. He stayed on the move, but I also noticed that he worked much less than the others, finding sly ways to stand back when his peers turned toward some more-difficult task. And I was fortunate enough to be watching when he took great pains to take possession of one of the smaller flat wooden boxes sent up from the basement, mark it surreptitiously with a faint chalk "X", and set it to one side.

As part of our work, we moved loaded boxes from delivery carts that had come from off-site storage areas, containing objects being brought in for new exhibits, and likewise we shifted boxes outward, to be carried away and back into storage. I was lucky enough to be watching when Todd Allen picked up the X-marked box and carried it to a furtive little driver who waited to one side, nothing else on his cart. He couldn't help looking around to see if he was being noticed, actually drawing more attention to himself than if he'd simply accepted the box without any indication that something was going on. He didn't see me watching – nor did he notice Isaiah, who was also looking with great interest. The furtive man laid the box in his cart, covered it with a dark tarpaulin, mounted the driver's seat, and departed.

This, I was certain, must be the activity that had worried Isaiah Beddings and, seeing it for myself, I also concluded that something illegal, or at least questionable, was afoot.

I also knew that I would have to return the next day and attempt to find out what Todd Allen was up to.

That night, I stopped by Foster's apartment to tell him that I needed another day in the Museum. I described what I'd seen, and he was in agreement that something wasn't right. "I spent my apprenticeship in that room," he agreed, "and there's no reason for a single box like that to go with a single driver. If there weren't so many new employees down there, they'd likely recognize which ones are the regular Museum-hired drivers who shuttle the big loads to and from storage."

After speaking with Foster, and turning down Violet's offer for a hot meal, I found a few of the neighborhood lads and hired them for the next day. This was a couple of years before I met Wiggins, and there was no thought then of organizing them into what would become the Irregulars – but as I occasionally used them, I did get more and more used to the idea, and then began to count on them for certain types of jobs. Following a cart through the streets of London was an ideal use of their special skills. Then I directed my steps to the wool shop, to report to Mr. MacGregor – but even though I was able to tell him about Todd Allen and the odd box, he seemed unimpressed with my progress, so I finished our conversation quickly and returned to No. 24.

I had neglected to recall that I was still wearing the guard uniform, though Mrs. Holmes was quick to notice it.

"So you've found a real job, then?" she sneered. "Your father will be pleased, I suppose."

"Are you spying on me for him, then?" I asked, forgetting my primary rule of avoiding any engagements with her at all cost. It was worth it, however, to see that she reacted with unexpected guilt, as if in mentioning

68

communications with my father, she had revealed something secret. I pressed my advantage.

"How quickly will you tell him?" I asked with apparent enthusiasm. "About my new job? It looks to be the start of a promising career." It was my hope that she would make a quick report, and that when the truth was discovered, she would lose all credibility. The plan was doomed, however, when she quickly progressed in a different direction.

"I'll tell him, all right," she said. "And I'll also mention that you're likely to lose the job in less than a week!"

She had outplayed me. By framing her news in that way, the subsequent report that I wasn't actually working at the Museum would be taken that she was correct, and that I'd been sacked before I could truly begin.

She was still baying and growling at me when I turned away and mounted the steep steps.

I was up early the next day, as I wanted to consult with Mycroft before my day at the Museum began. He didn't appreciate me arriving while still carrying out his morning ablutions, but I was able to snare some of his breakfast before he could eat it – not for the first time. Fortunately he had more than enough to spare, despite his bluster.

Unlike Mrs. Holmes the night before, he instantly perceived that the uniform I was wearing did not indicate that I'd found new employment, and I told him something of the case. He listened, but didn't turn his great mind toward offering any useful suggestions, as he also knew that I was there to see him for a different reason.

"If you continue living there," he said, cutting to the chase, "then you'll either have to learn to put up with her, or find more creative ways to get in and out without encountering her."

"You know that's impossible," I said. "She has a most meaningless existence, with nothing to do but rise up at any noise and start barking. She'd make a wonderful watchdog, but she's a terrible landlady."

"Nevertheless."

"Did you . . ." I had reached the central nugget of my concern. "Did you know she is reporting on me – to Father?"

"Of course I knew," he said. "Are you truly surprised? Just because he's cut you off doesn't mean that he stopped taking an interest in you, or caring about you – or hoping you'll come to your senses, according to his lights."

"But all he'll ever hear from her is the worst – twisted to present me in the worst possible manner!"

"And I," he said with a look of mostly concealed fondness, "will continute to counter whatever she tells him with my own more-positve reports."

I found that my jaw was agape. "Close your mouth," Mycroft commanded. "Surely you aren't surprised that I would also be enlisted to send news about you back toYorkshire. Father knows, as well as you do, that whatever I report will be factual and untarnished, compared to whatever the unfortunate Mrs. Holmes misinterprets or concocts. And never fear, Sherlock – on balance, what I've told father has been positive. And he's not as angry with you as you've feared. He only wishes to nudge you – most vigorously, I'll admit – back onto the path he laid out before you were even born. You have to decide whether you'll give in to him, or keep setting your own course.

"Now, aren't you due at the Museum soon?"

Foster didn't need to take me into the Museum that morning, as I was now already accepted as one of the new recruits. Knowing what to expect, I'd done a much better job on my makeup so that it wasn't a constant worry.

The day progressed much as had the one before, and I had time to recall Mycroft's words. There was much to ponder in them, but that would be something to examine at some other point, over a pipe. On this day, I had to pay attention.

Isaiah Beddings continued to watch Todd Allen, who continued to subtly shirk his tasks. As the day progressed, I began to fear that nothing would happen to advance my investigation. Then, in mid-afternoon, I saw that another X-marked box had appeared, apparently carried up from wherever all these other boxes came from. Clearly there was someone else involved in a different department, preparing the boxes and seeing that they were delivered for the next phase of the operation.

Over the course of a half-hour, Todd Allen worked around to pick up and carry out the X-box – and he took it over to the same furtive driver, who accepted delivery and laid it in the cart. My plans were in place, and I had the lads on either end of Montague Place ready to follow, whichever way the driver departed. But then I noted with horror that there were *two* carts of that type just then, both nearly empty and about to leave, and they wouldn't know which one it was. I raced back inside, grabbed my overcoat, hat, and scarf from the hooks along one wall, and ran back outside, thinking that whatever happened, it was unlikely that I needed to return to that temporary and uncompensated employment.

Luckily, Todd Allen had already returned inside and, in the milling confusion just outside the great door, I was able to get to the cart as the driver worked to turn it around and tie my scarf to the cart's back gate. No one seemed to notice, most importantly the driver, and in a moment he was ready to leave. Seeing that he and the other similar cart were both turning east toward Russell Square, I hurried out ahead of them and looked for young Garland, the boy watching on that side. He spotted me and came running over.

Out of breath, I hurriedly explained, "It's that one – with my scarf tied to it."

He nodded and, with nothing further to be said, set off in pursuit. I knew that the other boys would shift and follow, racing ahead and regrouping and adjusting their arrangement as the cart continued on its way.

Still in my borrowed uniform, I settled into a small teashop in Russell Square, knowing that I couldn't go back to No. 24 to wait for word, as the hateful Mrs. Holmes would never bother to let me know that a street urchin was waiting at the door with a message for me, and most certainly she wouldn't let him inside to deliver it upstairs in person.

In less than an hour, Garland was back, out of breath but with good news. "In the mews," he wheezed, "between Harrison and Sidmouth Street. Just near Regent Square. Martin and Lloyd are still watching."

I nodded, fished out some funds for Garland out of my earnings from the Bishop, and set off to take a look at where the X-box had ended up.

It was a narrow passage with empty stables on both sides. Many were padlocked, now used for storage of goods instead of shelter for horses. Knowing that many were likely now tenanted by costermongers, I wondered if the cart driver had that connection but, walking through the muse and casually glancing into the open stable, I saw that there was nothing like a costermonger's wares stored there – just a row of small empty boxes of the size that I'd seen marked with an X – and on a low rough-hewn wooden table, a stack of framed paintings!

I knew that I had to get a look at those paintings, but I was uncertain as to how. I was wearing my overcoat, so my borrowed guard togs were covered. Thus, if I stepped inside and initiated a conversation, there would be no indication that I had followed from the Museum. With no better plan, that's what I did.

The day was bright and bitterly cold, the temperature having dropped considerably overnight. Inside the chamber, the air felt twenty degrees warmer, though still bitter, but it was also quite dark, with only one lamp on the low table beside the frames. As I approached, I could see that they were all rather plain – like nothing that would have been hung in the Museum. Had I made some sort of mistake?

71

The driver had been talking to another fellow, over a foot taller, and dressed in an expensive-looking wool coat that looked almost warm enough for the January freeze. While much was hidden in the dim light, I could see that his hair was freshly trimmed, as was his short beard. He looked to be about fifty, and his voice sounded smooth and refined while he spoke to the driver, although I couldn't hear what was being said. He stopped speaking when he noticed my approach, turning smoothly to face me.

"What do you want?" he asked, and I could hear a trace of a German accent. "Be gone. This is private property."

"I'm just looking for my sister," I said, a whine in my voice, and continuing to approach. "She's been missing these three days. Disappeared just around here, she did. Thought maybe you might have seen her."

"We have not. Now get out."

But I kept walking closer to the table, sidling to one side to get a look at the stacked frames. I still couldn't see what they were, but in my inexperience, I suppose that I telegraphed my interest in the paintings too obviously. With a growl, and no other warning, the taller man took a step for me, suddenly swinging his stick, which I had not noticed him holding by his side.

It was lucky that I was able to lean back, as the weighted knob of the thing *swished* by my face with just a whisker's width of space. But in so doing, it connected with my false nose, knocking it askew and alerting the two men that I truly was not what I seemed, and worthy of their concern after all.

Then I was scrabbling backwards, trying to get away from the taller man as he pressed his advantage, swinging this way and that with his stick, and never a word being uttered by either of us. The little driver, however, started bouncing up and down as if he were at a prize fight: "Hit him!" he cried. "Hit him! Hit him!" – over and over again, as if the taller man needed this advice. In fact, hitting me was already his sole strategy.

I don't know how it would have ended if Garland and some of his friends hadn't been watching, having decided to see how this jolly affair progressed. In spite of their natural suspicion of authority, one of them sought a constable who soon arrived and waded in, swinging his own stick at the foreigner's head and blowing his whistle as he did so, summoning more of his brethren.

I didn't know any of them, and more importantly they didn't know me, so any explanation of who I was and what I was doing there was essentially useless. However, one of them did at least listen, telling the tall

72

man to be quiet when he attempted to have me arrested and removed without any further discussion.

In truth, I wasn't sure that I had any good leg to stand on. When I was allowed a chance to speak, and explain how I'd arrived there, and to direct attention to the stacked frames, I had a sinking feeling. One of the constables started standing them up, one by one, to show that they were all amateur and poorly executed paintings of circus clowns.

I recalled Foster telling me that some of the items that regularly left the Museum were donations of poor quality that, while of great value to the donor, held no actual value from the perspective of the institution. Were these, then, that type of object – amateur paintings that were donated and then rejected, culled by a wise curator and summarily sent away to whomever would take them? Had the X-marked boxes been so designated because they held clown paintings that were of interest to some private collector, to be packed separately and put into the care of the little driver? Was the tall Germanic man with the lethal cane actually a collector of clown paintings?

That seemed to be the case, as he was confirming that the paintings had been sent to him from the Museum, and that he had a special interest in that unique topic. Meanwhile, my thoughts raced as I tried to weigh whether or not such a tale could be true, and whether I had committed a major and embarrassing mistake.

And as I considered what was happening, the constable still holding one of the paintings happened to turn it over, so that I could see the back – and I saw the solution.

The clown painting that had been visible had been poorly mounted, as if it wasn't quite squared before being nailed to the wooden frame, and thus it had a small loose ripple in the canvas running diagonally across the front. But when the back of the painting was revealed, that canvas was stretched tight – nary a ripple in sight.

I knew that further examination was necessary – and that if I asked permission, it would not be given.

Moving suddenly, I stepped to the table and picked up one of the framed paintings.

"Here now!" growled one of the constables, moving to prevent me, while the tall man cried, "What are you doing?" Ignoring both of them, and feeling on both the front and back of that painting, I realized that I was correct. The tall man continued yelling, trying to stop me, and the constables were all barking warnings, but I ignored them and pushed the canvas out of the back of the frame with my thumbs, dislodging the painting and causing it to pop onto the table. The small nails used to tack the clown to the stretching frame were exposed – and also the fact that

73

underneath the clown canvas, the edges of a second canvas were just visible.

Just as I turned to show what I'd found to the constable in charge, explaining what it meant, the small driver bolted, which only served to confirm that something shady was going on. But Garland stepped forward and tripped him, and he sprawled for only seconds before he was dragged upright in the grip of two officers. Meanwhile, another placed himself beside the tall man while I worked the nails loose, peeling off the dreadful clown portrait to reveal an artwork of much finer quality – a landscape by one of the minor Dutch masters.

All of the clown pictures held the same secrets – lesser-known works from various Continental artists. The tall man, a German named Kreitzer, was a dealer who had set up the scheme whereby an agent of his named Daniels, working within the Museum, would identify lesser-known works that were in storage, as there was no room to hang them all in the Museum proper. He would reframe them underneath the terrible clown portraits and, now in cheap and unassuming frames, Daniels would log them as rejected donations, crate them and mark with an *X*, and then send them out by way of Todd Allen to the German dealer. Their operation had been going on for weeks, undetected, and they had become confident. There were so many stored minor paintings to steal that they had increased the deliveries to nearly daily. Dozens more works of the same value were found in Daniels' small basement room at the Museum, and there was really no defense when they were all tried and convicted later that winter.

With the thanks of the constables, and having given the one in charge one of my few cards so that I could be notified if needed, I once again expressed my appreciation to Garland, paid him more from my dwindling funds, and went around to MacGregor's shop to report. Though obviously disappointed after my previous visit the night before, he now seemed to be impressed – though it wasn't expressed in any effusive way.

"If you don't mind," he said in his northern manner, "I'll tell Isaiah that he doesn't have to worry about it any longer. It might embarrass him if we both let him know."

I nodded. The case was finished now, and how Isaiah found out what happened was of no consequence to me.

MacGregor then raised a thick eyebrow. "Your scarf," he said. "The one you tied to the cart – it seems that you left it behind."

I raised a hand to my throat. He was right – it had never occurred to me. As I considered whether it might still be in the mews if I hurried back, MacGregor raised a hand.

"Did it mean anything special to you?" he asked.

74

I shook my head. "Just something that I bought last fall, when the weather started to turn cold."

He nodded. "I saw it the other night. One tends to observe things like that, if you're in my profession. It was rather cheap, wasn't it?"

Without waiting for an answer, he turned to one side and reached across to a stack of wool scarves Taking one – a very fine one indeed – he shuffled back and handed it to me.

"We'll settle up what I owe you in a moment, but for now, take this – with my compliments, young Mr. Holmes . . . ."

"The scarf that you mentioned earlier," I said.

"This scarf," Holmes replied, waving a hand to the table where his Inverness, hat, and scarf were lying. "The one I lost had no sentimental value, but I wouldn't trade this one for the world."

I recognized it, of course, having seen it off-and-on for over twenty years. It was about nine inches wide and six feet long, fringed on the ends, and displayed a complex brown-and-black houndstooth pattern. I had long-ago noted that it was of the very finest wool. "This one is sentimental," I said, "but yet, you were willing to alter it – for that's the same scarf you've used in the past – that night on the docks, for instance, in '88, when we cornered a couple of the Rippers and you used the weights that had been sewn into the end as something resembling a Thuggee *noose."*

Holmes nodded. "When I asked, a few years later, MacGregor was more than willing to make the alterations necessary to add the weights. It's saved my life on more than one occasion. Yours too, as a matter of fact."

And then he abruptly stopped whispering, as there was a scratching sound coming from the rear door.

It was one of the easier captures we'd ever made: A bloodless runt of a fellow named Cyril Funt, who had conceived a hatred of MacGregor for not being willing to discount a hat to the price that Funt was willing to pay. There had apparently been a disagreement – though to hear MacGregor's later explanation, to him it had been so next-to-nothing that he barely remembered it. But Funt had brooded and festered after the encounter and, in his position at the nearby University of London dealing with various plants from beyond the coasts of England, he'd conceived the notion that he would taint MacGregor's stock, thereby ruining the store's reputation. It was a tedious little plan, poorly conceived, and he after he was caught, and when he'd lost his job and spent a few months in prison, he had an even greater grudge against the wool merchant.

"He will bear watching," advised Holmes that night, and MacGregor gave a dark nod.

Outside, with the little man in custody and MacGregor's shop once again buttoned up against the night, Holmes and I stood under a gaslight, facing the dark Museum across the way.

"Time for a pint?" Holmes asked, nodding down toward the Alpha.

My initial inclination was to shake my head. I was ready to head back to Queen Anne Street, as my consulting hours came early. Such a reply was on my lips when I suddenly changed it.

"Why not? Time for one, before they close."

I let him lead me inside, recalling the many times that I had been there, both as a medical student and during the short time after that when I'd had a practice nearby, and later in Holmes's company. Time was passing, but the old tavern never seemed to change, and it was a comfort, knowing that some places like that were always a fixed point and unchanging – or at least changing so slowly that they would seem to remain safe havens during the years of my own lifetime.

And as always, the beer at the Alpha was excellent . . . .

NOTES

1. Mr. Jabez Wilson's former pawn shop, 42 Charterhouse Square, London (as photographed by David Marcum, London, 17 September, 2013):

2. See "The Red Headed League", 25 October, 1890, and published in *The Strand* in August 1891.

3. For more details of the Chad Street residence, see *Enter the Lion*, 23-30 November, 1875. (Narrated by by Mycroft Holmes, and edited by Michael P. Hodel and Sean M. Wright)

4. The "Alpha Inn" is actually The Museum Tavern, located at 49 Great Russell Street, London, just across from the British Museum, and around the corner from both Holmes's former residence at No. 24 Montague Street and also Watson's first practice (before joining the Army) at No. 6 Southampton Place (now Southampton Place). The Tavern is sometimes called The Alpha Inn because of the various *A*'s worked into the outer woodwork – an example of which is shown in the photo below, within the oval inset. (Photo by David Marcum, London, 1 June, 2024)

5.   Holmes was born on 6 January, 1854. For those who consistently see him as fixed in middle age, he would have just turned twenty-one at the time of this narrative.

The Neopolitan Complexity
by Roger Riccard

Chapter I

As I have often mentioned in these little sketches of mine, my friend Sherlock Holmes is a consummate actor. He has several connections in London's theatrical circles dating back to his early days as a performer. Thus, he is regularly called upon by members of that profession in his capacity as a consulting detective. One such happenstance occurred in early April 1881.

I had just come down from my bedroom at the same time our landlady, Mrs. Hudson, was showing in a guest for my flatmate. Holmes, while reaching out to shake the gentleman's hand, turned to me and said, "Watson, may I introduce the very major model of a modern Major-General, Mr. John Napoleon of *The Opera Comique*. Mr. Napoleon, this is my friend, Dr. John Watson. Whatever you have come to tell me may be shared equally with him."

The actor was a bit startled at this pronouncement as he had just been about to give his name. "Have we met before, sir?" he said to Holmes.

The detective waved him to a seat, and he shook my hand *en route*. "Not formally," Holmes replied, "but I did observe one of your performances in *The Pirates of Penzance* late last year while I was on another case."

"And you recognized me now without my makeup? I hardly recognize myself when in costume."

"I have trained myself in the recognition of persons who attempt to disguise themselves. Certain facial features, especially ears and eyes, cannot be hidden by whiskers, and even though your costume is worn over some padding to add years to your true age, your general build is easily ascertained from the size of your hands and legs."

As I looked upon the fellow, I saw a clean-shaven middle-aged man in good, lean, physical shape, whereas the Major General in *Pirates*, as I recalled, was generally stout and adorned with grey hair, side-whiskers, and a large moustache.

"Well, you caught one of my rare performances then," said the actor. "As George Grossmith's understudy, I rarely got to perform the role. But I did recall your work on that case when I recently became concerned over my own situation."

79

"Tell us all about it," said my friend, "and please be precise as to detail."

Napoleon shifted in his seat. His chest heaved in a deep breath, and he let it out slowly as he prepared to deliver his statement. It was like watching an actor prepare to deliver a line on stage. "Just this past Saturday, after the evening performance, I was leaving the theatre and standing on the street attempting to hail a cab when I heard a loud retort and a chunk of brick in the wall behind me exploded into fragments. I naturally ducked and made my way to a recessed doorway. I then attempted to ascertain where the shot had come from.

"There were no alleyways or intersections from where a person could shoot and then hide. That at first led me to believe the shot must have come from a doorway, or possibly a passing cab.

"When I felt it was safe, I ventured out and examined the wall where the brick was gouged by the bullet. It was dark, and the wall was not well-lit at that particular spot, being just beyond the glow of the street lamp I had been standing near, so I could make little of it. I reported the incident to the local constable who took my information, said he would file a report at Scotland Yard, and that I should expect to hear from an inspector. When I went back to the theatre the next day, I looked at the wall again. The gouge was oblong, and at a slight angle. The shards of brick on the ground had been swept away. Later that day, I was contacted by an Inspector Bradstreet. He examined the scene and checked with the owners of the buildings across the street, but found no specific evidence. Frankly, he didn't seem all that helpful. He's thinking it may have been a stray shot from some other crime, or someone shooting a gun in the air in celebration."

"What time did this gunshot occur?"

"I left the theatre at ten-twenty, so about ten-twenty-five, I suppose."

Holmes nodded. "Very good. By the way, I hear Bradstreet is a good man. One of the brightest the Yard has to offer. Has anything else unusual happened?"

Napoleon wrung his hands. "Yes, Mr. Holmes, and just this morning. I found this slipped under my front door. I've informed Scotland Yard, but I wanted you to see it."

He pulled an envelope from his inner pocket and handed it over to Holmes, who took it eagerly. As was his habit, Holmes carefully examined the envelope first, even pulling his magnifier from his pocket to do so. As he began to mumble his findings, I thought it expedient to write them down, and took up pencil and paper to record his thoughts.

"Block printed with a soft lead pencil, as though trying to disguise handwriting. The stationery is cheap. One can almost read through to the note inside." As he held it close to his lens he gave a small sniff. "Perfume – or rather a cologne. Pleasant, but not alluring. Meant more to cover odors than to entice romance."

He took the note from within. It was a single sheet folded over twice. Again, Holmes examined the paper and determined it was the same stationery as the envelope and written with the same soft pencil, also in block printing. He handed it across to me.

"Doctor, do be good enough to read this aloud, and try to put yourself into the character of the writer."

This action would become a habit over the years. As Holmes later explained to me, he wished to concentrate on the tone of the letter and not be distracted by the clues coming at him through his other senses. Thus, he closed his eyes, and I read as follows in the stern and threatening voice that seemed appropriate:

Napoleon – You demon seed of the bastard of France! How dare you flaunt yourself in uniform on an English stage, pretending to be an actor when your true objective is revealed in the role you play. You seek to rule Penzance and expand your authority as the first Napoleon did in Europe. Thanks to him, my great-grandfather was impressed into the Royal Navy and killed by the French. His wife lost the farm, having no one to help her and her two-year-old son. My family has lived in near poverty ever since, all because of your ancestor! And now here you are, The Emperor reincarnate, in your army uniform, lying to pirates to save your miserable soul, and producing daughter after daughter to bear more of your tainted bloodline. You must be stopped! I shall be the instrument of God's wrath! Though I missed you the other day, the next time my aim will be true!

Chapter II

I handed the paper back to him, and Holmes examined the writing with his lens. "We are dealing with an extremely angry and disturbed mind, gentlemen. Possibly a woman. There are several indications that the pencil has pierced the paper from the pressure brought on by his or her emotions."

The actor responded with a loud burst of frustration. "Disturbed? She's crazy, is what she is! She doesn't seem to realize that Napoleon was Bonaparte's *first* name, not the family name that I inherited from my

81

ancestors in Naples. And obviously she's mixing up the play with reality. How am I to deal with this, Mr. Holmes?"

My friend looked across at his client and replied, "The presence of perfume or cologne doesn't necessarily indicate a woman. It merely suggests it. But think of your current acquaintances, no matter how remote. Is there anyone whom you have ever caught looking at you strangely or behaving oddly around you? It could be an actress, or a charwoman, or a laundress, or a fellow actor – anyone at all."

Napoleon bowed his head in thought, furrows etching themselves deeply above his eyes as he attempted to concentrate. "I am a widower, Mr. Holmes, and no one comes to mind. The ladies in my circle are all pleasant and quite friendly. Even my landlord's wife is especially flattered to have an actor of my station as one of her residents. As to my fellow actors, I can think of no one."

Holmes pondered that, then asked, "Has your landlady ever been flirtatious, or behaved in a way that would cause her husband to be jealous?"

"Oh, no, Mr. Holmes. She has been attentive to my needs as a tenant, and always with a smile, but she has never hinted at any romantic misbehaviour."

Holmes nodded and proclaimed, "Then I suggest the first order of business is to visit the scene of the attack. Are you game, Watson?"

"Quite so," I replied.

"Then let us be off," he said, standing. As he did so, he added, "Even though our quarry's marksmanship is off, we should be prepared to defend ourselves. Please do slip your army revolver into your pocket."

Armed with my six-shot Webley when we boarded the cab, I admit to being a bit thrilled at the prospect of adventure with my friend. After my army experience, I should have thought I would never again be comfortable in life-threatening situations, but there is an excited rush of blood-pounding that comes with such scenarios that can be quite addicting.

Napoleon directed the cab driver to the spot where his attack had occurred. Holmes asked the actor to stand exactly where he was when he heard the shot. He did so, looking anxiously at the buildings across the street. I too felt a responsibility to be on guard duty, so to speak, and regarded the scene with intense scrutiny and my hand on the grip of my pistol.

Holmes, meanwhile, stood at the kerb and noted the position of the scarred brick in relation to the actor's body. Then he stepped to the right, knelt, and examined the pavement. He held out his walking stick as if measuring the trajectory of some spot with the bullet mark on the wall. Then he stood and called our attention to another mark on the ground.

"Observe, gentlemen: The bullet that struck the wall did so at such an angle as to make a secondary mark here on the pavement when it ricocheted. Unfortunately, the bullet itself was likely swept away with the other debris, so we cannot ascertain its exact calibre. But see here, Mr. Napoleon – " He pointed to the gouge on the wall. "This height and location, being above your left shoulder by some two feet, indicate that the would-be assassin was likely using a pistol with which he or she was unfamiliar. As is typical of the untrained shooter, the shot went high and right, as that is the direction a pistol shot will kick, assuming a right-handed person. The width of the gouge indicates it was likely a .44 or .45 calibre pistol. The angle, as we can see from a triangulation of the ricochet mark, and the gouge itself, make the origin of the shot likely to be . . . *There!*"

Holmes turned and pointed his stick at the top of a four-storey brick building that was across the street and to the right of where we stood. There was a tailor shop on the ground floor with apartments above. We entered, and Holmes questioned the proprietor, who said he'd already told Scotland Yard that he didn't observe anyone go up or down the stairs, as the access to the upper floors didn't go through his shop, but through a separate door adjacent to him that was the stairwell for the upper tenants. He had access to that stairwell, as he lived on the first floor, but that was behind a closed door, so anyone could have gone up or down without his noticing. He also advised us that there was a back door on the ground floor that led to the alley behind the building where tenants could dump their trash. He told us that the top floor was currently unoccupied, and the tenant on the second floor worked nights as a watchman. On the night of the shooting, the tailor had been out to the theatre himself, but it was at the Criterion in Piccadilly, and he was late getting home, so was unaware of the incident until Inspector Bradstreet came to interview him.

We gained permission to use the stairs and proceeded to the top floor, where we found a built-in ladder for roof access. There were signs of chimney sweeps having plied their trade, but nothing incriminating any other persons. Once on the roof, Holmes motioned for us to stay back while he slowly approached the edge where the shooter likely would have positioned him or herself.

He scrutinized the flat rooftop. The slag atop the felt layers showed disturbance at the area where Holmes believed the shot had been taken. He called us over, and I could see footprints and a smudge where likely a knee had rested. But the indentations were so indistinct it was impossible to gauge the shoe size or type – thus, leaving open the possibility of the shooter being of either gender.

"Watson," said Holmes, "I'll not ask you to act out the role of the shooter, as I am sure this cold weather is exacerbating your war wound, but if I may borrow your revolver for a moment?"

I handed over my weapon, and Napoleon and I both watched as Holmes knelt and assumed a likely shooting position. The low wall surrounding the roof had provided perfect cover from the street, and a steady perch to rest the weapon upon. As our client and I stood behind him, we could easily imagine the scene. The spot where Napoleon had stood was near a street lamp, so he was well-lit. After the shooting, the assassin could have rushed down the stairs and out the back to escape through the alley, while any passersby would have been hiding or attending to the wounded man, had his or her aim been true.

Holmes stood, brushed off his knee, and said, "You are a fortunate fellow, sir. This was well-thought-out, which means the shooter knew your routine. Fortunately, his or her marksmanship was poor."

Napoleon swallowed hard. "You mean it's someone close to me?"

"Or at least someone keeping a close eye on you," Holmes countered.

Chapter III

"What should I do, Mr. Holmes?" Napoleon asked nervously. "There are still two weeks left in the run of the play before Gilbert and Sullivan's new production, *Patience*, opens on April twenty-first."

"Are you going to be in that one as well?" Holmes asked.

"I auditioned, but have been cast as understudy to Grossmith again, in the role of Bunthorne.

"I don't suppose Grossmith feels threatened by your continued presence at his heels?" commented Holmes.

"I hardly think so," said our client. "He's been a fixture in Gilbert and Sullivan's plays since 1877, and has always had excellent reviews. I was well-noted in one review for a performance I played in his stead last October, but it was hardly in the glowing terms he usually receives."

"Yes," said Holmes. "That was the performance I saw you in. I thought you quite excellent, which is why I brought up Grossmith's possible jealousy."

I asked a question at that point. "When you aren't fulfilling your duties as the understudy, what do you do during the play? Just stand by in case Grossmith becomes ill?"

"Oh, no, Doctor. I play one of the policemen."

"Ah, I see. Having never acted myself, I wasn't sure of the protocol for understudies."

"It is a unique position, but one to which I've grown accustomed to – though I still hope to land a leading part one day."

"The motto of every actor," stated Holmes. "But I suggest you go about your normal routine for now. Watson, if you would be good enough to accompany our friend here, with your pistol at the ready for the rest of today. I shall return to Baker Street, change to a less-recognizable persona, and meet the two of you at the theatre, where I'll introduce myself to the backstage manager. What time do you normally arrive, sir?"

"No later than six," Napoleon replied.

"Then I shall be there well-beforehand so as to scout out the situation. Fortunately, I have maintained my theatrical connections and know the backstage manager, Ed Whitmore. I can also enlist his aid in discreetly keeping an eye on things so that none of the other cast or crew are aware of our actions, in case our culprit is among them."

"You think one of my co-workers could be behind this?" asked the actor with some bewilderment. "I can't believe that. Besides none of them have ever shown signs of being this out of touch with reality."

Holmes shook his head. "Believe me, sir, if you had an understudy, he would be the first person I would suspect. You know how envious actors can get."

With that thought filling our minds, Holmes hailed a cab and saw us safely aboard. We trotted off toward Napoleon's flat, trusting that Sherlock Holmes would somehow solve the mystery of the actor's attacker.

In the cab, I asked our client, "Do understudies have understudies?"

"Usually not, Doctor," replied the actor. "At least, I've never heard of such a thing. If both the lead actor and their understudy are incapacitated, the performance usually gets canceled."

We arrived in due time back at Napoleon's flat. I exited the cab first, observing the neighborhood for any sign of a gunman. Seeing none, I indicated it was safe for our client to make his way into his building while I followed up, walking backward to keep an eye on the street. Once inside, we climbed the stairs to his first-floor flat and again, I took the lead, gun in hand, to open his door and clear the room.

This action, however, was met with a violent turn. I had only taken two steps when, from behind the open door, I was set upon by a tall individual who knocked the gun from my hand, tackled me to the floor, and we wrestled for advantage. My army training stood me in good stead, but my weakened leg betrayed me, and the attacker soon had the upper hand and was atop me ready to deliver a savage blow.

Fortunately, Napoleon reacted and dove into the fray, pulling the man off me and shouting, "Stop, Inspector! He's a friend. He's here to help!"

The full-bearded stranger stood, looked at the actor who nodded, and said, "This is Dr. John Watson. He works with Sherlock Holmes, and is acting as my bodyguard."

My attacker had the good graces to look chagrined, and reached a hand out to help me to my feet. Once I was face-to-face with the man, I found him to be nearly as tall as Holmes. His facial hair didn't extend to his scalp, as he was a bald individual of perhaps forty years. When he spoke, it was with a strong but contrite baritone.

"Sorry, Doctor. I am Inspector Bradstreet, Scotland Yard. When I found Mr. Napoleon not at home, I thought I would stake the place out in case the culprit returned to slip another note under the door. Naturally, when I saw a stranger with a gun entering so furtively, I assumed the worst and reacted. No hard feelings I hope?"

I brushed the dust from my coat and retrieved my revolver from the floor. I looked him in the eye and, seeing the honesty of his apology, replied, "I cannot fault you for your due diligence, Inspector. It's all right. No harm done."

The actor locked the door and waved us to sit down. He offered some brandy which I gratefully accepted, but the inspector turned it down due to being on duty. He then commented, "I've heard of Sherlock Holmes from Inspector Lestrade, but haven't yet met the gentleman, nor was I aware he had a partner."

I was struck by the word "partner", as I hadn't considered myself in that capacity. "I am not a detective myself," I responded to Bradstreet. "I merely share his rooms, and have occasionally assisted when he needed an extra hand or medical knowledge. My revolver is from my army days, as I was recently discharged after being severely wounded at the Battle of Maiwand. Holmes felt Mr. Napoleon could use an armed escort for the time being."

Bradstreet nodded. "A wise precaution. Where is Mr. Holmes, himself?"

"He has returned to our rooms to adopt a disguise which he will use to infiltrate the theatre and investigate the possibility of this would-be assassin coming from within the ranks of the theatre staff."

"Excellent!" declared the inspector. "I was planning on going to the theatre myself tonight. Now that I know you have things in hand here, I shall head over there now."

He rose and made for the door. With his hand on the knob, he turned back. "Keep taking precautions, Mr. Napoleon. A person this deranged may try anything, but we'll do our best to head him off."

His use of the male pronoun reminded me to convey Holmes's observation on the scent of the letter. "There was a perfume or cologne

86

fragrance to the note, Inspector. Holmes hasn't discounted the fact that the suspect may be a woman."

Bradstreet hesitated. "I wish you had brought the letter to us," he admonished Napoleon, "instead of just sending a note of its contents. I'll have to inform the constables on station around the theatre. Anything else you have to tell us?"

"Holmes is fairly certain the shooter was right-handed," I offered.

"Yes, I gathered that from the position of the bullet mark on the wall. Very well, I'll be off then."

By now it was approaching lunchtime, and my host rang the bell for his landlady. She came upstairs, noted there would be two of us, and returned to her kitchen.

Throughout lunch and into the afternoon, my host and I swapped stories about our careers. Napoleon told me of how he embarked upon acting. "I was studying history at Cambridge, intending to become a professor of such, when I joined the Amateur Dramatic Club. It was there where I felt we were making history come to life, and I was bitten by the acting bug. The thrill of performing. The accolades of the audience. The bond one shares with other actors. It was far more satisfying than writing dry treatises and giving lectures to students who rarely appreciate what the past can tell us."

As I had a captive audience, so to speak, I asked the historian a question that had always intrigued me. "Why do you suppose, sir, that there aren't more people who react as your adversary does to Napoleon? I've always thought of him as a dictator who would subjugate all of Europe into his empire. Yet there seems to be an admiration for him among certain segments of the populace of England." [1]

Our client looked up as if searching his brain for an answer, then back to me and said, "I believe it is partially due to the respect Wellington had for him. Wellington famously said that Napoleon's presence on the battlefield 'was worth forty-thousand men'. It was Wellington who saved Napoleon after Waterloo. When there were calls for him to be executed, he was strongly against it, and favoured giving him the governorship of Elba instead.

"The emperor is seen as a statesman and architect of modern France, as well as a great military leader. I believe it is these qualities that are admired by the English as well as the French. It is well-documented that he didn't commit the atrocities of so many conquerors of the past, and treated the enemy wounded with great care.

"You have to remember, Doctor, at the time British liberals and conservatives were on opposite sides of the Napoleonic question. Lord Byron, a champion of the liberals, criticized the victory at Waterloo, since it put a king back on the French throne. For him, Napoleon's defeat benefited only those who became rich at the expense of the poor. Prominent English churchmen also deplored the return of Catholicism to France, and the repression of the Protestants, as well as the reintroduction of slavery.

"Yet the conservatives saw danger if Napoleon succeeded. The fall of European monarchies was unthinkable to them. International politics was so much easier when dealing with multiple monarchies with whom you could form alliances to keep each other in check. If one government ruled all of Europe, what chance could England stand to resist it from imposing its will upon us?"

"Obviously," I stated seriously, "your attacker falls into this second camp."

"If my attacker's note is true, then his – or her – reasoning hasn't likely been thought out in the political sense. This person is merely reacting emotionally, and unstably in my opinion."

We whiled away the time until afternoon tea, when the actor announced, "You know, Doctor, lunch isn't sitting so well on my stomach. Anxiety I suppose. I don't feel like eating, and I cannot sit here any longer! Let's go to the theatre and discover what we may."

I had eaten the same meal as him and felt no ill effects, so I wasn't concerned about poison, and merely responded, "Good idea. A change in your routine could disrupt your predator's plans."

Chapter IV

Arriving at the Opera Comique, we immediately sought out the backstage manager, Whitmore, to ascertain if Holmes was there and what he looked like. Holmes had indeed arrived, and had been wandering the site looking for clues and observing people since one o'clock.

We were given his description, and soon found him up in the catwalks observing from on high. We kept our voices low so as not to be overheard. "Any luck, Mr. Holmes?" asked our client. "Does anyone seem suspicious?"

Holmes shook his head. "All appears normal for the day of a performance. Everyone is attending to their tasks. Performers are going over their lines. A surreptitious romance is occurring in a secluded spot between a stagehand and a young lady whom I presume to be one of your daughters in the play."

"Isabel Abbot," Napoleon commented. "She and Jordan Haas think they have everyone fooled, but the looks and slight touches exchanged between them are obvious to anyone paying attention."

"Would he be related to the well-known photographer of the same name?" Holmes asked.

Our client nodded and replied, "Yes, he is his son – Jordan Haas Jr., to be precise."

Holmes seemed to make a mental note and moved on. "There is a gentleman who arrived shortly after I did who also seems out of place. I haven't confronted him as yet, but I believe he must be Inspector Bradstreet of Scotland Yard from the fact that he showed some sort of identification to Whitmore, the backstage manager, and was given full access to the building. Apparently, Mr. Napoleon, they are taking your case more seriously than you supposed."

"Yes, we've met," I replied, rubbing my shoulder from where I had hit the floor. I explained our encounter with Bradstreet at Napoleon's flat, and Holmes nodded his approval at the Scotland Yarder's diligence.

"Well, let us go down, and I'll introduce myself. I would also like to examine your dressing table, Mr. Napoleon – just to ensure there are no traps or devices that might cause you harm."

We descended, found Bradstreet, and pulled him into a quiet corner where Holmes could introduce himself and maintain his *incognito*. "I've spoken to Mr. Whitmore," said the inspector. "I've confirmed there have been no strangers about – except for you, Mr. Holmes. If the perpetrator is here, it's someone Mr. Napoleon knows, even if it's just in passing."

The actor looked around the room. "I cannot imagine any of these people wanting to kill me."

Holmes hummed in thought and then said, "What if the shot was a deliberate miss, and someone was just trying to scare you away?"

Bradstreet responded to that. "What's the motive?"

"Just thinking out loud, Inspector," answered Holmes. "I just want Mr. Napoleon to approach his observations of his acquaintances from various aspects, not just as potential killers."

I chimed in at that revelation, asking, "Are there any women among the group who might have something against you? Or perhaps feelings towards you which you haven't reciprocated?"

"Not that I'm aware of," replied the actor. "As a recent widower, I have no desire to move on to a new relationship. I have received sympathy from my female co-workers, but nothing flirtatious. Besides, I would never get involved with any woman who was in the same production as me. If the relationship were to go sour, the work situation would become far too awkward."

"Well, let us check out your dressing area," suggested Holmes, "and see what we might."

Not having a leading role, Napoleon was assigned a table in one of the common rooms rather than a private dressing room. He shared this with several other actors whose dressing tables lined three of the walls, with the fourth being the entrance containing a wardrobe rack for their costumes, and a full-length triple mirror to ensure they were fitted out properly.

Holmes got down on his knees to check under Napoleon's table and chair, and he and Bradstreet pulled the table away from the wall to check behind the mirror. There proved to be no explosives or lethal devices of any sort, so the actor sat down.

"Is everything on your tabletop in order?" asked Holmes. "Nothing new or substituted?"

Our client looked over everything and that replied all was as it should be. I, again being unfamiliar with the theatre, asked a question about a particular item.

"What is that tin box labeled '*Neapolitan Skin Tones*'?

In answer, Napoleon lifted the lid and exposed a shallow tray of twenty various colours of flesh-toned makeup. It held every shade imaginable from clown-white face to sunburn-pink, through various beiges, several iterations of tans from light to dark, almost Negroid, and even some of an Oriental variation.

"This is my makeup kit, Doctor," answered the actor. "I can appear as a well-tanned soldier from the Middle East to a pasty-faced professor who rarely sees the outdoors. I have played a dark-skinned native, and once even a Himalayan guide. This other box," he continued, reaching for a larger container, "holds my various wigs, beards, and moustaches."

Holmes stayed the man's hand. "Wait! We should check the box before you reach into it."

Realizing the implication of Holmes's statement, Napoleon suddenly stood and stepped back. Holmes obtained some long pliers from Whitmore and gently pulled out each item. The rest of us held our breath expectantly, fearing some reptile, rodent, or poisonous creature would appear. Soon there was a pile of various styles and colours of wigs and facial hair stacked on the table, and fortunately, nothing dangerous reared its ugly head.

We all breathed a sigh of relief when this exercise concluded, but Napoleon was becoming unnerved. "This needs to stop gentlemen. I cannot go on living like this. Being afraid of shadows and having to worry about every little thing like opening a box."

He suddenly grabbed Bradstreet by the shoulders and shook him with a forceful demand. "You must do something, Inspector! You must put an end to this threat on my life!"

Bradstreet took his arms and gently pushed him away. "We are doing everything possible, sir. And with Mr. Holmes's help, and Dr. Watson guarding you, I am sure we shall capture this person."

"Before or after I'm dead?" said Napoleon as he sank sulking into his chair.

Chapter V

Not expecting an answer to his rhetorical question, the actor turned in his chair and set about applying his skin makeup. The hair would be determined after he was sure he wouldn't be needed as that night's understudy – a fact which he normally would have been made aware of by early afternoon, but one could never tell when an illness might strike.

While he was doing that, Holmes, Bradstreet, and I retreated to a quiet corner where we wouldn't be overheard. A thought struck me from Holmes's earlier comment. "Holmes, why did you come at one o'clock? When you left us this morning, it wasn't even eleven yet."

"I had a rare embarrassment of riches," he replied

At Bradstreet's puzzled look, he explained. "Inspector, your desk. I'm sure, has the files of several cases you are working on simultaneously. It is the lot of all Scotland Yard inspectors that they're overworked. At this stage of my career, it's rare for me to have two cases a once, and a definite boon to the rent money when I do. A client showed up as I was preparing my disguise, and took up a significant amount of time presenting her case. She was a very talkative woman and, while I appreciate details, she often wandered onto irrelevant tangents from which I had to steer her back to her original situation. I was finally able to extricate myself from her with the promise I would discuss her case with Scotland Yard if need be, which I have now done."

"But you've given me no details, Mr. Holmes," said Bradstreet.

Holmes shook his head. "It isn't a criminal matter. Should it take a turn in that direction I will inform you, but I believe it will be quite simple. Unlike this case," he said, nodding toward Napoleon, who was leaning into his mirror to catch the light.

"Have you formed any theory, Mr. Holmes?" enquired the inspector. "I'd much rather go on the offensive against a suspect than wait around hoping to catch someone in the act."

Suddenly a noise from the direction of our client caught our attention. Napoleon had stood up, knocking his chair backward onto the floor. He was grasping his chest, and then he vomited into a nearby wastebasket. Most of the other actors retreated from this spectacle, looking on in horror or confusion. One actress, however – Isabel Abbot as it turned out – came

91

forward as we rushed to Napoleon's side. As I bent over the now-unconscious form of our client, she said, "I'm a nurse. Let me take care of him. Go find a doctor!"

"I *am* a doctor," I replied, lifting his wrist to check his pulse, then checking his eyes while she put an ear to his heart.

"His heart is racing and his breathing is shallow," she replied.

Another actor approached, a large, older fellow, who asked, "Shall I call for an ambulance?"

"No time!" I shouted. "Hail a cab. We must get him to hospital quickly!"

Two men helped me get Napoleon into a four-wheeler and I ordered the driver, "The closest hospital – Hurry!"

As I was now gone with my patient, I must relate what Holmes later told me.

Miss Abbot, no longer concerned about the clandestine nature of their relationship, sought out Haas, who put an arm around her shoulders in comfort. Bradstreet went to question her while Holmes took to examining Napoleon's dressing area.

He checked the chair again for any exposed nails that might have pricked the actor's skin with some poisonous substance, but found none. He then went over everything on the table once more. The only items Napoleon had touched were a hairbrush to push his hair as far off his face as he could to apply his makeup, and the makeup itself. Holmes obtained a box from Whitmore and placed the hairbrush inside it, the makeup tin, and the sponges, pads, and brushes used to apply it.

As it turned out, the gentleman who had enquired about calling for an ambulance, was one of the play's pirates, Lionel Barry. He offered to help Holmes carry the box out so that the detective would have a hand free to hail a cab, but Holmes declined, saying he would wait for the gentleman he was visiting with, not wishing to expose Bradstreet's identity without his permission.

Soon the inspector returned to the dressing table, with Isabel Abbot at his side. "I've finished questioning this young lady and advised her of her rights, but I thought, as Mr. Napoleon's *friend*, you might wish to ask some questions of your own."

Holmes nodded his thanks to Bradstreet for not giving his identity away and turned his attention to the actress. She was a comely young lady of perhaps twenty years of age, with coils of light brown hair that fell to her shoulders. She played one of the Major General's nine daughters in the play.

"Miss Abbot," said Holmes, "you told the doctor you were a nurse. Is that true?"

She looked at my friend and replied, "Yes, sir. That is, I am studying to be one, and have almost completed my training. As there is no doctor on staff here at the theatre, I felt I was best qualified to attend to someone in distress until your friend identified himself."

Holmes nodded. "That was quick thinking on your part. Out of curiosity, tell me what you would have done, given the symptoms the victim was presenting."

She swallowed and tried to speak with conviction. "First of all, I would have let Lionel go ahead and call for an ambulance. I recognized right away that this was no mere first-aid incident. From John's initial reaction, I suspected a possible heart attack. After listening to his chest, I would have ensured his airway was clear, and then done as the doctor did while awaiting the cab – use the standard chest-pressure arm-lift method."

Holmes nodded. "Very sound, Miss. With the facts you had in hand, that would have been absolutely the right procedure. I'm sure you will make a fine nurse."

Holmes offered a farewell and started to turn, asking Bradstreet to accompany him outside, but the actress took his sleeve. "You will have the doctor send us word about John's condition?"

Holmes looked at the young actress with interest and replied, "Certainly, Miss Abbot. As soon as he knows something definitive."

Once outside, Holmes informed Bradstreet he was taking the items he had boxed up home to run chemical tests for poisons. If he obtained a positive result, he would keep the inspector informed.

"I can have our laboratory run those tests, Mr. Holmes," Bradstreet offered.

Holmes shook his head. "Scotland Yard's lab is far too busy, and time may be of the essence. I can have the results this evening. Let us just hope the dose Napoleon received will not prove to be his Waterloo."

Chapter VI

In the meantime, the hospital was running tests on my patient. In addition to the symptoms already noted on sight, his blood pressure was very high. It was nearly seven o'clock when the physician assigned to Napoleon, Dr. Wasserman, came to consult me outside my patient's room.

"We've identified the poison, Dr. Watson. It appears to be cyanide. But to have a reaction like this he must have been exposed to small doses over a long period. Has he exhibited any symptoms lately?"

"He complained of an uneasy stomach after lunch today, but I ate the same thing, and I'm fine."

"It likely wasn't in his food. What does he do for a living?"

"He's an actor."

Wasserman shook his head. "Then I can only surmise that this was deliberate. The theatre isn't a place where cyanide is usually found. It would be more likely if he worked in a hospital, or as a chemist or photographer. There are several manufacturing processes that use it, especially iron and steelworks, but I cannot see how an actor could receive this much exposure without it being deliberate. If not in his food, it might have been in his makeup."

"I'm sure that is being tested as we speak," I said with confidence in my friend's thoroughness.

"He wasn't suicidal, was he?" asked the physician, just to cover all possibilities.

"Far from it," I replied. "In fact, he's been threatened by some unknown person who has already taken a shot at him."

Wasserman started at this information, then said, "He'll need to stay in a private room so that no one else is at risk for contact exposure. I'll arrange for a guard outside his door. You say Scotland Yard is aware?"

"Yes, Inspector Bradstreet is investigating, and was there when Napoleon collapsed."

"Very well. I'll ensure he gets no visitors other than yourself or Bradstreet, and you'll need to wear protective garments while in the room while he is being treated."

"You'll need to include Mr. Sherlock Holmes on your list of visitors," I added.

Wasserman wrote it down. "Who is Mr. Holmes, and what is his relationship to the patient?"

"Holmes is the detective Napoleon hired to try to find out who is out to kill him. Once you've posted a guard, I'll leave here and report your findings, since it may assist his investigation."

Assuming Holmes would still be at the theatre working alongside Bradstreet, I returned there to report Wasserman's conclusions as to the poison. By now the play was in progress, but I found Bradstreet in the wings. He told me what had occurred after I left.

After informing me that Holmes had already gone home to test the items from Napoleon's dressing table, Bradstreet commented, "Cyanide, you say? Now, isn't that interesting? Isn't that usually found in hospitals?"

"Among other places, yes," I replied. [2]

He pointed to the stage where the actresses playing Major-General's daughters were performing the scene where the pirate apprentice, Frederic, was meeting them for the first time. Indicating Isabel Abbot, he said, "She isn't quite a nurse yet, but she has nearly completed her training, which is why she says she stepped forward when Napoleon collapsed. But what if

94

she were the one who brought the poison from the hospital and wanted to make sure no one else examined the victim too quickly? You did say that Holmes mentioned the possibility of a woman assassin."

I turned my gaze from the inspector to the actress. I had to admit she was of an age where her great-grandfather could have been impressed to fight in the Napoleonic War, but she hadn't appeared the least bit unstable, and seemed to have a genuine concern for our client's welfare when he collapsed – so much so that she disregarded her usual attempt to hide her feelings toward Jordan Haas. It didn't sit right with me, but I had been wrong before – especially when it came to beautiful women.

"What will you do?" I asked.

"I'll attempt to ascertain whether she was ever seen around Napoleon's dressing table. Then after the show, I'll take her to Scotland Yard for further questioning. You should probably get your information to Mr. Holmes as soon as you can."

I gave Miss Abbot one last look and nodded. "Very well. I suspect Holmes will want to see you first thing in the morning."

"I'll be at the Yard unless I hear that Napoleon is well enough to talk. Then I'll need to ask him some questions."

I reluctantly left him and obtained a cab for the short ride to Baker Street. I found Holmes at his chemical table. I informed him of Wasserman's findings, and he was pleased to hear it. "That coincides with my results thus far. I'm convinced the poison was in the makeup, and now I know exactly what to look for."

I then told him of Bradstreet's suspicions regarding Miss Abbot. He pursed his lips in a frown. "I should like to be there for that interview," he said. "I too have questions for that young lady. Why don't you have Mrs. Hudson put together a quick supper for you? By the time you have eaten, my experiments should be done, and we can go to the Yard together."

Within the hour we were in a cab southbound, and found we had arrived only a few minutes after Bradstreet's return from the theatre with Miss Abbot. We found them in one of the common rooms used for interrogation. Bradstreet was surprised to see us, but invited us in. I sat next to the lady while Holmes joined Bradstreet on the other side of the table.

"If I may, Inspector?" said Holmes, and when Bradstreet nodded, he continued. "Miss Abbot, my name is Sherlock Holmes, and this is my colleague, Dr. John Watson. Mr. Napoleon hired us to find out who is trying to kill him."

My friend let that statement hang there, waiting to see her reaction.

She looked to me as a fellow member of the medical profession, and I merely nodded. Then she turned back to Holmes. "Are you saying his collapse wasn't a natural medical issue? That he was attacked in some fashion?"

"Cyanide poisoning, in fact," stated Bradstreet, not wishing to completely let Holmes run the interrogation. "It was in his makeup."

"Cyanide?" she gasped, holding a delicate hand to her slender white throat while her head dipped toward the table in disbelief. Then she shot a look across at the detective and the inspector. "What about the rest of us? Is the entire cast in danger?"

To my mind, that statement immediately exonerated her, but then I'm neither a police inspector nor detective, jaded by years of dealing with deceitful criminals. "No, we don't believe so," Bradstreet replied. "Mr. Napoleon had been specifically attacked and threatened before. That is why we were there tonight. As a nurse – "

Holmes held up his hand to stay the inspector's next statement. "Bradstreet, I have a few questions of my own before you finish that thought."

The Scotland Yarder waved his hand to Holmes and took out a pencil and paper to record what was about to be said. Seeing this, the actress stiffened and asked, "Why are you writing this down? Am I a suspect?"

Holmes replied before the inspector could, saying, "You are what I would call a 'peripheral party'. [3] There is no evidence against you, but you did know the victim well enough to call him by his first name. You work with him, have access to his dressing table where the poison was found and, according to your statement, you are in training to be a nurse, which means at the hospital you have access to cyanide."

She leaned forward and started to protest, but Holmes interrupted. "There are other factors to this case, and we should discuss those first."

She sat back, crossed her arms, and said, "Very well. Ask your silly questions if you wish to waste your time, because I'm telling you I didn't do this!"

Holmes nodded then asked, "What time did you leave the theatre last Saturday night after the performance?"

She thought a moment, then replied, "About ten-forty-five. I had to wait a while for Jordan to finish his work, and we left together."

"Did anyone see you?"

"Mr. Whitmore saw me right before I met up with Jordan, but no one saw us leave together. We've been trying to keep our friendship secret. We didn't want rumours spreading around. Theatre gossip can be vicious."

"Where did you go?"

"There's a pub that's open late near my flat. We went there and stayed until they closed at midnight. And before you ask, Jordan saw me home and left me there. My landlady is very strict about no men coming inside."

"Did you happen to hear a gunshot around ten-twenty-five?"

"No," she replied. "But backstage after a show is somewhat noisy with scenery and props being put away and backdrops re-positioned for the next performance. Did this gunshot occur inside the theatre?"

"No, it was out on the street, not far away. Tell us about your family. What does your father do?"

She shook her head at this abrupt change of subject, but I knew it was a tactic of Holmes to not give her time to think and make something up. Thus, we were more likely to hear the truth.

"My father is a gunsmith, as was his father before him. My great-grandfather was in the Royal Navy, and his father was a farmer. I don't know any farther back than that."

Bradstreet's interest had perked up at this statement. The naval connection to her great-grandfather, and her likely having access to a gun in her father's shop, could certainly be considered circumstantial evidence.

"Interesting," said Holmes. "Does anyone else know of your family's connection to the Royal Navy?"

She shook her head again at this line of questioning, but replied, "Yes. There were several of us sitting around one day, and we got to talking about family members who had served in the military. I'm sure I mentioned my great-grandfather."

Holmes obtained the name of the hospital where she was training and then said, "One more thing." He pulled the envelope containing the threatening letter from his breast pocket, opened it, and handed it to her. "Do you recognize this writing?"

She glanced at it without actually reading it and said, "This is printed. It could be anybody."

"Do you recognize the scent on the paper?"

She held it close to her face and sniffed. "It smells like the cologne I use." Realizing the implication, she took time to carefully read the letter and cried, "I did not write this! I would never hurt John, and I certainly know he isn't related to the French Emperor! Whoever wrote this is mad!"

Holmes took the letter back and handed it to Bradstreet, saying, "Those are all the questions I have for now, Inspector. Miss Abbot, I would appreciate you not mentioning my involvement in this case to your fellow actors. Three is still a bit of investigating to do, and it would be preferable for now if they believe Mr. Napoleon's illness is due to natural causes."

She nodded her head in agreement, and then Bradstreet made several more enquiries, but could get nothing incriminating out of the young woman that would shake her alibi. Finally, he said she could leave, and asked if she would like a police escort to take her home.

"If he wouldn't mind," she said turning to me, "I should like Dr. Watson to see me home. I would like to discuss John's case with him."

I was caught off guard by this, but at Holmes's nod, I readily agreed. In the cab, her questions for me were strictly along the lines of the medical diagnosis and treatment options for Napoleon. My only question for her came as we stopped outside her flat. "Forgive my curiosity, but why do you call Mr. Napoleon by his first name? Are you close friends?"

She smiled. "He has become somewhat of a mentor to those of us who play his daughters when he steps into the Major-General role. He is almost an actual father-figure to us, whereas Mr. Grossmith virtually ignores us when offstage."

I smiled and thanked her, then exited the cab so as to help her out. As I did so, I heard heavy footsteps behind me and turned, my free hand reflexively going to the pocket where my Webley still resided. But I stopped when I recognized the young man approaching.

"Jordan!" cried Miss Abbot as she raced into his arms and hugged him tightly.

He returned her affection, but gave me a wary look as they parted. "Who's this?" he asked, with a bit of menace to his voice.

"This is Dr. Watson," she replied. "He's the one who took John to the hospital. He's working with the police to try to find out what caused John to take ill."

"Police?" exclaimed Haas with great surprise.

"Just some inspector butting in where he isn't needed." (She gave me a wink.) "But the doctor was good enough to escort me when I asked him to bring me home from Scotland Yard."

Turning to me, she said, "Thank you for your kindness, Doctor, and for answering all my questions about John's condition. I do hope you can cure him quickly."

"It's been a pleasure, Miss Abbot. We shall do our best. Good luck with your nursing, and with your acting career. Whichever you choose to pursue, I'm sure you will be exemplary."

Chapter VII

It was after midnight before I reached Baker Street again. Holmes, of course, was still awake, and the atmosphere of the room was starting to turn into a blue haze from the pipes he'd smoked since returning from the Yard.

After hanging up my hat and coat, I strode to the sideboard and I poured myself a brandy to help warm my insides after so much time out in the cold. I sat opposite my companion near the fire, and immediately he asked, "I presume you saw Miss Abbot safely home. Did she say anything of interest during your journey?"

"We spoke mostly of Napoleon's condition. She asked what the treatment options and prognosis would be. She exhibited both a curious and caring attitude which I would have expected from a nursing student, and said nothing that indicated to me she might be the poisoner. I dropped her at her door, and was confronted somewhat threateningly by her beau, Mr. Haas, as we exited the cab, but she explained the situation, and he was satisfied with my intentions as a protector."

Holmes nodded then continued his questions. "Setting aside your usual penchant for always believing the best about beautiful young women, what is your opinion of Miss Abbot and her involvement in this case?"

Taking umbrage at Holmes's blanket statement regarding my perceptions of beautiful women, I naturally defended myself first, as I thought it best to do so before giving my thoughts regarding the lady in question. "It may seem that way to you, as we've only known each other a short time, but I assure you, in my experience of women spanning three continents, I have certainly come across my share of conceited divas, abusive mothers, cheating wives, and mean-spirited ladies of title who should be stripped of their rank for the way they treat their servants. I will concede that I give women the benefit of the doubt until they prove otherwise, and I hope I never outgrow that habit.

"As to Miss Abbot, I know what you and Bradstreet must be thinking. She may have had access to cyanide. She may have had access to a gun. She certainly has access to Napoleon's dressing table. Her great-grandfather served in the Royal Navy, as the note indicated. She was the first one to react to our client's collapse – almost as if she were expecting it. The scent on the letter matches her cologne. Her alibi for the shooting needs to be verified. But let me remind you of something I've heard you say: 'There is nothing so deceptive as the obvious.'"

Holmes smiled. "So you were paying attention, even before you knew I was a detective."

I took a long sip of brandy and sniffed back at him, "I confess, at the time I thought you were talking about one of your chemical experiments. But it still applies, does it not?"

He nodded and answered, "Indeed it does. I would like to correct you on one point, however: I agree that it is highly likely that Bradstreet is thinking of all those things you mentioned as circumstantial evidence against her. I, on the other hand, see all those facts as evidence of a devious mind attempting to throw suspicion onto her and away from himself. As you say, she has become too-obvious a suspect."

"You are certain it is a man then?"

"I would be surprised if it isn't. While the letter appears to be from a deranged mind, I believe the actions taken by this person are those of a cunning individual, and that they aren't mentally unstable towards Napoleon at all. The scent was to lead us in the direction of a woman, and specifically to Miss Abbot, due to her great-grandfather being in the Royal Navy."

"If the letter was a ruse," I asked, "then what is the motive?"

"That is what leads me to believe it is a clever man. Unless our client is lying about a woman scorned, there is no woman with a motive in his life. Did you discover why Miss Abbot was so familiar as to call him 'John'?"

I explained that Napoleon was seen as a mentor and father figure to the actresses who played his daughters when he stepped into the Major-General role.

Holmes nodded. "Not an uncommon occurrence within the theatre, although that occasionally leads to hero-worship and feelings of what young women believe to be love. In his state of mourning, he may not recognize the feelings of one of the younger women towards him, and she may be feeling scorned.

"For the present, however, my primary hypothesis is to presume the motive lies within the ranks of his theatrical profession as an actor, rather than this spurious nonsense about being a descendent of Napoleon. That leaves us with the most common causes for crime among actors: Jealousy, envy, frustration, and hatred."

I shook my head in surprise. "You have developed a list of motives specific to actors?"

He folded his hands across his stomach and replied, "I have developed multiple lists of motives for a wide variety of professions. Just as you have lists of symptoms that lead you to diagnose specific diseases or conditions, I can often take the vast array of motives for crime and narrow it down to the most common for specific occupations, or ranks, or genders. It isn't one-hundred-per-cent accurate, but it does usually fall into the greater realm of probability."

"Does this list you've determined lead you to any specific individuals?"

"Generally, it could be any of the male actors. One of them may see Napoleon as an obstacle to their own climb up the ladder. Interestingly enough, based upon their recent pairing in two successive productions, it could even be George Grossmith."

This pronouncement took me aback, and I had to set down my drink before I spilled it. "Grossmith?" I cried. "He's been the lead actor for every

Gilbert and Sullivan production for – What? Five years now? What motive could he possibly have for eliminating an understudy?"

"Actors can be notoriously paranoid and insecure. Though unlikely, I cannot dismiss the possibility that Grossmith fears that Gilbert and Sullivan are grooming Napoleon to someday replace him."

"What will you do?"

"I've convinced Bradstreet to confine his investigations to areas outside the theatre for now. He'll be tracking down Miss Abbot's background, and verifying her alibi and the possibility of her access to cyanide.

"In the meantime, I shall don a new disguise. Fortunately, the *Opera Comique* is scheduled to have electric lighting installed for this fall season, and I can take on the role of a contractor inspecting the building and taking measurements. It will give me total access, and I can investigate the production personnel more closely."

Chapter VIII

The next morning, our first stop was the hospital to check on our client. Napoleon was responding well to the treatments and was awake when we arrived. Though weakened by the poison's effects, he was able to answer some questions for my companion.

"I am narrowing my list of suspects," said Holmes, "but before I proceed on the path I believe most likely, I need you to carefully think about the women at the theatre. I understand the ladies who play your daughters have formed a sort of attachment to you as a mentor. Is it possible that, in the fact that you are a recent widow, one of them may be confusing feelings of sorrow for you with feelings of love and admiration, and that they are disappointed that you haven't recognized and reciprocated those feelings?"

Napoleon's eyes stretched towards the ceiling, and I could see him physically tick off the ladies one by one on his fingers as he gave each a careful thought. Finally, he said, "No, they have been kind and sympathetic, but have shown no signs of wishing to step into my wife's place in my life. Miss Abbot is the most caring of the lot, but I believe that is just a natural aspect of her personality. She's training to be a nurse, you know. Besides, she has Jordan, and seems loyal to him."

"Very well," replied Holmes. "What about your working relationship with George Grossmith? Is there any resentment on his part towards you as his understudy?"

"George?" replied Napoleon. "I hardly think so. We have different interpretations of how we play the part, but George has nothing to fear from me. He is Gilbert and Sullivan's fair-haired boy."

Then the import of Holmes's question hit him. "Wait, are you thinking it's one of the other actors who is after me? Why?"

Holmes revealed his thoughts. "That's what I am asking you. Is there anyone in the troupe who could resent you for any reason? Someone else who thought he should get the understudy role perhaps? Or someone you've beaten out of a role in a past production?"

"I am not privy to everyone's audition, Mr. Holmes. I wouldn't necessarily know who I beat out for a role. As far as this production goes, I believe the only other actor who could have been considered would have been Lionel Barry, but he's too large for the part. The Major-General must be intimidated by the Pirate King, and a fellow of Barry's size wouldn't be believable as one who could be easily intimidated. I'm actually surprised he didn't get the role of the Pirate King. I think the fellow they cast is too young for the part, considering that Frederic is supposed to have been apprenticed to him for at least ten years. Certainly, the pirate should be forty or more to have been a captain at the time of Frederic's arrival. Yet this fellow they have in the part is but thirty, though his makeup does extend the look of his age."

"What is Barry's acting background?"

"Primarily Shakespeare. He was the ghost of the dead king in *Hamlet*, and Juliet's father in *Romeo and Juliet*, and King Duncan in the Scottish play. [4] Prior to this production, he was the understudy to the role of Sir Joseph Porter, First Lord of the Admiralty, in *H.M.S. Pinafore*. I believe that was his first non-Shakesperean part, and his first comedy."

"Wouldn't you getting this understudy role be a blow to him?" I interjected.

"As I said, he's physically too large for the part, though his voice would have fit well. No, I don't believe he's your man. He has always been friendly towards me."

Holmes continued to probe our client's memory, but he only came up with two other names. Henry Hillerman, the propmaster was one. Napoleon recalled an argument he'd with him about having to use real, full-sized police truncheons for the show since they were never going to hit anyone with them, and they were long and awkward to carry and dance with. It hardly seemed a worthy motive, though Hillerman did have access to the theatre's guns, which were real, but not loaded with bullets.

The other man was a theatrical agent, Delbert Kelso, who kept wanting to take over the management of Napoleon's career. "I saw no reason to give a percentage of my income to some irritable rascal for doing what I have already done all my career with great success. I sent him packing with the threat of a thrashing if he ever darkened my door again. But once more, that hardly seems like motive for murder, unless he is as mad as the person who wrote the note."

"I'll mention these men to Bradstreet so he can have them checked out," said Holmes. "In the meantime, I'm going to the theatre and see what more I may learn. Watson, I assume you'll wish to consult Wasserman regarding your patient's prognosis. Let us meet for lunch at noon, and we'll compare notes."

Just as Holmes was leaving, a slight commotion arose in the hallway. Someone was trying to get past the constable guarding Napoleon's door. I heard Holmes's voice, but couldn't make out the conversation so decided to see for myself. To my surprise, the visitor was Isabel Abbot.

The constable wouldn't accept Holmes's admonition to allow the lady through, saying he had orders from Bradstreet, but I stepped in and used my position. "As his doctor, I am authorising visiting courtesies to Miss Abbot. She is a close friend of the patient, and would be good for his morale."

The policeman hesitated, but after a stern look from me, he stepped aside and let her pass. Holmes thanked me for the assistance and left for the theatre, while I stayed and supervised the visit so that I could end it, should Napoleon become too weary and need rest.

At the theatre, Holmes, in a fresh disguise, let Whitmore in on his latest ruse and was given free access to the building. He learned that Kelso hadn't returned since being refused by our client, so that removed him from being a suspect. Holmes found an excuse as a contractor to examine the wall near Lionel Barry's dressing table, and when the big man came in, he engaged him in polite conversation, confirming all that Napoleon had told us, and also that he was perfectly content in his current role. It was steady work without the pressure of too many lines, which, at his age, was beginning to tell upon his memory.

While this discussion was going on, Holmes noted that Jordan Haas was engaged in conversation with one of the other "daughters". Suddenly he stormed out, much to the chagrin of the stage dresser who was setting up for the opening scene for the matinee performance.

Something about that reaction set off an alarm within Holmes, and he rushed out just in time to hear Haas order a cab driver to take him to the hospital where Isabel was visiting our patient.

At the hospital, I was pleased that Miss Abbot's attention was having a positive effect on our client. Though he was weak, her infectious good humour was like a tonic, supplementing the medicinal treatments he was receiving. However, after nearly an hour, I could see that he needed rest, and politely suggested that she should let him sleep.

She leaned over him to give him a kiss on the forehead, like a daughter would to a father, but at that moment Jordan Haas burst through the door, having knocked the constable out on the way. Seeing Isabel kissing Napoleon and noting my presence as well, he shouted a vile name at her and rushed at the bed.

I attempted one of my old rugby tackles and managed to throw him off stride, but it didn't knock him down. He caught his balance and reached for the young lady as I fell against the door-frame, momentarily dazed. Napoleon launched himself from the bed and threw his left arm around the thick neck of the outraged younger man who had just grabbed Miss Abbot's elbow. Grabbing his left wrist with his right hand, Napoleon got an elbow wrapped under Haas' chin as a chokehold, forcing him to lose his grip on the girl. With the strength of a madman, Haas clutched at the arm encircling his neck and tried to bend his body to throw the older man off. Instead, Napoleon tightened his grip as he brought his bare feet off the floor and wrapped his legs about Haas' waist. Miss Abbot was screaming at Haas to stop, but she couldn't physically get between the men, wrapped up as they were.

At that moment, Holmes entered the room, having paid his cab driver extra to rush through the London streets at breakneck speed. With our client blocking any attempt to land a knockout blow to Haas' head, or a kidney punch to his back, Holmes used both hands to drive the head of his cane into the stomach of the stage hand and knock the wind out of him. Haas went down, and Holmes helped Napoleon hold him on the floor while I grabbed a pair of darbies from the unconscious constable and we handcuffed Haas' arms behind his back and through the bedframe so he couldn't rise again. It took time for the younger man to catch his breath and, as he did, I helped Napoleon to a chair, as the exertion while under the effects of the poisoning was making it hard for him to breathe. Miss Abbot ministered to the constable who was finally starting to come around, and she also called down the hall for Dr. Wasserman.

Not wanting to risk loosening the handcuffs to move Haas, Wasserman instead moved Napoleon to another room and gave him something to help him breathe and sleep. But true showman that he was, the last thing he said to Miss Abbot before the drugs took effect was, "The show must go on, dear. You get yourself to the theatre. I'll be fine."

I escorted her out to obtain a cab and promised I would see her later at the theatre. While outside, per Holmes's request, I also sent a telegram to Scotland Yard, asking for Bradstreet to come make an arrest. I then returned to Holmes and our prisoner.

As soon as he saw me, Haas let out a stream of invectives condemning Napoleon and me for trying to seduce his girl. "She's mine, I tell you! You and that old man have no right to her!"

I looked at him blandly and replied, "Neither of us was attempting to do so. You have misinterpreted the situation entirely."

"Save your breath, Watson," said Holmes. "Remember that one of the motives I suggested was jealousy? He is blinded by his jealous wrath, and will not listen to reason until it passes."

I looked at the man, awkwardly seated on the floor, and asked, "If you truly love her, why did you plant clues during your attempts on Napoleon's life that would implicate her?"

"Because she was cheating on me!" he screamed.

I looked in confusion at Holmes, who merely shrugged his shoulders. "Save your breath, Watson. He isn't rational at the moment. Indeed, he may not have been for quite some time. It is an unfortunate effect of someone consumed by wrath."

When the inspector arrived, Holmes reported what had led him to follow Haas to the hospital and catch him in the act, so to speak, of trying to kill Napoleon.

"I was at the theatre speaking with Lionel Barry and, naturally, had my list of motives on my mind. I noticed a disturbance between Haas and one of the actresses. His irritation towards her wasn't logically motivated by any situation with the scenery or props – it was more of a personal nature – and this brought to my mind Isabel Abbot.

"When I saw him headed out the door, everything fell into place. He had access to the guns, and even those old flintlock pistols used in the play had a similar-sized bullet to the one that made the mark on the wall. Watson's description of Haas' attitude when he delivered Miss Abbot home last night coincided with that of a jealous lover. He certainly knew Miss Abbot's familial past regarding her great-grandfather, and had access to both her dressing table for the cologne, and Napoleon's to poison the Neopolitan makeup with cyanide he could have retrieved from his father's darkroom.

"All this was running through my mind as I was chasing after him, but it took me longer to obtain a cab than he, and so I was nearly too late. Fortunately, the Good Doctor and Napoleon were able to put up enough defence until I could arrive and improve the odds in our client's favour."

Bradstreet tipped his bowler back on his head and let out a low whistle. "That is some workman-like deducing, Mr. Holmes. That should wrap up the case nicely. It will just be a matter of whether he is sentenced to prison or the lunatic asylum at Hanwell. Thank you, sir."

He held out his hand and Holmes shook it with aplomb. Then the three of us, with the now-revived constable, unlocked the handcuffs holding Haas to the bed and then wrestled him back into them to escort him out to the police van Bradstreet had waiting.

Holmes elected to remain at the hospital and await Napoleon's next awakening while he sent me to the theatre to advise Whitmore that Haas wouldn't be returning to work and would have to be replaced. The matinee was just about to start, and I chose to stay out of sight of Miss Abbot. For the sake of her performance, I felt it better I should give her the details of Haas' arrest until the show was over.

After the final curtain, I found the young lady and explained what Holmes had concluded, and that Haas was under arrest for attempted murder. She sank heavily into the chair in front of her dressing table and fingered a small silver heart on a necklace she wore. After several seconds she took it off, looked at it longingly, and put it into a box. "Poor Jordan," she said softly. "He never learned what love is. He only wanted to possess me like some pet." She looked up into my face and implored, "Why is it that men don't mature until they reach John's age? They are such little boys wanting their toys."

Realizing that she had just insulted me, as I wasn't quite twenty-nine at the time, she caught herself. "I am sorry, Doctor. I didn't mean *all* men. You have been most gentlemanly. In fact, would you mind escorting me back to the hospital so I can check on John?"

I did so, and we found that Napoleon had just awakened when we arrived. Holmes was relating the conditions that brought about the confrontation with Haas, and that he was the threat to Napoleon all along, over a mistaken interpretation of Isabel's feelings for the actor.

As we walked in, Napoleon was just stating, "That's madness, Mr. Holmes! Isabel is sweet, kind, and beautiful, but she is a child. She could never replace my wife."

"Nor would I attempt to," declared the actress as we strode into the room. Napoleon had the good graces to look embarrassed, but she ignored his expression and continued. "I admire you a great deal, John, but I believe you would agree that we would both be better off with someone close to our own ages with similar life experiences."

"Well said, Miss Abbot," offered Holmes. "However, while I believe the doctor has greater experience than I in the art of love, I would make one observation: It is highly unlikely that you will find a man your age at a maturity level worthy of you. I suggest you set your sights a few years higher."

With that, he retrieved his hat and tugged my sleeve to pull me out the door to leave the father and daughter of Penzance to themselves.

NOTES

1. There is a note to this effect in Watson's case notes for his later story of "The Six Napoleons", edited by Arthur Conan Doyle and published in 1904.
2. Cyanide Poisoning: Misconceptions regarding cyanide have been ingrained into the literary world as cliché but are not, in fact, completely accurate. Such as:

   ☐ *"Cyanide smells like bitter almonds."* From the CDC: *"Cyanide is sometimes described as having a 'bitter almond' smell but does not always give off an odor, and not everyone can detect this odor."*

   ☐ *"Cyanide poisoning is not contagious."* From the State of Wisconsin Health Department: *"Cyanide can enter the body through skin when people handle the chemical."* In this story, since the cyanide is in the makeup, in theory, it could be transferred by touch to another person who touches the victim's face.

   ☐ *"Cyanide poisoning is always lethal."* From Johns Hopkins University: *"Victims may survive sublethal exposures."* Again, in this story, the dosage was minutely contained in the makeup and required more than a single application to be lethal.

   ☐ *"Cyanide wasn't used in medicine until the 1920's."* From the National Institutes of Health (USA): *"Cyanide was discovered in 1849 and later became part of the compound sodium nitroprusside, which was used to treat hypertension but not until the 1920's."* In this story, poetic license is used to assume it was being researched at the time in an attempt to find a more effective cure.

3. The term *"person of interest"* did not originate until the 1960's
4. An actor never utters the word *"MacBeth"* outside of a performance. It is considered a curse which brings bad luck upon the theatre. Thus, it is always referred to as *"The Scottish Play"*

The Boarding House Adventure
by Brenda Seabrooke

While sharing a flat with Sherlock Holmes, I'd become agreeably accustomed to our landlady Mrs. Hudson's excellent meals, and I'm sure they contributed to my feelings of well-being that October morning. Holmes had proved to be an interesting fellow, a brilliant detective in whose cases I'd become more and more involved as the months slid by. My wounds from the Battle of Maiwand, and the ensuing fever that so debilitated me, ceased to curtail my activities, and I awaited each new investigation with almost as much interest as Holmes.

We'd finished breakfast, lingering over coffee and the morning editions of the papers, when Mrs. Hudson entered.

"A tele – "

" – Telegram for me," interrupted Holmes as she handed it over and cleared away our dishes. "I heard the door."

Holmes read it and tossed it to me. "Thank you, Mrs. Hudson. Delicious as always. Watson, can you be ready in two minutes?"

"Two minutes? I'll try." I scooped up the telegram without reading it, jammed it into my pocket, and hurried to prepare myself for whatever might ensue. I joined him at the front door, where he already had a hansom waiting. I climbed in.

"Where are we going?"

"Camberwell," he told me and the cabman. "Torquay Terrace."

"What – "

"That is where the Charpentier's boarding establishment is located. You'll recall it from that affair last spring, when the American Mormons, Drebber and Stangerson, were staying there just prior to their deaths and our involvement. There's been a murder."

I pulled the telegram from my pocket and looked at it.

Please come at once. Murder is done.

Alice Charpentier

I handed it back to Holmes and he put it into his own pocket. "Alice Charpentier is the daughter."

"And I assume that one of her boarders is the victim."

"Never assume, Watson. You should know that by now."

"Right. Whatever is left must be the answer. Alice wrote the telegram, so she is alive. I feel certain if it were her mother murdered, she would have said so. Who then is left but boarders?"

"There was also a brother, if you'll recall. Possibly a handyman. A cook, a maid. The cat's meat man."

He had a glint in his eye.

"I understand," I replied. "A joke."

"Only a small one. Murder is no laughing matter, but without more information, we can't assume anything – except that there's been a murder at the boarding house and our help is needed again."

The cab halted in front of the establishment, a handsome red-brick building, perhaps originally intended as a private residence, but converted at some point, likely when the owners' fortunes frayed and they were forced to enter trade. Since the frontage was laid out like a commercial establishment, I rather thought the intention had changed before the dwelling was completed. The entry was enhanced with a white-columned portico. A decorative iron fence separated the structure from the street. Police vehicles stood around the frontage. A constable stopped us at the door. "Sorry, sir. No one can enter."

Holmes held out the telegram. "We were summoned by the family."

The young fellow peered at the telegram. "Mr. Holmes – I thought it was you. And you must be Dr. Watson. Sorry, sirs. Just following orders."

He opened the door for us to enter. "They're in the parlor."

Mrs. Charpentier, a widow, sat with her daughter on the sofa. The older lady's eyes were red from crying.

Alice held her mother's hand, and in her other a bottle of *sal volatile*.

"I'm not about to faint," Mrs. Charpentier was saying. Then, seeing us, she said. "Oh, Mr. Holmes. Dr. Watson. I'm so glad to meet you both, and thank you for coming so quickly! Please prove to that policeman I don't murder my boarders!"

"I shall be most happy to. We came as soon as we received your telegram. Miss Charpentier, can you tell us what happened?"

The girl, tall and attractive, nodded. "Mr. Raymond didn't come down for breakfast. I sent Marie to check on him, in case he had left early. His door was locked, and he didn't answer. She came down for the key and I went up with her, because Mr. Raymond never misses a meal. I unlocked the door and found him still in his bed, but he was dead." She spoke matter-of-factly and seemed calmer now. "Stabbed. The knife was still in him."

"How long had he boarded here?" Holmes asked.

"Five years," Alice said. "He was a nice quiet man. Had a job at the waterworks – something in clerking. Loved his stamp collection. Never married. He had no family."

"He had a cat," Mrs. Charpentier added. "I don't allow pets, except the occasional canary. He thought I didn't know. He let it in and out through the window. It climbed the tree behind the house. A nice thing. He called it Fluffy."

"Was the cat in his room this morning?" Holmes asked.

"No," Alice said. "I haven't seen her today. I often glimpse her in the garden and pet her sometimes."

"Was the window open?"

"It must have been if the cat wasn't in the room. She must have run away. Do you think the murderer climbed up the tree and came in through the window?"

"It's a possibility," Holmes said.

"What color is the cat?" I asked.

Before either of the ladies could reply, another constable entered. "Ma'am, they're ready to remove the victim."

"Oh!" Mrs. Charpentier clutched Alice's hand. "Poor soul."

"Who is in charge of this case?" Holmes asked him.

"Inspector Gregson."

"I'll go up and look at the scene first."

"Sir," the constable said, "I don't think you can do that."

"I'm here on Mrs. Charpentier's behalf."

"The inspector doesn't like lookers."

"This is Sherlock Holmes," I said as Holmes was already halfway down the hall. The constable and I followed him to the stairs.

"Sorry, sir," the officer murmured. "I didn't know." He looked at me. "You must be Dr. Watson."

"I am."

"Heard of you. You was at Maiwand. My uncle was there."

"Was he?"

"He's still over there."

"Alive, I hope."

"Oh, yes sir. He weren't even wounded."

"Lucky man."

"He's coming home at Christmas on leave. I'll tell him I met you." He saluted and I returned his salute, though it wasn't military protocol.

Holmes took the stairs two at a time. I could only manage one.

The victim's room was at the end of the hall, where Gregson stood in the doorway, directing two men from the morgue.

"Halt!" Holmes's voice commanded, echoing in the hallway. Gregson's head jerked up at the sound. He was one of the better inspectors at the Yard, but he had a certain self-importance, and often took the surface as fact, to his later chagrin.

"Mr. Holmes! What are you doing here?"

"Mrs. Charpentier summoned us. Good – I see the body is still *in situ*."

The man lay on a narrow bed with covers thrown back. He wore a blue striped nightshirt that bore a dark red stain in the upper left quadrant from which a knife protruded. Apparently the victim had been sleeping, and hadn't awakened as the knife entered his heart. He'd been small in life, but now, with the loss of blood, he was even smaller. His brown hair was almost hidden under a night cap that matched his sleepwear. A blue robe lay on a chair near the bed.

The top of a nightstand held a half-glass of what appeared to be water and a pair of spectacles. I picked them up and looked through them. "He would have needed to wear these all the time."

The room held a desk, a bookcase with several volumes for the stamps he collected, an easy chair with an ottoman, and a table with a lamp for reading. There was a rag rug in front of the fireplace. A china cup and saucer sat on the table beside a book: *The Pickwick Papers* by Mr. Charles Dickens. A bureau was along one wall with a tin of cocoa on top. Its drawers containing some of the dead man's clothing. A chifforobe held a suit and the rest of his meager wardrobe. He'd had just enough to wear, a job, some stamps, and a cat. A man living on the margin, but he no doubt thought himself to have just enough for his needs and considered himself lucky – until the previous evening.

Holmes opened the cocoa tin and sniffed. He then scooped some of the powder with a silver spoon into an envelope from his pocket and surveyed the room. "Not much to see. His pocket-watch is still here. Nothing seems to have been disturbed. His whole life was spread around him."

"An unremarkable life," Gregson said.

"It was cozy and comfortable," I said. "A snug room, excellent meals, an absorbing hobby, books, a pet to love. He didn't have much, but his needs were met."

I appreciated Mr. Raymond's nest. I'd lived alone in a less-than-cozy hotel room off the Strand before moving into the Baker Street rooms. He made a little home for himself in this boarding house of disparate souls.

Holmes bent and retrieved something from the floor of the chifforobe, dropping it into another envelope which he also pocketed. In a bureau drawer, he found a false bottom with an envelope under it containing Mr. Raymond's small savings. Gregson was clearly miffed at missing that.

When Holmes finished his inspection of the room, we returned to the parlor. Gregson joined us. There, Holmes questioned the landlady about the other boarders.

"I have ten rooms to let, eight upstairs and two down. In a pinch, we can let my son's room short-term with his things stored in the attic while he's away on sea voyages."

"Where is he now?" I asked

"The last message we received from him," Mrs. Charpentier answered, "the ship was in Cairo."

"Safely away from Inspector Gregson," Alice added, with an edge to her voice as she glared at the policeman. I recalled that Gregson had arrested the lieutenant for a short while the previous March, certain that he was the killer in the "*Rache*" murders, as some of the newspapers had called them.

Mrs. Charpentier and Alice then told Holmes what else had happened before we were summoned. "The inspector questioned the boarders and allowed them to leave for their jobs."

"They needed to go to work," Alice explained.

"It isn't as if it were a family death," Mrs. Charpentier added .

I made a chart in my notes to show where the boarders' rooms were. Three of the ten rooms weren't presently occupied, leaving seven boarders: Miss Myrtle Quinney, a middle-aged clerk at John Barnes Department Store in Finchley Road, had boarded since 1868. Miss Josephine Hufford, a milliner at a pricey shop, moved in during 1876. Mrs. Jane Potter, a youngish widow, had boarded for a year-and-a-half, and was saving her money to move to Brighton. In fact, she had gone down there two days previously to look for a situation.

"Is her room re-let while she's away?" Holmes asked.

"No. She's only been gone for a short while, and she pays by the week."

Mr. Harry Ambrose had a position at Charteris Publishers. Mr. William Sherman was in banking and soon to be married. University Professor Johan Dieterich from the University of Heidelberg in Germany was a translator of German documents, and sometimes gave lessons. He always dressed rather shabby and seemed to be struggling to make do. The professor had left the day before, a Monday, to travel down to Manchester to discuss a permanent position.

The seventh boarder was the late and unfortunate Mr. Raymond.

The professor and Mrs. Potter were away, looking for their futures, and the remaining boarders were now at their places of work – everyone but the victim, who was on his way to the morgue. We took our leave and paused with the inspector outside.

"Rum business, that," he said. "Vicious murder. I sent a telegram. Young Charpentier is indeed in Cairo – more's the pity."

"You surely couldn't think he would commit so heinous a crime in his own mother's boarding house?" I said.

"There's something suspicious about that Frenchy."

"The admiralty deems him a fine young officer," Holmes stated, "and despite his parents being French immigrants, he was born in this country. I checked, during the affair last spring."

"Why do you think the murderer was an outsider?" I asked.

"Footprints around that tree against the house," Gregson replied. "It stands to reason that's how he got in. And the fresh mud we found on the rug matches that around the tree." He smiled with satisfaction.

"Congratulations, Inspector," I said.

"I'm going back to the Yard. There's naught to be done here. The murderer came from the streets. He climbed the tree to gain access to the victim's room. We'll be concentrating on this area. This isn't the first housebreaking in Camberwell. There has been a spate of them these past few months. That's what this is. Mr. Raymond had the misfortune to awaken and was killed for it. You may interrogate the boarders if that will please the ladies."

"Good of you, Inspector," Holmes answered. "That will not be necessary since you don't suspect any of them."

Gregson acknowledged this with a nod and boarded the waiting police vehicle. I shook my head as the horses entered the roadway at a brisk pace and disappeared around the next corner. "Sometimes he can be insufferable."

"It seems he hasn't recovered from being wrong about Lieutenant Charpentier in the Drebber case," Holmes said, "and now he is wrong again. Oh – Young man! Just a moment please."

"Yessir." A lad about ten, with a cherubic smile, wandered over.

"What is your name? Do you work here?"

The boy nodded. "I'm Ned. I fill baskets with coal, light fires, run errands." I hope that he sometimes attended school.

"Could you answer a question for me?"

He cocked his head. "I could try."

"Did you procure a hansom to take Mrs. Potter to the station on Monday?"

"I did sir."

"And Professor Dieterich as well?"

"No. He said he was going to the German Embassy first to drop off some papers."

"Excellent. And did you seem him when he left?"

"No, sir. Leastways, I didn't see 'im leave. He was here for his meal the night before, though, 'cause I helped Marie serve."

Holmes thanked him and gave him a coin. "Watson, let's take a look at the back of the house. I believe it connects with a mews."

We walked the narrow path around the house. The kitchen entry was on the opposite side. In the back garden, the tree used by Mr. Raymond for a cat ladder flung one sturdy branch up to the window of his room. "Look at that." Holmes pointed at the ground with his stick. The mud from Sunday's rain was churned up by footprints around the tree.

"How could he tell somebody went up the tree from that mud?"

"Those are police footprints. Gregson no doubt saw the ground when the footprints weren't obscured. And of course, there is the mud found in the victim's room."

I eyed the tree. "Could a man climb that tree? What is it anyway? I haven't seen its like."

"A Paulownia from China," Holmes said. "Sometimes called a Princess Tree, or an Empress."

" I don't think the cat would have any trouble going up and down that tree."

"I climbed a few of them in my early years."

He tested the tree's limbs. They held firm even for his tall frame. He caught the lowest limb and swung himself up. "Not difficult. Try it."

"I haven't climbed a tree since I was a lad. I see no need to resume it at my age."

Holmes laughed as he jumped down, adding his own footprints around the tree and retrieving his stick where he'd leaned it against the house.

"I wonder where the cat is." I looked around the garden, the shrubbery biding its time while huddled against the autumn cold.

"It may have been in the murderer's way. He may have dealt with it."

I nodded. "He killed a man. A cat would've been nothing to him."

"The man was also nothing to him. But killing a cat might be messy."

"Have you decided the murderer is a man?"

"It could've been a woman," he said, "but not likely. That knife went in with a great deal of force behind it, all the way to the hilt. I would expect a man to plunge it that way, though a strong woman could as well."

Our next stop was the German Embassy at Carlton House Terrace, bordering St. James's Palace. A man fitting the professor's description had been there the morning before, but no one knew anything of him, or how long he stayed or who he visited. No package of papers had been logged in.

Holmes nodded as if he had expected no less.

Outside the embassy, none of the cabmen drawn up awaiting fares recollected anyone fitting the professor's description, nor did any recollect fares going to a train station that morning.

"That wasn't helpful," I said as we returned to Baker Street, after first stopping at the post office for some time while Holmes sent a number of telegrams.

"On the contrary, it was very helpful."

"I don't see how. It didn't prove anything."

"Sometimes, Watson, things are proven by what *isn't* there."

He refused to further elucidate and, after a sumptuous lunch, I was less inclined to think about it. Meanwhile, Holmes spent time at his chemical table until a sheaf of telegrams arrived. He glanced through them and stuffed them into his pocket. Then he quickly finished his work and went into his room. I settled by the fire with a cigar as Mrs. Hudson brought coffee. Before she could pour a cup, a strange man exited Holmes's room. He had black hair parted in the middle and a matching mustache. Spectacles perched on his nose. He wore checked trousers and a striped waistcoat with a good watch and chain, and he struggled into a russet coat as he walked. He appeared more rounded than Holmes usually did, and I suspected padding under his outlandish clothes. He carried a large carpet bag.

"Who are you, pray tell?" I asked, half in jest, because no end of personas lived in that chest in his room.

His voice was higher when he replied, and he lingered somewhat on the ends of his words.

"I am Bertram Kayden-Pryce – with a *Y*. I am a clerk, recently widowed, needing a change of venue. I'll be boarding at Mrs. Charpentier's while I find work and settle in. You, on the other hand, may be yourself with a slight name change, and perhaps a tweedy jacket. Dr. – Your name, sir?"

"John Weston will do nicely," I said, getting into the spirit.

"Pack your things, Weston," Holmes said in his own voice, downing most of a cup of coffee. "Not too much – I doubt this will take long. Mrs. Hudson, we'll not be here until tomorrow or the next day."

Holmes went first to rent a room and explain to Mrs. Charpentier and Alice that we were in disguise. I took time to enjoy my coffee so that we didn't arrive in tandem.

My story was that I had come to London to join a practice as partner with an older man who was retiring for his health. I was waiting for him to finish up and looking for a flat so that my family could join me.

I explained all of that later that night to the company of the remaining boarders – minus two, but plus one new clerk – at the evening meal, a nicely cooked joint with many bowls of vegetables, and a sponge cake for dessert.

"Two new boarders on the same day," Miss Quinney said, her eyes on Holmes, who continued to eat his cake as if she hadn't spoken. It was rude of him. "Where did you come from? "

"Miss Quinney asked you a question," I said to Kayden-Pryce.

He put his hand to his ear. "What did you say?"

I repeated the question.

"I'm sorry. I have a hearing problem on that side. I clerked in a factory, and all that machinery noise affected my hearing.

Instantly Miss Quinney was ready to take care of the poor man.

"I'm surprised you would come here," she said, "to so dangerous a place."

"Dangerous?" I lifted an eyebrow. "In what way 'dangerous'?"

"You won't have heard of the murder done here."

"Is anyone here under suspicion?" I asked with concern.

"Oh, dear me, no."

"None of us would harm dear Mr. Raymond," Miss Hufford said.

"Or anybody else," Mr. Sherman added.

"We're a peaceable lot," said Mr. Ambrose.

"That nice inspector thinks it was an outside job," Miss Quinney confided.

"What does he think happened?" I asked.

"Somebody climbed the tree and came in the window that Mr. Raymond keeps – *kept* – open at night for that wretched cat," Mr. Sherman said.

"I don't know why that sweet little Fluffy bothered you," Miss Quinney said.

"My breathing is affected by cats," Sherman growled.

"He never lets her into the rest of the house. She stays in his room and climbs down the tree into the garden, where she takes care of any rodent problems."

"It isn't just me," Sherman protested. "The professor has the same reaction. I thought he might not be able to travel on Monday because of it."

"I noticed the same thing," Mr. Ambrose said. "He was coughing prodigiously at breakfast Monday."

"Inspector Gregson thinks it was a robbery gone bad," Miss Hufford said.

Talk turned to suspicious men they'd noticed on the streets or in the vicinity.

"You just knew he was up to no good, skulking about in the shadows like that," Miss Quinney said with a shiver, recalling one of them.

"How could you tell?" Miss Hufford asked.

"My dear," Miss Quinney replied quietly, "he had *tattoos*."

Mrs. Charpentier had told us that the boarders often gathered in their parlor to continue talking and sometimes played whist and other games, but tonight they each had a cup of tea and then trickled away to their rooms. Holmes and I remained by the fire, where we were joined by Alice and her mother.

"What are your thoughts, Mr. Holmes?" Alice asked softly. "I mean, *Mr. Kayden-Bryce*, now that you've met the boarders?"

"You surely can't suspect them!" Mrs. Charpentier said.

"The inspector questioned them briefly this morning," Holmes said. "He was very quick and passed his judgment on the crime. Now he will try to find suspicious characters in the street, but that will not reveal the murderer. However, I hope that your lodgers will lock their windows and put chairs under their doors. I said as much tonight."

I was more than ready to retire for the evening, but Holmes showed no inclination to finish talking with Mrs. and her daughter. Holmes asked what initially brought them to England.

"The firm my husband was with was failing – something about investor's money. It had gone astray, and Charles was afraid he would be accused. He resigned, we sold everything we had, packed what we could, and left in the night. I remember being ill on the ferry across the Channel. I didn't know if the cause was the choppy water or sorrow for leaving our home. We came here and rented rooms. The owner then, Mr. Helton, was so kind. He took us in and treated us like family. He didn't offer meals then, so I began cooking and, when he died, he left the house to us. This was many years ago, and we've been here for quite a while. Arthur and Alice were born in this house. When my husband passed away . . . ."

After conversation of this sort had continued for a while, I was glad when the ladies finally rose to depart, Mrs. Charpentier saying, "We must leave you gentlemen. This has been a long, exhausting day."

We waited until they were in their rooms before we took ourselves upstairs to ours. Mine was across the hall from Holmes, who was next door to the murder room at the corner of the house. The night was quiet, and I was soon asleep.

117

The following day, the boarders were subdued at breakfast. "I trust you're all well rested," Mrs. Charpentier stated as she poured coffee.

Several nodded, though Miss Quinney said she hadn't expected to be. I suspected the boarders slept well from exhaustion.

After they left for work, Holmes removed his disguise and we went to see Inspector Gregson to find out if he had any leads. He wasn't in, but Inspector Lestrade saw us in the hall and said there was no news. The autopsy report wasn't complete yet.

Holmes sent off more telegrams on the way to lunch at the Holborn.

Over dessert, he asked me an age-old question: "Why do you think people kill?"

"Outside of wars, do you mean?"

"Yes, although it must be difficult for some to tear out into a battlefield to kill."

"It isn't hard at all when the enemy is rushing forward to kill you."

"Yes, yes. The basic instinct for survival takes over in today's battles, but in the past they stood in formation and shot at each other while one army advanced on the other."

"It is difficult to understand. But armies aside, to answer your question, people kill in anger. For vengeance. For money – to either inherit or steal. Or someone is hired to kill. For hatred. Jealousy."

"And some kill for the thrill of it."

"Yes, I suppose some do, but I haven't come across that."

"I hope you never do."

"Do you think this present case was such a 'thrill' killing?"

"I hope not."

"Have you a clue as to what the motive was?"

"Not yet. I know it wasn't thievery. Raymond's gold watch was on the bureau and his savings weren't touched. He had no family, so that rules out inheritance – "

"That you know of."

"True. And most likely vengeance is ruled out as well."

"What about a crime of opportunity?"

"A killer skulking through the night looking for a way in to commit random murder? I can't rule it out, but it doesn't sound plausible. The victim gives every appearance of being a gentle soul, the sort that doesn't engender the passion required to generate the rage needed for a killing. We need more information."

We returned to our Baker Street flat where replies to more of Holmes's telegrams awaited. He read them standing by the table. He then made a tidy pile of them and then resumed his disguise. I suggested he change into a different shirt, which he did, and we returned to Torquay

Terrace, where we found that Mrs. Potter was back from Brighton with the news that she would be sharing a cottage with a widow there as soon as she could pack and leave. "Tomorrow or the next day."

She was petite with fair hair and blue eyes, and popular with the boarders who would, I suspected, miss her bonnie face at the breakfast table.

Our boredom was broken by a message from Lestrade. The autopsy report was in. We hurried to the Yard, and Holmes removed his disguise while we were in transit.

Lestrade met us by the entrance. "He's in a right state, is Gregson."

"What did the report say?"

"That the victim had drank cocoa laced with a sleeping drought."

"It was premeditated then?" I asked.

"I wouldn't say that yet," Lestrade answered. "He could have taken the sedative as a sleep aid. The cocoa powder is being tested."

"You will find the sedative there," Holmes said.

"How do you know that?" Lestrade asked.

"Because I already examined the powder in the tin. The chocolate was easily separated from the powdered sedative. It wasn't poison, so it had to be a sleep aid."

"What does that prove?" Lestrade asked.

"Watson?"

"That the powder mixed with the chocolate was, in fact, to induce sleep," I replied.

"But we don't know if Mr. Raymond put it in, or the murderer," Holmes said, "but my money would be on the murderer, and that rules out a housebreaker as the killer."

"But not a murderer looking for opportunity," Lestrade noted.

"It's still a possibility," Holmes replied, "but it would have to be someone familiar with the boarding house. Come, Watson. We have work to do."

In the cab, I waited to hear his explanation. It wasn't forthcoming. Holmes leaned back and closed his eyes. I thought of the boarders. I couldn't think of even one that might have done murder.

Once again in our disguises, which was easier for me to accomplish than Holmes, we returned to the boarding house in time for the evening meal.

"Did the professor say when he was coming back?" Holmes asked Miss Hufford seated on his right.

"Let's see. He left Monday morning. This is Wednesday. Maybe he was planning to see friends for the weekend. Maybe he'll be back on Sunday night."

119

Mr. Sherman helped himself to potatoes. "Yes, he mentioned Sunday."

"Oh. that's a shame," Mrs. Potter said. "I won't have a chance to tell him goodbye. I'm leaving tomorrow. I finished packing, and the removal van is coming in the morning. I do hope you'll all visit me when you come to Brighton."

Talk turned to seaside visits, and life went on for the resident boarders. Mr. Raymond was gone with hardly a ripple.

Holmes called me to his room when we retired. "Something may happen tonight," he said softly. "We must be on the alert. Keep your Adams handy."

I went to my room and put my gun in my pocket. Returning, I scratched on Holmes's door and he let me in.

"I suggest you sleep for an hour or so. Nothing will happen until the house settles down."

Holmes turned the light low and sat in the comfortable chair. I sat on the bed then swung my legs up and tried to stay awake –

– I awoke with Holmes shaking my shoulder. Very softly, he whispered, "He's here."

I eased up and stood behind Holmes. He'd turned the light out and opened the door a crack. I couldn't see or hear anything in the silent darkness until a floorboard creaked in the hall. Someone was moving in the vicinity of my door.

Inch by inch, the person moved past my door until he was even with the washroom and the stairs on the front.

Holmes slid out the door with me behind him, my finger curving around the trigger of the Adams in my pocket.

We crossed to the far side of the hall, close to the wall. If the intruder turned to look behind him on the other side, he might not see us. Ambient light came from the window above the stairs on the front of the house, cast by the streetlight beyond. It wasn't much, but it allowed us to see the intruder as he stopped at Mrs. Potter's door. He had something in his hand. A key. He pushed it into the lock and turned it slowly. The clicks sounded loud in the silence.

He turned the knob and opened the door slowly. He stepped into the room and slipped something out of his pocket.

"Now!" Holmes hissed and sprang after the intruder, into the room.

I heard a shout, then a crash, and when I gained the room I saw a man sprawled on the floor, and Holmes standing on a man's hand which clutched a knife with a long thin blade.

Holmes increased the pressure. The man's fingers flopped open and the knife slid down. I leaned forward and picked it up with my

120

handkerchief. I didn't like to touch instruments of intimate killing. The blade was thinner than a stiletto and had Eastern writing on the handle. I placed it in my pocket, keeping my Adams trained upon the prisoner.

Mrs. Potter had awakened and, seeing us crowded into her room, let out a scream while clutching her quilt. "Help! Help!"

"Thank you, Mrs. Potter."

"Who – who are you?"

I noticed that Holmes had changed back into himself as he replied, "I am Sherlock Holmes. This is my colleague, Dr. John Watson. And this person on the floor is the former Professor Johan Dieterich, late from Heidelberg and Manchester. Watson, would you keep him covered?"

While I trained my weapon on the killer, Holmes removed some cords from his pocket and tied the man's free hand. He then pulled it behind the man still lying on the floor and jerked the one he'd been standing upon to bind it with the other.

By then, the doorway had filled with the rest of the boarders, Sherman and Ambrose and the Misses Hufford and Quinney all making remarks and questioning Holmes. Behind them were the mother-and-daughter landladies. "Who are you?" Miss Hufford demanded.

"My name is Sherlock Holmes. This is Dr. Watson. I'll explain everything in due time. Let's go down to the parlor."

We went down the stairs and into the boarders' parlor. Holmes had brought the prisoner and bound him to a chair. Only then did I put away my weapon. Holmes took out a pencil stub and scrap of paper and wrote a note. Looking around, he saw the young boy lurking in the hallway. "Ned, take this to Scotland Yard. Ask for Inspectors Gregson or Lestrade. Off you go now! Take a cab if you can find one." And he gave Ned a coin. The lad scampered off, excited to have a part in catching a criminal.

The room was quiet as we stared at the housebreaker and likely murderer of Mr. Raymond, and he stared back at the boarders. He was a stocky man, somewhat less than my height. He wore a trim graying beard and mustache. His hair and eyes were dark brown. His thin lips twisted in a sneer. He wore dark clothing, which was no doubt his skulking costume.

Mrs. Charpentier, her daughter, and Marie the maid went to the kitchen to organize some refreshments, since it was clear we would not be returning to bed this night.

"I always thought meanness lay behind his charming manners," Miss Hufford said.

"But why did you want to kill me?" Mrs. Potter asked. "I never did anything to you. We always conversed pleasantly when we met."

Dieterich snored again, and I thought Ambrose would arise and attack the killer, but Mrs. Charpentier arrived with tea and biscuits, for

121

which I had great appetite. (Catching criminals takes a lot of energy. Lestrade was always grateful for a bite when he stopped by our flat.)

The boarders were occupied with their tea. The murderer was busy with his sneering and trying to find ways to escape.

When the knocker sounded on the front door, Holmes asked Ambrose to answer it, and he soon returned with Gregson, two stalwart constables, and Ned. "They give me a ride in the p'lice wagon," the latter whispered to me. "Can I have a biscuit?"

I nodded as Holmes greeted the inspector, who replied, "What have we got here?"

"I shall now explain," he said, speaking not to the inspector but to the boarders. "As you know, Mr. Raymond, who lived here, was murdered Monday night. What you didn't know was Mrs. Charpentier and Miss Alice engaged my services to discover who killed Mr. Raymond. To prevent alerting the murderer, I stayed here in disguise. Dr. Watson had no need of a disguise, but he did use an alias."

"What's an 'alias'?" Ned asked, his mouth sticky with crumbs.

"A different name," I whispered back.

"We discovered Mr. Raymond's cocoa tin also held sleeping powders. Was he in the habit of taking a sleep aid?"

"Not to my knowledge," Miss Quinney said. "He took a cup of cocoa before retiring, but never anything for sleep."

Inspector Gregson made a note of her remark.

"The murderer climbed the tree outside the window. Mud was found on the rug in Mr. Raymond's floor – the same mud found around the tree. He may have thrown the cat out the window as well. We can only surmise Mr. Raymond awoke, but the murderer silenced him with a knife to the heart before he could cry out. The killer then left the same way he came in, but he didn't take anything, not even the gold watch lying on the bureau. Mr. Raymond was discovered by Mrs. Charpentier and Marie on Tuesday morning."

"Do we need to rehash all of this?" Gregson said. "It was a robbery gone bad. We established that."

"Did we?" Holmes countered. "Then who was this killer, and why did he choose this house?"

"We established that too," Gregson answered. "He's the housebreaker. Hitting houses all around. He ran into trouble here and got caught. If you're in that line of work, you should know not to hit the same house twice in one week."

"Perhaps. But *perhaps* that isn't what happened." He emptied his pockets of telegrams. "We established early that none of the five boarders nor staff were responsible for the murder of Mr. Raymond. Two of the

122

boarders were away from Monday until after the murder. Mrs. Potter returned with the news she was moving to Brighton. The professor was away for the week."

Holmes took a sip of tea.

"Dr. Watson and I were waiting for the killer to make another move. We had reason to believe he would. Tonight he did just that. This man was caught with a knife in the room of a sleeping boarder."

"That's an excellent recital, but what is this man's motive for returning to this house? In my experience, murderers seldom do that."

Holmes held up the stack of telegrams. "We didn't know at first, but information began to trickle in via the wires. First and foremost, the University in Heidelberg has no record of a Johan Dieterich, either as a student or as a professor.

"I talked to Mrs. Charpentier. Her husband worked for a company in Rouen. The company was in trouble. Money was missing. Her husband was afraid he would be blamed for theft. He sold everything the family had and they came to England. I have verified that they stayed in this boarding house. Mrs. Charpentier began serving meals and the owner, William Helton, willed the house to them when he died.

"I sent telegrams to the police in Rouen and learned that another colleague was caught with some of the missing funds." He then pointed at the tied prisoner. "*This man.* Monsieur Jean Leon."

"That was a lie!" cried the man who had pretended to be a professor. "I never took that money!" he shouted, attempting to rise, but the cords held firm. "It was planted in my desk!"

"That's enough of that," Gregson said.

"The money wasn't found in your desk," Holmes continued as if there'd been no interruption. "It was found in a bag belonging to you, in your room. The Rouen police named *you*, Monsieur. *You* spent ten years in prison learning how to make keys, pick locks, and other handy skills from the criminal world. *You* were recently released and, just a week later, you showed up here and became 'Herr Professor' – a good disguise unless you were required to actually speak German."

"But if it's some kind of revenge," Gregson asked, "then why didn't he kill the Charpentiers?"

"Yes," Miss Quinney said. "What did he have against poor dear Mr. Raymond?"

"When Leon arrived, he discovered that his old co-worker, Mr. Charpentier, was long deceased, and that his family now owned this substantial house. Young Charpentier is a naval officer – while Leon had nothing after ten years in prison. He vowed to make the boarding house so dangerous that no one would stay there. He chose Mr. Raymond as his first victim – perhaps he was easier to kill, perhaps for some other reason. I don't know why he chose Mrs. Potter to be the second victim. Maybe he thought that the killing of a woman would be worse than another man."

"Why did you think it was the pro – the man posing as a professor?" Mr. Ambrose asked. "Why him and not, say, me or Sherman?"

"The professor was away, it's true, and normally wouldn't have come under suspicion, but for one thing: He was said to have adverse reactions to cats – and yet I found a white cat hair on the floor of the professor's room." He looked at Mrs. Charpentier. "I searched all of the boarder's rooms at different times over the last day or so. If he reacted adversely to cats, then he wouldn't have had a cat in his room. Thus, the hair had to be from Fluffy, Mr. Raymond's white cat, acquired on his clothing when Jean Leon threw her out the window.

"This crime happened in two parts. The first part was on Monday morning when everyone was dressing for the day. Do you remember when this man disguised as the professor came down to breakfast?"

He waited expectantly, but nobody spoke up, with some shaking their heads. "His plan worked. He waited until everyone including Mr. Raymond went down to breakfast. Then he walked to the end of the hall and opened Mr. Raymond's room with a key he acquired, likely made from the pass key – one of his prison skills. He emptied sleeping powder into the cocoa tin and shook it up. Possibly some of the white cat hair got onto his clothing then, or maybe he had other reasons at other times to reconnoiter there.

"I found a smoking jacket in his room. Did he usually wear it to breakfast?"

"Yes, he did," Miss Hufford said. "I asked him about it once because he didn't appear to smoke. He told me it was more comfortable when he was working in his room."

Holmes nodded. "That garment, hanging in his room, also had cat hair on it. After breakfast, he exchanged it for his coat and then left on his supposed trip to Manchester. In reality, he had a room somewhere nearby, and it was there that he shed his professor disguise. He returned Monday night, climbed the tree, opened the window wider, and stabbed the sleeping boarder. The cat may have scratched at him and he may have thrown it out of the window. He then returned to his other rented room and awaited events. Tonight he returned for the second murder. He didn't bother giving Mrs. Potter sleeping powders, and I don't know his plan for the remainder of the boarders. I'm happy we were able to thwart him and to save Mrs. Potter."

"Where's your proof?" Leon sneered.

"Here." Holmes gave Gregson the stack of telegrams, and an envelope containing the cat hair from the man's floor and clothing. And I gave him the knife, with the stipulation that I'd like the handkerchief wrapping it returned.

With the murderer taken away, the boarders were wide awake and ready to talk. Holmes and I made our escape. I was tired, though I didn't think that Holmes was.

"What put you onto him?" I asked as a hansom returned us to Baker Street.

"It was too convenient for him to be away for such a long time. He was almost penniless. No doubt some robberies can be attributed to him, but a week in Manchester could be expensive for a man who as a professor must keep up appearances. I thought it worth delving into after I heard Mrs. Charpentier's story."

"Fortunately for Mrs. Potter you did."

As I was readying for bed, I heard the notes of a violin downstairs in the sitting room.

Mrs. Charpentier sent Holmes a cheque the next day, and a note thanking him profusely. She ended with the news that Fluffy had returned and was now going to Brighton with Mrs. Potter.

"In a way," I noted, "Fluffy saved her life."

"Indeed," Holmes said.

The Wolf of Kensington
by Mike Adamson

After a damp, grey start to spring, the burgeoning sunshine and warmth of the middle of May 1884 came as a reward to the weary. The papers reported temperatures reaching the upper seventies, even the lower eighties, here and there in the country, and London basked in the delights of the season. I spent much of my time in Regent's Park, sitting under a tree in its new green leaves and working on my notes, for at this time I was determined to do best justice to the cases of my friend, Mr. Sherlock Holmes, in many of which I have had the honour to participate. We had entered our fourth year in residence at Baker Street, and the pace of Holmes's life was a rhythm into which I had settled. Moments of haste and desperate action were interspersed with those lulls in which it seemed the criminal classes of London had taken a holiday, and Holmes despaired of finding the challenge he craved.

After I walked home from the park in the afternoon on one such day, I encountered a fellow upon our doorstep who seemed to be gathering his courage to pull the bell. He was a rangy young chap with a wide and innocent sort of face. I had learned to read the language of the body well enough to recognise his tension.

"Pardon me, sir, but are you seeking the services of Mr. Sherlock Holmes?" I asked.

He doffed his derby at once. "I am indeed."

I offered my hand. "Dr. John Watson. I share rooms with Holmes. Do come up."

Escorting him upstairs, I was pleasantly surprised to find Holmes engaged in research at his chemical bench. Some substance bubbled in a glass vessel over a burner.

"Holmes, we have a guest," I announced, and the gentleman presented his card.

"Do excuse the general untidiness," Holmes remarked, glancing at the card. "Mister Kemble. Be seated and tell me in what way I might be of assistance."

I offered lemonade for our guest, took my seat by the room's unlit hearth, and noted the proceedings as Mr. Peter Kemble began.

"Gentlemen, I have reason to believe my father's life is in danger."

"You interest me already," Holmes said with a smile. He reached for his pipe and black shag, then reclined in his chair in the posture that I knew denoted his absolute concentration. "Go on. What leads you to suspect this?"

"My father is Mr. Philip Kemble of Kensington, a businessman of some standing and repute. He has done very well for the family – I grew up in a fine house whose back garden overlooks the woods of Holland Park. Now, my young children visit their grandparents in this wonderful place, and are their joy. But lately, Mr. Holmes, my father has received threatening messages of the most awful sort."

"Do they seek to extort financially?" Holmes asked bluntly.

"No. That's the strange part. They merely forecast doom. *His* doom." Kemble took a sip and seemed truly perplexed. "I was present when they first arrived – I have barely left his side since – and advised my father to lay the matter before the police, but he shrugged it off as nonsense – merely some lunatic seeking momentary notoriety, which he refuses to indulge."

Holmes removed his pipe from between his lips and directed his comment at the ceiling. "Would you say such behaviour is typical of your father?"

"By no means. I have always considered him to be a prudent and cautious man who evaluates any jeopardy with great seriousness."

"Make a note of that, Watson," Holmes murmured, closing his eyes. "Does your father know you are approaching me on his behalf?"

"No, sir, he has no idea. I fear he would be most displeased."

"Very well. Pray, continue."

"So far, there have been three messages, each of the same general character. The first, received in April, was composed of letters cut from the newspaper and pasted together. The unknown correspondent always writes thus."

"What did it say?"

Kemble took a notebook from an inside pocket and read aloud: "'*Your time has come, Kemble. All good things come to an end, and your days as a king are running out.*'"

"Hmm." Holmes drummed his fingers on the arms of his chair. "Straight to the point. No demands for largess to deflect the oncoming doom. Merely the implication that it is inevitable. It declares, of course, that Mr. Kemble knows what it's about."

"How can you be sure of that, Mr. Holmes?"

"Come now. It's as plain as a pikestaff. If he did not know, the message – which is otherwise ambiguous – would be pointless. Self-evidently, the writer knows your father, and something about his past. Mr. Kemble's dismissal of this as nonsense as good as confirms it. He has no intention of sharing the details with his family or of drawing the matter to the attention of investigative bodies."

"You're suggesting that my father has something to hide?"

"Smoke is rarely present without fire, and this approach doesn't resemble simple extortion. The writer seems less interested in the family fortune than in the satisfaction of doing damage." Holmes blew a last smoke ring. "Do I agree that your father's life is in danger? Most certainly."

"Then you'll take the case?"

"To be sure. However, I must caution you at the outset that your preconceptions about your father may be challenged at some point. Are you prepared for this?"

The question took our guest aback, and he swallowed hard before pressing on. "I would be remiss in my duty if I took any other course. If grievous mischief is intended, we must get to the bottom of it."

"Splendid." Holmes came to his feet with a bound and extended a hand. "We shall make inquiries forthwith. Do you have the text of the other notes?"

Peter Kemble tore a page from his notebook and passed it to Holmes. "These are the messages, verbatim, with the date of receipt in each case."

"Do the messages themselves still exist?"

"I'm afraid not. My father burnt them promptly, though I was able to glance surreptitiously at them. I felt that a record of their content might be valuable."

"Quite correct. A pity. It would have been illuminating to examine the paper and envelopes, despite the hand being inaccessible." Holmes shrugged with a quick smile. "No matter. We must work with what we have. However, I will ask you to remain with your father in the forthcoming days, upon some pretext. Should a fourth message arrive, you must intercept it before your father reads it. I *must* see it."

With his assurance on this score, I took Kemble's address and showed him out. No sooner had I ascended the stairs once more than Holmes thrust a hat and stick upon me.

"No time to waste, Watson. Kensington!"

Holland Park – the road, as distinct from the woodland – is a circuit off Uxbridge Road in the fashionable West End, and the wealth of the residents there is evident at first glance. No terrace accommodation. Not even the four- or five-storey Georgian standard. Impressive, fully detached houses stand upon their own generous plots, where trees line the approaches. A cab dropped us by a footpath leading into the park proper, whose forest runs south towards Kensington Road, and we found the

Kemble residence. Strolling by the frontage in the late afternoon light, we took in a tall façade of stone and glass with mock classical columns, the whole giving the impression of a stately and relaxed way of life.

"One can almost smell the money," I mused quietly, my stick striking upon the paving stones. I raised my hat to a governess with her three young charges, returning to her place of employment after a stroll among the rustling woodland behind the houses.

Holmes raised a dark brow at me. "Indeed, one can. And I find it quite impossible to believe that money doesn't play a part in this business. It is, as churchmen so often remind us, the root of all evil, and such conspicuous wealth evokes both envy in those who do not have it, and simple hatred in those who have been, shall we say, *deprived* of it. The tenor of the messages would seem to suggest the latter."

"And Kemble's unwillingness to acknowledge the problem? What of that? If he knows what he is being taken to task about, and it is a serious affair, how can he shrug it off?"

"All excellent questions," Holmes agreed. "No man who lives in such style is without resources – of whatever sort – and I would be surprised to discover that measures aren't already in hand, albeit of a kind upon which the police would doubtlessly frown."

"So, he's making light of it in front of his family while taking his own steps?"

"This seems logical." We passed eastward along the street as we spoke and, at the far end, discovered a further pathway into the park. Before I had spotted the figure upon a bench under the spreading trees, Holmes raised his stick in greeting. "Good afternoon, Inspector."

We were quite alone, so the indiscretion of the announcement was permissible. The tall, burly figure of Inspector Bradstreet rose, folding a newspaper under his arm. He was a twenty-year man, like Lestrade. Indeed, he had joined the force just the year after Holmes's most frequent sparring partner.

"Mr. Holmes." His bass voice rumbled through his whiskers. "This cannot be a coincidence."

"I fear not. You, too, are observing the comings and goings at Holland Park? I have the honour to hold a commission of investigation into affairs at the Kemble household. And yourself?"

Bradstreet nodded. "Comings and goings, indeed. Kensington is one of my old 'patches', as you're probably aware. When known felons were seen consorting in a riverside pub with a man we identified as the chief coachman serving the banker, Phillip Kemble, it seemed only right to keep an eye on affairs." He gestured into the park, and we strolled beneath the new spring's leaves. "I'm a practical man, Mr. Holmes, not given to opportunism. I leave that sort of thing to my colleague, Mr. Lestrade. So, perhaps we could both advance our investigations by reviewing what we know?"

"An eminently sensible suggestion, Inspector. I shall rise to the moment by informing you of threatening messages received by the master of the house, which he chooses to dismiss but which were just a few hours ago brought to my attention by Mr. Kemble, Junior. Extortion doesn't seem to be the motive at this point."

Bradstreet raised a brow. "You do surprise me, Mr. Holmes. Wealth defines the people in this neighbourhood. Over what else could they possibly be victimised?"

"An interesting choice of words, Bradstreet. It defines Kemble as the victim, but from other perspectives, he might *perhaps* be a perpetrator." Holmes raised a hand to forestall comment. "Allow me to explain. Mr. Kemble is a banker – with Gablehouse, I believe, off Cornhill Street. Now, while there is no suggestion of impropriety or sharp practice on behalf of the bank at this time, one might quite naturally suspect such as a motive. If a small investor lost his life's savings in some venture and perceived the bank to have taken advantage, or to have been merciless in its dealings, or indeed to have mismanaged affairs and precipitated the loss – *there* is a strong reason for a personal attack upon one of the bank's directors."

"Indeed. We've made confidential inquiries among the other trustees, but no one has been threatened. Nor have we made them aware of the details of this situation."

"So, the threat is directed personally at Mr. Kemble. What do we know of him as a man?"

Bradstreet shrugged his ox-like shoulders. "He's the quintessential London success story. He was born in 1826 to a good family in Kent, and served in the army briefly before transferring to the police. Oh, yes, he's one of our own."

"A Scotland Yard man?" I asked, pencil poised over my notebook.

"Not *that* close to home. He was actually with the colonial constabulary. He served for several years as a lieutenant, in charge of a ragtag squad of troopers in the high country of Victoria, down in Australia. He spent the early 1850's chasing outlaws – 'bushrangers', as they say – and guarding gold shipments."

"My word, what a colourful career," I remarked, wondering quite how to record all this.

"Apparently, it was a life of great hardship and privation. I heard Kemble speak once after a police dinner in the City, and he described his pursuit of violent, desperate criminals in harsh country and the most appalling weather, heat and cold alike. It was all very 'Wild West', as the penny-dreadfuls call it."

"So," Holmes went on, "a hard man who is no stranger to privation. And his fortune?"

"He saved his pay and invested wisely, made some shrewd transactions in the Colonies, and had a stake to begin in business when he came home in . . . '58, as I recall. He brokered some transactions between Australian contacts and the Gablehouse Bank. Became personal friends with the chairman of the bank during bridge and polo sessions, and married the man's daughter. The rest is history."

"A long and chequered career," Holmes mused. "A policeman on one of the Empire's wilder frontiers, trying to enforce Her Majesty's Law in a land at that time heavily populated with convicts and the descendants thereof. And now, someone – as yet unknown – has an axe to grind with ex-Lieutenant Kemble of the Victoria Police."

"We shan't let the blade fall," Bradstreet murmured.

Holmes nodded thoughtfully, and I knew his mind was already several scenarios ahead, advancing beyond the facts and seeking patterns that best reflected what we knew. He had spoken the truth to young Peter Kemble. Clearly, delicate matters were in play, and the outcome might not be pleasing to all.

"Patrick Brand," Holmes mused as we watched Kemble's driver step out of the carriageway of his master's home.

He was a thickset fellow in a dark coat and hat and had a face like a prizefighter. We sat in a growler along Holland Park from the Kemble property. When Brand put best foot forward, Holmes tapped on the ceiling, and we followed at walking pace.

"A curious figure," Holmes went on. "An ex-criminal in the employ of an ex-policeman. There is, of course, history between them. According to sources in the City who shall remain nameless, Kemble sought out Brand as a reliable chap to serve his household."

"Isn't that rather a contradiction in terms?" I mused, watching the hurrying figure ahead.

"Not really. Kemble knows criminals. He knows how to appeal to them, and to recognise one who has been rehabilitated. We may assume Brand belongs to the latter category. His skills have doubtless been useful, and as a driver, he is frequently entrusted with the Kemble grandchildren."

"Why this sudden need for Brand to associate with his old sort of colleagues?"

"There are a number of possibilities," Holmes mused as our cab turned at the end and drew in to arouse less suspicion. The driver was well paid and knew this game, having transported Holmes often enough. "Brand may have chosen to bite the hand that feeds him and is involved willingly with the party who wishes Kemble ill. Or he has been coerced into cooperating."

"Then shouldn't Bradstreet simply arrest the fellow and get the facts out of him?"

"Patience, Watson. We haven't yet exhausted the possibilities. A third scenario sees Brand loyal to Kemble and exploiting his old contacts very much for his master's benefit."

"You mean those private measures you spoke of?" I nodded over the implications, jotting quickly.

The coach pulled out to follow Brand, who was almost up to the main road. He turned left, and as we reached and negotiated the corner, we watched him snare a hansom. Our driver fell in a good distance behind the other vehicle. Uxbridge Road became Goldhawk Road, and we followed the gleaming rails of the tramway west and south, where Shepherd's Bush melds into Hammersmith.

"We seem to be on our way to the waterfront," Holmes observed ten minutes later. "Officers of F Division observed Brand there while they happened to be keeping watch on a group of dockworkers. Criminal records all – larceny, violence, the usual – men known to be for hire in the underworld, who usually earn their extra-legal shillings as enforcers for the shadier elements behind the dock trade. That night, they cosied up with Patrick Brand. The F Division men overheard nothing, but Brand bought the drinks, and they spoke, if not like old chums, then as equals."

I sighed over my notes. "It would be easy to see them using him to gain some sort of entrance. Brand works for a rich man in a neighbourhood of rich men. The pickings are too obvious."

"Just so. *Too* obvious. Merely because such powerful and influential figures are involved, police vigilance is high in that area. Magistrates are notoriously hard on thieves who trespass with intent to burgle the well-to-do. Your common thief leaves such places to the elite of his trade – cat-men, who can enter almost-fortified residences and make off with goods that are dashed hard to dispose of. No, the roughs around the docks are a different class of criminal, and unless Brand is posing as an inside man to facilitate thievery, their business is of a different sort."

"What did the F Division officers have to contribute?"

"They are engaged in investigation of organised crime in the poorer parts of the West End. There are several brewers and distillers on the river near Chiswick Eyot, and corruption has been suspected for quite some time. The men under observation are in the common employ of figures higher up. At this point, however, that appears to be an entirely separate case. I would expect some prior connection to present itself between Brand and those he has approached."

The hansom ahead rolled by St. Peter's Square, then followed Eyot Gardens down to Chiswick Mall, which runs like an esplanade along the shore. Holmes tapped the ceiling, calling directions for the driver to thread through to Standish Road and approach the river from the north.

"He can only be heading for The Old Ship Inn, the very same public house in which he met his comrades last time. This is it, Watson. I must approach by stealth. His cab will drop him at the corner of Black Lion Lane, from which he takes a footpath to reach his destination."

As he spoke, Holmes opened a valise, swapped his deerstalker for a county cap, and swiftly applied a facial disguise of whiskers, bushy eyebrows and spectacles. The carriage dropped him low on Standish Road, a hundred yards from the pub that nestled between the offices of the West Middlesex Water Works and the corn maltery of the Albert Mills. With instructions for me not to wait, he walked into the gathering dusk with the rolling gate of an old sailor.

I *hmphed* softly in frustration, for I had yet to fully accustom myself to Holmes's eccentricities, and to the monologue of our intellectual exchanges being punctuated by the exigencies of circumstances. I would see him again when he had gathered the information he was seeking, and until then, my thoughts were my own.

A tap and a soft call sent the driver back northward, and I entertained thoughts of supper as I added to my notes.

Holmes returned by cab at late evening, and I laid aside an astounding new work by that celebrated Frenchman, Jules Verne, so that we might resume our consideration of the case. I had reserved some supper for my friend – the makings of tea with bread and butter – and Holmes quickly shed his disguise before joining me.

"Progress?" I inquired as the kettle boiled on the hob and I set out cups.

"Adequate. I have left a message, which Bradstreet will receive in the morning. In my guise as a retired seaman and in the poor light of the public house and general inebriation of its patrons, I blended well-enough with the rivermen. While playing darts and skittles with them, I kept my ears open, and Brand was certainly in discussion with the dockers once more."

Holmes sat and took tea with me, leaning forward a little. A glint in his eye assured me that he had indeed made a useful connection. "You know me well enough by now to know I never leave things to chance."

I nodded my agreement as I buttered fresh, crusty bread.

133

"However, there are occasions when one may be forgiven for dangling a lure, as it were, to see if the fish are biting."

"Were they?" I asked, already knowing the answer.

"Cautiously at first, but they displayed a very definite interest. Remembering Phillip Kemble's service in the Colonies, I dared to affect the Cockney-like accent of our austral kin and, in rather short order, one of the roughs approached me – in a genial and companionable way, certainly, but with an undeniable element of urgency. Sensing in my air a fellow sailor, he chatted for a while about matters maritime before steering the conversation to my Australian character. He was interested to know when I had arrived and if I knew any other Australians presently in London."

"As you say, a very pointed interest," I said, passing the buttered bread. "An Australian connection, then."

"And, as the very sound of an Australian accent sparked interest at once – such that they must approach a stranger and seek to know him – we are left with an inescapable conclusion: Their quarry is indeed an Australian personage, and obviously, they have yet to locate him. Thus my message to Bradstreet, seeking a Customs check on all arrivals from the Colonies in the six weeks up to the middle of April."

I raised a brow. "That could be a considerable number."

"Perhaps, perhaps not. The first threatening message reached Kemble in the weeks following the arrival of the season's last wool clippers from Australia. As we know, these are the fastest ships in the world and carry a few passengers in addition to their rich cargoes. Liners are much slower, their arrivals less frequent. I'm hoping an inspection of those passenger lists will bear fruit."

"If so, we'll have a candidate for Kemble's heckler."

"But the pursuit will have only just begin," Holmes added reflectively. "If I had come halfway around the world, I would not be careless in my dealings where the law is concerned." He thought for a moment, reaching for his pipe on a sideboard and taking it unlit in his teeth for a moment. "And I confess an abiding interest to know what drives any human being to such a voyage – such a mission, if you will – for I am certain that this affair, couched in harassment and threat though it may be, has a deep, ultimate significance."

Society provides various means for one person to learn about another without them ever being aware of the scrutiny, and the more prominent or famous the person, the easier it has become to do so. The following morning, Holmes visited the Reading Room of the British Museum to look up Phillip Kemble, ex-Lieutenant Kemble of the Victoria Police. He appeared in the *Who's Who* volumes of London published since his return from the Colonies. He was mentioned in the *Australian Parliamentary Papers* volumes as being instrumental in various operations against the criminal elements of the antipodes, and the general summary of his record with the service was available for consultation.

"An accomplished man," Holmes remarked as we began lunch while Mrs. Hudson's footfalls receded upon the stairs without. "Our Mr. Kemble served five years in a difficult station, endeavouring to keep order among settlers, the last of the convict population, and the floods of prospectors passing through. These were the days of the Victorian Gold Rush. As you might imagine, banditry was rife in the wild countryside and upon the muddy tracks and dusty ways that passed for highroads. His record is not without blemish, though."

"What sort of blemish?" I asked, pouring tea from the porcelain pot.

"Heavy-handedness in pursuit of his duty. He got results, which tended to overcome complaints, but those complaints remain a matter of record – property damage and loss, injuries, and troopers lost in the line of duty. There were calls for inquiry into the conduct of his affairs, but they came to nothing."

I pondered this for a moment. "It's more than easy – it's *natural* for a man in a position of power to overstep the mark when devoid of oversight. I remember times in India, on the way up to Afghanistan, when officers entrusted with duties among a native population were largely cut off from contact with their chain of command for long periods. It takes a very superior sort of man to rise above the impulse to overstep his own authority – like the Naval captains in the bad old days, who exercised the letter of their commissions and ran their ships as private fiefdoms with the power of life and death over their crews. The Admiralty was wont to shrug off charges of excess and brutality. Sometimes they were right to do so, but not always." Frowning, I stirred my cup. "I wonder if Lieutenant Kemble was another Bligh? Out of sight, out of mind. The only instrument of authority over a vast territory. The odds are high of a man losing his sense of proportion out there and becoming exactly the sort he was set to catch."

"I find myself in agreement, Watson, especially when we consider the economics of the situation. A Victorian Police lieutenant's pay in the 1850's was generous – I looked it up. Kemble would have been drawing some thirty-six shillings weekly, that figure mounting somewhat throughout the years of his service. On average, he would have earned around a hundred-pounds-per-year in a position of such responsibility. Assuming he never spent a penny, he would have brought some five-hundred pounds back to this country from his legitimate earnings."

"Half that, at the *absolute* most," I amended with a sour look. "Between food and drink, the 'necessaries' of his profession, lodgings when away from duty, transport, staying well-dressed. It all mounts up, and I don't see any man saving more than half, even of a generous income."

"Then where did he come by *twelve-thousand* pounds to invest upon his return?"

My brows must have risen dramatically.

"Just so, Watson. That was the sum of his investment with the Gablehouse Bank, which caught the attention of its directors and helped launch Kemble into London society."

"A working police officer couldn't hold two careers – it would be a conflict of interest. In practical terms, he could spare neither the time nor the energy to wade in streams and pan for gold, so honest toil is unlikely to be the source of his largess." Arms folded, I sat back. "That leaves speculation – investment in enterprises out there – or gambling. Was he adept at taking money from others at the card table?"

Holmes shook his head as he buttered toast. "Private gambling was illegal in the colony. Oh, horseraces and boxing booths, certainly, but private card schools – absolutely not. Kemble was the one charged with closing them down."

"His legal options for amassing wealth like that are growing thin. What about winnings at the racetrack? Maybe he knew his horses and was a clever punter."

"That is worth assessing, and I know just the man to consult. But on these points, nothing specific is stated in the public records. Merely that he 'encountered success in the Colonies' and built upon it with wise investment in the old country." Holmes adopted the cynical look I knew so well. "As you say, the temptation to emulate the criminal while hiding behind the respectable face of authority is the very song of the siren. I need to learn more about Kemble. I want to know who he was *before* he went to Australia. He came from a good family and studied at Eton and Trinity, so I don't anticipate undue difficulty in filling in the missing dimensions of his character."

During the afternoon, further elements presented themselves when a large envelope containing two items arrived from Scotland Yard. The first was a note from Bradstreet to the effect that the Customs Service had reported that they received the same request some weeks earlier, but declined to cooperate since it didn't come through correct channels.

Holmes raised a brow at this news. "Kemble, obviously. An ex-policeman, thinking like a policeman – trying to gain access to the

136

resources of government and perhaps calling in favours. We may be thankful that the Customs Service is more autocratic than that."

The other contents were several sheets of writing paper: The passenger lists of ships reaching the Port of London from Melbourne, Sydney, Newcastle, and Perth. They weren't long. Those clippers were cargo ships first and foremost. None carried more than two or three passengers. That greyhound of the ocean, *Cutty Sark,* had hosted two, and made port the week before the first message was received.

The list was annotated with what was known about the arrivals: Businessmen whose trade demanded their presence rather than the usual conduct over the lines of telegraphic relay. A military man retiring to his home estates. A courier bearing urgent dispatches from the Australian Governor General to Westminster, and so forth. Of all those who landed by express passage, only one stood out as unknown: An ordinary citizen without connections in Britain. He was no figure in industry, government, or services – just a chap from the backcountry of Victoria who had joined the ship in Newcastle, New South Wales, and alighted at the London Docks in Wapping. He took his valise, walked through Customs into the bustling city, and at that point vanished from official attention.

"His very anonymity raises a question," Holmes mused, standing by the window with his unlit pipe between his teeth. "Who is this *Percival Morse*? It would seem he had no difficulty finding the price of his voyage, so he is of some means in his own country. Her Majesty's Customs Service had no qualms about admitting him to this one."

"He could be anywhere, Holmes," I remarked a little despondently.

"This is a city of over five-million persons, not counting the outlying villages and townships, so finding a single individual among them is like looking for one particular pebble on Brighton Beach. However, Morse shared a cabin aboard ship with a Herbert Drew, an agent for the Australian wool merchants bound for talks with the corresponding London organisation. Drew should be easy to track down. If Bradstreet could organize for us the services of an artist, we shall have a usable likeness quickly enough. One cannot spend ten or eleven weeks in someone's company without learning their features quite well."

Before we could act on this, the bell announced a visitor, and in moments, Peter Kemble had joined us. Doffing his derby, he produced an envelope. "You wanted to see a fourth message, if one should arrive, Mr. Holmes. I was able to intercept it."

"Splendid!" Holmes held the envelope to the afternoon light. "Watson, make a note: A standard stock such as hotels might purchase. No watermark, so possibly a cheaper place of accommodation." A sniff at the glued edge produced further observations. "A whiff of tobacco, but nothing singular or overpowering." He took up his letter opener and ran the blade along the top edge. "The missive within uses what looks like butcher's paper." Sliding the sheet out, he unfolded it by the window. "Once again, words and letters, cut from a newspaper and pasted together. *'Your time is running out, Kemble. You didn't think you could run forever? Privilege will not shield you.'* This is more to the point – it sounds ever more like remonstration over a grievance."

"Have you any clues, Mr. Holmes?" the young man asked plaintively, obviously somewhat taken aback by the implications of Holmes's words.

"Only that we suspect an Australian connection at this point. We have a man in mind and are on his trail as we speak." Holmes pocketed the letter and reached for his coat. "You must excuse us, Mr. Kemble. Our next stop is Scotland Yard."

Hailing a cab in Park Place, we made haste for Whitehall. "We have a possible grudge going back decades," I observed. "Why pursue it *now?*"

"There could be many reasons. Remember, Phillip Kemble retired from the colonial force over twenty-five years ago before returning to England. It might be that his assailant simply lost track of him and learned his whereabouts just lately, perhaps serendipitously. We already have a large part of the *how*. I am interested to know the *why*. Surely, all will become plain at that point."

Baker, Oxford, and Regent Streets were our route, and in no time, we were alighting at Scotland Yard in Whitehall Place. The name and face of Sherlock Holmes weren't yet second nature to the Metropolitan Police Force – other than as the bane of some officer's professional pride. Inspector Bradstreet had left word with the reception sergeants that he was working with Holmes on an urgent matter and, at their prompting, he came down to join us.

In the fresh afternoon air, we strolled eastward towards the river, past the great railway span of Hungerford Bridge, and paused by the noble pillar of the statue of General James Outram. Bradstreet hooked his thumbs into his waistcoat pockets and Holmes and I took a smoke.

"Here's the thing," Bradstreet began in his bass rumble. "There's some at Scotland Yard who are of short temper where the name of Sherlock Holmes is concerned, so it's probably more productive to meet outside. I assume the passenger lists I sent earlier have borne fruit."

"We have a candidate," Holmes replied. "Percival Morse, from Australia. You could search the registers of London's hotels, but I would assume he is lodging under an alias – Indeed, the name given to the shipping company might also be false. However, we learned of someone who knows Morse on sight. Could you connect us with an artist to secure a likeness?"

"Done," the inspector said with a nod. "Anything else?"

Holmes produced the fourth message. "You may want to log this in as evidence, Bradstreet. It seems matters are approaching a cusp."

"I'll trust you to call us in when the moment arrives." In a cautionary tone, he added, "It is a police matter, after all."

"You have my word, Inspector. Would you care to accompany us to the woolsheds at Wapping? Excellent. Then, a telegram to the managers is the next step."

It transpired that Herbert Drew had concluded his business in London some weeks before and retired to the country, near Oxford, to visit family for the months until the new season's voyages began, when he could take a berth on a clipper outbound for Australia. The wool merchants were able to give us an address, and at once we dispatched a telegram. Bradstreet looked up an artist but declined to make the journey with us, leaving us free to pursue the verity of our impressions regarding the odds of Kemble coming by his fortune through the means of gambling.

As afternoon wore towards evening, we took our leave and enjoyed a brisk walk up Northumberland Avenue to Trafalgar Square before making our way along the busy thoroughfare of the Strand. Holmes knew a man he had had cause to consult on affairs of the turf. When not posting odds at Kempton Park, Royal Windsor, and the other great racing venues serving the metropolis, the man would usually be found at the Coal Hole – a public house said to be built upon what had once been the coal cellar of the Savoy Theatre, the imposing bulk of which rose behind it.

Jeffrey Cousins was a bookmaker, as wise in the lore of the track as any man alive, and I had to smile as Holmes pointed him out in the quiet bar. Cousins was of advancing middle years, with silvering hair tucked under a wide-brimmed hat. A fur-collared topcoat lay folded at his side, and he sat in a corner booth, inspecting a form guide with an overflowing ashtray and an almost-empty ale glass before him.

The first he knew of our presence was when Holmes set a fresh glass of rich amber fluid before him, and he beamed a smile. "Mr. Holmes, as I live and die! It's been a long time, sir!" His Cockney twang was broad and pleasing – Fulham, I thought.

"Busy times, Jeffrey. Not a moment to socialise." Holmes introduced me as I brought over two tall glasses of stout, and Cousins invited us to join him.

"What brings you in search of a humble bookie, Mr. Holmes? I've seen your name crop up in the papers now and then – some *rum* cases you have investigated!"

"I am upon such business at this very moment, and would appreciate the professional opinion of a master of trackside intrigues."

Cousins smiled with a wave of denial. "I'm just what a lifetime in the trade has made me."

"A walking encyclopaedia of odds, records, form of horse and jockey, who wagered what, who is a wise punter, and who is anything but."

"You do me honour, sir." Cousins took an appreciative pull at his fresh glass. "And which of those would you be after?"

Holmes shot me a glance and thought for a moment. "You've been in this business a long time, Jeffrey. Cast your mind back to the Fifties."

"Right cutthroat days, they were. But with the end of public hangings, people needed some other form of entertainment, so they flocked to the tracks. Good for me."

"Think of country race meetings. The case in point is actually down in Australia, but the mechanics of wagering are no different." Holmes took a long drink and set his glass down. "Could a man earning a hundred-pounds-a-year turn it into at least ten-thousand – and do it on the quiet?"

"Over what period?"

"Five years, no more."

Cousins's brow furrowed in thought. "It can be done, certainly – but it takes either a brilliant understanding of the sport or God's own luck." He smiled conspiratorially. "Spare me no detail, Mr. Holmes."

What we knew of Kemble's remarkable gathering of largess didn't take long to outline, and Cousins lit a fresh cigar as he listened. "Hmm. Knotty problem there, Mr. Holmes. The strategy of a careful punter is to lay multiple small bets to hedge the odds at every race meeting he can get to. He has to fight the temptation to go for big scores, because the odds run against him. If he's satisfied with less, each-way and favourite-for-a-place are almost guaranteed to return him something every time. But you're talking about a sportsman winning a hundred-twenty *years'* wages in five. As I understand it, there aren't enough country races in the Colonies to stand a chance, even supposing your man had nothing to do but travel and gamble. You tell me he had a demanding job at the same time?" Cousins shook his head. "Not unless he had the luck of the Devil – a string of hundred-to-one outsiders that all actually came in. The process takes longer, and the larger the bets get, the bigger the risk. But you can only accumulate faster with big wagers."

"What about the single stroke of divine luck?" I suggested. "The long odds that come up, the large wager at the right time – ?"

Cousins plumed blue smoke and gave an eloquent shrug. "I'm not saying it doesn't happen, Dr. Watson, but we're talking very large sums here. A hundred-pound bet on a horse coming in on hundred-to-one odds would get you there, but think about what you're suggesting. Only the most arrogant and desperate toff who doesn't know the value of money

140

would lay a wager like that – and probably blow his brains out in the *likely* eventuality he loses. Bookies rub their hands in glee when they see a mug like that coming. It's free money. But your man doesn't sound like a total gully who'd throw away a year's wages on an infinitesimal chance. Even today, it'd take every bookie at the track to cover the bet if the unthinkable should happen and that horse actually came in first. No responsible bookie would even take the bet if there was a ghost of a chance of it coming up – If it does, he isn't just bankrupt. He's probably *dead.*"

"What about working through agents?" Holmes proposed.

"Put up the stake money, and pay a professional gambler a commission? That's always possible. On a busy day of racing in this country, all manner of miracles can occur. A four-horse accumulator – laying winnings from each on the next – can turn a few bob into hundreds of pounds. Always worth a shot, but there's a lot of luck involved. Your man doesn't sound like the sort to trust in luck, which kind of wagers against him building a fortune at the track in the first place." Cousins sat back, glass in one hand, cigar in the other. "If you want my professional opinion, gents, it can't be done – not by this fellow, with the time and resources he had. I've seen fortunes rise and fall, and winners going up like a skyrocket. But greed *always* gets the better of them. Without fail, they think their winning streak will last just one more flutter, but all streaks end, and only the bookie benefits from that last bet. No wonder they call this profession 'a license to print money'."

Holmes and I shared a glance, and I knew he had the information he had come for. He shook hands across the table. "Thank you, Jeffrey. You have contributed to a villain's demise."

We walked out onto the Strand in the early evening and wandered along to Simpson's for dinner. Holmes was pensive. "The mechanics of the racetrack or boxing booth – the only legal public wagering in the Colonies – were dead against Kemble. Let us not forget that, had he won his capital fair and square, he could have converted it into sterling and drawn it in London through the banking system. But I inquired, and no record of such a transaction exists. I'm satisfied to say that the origin of Phillip Kemble's fortune remains shrouded in mystery, and therefore suspicious."

We enjoyed an excellent meal and took a hansom home as dusk thickened over the old city. Upon our return to Baker Street, we found a telegram awaiting us: A reply from Herbert Drew, securing us an invitation to visit him tomorrow. Holmes hurried along to the post office to dispatch a note to Bradstreet, confirming our need for his artist.

Bright and early next morning, we met Bradstreet's artist at Paddington Station. A rangy young chap with red hair fringing his neck beneath a bowler waited in the public concourse, a portfolio – obviously of art materials – in hand. Having been briefed on the duo to expect, he waved a greeting.

The day's excursion was a pleasant escape from the city to the spring green of the farms and dales. I treated it as an outing, allowing Holmes to remain focused on his case. There was nothing to do but read the papers and chat with the artist who shared the first-class carriage. Scotland Yard had funded him only for third class, but Holmes made up the difference with that delightful and slightly baffling disregard for money he often displayed. The *things* money could buy had far greater meaning to him than mere figures in his bank account.

As an art school graduate who provided the basic life sketches from court proceedings that were rendered as engravings to appear in *The Police Gazette,* Bernard Cope relished the chance of a country journey rather than yet another session at the Old Bailey or the Uxbridge Magistrates Court. Of that reserved demeanour that befits one who is always present in court but never heard, he had quite a quick wit and was a sharp student of human nature. He had seen and depicted all types, and I found him a personable fellow who looked forward to this commission.

Our object was twofold: To obtain the portrait from Drew's memories of Morse, but also to draw out what the gentleman could recall of the fellow. To this end, Holmes interviewed him while Cope sketched, in a sunny parlour to one side of a neat detached house in Iffley, some miles south of the quaint university town. Drew was a bluff, plain-speaking man, browned by the southern sun, whose accent carried the broad Cockney-like strain of the antipodes. He was happy to assist the police and sorry to learn that his travelling companion might be up to no good.

"He was the quiet sort," Drew told us as a young maid servant set out tea. "There isn't much room on those ships, as you'd expect, so you're pretty well cheek-by-jowl with other passengers. You keep to yourself, let the crew get on with running the ship, and just hang on for dear life in the high latitudes – seas like I never imagined existed." Memories consumed him for some moments. "Dinner in the captain's mess a couple of times a week, of course. We played bridge with him and his first officer more times than I can remember. Morse was a very reserved chap. You could hardly get a word out of him, but when I asked him why he was coming to England, he said he was looking up old friends. Fair enough, but he wouldn't be drawn on the point. I soon learned to let him be. Me? I'm the garrulous kind. I'll talk the backside off a donkey, but it made for a lot of one-way conversations, I'll tell you."

All the while, Cope was seated a little apart from us, sketching on a pad in his lap. Pencils and charcoal sticks flew in his fingers as he worked from Drew's description, regularly turning it to the gentleman for judgement and improvement. Morse, as Drew recalled, was a strong country fellow with features thickened by harsh weather and likely a fondness for "grog", as alcohol in general is still commonly called "down under". He wore a neat moustache, and his dark hair had thinned at the front. His eyes were narrow and hard, and in the face that emerged from the sketch pad, I saw someone who carried the weight of the world upon his shoulders. Certain lines, etched deeply around eyes and mouth despite his young age – which was probably little more than thirty – spoke of hardship and embitterment, supporting the view of him as a man upon some grim mission.

"What can I say?" Drew sighed, giving a huge and expressive shrug. "We shared a ship for months through fine weather and foul, and at the end of the day I couldn't tell you much about him, other than that he's from Ballarat in Victoria, born in a gold-digging camp during the rush, worked as a shearer and a blacksmith in his time and has family here. Somewhere in Nottingham, he said, though they haven't shared more than a few letters in generations. As to what would bring him to this country – if not to look up someone – I couldn't say. He had papers, of course, but he kept them safely locked in his luggage."

Holmes nodded over these details as I took notes. "Thank you, Mr. Drew. You have been most helpful. Now, how close a likeness do we have?"

Cope turned his sketch pad once more. With spectacles upon his nose, Drew inspected it closely. "That's very good, Mr. Cope! I think you've captured him. I'd put my hand on the Bible and swear that's a true picture of Percy Morse."

"Thank you, sir." Holmes rose with implicit finality, and I finished my tea I one gulp, knowing we were bound for London on the next service.

The train had us back at Paddington by mid-afternoon, and Cope promised that the police print shop would produce handbills as fast as humanly possible. We parted at the station, and with Bradstreet's caution in mind, Holmes was reluctant to show his face at Whitehall Place again. We stepped out into Praed Street to seek a cab, and he declared his intention to mount one further expedition.

"It's time to learn who Phillip Kemble was as a young man. This means a foray west to Eton, in some suitable guise, to consult their registers and yearbooks – an inspector from the county school board, perhaps. My best course of action is to locate long-serving masters who

143

may remember him and skilfully extract some reminiscence to provide the perspective I yet require."

This demanded Holmes assemble the elements of a new identity, and he selected suit, coat, and props, such as a briefcase and umbrella, from his copious supplies at Baker Street. The persona he cultivated was that of a plodding, methodical civil servant who had unearthed some discrepancy in departmental records going back thirty years, necessitating an inspection of Eton's own records to sort out the situation. As it was a low-key, unofficial visit, he wouldn't be required to give advance notice or present ministerial permission for his inquiry.

We spent a convivial evening with the case firmly set aside, and I was glad of the diversion. Holmes was a past master of the art of separating matters over which he could exert some control from those over which he could not. Once a case had reached an impasse for want of fresh information, he could remove his attention from it in the most remarkable way. We took dinner in the City, returned to a quiet evening with tobacco and reading materials, and retired with the expectation of fresh developments upon the morrow.

Holmes was away to Paddington for the Windsor train to Eton train before I rose for breakfast, and I didn't anticipate his return until late. I appreciated that he must ingratiate himself with the staff, gain access to records, then talk his way to the impressions he sought, which could take some considerable time.

Nevertheless, his key turned in the lock with hours left in the long, late-spring day, and when he had washed away the facial attributes he had affected, he told me of his findings over tea and biscuits. "The ledgers are a mine of information. As I was very kindly left alone in the basement archive to seek my spurious discrepancy, I was quickly able to locate and view Phillip Kemble's personal record. It was illuminating, to say the least."

"Did you learn what sort of man Britain bestowed upon the Colonies?"

"I did indeed, and I'm unsure if it was a gift." Holmes sipped his tea with pleasure before continuing. "Kemble, as we know, comes from a landed family in Kent and has always enjoyed privilege. He was certainly a bright student, but he was part of a group suspected of academic dishonesty to boost their grades. Nothing was proven, but neither was it forgotten. He was an arrogant young man, flogged twice for fighting with other students, which he called 'matters of honour'. He rather styled himself the dashing sort, one of those upon whom good fortune always smiles." Holmes took a biscuit and paused for a moment's enjoyment. "After lunch, I was entertained for a time by an elder master who recalled him, and I steered the conversation to embrace the group to which Kemble belonged.

"Apparently on the one hand, he had the well-spoken graces of a gentleman, and on the other, the lack of scruples we would associate with the *opposite* end of the social spectrum. He wagered. He was tough and knew how to use his strength – and not just on the playing fields. He brought young women into the college and was known to supply alcohol to fellow students. Any of these things would have earned severe discipline. Collectively, they could have amounted to expulsion. But Kemble was clever – clever enough for there to always be doubt as to who was behind any particular goings-on."

"He was smart, he was strong, and he had little time for rules," I observed. "Doesn't that make the police a rather unusual choice of career? I'd have thought a professional gambler would be more his cup of tea."

"In a sense, he *was* gambling – wagering his own life and liberty against his skills to thwart the system for his own gain. Perhaps he was compelled to leave Britain, and the Victoria Police was a means to escape the consequences of some act or other. If so, this will come out in due course. But the picture I now have is of a skilful and confident young man for whom rules came second to simply winning, and he took this attitude into the police academy.

"The service was, then as now, desperate for promising recruits. Kemble's native toughness would have made him an excellent candidate for officer selection, in the belief that the force would smooth off his rough edges. Then came his application for the colonial constabulary, and he was commissioned into a situation where he was in charge. He became the only active officer to enforce the law, under the auspices of a magistrate who wasn't always even in the territory."

"For such a personality," I whispered, "it must have been a dream come true."

"For Kemble's sort of mind? I'm sure of it, Watson. As certain as I am that our Percival Morse has come here to redress some grievous wrong, and while it is imperative that we prevent any ultimate sanction Morse may have in mind, it also goes without saying that Phillip Kemble's offences, whatever they might be, are overdue for an airing before the law."

I nodded slowly, my expression sombre. "That isn't going to please his son, who obviously has great affection for his father and came to you seeking to protect him."

"An awful irony, indeed, and I regret that it is so. But I cannot protect Kemble from the legal ramifications of actions long past. If my suspicions are correct, whatever Morse's intentions may be, Kemble has brought them upon himself."

"What's the next step, then?"

My friend managed a smile. "To build a tiger trap."

Scotland Yard had the handbills out in good time. In pubs throughout the West End, bobbies on the beat asked after anyone matching the description. It was never easy, as people in the poorer districts often see themselves as adversarial with the law and might not help even if they know *exactly* who is being sought. But someone would find that face familiar eventually, and we had to allow for Morse now using some facial disguise.

But Holmes was, as ever, both more direct and more devious. He ran an advertisement in the personal columns of the papers: *Mr. Morse, Threats will not avail you, but the law will be served. Reply via this column tomorrow if you wish to discuss your grievances. H., Esq.*

We watched the papers like hawks the next day, but nothing emerged. When Bradstreet called around, he had no information to report from his men's canvassing of suburbs from Kensington to Chiswick.

"We must draw out our man," Holmes said, concluding a roundup of matters for Peter Kemble that afternoon. "As you can see, Scotland Yard are on the lookout for an Australian whom we suspect of being behind the threatening messages. We cannot confirm or deny this until we have interviewed Morse, but he is being particularly circumspect. I propose that we offer him a target: Your father."

"Father will never agree to participate, Mr. Holmes. He would be mortified to know the matter is being investigated at official levels."

"Things have gone too far for us to back out," Holmes replied softly. "It actually became an official case the moment your father applied to the Customs Service for a surreptitious check of their records – and he must have suspected it would. It was only his presumption that he would get away with such a move under the so-called 'Old Boys Act'. That he was willing to use his coachman to discreetly approach underworld roughs suggests he is recruiting force to his side of the sort that asks no questions. None of this can escape police attention now." Holmes sank into a chair with a somewhat disinterested smile. "If you would prefer, we will place the matter formally before Inspector Bradstreet, and I can desist from my own inquiries."

Peter Kemble seemed somewhat agitated at the suggestion and, glancing between Holmes and the inspector, quickly shook his head. "Not at all, Mr. Holmes. I trust you to do whatever is required to find the most equitable resolution for all concerned."

146

"Excellent!" Holmes slapped his knee as he bounded from the chair. "Then I require you to do something for me."

"What's that, Mr. Holmes?"

"Let it be known that your father will be walking on Shepherd's Bush Common for his health each evening."

Kemble's brows knitted in consternation. "To what end, sir?"

"To offer our wandering antipodean a target he cannot refuse – and take him in the act." Holmes's stare was sharp. "I must warn you that there is as much jeopardy to whoever poses as your father as there would have been to the gentleman himself. The object is, of course, to intercept Mr. Morse before he can do any harm."

"And pass him into police care?"

Holmes smiled, an expression I knew well. "Of course. But I believe we can depend upon Inspector Bradstreet's inclusion of us in the interrogative procedure."

Bradstreet nodded silently.

The younger Kemble shrugged his shoulders. "Whatever you need, Mr. Holmes. I confess, this matter has become a millstone around my neck, and I desperately want it cleared up."

"Very well. I give my word that every precaution will be taken to assure everyone's safety. Hopefully, we will end the night with Morse in custody and a clear picture of the events prompting him to take these extravagant actions."

"Father will learn of it," Kemble said with a resigned look. "There'll be Hell to pay."

Holmes nodded. "Then perhaps the time has come to have it out with him. Inspector Bradstreet may as well be present to reinforce the point that matters have gone beyond any casual dismissal."

That evening, we found ourselves guests in the drawing room of the grand house in Holland Park. Phillip Kemble received us after dining, and his expression couldn't have been more confident or self-assured. He glanced once at his son and made a perplexed face before summoning his butler to serve sherry, which Inspector Bradstreet politely declined on our behalf.

"Whatever is this about, gentlemen?" Kemble began, folding his hands across his middle in a comfortable armchair. Drink and good food had thickened his body, but I still saw the same man who was depicted in the old portrait photograph that stood upon the white grand piano: A narrow-featured chap with a moustache and long, fair hair, and a keen, penetrating look framed by the collar of a police jacket. "Not that silly business of the threatening notes, surely?"

"I'm afraid it is, sir," Bradstreet rumbled, thumbs hooked in his waistcoat pockets, fishing out his warrant card, which he presented. "Bradstreet, Scotland Yard. And we're taking the matter very seriously indeed. May I present Mr. Sherlock Holmes and Dr. John Watson, who have assisted the police with our inquiries on a number of occasions over the years."

Kemble managed a chuckle and a dismissive shake of his silvering head. "However did this business come to your attention? I threw away those ridiculous notes as they arrived."

Bradstreet filled him in on the organised crime boys' chance observation of the meeting in the The Old Ship pub. "When the coachman of a distinguished City gent is seen in conference with known bad lads, we tend to suspect that *something's* afoot. It didn't take much to ferret out the business of the letters from your son." Bradstreet raised a hand as Kemble's expression darkened. "He was concerned for your well-being – and from our perspective, he has every right to be."

Neatly done, Bradstreet, I thought. He had just sidestepped the entire aspect of Kemble, Junior approaching Holmes directly.

Kemble wore a strained look. "Clearly, I must have words with my coachman, if he is consorting with such types once more. I brought him up from the gutter, so to speak, and would be most disappointed if he has let down my confidence in him." He sighed, as if the situation were too silly to be taken seriously, and gestured at chairs around the room – humouring us for the sake of good manners. "Do tell me all about it, gentlemen."

Stepping aside, Bradstreet turned the interview over to Holmes. My friend promptly presented one of the handbills. "Does this face mean anything to you, Mr. Kemble?"

It received a reasonable inspection before Kemble shook his head in a definite no. "Not a thing, I'm afraid. Who is this?"

"A gentleman from the Australian colonies who arrived in London not long ago. Percival Morse, by name."

At this, Kemble's eyes narrowed just a little.

"I did not, in fact, expect you to recognise the fellow," Holmes admitted. "If your paths ever crossed, it would have been half-the-world away, and Morse would have been but a child."

Kemble hesitated just for a second, but the stumble was clear enough. "During the years of my service in the Victoria Police, then."

"Just so. We believe Mr. Morse is behind those notes, and that he is merely biding his time for the opportune moment – *to kill you,* Mr. Kemble."

Now, Kemble frowned long and deep. "A *vendetta?*" No one spoke as he collected his thoughts. "I won't say I left the colony without enemies. Every police officer knows he runs the risk of retribution for merely doing his job. Those were wild lands, indeed. I brought in bushrangers, runaway convicts, murderers, military deserters . . . I sent more than I could count to the flogging triangle and the gallows, just like any other policeman in the Colonies. That's *how* it was done. I find it difficult to believe that anyone could be so monomaniacal as to nurse a grudge for thirty years. You're sure about this?"

"As sure as we can be at this point," Holmes went on. "You might not feel that your life is in danger. We cannot compel you to accept police protection, but we feel it would be highly unwise of you to refuse it."

Kemble weighed Holmes's words for a long moment. "Very well, gentlemen. What do you propose?"

"That from this moment forth, no risks are taken with your personage," Bradstreet began. "And that your family is also subject to the greatest possible caution. We don't want a kidnapping to substitute for an attempted assassination."

"Indeed not," Kemble agreed.

Holmes smiled thinly. "And as our man seems to be keeping very much to himself in this town, entrenched deeply enough to have escaped notice as yet, it is our intention to entice him into giving himself away."

Kemble responded with a smile and nod. "I'll wish you excellent hunting, gentlemen, and look forward to hearing what this scoundrel has to say for himself."

Our meeting was essentially over with Kemble's acquiescence. We paused in the hall as the butler presented hats and canes. Holmes and I glanced back and saw Kemble's black expression, which was barely ameliorated as he surveyed his son.

But before we could depart, the lady of the house appeared – an elegant woman in her middle years, with the assurance and poise afforded by a lifetime of unchallenged privilege. She wore a silver-grey gown, and her auburn tresses were piled high. Respectfully, I removed my hat once more.

"Gentlemen, I couldn't help but overhear at least something of your discussion," she began in a smooth contralto. "I confess, I am concerned. We are to be restricted in our movements and accompanied by guards?"

"The only sensible precaution, ma'am," Bradstreet explained in a gentle tone. "Until we have this fellow in hand, there's no telling what he might be capable of. Better safe than sorry."

"This is understood and appreciated, Inspector. But for what reason could he wish my husband ill? I have had the honour to share Philip's

149

company for a quarter-of-a-century, and I can assure you that there is no finer man, no truer partner, and no more loyal officer to Her Majesty. If Phillip gathered enemies in the performance of his duty, he can only be held blameless."

"A stirring testimonial, Madam," Holmes replied with a winning smile, "but matters must play themselves out. Your husband's nemesis will have a story, which Scotland Yard and our humble selves will be most interested to hear."

"Then I will wish you Godspeed, gentlemen," she offered, "in the confidence that your findings will condemn this rogue from the Colonies beyond all redemption."

As we stepped out into the evening air to find our coach waiting in the street, I gave Holmes a canny look. "You set him up," I whispered.

"By informing him of our plans. If there is now the *slightest* interference in the operation to decoy Morse, we know precisely where it originated. As of this moment, beyond the three of us, only the Kembles are aware of our intentions."

Shepherd's Bush Common is a triangle of mowed lawns, bisected by pathways and framed by trees, at the convergence of Uxbridge Road on the north side and Goldhawk Road to the south. In the lengthening evenings, many stroll there after a day's work is done. People walk their dogs, and others sit to enjoy the sunset hours as the horse-trams rattle by on each main road.

At our request, young Peter Kemble had walked there with his father just once – an unusual sight for one of Holland Park's denizens to mingle with ordinary Londoners. But each evening the solitary figure in coat and hat, having been dropped by a driver, took a turn around the common in no great hurry. None of the passersby looked closely enough to realise it wasn't a man of mature years at all, but a fit young fellow adorned with a quantity of facial makeup.

Holmes had designed the disguise. Scotland Yard obtained the services of a professional artist, who applied it each evening after the young police officer – a volunteer – arrived at the Kemble house in the guise of a deliveryman or tradesman. Shortly after, he would emerge, posing as Kemble Senior, and step into his carriage for the short drive.

For two evenings, nothing happened. Holmes and I walked upon the common with a sense of anticlimax – Was Morse never to show his hand? We could hardly present him with a more appealing target.

"If he doesn't take the bait," I wondered as we strolled, fifty yards behind the decoy, "what does it mean? That Morse was never sincere in his threats?"

"Perhaps," Holmes said in a musing tone. "Or perhaps he has seen through our ruse and knows it is a trap. We can only keep the offer in play so long. Besides, if the latter is correct, Morse will easily intuit that most of Scotland Yard's strength is concentrated here. Remaining at the house, Phillip Kemble has minimal protection. If he were so disposed, Morse could enter over the back fence from the park, gain entry in any way necessary, do his vile business, and leave the same way."

"He'd have to overcome the bodyguard, and in his day, Kemble was used to lethal action. I doubt he'd go down easily."

"All excellent points, Watson, bringing us back to the puzzle of Morse himself. To come all this way on a thirty-year-old vendetta, he must be willing to make the final sanction, even at cost of his own life, whether in the attempt or upon the gallows. But he displays the caution of a spider in its web: Forever watching from the shadows and biding his time, which speaks to me of a man who would rather not lose his life at all, if he can help it."

"A tortured position to be in," I said in agreement. "Unable to set aside the wrongs he perceives, unable to obtain redress by any means other than resorting to crime, yet having much to lose should he manage anything less than the perfect assassination."

"And such is usually the province of highly skilled professionals – ex-military men, perhaps, or a member of an organisation that is more shadowy and less accountable. That such an individual was *not* contracted to perform this assassination suggests Morse either cannot afford such an employee, or ultimately intends no more than harassment." Holmes shook his head. "This is a personal grudge – it can only be. There is no hint of entanglement with any other entity, private or governmental, nor does the bank seem to be involved."

We were pondering these mysteries when our decoy turned at the corner of The Lawns Street to make his way up towards Uxbridge Road once more, and a figure rose from a bench under the trees fringing the park, carrying a folded newspaper in the way one might – perhaps – clutch a pistol under its concealment.

The fellow was nondescript, in coat and hat, and with unhurried grace, he moved past the lamplighters in the gathering twilight. The common was now emptying out as day reached its end in flurries of colour to the west, where open ground runs on beyond the rank of fine houses, towards Shepherd's Bush Station, on the Hammersmith and City line.

With a sense that things were moving at last, we fell in behind the newcomer, Holmes raised a hand to send a tic-tac signal, unseen by our quarry, to the plainclothes police officer who posed as a gardener working near the public convenience on the corner of Uxbridge Road. At once, the officer took a hessian sack from his cart and began to empty a dustbin – the signal that the decoy would interpret to mean he was being followed, whereupon he would lead his pursuer into a well-thought-out trap.

Now we'll get to the heart of the matter! I thought, slipping a hand into my pocket for the butt of my revolver. I matched Holmes, stride for stride, as we passed the drinking fountain and continued along the line of plain trees in their new green. Lights glowed from many a window, and, nearing the northern corner of the park, we heard the hiss of the streetlights' mantles. To all intents and purposes, this was a peaceful evening like any other.

The decoy left the park with a brisk step, paused at the kerb, then crossed Uxbridge Road towards the tall and welcoming façade of The Defector's Weld public house. Now, had anyone cared to notice, other figures moved all around the park, melting away and crossing the main road as if also bound for the pub. The clop of hooves, the merry jingle of harness, and the cries of coachmen along the thoroughfare were a profound normality that seemed to deny the crux to which matters were swiftly moving.

Holmes and I broke into a run to close up while the man shadowing our decoy also stepped into the road. On the far side, the decoy passed by the tall front door of the pub, turned into Wood Lane, and made for the pub's yard. I knew that, east of us, officers were taking the public right-of-way that leads through to the back yards of houses flanking the pub on the main road, providing access for dustmen. At a flat run, they would be in place in one minute to box in Morse – if indeed it *was* Morse.

Some nagging concern twisted my belly as we hurried after our men, something I couldn't name yet – a sixth sense I had learned to trust as far back as the Subcontinent. I hunted for words at which Holmes, the eternal rationalist, would not scoff. As affairs unfolded, I had yet to frame my misgivings when a shot rang out from the pub's yard.

"Great Scott!" Holmes exploded, and ran headlong through the traffic on Uxbridge Road, his pistol appearing in his hand

Loafers by the door of The Defector's Weld hunched down as they realised something dire was happening. Police whistles shrilled at once, and I drew my revolver as I crossed the road between traffic at a dead run. My old wound twinged uncomfortably with the sudden exertion, but Holmes and I reached the far side, passed by the cheerful illuminations of the pub's front windows, and in moments were at the corner of the yard, where tall timber gates stood open.

Another shot rang out, and bricks splintered over Holmes's head. A scream went up in the taproom, and we heard roars of consternation. I imagined people hugging the floor and crawling under tables for protection as the barman went down behind his counter. But a second later, Holmes darted across the gateway, fetched up against timbers on the other side, and together we presented our weapons to the mystery in the pub's loading yard.

Throwing a glance around the corner, I spotted our decoy crouching behind the barrels, apparently unharmed, a Bulldog .38 in his hand. The man who had followed him, however, was on his knees beside the inclined hatchway to the cellar, one hand covering a red stain upon his left shoulder. As I watched, a round sparked from the iron lamp standard over his head.

"By the fence!" Holmes shouted.

At the next shot, I caught the muzzle flash. One, possibly two, gunmen were well-entrenched behind a stack of crates. Only by some miracle had our decoy evaded sudden death. He must have walked into their very sights. Indeed, these men must have used the alley between the gardens, perhaps intending to come up behind their prey, if he had continued along Wood Lane. That he had turned into them was both their luck and their conundrum: They were now trapped between our guns and those of the constables behind them – the officers who had moved in to intercept Morse once the decoy led him into this yard.

Who were these interlopers? We had organised a nice, simple trap in which the chief danger lay only in apprehending Morse before he could act. All the decoy had to do was draw his weapon and "bail up" Morse when he entered the yard. Out of public sight, neat as you like, constables were situated to box in our quarry before he could blink.

Now Morse was injured, while unknown gunmen remained intent upon dispatching him.

Holmes and I chanced a shot each, but we couldn't blaze away for fear of sending rounds down the alley, where Bradstreet's men were doubtlessly crouched, working their way forward. A gate dividing the alley from the yard stood wide – Bradstreet had seen it unlocked earlier to give his men quick access.

This was the kind of mess Holmes put down to random factors, and which I, as a military man, half-expected. As every commander knows, battleplans aren't worth the paper they're written on, because events invariably fail to follow the script – even the simplest.

Bradstreet appeared at my side, a .38 in his beefy fist, and bawled into the yard with a voice like a foghorn. "This is Inspector Bradstreet of Scotland Yard! Whoever you are, throw down those guns! You've nowhere to go!"

Hysterical voices from the bar, and the whinny of a horse, punctuated the following silence. The next shots cracking through the evening weren't aimed at us. There was a commotion in the alley as men looked for a way out: A couple of shots – a long pause, then one more. Silence. I had caught Holmes's eye and spread my hands in a helpless gesture, when voices called out, and it seemed the way was clear.

In the yard, we found our decoy by the barrels, peering down the alley. At once, I went to Morse to inspect his shoulder. In the light of a hissing gas-lamp, I saw it was indeed the man so well described to us by his cabinmate from the *Cutty Sark*, and though he was grey-faced with shock, his wound was superficial.

"You'll live," I muttered, looking up as officers appeared in the yard, lanterns held high.

At their flurry of shouts, Holmes accompanied them into the alley. I followed, and found the two men sent to box in Morse – both down, one with a contusion swelling his face, the other with a bullet wound to his side.

"What a mess!" Bradstreet exclaimed, setting his weapon's safety catch and sliding it away under his jacket.

"Not at all, Inspector," Holmes replied, rising from the injured officers. "We have Morse. He is quite well enough to answer a few questions, and the mere fact that this operation was targeted by others informs us with pellucid clarity that a deeper dimension pervades this whole case."

"And what would that be?" the inspector asked gruffly.

"Oh, I expect Morse can elucidate that point, Bradstreet. I would be delighted if you would arrange matters so that we could manage an hour with him at the earliest possibility."

At half-past-ten, I accompanied Holmes and Inspector Bradstreet into an interview room at Hammersmith Police Station, just off Broadway. As attending physician, I had accepted the task of patching up Morse. Our Australian guest had received no more than a graze to his shoulder, a nasty enough injury that would certainly leave a scar. Having administered something for shock, I sterilised, stitched, and dressed the wound. Indeed, a hot cup of tea with a shot of brandy was as effective as anything.

With Morse wrapped in a police blanket in lieu of his ruined coat, we came together around a table. A uniformed officer closed the door and put his back to it. Another, seated at the end of the table, opened a notebook and prepared to take down the interview. To open proceedings, Bradstreet showed his warrant card to Morse.

"Mr. Percival Morse of Ballarat, Victoria, in the Australian colonies, you are under arrest and charged with malicious mischief – specifically the making of dire threats – and upon strong suspicion of the intended murder of Mr. Phillip Kemble. Do you understand?"

Morse was thin-faced and wore an expression as if the weight of the world had bowed his shoulders for many a year. He simply nodded and gave a little shrug of his shoulders. "Is it a crime in this country to be *supposed* to intend some misdeed, Inspector?"

"It is, when that crime is murder," Bradstreet began ominously.

"I think you're confusing *intent* with *attempt* there. And I have *done* nothing."

"That's a fine distinction, and I know some magistrates who would take a very dim view of it as a defence."

Holmes cleared his throat. "Gently does it, Inspector. In fact, Mr. Morse is correct in that the only offence he has committed upon English soil is to send some vaguely threatening notes. It is merely our construction, based on those notes and his behaviour this evening, that further harm was his object." He gave Morse a cold look. "You *were* responsible for the notes, were you not?"

Morse nodded readily. "I pasted some cuttings together and sent them to someone I know."

Bradstreet was only slightly put out by the interjection. "Mr. Morse, may I introduce Mr. Sherlock Holmes, who has made it his business to assist the police with our more bizarre cases. Dr. Watson, you have already met. These gentlemen have an interest in this matter, having been engaged by Mr. Kemble, Junior for the purpose of getting in the way of whatever malice you intend regarding his father."

Morse remained silent and, after a moment, Holmes placed an open box of small cigars and a box of matches on the table. "Feel free, gentlemen."

As we availed ourselves of the rich tobacco, a knock heralded a sergeant bringing in a wooden tray with mugs of tea. When we were all thus supplied, Bradstreet gave a pensive smile. "Let's start again, shall we? Mr. Morse, do you know why you're being held?"

Now Morse looked up with a hard, cynical set to his lips. "Because the law is always on the side of the likes of Kemble."

I took down his words verbatim, sensing that the short, pithy denunciation of justice was very much the key to this affair.

Holmes laid a hand on Bradstreet's sleeve and exhaled a blue plume towards the gaslights. "How old are you, Mr. Morse?"

He blinked, somewhat blindsided by the question. "I'm thirty-four. Why, Mr. Holmes?"

"You must have been only a child when you last crossed paths with Lieutenant Phillip Kemble of the Victoria Police."

I saw Morse's eyes narrow, and a sudden hardness come over him at mention of the name, and realised Holmes had skilfully struck a nerve.

155

In the silence, Holmes sat forward and met him eye to eye. "Mr. Morse, please tell us why you hate Phillip Kemble with every fibre of your being."

He took a long drag at his cigar and nodded slowly. "And at last, we come to it. It must be said, supposing I face a year behind bars and the birch for slander."

"In your own time," Holmes whispered, and I waited with pencil poised for the tale to come.

"You're right. I was just a child when the name 'Lieutenant Kemble' came to mean everything *wrong* – everything vile and cruel in my small world. I was born in Cockatoo Springs, a muddy street of tents serving the gold diggings. My father was panning the creeks for gold dust, and my mother made what home she could. You had to be hard to call canvas and a bit of timber your home, and what I remember most is the cold and wet of the high country, and never having a full belly. But we were honest folk. I watched my father work himself into an early grave, wearing himself away, trying to make that stream give up enough gold to buy our way out of poverty.

"Then, one day, the troopers rode in. I was too young to really understand, but they were hard men, up there on their horses, giving orders and making threats. Permits, taxes, fines – it was always money. *Money.* Pay for this, pay for that, pay your dues. Never lip the troopers, else you'd find yourself having 'accidents', committing misdemeanours that'd get you more fines. Any hint of resistance – I saw men clubbed down and taken away to face three months, or six, on a chain gang, slaving to clear roads through the bush.

"And you weren't given much choice. It was safer to pay the coppers in advance than have anything happen. You know, bushrangers and the like could strike at any moment, and the troopers had to be there to stop them. The best way to keep unfortunate *incidents* from happening was just to settle with the officer in charge first."

"Protection?" Holmes mused.

"Call it what you will. My father always paid up and kept his mouth shut for the sake of his family, but he talked bitterly with his friends about how they were breaking their backs to make coppers rich. All kinds of sedition, certainly, but they'd never lift a hand to a trooper. And one day he was face-down in the stream with a gash in his head. Plenty of hoof prints round the diggings, but nobody would come forward to say what happened. *Accident*, they called it. But we knew – me and my mum. Kemble's boys had been round to make an example of a troublemaker.

"And that was just the start of it. Nobody was safe from them. Those who ran the few shops in town had to pay them off as well. The bar, the general store, the knocking shop. Paying was the surest way to keep tents from mysteriously catching fire. Lieutenant Kemble was coining it – taking two, three pound a week from Cockatoo Springs alone, we reckoned. There were other towns in his area, and gold disappeared from miners' billets. More than once, a man panned that creek for a twelve-month only to find himself in some trumped-up trouble, and buying his way out of it with the proceeds of a year's backbreaking labour.

"Then there were the payments made 'in kind'. The food and drink they helped themselves to from our tables. And other things. Miners got very good at hiding their daughters."

An uncomfortable thrill went through the room and I sipped my tea, resting my writing hand for a moment. I had to admit that Percival Morse was a very convincing witness who had me believing him with the very sincerity of his speech.

"I was about six and orphaned for a year when Lieutenant Kemble took a shine to Mum. By then, she was working in the bar to keep the canvas over our heads. He called it 'protecting her' – looking out for a widow in a hard world. That's what I was given to believe at that tender age. But one day, I grew up and understood what was happening. It's a miracle I don't have a brother who looks just like that bastard." Morse took a deep drag at his cigar, and we let him have his moment. "Mum passed away of consumption in '79, coughing her lungs out in a cold, stone hospital.

"Before she died, she told me the truth. I'd already guessed much of it. How we were kept down in the muck, and no matter how hard we worked, we'd never get out. Well, I left Cockatoo Springs when I was twelve to work as a drover moving mobs of sheep, and it was the best thing I ever did. I made enough to move Mum to a house in Ballarat, but the hard life round the diggings had done its worst. Her health was never right again.

"Don't even ask about the Australian police. Investigate one of their own? They'd flog you for even suggesting it. I'm not saying dirty coppers didn't get what was coming to them in the end, but not *this* one. Kemble was too clever by half, and too many others owed him their silence. For the miserable beggar in the street, there was no law.

"And who did we have to thank for these lives wasted in sweat and toil, to no end? *Lieutenant Kemble.* The man who used the entire place like his private piggybank and probably paid off his superiors to look the other way. The one who beat, flogged, murdered, and raped his way to the honourable retirement of a gentleman. He turned up in an Australian newspaper last year: *Ex-Victoria Police Officer Makes Good* – that sort of thing. They gave his address as Kensington, London, and after that, it was just a matter of making the voyage and looking him up."

After a long silence, Bradstreet coughed and tapped ash from his cigar. "What would you have done, had you caught up with Kemble?"

"You mean, instead of your decoy?" He gave a cynical smile and spoke with grim precision. "Beat the bastard within an inch of his miserable life. One thing a hard life teaches you is – how to *be* hard. You didn't find a weapon on me, did you? Not a gun, not a knife. I don't need them. After all these years of soft living, Kemble wasn't going to hold me off, toe-to-toe. I would've given him a long-overdue taste of what it's like to be on the receiving end of what he and his troopers dished out for years." He inhaled smoke and seemed to have reached the end of his dissertation. On a sour, bitter note, which I could only surmise also stemmed from experience, he said, "There, it's all said. Now, if you want the back off me for speaking out of turn, you have at it."

A knock, and the uniform man opened the door. A sergeant stepped in, bent to Bradstreet's ear, and whispered. The inspector regarded him with a raised brow, then whispered in return, and as the sergeant hurried to carry out his instructions, Bradstreet beckoned Holmes and myself into the corridor.

With the door closed once more, he put his big fists on his hips. "A body was just found on the common land behind Tadmor Street, a couple-of-hundred yards from the scene of that shootout, with a gunshot wound to the thigh. Looks like he bled to death. One of our boys in the alley swears he put a bullet in one of the two who made it away. I just ordered the bullet recovered and checked against the police sidearm involved. If the calibre matches, we have one of those sent to kill our Australian visitor."

Holmes nodded with a kind of pensive certainty. "At the earliest possible moment, please have the officers who observed Brand and his cohorts at The Old Ship view the body. If they identify him as one on their own watch list, we have our connection, and it's a strong one." He gestured at the door. "Follow my lead, Bradstreet."

We returned to the interview room, resumed our seats, and Holmes leaned forward with an intense focus upon Morse. "Mr. Morse, do you have any idea who tried to kill *you* tonight?"

Morse stubbed out his cigar and shook his head emphatically. "I didn't get a good look at them, but in any case, I know no one in London, Mr. Holmes."

"Oh, come now. You know at least *one* man."

Morse blinked in surprise. "But how would *he* find me? I was careful – On my *life,* I was careful."

158

"In retrospect, while sending the notes was meant to subject Mr. Kemble to a torment of uncertainty under some undefined threat of dire retribution, they also warned him. You must have known he would take action if he could."

"I knew he'd try. It was a question of how much he could know. He'd never recognise me – I was only eight when he left Australia."

"He knew enough to take steps." Holmes waved a hand in dismissal of the point.

Bradstreet huffed a sigh. "This is all very well, Mr. Morse, but look at it from our point of view. A visitor is accusing a pillar of our community of being the worst scoundrel unhanged. You've offered no proof. At this point, it's all he-say. Of course, we can't act on it."

Holmes caught my eye, and I knew what he was thinking: The mere fact an attempt was made to silence Morse lent credence to his story. "The inspector is correct, Mr. Morse. While there are certain attendant circumstances that also factor in, we have only your word as to Mr. Kemble's behaviour while in uniform thirty years ago." He rubbed his hands together with a thoughtful look. "Nevertheless, I believe you. I find it incredible that anyone should go to the extent of travelling halfway around the world and attacking a man he has never met if there were no underlying cause of the direst sort.

"In your account, I see ample motivation for your actions. Understand, however, that revenge cannot be permitted. There is due process, and whatever occurs must do so within that framework. Now, I'm sure that sending a few silly notes can be overlooked. They are worth a reprimand at most." He leaned forward earnestly. "But I will promise you this: If it is within my power to do so, I will bring Philip Kemble to answer for his actions in the Victorian colony. I cannot promise to what extent he may be prosecuted or what restitution is even possible after so long, but he will *not* go forth with a spotless character. If there were something concrete – checkable – that would cast doubt on his claim to an unblemished record during and after service, we might be able to pursue that point."

Glancing from Holmes to Bradstreet and back, Morse gave a small shrug. "You mean, like the diamond?"

My gaze went to Holmes, and my expression must have been worth a thousand words, for he set a hand on my arm for a moment.

"Mr. Morse," he said, "you are well aware of the penalties for slander, and I doubt anyone would engage in such an expedition as you have without ultimate belief in the verity of their own case. I will do you the courtesy of accepting what you tell me. And with your assistance, we shall dispatch this wolf in sheep's clothing that has haunted the byways of

159

Kensington." He folded his hands with a grim smile. "Now, you mentioned a diamond. You have my undivided attention . . . ."

"Did you sleep well, Watson?" Holmes asked, more buoyant than any man had a right to be after a night spent in the dubious accommodation of a holding cell.

With the first light of dawn as yet barely blueing the window, I ran a borrowed razor over my jaw in the lavatory at Hammersmith Police Station and shook my head with a rather put-out look. "Missing my billet at Baker Street, if you want the truth." The facilities for prisoners were an insalubrious accommodation, but their meagre hospitality had been preferable to journeying home, then back to the West End, a matter of hours apart. "That's the first time I've ever spent a night in the cells, and the one consolation is the fact the door wasn't *actually* locked."

Holmes laughed as he rolled up his sleeves at the next sink for his morning ablutions. "Chin up. We've made progress. Why, Bradstreet sent a message with the morning tea – the body found near Tadmor Street *has* been identified as one of the dockers the coachman approached at The Old Ship. Given the way we left matters when we interviewed Phillip Kemble . . . ."

"It's difficult to reach any conclusion other than that the coachman petitioned them on his master's behalf, and Kemble employed them to intercept Morse at any cost." Rather pleased with the succinctness of my summary, I rinsed the razor. "Kemble was taking a dreadful risk, though. He must have known that if the dealings at The Old Ship could be tied back to him in any way, his position would become precarious."

"A measure of his desperation." Holmes lathered up, and I passed him the razor. "He must silence Morse to prevent the story coming out, but now that it has been told and entered into official record, the accusation has been made. He will deny it, obviously, relying on the paucity of tangible evidence from three decades ago. However, the fact the hired roughs both failed to kill Morse *and* allowed themselves to be connected, however tenuously, back to Kemble, will put the cat amongst his particular pigeons."

"I imagine he is a very frightened man today," I said, patting dry with a rough towel. "And this business about the diamond?"

"My first inquiry of the morning – it certainly answers a great many questions." As he spoke, Holmes rasped the blade over his jaw with swift, precise strokes. "Think of it: There's Kemble at the end of his five years' service, determined to come back to England and live on his ill-gotten gains. Most of what he amassed illegally would have been in coins, gold dust, and nuggets. But gold is heavy. He could hardly fill his luggage with it.

"Converting gold to cash would have attracted attention and left him vulnerable to theft. Depositing it into a bank account and redrawing it from a London branch would have made his fortune a matter of record, and thus open to question. *Officially*, his savings amounted to little more than one-hundred pounds, according to his bank in Melbourne, whose manager this morning replied to Scotland Yard's telegram. That sum was drawn here in London, all neat and tidy. But where did he come by twelve-*thousand* pounds to invest in the Gablehouse Bank?"

I smiled as I drew on my shirt. "Lieutenant Kemble converted his stolen gold to a more compact form of currency – a precious stone, something he could carry on his person at all times between Melbourne and London."

"Precisely." Holmes paused to rinse his face and reach for a towel. "Risk was always involved, but his sort thrives on it. During the old days of the East India Company, it was common practice for soldiers returning from the Subcontinent to consolidate the plunder of a violent career into precious stones and stitch them into the lining of their regimental jackets, to be realised as capital when safely home. Kemble knew all the tricks.

"According to Morse, the Australian papers of the day described a diamond worth over ten-thousand pounds. It was the prized possession of an industrialist in the colony, a shipbuilder on Port Phillip Bay, as he recalls. In later years, Morse read the papers from the publishers' archive, where the stone was often mentioned – until 1858, when all trace of it vanished. Coincidence? I'll offer short odds we shall discover that a diamond answering the same description and carat weight came into the possession of the Gablehouse Bank soon after."

I fixed my tie and drew on my jacket. "Gablehouse will be tight-lipped about their assets. It would take a court order to open their books."

"Hopefully, we will not need to actually see the stone in question." Holmes finished drying his hands and began to sort out shirt and tie. "Merely our knowledge of the transaction should provide reason enough for us to confront Kemble regarding his past deeds."

"And then we shall see how strong his nerve is," I mused.

The sudden disappearance of Kemble's coachman came as no surprise. The Scotland Yard bodyguards at the house on Holland Park reported that Patrick Brand had been absent since the previous day. Kemble hired a vehicle to take him into the City on business, but the bodyguard travelling with him found nothing untoward in Kemble's activities.

161

At a meeting around noon, Bradstreet brought us up-to-date on matters. "Given that we have Morse in custody, there's really no reason to prolong watching Kemble, is there, Mr. Holmes?" His eyes narrowed. "Unless you suspect that some threat remains – ?"

Holmes issued a noisy sigh through flared nostrils. "Danger, no, but there is some benefit to be gleaned from leaving the Kemble family in a state of mild unease for a while yet. So long as Kemble is under guard, he will assume *we* believe the threat exists. That is to our benefit. It lulls him into the belief that matters have yet to shape themselves, one way or another."

"And the coachman who hired in the roughs?" Bradstreet went on, "Brand, himself an ex-con, in a position to know the workings of the underworld – Where's he got to? I expect Kemble paid him off merely to stall our progress."

"More than likely," Holmes replied as if the point were beneath consideration. "I doubt we would find the fellow anywhere in London at this time. No matter, he'll keep – his part is but a minor detail. More important is the matter of the stone."

"What did you learn, Holmes?" I asked with interest.

Holmes had departed Hammersmith by an early hansom and only just returned. "Much of importance. As you know, the Customs Service records the entry to and exit from this country of items of high value, and Scotland Yard's automatic check of records indicates no such stone being officially admitted to England in '58. However, there are other forms of record. The Gablehouse Bank was established in the 1780's, using a board of trustees to manage its assets, and to oversee the equitable operation of the original trust fund upon which the bank was founded. Its role is less crucial a hundred years on, but the board remains part of its business structure and continues to account for those assets."

Holmes was warming to his theme – I saw a gleam in his eye. "While you were quite right in saying, Watson, that it would take official leverage to get them to open their ledgers, any bank styles itself as an institution of rock-solid and monolithic nature, and Gablehouse has indulged in the occasional boast to attract new investors.

"I located a brochure of 1870 in which they refer to their gold reserve, available for international on-paper trading – a mere shuffling of bullion from one part of a vault to another to represent bulk transactions. They also spoke glowingly of their property investments and various treasures, all of which contribute to the bank's total resources. One such treasure was a diamond, of the value that concerns us. And, yes, it was an 1858 acquisition."

162

Bradstreet smacked his fist into a palm. "We can subpoena the details. A pound gets you a penny that Gablehouse accepted it in all good faith as a deposit from Phillip Kemble."

"How quickly can you accomplish this, Inspector?"

Taking his bowler from a hatstand, Bradstreet consulted his watch. "Give me two hours."

"If the information confirms our suspicions – " Holmes smiled wolfishly. " – we can retire the guards this evening. Indeed, we may inform Mr. Kemble that Mr. Morse is no longer a threat – and of a great many further details, none of which will be of any comfort to him."

Our appointment with the Kembles was arranged for eight o'clock, after dinner. During an afternoon visit, Bradstreet informed Mrs. Kemble that the danger was past, withdrew the bodyguards, and promised to return that evening to inform Kemble, who would by that time have returned from the City, of the details of the affair.

Two coaches rumbled out to Holland Park in the twilight, and my stomach knotted in anticipation of the scene about to unfold. My notebook and pencil seemed wholly inadequate, but I determined to do my best to record my impressions of the event. I rode with Holmes and Bradstreet and, at the invitation of both, Percival Morse sat quietly, in clean suit and coat. A flowing false moustache from Holmes's copious supplies served as a facial disguise, catering to the possibility that Kemble had seen one of the handbills. Morse must remain silent, lest his accent give him away, and would be introduced simply as another detective.

To make the arrest, a sergeant and two uniformed constables rode in the second coach. When we alighted in the gentle evening air, while lamplight bathed the frontages of the magnificent houses and sunset faded in the west, the fellows in blue waited outside for Bradstreet's word.

The butler admitted us, but cast a concerned eye over the silent figures at the foot of the steps. I think the elderly servant knew then that matters had taken a decidedly ominous turn. Hats and sticks went onto a hall rack, and in moments, the banker received us in his study.

Kemble sat at an enormous desk, where the geometry of a bay window framed him as if designed to magnify the importance of the person occupying that chair. I perceived the ego of a man who indulged in showmanship. Kemble *needed* to intimidate others – to be feared and respected. Being a member of the board of a major trading bank suited that ego to a *T*.

"Good evening, gentlemen," he began with a gracious smile. "Do be seated. Surely you'll take sherry?" Kemble raised a hand to summon the butler, but Bradstreet politely declined. "All business, eh? Very well. Pray continue. I'm all ears."

Something in his tone suggested that he knew perfectly well that when a policeman refuses a social libation, it is usually because he is on duty – which didn't bode well for Phillip Kemble.

Peter Kemble entered and stood to one side, appearing very much the dutiful son. I briefly noticed Mrs. Kemble in the hall, hands clasped, her expression curious but troubled. Bradstreet had given the family to understand that they were out of danger, but the lady must have read in our manner some foreshadowing that this matter hadn't yet reached its crux. In the goodness of her nature, she believed her husband to be blameless and could not, as yet, be expected to understand our intentions.

"Mr. Kemble," Bradstreet began, "as before, Mr. Holmes and Dr. Watson are present as concerned agents in this investigation. May I also present Inspector David Mayhew of the Yard."

Percival Morse smiled a silent greeting and displayed a borrowed warrant card.

"Now," Bradstreet went on, "as I said earlier, we are satisfied that no further danger exists to your family. The miscreant was, in fact, intercepted yesterday evening in Shepherd's Bush and has been interviewed at length. The gentleman is a visitor from Australia and, after his activities here, will doubtless be packed off back to Australia forthwith."

"Excellent," Kemble said with a smile. "Good work, gentlemen. You have my thanks."

"The circumstances surrounding this affair are most peculiar, however," Bradstreet added. Then, after a theatrically long pause, "Perhaps Mr. Holmes would like to go over the details."

"Thank you, Inspector." Rising, Holmes stood a little apart from the group, the better to address them. "Mr. Kemble, the decoy operation we staged from this address was successful. The suspect, Mr. Percival Morse of Ballarat, Australia, was arrested after following, with apparently ominous intent, a courageous police volunteer. The plan was to lure Morse into a reasonably private spot where officers would close in and make the arrest. Things didn't go quite as planned. A third party was in attendance." He paused to study Kemble's reactions. "Indeed, the only violence offered was on the part of these newcomers."

I also studied Kemble's features closely and acknowledged that he was a master of self-control. He gave little outward sign of the thoughts and anxieties that must, even now, be swirling within him. Holmes went on to describe the scene of the shooting, and how both Morse and a policeman were injured.

"The mysterious assailants made good their escape down the alley, having got through the constables by brute force." Now Holmes changed tack slightly. "Mr. Morse was not seriously injured, and received treatment at Hammersmith Police Station before providing a verbal statement, which has since been formalised. We wanted to know what his relationship with you might be to prompt his actions against you, and he gave us a more-than-complete picture." Holmes paused once more, watching for some reaction.

Kemble sat back, his genial smile unchanged, and spread his hands in a perplexed gesture. "I fail to see what sort of relationship we could possibly have. I've never met the man."

"Not quite true. He would have been a child when you encountered the Morse family at the gold-diggings named Cockatoo Springs."

Now, Kemble nodded with a pensive look. "I remember it. A shanty above a creek where small claimholders panned for gold dust. Quite a lawless place. One of several on my usual rounds." His good humour was visibly eroding. "What is the significance?"

"Mr. Morse alleges that your troopers murdered his father."

"What?" Kemble gave a bark of laughter. "Oh, this is really too much. I'm not saying troopers didn't step out of line, but when they did, they were soundly disciplined. Any allegation of murder went before the regional magistrate, and I recall no such proceedings."

"He doesn't claim that allegations were made. Mr. Morse alleges that the people of Cockatoo Springs were terrorised by you and your men into tolerating your brigandage."

"*Brigandage?*"

"The protection game. False and vexatious charges, using the law to further your own fortune. The theft of everything from gold dust to the virtue of women and children. Morse alleges that his father was killed as a warning against the fomentation of dissent against these outrages."

Coming to his feet, Kemble thumped the desk with a balled fist. "This is outrageous! I was a loyal officer of the Victoria Police, and my record speaks for itself! How dare you come into my home with the scurrilous accusations of a colonial – a criminal – and offer them to me?"

"Oh, we have a great deal more than accusations," Holmes replied softly. "There is the matter of the diamond."

"Diamond?" Kemble subsided slightly.

"The Barclay Diamond. I'm sure you remember it. It was famous in Melbourne, one of the treasures of the well-to-do – until it quietly departed from public notice around the time you returned to England."

Kemble shook his head in bewilderment. "Obviously, you're aware I deposited that stone with my bank. It constituted the investment that

165

eventually propelled me onto the board." He sneered. "You aren't suggesting I purloined it from Barclay as the crowning offence in my reign of terror in the Colonies, are you?"

"Did you legally purchase the stone?" Bradstreet asked bluntly.

Kemble stood with fists on hips and stared daggers at us, then opened a desk drawer. Taking out a key, he bent to the sturdy iron safe that was installed at one side of the window and removed a folder. He ruffled through the contents before presenting two documents. "There, Inspector. The bill of sale from Mr. Barclay in Melbourne, notarised by a witness, and Gablehouse's receipt for its deposit."

Bradstreet studied them for a moment and nodded with a grim smile. "The precise description of the stone and calculated carat weight exactly match the information we obtained from Gablehouse earlier." He folded the papers and placed them in his inside pocket. "These documents are material evidence."

"Evidence of *what?*" Kemble threw up his hands. "They support my position that I have done nothing wrong."

"But how did you come by the ten-thousand pounds to buy the stone in the first place?" Holmes asked softly. "We already know that savings from your wages amounted to – " He glanced at me.

I thumbed back in my notebook. "One-hundred-and-two pounds, twelve-shillings-and-fourpence," I supplied.

"On the face of it, you saved about twenty-per-cent of your gross income during the years of your service. This is quite reasonable for a prudent man in a well-paid position. Yet it was only *one*-per-cent of the price of that stone."

Kemble set down the folder and sank onto the corner of his desk. "Inform me, if you would be so kind, under what obligation I must answer these questions."

Holmes and Bradstreet shared a quick glance, and the latter continued, "At the moment, we are asking you to account for apparent discrepancies – very wide ones – in your financial history. I can make it more official if you prefer to continue this discussion at Scotland Yard."

At this point, young Peter Kemble stepped forward, hands raised. "Gentlemen, gentlemen, please. This is quite ridiculous. You are accusing one of the finest officers ever to serve Her Majesty of being an utter scoundrel, and doing so on the say-so of a man who is himself an admitted criminal. I ask you – how could you possibly take his word against my father's?"

"Mr. Percival Morse made a very convincing case," Bradstreet replied mildly. "To date, his only criminal act is sending those notes. Given that, upon arrest, he wasn't in possession of a weapon, the notes

166

constitute a misdemeanour. By his own admission, he intended harm to you, Mr. Kemble, but the law doesn't cover *ill thoughts*. However, his assertions and his reasons for coming halfway 'round the world to find you raised a great many questions – such as why, if the stone's purchase was perfectly legal, did you not declare it upon entry to this country?"

Kemble snorted a laugh of derision. "The British Empire functions as a commonwealth. There are no duties or tariffs upon imports and exports between its members."

"Nevertheless," Holmes countered, "the Customs Service keeps track of the movement across borders of high-value goods. Why didn't you disclose your ownership of the stone to the authorities at point of entry?"

Kemble had no answer this time, and I saw in his silence a certain edge of desperation. The set of his jaw and the gleam in his eye spoke volumes as to his anxiety.

"Is it because you couldn't account for the income to obtain it in the first place?"

"I had some luck down in the Colonies," Kemble growled. "I engaged in the odd business deal. No conflict of interest with my position as a police officer. I recall purchasing sheep and undertaking to get them to market, on more than one occasion. I was a silent partner in a tavern on the Ballarat Road, where the investment of fifty pounds earned hundreds in return. And I had some handsome winnings at the odd sporting event. Dribs and drabs, but it all added up." He gestured at the safe. "Several documents here will support this – my deed of partnership in the tavern, for instance."

"Still, to reach five figures . . . ." Holmes was unconvinced. "At no time have you mentioned the services of a chartered accountant."

"My territory was in the back of beyond. Our doctor was a sawbones and our lawyer a reject from the Melbourne bar. We never saw a dentist. As to an accountant – upon his honour as a gentleman, a man was expected to keep his own ledgers in good order."

"The income of one-hundred-and-twenty *years* is a fortune of remarkable proportions for any man to accumulate, much less in his spare time. Supposing it was amassed by entirely legal means, why would you take the dire risk of carrying a valuable stone on your person when you could have deposited your earnings in Melbourne and simply drawn them from a corresponding London bank? This method was created to avoid the vulnerability of cash and valuables to theft. I cannot imagine a police officer choosing not to use it . . . unless for reasons he preferred to conceal."

Kemble waved a dismissive hand as he returned to his seat. "So I chose to do it the adventurous way. I *was* an adventurer in those days. It took an adventurer to go out to Australia and put on a uniform that made you a target for every criminal in the bush with a pair of cap-and-ball pistols in his belt. If I omitted to make it a matter of public record that I made good out there, it's hardly a grand tragedy. If you're trying to validate Morse's claims against me, you'll have to do a lot better than that, Mr. Holmes."

I experienced a sinking feeling. In four years, I hadn't seen Holmes bested in his summation nor led astray in his convictions, both logical and instinctual, regarding where blame lay.

Holmes let a long pause go by, then steepled his fingers and began again. "Where is your coachman, Patrick Brand?"

"Brand? The deuce if I know. The fellow didn't turn up for work yesterday. I'm somewhat concerned for him."

Bradstreet followed Holmes's lead a moment later. "Two weeks ago, Mr. Brand was seen in The Old Ship pub, consorting with known roughs from the dockers' underworld."

"Was he, by God?" Kemble snorted, tossing his head. "If he's backslid to his old ways, I'll have to let the man go."

Bradstreet warmed to the narrative. "Further to this, do you recall the third parties mentioned earlier as being present when we apprehended Mr. Morse? Two men attacked Morse with, we believe, intent to kill. They escaped by going through two of my men, one of whom was beaten and the other shot. But one of my boys got off a shot of his own and plugged one of their assailants in the leg. Well, we found a body near Tadmor Street with a bullet in the leg. The round was extracted and compared to my man's revolver – no question, same calibre. Would you be surprised to learn that the body was identified as one of the dockers Mr. Brand approached?"

Silvering brows rose, and Kemble nodded. "Very surprised, and more than a little troubled."

"We are naturally eager to interview Mr. Brand," Bradstreet added. "As an ex-convict, he knows he can expect little leeway, and it's in his interests to tell the unvarnished truth. The questions uppermost in my mind are: Did he engage those dockers to eliminate Mr. Morse? Why would he do this? And where did he find the hefty price of their hire?"

"I would also like to know these things." Kemble's agreement was smoothly professional.

Yet the words seemed to mask a growing anxiety. I saw his hands trembling and heard an edge in his voice, and my knowledge as a medical man told me he had a lot to be afraid of.

"It is only a matter of time," Holmes added. "Brand cannot remain anonymous forever. He will resurface, either here or in some other city.

His description has been circulated. Sooner or later, he will be available to answer those questions, and we shall know upon whose behalf he set in motion an attempted murder – which, you note, is a far more tangible offence than some mere *intended* ill. In the eyes of the law, ordering and financing an attempted assassination is as good as performing the deed with one's own hands."

Kemble could mount no response this time. From the corner of my eye, I noticed his son's blanched face, as though Peter now blamed himself for ever approaching Holmes.

"There are only two possibilities," Holmes went on. "Brand engaged the roughs on his own initiative and for his own purposes, or else he did so at the bidding, and likely financing, of another. Assuming Mr. Morse's allegations are true, the only concerned party who could benefit from silencing Mr. Morse is yourself, Mr. Kemble."

"I know nothing about any attempt to silence Morse."

"Why would Brand act on his own?"

"Perhaps perceiving a threat – real or otherwise – he would do so out of loyalty to a man who has been good to him."

Holmes allowed himself a nod and smile. "In fairness, I have witnessed such loyalty at work. I'm sure it is a question my friend Bradstreet will be pleased to put to Brand when the time comes. Until then, Mr. Kemble, your status is quite in flux. If the coachman confirms your position – gallantly taking the blame for attempted murder upon himself – he puts us in a difficult position. But as you are well aware, a policeman can usually tell when he is being lied to. The alternative is that you acted in your own interests, employing Brand as a go-between to silence Mr. Morse before his allegations could be heard. Do you deny this?"

"Most strenuously."

"Let me tell you how I believe matters played out." Holmes spoke quietly, thumbs in his waistcoat pockets.

"You seem determined to."

"You were everything Percival Morse claims you were. That most despicable thing, the smooth-spoken gentleman who wields the social graces like a weapon, plays the game of culture and hierarchies with the ease of one drilled in such things by the public school system, yet despises rules and believes they apply only to lesser beings than himself. Your record at Eton certainly supports young Morse's view.

"In Australia, you found rich pickings. As the only officer of the law in hundreds of square miles, there were none to oppose you. You prospered off the backs of the miners, prospectors, and small traders who fought to scratch a living out of the wilderness. You stole at will. All force lay in your hands, and you were the sole arbiter of truth. Your magistrate automatically took your side in all things, relying, as he did, upon you to do the physical labour of law enforcement.

"You amassed capital rapidly through the protection game and outright theft, manipulating the law for your own ends. This provided ample stake money for small business enterprises – the inn you mentioned, the livestock trading, doubtless many others, and, of course, the wagers. Not one of these things is illegal, but the bedrock of your fortune is the simple fact that *hundreds* of people worked for you, tithing to you on an ongoing basis. After five years of all these measures operating at full force, you had a considerable fortune – none of which you deposited in a bank, so your illicit income remained strictly out of official records.

"When the time came to return to England, you converted that fortune into gemstones – one in particular, the way military men did in the old days to syphon the wealth of India into this country one emerald at a time. You purchased the stone legally, but Mr. Barclay asked no questions – for reasons that remain moot at this point. You didn't declare it upon your return, in order to keep it out of official records, and the officers at Gablehouse were so mesmerised by the investment that they chose not to inquire too closely. I assume they viewed the bill of sale, and were duly satisfied.

"Come forward twenty-six years. Those grim times, far away, were suddenly brought back into focus by certain threatening notes – notes whose significance only you, Mr. Kemble, could understand, for they called you out as the black-hearted scourge of those hills, upon whose very shadow people spat. The respectable Phillip Kemble couldn't have this tale told, for obvious reasons. Mud sticks, as they say. Better to keep it unuttered.

"The Customs Service received a request to provide information about passengers arriving from Australia, which they declined. That was you, making a discreet inquiry. Then you sent Brand, your rehabilitated felon, to recruit the sort he used to run with long ago: Hard men who were not averse to doing grievous bodily harm, or worse, for pay. We made no secret of the fact that we had identified Mr. Morse. I recall your facial reaction when the surname was mentioned, as if you remembered a family by that name perfectly well.

"One cannot, of course, take a momentary reaction into court as evidence. But with us running the decoy operation from your very home, you could hardly be unaware of where and when we would be casting our net for Mr. Morse, and thus, you knew precisely where to send your hired hands to get to him before we could. We took care to ensure that you were the *only* one to know this. In fact, you informed Brand, whose roughnecks were in the right place, at the right time. Still, it all went wrong for them –

one dead and one on the run, while Brand has conveniently disappeared. He also could be dead, for all we know at this point."

"A fabulous tale, Mr. Holmes," Kemble said with a deep nod. "It has its own peculiar logic, I grant you. But the burden of proof lies with the accuser, and so far, this is a theory. There is nothing – *Nothing!* – to tie me to alleged improprieties in the territory of Victoria. Supposing you went down to Australia and searched for a year to find anyone who might have been involved, their testimony would still be hearsay, unless multiple witnesses corroborated each other's stories." He gave us a confident smile. "Good luck on that score. While you're there, I can give you a list of brother officers whom I am quite certain would speak on my behalf against this nonsense . . . assuming, once again, they still live to comment at all."

A heavy silence filled the room, and I watched young Peter Kemble relax somewhat. His father's certainty seemed to reassure him, and I was genuinely sorry that we had brought this tragedy to his doorstep. But I couldn't let myself forget the countless people whom Morse claimed to have been brutalised by this smiling fellow.

At last, Holmes sighed. "Mr. Kemble, for what possible reason would Mr. Morse spin his incredible story if it were a fabrication?"

For a long moment, Kemble stared at the pen set before him on the blotter. His eyes went to a photograph of his family in a gold frame, and to his old service revolver in its polished brass holder. At last, he shook his head. "I can only speculate. Children are impressionable creatures, and the shock of his father's passing must have been terrible. If he heard his neighbours laying blame, it could very well have taken root in his mind and become a hard fact for him, when it was in reality very much the opposite – merely the supposition of embittered people."

"Why were those people bitter, Mr. Kemble?"

"Miners are speculators. They bid their health and youth on the gamble that the river will reward their efforts. For many it does, but such deposits are fickle things. I watched one fellow take a rich yield from his stretch of creek, yet his neighbour, working a claim just a hundred yards on, could extract only a pittance. That's the luck of the draw. Providence can be cruel, and nothing is more natural than that those who get the thin end of the wedge will seek someone to blame." Kemble gestured loosely at his own chest. "The face of authority is a handy target."

Bradstreet shifted in his chair with an impatient grumble. "This is reasonable, but we have to deal in facts, not speculations. The *fact* is that someone tried to kill Mr. Morse, and any jury will see that as essentially an admission that what he claimed about you, Mr. Kemble, is the truth. Regardless of whether anything might ever be proven against you concerning those allegations, it'll only take Mr. Brand's testimony to

171

determine at whose behest he organised the attempted murder." He sat forward with a hard look. "Rest assured, we *will* get the truth out of Patrick Brand."

Kemble subsided, resting back in his chair, rubbing his hands slowly together as if in deep thought.

After a moment, his son gave a soft cough. "Father?"

The ex-Lieutenant glanced up with a smile, now devoid of all recrimination for his son's actions in bringing this investigation upon him. "Not now, my boy. Just be at peace. All will be right. I promise you that much."

Bradstreet rose ponderously, followed by myself and the silent, disguised Morse. "Mr. Phillip Kemble, I am placing you under arrest on suspicion of the attempted murder of Mr. Percival Morse. I'm sure you know your rights very well indeed, and you will be able to contact your chosen legal representative in the morning. You'll have to come with us, I'm afraid."

Kemble, Junior was pale as a ghost. "Father, I'm so sorry – I thought I was helping you."

"It's all right, my boy," Kemble said softly as he rose, patting his son's arm. "Don't worry. Due process, and all that." After a long, distracted pause, he gave a small shrug. "It's about reputation, you see. How we are considered by our peers. How we are dealt with by the public press. Our standing in society." He smiled once more, an introspective expression. "Some things just won't do." With this cryptic whisper, he nodded at the door to the left of the study. "May I get my coat?"

"Of course." Bradstreet was happy to be entirely polite.

I glanced at Holmes, who wore a troubled look. He had made a less conclusive argument than he preferred, and conviction depended upon Brand's testimony – should the coachman take blame upon himself to protect his master, Kemble might be untouchable. All the same, there would be talk, a real to-do in the papers. Even assuming he came through it unimpeachable, it would probably cost Kemble his position with Gablehouse.

The door opened upon a deep closet – more a storeroom for odds and ends – and I thought it strange that such a chamber should have a gaslight. I thought it doubly odd when Kemble turned up the light, and the door closed behind him. A second later, we heard a bolt locking.

In a heartbeat, Holmes was halfway across the room, taking Peter Kemble by the elbow. "Is there another way out of that chamber?"

"No, Mr. Holmes. That's Father's filing shelves for paperwork. His old uniform hangs there." The young man swallowed, and his expression tightened with dread. "He keeps a pistol in there."

My heart sank with the natural horror one feels at such implications. With a grim look, Morse crossed himself. Holmes and Bradstreet tensed with dreadful anticipation, and my friend knocked sharply at the door. "Mr. Kemble, do come out. There is no call for anything precipitate at this time. The matter has some way to go before every question has its answer. There is as yet no guarantee of any particular outcome."

A long silence followed, in which I found myself hoping that the next sound would be the bolt, as Kemble listened to reason. But no matter what brutal code he had lived by, it seemed Phillip Kemble was a gentleman at the last. All we heard from the closet was the shocking report of the pistol.

Peter collapsed into a chair, close to fainting in shock, and pounding footsteps approached from the hall. Bradstreet put his shoulder to the door and, in three crashing impacts, burst it in with a splintering of wood. But a sorry sight greeted us, and the sergeant and constables who had waited outside were in time to see only slow red drips from amongst sandy hair – the vacant ruin where a man had been moments earlier.

A welling scream announced Mrs. Kemble. Holmes turned, asking me to intercept her, but the lady had already seen the worst, and she had overheard enough to know half of what had happened. She understood only that the man she had loved and trusted had been taken from her by these terrible circumstances, and through her tears, she berated Holmes with a flurry of partly formed words, beating her clenched fists upon his chest.

His face a mask of control, Holmes stood stolidly until Bradstreet and I took the distraught woman by the arms and urged her away to a chair, where she collapsed in wracking sobs. The inspector spoke to his sergeant, who left at once to summon the divisional surgeon to pronounce death, and the constables gently cleared the room, ushering mother and son and the hovering butler into the hall. The door closed behind them.

Holmes and I would be taking part in lengthy discussion on these matters, as would Morse – who, to his credit, was trembling like a leaf, far from gloating over the moral victory the evening's events might have constituted. We stepped into the street and quite automatically stuffed and lit our pipes, eager for that first soothing rush of tobacco. Under the glow of the gas standards, Holmes looked off into the night sky for a long while, then mustered a comment from somewhere deep down.

"There are times, Watson, when I despise my profession."

"You weren't to know he would take such an option."

"Do the honourable thing? It's what gentlemen have always done. And in so doing, he confessed to every allegation Morse has made. We may take it as read that Kemble commissioned Brand to arrange the attempted killing last night, and that there was nothing he wouldn't have

173

done to prevent the truth of his reign of terror in the Victorian goldfields from coming to the attention of London society.

"My deepest sympathies are with the family, who never knew the brigand – only the solid patriarch, the respected father. I have robbed them of that figure, that memory, and I regret that the cold mechanics of deductive reasoning make no allowances for those who will be injured, incidental to the unfolding of logic." Holmes plumed smoke into the night. "I just hounded a man into his grave, Watson. That was not my intention, but merely to seek justice, in whatever measure, for the hundreds whom he brutalised."

"And you have done so," I added at once, firmly but kindly. "After so very long, it was likely impossible to tie Kemble to specific acts, much less secure any sort of compensation for his victims. His suicide may very well be their only satisfaction." I clapped a hand on Morse's shoulder, where he stood at our side. "How do you look upon it, sir?"

Morse coughed, finding his voice at last, and sighed. "Part of me is glad to see the end of him, but another part is so sorry to see what it did to his family that I might just as well not have bothered making this voyage. I'll have to square it with my conscience as to what I've done here. I came to London willing to face gaol, if I could have the satisfaction of beating Kemble to a pulp in the names of everyone he ever rode down, roughshod. And now?" He glanced back at the tall house, from which we heard sobbing, a thread of despair on the breeze. "I don't know."

"Perhaps justice has been served the only possible way," Holmes said gruffly. "I'm sorry, gentlemen. I shan't be good company for some while to come."

"I understand," I whispered, and left him to himself.

In the amber glow of the gaslights, we waited for Bradstreet to join us among the rustling trees of a suburb where, I thought abstractly, such crime might never have visited before. Yet almost at once I rejected the notion, with a sudden, repellent suspicion that all of the ostentatious wealth around us was probably tied – more often than we might ever care to acknowledge – to the wages of one sin or another.

In the Flesh
by Elbert Henry Smith

Mycroft Holmes shoved his body through a large crowd of degenerates. He was not an enthusiast of the penny gaff, as he thought that they harbored the underbelly of London society, but on this day, he had come here out of curiosity. Rumors of a half-man and half-elephant had been spreading around town like wildfire. People had been lining up into the next streets in order to obtain a glance at this monstrosity, and it was up to Mycroft to look into it. Weaving through the crowd was quite easy for him. He was a large man and everyone had to make way when he got close.

Mycroft was finally able to take a look at the stage. A group of Chinese acrobats and then a magician were still on before the Elephant Man was to make his grand entrance. He watched on as the Great Móshù Jiā carefully placed a young woman into a small box on a table and pulled out a saw blade. He showed it to the audience and cut a piece of silk in half. The audience stared on anxiously. "A smile dispels many worries," Móshù Jiā said. The girl in the box smiled at the crowd. "I shall now do the unbelievable," Móshù Jiā continued. "I will cut my assistant in half with this blade, and yet – *She will not die!*"

Móshù Jiā walked closer to the table and, with a mighty shove, forced the blade through the girl. Everyone gasped, the girl on the table played dead for a second. Someone screamed in the audience, and the girl looked up and waved. Móshù Jiā moved the second half of the table around as she moved her arms and legs. He closed up the table and removed the blade. The girl opened the box she in which she was resting and got off the table, put back together and waving again. "See, she is safe!" Móshù Jiā cried as the audience cheered. "You have seen a miracle of the gods, in the flesh."

Mycroft looked on in distaste. "Rubbish," he said.

"What?" someone nearby asked. He turned around to see a rather dashing young gentleman of medium height and build, with nicely kept wavy hair. The man was clapping for the performance, all the while looking at Holmes in disbelief. "That, good sir, looked like a miracle," the man said.

"Cheap parlor tricks," Mycroft countered. "I've seen that act countless times. He has two assistants on the table. Both are curled up inside the box. It's really basic, old chap."

The man looked at Mycroft and tilted his head, as if he was trying to remember something. "You know, I've had a lot of detectives and other police officers come through my place of work. You look rather familiar to me. Are you Sherlock Holmes?"

Mycroft peered at him with some discouragement. "No, and please do not make that mistake again. I am his brother, Mycroft."

The man laughed. "I'm truly sorry, Mr. Holmes. Please – accept my apologies. My name is Christopher Andrews."

The man reached out to shake his hand, and Mycroft reciprocated.

"You seem like a well-to-do kind of chap, Mr. Andrews. What brings you to such a den of thieves?"

"I'm a surgeon over at the London Hospital. I come here sometimes for a bit of beer and skittles."

"To each his own, I suppose. I'm rather interested in the next performance – this Elephant Man."

"Ah, you and half of London sir."

"Do you think he's real?" Mycroft asked.

"Oh, yes. I've seen him here before. He's as real as it gets."

"As a man of science and medicine, what do you think is wrong with him?"

"I'd say that our dear fellow suffers from enlarged tumors all over the body. But that's just a guess."

"Indeed. Most fascinating."

"I've tried to get him to let me examine him, but he won't allow it. I told him that maybe I could help ease his way of living, and he still denies me."

Andrews pulled out his watch. It was a peculiar timepiece, engraved with three monkeys: One covering his eyes, one covering his mouth, and the last covering his ears.

"I say," said Mycroft, "that's a wonderful pocket-watch you have there."

"Thank you. My grandmother had it made for my grandfather. After he died, she gave it to me on my first day at university." He looked at the time and replaced the watch. "He should be coming on stage very soon."

The curtains closed and a hush fell over the crowd. A man stepped out. Tall, and thin, he fixed his top hat on his head and took a swig of whisky. "Hello! I am Tom Norman. I want to thank you for coming tonight, and hope you have enjoyed the show. I think we all know why you're here. The tales of this man are legendary. Some say he was a beast formed in the Pits of Hell. Others say he's a poor love child of bestiality. Tonight," Norman proclaimed, "we'll let you decide. I present to you the one, the only . . . *The Elephant Man!*"

The curtain pulled back to reveal a small deformed man sitting in a chair. He was shirtless for all to see. Overgrown masses littered his body like a vicious disease. His head was massively deformed, and he had one clubbed arm. The women in the audience screamed. Mycroft's eyes widened. He had never seen anything like this in all his life. Meanwhile, Andrews smiled and tried to get closer to the stage.

The Elephant Man looked around as much as he could. He was clearly frightened of the people, some of whom began to throw trash at him. Others tossed bottles. Norman stepped forward to calm the audience down.

"Now please," he cried. "Be respectful! Our man here has seen the dark side of the world. Can we not afford him some kindness?"

The crowd simply booed him. At that moment, the deformed man stood up and limped towards the edge of the stage. Then he began to speak:

> " *'Tis true, my form is something odd,*
> *but blaming me is blaming God.*
> *Could I create myself anew*
> *I would not fail in pleasing you.*
> *If I could reach from pole to pole*
> *or grasp the ocean with a span,*
> *I would be measured by the soul.*
> *The mind's the standard of the Man."*

The crowd paused and became quiet, suddenly not knowing what to say. Mycroft smiled, thinking that the Elephant Man, for whatever he was, must be a kind soul. Additionally, he must be somewhat educated, quoting Isaac Watts.

The curtain then closed and, after a few moments, the crowd dispersed. Mycroft said his goodbyes to Andrews and went backstage to meet the Elephant Man. He walked down a hall and noticed Tom Norman standing outside of a room. Mycroft casually walked up and greeted him.

"Hello, my name is Mycroft Holmes. I enjoyed your presentation immensely tonight."

"Thank you, sir. Did you say, Holmes? Are you – ?"

Mycroft interrupted him. "Yes, he's my brother – younger brother. I am quite curious about your 'Elephant Man'. I wondered if there was any way I could have a chat with him?"

"I don't see why not. He might enjoy talking to someone famous. Besides, he's already spoken to some authorities earlier."

"Interesting. Did they say who they were?"

Norman nodded. "A couple of coppers. Said they wanted to question him about some murders."

"Well, let's hope they get the right man."

Norman opened the door to reveal the Elephant Man sat on a stool, reading the local newspaper. Both Norman and Mycroft walked in. Norman reached for a bottle on a nearby table and took a swig of whisky. "Oi," he said. "Sherlock Holmes here to see you."

Mycroft looked annoyed.

"You . . . you are Sherlock Holmes?" the Elephant Man asked.

"I'm afraid not. I am his brother, Mycroft. May I ask what is your name?"

"My Christian name is Joseph. Joseph Merrick." Although difficult to determine from his appearance, his voice sounded young, and Mycroft thought that he might be in his early twenties. "I have to admit," said Merrick, "I'm an avid follower of your brother's work in the newspapers."

Mycroft nodded. "Thank you, I will mention it to him." He looked over at Norman. "May we have some privacy?"

Norman nodded and, taking the bottle with him walked out the door. Mycroft then sat down on a sturdy chair near Merrick. He smiled, but it was a sympathetic smile. Merrick looked him over, trying to see what kind of man he was.

"Do you find my appearance revolting, Mr. Holmes?"

"No, I find it fascinating. Have you been looked at by any doctors?"

"No, not as of yet. One has visited me here in the past – a surgeon, Dr. Christopher Andrews. He seems a nice fellow, and says he wants to study me."

"Ah, I met him out in the audience tonight. Do you think that you'll let him?"

"Yes, though I don't know what good it will do. I don't see him curing my ailment. May I ask, why are you here?"

"I wanted to see if the rumors were true."

"What – that a grotesque freak walks about in London town? Well, I think you have your answer."

"Mr. Norman said that the police have been here."

"Yes. A young woman was brutally murdered. They said that someone gave them my description."

"Ah. So they think you might have some involvement."

"What do you think Mr. Holmes? Do you think I killed her?"

"I don't know anything about the murder, but I'm a pretty good judge of character, and I have somewhat dabbled in investigations in the past. No. Based on my initial impressions, I don't think you're a murderer. You seem like a man who has been dealt a bad penny in life, with the way your muscle structure is, you wouldn't have the strength to kill someone."

Mycroft Holmes stood. "If you don't mind, I would like to come again tomorrow night. It's getting late now, but I'd like to carry on with our conversation."

Merrick agreed, and Mycroft opened the door to find Norman, who walked back into the room with Merrick's coat and hat. "Time to go, Joseph." Merrick stood as well, and he slowly put on his coat. Norman then placed a large sack with two eye holes over his face.

"I would enjoy seeing you again tomorrow immensely, Mr. Holmes," said Merrick, his voice muffled. "Perhaps you can tell me something of your brother's adventures?"

"Quite possibly," Mycroft replied. He smiled again and then left the penny gaff, stepping back out into the gray, smoke-ridden London streets, where people were going about their business on this busy late night. As Mycroft wandered back to his home, he wondered what Joseph Merrick would be doing tonight if he wasn't "The Elephant Man"?

Leslie Ann Wagner stood just outside an alleyway, waiting for customers to walk by. She was all dolled up in her best dress and makeup. She fiddled with her long curly black hair and watched as her friend Delia tried her best to lure men to come back with her. Tales had been going around that someone was up to no good, out there cutting up the girls. Delia had to keep a close eye on Leslie because she was new, and she didn't want her to get hurt. Finally, a man approached Delia. He whispered in her ear and caressed her body. She smiled and played along. The man gave her a cigarette, and she walked over to Leslie.

"You all right, Love?" Delia asked.

"Would be better if I was getting some work tonight."

"Don't worry," Delia said as she laughed. "You're young and beautiful and haven't been touched. Men will be banging down the door soon."

"Better not leave your man for too long," Leslie replied.

"Look, I'll be back in a few."

She walked away with the strange man, and Leslie stood there watching everyone going by. She received a few glances here and there, and a few smiles as well, but nothing of real interest. Then she suddenly heard a bottle break in the alley and turned, going to see what had happened.

Leslie cautiously walked back into the alleyway. "Hello? Is someone there?" she asked. A rat unexpectedly scuttled across the ground and she jumped. She then gathered her composure and sighed. Suddenly a man came forth out of the darkness. He wore a sackcloth over his face, an old

dirty hat, and an old dirty jacket. Leslie backed up, now very frightened.
The man produced a scalpel from his pocket.

"You're him, aren't you? The Elephant Man."

The man stepped forward and pushed her against the wall. He placed
the scalpel against her neck.

"Please don't do this!" she cried.

"Mummy . . ." he quietly whispered. Then he slit her throat, and an
eruption of dark red blood poured down her neck. She gasped for air and
slid down the wall. She looked up at him, trying to grasp enough air to
breathe. Then the masked figure bent down and started to cut off her face,
her like a butcher carefully choosing where to slice, like a painter looking
for the perfect stroke. He looked into her eyes as he removed the flesh. He
stood up and held the skin close to his own face. "Yes . . . Mother," he
whispered. As he heard people walk by the entrance to the alleyway, he
slid back into the darkness, unnoticed . . . .

The next day, Mycroft entered through the back of the penny gaff and
made his way through the people getting ready for the show. At Joseph
Merrick's dressing room, he knocked on the door, and it opened just a little
– enough for him to see inside. Tom Norman was sitting in Merrick's
chair. Mycroft walked in, a bit confused about the long sad face Norman
had while he stared down at the newspaper.

"Is everything all right?" Mycroft asked.

"No, it most certainly is not!" Norman tossed the paper on the table
in front of him. The headline read: "*London Face Ripper Strikes Again!*"

"Another dead girl," Mycroft noted. "Where is Merrick?"

"The police came earlier and took him away. What am I going to do?
He's my main attraction!"

Mycroft grew angry, leaving the room and slamming the door. He
walked down the hall straight past Christopher Andrews, who seemed to
also be on his way to Merrick's dressing room.

"Mr. Holmes. Nice to see – " Before he could finish his sentence,
Mycroft walked past him and into the street. He knew that Merrick was
innocent of this crime. He wasn't one who normally cared to involve
himself and solve murders like his younger brother, but he felt that Merrick
was owed some justice in this life. He was determined to help him as much
as he could.

After a telephone call to locate Merrick, Mycroft made his way to
Bishopsgate Police Station, hoping that the detective on the case had a bit
of intelligence to him, and that he wasn't simply looking to make a name
for himself. Entering the building, he was reminded of the penny gaff –
two sides of the same coin. He walked up to the front desk where a young

bobby was chatting with a prostitute. Mycroft overheard their conversation as he approached.

"Look, Love, you gals have nothing to worry about!" the bobby said. "We've caught the killer."

"I heard you got the wrong man," replied the prostitute. "Word is you're trying to keep it all hush-hush."

Mycroft walked forward and cleared his throat, interrupting the conversation and looking at the bobby with a stern expression.

"Mycroft Holmes, I'm here on Crown business, and I wish to speak to the detective in charge of this case."

The bobby looked at him and nodded. "Yes, sir. Follow me." Then he led him to the back of the station where they both heard a loud commotion. The police officers are standing around, celebrating the quick capture of Joseph Merrick. The bobby stepped closer and spoke loudly over their conversation. "I have a Mr. Mycroft Holmes here to see Inspector Lucas Henry." The group scattered, leaving a sharply dressed man in plaid trousers and a frock coat. He had been the middle of mocking the way that Joseph Merrick walked when he noticed Mycroft staring at him.

"Inspector Lucas Henry, I presume?"

"What's it to you?" the inspector replied.

"As your policeman stated, I am Mycroft Holmes, I'm represent The Crown, and I need to speak with you regarding the Face Ripper investigation."

Inspector Henry didn't speak, taking a moment to light a cigarette. Then: "You're a bit late for that. We nabbed the bloody -------." And he laughed.

"You have got the wrong man, Inspector Henry. The murderer is still on the loose – "

Inspector Henry interrupted him. "Look, I'm well aware of your brother. I read the newspapers. Sounds to me as if he gets in the way of proper investigations." He walked over to Mycroft, standing face-to-face, taking a puff of his cigarette and blowing smoke into Mycroft's face.

"That ain't happening here. You get what I mean, Guv?"

"I demand to see Mr. Merrick, and this case is not closed. If you do not cooperate, I will have you jailed for obstructing justice."

Inspector Henry gave him a sour look, and then looked toward the bobby. "You – take him down to the prisoner, and then get back to the desk."

The constable nodded as he led Mycroft downward to the cells. It was dark and dreary like a dungeon. When they reached the end of a hallway, Mycroft saw Merrick sitting alone in a cell. The officer opened the door and let Mycroft in, whereupon he observed that Merrick seemed to have been beaten.

"Mr. Holmes, you came to see me?"

Mycroft was very angry. He sat down next to Merrick. "What happened, Joseph?"

"They tried to get a confession from me, but I didn't do anything. They said I killed several girls and peeled the flesh from off their faces. Who would do such a thing?"

"Someone with a sick mind – which is not you. I know you did not do this, and I will prove your innocence."

"How, Mr. Holmes? It could be anybody. London is a big place, and I know how the public views me. They think I'm a monster – a monster that is capable of anything."

Sadly, Mycroft knew that he was right. He was aware from reports that he'd read that there were no clues, but he had to keep Merrick's hopes up. "I will get you out of here, Joseph. Put your trust in me."

Superintendent Murphy called for the constable who had first spoken with Mycroft. He'd heard of the commotion with Inspector Henry and wanted to know what was going on.

"Can you tell me why this man is here?" Murphy asked.

"Yes, sir. It's Sherlock Holmes's brother – Mycroft Holmes. Said he works for the government, and is investigating the Face Ripper."

"I see. A government agent?" The constable nodded. "Sherlock Holmes?"

"No, sir. His brother – Mycroft."

"Tell the inspector to get in here at once," Murphy said. The constable nodded and then left.

Inspector Henry walked into Superintendent Murphy's office. He was beginning to understand that he might have overstepped his authority with Mycroft Holmes, and was now in for a browbeating. Murphy looked up from his desk and stroked his long mustache. "Lucas, sit down,"

The detective pulled up a chair and leaned back, smoking a cigarette.

"Listen to me," said the Superintendent, "and listen carefully. They have just found another dead girl – murdered *after* you arrested Merrick."

Inspector Henry looked up at him. "You're lying."

"Afraid not. You have the wrong man – but I want to keep him for a while. I want the public to have a little confidence in our abilities to catch criminals. And I want you to get down to the morgue, and take that Holmes fellow with you. Don't stir any trouble with him – he's much more powerful than you realize, and the last thing we need is the Government prodding around in this."

Henry stood up and put out his cigarette. As he did, he saw Mycroft, back at the front desk, speaking with one of the officers. "I don't like him. He walked in, thinking he owns the place."

"Well," replied Murphy, "let him believe what he wants until he's out of our hair."

"But sir, he's only going to get in the way! I have a friend at the Yard, and he says the the other Holmes – Sherlock – always has his nose in their business. I – "

Murphy quickly interrupted him. "Do as you are told. If you spoil this, there will be consequences. Do you understand?"

Inspector Henry nodded.

Mycroft was angrily berating the desk officer. "I want him released immediately! That man is innocent, and his only crime was to allow himself to be taken into custody."

Inspector Henry walked out of the superintendent's office. "All right, all right, Mr. Holmes. Just calm down. It seems that we got off on the wrong foot."

"Wrong foot? Wrong foot? You arrest a disabled man who could not have committed the crime – "

"Witnesses said that the killer was seen wearing the same kind of sack over his head as Merrick."

" – You beat him," continued Mycroft, "and accused him of murder, and you say that it's 'the wrong foot'?"

Mycroft paused to take a breath, and Henry replied, "The case is still open, and we're looking into other possibilities." He lowered his eyes. "We just had another girl just come in – murdered. *After* we arrested your friend. Come with me, and help me solve this."

"What about Mr. Merrick?" Mycroft asked. "Clearly he is too weak to commit these crimes, and now another has happened while he was in your custody."

"And unfortunately, we're going to have to keep him a little longer. I promise you, though, that if he didn't commit the other murders, then we will let him go."

Mycroft nodded regretfully, and Inspector Henry led him down to the morgue.

They were greeted by a doctor wearing an apron covered in blood. He looked like some crazed butcher with blond hair and muttonchops. He smiled and reached his hand out to greet Mycroft. "I heard you were in the building. It's an honor. I'm Jack Temple."

Inspector Henry stepped between the two, wondering at Temple's respectful attitude toward Mycroft Holmes. "All right, enough of this. Let's see the lady."

Henry walked over to the body. Temple had already performed the autopsy.

Mycroft looked at the poor girl's missing face. The killer had left everything else – the eyes, the tongue – all intact.

"Has the missing . . . has her face been found?" Mycroft asked.

"No," Temple said. "Just like the others. I have no idea what he does with them."

"He collects them," Mycroft stated. Temple and Henry both look at him in disgust. "Why else? Why go to these lengths to cut off someone's face if not keeping it as some memento."

Temple looked at him. "Funny thing is, all the victims had the same look: Long, curly black hair, and fair skin."

"Jilted by a former lover perhaps, who also had those features?" Mycroft pondered. "Fixated on them. Or possibly his mother . . . ."

"Where are you getting all of this Holmes?" Henry asked.

"It's basic psychology, Inspector. We're dealing with someone who is very ill." He looked down and then held his hands over the dead girl's head, gently gliding his hands several inches over the cut marks. "Look at the way the face was cut. This man knew what he was doing. This isn't some half-crazed butcher. No, to him, this was like a work of art. A Rembrandt of mutilation."

"What are you suggesting?" Henry asked.

"We are dealing with a surgeon. Someone with great skill. Tell me, Temple," said Mycroft, "was there anything found with the body?"

"Yes, there was this." Temple reached onto the surgeon's tray and produced a pocket-watch. "Quite unusual. It has three monkeys engraved on it."

Mycroft stepped back in shock. "I have seen this before."

"I had to break her fingers to get it out of her hands," Temple said. "She didn't want to let go – even in death."

Meanwhile, Mycroft paced back and forth, working it out in his head. Normally this wasn't his line of country, but Merrick's life was on the line. It had to be Christopher Andrews. *Of course*, he thought. *It's the only reason he's interested in Merrick – as the perfect scapegoat!*

"You recognize it," Henry prodded, but Mycroft wouldn't answer. He was thinking.

"I swear, Holmes," Henry exploded, "if you're just mucking about, I'll put a stop to your little circus."

Temple walked over to Henry. "Leave him be. He's sorting it. Give the man some space."

Finally, Mycroft seemed to reach a conclusion. "Come, Inspector Henry. We must go to the London Hospital at once." Mycroft hurried walked through the door, and Henry followed closely behind.

Andrews slit the throat of another young lady.

This time, he was closer to the hospital than he would have preferred. He was getting more and more careless with each killing. Losing his pocket-watch, and now, instead of wearing a sack like Merrick, the only thing hiding his identity was a handkerchief worn across his face. He dug the scalpel into this woman's neck and she fell instantly to the alley pavement. He carefully cut off her face and held it to the light. *Christopher,* he heard his mother say, inside his head. *You've been a naughty boy! Another girl? She will never replace me!*

"Stop it!" he cried. "I'm a good boy! I am a good boy!" Bottles rolled in the alley, and an old man crawled out of some litter on the ground.

"What's wrong, lad?" he blustered. Andrews ran away in fear.

Mycroft Holmes and Inspector Henry walked into the administrative area of the hospital, having already confirmed that Dr. Andrews was not in the building. A woman at a desk smiled as Holmes rushed toward her, and then the smile vanished at his urgent tone. "I need someone to provide the address of Dr. Christopher Andrews," Mycroft said. "Immediately."

"I'm sorry sir," the woman replied, "but we aren't allowed to give out that information."

Henry stepped forward. "Look: We are the law, and you are interfering in a police investigation. Now, go get someone with a lick of sense, and we'll be waiting right here."

The woman gave him an angry look. Suddenly a man called from down a nearby hallway.

"Mycroft! Mycroft Holmes!" The man quickly walked down to join Mycroft and Henry. Mycroft looked at him and instantly recognized an old friend.

"Archie! Archie Davis, as I live and breathe!" Mycroft said as the two men shook hands. "Inspector Lucas, this is Archie, an old chum from university days." Turning back to Davis, he asked, "How have you been?"

Davis smiled. "Head surgeon over this area. Is there a problem?"

"Yes. We're looking into one of your men, Dr. Christopher Andrews. We need to speak with him, and he isn't here. Can you help us find his address?"

"Chris? Yes, he's a good friend of mine. Hope he isn't in any trouble."

"I can't go into it," Mycroft replied, "but it is of the utmost importance we reach him."

"Come along then," Davis offered. "I know where he lives. I'll take you there."

Andrews finished sewing the last piece of human flesh onto the tapestry he'd created. He stepped back and gazed upon the shrine he had made to his mother. All the women he had murdered – he had sewn their faces into a macabre tapestry hanging on the wall. And suddenly they all began to talk to him. One by one, they chastised him, each face seemed to be a voice-piece for his mother. Andrews fell to the ground, cupping his hands over his ears and yelling at the top of his lungs. "Yes, Mother, yes! I will do better next time." He then walked over to his closet and opened the door where another young, dark-haired beauty was tied up and gagged, brought here because the streets were becoming too dangerous for his work. He pulled her out and threw her to the floor. He removed the gag and, before she could scream, he placed a scalpel under her chin.

"Quiet now," Andrews said, "or I'll slit you from ear to ear."

"Please sir!" she cried. "Let me go! I have done nothing to you."

"Listen to your lies! What else should I expect from the mouth of a streetwalker?"

"Streetwalker?" she cried. "I'm no prostitute, My name is Anna Price."

"More lies! When will it end?"

"No, it's true! I was waiting on my father to come out of the butcher's. Please sir – I am to be married soon. I don't want to die! I have so much to live for!"

Dr. Christopher Andrews spat in her face. He dragged her over to the tapestry, and when she saw it for the first time, she screamed, in spite of the killer's warning not to. Anna looked on in pure terror as she gazed upon the faces of his poor victims, displayed in such a vile manner.

"See, Mother?" whispered Andrews. "Here's one that is pure – untainted by the touch of a man." His mother's voices kept speaking to him. They wanted him to kill her. Andrews grabbed his forehead in anger. "Why? Why? She is what you wanted," He looked at the faces, and they began to move when he spoke. *She still won't do, boy. She must go like all the rest. This is your Mother's will.*

Andrews held the scalpel to the girl's neck "Your will is my command," he breathed.

Then he heard a knock at the door. "Christopher Andrews!" Inspector Henry yelled. "Open up! It's the police."

Anna screamed again, and Henry bashed the door in.

Mycroft, Henry, and Daws rushed into the room. Even as they did so, Andrews pivoted and fled out the open window. Mycroft quickly followed after him.

Inspector Henry and Dr. Daws bent down to comfort the young lady while she continued to scream hysterically. Meanwhile, Mycroft had followed Andrews out and onto a ledge that ran a few feet and onto a nearby roof. Mycroft had just reached the flat open space when Andrews jumped on top of Mycroft. The struggle was short, Mycroft giving Andrews a good wallop across the face, even as the doctor reached out with his scalpel and held it to Mycroft's throat. They froze in that position.

"You've ruined it, Holmes! You ruined the whole damned thing!"

Mycroft held the doctor's arm, trying to overpower. "Andrews," he said urgently. "*Christopher – Stop!*"

Hearing his first name, Andrews paused for a moment. Then, as if coming back to himself for a moment, he backed off for a few steps.

"Christopher, it's over. Throw down the scalpel."

"I can't!" Andrews breathed. "I can't, Holmes! She cries out to me. Everywhere I go, I *see* her! And she wants me to *kill*!"

"For God's sake man, who wants you to kill?"

"My *mother*! She won't leave me alone! Even in death." Andrews closed his eyes. "I see her everywhere, and I must kill her!"

"Come back with me, Andrews," Mycroft said softly. "You are sick."

"What would I do? I'll hang. And if they judge me insane, will I live the rest of my life behind bars? The man who mutilated women? I would be no better than old Joseph Merrick himself."

"Merrick is a good man with a bad illness. Just like you. He would want you to turn yourself in as well."

At that moment, Inspector Henry climbed up on the roof after Mycroft. He had his gun aimed at Andrews. "Don't worry, Guv. I've got him."

Holmes quickly turned around long enough to yell, "Wait! Don't shoot him, Inspector!" Then he heard a cry and looked back at Andrews, in time to see the doctor leaping from the rooftop. Holmes cried out in anger as Christopher fell to his death on the busy street below.

Holmes shook his head. He had thought that, possibly with proper care, Dr. Andrews might have had something of a life in an asylum, if he wasn't hanged. There was still a chance that he could have done some sort of good. It all seemed such a great waste of human potential.

Meanwhile, Inspector Henry looked over the ledge and nodded his head. "Good riddance."

A few days later, the rain poured down heavily over London. Mycroft made his way back to the Bishopsgate Police Station. As he walked back through the building, the various officers gave him nods of respect. He found Inspector Lucas Henry's office, where he was surrounded by some of his police chums. Once again, Henry seemed to be mocking someone as he told another one of his stories to the group. However, they all scattered once Holmes reached Henry, who looked him up and down with a scowl on his face. He then sat back and relaxed in his chair.

"Well, well. Welcome back. What can I do for you?"

"I just wanted to see how everything has turned out."

"Well, we had to let old elephant-ears go, so you'll be happy about that. We returned Anna Price to her family. Christopher Andrews though – Well, we gave him over to the coroner's office. They said they wanted him for research."

"Very good," said Mycroft. "I'm glad you did right by Mr. Merrick."

Henry lit a cigarette, took a piece of paper off his desk, crumpled it up, and dropped it back on the desktop. "Look – Don't get all sentimental on me, Holmes. If Merrick had done the deed, I would have still locked him up and thrown away the key. No one is above the law."

"Quite right," Mycroft said.

"There's still one thing that I still don't understand." Henry leaned forward. "Why? Why did he do it? I still can't wrap my head around it."

"*Dementia Praecox*," replied Mycroft. "It's a new term going around for mental illness, first used just a few years ago, in 1880 by German psychiatrist Heinrich Schüle. In each one of those victims, Andrews saw the face of his mother, who must have abused him when he was young."

"Right barmy, if you ask me," Henry said. "Whatever happened to old criminals cutting each other up in seedy parts of town? That's my kind of case."

"I take it that you aren't happy unless you're shooting at someone."

The inspector stood up and held out his hand. Mycroft looked down and smiled. He thought that possibly Henry was all right in his own small way way. He shook the inspector's hand.

"What will you do next, Holmes?" Henry asked.

"I'm going to take in a show," Mycroft said as he walked out. He walked by the front desk, which had a long line of criminals, thugs, and prostitutes waiting to be seen. He saw the constable who helped him earlier. He patted him on the back. "Keep up the good work, lad."

Later that evening at the penny gaff, a red velvet curtain pulled back to reveal the Elephant Man. People in the audience gasped as he sat in a chair with no shirt on. He looked out into the crowd and saw Mycroft Holmes. The Elephant Man stood and hobbled to the front of the stage. People were amazed by what they saw. In that small penny gaff in the Whitechapel Road, they were all in attendance to history in the making. Joesph, the Elephant Man recited a poem:

> *"'Tis true, my form is something odd,*
> *but blaming me, is blaming God.*
> *Could I create myself anew*
> *I would not fail in pleasing you.*
> *If I could reach from pole to pole*
> *or grasp the ocean with a span,*
> *I would be measured by the soul.*
> *The mind's the standard of the Man."*

Mycroft raised a glass of ale and cheered. The crowd looked around, and this time, instead of booing or hissing, they too started to cheer. By the end of his show, Joseph Merrick had received a round of applause. Tom Norman clapped and patted the young man on the shoulder.

Merrick turned to the crowd. "Thank you."

The Question of the
Rival Criminalist
by Will Murray

My good friend Sherlock Holmes and I were enjoying a comfortable afternoon in our Baker Street sitting room one day in the middle of November in the year 1884 – I, reading a magazine, while he was cutting items from the previous day's newspapers for his ever-growing collection of oddities. The hearth was blazing, which added to our enjoyment of creature comforts, for it was quite cold.

Our friendship was sometimes one of long silences peppered with intriguing conversations. This suited our natures, although we were as unalike as two men could possibly be – except, of course, that we were both staunch Britishers.

Silence is conducive to reading, but it's also productive to getting along well.

Holmes broke this particular silence with a question

"My dear Watson, are you familiar with the term 'red herring'?"

"Yes. It's a herring that has been baked."

"I'll not fault you for a correct answer, but I would like to point out that your answer is only nominally correct."

"Is that so?" I replied. "I seem to have encountered the term in another context, but am afraid that it eludes me at the moment. Kindly enlighten me, if you would."

"'Red herring' is a figure of speech that comes to us from the journalist William Cobbett, who penned a presumably fictitious account of dragging a red herring along the ground to throw certain hounds off the scent of a hare, the fishy odor confusing and foiling the otherwise unerring canine scent. Since that day, the public has embraced the term as a euphemism for a ruse or a false report intended to distract from an important truth. Writers of detective stories have taken to using it to label a false clue planted in order to deceive investigators. And the reader, I might add."

"Now that you mention it," I stated, "I have come across the term in that particular context. I'm not sure I fully understood it, but now I do. And for that, I thank you."

"Think nothing of it."

"Why do you bring up the subject?"

"For no other reason than curiosity. I know that you're very knowledgeable in your field but, outside of it, your fund of facts is rather in the way of a sack of odds-and-ends."

"As a medical man, I pay the greatest attention to things that are discovered in my field. It sometimes leaves me little time for outside exploration – unlike yourself, a voracious reader and explorer of virtually all of the byways of modern man."

"True. I cannot claim to be a specialist, but more of a generalist. But by being a generalist, I carry in my brain a great deal of knowledge about a great many things which is indispensable for me in my work."

After that, Holmes fell silent. He seemed to have no other reason to bring up the question than his own explanation offered. I imagined that something he read had prompted him to open up the subject. I returned to my magazine.

Not an hour later, however, the entrance door to the ground floor below us could be heard opening and closing, and Mrs. Hudson, our landlady, was greeting a caller who then came tramping up the stairs.

"That sounds like young Wiggins," remarked Holmes.

"How do you know that it's him who is calling?"

"From the peculiar way he stamps his feet. He was born with a deficiency of toes on his left foot, and it impedes his walking sufficiently that the sound of his arrival is unstable."

"Very good," said I. "But what if he hadn't had such a deficiency?"

"I'm certain I would have recognized the cadence of his stamping feet, the speed at which he climbed the familiar stairs, or some other telltale trifles."

Upon hearing a brisk knock, Holmes invited our guest in.

I wasn't surprised to see Wiggins, who was the official leader of the Baker Street Irregulars. He was a typical street Arab, rather unkempt, but a bright lad nonetheless.

"Hello, Mr. Holmes," he greeted. "Doctor. I trust that I'm not interrupting your afternoon."

"Not at all, Wiggins. What have you brought me?"

"There is a man, Mr. Holmes, who fancies himself as your opposite."

"Do you mean that he is a criminal?"

"No, not exactly. He doesn't seem to commit any crimes."

"If that is the case, then, how is he my opposite?"

"Because, sir, he considers himself to be a consulting *criminalist*."

"Have you not just contradicted yourself? You told me he isn't a criminal."

"He doesn't commit crimes. He *advises* those who commit crimes."

"Kindly elaborate."

"He fancies himself as a man who advises criminals on how to commit their crimes so that they aren't captured by Scotland Yard – or Mr. Sherlock Holmes. Particularly the latter."

Holmes paused to absorb this curious statement.

"I see. And what is this man's name?"

"He calls himself Reynard Renbourne."

"And where can this Mr. Renbourne be found?"

"That is the rub, Mr. Holmes. He cannot be found in any place in particular, for he moves about. He can sometimes be seen loitering in this pub, or that tavern, and other such places, but never in the same place twice in a row. He is very guarded and canny that way."

"And how do you come to know this man?"

"I'm hearing talk of him. Among The Element."

"The criminal element, I'm sure you mean."

"Exactly so, Mr. Holmes. The criminal element is all agog about this man. You see, they pay him for his advice. Sometimes he takes a percentage of illicit gains. The Element is quite pleased with him."

I spoke up at this point. "I've never heard of anything quite so outlandish."

"And I rarely have, either," allowed Holmes. "But I don't doubt this young lad's story."

"Thank you, Mr. Holmes," said Wiggins.

"What does this individual look like?" Holmes asked Wiggins.

"I haven't seen him, so I can't say, but if you're a criminal, and you know other criminals, he isn't difficult to find."

"Alas," averred Holmes, "I am not a criminal, so I cannot proceed along that sordid path."

"Perhaps I could," offered the young man eagerly.

"How do you mean?"

"I mean that I could pretend to intend to rob a store, and ask Mr. Renbourne how best to go about it so that I'm not caught."

"This will require some thought," mused Holmes. "I don't care to place you at any risk. Also, in order to bring this man's career to a conclusion, he would have to be found to be complicit in a crime."

"From the talk here and there, Mr. Renbourne is complicit in many crimes."

"Proof is another matter," Holmes murmured thoughtfully. "Tell me, Wiggins, are you quite certain of the term used to describe this Renbourne. You said he was a *criminalist*. Would you mean *criminologist*?

"No, the term was 'criminalist', although I don't know what it means.

"'It signifies one who studies crime and criminals. A criminalist is one who is an authority on the law as it applies to criminals."

"By his vocational choice," I noted, "this man is neither."

"He may have simply adopted a term he found to be exalting. He is, after all, of a low character."

"That he is," I agreed.

Holmes took a shilling coin from his mouse-colored dressing gown and gave it to Wiggins, saying, "Keep your eyes and ears sharpened. See if you can learn more of this man, and especially of his whereabouts. I would be most keen to meet a criminal who availed himself of Renbourne's services, but I doubt that one could be persuaded to pay us a visit."

"I can ask about, sir," said Wiggins, eagerly pocketing the coin.

"Better that you do not," cautioned Holmes. "We don't wish to tip our hand in advance of any effort we may undertake against this man. Now run along."

Wiggins left as noisily as he arrived.

Turning to Holmes, I asked, "Will you be informing Scotland Yard of this unsavory personality on the London scene?"

"Not as yet. I prefer to learn more and keep the matter close to my vest. Lestrade and his fellow detectives are apt to trample all over the fertile ground of a proper investigation if they become involved precipitously. I'll inform Scotland Yard when it seems correct to do so."

"Do you see this as a personal challenge?"

"I haven't yet formed such an opinion, but if this man has gone into business for the express purpose of foiling my own consultancy, I'll take this as a *professional* challenge. In any event, Reynard Renbourne, whatever he may be, is fair game."

And there the matter rested for three days.

Nothing of consequence transpired during that time, but then something remarkable happened.

I had been out for the afternoon and had been caught in the cold rain without my umbrella. Hailing a hansom cab, I made haste to return to Baker Street. Letting myself in, I tramped up to the first floor and entered.

"My word!" I exclaimed upon realizing that a stranger was seated in my customary chair.

There was no sign of Holmes in the sitting room.

"I beg your pardon," I inquired, "are you waiting for Mr. Sherlock Holmes?"

"Is it not obvious?" replied the stranger in a gruff voice.

I couldn't tell his height, for he was slumped in my chair. I wouldn't call him slovenly in appearance, but his coat had a slightly threadbare

193

appearance. His grey cloth cap sat on his lap, looking as if it had given up on life.

As to his features, they reminded me of Wiggins's own, for they could use a good soapy scrubbing. His hair was the only neat thing about him. It was combed quite carefully back from his brow.

The fellow eyed me in an accusatory way.

"I presume that Mrs. Hudson let you in," I asked, ignoring the man's uncouth manner.

"I'll not contradict your suggestion," said the visitor in a sharp tone. "Now tell me, where is Mr. Holmes? I have been waiting for more than ten minutes, and my appointment was for two o'clock sharp."

I gathered up my own dignity and remarked in a level voice, "I cannot answer your question, for I don't know where Holmes might be. As you can see, I have just returned from an afternoon of errands."

"Well then," said the man, rising in his seat, "I will not be trifled with. Nor will I wait more than five minutes longer."

"That is your business," I told the fellow. "I'll not stop you."

I felt rather uncomfortable under the scathing regard, and since he had taken my customary chair, I was a bit at a loss as to what to do with myself.

Finally, I took the chair that was normally reserved for visitors. It felt awkward to do so, but such are the vicissitudes of personal habits. One wouldn't think that being forced to sit in an unaccustomed chair would put me out so much, but it did. No doubt it was the man's gruff manner that also contributed to my discomfiture.

Settling into the visitor's chair, I remarked, "I'll not ask your business, since it's none of my business."

"Nor would I tell you," rejoined the other in a clipped tone. "It is confidential."

"I must advise you that, should Holmes return during your stay, he is in the habit of discussing his cases in front of me. Unless I'm asked to leave the room, I imagine I shall be privy to your consultation with him."

"In that case, since I value my privacy, holding it to be inviolate, I will take my leave."

"It's entirely your affair," I returned in an even tone, even as I felt relief that the uncouth fellow was quitting our rooms.

I was surprised when the man stood up. He was taller than I imagined. His shoulders were slouched and his head seemed to tilt forward as if his neck was too weak to hold it up straight.

As he strode for the door at the top of the stairs leading down to the street, I was polite enough to inquire, "Shall I inform Mr. Holmes that you paid him a call?"

"It makes no difference to me whether you do or not," shot back the rough voice.

"I imagine he knows your name, if you had an appointment with him."

"The name is Nettlesmith. Nigel Nettlesmith."

"Very good. I shall tell him you were here in a punctual manner."

"Before I go," said the man, pausing in mid-stride, "I have a question to put to you, good sir."

"And what is that?"

"If you will recall, I informed you that I arrived at two o'clock on the dot."

"You did," I acknowledged.

"Yet you didn't question this statement."

"True. I did not. Why would I?"

"Because, if you had been a more observant individual, you would have questioned me as to why my cap and coat were not wet, for if I had arrived at two o'clock, as I claimed, I would have come in out of a pouring rain."

It was a profound shock that I absorbed these words. It wasn't the words themselves that drew me back to my feet in consternation, but the alteration in the visitor's voice.

It was no longer gruff and suggestive of the East End. No, this was the supremely recognizable voice of Sherlock Holmes himself!

"Holmes?" I exclaimed.

"Unless you think someone could impersonate my voice with uncanny faithfulness," drawled my friend, "I must admit to the truth."

Smiling thinly, Holmes claimed his velvet-lined chair by the hearth and took up his black clay pipe.

"I am taken aback by your boldness, I confess," said I, "but what is the meaning of this disguise?"

"Quite simply," declared Holmes, waving me to take my own chair, "I had donned the personality of Nigel Nettlesmith with the thought of making the rounds of various disreputable public houses in the hope of locating this man Renbourne, when the rain commenced with such force that I realized that I should keep indoors. So I'm putting off my plan until the downpour abates, as it must eventually."

"I see. And you couldn't resist the impulse to needle me on my lack of observation, I take it."

"Your lack of observation," said Holmes dryly as he charged his pipe, "was so obvious I couldn't help but remark upon it. Really, Watson, this is disappointing, even for you. Surely, you should have noticed that I was too dry to have come in out of the rain in the last twenty minutes."

"Yes, yes," I said impatiently. "Now that you bring it to my attention, it is abundantly clear, but I was so put off by your difficult manner, and the surprise of finding a presumed client of Sherlock Holmes present in these rooms and yourself being absent, it rather threw me."

"Perfectly understandable. And I consider our exchange an admirable test of the utility of Mr. Nigel Nettlesmith as a personality for ferreting out Mr. Reynard Renbourne – for if you couldn't tell that it was me, how could my opponent?"

"You make an indisputable point," said I, lighting a cigarette as I once again enjoyed the familiar comfort of my chair.

As the room filled with the pungency of tobacco smoke, I studied Holmes. Even though it was the familiar voice coming from somewhat unfamiliar lips. I nevertheless marveled at the art with which my friend had transformed himself into an entirely different entity. I have remarked before that the stage lost a great performer when Sherlock Holmes chose to turn his formidable skills in other directions. Never was it more true.

"Have you formulated a definite line of attack?" I asked him.

"I have not. Since Renbourne doesn't hold court in any single specific place, I must beat the bushes, as it were. And hope to flush him out."

"Once you do that, what do you intend to do?"

"I'm not certain, but I'm thinking of hiring Renbourne to advise me on a rather delicate undertaking. A criminal undertaking, of course."

"And what planned crime do you propose to lay before him?"

Holmes took a long drag on his pipe before replying. The answer came out in a gush of tobacco smoke.

"I am contemplating a murder."

"Ah," I said. "That should snare him. Have you thought far enough ahead to have a victim in mind?"

"I have." Holmes regarded me with his level gaze. *"You,* Watson.

"I beg your pardon!" I exclaimed

"The man I intend to murder is none other than yourself," stated Holmes with characteristic coolness.

Here, I'm afraid that the cigarette fell from my lips, and I was busy slapping at the resultant sparks while I fumbled for the fallen smoke.

After finding it, I demanded, "Why in God's name would you plan to murder me?"

"In case I'll be in need of a *corpus delicti* in the furtherance of drawing my net around Renbourne."

This comment left me rather aghast, as one might imagine.

"I hope it will not come to that," I said fervently.

"Perhaps not," murmured Holmes quietly. "But should I be in need of bait, I trust that you'll provide a suitable cadaver."

"Only insofar as a ruse is concerned," I insisted. "I trust that I'll not necessarily be truly deceased in order to further your scheme."

"That goes without saying," Holmes commented as he smoked away.

I must once again confess that, even though it was the familiar voice of Sherlock Holmes talking about my planned murder, having these pronouncements come from a completely alien personality gave me an uncomfortable sensation.

I am not an imaginative man, but for a chill moment, the thought crossed my mind that I was having a conversation with someone I didn't truly know and who was mimicking Holmes's distinctive voice . . . .

Over the following days, I grew accustomed to Holmes donning the unpleasant attire and demeanor of the imaginary Nigel Nettlesmith as he prepared himself to go out on his quest for the remarkable Reynard Renbourne.

From time to time, Wiggins showed his dirty face and tendered his reports to Holmes. Wiggins was at first confused by the miserable apparition that was Nettlesmith, but he soon grew accustomed to finding the nonexistent fellow in Holmes's place.

One day, Wiggins came in with a report that Holmes found useful.

"Word is getting around town that Mr. Renbourne the Criminalist will be holding forth at The Black Lion Tavern in Chelsea.

"Is the fellow announcing his relocations in advance then?" asked Holmes.

"Apparently he is in need of a fresh clientele," said Wiggins. "He's letting it be known where he can be found, but only among The Element."

"Very good. I'll beard this bold fox in his new den. It will save me the trouble of haunting other public houses, as I've been doing without success."

Wiggins suggested, "Could this be a trap?"

Holmes considered this. "I don't think that Renbourne knows that I'm on his trail, so no, I cannot imagine it's a trap. But it's a point worth keeping in mind as I go about my search. Thank you for the suggestion, Wiggins."

"Think nothing of it," replied the youngster. "I'm only keeping your interests uppermost in my mind."

As the light began fading in the late afternoon, Holmes departed the warmth of our sitting room. He hurried, for he didn't want to be seen leaving Baker Street as Nigel Nettlesmith, even though that personality had no formal existence. Holmes was, if nothing else, quite thorough in his precautions. The criminal element wasn't foolish enough to watch

221b Baker Street in hopes of spying on his investigations, but among that lowest of lower classes, word travels, swiftly and all but silently.

As always, Holmes took the precaution of hiring the third cab in the rank, lest he fall into a patient snare like a fly into a spider's web. He returned rather late that night and threw himself into his chair with barely a nod in my direction.

After assembling his pipe and mixture of black shag, he took a preliminary draw, threw his head back, and released a long plume of smoke in the direction of the ceiling, watching it disperse in contemplative silence.

Finally, he deigned to acknowledge my presence.

"Watson, I have observed my man closely."

"Did you not approach him?"

"Bearing in mind Wiggins's admonishment about a trap, no. I took the precaution of only watching."

"What did you make of him?"

"From his manner of declaratory speech and general deportment, I took him to be a former barrister. There is no mistaking the type. There was a lean and almost-wasted look about him, especially around his eyes, that I also knew well, for it suggested that he had seen the inside of a prison in recent years. If I'm correct, this narrows down the possibilities, for I don't think that 'Reynard Renbourne' is his Christian name."

"I see," said I. "So he is a criminalist, after all."

"After a fashion," agreed Holmes. "One who went bad in the past and has now found a new way to cash in on his now-useless Law Certificate of Practice. I didn't recognize his face, but I'm not acquainted with every London barrister who fell afoul of the law. I don't think he's much over forty, so it shouldn't be difficult to draw up a list of possible suspects. Lestrade, no doubt, will be helpful in that direction."

"Will you approach him tomorrow?"

"That is my plan, but I may not follow it precisely."

"Why not?"

"It will depend on whether or not Renbourne is approached by another. For if he can be proven to have aided and abetted in the commission of actual crime, it will be better than advising a murderer who doesn't plan to carry out his murderous intentions."

"I see. Well, good luck. I would rather not be involved, if it's at all possible to avoid it."

"We will see, Watson," murmured Holmes. "We will see."

Holmes left in the person of Nigel Nettlesmith the following afternoon and was gone until the middle of the evening.

Upon his return, he swiftly removed his disreputable garments, drew on his colorless dressing gown, and took up his habitual chair by the hearth.

"I am eager to hear the results of these nocturnal endeavors," I invited.

"Renbourne failed to turn up." Holmes's voice carried an echo of the frown on his face.

"What do you make of that?"

"I don't yet know. It may not be significant. Perhaps he found The Black Lion to be not to his liking. Perhaps he understood that if word is out that this was his new habitat, he is being careful, but I understand that the man is wily. I'll try again tomorrow in the hope that my luck will be better."

"This is profoundly disappointing," I exclaimed.

Holmes shrugged slightly. "In the game of cat-and-mouse, there are many gyrations and reversals. This may be only a temporary turn of events."

But again the next night, Reynard Renbourne wasn't to be found at The Black Lion.

Holmes returned, rather downcast of countenance and carriage.

"Conceivably," I reassured him, "the fact that you have seen his face means that you are better prepared to recognize him again."

"True, but I'm disinclined to make the dreary rounds of London's pubs on the chance that we'll encounter one another again. It's a rather roundabout way to go at something that is best tackled directly."

"I'm sure that the Irregulars, given his description, can assist mightily in this search."

"Yes, no doubt. I think I'll pay a call upon Scotland Yard tomorrow. It's time to talk to Lestrade about this growing vexation."

"I would like to hire Mr. Renbourne to advise me in a proposed murder."

Inspector Lestrade nodded somberly. "Yes, that would definitely lead to a conviction. Particularly since you will be testifying against him.

"And I'm to be the victim," I interjected.

Lestrade was apparently unmoved by my admission. "I see. I place no official restrictions on your pursuit of this investigation. Scotland Yard stands ready to help if its assistance is necessary."

"Thank you, Inspector," said Holmes, rising to go. "I'll inform you of my progress as circumstances permit."

"Good luck with your hunt."

"I hope," said Holmes sincerely, "that luck has little or nothing to do with it. This is a job for brain work. Now I must apply myself to the task in earnest."

Regrettably, I must report that Holmes utterly failed to pick up the scent of the disbarred barrister purporting to be Reynard Renbourne. Despite setting Wiggins and the Irregulars to searching high and low, no further reports came back of his furtive activities. Nonetheless, Holmes persisted in his own search.

Returning to Baker Street one evening in the shabby attire of Nigel Nettlesmith, Holmes dropped into his customary chair by the hearth and announced, "I fear Wiggins was correct in warning me about a trap, for the trail has gone utterly cold."

"Perhaps it's just a matter of perseverance," I said in an effort to encourage my downcast friend.

Holmes shook his head gravely. "No. Hindsight leads me to conclude that I fell into a clever trap, one that is now painfully obvious to me. Kindly remind me to reward Wiggins with a gold *Jimmy O'Goblin*, would you?"

"I don't see where the trap lay," I asserted, "never mind how it was sprung."

"No," Holmes said heavily, "I imagine that you would not. Permit me to lay it out for you."

Holmes reached for his cherry-wood pipe, which indicated that his mood was foul. He spoke as he filled the bowl and set it alight.

"In plying his trade in various public house and taverns, our Mr. Renbourn had been in the habit of moving about. News of his availability to be hired traveled within severely constrained circles. The fact that he announced in advance that he would be holding court at The Black Lion was meant to reach my ears, were I listening. Which, of course, it did. Like a witless amateur, I donned my disguise and blundered properly into the trap. No doubt Renbourne noticed that I was scrutinizing him, despite my efforts to conceal that fact. This informed him that I – or at least some interested party – was hot on his trail. Unquestionably, he has decamped. To where, it is difficult to say, but I doubt that he is in London any longer."

"So what will you do?" I inquired, quietly relieved that I was released from my agreement to become the nominal victim of a murder plot.

Holmes had his pipe going strong, and was now puffing away most energetically. He didn't answer for quite some time, but when he did, he said the following:

"If I cannot find the man, perhaps I can identify the crime that resulted from Renbourne's most recent consultation.

"I see. Do you think that will lead you to him?

"It seems doubtful, but if I can't lay hands upon this self-proclaimed rival, I can at least damage his reputation among The Element by foiling one of his schemes.

"It sounds to me as if you must pay another call on Scotland Yard."

"Exactly. I commend your insight. I must seek a crime that has baffled Scotland Yard. Only by such means may I get back on the scent."

At that, Holmes fell to claiming the evening newspaper and perusing it most diligently. I understood that he was already seeking reports of a crime that had inexplicable qualities to it.

The next morning, Holmes and I were cordially received in Inspector Lestrade's office.

"I'm forced to admit defeat," Holmes stated candidly. "I believe that Mr. Josiah Graysmark, alias Reynard Renbourne, has left London, having cleverly deduced that I was on his trail."

"Could he know that to a certainty?" asked Lestrade.

Holmes nodded. "Even though I was in disguise, his boasting that he was my opposite, coupled with the fact that he had announced that he could be found at The Black Lion on a certain night, could only have been conceived as a lure to test my interest in him. Renbourne – I prefer to call him that – may not have penetrated my disguise, but he recognized in my attentiveness that I had a compelling interest in him. He may have concluded that I was merely an agent of Scotland Yard and not myself. But it is of no moment. He has flown the coop, as it were. I face a blank and obdurate wall, except for one possibility."

"What is that?" asked Lestrade.

"It may be possible to get on his scent once more if I can find his most recent client. Tell me, Inspector, has there been a recent crime of significance that has proved baffling to Scotland Yard? One that might be outside of the ordinary."

"Many cases are initially baffling," said Lestrade rather defensively, "but in time, we do solve a great many of them, as you know."

"This crime would either be quite recent," suggested Holmes. "Or perhaps it's yet pending."

"There was a murder a fortnight ago that has some peculiarities."

"Would that be the murder of the cooper, John Singleton?"

"Yes. He was discovered at home, bludgeoned in the most brutal way. We found boot tracks coming and going from his house. The peculiarity is that the impressions belong to a woman's boot. It's an unusual thing for a woman to bludgeon a man to death – never mind the issue of motive, which is so far opaque."

"I've read of this murder," acknowledged Holmes, "but not about the female boot prints."

"We are keeping that out of the newspapers for the moment."

Holmes nodded in understanding. "Do I have it correctly that the victim is unmarried, but has a household maid?"

"Yes. We've questioned the maid, who seems entirely distraught, for she was asleep in her room on the night of the attack. She hasn't been ruled out. A motive pointing in her direction seems difficult to conceive. Also, she is rather slender and so appears to lack the muscular power to commit so brutal a murder."

"Quite," murmured Holmes. "The victim had a partner in his business. What of him?"

"Mr. Avery Murcott. We've questioned him, of course. He's admitted to some business difficulties, but nothing that would rise to the occasion where cold-blooded murder would solve them."

"Have you photographic evidence of these boot tracks?"

"Of course. Let me find them."

In short order the inspector produced the evidence and Holmes studied the images closely, taking out his glass to see some of the finer details more clearly.

"Unquestionably," he said, "these tracks were created by boots made for a woman – but a woman didn't wear them on the night of the murder."

Lestrade looked skeptical. "What's this?"

"Do I need to repeat myself?" countered Holmes. "A woman didn't wear these boots. It's obvious to me, even if it isn't to Scotland Yard."

"How can you assert that so baldly?" demanded the inspector.

"Kindly examine the impressions under my glass. You'll see at certain points where the wearer of the boots stepped awkwardly and seemed to have bent his ankles painfully in one direction or another, causing him to all but stumble. This wouldn't be the case with a woman stepping in her own boots, but a man wearing a borrowed pair of women's boots to conceal his cowardly act would certainly have difficulty walking, and even more difficulty running away from the scene. I note from these photographs that the departing boot tracks show the greatest clumsiness. In short, these boot tracks are a clever red herring."

Lestrade studied the photographs, then looked up and admitted, "I don't quite see what you are able to perceive, but I can see how you have reached that conclusion."

"I must also call your attention to another feature you have failed to notice," added Holmes. "Observe this straggling line of round holes in the earth. They suggest the assailant, while approaching the Singleton residence, walked with the aid of a cane. That a woman requiring a cane would be capable of bludgeoning a man to death seems improbable to me. Tell me if I am in error, Lestrade, but I'm inclined toward the belief that the murder weapon hasn't yet been discovered?"

"It has not," admitted the inspector. "How did you deduce that?"

"From the fleeing footprints. Or shall I say, from the absence of accompanying walking stick marks, which clearly contributed to the murderer's difficulty in departing the Singleton home. Let me suggest that the house and immediate grounds be searched for the missing cane, for I firmly believe it to be the missing murder weapon."

"The truth has been in our hands all along, but we didn't recognize it," Lestrade declared. It seemed to me that the inspector didn't know whether to praise Sherlock Holmes, or berate himself and his detectives.

Holmes continued, "This seems to be a simple case, Lestrade. You stated that you interviewed the business partner. Personally?"

"I did."

"Did he show any difficulty walking?"

"Not that I can recall, but we conducted the interview in his office, and he was seated for most of the occasion."

"Let me suggest that you pay this man another call. I'll be happy to accompany you. I would like to talk to him about Reynard Renbourne, once he provides his confession."

Lestrade now looked a trifle taken aback. "You seem rather confident in your deduction," he remarked.

"It is a sound one, and I wouldn't be surprised if the boots were stolen from the murdered man's house and belonged to his maid. Did you ask her if she is missing any footwear?"

"No, I did not. My interest was in her guilt or innocence, but this is a new wrinkle. And worthy of pursuing."

We straightaway hired a Clarence and were soon at the murdered man's modest home in Chelsea.

The maid appeared to be surprised to see us, but let us in nonetheless. She was a painfully slight thing. The thought of her murdering a man struck me as improbable in the extreme.

"Miss Fenwick," began the inspector, "I have brought Mr. Sherlock Holmes and his associate, Dr. Watson, with me. Mr. Holmes has a theory as to the murder that would appear to exonerate you, but it turns on one possibility."

"And what is that, sir?"

"As you know, the murderer wore women's boots, and we have tentatively concluded that the murderer was a woman. Mr. Holmes has suggested it was a man wearing a woman's pair of boots. Would you be able to account for all of your boots?"

The maid looked hesitant. I could tell that she was considering whether or not this was a trap, but if it was, her better nature caused her to reply, "I'm not aware of any missing boots, but I'll look."

We were left alone in the parlor for some minutes. Soon, the maid came back, she was flying.

"My winter boots! I cannot find them!"

"Winter boots are often worn over heavy wool stockings," Holmes said, "and therefore might fit a man if he were barefoot. I think we have the first clue pointing in the direction of the true murderer.

Inspector Lestrade spoke up. "I'm afraid that we must search the house for the murder weapon, which we now believe to be a cane or walking stick with a head of brass or silver."

"That will not be necessary, Inspector," interjected Holmes, rising and striding toward the hearth. He selected a stout poker and began rooting about among the pleasantly smoldering logs therein. In time, he unearthed a misshapen lump of charred metal. Carefully knocking this onto the stone flags before the fire, he pointed downward.

"You cannot help but recognize the much-dented brass knob of a gentleman's cane," he asserted.

Bending down, Inspector Lestrade studied the smoking object.

Holmes added, "No doubt the killer, after completing his grisly deed, broke the blood-soaked stick in twain and threw the halves into the rear of the fireplace, where they landed behind the burning logs, knowing that they would shortly be consumed – all but this telltale globe of dented brass, which is evidence of the ferocity of the murder."

"There can be no question about it," said Lestrade, standing up with the evidence cradled in a handkerchief, for it was still too hot to touch. "Very good work, Mr. Holmes."

Holmes nodded. "Whether the murderer disposed of the weapon in this manner for convenient destruction, or to cast suspicion upon the maid if the remnants were ever discovered, only he can say, but I suspect the former motive."

We thanked the relieved maid and took our departure.

The carriage next took us to the office of Singleton and Murcott, Coopers, where a sign painter was altering the signage so that it only showed the name of the single surviving proprietor: *Avery Murcott*.

Entering, we saw a mild shock cross Murcott's ruddy features.

"Inspector Lestrade!" he exclaimed. "What brings you here?"

"It isn't what brings me here, but what I bring," rejoined Lestrade in an officious tone. "May I introduce to you Mr. Sherlock Holmes, of whom no doubt you have heard, and his associate, Dr. Watson. Mr. Holmes has formulated a new theory as to the murder of your partner."

"I see," said the man, not rising from behind his desk. "Well, I am keen to hear it."

Holmes spoke up. "A new clue has surfaced. It's my understanding that you are at least, in theory, a suspect. I believe I can disprove that possibility, if you will indulge me."

A slight look of relief caused Murcott's features to quiver.

"Why, I would be happy to accommodate you, Mr. Holmes. I've read so much about you in the newspapers."

"Very good," returned Holmes. "If you'll step outside and into the daylight, I'll explain my theory to you."

"Is daylight necessary?" asked the man.

"Daylight," replied Holmes, "exposes everything. Lies. Deceit. Subterfuge. From it, all shadows flee. And so is revealed the truth for all to see."

"Very well then," said the man, rising from his desk.

Holmes courteously opened the door to the street and we all watched as Avery Murcott made his way across the office floor. He walked rather gingerly. As a physician, I could tell that his left ankle was weak. He might have been suffering from a slight sprain.

No doubt Inspector Lestrade noticed this as well, but he gave no indication of suspicion.

Out into the light of day, Holmes said, "Unless I'm very much mistaken, the perpetrator suffered certain indignities during his escape. These indignities can be found upon his person. One only has to peer into the correct crevice, as it were."

Murcott blinked rather stupidly. "I'm afraid I don't follow you, Mr. Holmes."

"If you will be so good as to remove either of your shoes and the underlying stocking, we can establish your innocence for once and for all."

The look that came over Murcott's features was more than equivalent of concern. The man all but quaked in surprise.

He regarded Holmes with his dark eyes and compressed his lips, as if fearing to speak.

"You will have to explain yourself, my good sir," he muttered, "because in this moment, I am very confused."

"We believe that the murderer wasn't a woman, but a man wearing a woman's winter boots."

Murcott forced a smile. It wasn't genuine. "Oh, I see," he said vaguely. "Quite." The pallor that came over his ruddy features effected a remarkable transformation. Hesitancy took hold of him briefly.

Then, rather foolishly, he turned on his heel and attempted to flee.

It did no good, of course. Both Holmes and Inspector Lestrade easily overhauled him, and each taking him by one shoulder of his coat, preventing him from escaping.

"I'm arresting you in the name of The Crown," scolded Lestrade. "The charge is capital murder. I don't think there is any necessity to name the victim, for he is well known to you."

"But you have no proof!" shrieked Murcott. "Unhand me at once!"

"Once we get your shoes and stockings off," said Holmes confidently, "I'm quite certain we will have all the proof we require. In your haste to cover your tracks, you availed yourself of footgear of convenience, and not ones that properly fit your feet. Since it's often that women's feet are more narrow than that of adult men, it's to be expected that you dispensed with wearing stockings in order for your feet to fit the feline items. The stolen boots chafed your bare feet as you crept about in them. Running from the murder proved painfully difficult. The proof will, I expect, still be found on your naked feet."

Avery Murcott didn't faint. The newspapers reported that, but it was mere sensationalism. In truth, his knees grew weak and fearfully wobbly, and he had to be held up by Holmes and Lestrade as he was escorted to the waiting carriage.

At Scotland Yard, with the dented and blackened brass cane-head set before him, Murcott was formally charged, and his shoes and stockings removed. The blisters were quite alarming. As a physician, I examined his left ankle, which was swollen.

"Sprained. But not badly."

"Murder is something we cannot countenance," said Lestrade grimly. "But we may show mercy if you give us your full confession."

"And tell us everything you know about the man who calls himself Reynard Renbourne," added Holmes

This statement made Murcott's scowling features quirk up

"How the devil did you know about him?"

"You might say," stated Holmes, "that Reynard Renbourne led me to you, albeit in a roundabout way.

The suspect didn't know what to say about that. His head sagged forward on his shoulders and despair overtook him.

Avery Murcott unburdened himself in hesitant stages. He spoke of his desire to rid himself of his partner, for the joint business was struggling and couldn't support two owners. Buying Singleton's half was financially out of the question. Nor would the other man sell. And so they quarreled, until murder seemed the only fiscally sound solution. But first, there was the necessity of shifting blame away from himself. He had learned of Reynard Renbourne and had found him in a certain public house. The man

206

advised him that there was no legal way to commit murder, but many ways to conceal his guilt. One of them was to suggest that he wear women's boots, but not boots that belonged to any member of his family. Since Murcott had often visited the home of the deceased, he knew where the maid's boots were stored and managed to steal them out during a past visit.

Returning later, wearing the boots and helping himself along with a brass-headed cane he'd purchased for the express purpose of slaying John Singleton, he committed the murder and found himself stumbling and bumbling in the ill-fitting boots during his escape, but he couldn't remove the boots until he was safely at some distance from the murder scene, and so suffered fierce blisters and a sprained ankle.

We listened attentively to all this, and in truth learned very little about Josiah Graysmark, alias Reynard Renbourne, that we didn't already know.

At the end of it, Holmes said, "Well, Lestrade, at least we have cast a shadow over Renbourne's expert advice to the criminal element."

"At the very least," agreed the inspector. "Will you pursue the man?"

Holmes demurred. "Without a definite trail, I'm afraid for now that it would be pointless. But you can rest assured that I'll keep my eyes and ears open for another crime that has baffling aspects. I have no doubt that Reynard Renbourne has taken up residence in another city or town and is poised to resume his rather unsavory consultancy. Once I again have his scent, I will be hot on his trail. You may count on that."

And there the matter rested for a considerable period of time. But that wasn't the end of Sherlock Holmes versus Reynard Renbourne. Not at all. Nevertheless, that is a story for another occasion. One I intend to tell sooner rather than later . . . .

The Adventure of the
Deadly Bird
by Tracy J. Revels

Not every visitor to Baker Street was a welcome one. When my friend's fame was at its highest peak, we were occasionally annoyed by individuals whose goal was not to seek Sherlock Holmes's aid in clearing up their problems, but simply to make the acquaintance of the celebrated detective. This led to the rapid ejection of many impertinent fellows who carried the print of my boot on their posteriors for some days afterwards. Holmes and I developed a code. If he drolly muttered the words "I have never heard a more fascinating tale," I knew it was my duty to escort the wearisome guest out.

More than once, Holmes simply rose and strolled to his deal-top table, where he ignited an explosive chemical reaction. This usually sent a false client rapidly down the famous seventeen steps and out into the street. One afternoon, the trick was almost necessary to free ourselves from two young men, a Mr. Grant and a Mr. Lee, recent university graduates, who arrived at our chambers claiming they wished Holmes to investigate a murder.

"Whose murder?" Holmes asked respectfully. Mr. Lee, the larger of the two, a burly youth clad in a sartorial display of wealth without taste, jumped from the divan, frantically waving his arms.

"Mine, Mr. Holmes! I know I shall be done away with. Jimmy here intends to kill me because I'm in love with his sister. Oh sir, help me, please!"

I showed the rascals the door, and none too gently. But much to our surprise, an hour later, one of them returned, the very picture of an honest penitent, his hat held in his hands.

"I've come to humbly beg your forgiveness, sir. I tried to talk Bernard – I mean, the Viscount – out of coming here, but he insisted on the jape, including the use of false names. He is the Earl of Clayton's heir and, I am ashamed to admit it, a suitor for my sister's hand."

Holmes considered our guest with hooded eyes. "And what is your elevated title?"

"None, sir – I am a person of utter insignificance. I'm merely James Morton. My friends call me Jimmy."

"I would hardly call the son of one of England's richest men a person of 'insignificance'," Holmes replied. Indeed, the name of Morton was a celebrated one, for William Morton, the boy's grandsire, had risen from the grim pits of the coal mines to become a merchant prince, with business interests across the Empire, and his son, Alexander Morton, was equally famous for parlaying the family's nautical trade into the establishment of great shops and galleries. James Morton – perhaps twenty-five years of age, slender, modest, and gentle-faced – blushed to the roots of his blond hair.

"It is true that my family has prospered, but to hear the Viscount tell it, we are still little better than village shopkeepers."

Holmes was clearly intrigued. "Why are you friends with such a callous example of the British nobility?"

"Because my father wishes it. Forgive me, sir, I do not mean to impose upon your time, but I have read that you offer advice to those in strange predicaments. Perhaps you can help me as well. You see, sir, I would gladly murder my erstwhile 'friend', even if I knew I would hang for it."

"This is surely an unparalleled occurrence in these rooms," Holmes replied. "Do write this down Watson: A murderer is confessing to his evil deed prematurely."

His words were light, and his smile clearly reassured the youth, who settled upon the divan and began to slowly turn his hat around in his hands. Holmes rose and poured him a libation.

"Tell me, Mr. Morton, what has your titled companion done that makes him deserve death?"

"I could list a thousand things, Mr. Holmes. I have known Bernard – He wouldn't approve of that familiarity, but he isn't here! – since we were children. The old Earl has a hunting lodge near our own, and Bernard and I attended Eton and Oxford together. Bernard has always been selfish, and prone to cruelties. More than once I have stopped him from tying cans to cats' tails or maiming helpless puppies. Once he stole coins from a blind beggar, and I had to empty my own pockets to make amends to the poor fellow. Were it not for my interventions, Bernard would have set fire to the rooms of our university tutor or tossed his precious books into the River Cherwell. It seems I have spent my whole life protecting innocents from Bernard's meanness.

"But you see, Mr. Holmes, Father's greatest ambition in life is to have one of his offspring marry into the nobility. Of course, it would do me little good to wed a noble lady, even if one would have me, for I wouldn't share her title. Instead, my sire's hopes lie in becoming the father-in-law to a titled man. He has urged me, since childhood, to befriend boys of rank, to support his goal of social elevation for his daughters.

"This has been painful for me. I am not a gregarious individual by nature. Nor do I appreciate Bernard's constant antics and his slurs upon my heritage. I would be happier working at the register of one of Father's stores than feigning interest in Bernard or any other young nobles of my acquaintance. But there are my sisters to think of."

"And they have their sights set on wearing tiaras?" I asked.

Young Morton sighed. "I have five sisters. Agnes is my elder by six years. She had a glorious debut in society, but shortly afterward was struck down by rheumatic fever, and nearly died. The disease stole her beauty and left her half-crippled. It is likely she will remain a spinster. Elizabeth is three years older than I, and from childhood she demonstrated an intense religious disposition. Though our family is of Anglican stock, Elizabeth became fascinated with Catholicism. Father sent her to Rome, supposedly for instruction in art, but she returned a committed Papist. She will undoubtedly take the veil when Father dies. Jael is my twin, and Rebecca is three years younger than us. Our mother passed away ten years ago, just after the birth of our youngest sister, Martha. Thus, the family's focus is on Rebecca, the one daughter who is of age, attractive, and eager to, as you say, wear a tiara."

Holmes frowned. "What of your twin?"

"It pains me to tell you her story. Jael is the most sweet-natured girl you can imagine. Naturally, we share a special bond. Just after her debut, she met Lord Zaltair, a man twenty years her senior. Despite the gap in their ages, there was never a better-matched pair, and he was the entire world to her. Our family celebrated their engagement with a trip to Brighton. We were playing about in the surf when Lord Zaltair was knocked down by a wave and swept out by a current. The fellows in the water tried to save him – even Jael rushed forward, would have thrown herself after him had not Elizabeth and Rebecca held her back. But when he was at last plucked from the ocean, my sister's betrothed was dead. Jael watched it happen helplessly, and since that moment, she hasn't spoken. Her mind was affected, in a way no physician or alienist can treat. My dear sweet twin sits beside the fireplace in the ladies' parlor, clad completely in black, endlessly sewing, showing little interest in our affairs. The entire family has given up hope of her recovery."

Holmes nodded his understanding. "But Miss Rebecca wishes to be a Lady – or perhaps a Countess?"

"You may have heard that the old Earl isn't long for this world. He is currently in Baden, taking the waters. Bernard has confided to me that he doesn't expect his father to return. Is it not a mark of Bernard's despicable nature that he cuts capers in London instead of attending his ailing father?"

"Is there an understanding between the Viscount and your sister?"

"Nothing formal. Bernard has toyed with her affections, while I have urged her to be more attentive to other suitors. Rebecca has caught the eye of Sir Henry Lionel and Lord Fewell, both good and handsome men. I would gladly embrace either as a brother-in-law. But Rebecca is as hard-headed as she is pretty, and she aims for a grander title. I have told her everything about Bernard, painted him in his true, hideous colours. She claims her love will change him, and threatens to tattle to Father if I, in any way, interfere in their romance." The young man shook his head. "There is nothing for it, sir, except Bernard's untimely death!"

Holmes spoke low and firmly. "You have come to me for counsel – Let me advise against murder."

James Morton managed a rueful smile as he rose and offered a hand. "I was quite afraid of that. I shall do my best not to kill him, but I will make no promises."

Time passed and we thought little more of our apologetic guest. We saw the notice of the Earl of Clayton's death, and a few weeks later the newspapers reported that Mr. Alexander Morton was travelling to New York to open a branch of his famous department store in that city. Two days afterward, a note was brought up to our breakfast table. Holmes read it and dropped his napkin.

"The kippers must wait, Watson! The new Earl of Clayton has been murdered in the house of his best friend – the very youth who expressed his desire to slay him."

This startling information saw us reaching for coats and hats. Holmes hailed a cab which delivered us to one of the most fashionable addresses in Mayfair. A constable stood guard at the door, and a pale-faced butler led us up to a small parlor on the first floor, where we found a sad, pathetic scene.

The young earl was stretched out beside the fireplace in the windowless chamber, clad in only his nightdress, a deadly wound obvious on his right temple. His left arm was extended, and just beyond the fingertips lay a brass candle holder and a detached, rather thick white candle. The body was sprawled across a thick gold-and-blue rug. I looked about, gaining the impression this chamber was the special retreat of the home's ladies, for there was a chair and sewing table in the right corner beside the fireplace, and a harp near the door. Across from the instrument was a *prie-dieu* and, in the left corner by the fireplace, a tall stand with a brass birdcage, in which a sizeable gray parrot dozed. A love seat, a low marble-topped table, and a pair of dainty chairs completed the décor. Holmes immediately turned his attention to the body, while I addressed the detective who stood beside it.

211

"A tragic morning, Inspector."

"Indeed, it is," Inspector Lestrade of Scotland Yard grumbled. "It's bad enough when a pair of common blokes beat each other senseless in Whitechapel, but when a young Earl is done to death in the bosom of his prospective wife's family, there's bound to be a scandal."

"Ah, so the late gentleman finally proposed to Miss Rebecca," Holmes said.

Lestrade had been flipping through his scribblings. At this comment, he started and nearly dropped his notebook on the dead man's head.

"Here now! I believe you are the Devil himself, Mr. Holmes. What else have your imps told you, to get you ahead of the game?"

"Very little, Lestrade. We are merely in possession of some interesting particulars about the Morton siblings, having met the young gentleman previously. Please tell me what you have learned."

Lestrade looked unconvinced, and I was again reminded of how lucky my friend was to have been born long after the days of witch-hunts and inquisitions.

"The facts are these: The Earl arrived yesterday, alone, with not so such much as a valet attending him, to visit with the Mortons. Old Mr. Morton is in America, and the Earl took advantage of the patriarch's absence to propose to Miss Rebecca over the family dinner table. Toasts were drunk and later the family engaged in various amusements until the pious sister – I have her down as Elizabeth – demanded the ladies retire to bed. The two gents sat up in the study until nearly midnight."

"When did their fight occur?" Holmes asked.

"Fight?"

Holmes had been kneeling beside the body, subjecting it to his usual close inspection, checking the hands, the feet, and the strangely shaped wound upon the temple. He now pointed to the gentleman's damaged nose and left cheek.

"He got that when he fell," Lestrade said.

"I have made a study of bruising, both before and after death. This injury occurred *before* the Earl's brain was fatally pieced. It has all the marks of a fist applied with pressure, not a tumble to a very soft carpet."

Lestrade jotted the fact in his notebook. "Certainly, that adds more mystery. James Morton didn't mention a brawl. He claims they both went to bed as the clock struck twelve."

"And when was the body found?"

"At five-thirty, when the maid came in. She discovered the corpse when she turned on the gaslights."

"She disturbed nothing?"

"She says her only other action in the room, upon finding the body, was to scream, and then to shut the birdcage, which was open."

"Intriguing." Holmes looked around. "Have you gathered up the feathers?"

"I saw none."

"Had there been a fire the evening before?"

Lestrade scowled. "The hearth was empty of any coals or ash, and the night was oppressively warm, so I would say it was unlikely."

"Where is James Morton?"

"In his room. I ordered all the young people to their chambers and have stationed a constable to watch the servants in the kitchen."

"There was no one else in the house last night?"

"Not to anyone's knowledge. And before you ask, no disturbances were heard."

"Very well. Would you have the kindness to fetch young Mr. Morton? I have a few questions for him."

"As do I," Lestrade muttered, and exited the room. Holmes snagged my sleeve and drew me toward the body.

"What do you make of this wound, Watson?"

Delicately, I separated the stray hairs and considered the mark. "He wasn't shot or bludgeoned, obviously. The temporal lobe was fatally pierced. This is a stabbing . . . though I am at a loss as to what type of blade was used."

"It appears wedge-like in shape," Holmes said, examining it closely with his lens. "It isn't the clean and efficient entry of a dagger or an icepick. And I see nothing in the room that matches it. We will need to envision what isn't here."

Before I could ask him to explain, we heard footsteps outside the door. Holmes rose, addressing the young man we had, only weeks before, hosted in Baker Street.

"Greetings, Mr. Morton. I am saddened to become re-acquainted under these circumstances."

"As am I," the youth said. He had dressed haphazardly, his shirt untucked and his hair uncombed. "My God, for it to come to this."

Holmes instructed him to sit on the loveseat, facing away from the corpse. My friend wasted no time in coming to the crux of the matter.

"You must be honest and forthcoming with us. Why did you quarrel with the Earl last night – furiously enough to strike him and break his nose?"

Morton gasped, and then looked down, guiltily, at his right hand. His knuckles were raw and bruised.

"Mr. Holmes, Inspector, Doctor – I swear I will tell you everything, though it may take me to the gallows. Yes, I struck the Earl – Bernard. I'll be damned if I'll give him any title – just before midnight, and I broke his nose. But if you had heard the vile things he said, about my own dear sister . . . You wouldn't blame me."

I saw Lestrade scowl. Holmes perched on the opposite chair and nodded for Morton to continue.

"None of us were expecting Bernard. We all assumed he was still mourning for his father, and in Hampshire, settling the estate. When he arrived, I had the servants pull together as grand a supper as possible under such short notice, and even told the housekeeper fix up a room for him, when he said he wished to stay with us. Far from being saddened by his recent bereavement, he was filled with brags and boasts of all the things he would do, now that he was Earl, and he got rather in his cups before dessert was brought out. You met him, Mr. Holmes. You saw his flair for the theatrical. He dropped to one knee and proposed to Rebecca, who was all atwitter. They would need Father's blessing, of course, but there was no question of that! We drank a toast to them, finished our meal, and retired to the billiards room. An awkward hour followed."

"In what way?" Holmes asked.

Morton stared down at his wounded hand. "In that the proposal made only Rebecca happy. Agnes is resentful that her younger sister will wed first, and Elizabeth doesn't approve of Rebecca being married to someone not of the Roman faith. You know my feelings on the matter, and Jael's thoughts remains a mystery. Perhaps little Martha would have lightened the evening, but she has gone away to America with Father. I tried to be a good host, to interest them in a game of cards or even charades, but my elder sisters were petulant, and Jael returned to this parlor to sew, as she does every evening. Bernard and Rebecca sat uncomfortably close. More than once I had to speak sharply, to prevent Bernard from becoming too familiar with Rebecca in our presence. At last, Elizabeth compelled the girls to go to bed and I took Bernard into the study for a nightcap. He spoke before I could pour us a drink.

"'Here now, Jimmy – Let us be clear. Man to man. I know you have never approved of my love for Becky, but the thing is done. I suggest you improve your attitude toward me.'

"It was all I could do to be civil. I told him I wished the pair only happiness, but I also hoped Bernard would amend some of his bad habits before he and Rebecca wed. He laughed at me.

"'It is not for a mere commoner like you to tell me how to behave! I am an Earl, and you are nothing but a shopkeeper's son. You should be grateful that I find Becky so delicious. As for my bad habits, let me assure

214

you I shall do *what* I please, *when* I please. My bride will learn her place, and quickly.'

"At that, sir, he began to tell me exactly how he planned to treat Rebecca once they were married. He has always been coarse in his speech, disrespectful to ladies, but this . . . It was vile and filthy, and I shall not repeat it, even if I am executed for my silence. I will say only that I reached a point where all honor seemed at stake, and it was at that moment I struck him. He fell with a thud, blood shooting from his nose, but he got up laughing and waving his hands. That was his way – to make a mockery of things when he was bested and chastened.

"I helped Bernard up and half-carried him to the bathroom to tidy himself. You will find bloody towels there, and his clothes as well, which I intended to have laundered this morning. He was giddy with laughter, telling me he meant no harm, saying we should always be the best of friends, as well as brothers. I thought, foolishly, that I had made a point he would not forget. I saw him tumble into bed. Then I retired to my own room for the rest of the evening."

"And you heard nothing afterward?" Lestrade asked.

"Nothing until this morning, when the maid began screaming."

Holmes had risen and was now staring at the birdcage. "To whom does the parrot belong?"

Lestrade scowled. "For pity's sake, Mr. Holmes, what does it matter?"

"The maid said the cage was open this morning," Holmes replied. "Is it your pet, Mr. Morton?"

"No sir. That is Georgie, and he belongs to Father. This isn't his regular room, but Sarah, the chambermaid, moved him yesterday while she was cleaning Father's room with some chemicals which she feared might disturb the bird. Georgie was the property of sailors for some years, and to be frank, he learned a many vulgar expressions, which makes him a perpetual embarrassment."

"Yet he must have witnessed the murder," Holmes said. "Didn't you, Georgie?"

The creature came alive, ruffling his feathers and bouncing on his perch. He clearly recognized his name.

"Naughty boy! Naughty boy!" he squawked.

Lestrade looked between the parrot and young Morton. He rubbed his chin thoughtfully and called for his constable.

"Macintosh, take this young man back to his room, and then find out where the servants keep the bird's food."

Morton shot us a sad look, but Holmes advised him to go along quietly.

215

"You have no objections to me interviewing the servants and the young ladies?" my friend asked the inspector.

Lestrade pressed a hand to his brow. "Be my guest, Mr. Holmes. Just be warned – the girls consist of a hypochondriac, a fanatic, a maniac, and a hysteric. I had a painful hour with them before you arrived."

Holmes nodded, but as we reached the door he turned and drew my attention to the mantel above the fireplace. "Did you note it, Watson?" he whispered.

I was uncertain what I was supposed to observe and said as much when we exited into the hallway.

"The candle beside the Earl doesn't belong in this chamber. There are two slender red candles in delicate crystal holders on the mantel. They don't match the brass holder and the much thicker white candle upon the rug. There are drippings on the mantel, but only from the larger candle. The others are new, their wicks never lit. There is gas lighting in the room, which was not, to our knowledge, utilized, though certainly a murderer could simply have extinguished it upon his departure."

"I presume the candle was snuffed out when the Earl fell."

"No. That is another singular feature. The flame left a visible burn upon the rug. It was quickly stamped out, for otherwise it might have turned into a conflagration."

"Only the murderer could have done so!" I saw hope dawning. "And he would likely have wax upon his shoe."

"Perhaps," Holmes agreed. "But presently I am more interested in why the young Earl brought a candle – most likely from his bedroom – to the parlor and left it burning. If we work on the theory that he never ignited the gaslights, then a world of possibilities is suggested. Come, Watson, we have more to learn."

The staff of the Morton home had nothing of substance to add. There was a butler and a housekeeper, as well as four young maids, all of whom slept in chambers on the mansion's third floor. They had completed their duties by eleven and retired to their beds, with only the butler, Woolsey, staying awake for another hour. He had heard the altercation in the study and seen his young master supporting his friend up the stairs, but had chosen non-intervention as the wisest course when his master did not call for aid.

"I went to my room immediately afterward, sir."

"Did you not think it strange that the lads were quarreling after such a happy occasion?" I asked.

Woolsey barely suppressed a sigh. "Forgive me if I am forward, sirs, but no one in this household, except for Miss Rebecca and the elder Mr.

Morton, was fond of the Earl. He had been sharp with all of us and played many a cruel prank. I hoped Master James had made him aware that his meanness would *not* be tolerated. It seemed best to allow the young men to sort it between them." The butler looked over his staff in a benevolent fashion. "Poor little Sarah hasn't stopped shaking since she discovered the body."

Holmes thanked him and together we climbed the stairs to visit the sisters. The staff had told us that Miss Agnes and Miss Elizabeth shared a room, while Miss Rebecca and Miss Jael had individual chambers.

"We shall take them in chronological order, I think," Holmes said, gently rapping on the elder siblings' door. It was opened by a woman dressed in a simple blue gown with white lace pinned about her hair. A massive silver crucifix hung from her throat. Holmes offered a short bow.

"Forgive us for disturbing your devotions, Miss Elizabeth," he said, and I noticed that her skirt was wrinkled, as if she had just risen from her knees. Holmes offered a quick introduction which the girl received with downcast eyes. Her sister emerged from behind a poster bed, using a crutch to aid her painful, slow movements. She has the sallow skin and labored breathing of the perpetual invalid. She took her younger sister's arm protectively.

"When will they let us go? You would think we were common criminals, confined to our rooms like this, not even served breakfast."

"I will see that refreshment is brought up shortly," Holmes said. "I have only a few questions to put to you."

"Oh, please hurry and ask them," Miss Agnes begged.

"Very well. Did you wish your future brother-in-law dead?"

Miss Elizabeth gasped and clutched her crucifix. Her sister leaned heavily against the crutch.

"The Earl has never been my favorite person," Miss Agnes snapped. "Just last night, he hopped around the room, mocking my tortured limbs, claiming I fake my illness to win sympathy because I am an ugly old maid."

"Aggie!" Miss Elizabeth whispered, her fingers crabbing tight on her sister's arm.

"No, I shall tell the truth! I'm not sad the Earl is dead, though I pray Jimmy didn't kill him. Our brother has said it more than once, that he might do the Earl in to keep Rebecca safe. Whoever murdered the Earl has spared Rebecca a lifetime of suffering. It was the best thing that could happen for her, though she's too stupid to see it!"

"Two titled men died who would have wed Morton girls," Miss Elizabeth whispered. "This family is cursed! Our sins are coming home, we must seek forgiveness. Oh, why can you not see the way to the true church, which alone can redeem our lost souls?"

Miss Agnes glared at her. I had the impression this was a long and unpleasant argument between the young women. Holmes thanked them and promised to have breakfast delivered in the hour.

"Is she merely pretending?" Holmes asked, as we made our way down the hall.

"I would not wish to say for certain, without an examination," I answered, "but her walk appears that of a true sufferer, and disease has greatly aged her features."

"I shall take that as confirmation the lady is not dissembling," Holmes said. He knocked on the second door, but there was no answer. Holmes paused in thought for a moment before moving on to the final room, Miss Rebecca's chambers.

Lestrade had clearly been concerned about the young woman's distress over the loss of her fiancée, for the door was opened by her maid, whom Lestrade had allowed to remain with her. We had come in the middle of the lady's *toilette*. Miss Rebecca Morton was seated before a mirror, wrapped in a heavy dressing gown, with her long auburn hair streaming about her shoulders. She was the fairest of all the young women we had met, with ivory skin and a pretty blush to her cheeks.

"You are the gentlemen Mr. Lestrade said would come to help him." The lady's voice was hoarse and rough from long bouts of weeping. She turned on the chair, her fingers nervously touching the heavy black velvet choker she wore around her throat. "I will tell you what I told him: I truly had no idea Bernard – the Earl – had come with the intention of proposing to me. Yes, we had spoken of our future together, but I didn't imagine he would be so impetuous. It was hardly romantic, and afterward, we sensed my siblings were jealous of our happiness, so I felt it best to retire along with my sisters Agnes and Elizabeth. Agnes called to Jael to follow us to bed, as she always did. I was asleep before midnight, and knew nothing more until this morning, when the maid began screaming in alarm."

Holmes asked the lady to send her attendant to fetch breakfast for her sisters. At first, I thought Miss Rebecca would refuse, but then she hurried the young girl along.

"Miss Morton, please forgive me, but you aren't being truthful with us," Holmes said, his voice firm and paternal. "If you don't speak honestly, it is likely that your brother will go to jail, and perhaps even be convicted and hanged, for the death of your lover. Is that what you wish? If not, then avail yourself of this one opportunity to make the matter clear. You met the Earl last night, after all your siblings and servants were in their rooms. What happened during that assignation?"

The girl went so white I thought she would faint. Her hand closed around the baroque pearl that hung from her choker.

"I . . . do not understand."

"Very well," Holmes replied curtly, "your false posturing will condemn your brother. You truly have nothing to say? Then we shall depart."

"No! No, please . . . I am so ashamed!" The girl trembled and seized a handkerchief to daub at sudden tears. "You may not believe me even if I do speak the truth."

"The evidence, Miss Fox, never lies. If your words match it, I will know you not dissembling."

The girl dropped her hands into her lap. "Everyone was rude to us after dinner. They would not permit us to be alone. Bernard whispered to me to join him in the ladies' parlor when the clock struck one, so that we might have some privacy to celebrate our betrothal. I found him waiting there in his nightshirt. There was no fire or light, only a candle upon the mantel. He embraced me, and it was then, in the flickering light, that I saw the bruise upon his face and the injury to his nose. I asked what had happened.

"'Your damn brother,' he snarled. 'He will be a problem to us. Perhaps I shall order an accident to befall him. You would like that, wouldn't you?'

"Sir, I suddenly realized what a foolish thing I had done, how terribly compromised I was. The Earl was still quite drunk. He reeked of whisky. His breath was foul. It was folly to agree to meet him in this state, when my virtue might be questioned. I pushed away from him, saying we could talk in the morning, when he was sober. He demanded a kiss. When I said no, he seized me in grasp and . . . and . . . ."

She reached back and unfastened the velvet accessory, allowing it to drop to the floor. Her pale throat bore telltale bruises and scratches from her mistreatment.

"I fought back. I have always been the most athletic of the family, and when I struggled, my knee struck a spot which gave him great discomfort. He released me and I flew back to my room, locking the door behind me. I fell on the bed and cried myself to sleep, knowing I would immediately break off my engagement."

"And that is all?"

"It is. We were alone in that dark room, though I heard the squawking of Georgie nearby. He is a wickedly clever bird. He had probably unlatched his cage again. He can do so at will, we have learned, but I did not see him."

Holmes nodded. "Thank you, Miss Morton, for your honesty. I am sorry to force you to recall such an unpleasant encounter, but murder has been done and the truth must prevail."

"But who . . . Oh sir, please . . . It cannot be Jimmy! I know he hated Bernard, and now I know he was right to hate him. Please, say it wasn't dear Jimmy. I cannot lose my brother!"

Holmes merely bowed without a reply. We left the lady dissolved in more tears as we returned to Miss Jael's door. Holmes tapped lightly, then spoke against the portal.

"Miss Morton, my name is Sherlock Holmes, and it is imperative that I have an audience with you." My friend waited a few seconds before adding, "It concerns your bird."

"*Her* bird?" I whispered. "No, the parrot belongs to her father."

The door was suddenly opened by a young woman dressed completely in black. Her face was a perfect copy of her twin brother's countenance, gentle yet resolute. Her blond hair was pinned back in a tidy bun. She considered us for a moment and waved us inside.

Miss Jael's chamber was neat, with a host of sewing projects set on frames and forms. Clearly, the silent young woman was industrious. She sat on a chair by the fireplace, and Holmes took the opposite one. He spoke softly but firmly to her.

"Your brother has made us aware that you don't speak because of the great loss you have suffered. Therefore, I will respect your reticence and simply tell you what happened last night. You may interrupt me if you choose, or if I err. Even a raised hand will stop me. But we must have the truth, or justice shall be miscarried. Will you listen?"

The girl nodded, fastening her gaze on my friend's face.

"You bear your sister Rebecca no ill-will, but over time you made many observations about her beau, the late Earl. You saw beyond his title for the mean and cruel man that he was. Last night, your heart sank when he proposed to your sister, but you dared not intervene, for her life was her own to live. Knowing the Earl was often spiteful and prone to tease, you removed yourself from the billiards room and retired to the ladies' parlor to sew. Like many talented seamstresses, you require no light, you could work even if blindfolded, for your hand knows where the needle should go. The darkness of the chamber fit your depressed and lonely mood. You never went up to bed, even when your sisters called you. You were absorbed in your work and your thoughts, perhaps in your memories of your own lost beloved, who was a far better man than the Earl."

To my surprise, the girl gave the slightest of nods. Her eyes had begun to glisten.

"You had lost all track of time when, to your surprise, someone entered the room with a candle and placed it upon the mantel. It was the Earl, and you shrank back further into the shadows. You were clad as you are now, all in mourning black, and in his clumsy, intoxicated state, he didn't perceive you. Moments later, your sister Rebecca came into the chamber. You saw the pair embrace, you heard them quarrel, and you witnessed the moment he throttled her. Before you could move, your sister wounded him, and he doubled over in pain while she fled.

"You remained stationary. The Earl rose and took down the candle. At that instant, you sprang to your feet and savagely plunged the beak of your sewing bird into his temple, sending him to God."

I gave a startled gasp. The young woman simply stared at Holmes. At last, she rose and walked silently to a large sewing basket which was lying upon her bed. She pulled an instrument from it, returning to place it in Holmes's hands.

It was a brass figurine shaped like a bird and perched on a heavy stand with a stout clamp. Its sharp beak was set on a hinge, enabling it to hold threads tightly. The beak was bloodstained.

Miss Jael spoke at last, her voice weak and fragile after so many years of disuse.

"He said horrible things to Rebecca, and worse after she ran away. He vowed to shame her and force her to wed him, then beat her and use her cruelly until he broke her. I had studied him for years – I knew he would do what he said. I had only seconds to act and save my sister. The candle almost set the rug on fire, but I quickly stepped on it and put it out." The young woman sat down. Her face was remarkable, for it was peacefully composed, with no sign of horror or regret. "I understand that I will hang, sir. But Rebecca will be safe, and I shall be in Heaven with my blessed Lord Zaltair. Nothing else will matter."

I saw at once what Holmes had deduced – the "sewing bird" was a perfect murder weapon, and the hand that bore it was a determined one. Holmes rose and gently patted the girl's shoulder.

"Say nothing to anyone," he advised. "And do not despair."

We went out and closed the door. Holmes gave a sad sigh.

"Concluding this case will bring me no pleasure, Watson."

I nodded my understanding. It was difficult for me to feel anger at a girl who had acted to protect her sister from a monstrous man. Yet at the same time, we couldn't have her brother falsely accused, or the other sisters, or one of the servants. We were halfway down the stairs when Lestrade emerged from the parlor, waving his notebook over his head.

"Congratulate me, Holmes! I've found the killer!"

221

Holmes quickly placed the weapon behind some flowers on a hallway table. "Indeed? That was fast work, Lestrade."

"And clever work as well – though I will give you credit for drawing my attention to the culprit."

"Who is . . . ?"

"Georgie! We shall call this 'The Case of the Deadly Bird!'"

Holmes slapped one hand over his mouth. A moment later, he recovered, and spoke in the most obsequious of tones.

"Please instruct me how you came to this remarkable conclusion."

"You noted that his cage was opened, and that the fowl was a witness to the affair. I posed some questions to the rascal, and he gave very interesting answers – 'Georgie bad! Georgie bad!' – and . . . Well, I shouldn't repeat the other language. It was rather risqué nautical speech."

"The bird confessed?" I inquired, with a quick glance at Holmes.

"Yes," the inspector chuckled, "though his statement is hardly evidence that would stand in court. This, however – "

Lestrade held out his right hand, which he had wrapped in a handkerchief. He pulled the linen back, revealing several vicious wounds.

"I was merely trying to give the beast a cracker and see what he did. A rather good match for the Earl's fatal assault, wouldn't you say? Yes, here is exactly what occurred: The Earl, an hour or so after his quarrel, came down to the parlor. Perhaps he couldn't sleep. Perhaps he was seeking some medicine and wandered into the wrong room. He came with a candle and did not turn on the gaslight, for his head was pounding and disordered from the beating. He saw the parrot in its cage and decided to toy with it, unlatching the cage to do so. The parrot flew out and attacked him, with fatal results."

Holmes stared at Lestrade for a long time. Lestrade bristled.

"Do you have a better theory of the case, Mr. Holmes? One that can account for the singular nature of the wound?"

"No, Inspector. Clearly, I lack your imagination."

Lestrade appeared stunned by my friend's admission. A moment later, he turned giddy. He hopped about like a schoolboy.

"Yes! Yes, I knew it was rather outlandish, but it covers all the facts. Well, we will make bloody bird pay for his crimes."

Lestrade went back into the parlor. I looked to Holmes, who gave a quick shake of his head and put a single finger to his lips, dropping it as the inspector emerged with the parrot in its cage.

"The Earl's body was removed while you were upstairs. Now, all that remains is to haul the culprit to Scotland Yard!"

Holmes stepped closer, bumping into the inspector, begging Lestrade's pardon as he leaned over to put his face close to the cage. Georgie squawked and offered up some most appalling epithets.

"Gracious me, he does sound like a killer. Let us get a carriage. Watson?"

I hurried outside and flagged down a four-wheeler. Holmes slid inside with the cage next to him. Lestrade was perched on the carriage step when Holmes asked if he might consult the inspector's notebook before we began our journey. Lestrade reached into his coat pocket.

"Why . . . Blast! Where is it? I was sure I had it a moment ago. I must have dropped it in the hall."

"We shall guard the prisoner," I laughed, slipping onto the opposite seat as Lestrade trotted back inside. When the inspector passed through the doorway, Sherlock Holmes did a wonderful thing.

He opened the cage door and let the parrot out.

The grey bird immediately hopped onto the carriage window, shot a grateful glance at his liberator, and flapped off to freedom.

"A thousand apologies, old friend," Holmes said, one instant before launching into a tirade of vitriol and abuse loud enough to be heard to Windsor Castle. He called me many things, the most flattering of which was "Clumsy oaf!" Lestrade, who had just emerged from the mansion, came running over.

"Good Heavens, what's – *Where's the bird*?"

"Watson, like a fool, jiggled the cage and the door popped open. The beast was gone before either of us could seize him. I've never seen a more careless 'guarding of a prisoner' in all my days."

Lestrade's face went rigid with horror. He stepped back and stared skyward, as if he could locate his villain soaring in the air over London. Holmes beckoned him to sit inside the carriage, reaching over to pat his knee.

"It was a freakish accident. Clearly, the Earl met his death through provoking a dangerous animal. He unlocked the vicious parrot's cage in the middle of the night, when all were asleep, so the Morton family cannot be blamed for his demise. Admittedly, it is a tragedy, but since the Earl was unwed and without heirs, I think the scandal will be a mild one. I shall make a full report as well, acknowledging your brilliance in the matter. Watson and I will confess to our incompetence which led to the release of the captive. The solution will, at the risk of a terrible pun, be another feather in your cap! There, there, Inspector . . . Do not cry. The killer will never strike again."

"Were you afraid they would execute Georgie?" I asked that night in Baker Street. Holmes chuckled as he poured me a glass of port.

"Such would have been a great miscarriage of justice. But I was more concerned that a clever police doctor would note the wound to the late Earl's temple didn't precisely match the parrot's beak. Lestrade was so attached to the novelty of his theory he lost sight of the reality within the home. He apparently never noticed, as I did immediately, that Miss Rebecca was going to extremes to hide the marks on her throat. When a lady dons an accessory more appropriate to a night at the opera than a morning at the breakfast table, one knows something is amiss. And in my study of the parlor, I noticed deep scratches upon the sewing table by the fireplace, where the sewing bird had been anchored by a clamp and roughly snatched free."

"Now I understand what you meant about seeing what wasn't there – and immediately envisioning the sewing bird and how it fit as a weapon. But by all that is wonderful, Holmes, whatever made you think of it? It is such a feminine device."

Holmes lifted his glass to his lips. "My mother had one. I can still picture it next to her chair, holding the threads tight."

I stared at my friend. Of course, he had a mother, yet this was the first time I could recall hearing him speak of her. There was something sad about his face in that moment.

"I do have some moral qualms," Holmes continued. "One must not condone a murder. Even repulsive gentlemen have the right to live. And yet . . . Had I seen a beloved sister almost strangled, and heard such vulgar words and threats leveled against her, would I have hesitated, with a deadly weapon close at hand? I cannot say that I would, especially if my mind was already disordered by a terrible loss. Ah, but I hear the bell and I am certain it is young Mr. Morton, who I have asked to call upon me tonight. I shall lay it all before him and suggest he and his sister Jael would do well to travel to America and serve as the representatives of their family enterprise in that new county. A change of scenery would certainly benefit his twin. I will also advise the youth to acquire a new pet to present to his father, who will be grieved to learn of the loss of his cheeky bird. Ah, Mr. Morton – do come in."

The Adventure of the
Scottish Coffins
by David MacGregor

"Coffins? In Scotland?" I found myself blinking in the morning light streaming through my bedroom window as the indistinct form of Sherlock Holmes stood at the foot of my bed.

"Indeed," returned Holmes. "They are awaiting our attention in Auld Reekie."

"Edinburgh?" I had managed to struggle to a seated position. "Whereabouts in Edinburgh?"

"Well, there's a bit of a story I will need to relate to you, but they were originally found hidden on Arthur's Seat, and since I suspect that we will be unable to convince an extinct volcano to make its way to London, I suppose we must venture north to investigate. Now then, if you would be so kind as to shift yourself with a modicum of alacrity, we should be able to catch the Flying Scotsman and have you in Edinburgh in time for tea."

With that, Holmes disappeared, only for his head to appear around the edge of my door frame a moment later. "No time for breakfast, but we'll get some haggis and whisky into you once we arrive."

Truth be told, the prospect of haggis for tea was not likely to rouse me from my bed with anything approaching the alacrity that Holmes had just requested, but the additional elements of a crime to be investigated and the possibility of a tasty dram or two did the trick.

Once my feet were on the floor, and having taken a moment or two to ease the stiffness out of my joints, I began rapidly assessing what I would need to have with me for this spontaneous excursion. Having experienced the vagaries of Scottish weather during my time studying medicine at the University of Edinburgh, two tweed jackets and a mackintosh were soon nestled into a travelling case, with a sturdy pair of wellies joining them a moment later. Reasoning that anything I had forgotten could be quickly procured at any of the fine establishments lining Princes Street, I soon presented myself to Holmes at the very moment Mrs. Hudson rounded a corner and regarded Holmes and me with some surprise.

"You're quite right, Mrs. Hudson," said Holmes, jumping straight into the middle of the conversation without wasting time on any preliminaries. "We are off to parts very well known. Scotland, to be precise. Your deductive faculties do you proud. Now then, during our absence, I will kindly beg you to use your Herculean powers of self-control to not enter our rooms and tidy up. I have a very delicate experiment in progress, and even the gentlest zephyr generated by the opening of the door is liable to set me back three weeks of research. Do I have your word on that?"

"Why, yes," Mrs. Hudson nodded her agreement. "Of course. Was it Scotland you said?"

"Aye, Lassie." I struggled to control an outburst of mirth as Holmes continued with his version of a Scottish brogue. "It's a bonny wee land just north of here on the verge of becoming civilised. We won't be but a day or two. Come along, Doctor."

Less than a minute later, Holmes and I were seated across from one another in a cab, rattling our way across London in good time.

"Should I even ask what that was about?" I began.

Holmes offered a good-natured shrug and smiled. "Being able to speak in various languages and accents is occasionally part of my vocation. One must keep in practise."

"And was it really necessary to come up with that nonsense story about your delicate experiment?"

"I'm afraid so," Holmes leaned back and tented his fingers together. "You haven't made a study of the inner workings of Mrs. Hudson's mind as I have. Were I to simply instruct her not to enter our rooms in our absence, I guarantee you we would have returned to a scarcely recognizable scene. Books would have been reshelved, papers would have been tidied up, and so on."

"Surely not."

"For the first few hours of our absence, Mrs. Hudson would have obeyed my command to the very letter, but soon enough, chinks would have appeared in her armor of resolution. It would begin with her thinking to herself that a quick clean couldn't hurt anything. This would then progress to ruminating on my reasons for asking her not to enter our rooms. Did I, perhaps, think she was incapable of tidying up a room properly? Was this a commentary on her house-keeping skills? Was she getting on a bit and I simply didn't wish to inconvenience her? Well, that simply wouldn't do. She would show me. She would show both of us. And we would have returned to immaculate rooms wherein every surface would be polished, every wayward crumb would have been swept up, and it would have taken us a good month to return matters to our preferred conditions."

"Good God," I muttered. "That was a narrow escape then."

And as I observed the brow of Holmes shaping itself into a small furrow, I cast my glance outside at the swirling colors of early morning London, happy as always to be moving, and with a specific destination in mind. In short order, the cab delivered us to King's Cross Station, where the gently puffing Flying Scotsman seemed to be patiently waiting our arrival, as it was only moments after we boarded that I felt the lurch of the train moving forward as we settled into our seats.

It was only now, with my morning fog well and truly cleared, that the full meaning of Holmes's rousing words came back to me in a rush. "Seventeen coffins, Holmes? Did I hear you correctly?"

"Allow me to be more precise. Seventeen coffins were originally found, but then they all mysteriously disappeared, the theory being that they had passed into the hands of private collectors."

"Private – ?" I could scarcely conceal my astonishment. "Who on earth would possibly want to collect coffins?"

Ignoring my question, Holmes continued on. "However, eight of these coffins reappeared just yesterday, and are currently awaiting our examination at the Museum of the Society of Antiquaries."

"I see," I began, trying to fashion some semblance of order out of the bizarre array of facts that Holmes had flung about in scattershot fashion. "These are relics of some kind? Coffins going back to the days of the Celtic tribes, perhaps? Were they the result of some battle or human sacrifice?"

"Not at all." Holmes's gaze was now fixed on the rapidly passing scenery outside our window. "They were originally discovered in late June of 1836. A group of young boys had taken themselves up Arthur's Seat to do some rabbit hunting, and in the manner of small boys everywhere, their enthusiasm and insatiable curiosity led them to turn over every boulder and investigate every nook and cranny that they could find. Well, they found far more than they could have ever bargained for. No fewer than seventeen coffins, carefully concealed within a cave on Arthur's Seat."

"Presumably you received a communication regarding the reappearance of these coffins?" I asked. Not deigning to shift his gaze from the window, Holmes nodded almost imperceptibly. "Inspector Murdoch?" I hazarded.

"The very same," answered Holmes. "Good man. It shall be pleasant to see him again."

Now then, to provide my readers with some context for a case to which I have never referred, Holmes was speaking of events that had taken place four years previously, also in Edinburgh, but an urgent medical matter had precluded my accompanying Holmes. It was either an unfortunate accident or a nasty bit of business involving an enterprising gentleman by the name of Alf Smith, who had made a fortune for himself

228

by contriving a new acid formula to aid in the tanning of leather, and had built himself a factory on the banks of the River Mersey in Manchester. His labour practises and policy of dumping used chemicals directly into the river had not endeared him to the local inhabitants, so he used a portion of his fortune to buy himself a large estate and ruined medieval castle outside of Edinburgh, and upon his visits to the city, had begun styling himself as Laird Dalhousie. This had been irritating enough for the local inhabitants, but their ire steadily grew as the self-minted Laird began appearing in public in full Scottish regalia, from his kilt right down to his sporran, with a *sgian-dubh* tucked inside one of his socks. When visiting pubs and engaging the locals in various spirited discussions, he had the habit of pulling out this small dagger and driving it into the table for emphasis.

Increasingly exasperated at the lack of respect he felt that his newly acquired real estate should bring him, the breaking point came on a rainy evening at Deacon Brodie's Tavern. In the midst of a heated political argument, to the astonishment of everyone present, Alf Smith, the born and bred Mancunian, had begun speaking with a thick Scottish brogue. Accounts from this point on differ, but they agree that various chairs and stools had been raised over various heads, and that Laird Dalhousie had fled outside into the teeming downpour. In his panic, he ran in the direction of Arthur's Seat, with several of the more incensed tavern patrons in hot pursuit. In the end, Alf Smith, the erstwhile Laird Dalhousie, had never been seen alive again. His body was recovered from some tangled brush on the steep slopes of Arthur's Seat the next morning, and on the basis of his title alone, local officials had encouraged Inspector Murdoch to call in an outside authority, who arrived in the person of Sherlock Holmes.

The coroner's report revealed no wounds upon Laird Dalhousie's body, and concluded that he had died of exposure as the cold rain had continued to fall during the night. Had he been chased or pushed off the edge of the path? The steady rain had thoroughly effaced any and all footprints that might have assisted Holmes in his enquiry, and to a man, the patrons of Deacon Brodie's Pub had quite cheerfully provided alibis for one another. The most striking thing about the case from my perspective was that, upon his return to London, Holmes had described Inspector Murdoch as a gentleman who was "observant, diligent, and keeps his own counsel." This alone put him streets ahead of the police personnel typically encountered by Holmes, and as the Flying Scotsman sped its way north, I found myself quite looking forward to meeting this exemplar of his profession.

In the meantime, my stomach let loose a low growl to express its unhappiness with being empty, and I saw Holmes smiling across at me.

"I do apologize for rushing you off like this and disturbing your morning routine, Watson. Particularly your need to feed at regular intervals."

Was that a glint of amusement I saw in Holmes's eye? If it was, then I was perfectly prepared to amuse myself at his expense in return.

"No bother at all," I assured him. "I'll just take myself off to the dining car and see what they have."

Rising from my seat, I was gratified to see the faintest expression of bewilderment cross Holmes's face, and almost in spite of himself he uttered, "Dining car?"

"Part of the recently completed modernisation on the Flying Scotsman," I explained. "Not only did they add corridors between the cars, but they also installed heating and added dining cars. I do like to keep up on our advances in transportation. Eminently civilised, wouldn't you agree?"

"Quite," nodded Holmes. "Come to think of it, I wouldn't mind a spot of tea myself."

"Well then, join me," I said as I slid open the door to our compartment, and a moment later Holmes and I were strolling through the swaying carriage towards the nearest dining car. As we sat down and were presented with menus, Holmes surveyed our surroundings and fellow passengers, giving a nod of approval.

"Very nice," he began. "The last time I took this train, there was a half-hour stopover in York for lunch, which I thought was a ridiculous waste of time. This is, as you say, much more civilised."

I nodded, my attention more fixated on the menu than Holmes's approbation, and twenty minutes later, as I delved into my second quite acceptable soft-boiled egg, Holmes turned his attention from the window and enquired, "Did you ever have the pleasure of ascending Arthur's Seat during your university days?"

"No," I answered. "I wasn't in Edinburgh to go hill-climbing, I was there to study medicine. I did know several fellows who enjoyed taking the local girls up there. Apparently, the uneven walking paths afforded many opportunities to offer a steadying arm or hand."

"And presumably the young maidens saw to it that they were suitably unsteady."

Not for the first time, Holmes's cynicism regarding the world of courting and romance raised its head and, not for the first time, it led me to wonder where the roots of his dismissive and contemptuous feelings for the softer emotions lay. Past experience allowed me to say with absolute certainty that any enquiries along those lines would be utterly fruitless, so

I spread a good dollop of Robertson's Golden Shred Marmalade on my toast and allowed my gaze to wander to the passing scenery.

We passed the next minute or two in silence, but I was well aware that Holmes's mind was spinning at its usual rate, and I took it upon myself to see if I could somehow deduce his current train of thought. He had just mentioned Arthur's Seat. Therefore, it made perfect sense that he was still musing upon that topic, so with another eight hours ahead of us on the train, I saw no harm in hazarding a guess.

"I quite agree," I announced.

Holmes looked at me in surprise. "What's that?"

"The fact that the Scottish Lowlands are home to an extinct volcano is quite remarkable. Very remarkable, indeed."

"Ah, yes," Holmes nodded. "The etymology of the name, Arthur's Seat, is obscure, but geologists estimate its age to be greater than one-hundred-million years old. It provides excellent panoramic views of the city of Edinburgh and surrounding countryside, and was described by native son Robert Louis Stevenson as, '*a hill for magnitude, a mountain in virtue of its bold design*'."

I smiled at Holmes, more than a trifle pleased with myself, "I fancied that's what you were thinking about."

"When?"

"Just now."

"Oh, I see. Actually, I'm afraid my thoughts had strayed into criminal realms – specifically, crimes associated with the city of Edinburgh."

"Any crime in particular?" I asked.

"Burke and Hare, of course," answered Holmes. "Surely you would agree that the murderous careers of those two bold entrepreneurs rank among the very worst atrocities ever committed in these Isles. Also quite instructive when considering human behavior in its more extreme manifestations."

"In what way?" Dabbing at the corners of my mouth with a white linen napkin, I took another sip of tea and leaned back in my chair. "I can't say I'm overly familiar with their crimes, aside from the fact that they were as sensational as they were horrible."

"Then allow me to fill you in. It will enable you to be a more active participant in our investigation." Holmes produced a pipe from one of his pockets, along with a pouch of tobacco. A few moments later, a gentle puff of smoke made its way towards the ceiling of the dining car, and Holmes proceeded to embark on a tale of intrigue and murder.

"The events took place in 1828, and were a direct result of the needs of one Dr. Robert Knox, a Scottish anatomist and ethnologist whose career ended in disgrace. He was, by all accounts, an extremely intelligent yet extraordinary unpleasant individual, perhaps due to a severe bout of smallpox as a child, which had left him severely disfigured. After graduating from the University of Edinburgh, he toured the world as a physician for hire, but eventually returned to Edinburgh, where he joined an anatomy school in Surgeon's Square in 1825.

"Now then, prior to the Anatomy Act of 1832, anatomists and their students were forced to rely solely on the bodies of criminals who had been condemned to death and dissection by the courts. These weren't in abundance, and the so-called 'French Method' of teaching anatomy required one body per student, so to make up for the shortfall in corpses, the practise of grave-robbing grew in popularity. After the death of a loved one, families would have to set up a vigil near the grave to prevent it from being violated, and it is here that one William Hare enters the picture.

"There is no record of him being accused of grave-robbing, but in late 1827, an indebted lodger passed away under his roof, and Hare subsequently sold the body to Knox, who by that time had amassed more private students than any other physician in the city. This event apparently set the wheels turning in Hare's mind, and after consulting with his friend William Burke, they joined forces to begin murdering poor people in the city's Old Town and delivering the bodies to Knox, whose dissection theatre was described as a 'charnel house'. Known as the West Port Murders, Burke and Hare collected eight to ten pounds per body, which was quite a tidy sum of money to be spent on all the delights that Edinburgh had to offer, up until the day they were both arrested. Questions?"

The abruptness of Holmes's query caught me off guard, and it took me a moment to collect my thoughts and ask, "Presumably both scoundrels were hanged?"

"Not at all," answered Holmes. "The case against them was actually quite weak, and it was only when Hare turned King's Evidence that Burke was convicted and hanged in front of a crowd estimated to be at least twenty-five thousand people. Appropriately enough, he was then publicly dissected at the University of Edinburgh's Old College. His skeleton was given to the Anatomical Museum of the Edinburgh Medical School, and reputedly a pocket book was bound with his tanned skin, an unusual but by no means unique practice known as *anthropodermic bibliopegy*. It's currently on display at the Surgeons' Hall Museum. I'm must confess that I'm disappointed to learn that you aren't aware of these admittedly insalubrious details."

"I was in Edinburgh to learn the art of medicine!" I replied somewhat heatedly. "Not to gawk at some macabre souvenirs! And what about

William Hare then? He was the instigator of the entire affair. Was his skull made into a chalice and his bones into some kind of musical instrument?"

"Better than that, Watson," answered Holmes. "Much better than that. No one knows."

"No one knows what?"

"What happened to William Hare. He was promised immunity to provide testimony against his former partner, and he was last seen heading south towards England. His ultimate fate remains unknown to this day."

This put me back on my heels, as it were. Was this the purpose of Holmes's desire to visit Edinburgh? To somehow pick up the trail of William Hare and determine his eventual fate? But no. We were heading north to view some coffins. Holmes had said as much. How had the conversation veered into this unpleasant direction? Before I could begin to assemble my thoughts to ask further questions, Holmes interrupted me.

"There is one more feature to the Burke and Hare case of which you should be aware – that is, their number of victims."

"It was . . . ." I began to rack my memory, but with no success. "I can't remember the precise number, but it was not insubstantial."

"Sixteen."

I stared at Holmes. Now it was all coming together in a rush. Seventeen coffins found on Arthur's Seat and sixteen victims of Burke and Hare. They couldn't possibly be connected, could they?

"The number may be slightly fewer or slightly more," added Holmes. "Burke and Hare proved to be peculiarly reticent when it came to providing precise figures, as was Dr. Knox."

"Whatever happened to this Knox fellow?" I asked.

"He was never prosecuted," said Holmes, "arguing that he was entirely unaware of the murderous activities of Burke and Hare. He was merely the happy recipient of the extremely fresh corpses they provided. However, his dark reputation in Edinburgh made life difficult for him, so he subsequently removed himself to London where he wrote two popular books: One on salmon fishing in Scotland, and the other on ethnology and race. He was particularly keen on the idea that Irish Catholics should be utterly eradicated from the face of the earth for the benefit of humanity."

Holmes paused as he took in my shocked expression. "And that, my dear Watson, is why human beings will remain a never-ending subject of study, speculation, and grief to one another."

By the time we arrived at Edinburgh's Waverley Station, I had decided to give up on making any sense of this mad journey, and allow Holmes and time to reveal what they would reveal. As various disembarking passengers hurried to meet friends and relatives, I spied a small, unmoving figure at the back of the platform, and somehow conceived the idea that this must be none other than Inspector Murdoch as I had pictured him in my mind. To my pleasant surprise, I was proved correct, as Holmes grasped my elbow and led me towards this paragon of Scottish policemen.

"Inspector Murdoch," began Holmes, "this is my friend and colleague, Dr. Watson, without whom I would be utterly lost. Watson, this is the estimable Murdoch."

He couldn't have been much over five feet tall and weighed no more than ten stone, but his crystal blue eyes held mine unwaveringly as he shook my hand and I felt the rough skin of a man who had been raised doing more than his fair share of manual labour.

"Coffins or hotel?" asked Murdoch in a soft Scottish brogue.

"Coffins, of course," answered Holmes. "As you can see, we haven't much baggage and can carry what we have with us."

As we settled into the carriage provided by Murdoch, Holmes looked at the small figure sitting across from him with a smile. "Now then, I would imagine that it isn't every day that eight coffins magically appear on your doorstep."

"No indeed," answered Murdoch. "And it was scarcely a minute later that I composed a telegram to be sent to you. I felt quite certain you would find the news, shall we say, of interest."

"And here I am," answered Holmes.

"Here you are," repeated Murdoch.

"You have your opinion," ventured Holmes.

"I do," replied Murdoch, "but should be glad of yours."

"And you shall have it."

The two men nodded at one another, and the remainder of our journey was passed in silence until we pulled up outside the Museum of the Society of Antiquaries. As we approached the entrance, I observed the Coat of Arms of the society emblazoned with the St. Andrews Cross near the top of an archway. It was clear that our arrival was expected, as one doorway after another was opened for us, until we arrived at a small room at the end of a long corridor.

It was Murdoch himself who produced a key and pronounced, "The coffins of Arthur's Seat, gentlemen." With that, he opened the door and ushered us into a space not larger than a small bedroom. There would scarcely have been room for eight coffins, and as I looked around, I discerned none at all. The day had begun with some degree of discombobulation, and as I stood there looking around in bewilderment, I began to suspect that this was nothing more than some grand joke concocted by Holmes with the assistance of his friend Inspector Murdoch. Just as I was on the verge of expressing my exasperation and outrage,

Murdoch lifted a cloth from a small table, and as he whisked it away, I observed to my astonishment eight miniature coffins. Each one could not have been more than four inches in length and perhaps an inch or two across. In an instant, Holmes had brought out his magnifying lens and was examining the exteriors of the coffins with the utmost concentration. Small, involuntary sounds began to emerge from Holmes, and as I glanced at Murdoch, I saw a small smile on his face.

When Holmes removed the lids from the coffins, my astonishment grew, for inside each coffin was a small figure. Each of these figures was examined in turn by Holmes with painstaking attention to the figures themselves, as well as to the various styles of clothing that had been glued and stitched onto them. This analysis went on for several minutes, at which point, without a word, Holmes turned and handed his magnifying lens to me. I dutifully bent over to conduct my own examination of the coffins and figures, all the while highly conscious of the fact that the odds of me perceiving anything that had escaped Holmes's attention were very slim indeed. However, the fact that Holmes had been kind enough include me in his investigation filled me with pride, and I was especially pleased that this small gesture would elevate me in the estimation of Inspector Murdoch as well.

To my eye, the dolls all seemed to be representations of adults, with roughly carved features that didn't betray the hand of an especially skilled artisan. Some of the figures were without arms, presumably for the simple reason that they wouldn't have fit into the coffins otherwise. I observed what appeared to be spectacles drawn onto one or two of the faces, but beyond that failed to discern anything particularly remarkable. After what seemed to me to be a suitable amount of time for a thorough investigation, I handed Holmes his magnifying lens. Rather than launch into a lengthy disquisition of my thoughts, I reasoned that given the situation and the company, this might be a good time to keep things brief.

"Fascinating," I offered.

"Indeed," confirmed Holmes. "If you might give us a chance to change into more suitable clothing, Murdoch, I would like to see where these coffins were found originally."

"Of course," answered Murdoch. "I arranged for accommodations at The George Hotel. I trust that will meet your needs."

"Excellent," replied Holmes. "Then Watson and I will join you at Arthur's Seat in one hour."

By the time we reached our hotel, a fine, misting rain had begun to settle on the city, and so it was that when we joined Inspector Murdoch at the foot of Arthur's Seat, I was fully clad in my mackintosh and wellies for the trek ahead. It wasn't a particularly arduous climb, for Arthur's Seat presents the hiker with gentle slopes swathed in brilliant green, and walking paths have been worn into the side of the hill thanks to the countless travellers over the centuries who have been lured by humanity's urge to climb to the top of the highest peak in the vicinity.

We were only ten minutes into our ascent when Holmes and Murdoch paused to look over a precipice that plunged down into a sea of heather and brambles. I immediately assumed that this was the spot where the late Laird Dalhousie had met his fate, an assumption that Holmes quickly verified as he turned to Murdoch.

"No further news on what happened to his Lairdship?" he asked.

"None," answered Murdoch. "As far as the locals were concerned, it was as if nothing at all had transpired, although I will say that more than the usual number of toasts were offered in the city's pubs."

Murdoch picked up a sizable stone, glistening from the rain, and with a gentle motion tossed it down into the chasm of foliage beneath us. It rustled a few leaves before it was swallowed up, presumably to remain untouched by human hands for the next few centuries.

"It's a natural thing for our arrival into this world to be celebrated," mused Murdoch, "but when your departure is celebrated even more, it's fair to say that your time on earth was not well spent."

With that, Murdoch resumed his upward climb, Holmes and I following him, until we rounded a corner and Murdoch led us to a cleft in the rock that opened up into a very small cave.

"Originally," began Murdoch, "this cave was hidden behind three slabs of slate that the boys were able to move to gain access. And it was here they found seventeen wee coffins. They were arranged in three tiers, two tiers of eight, and then a single coffin placed on top."

Holmes inspected the cramped space closely, then ventured back outside the cave to get his bearings.

"North-east side of the hill," he began, "the pieces of slate not only protecting the coffins from the elements, but also from prying eyes. Were it not for the curious boys, they could have remained here undetected for decades, if not centuries."

"Shall we retire to Deacon Brodie's for a pint or two to discuss the matter?" asked Murdoch.

"Capital!" replied Holmes, and as he glanced at me, I nodded my enthusiastic agreement, especially at the prospect of a pint accompanied by a meat pie or an old favorite from my university days, bangers and mash.

The tavern was only half-full when we entered, and as my eyes adjusted to the dimness, I became aware that everyone in attendance had turned our way as we sat down at a corner table near the fire. The presence

236

of Murdoch appeared to assure the locals that Holmes and I weren't strangers looking for trouble, and it seemed we had barely sat down and divested ourselves of our damp garments when three pints of bitter appeared, followed by an assortment of meat and pork bridies. There then followed several minutes of silence as we turned our attention to the food and drink, but at length Murdoch pushed his chair back an inch or two with a satisfied sigh and glanced at Holmes, who was in the process of lighting his pipe.

"I will take it for granted," began Murdoch, "that you have already formulated your own theories, so I will offer you my impressions and see to what extent they coincide with your own."

"That will be fine, Murdoch," answered Holmes. "I was hoping for as much."

"Then let us start with the Lilliputian coffins themselves," said Murdoch. "At one point in time, they weren't in existence, yet some event or series of events, prompted an unknown individual to create them. I say 'individual' because I feel certain that they were the product of a single hand. There is a marked similarity between all of the coffins, and while the figures inside them vary, I note the same carving marks, presumably made by the same carving tools. What sort of tools were they, and what sort of person would have had access to those particular tools? Taking together the iron embellishments, the type of nails used, and the carving marks made by a sharp, hooked knife, they are all consistent with the implements typically used by a cordwainer."

"Or perhaps a cobbler," added Holmes. "And to my eye, all of the coffins appear to have been carved from the same piece of wood."

"Agreed," said Murdoch, "which indicates they were likely manufactured at approximately the same time."

"Does the upright bearing, flat feet, and swinging arms of the figures suggest anything to you?" asked Holmes.

"It would support the idea of toy soldiers," answered Murdoch, "save for the variations in attire or costumes. Recall, if you will, the figure with the high starched collar and matching coat and pants with blue stripes. Before your arrival, I did take the liberty of consulting a local haberdasher whose family have lived here for the past two centuries. He was able to confirm that the styles of clothing on the dolls were consistent with the late 1820's and early 1830's."

"Excellent work," nodded Holmes. "So then, let us turn to the rationale behind the creation of the dolls. They were not an inconsiderable amount of labour, so why create them only to hide them away?"

"There is the possibility of some association with witchcraft and demonology," offered Murdoch, "the idea being to entomb the likenesses of people the creator wished to destroy."

"In ancient Saxony," added Holmes, "there was a tradition of burying effigies of departed loved ones who had died in distant lands."

"There is also a superstition among some sailors," continued Murdoch, "in which they ask their families or wives to give a proper Christian burial to an effigy of them should they be lost at sea."

"Which brings to mind the old German seafaring tradition, in which small dolls or mandrake roots were the kind of talismans kept in small coffins and sold as lucky charms to sailors about to start a voyage," said Holmes.

A moment of silence fell over the table, and it was then that Holmes turned to me. "Watson? You have seen everything that Inspector Murdoch and I have seen. Have you developed any theories?"

As pleased as I was to be included in the discussion, I wasn't prepared to offer any answer that I felt would provide a definitive solution to the mystery. Still, I was among friends, and aided and abetted by the courage of two pints, I spoke my mind.

"There is the old saying that for a carpenter every problem is a nail and every solution is a hammer. As detectives, you're both drawn to, shall we say, somewhat dark conclusions when presented with a mystery. But perhaps there is nothing evil or nefarious about these figures at all. Besides their bizarre appearance and the fact that they were hidden in an extinct volcano, let's not lose sight of what they are: *Dolls*. Dolls are for children, yes? Perhaps some shoemaker put them together for a young child as a present, then didn't want to risk having them found in the house, so he hid them on Arthur's Seat, but then some tragedy befell him, so there they sat until they were discovered."

As I inwardly braced for some kind of dismissive comment from either Murdoch or Holmes, instead another silence fell upon the table, before Murdoch examined the dregs of his glass and declared, "That is a possibility. Or perhaps the dolls were simply part of some macabre practical joke, the best of which unfold when the perpetrator is nowhere near the scene. But what about you, Mr. Holmes? You've heard the theories of Dr. Watson and myself. Have you one of your own?"

"I do," said Holmes, sending a puff of smoke towards the ceiling. "My theory is one of context. That is, one that depends on the series of events that would have led to the creation of the dolls. I fear it isn't a theory that I will ever be able to prove, but I feel quite certain that the manufacturing of the dolls and their subsequent placement on Arthur's Seat was the work of none other than William Hare."

At this, Murdoch and I exchanged a glance as Holmes took another puff on his pipe, then leaned back in his chair and fixed his gaze upon the ceiling.

"Do go on, Mr. Holmes," said Murdoch.

"As Watson will tell you, my interest in crime and sensational literature is longstanding, and the crimes of Burke and Hare have always exerted a certain fascination. William Hare and William Burke were both Irishmen who wound up in Edinburgh and formed a friendship, no doubt based in part on their common backgrounds. Hare and his wife or partner ran a lodging house in Tanner's Close and, when a lodger died owing rent, it was only natural that Hare would bemoan this loss of income to his friend Burke. They soon landed upon the happy idea of selling the lodger's corpse to Dr. Knox for a tidy sum, where they were informed that fresh corpses were always welcome.

"Following this, I would argue that Burke took the lead in this partnership. While they often teamed up to end the lives of other unfortunate lodgers, in his confession, Burke noted several occasions where he was the sole perpetrator. He had no qualms about killing and he was quite adept at it. He took a special pleasure in suffocating intoxicated women. As the old rhyme describing the roles of Burke, Hare, and Knox went:

> *Up the close and doon the stair,*
> *But and ben wi' Burke and Hare*
> *Burke's the butcher, Hare's the thief*
> *Knox the boy that buys the beef.*

"As I related to Watson on our journey here, with the promise of immunity dangled before him, it was Hare who testified against his old partner, and Burke was subsequently hanged, with Hare reputedly making his way to England, where he no doubt changed his name and disappeared from the historical records. And I would wager that it was during this period, as he strove to keep his anonymity, that the enormity of his crimes began to weigh on his conscience. No fewer than sixteen people hadn't only been murdered, but then denied a proper Christian burial as they were dissected into pieces by Knox. And so William Hare began to roughly carve the figures we have seen with his unpractised hand. He clothed them, enclosed them in rough-hewn coffins, and then made his way back to Edinburgh, no doubt in some kind of disguise. He couldn't risk being seen in the city proper or being caught digging small graves in a cemetery, so he made his way up Arthur's Seat, found a suitable cave protected from the elements, and deposited the coffins there."

"But Holmes," I objected, "there were *seventeen* coffins, and only *sixteen* victims."

"Two rows of eight, Watson," answered Holmes, "with a single coffin placed atop them. The sixteen coffins represented the victims of Burke and Hare. The single coffin, of course, would be for his erstwhile partner, William Burke, whom he betrayed to the hangman's noose and then the anatomist's dissection table."

At this, Murdoch and I looked to one another, then back at Holmes, marvelling at the tale he had just told. It was a long and convoluted chain to be sure, but every link rang true.

"Merely a theory," added Holmes, "and we will never be able to verify whether it is true or not. Still, it has been a pleasant day of adventure nevertheless. Perhaps a dram or two of whisky to round off our day, gentlemen?"

This most excellent suggestion was immediately acceded to, and it was some time later that we said our good-byes to Inspector Murdoch and made our way to The George Hotel, where a soft bed and dreamless night awaited.

The next morning found neither Holmes nor myself particularly interested in conversation, and we arrived at the Waverley platform for our return journey aboard the Flying Scotsman in relative silence. Once settled into our seats, I observed Holmes's heavy lids drooping, and I must have dozed off myself, for it was a full three hours later that I awakened to find us speeding through the English countryside on our way back to London. Holmes had recovered somewhat as well, as he had procured a newspaper and was absorbed in an article of some kind. Waiting until he turned the page, I asked the question that had occurred to me the previous evening, and now seemed to demand an answer.

"Why, Holmes?"

As Holmes dipped his newspaper, I saw that his grey eyes had resumed their typical alertness. "What's that?"

"Why did we travel to Edinburgh? There was no crime to investigate, and even if you had somehow managed to forge a definite connection between those dolls and Burke and Hare, the crimes and the people who committed them are ancient history. So why make the journey at all?"

Holmes thoughtfully folded up his newspaper and regarded me with a steady gaze. "Not an injudicious question, Watson, so one that I will attempt to answer fully. First, I would draw your attention to the value of movement for its own sake. Mind and body tend to stagnate if we stay in one place for too long. In the case of London, it is a city that is quite refreshing to leave, and then there is the added benefit that one sees it more clearly, in all its splendour and squalor, upon returning.

240

"Then there is the always edifying practise of studying crime in all of its manifestations. So then, let us divide criminal activities into two categories: Crimes of passion and crimes of profit. Invariably, crimes of passion are more easily solved because no planning or foresight has gone into them. They occur in the heat of the moment and the perpetrator is invariably apprehended quite quickly. Contrast this to crimes of profit, where the planning may be rudimentary or extremely complex, but these crimes are committed with some degree of mindfulness in the hope of not being caught or punished in any way. They are typically committed by men who focus almost exclusively on what benefits them, and they are unmindful or disinterested in how their actions might affect other people. For them, there really is no concern regarding what is right and what is wrong. It is simply a matter of what they can get away with.

"It is these depraved individuals who are the implacable enemies of every society within which they exist. Men not dissimilar to you and me in appearance, but oceans away from us in terms of values and common decency. They are predators, and their prey is their fellow human beings. This tendency is clearly exemplified in the activities of Burke and Hare. They bore no malice towards their victims. Theirs was a business enterprise, nothing less and nothing more. Indeed, in terms of business philosophy, their practices weren't dissimilar to the practices of the late Laird Dalhousie."

"Come now, Holmes!" I expostulated. "You can't compare the two. Burke and Hare were murderers and Laird Dalhousie was a businessman."

"A businessman quite content to poison his own community to increase his profits," answered Holmes. "Happy to use child labour and equally happy to pour the toxic dregs of his factory into the River Mersey, with not a single care how those corrosive chemicals might affect the communities downstream. Beware of esteemed industrialists and captains of industry, Watson. All too often, forests, rivers, and other human beings are simply commodities to be used up in their view of the world. As the French novelist Balzac expressed it: '*Behind every great fortune lies a great crime.*' And as the twentieth century gathers steam, you can be certain that technology and industrialization will enable unscrupulous men to further indulge their darkest urges, even at the risk of eradicating humanity itself. That is why it's important to understand where that criminal impulse arises, how it grows, and to what it can lead. To turn a blind eye to the activities of these men is to condemn our own species to oblivion. You may count on that."

"That's a terribly grim prognostication, Holmes," I said.

"Indeed. But picture men like Burke and Hare as the heads of government and industry, in charge of increasingly powerful machines and weaponry, and I fear that the future is bleak. In the meantime, we do what we can, old friend."

Holmes turned his gaze to the passing scenery and I observed an almost wistful expression upon his face. When he spoke again it was in an almost inaudible whisper.

"We do what we can."

The Return of the
Rival Criminalist
by Will Murray

It was one of those dreadfully hot days in the summer of 1885 when I tramped up the stairs to the Baker Street sitting room where Sherlock Holmes and I shared quarters. I recall that I was sweltering. The air was also quite humid. I could not wait to remove my coat.

Entering, I discovered Holmes seated in his customary chair by the cold hearth. He was industriously scaling the bowl of his briar pipe with a silver tool. Occupying a facing chair was an unkempt and unwashed young man I had come to know as a frequent visitor.

"Why, Mr. Wiggins!" I exclaimed. "What brings you here on such a hot and insufferable day?"

Wiggins, he of the dirty face, who was the leader of the gang of street Arabs known as the Baker Street Irregulars, turned his face to me and smiled toothily in greeting.

"Greetings, Dr. Watson. I was just telling Mr. Holmes the news."

I lowered myself into my accustomed chair and loosened my neck tie.

"I'm interested in hearing it as well," I remarked. "Whatever it might be."

Turning his attention back to Holmes, Wiggins said, "It's more than a rumor, Mr. Holmes. The scoundrel is back in London."

"Are you certain of your information?" inquired Holmes.

"It has gotten around among The Element that the man has hung his shingle in this place and that other place. As you will recall, he doesn't show his face in the same place very often."

I knew by the term "*Element*" that Wiggins meant the criminal element.

"You are certain it was Reynard Renbourne?" asked Holmes.

Wiggins nodded eagerly. "The description is exact, except that he has shaven his mustache and he wears his hair quite short now. But it is he. I saw him entering The Spotted Dragon tavern with my own eyes."

"I see," returned Holmes, casting the scraped dottle into the hearth with a practiced toss of his briar in that direction. "This is intriguing news."

I thought so, too. It was clear about whom they were speaking. The previous year, Renbourne, who had once been a disgraced barrister named Josiah Graymark, was making himself available to the criminal trade as a

243

consultant of sorts. He called himself a *criminalist*. Using his knowledge of the law, he was carefully advising his clients on how to avoid capture by Scotland Yard or notice by Holmes. The man had the temerity to call himself Sherlock Holmes's opposite, and fancied himself his rival. This drew the professional wrath of my friend Holmes, who endeavored to bait Renbourne into becoming complicit in a crime. However, the man proved to be too clever, and he escaped London unscathed, one strep ahead of Holmes and Scotland Yard.

The only solace Holmes received was that he had solved a baffling murder which Renbourne had helped plan. But this was insufficient to satisfy my friend.

It appeared that, against all common sense, Renbourne had returned to the city.

Addressing Holmes, I remarked, "I imagine that you'll resume the hunt at this point."

"Indeed. But I must advance carefully. Beyond any doubt, Renbourne will be alert for any signs of renewed interest on my part in his illicit activities."

"Can he not be arrested for the complicity in the murder of John Singleton, the cooper?" I wondered.

"He can. We have the testimony of the murderer that Renbourne advised him in certain details, thereby making the fellow subject to arrest on those grounds. But Renbourne is a disbarred and disgraced barrister. We must keep that uppermost in mind. He will without question attempt to weasel his way out of the toils of the law. It would be better if we capture him in the act, with a witness."

"What do you propose?" I asked.

"Why, Watson, have you so soon forgotten my original plan?"

I hadn't quite forgotten, but I had put it out of my mind. Now it came back to me. I all but shuddered, for I recalled that Holmes's plan involved a plot to murder of none other than myself.

Fortunately, I thought of an objection. "See here, Holmes: If you were to seek out this person in one of your imaginative disguises and attempt to inveigle him into a plan to murder me, would he not become suspicious? For it is well known that the famous Holmes is often seen in the company of Dr. John Watson. Why, just mentioning my name would give the show away. Would it not?"

"I've thought of that. You are quite correct. I cannot name you as the intended victim. But that doesn't mean you cannot *stand in* for said victim. This is a problem that can be solved by the application of careful disguise. I will create one, and then I'll devise another for yourself."

I didn't like the sound of that, for it promised personal peril, but I had previously agreed to the scheme, so I kept my deeper reservations to myself.

"Of course," I declared. "I'm always ready to help you in your endeavors."

"Very good." Turning back to Wiggins, he handed the little fellow a sovereign coin and instructed him carefully.

"Return to the streets, my good Wiggins. Keep your eyes sharp and your ears wide open. Do your best to learn of Renbourne's activities. Let me know where he can be found."

Wiggins bobbed his bare head in agreement, but also said, "It's known that where he can be found is only a temporary encampment. The next night will find the fellow somewhere else."

"I understand perfectly," said Holmes. "The base fraud doesn't seem to return to the same haunts very often, if at all. That means once he has been seen in this tavern or that other public house, it may be crossed off the list. We may be able to isolate his next likely temporary office through a simple process of elimination."

"Very good, sir," said Wiggins, standing up and taking his leave.

After Wiggins had departed, I turned to Holmes and inquired of him, "Have you a definite plan of action?"

"Beyond the obvious, no, I have not. Our opponent is a cagey sort. Renbourne not only owns the mind of a man versed in legalities, but his brain has taken a criminal turn. I wouldn't want to make a misstep."

"Perfectly understandable," I returned. "So you'll await the reports that are sure to come from Wiggins?

"If nothing better turns up."

"Will you inform Lestrade of your endeavors?"

Holmes frowned thoughtfully. "I think not. I prefer to hold that option in reserve. My aim is to entrap Renbourne. Regrettably, the police are more than apt to complicate any snare I devise, if not foil it through clumsiness."

"I fail to understand your motives. Surely, Scotland Yard has enough on the man to take him into custody without further machinations on your part."

"I have explained my reasoning," returned Holmes as he charged his briar with tobacco. "You must understand that this has become a personal matter. Renbourne fancies himself to be my rival and, according to his lights, a worthy opponent of mine. This offends me greatly. I view the rivalry as a game of chess. I will checkmate him on my terms and no other."

I understood perfectly. I couldn't help but feel that I was a mere pawn in this game of wits. But I swallowed that qualm unspoken.

And there the matter rested for several days.

I didn't see Wiggins for nearly a week. When he returned, the lad was bursting with information.

"Mr. Renbourne has taken up a table at The Rising Sun on Cloth Fair, in Smithfield, Farringdon Without."

Holmes glanced toward the mantel clock and his lean features settled into pensive lines.

"I don't think there's time to put my plan into action tonight, for the hour is growing late and Renbourne won't remain at The Rising Sun much longer."

"Not necessarily," returned Wiggins excitedly, "for I'm told that Mr. Renbourne has held forth at his table for the last two nights."

Holmes lifted a surprised eyebrow. He took the fuming briar from his clenched teeth and made an interested sound deep in his throat.

"This is a change of habit, indeed," he remarked. "I think my supposed rival is becoming desperate for trade. Never before has he remained in one spot more than a single evening. It bodes well for him returning to The Rising Sun tomorrow when the sun begins to set."

Turning to me, Holmes declared, "Watson, we must begin to experiment upon your features forthwith."

"I beg your pardon?"

"I intend to make you look like someone other than Dr. John Watson. In fact, I plan to make you look like *two* other individuals."

"My word!" I explained. "Why two and not one?"

"Because you are going to hire Renbourne to assist in killing *yourself*. And inasmuch as you must wear the face of a would-be murderer, as well as that of his victim, I must contrive to provide you with two separate presentations. We'll decide upon your wardrobes later. But for the moment, the malleability of your countenance is what interests me."

Handing Wiggins another sovereign and thus dismissing him, Holmes brought out his box of theatrical disguises. He insisted that I remain in my chair while he fussed about the contents and examined this item and that in the flickering gas light.

It was a weary evening I spent as various whiskers and wigs were applied to my head, and other contrivances inserted into my nostrils to dilate them. I found the entire ordeal abominable. But I stood for it, since I knew it was for a good cause.

Finally, Holmes was satisfied with one of his facial concoctions. I looked at myself in the mirror and didn't care for the profusion of muttonchop whiskers, nor the way my nostrils were grotesquely distorted. The whiskers served to all but conceal my lips, and a brown bowler hat was placed on my head so as to obscure the configurations of my brow.

I suppose that I would have been more thunderstruck by the transformation, but I was extremely tired of the gyrations leading up to the final result.

I went up to bed wearing my own features. And was glad for it.

The next day, Holmes coached me in my role.

"You are a haberdasher, Watson. Your name is Philby – Alan Philby. You wish to have your brother-in-law removed from this world, and are willing to do the deed yourself – but you cannot afford a misstep."

"And what is my motive for doing this?" I asked dubiously.

Holmes pondered a moment. "Your marriage is in a precarious state, and your brother-in-law is having a strong influence on your wife. You fear that she is going to leave you. Divorce would ruin you. It is motive enough, I should think."

"And what is the name of my untrustworthy brother-in-law?"

"George Smithers. It is imperative that you keep the two names straight. Explain yourself slowly and carefully as you ingratiate yourself into Mr. Renbourne's confidence. The fact that he is holding forth at The Rising Sun beyond his usual term of occupancy suggests that he has been putting the word out, but failing to attract paying customers."

"Where will you be when I make this assignation?"

"I would rather not say – simply because I haven't decided. Renbourne pierced my previous impersonation as Mr. Nigel Nettlesmith. It isn't inconceivable that he would penetrate a different one. More to the point, I don't care to have you looking around, seeking me, no matter how covertly you do so, so I'll not vouchsafe to you that I will be present. Remember that it is our purpose to gull Renbourne into a criminal conspiracy, not to capture him on this occasion. He must be drawn into our web carefully, lest he escape like a common bottle fly."

"I quite understand."

Holmes went about his careful business of transforming me into the purely imaginary Philby, and then rummaging around among his wardrobe for suitable attire.

When I left Baker Street, I was the picture of a London businessman. I felt awkward, but was confident in my disguise.

A hansom cab conveyed me to The Rising Sun pub on Cloth Fair in Smithfield, which sat under the looming edifice that was St. Bartholomew the Great Church. By the time I arrived, the sky was growing dusky, and I steeled myself to enter.

The place wasn't very busy, owing to the early hour, but six customers were frayed around the smoky interior redolent with the pungent aromas of diverse types of tobacco. My gaze swept the tables.

I had only an imperfect idea of what Renbourne looked like. Holmes had described him to me, but as Wiggins explained, the rogue had made certain alterations calculated to obscure his identity. I pushed inside carefully and looked about the dimly-lit interior of the public house.

I spied what I thought to be the furtive fellow and drifted over to a table not far from his. After ordering a pint of stout, I settled in and drank slowly.

This gave Renbourne time to become accustomed to my presence. From time to time, I glanced in his direction and saw that he was studying me with his uneasy eyes. But of course he would. He was sizing me up as a potential customer.

I took him to be somewhat more than forty years of age, although his greying temples suggested a man of fifty. He possessed a bit of a haggard air consistent with a man who had served time in prison, as well as a fugitive criminal who dared not let down his guard. All of this lined up with the description Holmes had given me. The one difference was that he no longer wore his grey mustache. Wiggins had reported that he was now cleanly shaven.

At length, I spoke up in a voice that didn't carry far. I gave my delivery a slightly Cockney twist without overdoing it.

"Would you be the Mr. Renbourne I have been hearing so much about?" I inquired.

"I will not deny it," replied the man.

I nodded somberly. "Would you like to join me?" I asked.

"I rather prefer that you join me, for I'm quite comfortable in my present seat."

I took up my glass and went over to him, and so we were face-to-face at last.

The fellow looked pale and dissolute. I imagined that he slept much of the day away. He certainly didn't look like a man with an honest trade, much less a former barrister.

"I understand that you advise men with certain . . . *difficulties*?" I queried.

Renbourne simply nodded gravely, his eyes never leaving my face.

"I have a difficulty. And it is a delicate one."

I looked around to make sure no one was within earshot. Renbourne did likewise.

"I'm adept at resolving difficulties," he stated, "for I possess the type of logical mind capable of untangling them. For a price, of course."

"Of course," I returned. "Here is my issue."

I lowered my voice still further. "I'll not give you my name, except to say that my first name is Alan. Presently, I am having trouble in my marriage. I believe I can navigate my way through these troubled waters, except for one sticky issue."

"Marriage counseling isn't among my skills, but I'm prepared to listen to you to the last," returned Renbourne quietly.

"As I said," I continued, "I believe I can manage my own personal affairs. The problem lies with my brother-in-law, my wife's elder brother. They are quite close and remain so. I believe he's supporting her thinking that she might be better off without me."

"I see. He is an obstacle to your continued marital bliss."

"He is a dire threat," I said emphatically. "And I must be rid of him."

"What does he do for a living?"

"He drives a growler. This irks me, for I consider him to be below my station in life. Yet he is attempting to undermine me with my own wife."

"And so he must be eliminated," prompted Renbourne.

"Quite so," I said hoarsely. "But the plan must be foolproof."

"No plan is entirely proof against misadventure and ill luck," returned Renbourne. "But just as one can caulk a ship's hull against leaks, it is possible to make a plan that is highly resistant to failure."

"I'm listening," I said quietly while taking another sip from my glass.

Renbourne leaned forward conspiratorially. "It is always best to arrange matters so that events appear to be accidental. Given the man's livelihood, contriving an accident involving his carriage or horses would seem to be the best approach."

"Yes, yes, I can see that. But what do you propose?"

"Perhaps you might endeavor to weaken the spokes of his wheels with a hand saw so that when the growler executes a sharp turn, the wheels come apart and precipitate the man onto the cobbles. Conceivably, he might be run over by any horses that happen to be following his carriage."

"That sounds rather chancy," I remarked.

"True. It requires as much luck as skill. Perhaps more so. But it could be worth the effort. He isn't likely, should he survive, to think that he is the target of a murder plot."

"I think I would prefer something more certain," I pressed. "I fear I haven't the nerve for a second attempt should the first fail."

"Very well. I don't recommend this course of action, but here it is. If you can hire him some dark night, preferably on a rainy or foggy evening, you could fire a pistol from the comfort of your carriage seat into his spine. Make sure the caliber is sufficient to pierce the carriage body and penetrate his back. And finish him off with a shot to the head for good measure. But before you leave the scene, you must take his wallet so that, by all appearances, he has fallen victim of a common robber. Proper disposal of the incriminating pistol is of the highest importance, which I leave to your own devices. Of course, you must dress in a manner entirely unlike your own and disguise yourself as much as it is possible to do so."

"I could shave my whiskers," I suggested.

Renbourne shook his head violently. "No! Shaving your whiskers – either before or after the murder – would only call attention to yourself. Scotland Yard is quite canny in these matters. They would ask you why you did so. A ready answer, no matter how well thought out, wouldn't absolve you. You might not be the chief suspect, but something so out of the ordinary would call attention to you in a way that Scotland Yard wouldn't ignore."

"Very good," I said sincerely. "That is very wise of you. I will simply disguise myself."

Renbourne had barely touched his drink, which I took to contain bitters, a fact I took to signify a state of temporary poverty. Now he took a long sip and placed the glass on the well-worn oaken table.

"And now I must ask you to quietly and unobtrusively pass to me the sum of twenty-five pounds," he said in a low tone of voice.

This wasn't unexpected. Holmes had prepared me for the eventuality. Wiggins had informed us of the price Renbourne would demand.

"Alas, I have but ten pounds on my person. However, I'm so pleased with your advice that I'm prepared to bring the balance to your table tomorrow night, if you will simply be patient until then."

Reynard Renbourne regarded me silently for some moments. There were queer lights in his eyes that I couldn't read. I imagine that he was measuring me. I also imagined that he was weighing the risks of coming back for the balance of his fee. Holmes had counted on this.

At length, he said quietly, "I am prepared to operate on the terms you state. I assume you will not undertake the difficult task between now and then."

"No, of course not. It will take careful planning."

"Very well. Come tomorrow night at seven o'clock. No earlier or later. I am growing weary of The Rising Sun and plan to move on to fresher pastures."

Slipping him ten pounds and rising from my chair, I said, "I would shake your hand, but it wouldn't be appropriate under the circumstances."

Renbourne gave me a kind of half-hearted salute that didn't rise beyond his shoulder.

"Good night, sir," he said dully.

"Until tomorrow evening," I returned.

With that, I took my leave and found an available hansom cab to whisk me back to Baker Street. When I pushed into our sitting room, Holmes greeted me with an uplifted face that was marked by an expectant curiosity.

"What news?"

"Success! Your rival has presented me with a solid plan for the murder of the imaginary George Smithers. I am to hire his growler while in disguise and, at an appropriate spot, fire a pistol bullet into his back and relieve him of his wallet before disappearing into the night, thus making it appear that he fell victim to impersonal robbery."

"It isn't a particularly brilliant plan," remarked Holmes dryly, "but it has its features."

"I gave him ten pounds, with the promise of another fifteen tomorrow. He insisted that I return to The Rising Sun at seven o'clock sharp. I don't think he will wait much after that, for he seems eager to push on. Perhaps to quit London altogether."

"Very good. You played your part to perfection. You will go to the Rising Sun tomorrow night and consummate the deal, and I shall accompany you."

"Of course," I suggested, "you'll inform Scotland Yard in advance."

Holmes hesitated briefly. "I'll make certain arrangements for the apprehension of Mr. Renbourne. But I must confront him first, for it is a matter of personal honor. Nevertheless, I'm pleased that we have him ensnared so perfectly. The man is quite intelligent, but he appears to have become desperate. That will be his undoing."

Holmes smoked quietly for some time. He appeared satisfied with his plan.

For my part, I was quite pleased with myself. But then a thought occurred to me.

"Holmes, if we're to finish this business tomorrow night, of what use is the second disguise, that of George Smithers?"

"It is part of my plan. You'll recall that Renbourne fancies himself as my opposite and rival. I intend to teach him a lesson. When you return to The Rising Sun, you will not be Alan Philby, but George Smithers, the intended victim."

"I don't see the point of that," I said doubtfully.

Holmes smiled a rather secretive smile.

"No, I suppose that you don't. But I'll explain it to you tomorrow. For now, I prefer to contemplate the satisfactory culmination of my plan."

As one might imagine, this left me rather befuddled. But I understood Holmes's sometimes recondite ways, and chose not to press the matter.

The next day was quite ordinary, but by the time evening approached, Holmes brought out his box of theatrical disguises and proceeded to give me an entirely different face than that of Mr. Alan Philby.

Here again, whiskers played a large role, but they were very different. He did some other things, some of which were uncomfortable. My complexion was made red and rough, as would befit a man who drove a growler for a living. When I stood up and looked into the mirror, I wasn't quite so startled as before, but the change was still noteworthy.

Once Holmes had furnished me with suitably shabby attire, I pronounced myself ready to make the rendezvous.

Leaving Baker Street, we walked down the street to where a rank of cabs stood waiting, and Holmes prudently selected the third in line. This was a growler, not the customary hansom cab he usually preferred, owing to the fleetness and agility of those light carriages in negotiating London's many narrow byways. I thought nothing of it, for I understood that he required a carriage in which could lurk unsuspected for a time. An open hansom cab simply wouldn't do.

During the ride, Holmes laid out the scheme for me.

"You will enter the establishment without me. Go directly to Mr. Renbourne's table where you will confront him, announcing that you know everything about the plot to murder yourself. No doubt Renbourne will be startled in the extreme and not know what to do. At which point, I will swoop in and make a proper arrest."

"Would that not be the proper province of Inspector Lestrade?" I asked.

"Normally, yes, but you understand that this is a personal matter. I wish to apprehend the blackguard myself. And to make it clear that he has stirred my ire and consequently reaped the regrettable rewards of doing so."

"I see," I returned. "Yes, such a performance is sure to throw Renbourne off balance, making his capture a matter of form."

Holmes's plan seemed impervious to failure, and I trusted that it would come off without complications. He told the growler driver to stop around the corner from our destination. Then he sent me ahead.

"I will follow directly," he promised. "Do not fear for your safety, for I've brought my pistol."

"I trust that it won't be necessary to use it."

"One never knows," replied Holmes.

Leaving the carriage, I walked up Cloth Fair Street and entered The Rising Sun. My eyes went to the table where I had last seen Reynard Renbourne. I was slightly taken aback not to find him seated there. It was two minutes short of seven o'clock. This probably signified that the man was still on his way. No doubt the knave intended to take the remainder of his fee and depart as soon as possible. I was forced to take a table and await his entrance while I nursed a glass of stout.

But that entrance never came. The appointed hour came and went. Then it was half-past-seven. By eight o'clock, I felt certain that Renbourne wasn't going to show his face.

Holmes entered The Rising Sun at quarter-past-eight, came directly to my table, and sat down.

"There's no sign of him," I said quietly.

"The man is canny. Perhaps he smelt a trap."

"What will you do?"

"If he comes in now and spies me, the game is up. I'm going to step out. You may follow or tarry longer, if you wish. But I think for tonight at least the cause is lost."

"I quite agree," I stated quietly. "We should go."

During the dispirited journey back to Marylebone, Holmes fumed rather noticeably.

"This Renbourne is the most vexatious adversary I have encountered in some time," he said tightly. "He has the annoying knack of slipping free of my best snares, as if my mind is an open book to him."

Recalling the clever rogue's escape from one of Holmes's traps during their prior clash, I could hardly disagree.

"Inasmuch as he offers to advise his unsavory clients in the avoidance of your investigative notice," I suggested, "conceivably he had made a deep study of your methods and thinking."

"Rot, Watson!" snapped Holmes. "The bounder wisely takes no chances with his liberty. And in the exercising of ordinary precautions, he simply experiences runs of ill-deserved luck. But they are sure to run out. And when they do, I shall have my man."

I didn't offer my private opinion that my good friend appeared reluctant to give his confounding foe the proper credit where it was due. I suspected that I was correct in my estimation and Holmes simply refused to see it, so greatly was he offended by the criminalist's temerity in holding himself up to be a rival and counter-force to London's leading consulting detective.

After returning to Baker Street, we sat down and availed ourselves of different brands of tobacco. Holmes settled down with his black clay pipe while I enjoyed several cigarettes.

Neither one of us spoke for the better part of an hour.

I was at the point of asking Holmes what he might do next when he volunteered his next maneuver.

"I intend to place a notice in the agony columns of *The Times* in the hope that Renbourne reads them. I'll use your assumed name and offer to meet the man at another public house to settle the outstanding debt."

"If he feared to return to The Rising Sun," I pointed out, "why would you think he would make such an assignation?"

"I don't know that he would. But I cannot think of another certain way to reach him that isn't long and laborious. If the man is as desperate as I believe, given your report that he nursed a single glass of bitters during your meeting, he may well be tempted."

"He would also be quite chary."

"No doubt, no doubt. But let us see what happens when we bait the hook. Don't forget that Renbourne is in possession of incriminating facts concerning the murderous plans of Mr. Alan Philby in regards to the fictitious George Smithers. He would naturally assume that Philby would be eager to pay off the outstanding sum, if for no other reason than to avoid future blackmail."

"I see your logic."

"Let us trust that Renbourne hasn't already departed London. Otherwise, we may never locate him."

Holmes did as he said he would. Being the thorough sort, he placed notices in the agony columns of several London newspapers. After that, we waited.

After three days, an answering notice appeared. It said, simply:

Philby – I would be pleased to share a pint of stout with you at The Fortune of War.

After reading this, I noted, "He doesn't specify a night."

"Renbourne is highly cautious, as well as canny. You are expected to show up at The Fortune of War tavern until he feels it safe to put in an appearance. Note that the spot isn't far from The Rising Sun. Perhaps he has a room in, or possibly adjacent to, that neighborhood."

"I imagine that for this plan to properly succeed," I declared, "I must revert to the personality of Alan Philby."

"There is no better way," agreed Holmes. "I had hoped that my original plan would work out to my satisfaction, but this will be enough to capture the man. You are able to testify as to his willing participation in a murderous scheme, and that will be sufficient to charge him at the dock."

For four consecutive nights, Holmes and I hired a growler to take us to The Fortune of War, where I took a table in expectation of Reynard Renbourne's reappearance.

Holmes remained outside. He had become quite friendly with the driver of the growler, and hired the same man for each evening's trip so that he could sit quietly in the cab rank and not be noticed.

By this time, Holmes and I had grown weary of applying the accouterments of George Smithers each night to no avail. I was equally weary of the repeated nightly ordeals.

"Confound the vexatious man," Holmes fumed. "I'm afraid that I must have you show up as Philby, for the appurtenances of George Smithers have been ruined by excessive use."

And so I submitted to becoming Alan Philby once more by an inordinately peeved Holmes, who denounced Reynard Renbourne as a stubborn thorn in his side for perpetually foiling his carefully-considered schemes.

"So much for you clever ploy to waylay your quarry as George Smithers."

"I will just have to make do," muttered Holmes. "All is not lost, Watson."

It was upon the fourth night that Reynard Renbourne entered the establishment.

He wore his shapeless brown hat low and kept the wide brim turned downward to shade his features in the dimness of the public house. I noted that he had grown a thin beard and mustache since I saw him last. They were quite grey.

When he spied me, Renbourne came directly to my table. Placing a vertical finger in front of his compressed lips, he admonished me to keep silent. Taking the seat opposite me, he said quietly, "You know what I came for."

"I do." I had the money in a small purse and gestured that I would hand it to him under the table. This I did.

"It is good doing business with you," he said. "I had doubts, Philby, but now I see that you are an honest man."

"Honest, true," I remarked in an undertone, "but not entirely so."

Renbourne gave a light little laugh. It seemed incongruous. He hadn't taken off his hat. But now he touched its brim in a sort of goodbye salute. Standing up, he turned to go. But before he could reach the door, the way was blocked.

A man stood in the doorway. He was dressed as I had left Holmes, but he didn't wear Holmes's face. His features were ruddy and his eyes dark and piercing. They looked in Renbourne's direction with an accusatory fire.

"So!" he exclaimed. "I find you here, my dear brother-in-law. And do not think I don't know your game! You intend to murder me – and this dastard is your accomplice!"

Hearing this, Reynard Renbourne came bolt upright and made a stumbling charge for the door, which Holmes blocked. For it was indeed he.

The altercation was brief and rather muscular. I had no doubt that Holmes would come out on top except that Reynard Renbourne slipped a knife of some sort from a pocket and used it to slash at the obstructing man, cutting him on the back of his wrist rather severely.

"My God!" I exclaimed, rising to my feet.

With a cry of blind anger, Renbourne elbowed Holmes aside and somehow managed to break out into the night.

Rushing up to Holmes, who had dropped to one knee, I pulled out my handkerchief and began bandaging the bleeding wrist as expertly as I could.

"Holmes – he has cut you!"

"Yes," Holmes shot back. "And more severely than I would care to admit, for the strike prevented me from drawing my revolver. I underestimated the ferocity of his fear. He was determined to escape at all costs."

Outside, I could hear a carriage departing with alacrity, making its familiar growling noise on the cobbles.

Having bandaged Holmes's wrist, I rushed to the doorway and saw the growler we had hired wheeling away. Inside was Reynard Renbourne. The angry fellow was staring back in my direction. There was no question that it was him. His glare was filled with baffled rage.

"He's getting away!" I cried.

Holmes stood up, examined the bandage and seemed unperturbed.

"Do you not intend to give chase?" I demanded.

"There is no rush. But we will hire a cab and go directly to Scotland Yard."

I was nonplussed, to put it mildly.

"Should we not find a policeman? The man is escaping once again."

"No," Holmes said coolly. "Not escaping. However, let us find a cab. I'll explain everything on the way to our destination."

Soon, we were clattering along London's cobblestoned byways. Holmes was examining the bandage critically and tightening it. The worst of the bleeding seemed to have abated.

"Don't worry," he stated calmly as he removed the false elements that had so altered the hawk-like cast of his countenance. "It will heal. As for

Reynard Renbourne, perhaps you noticed that I had made friends with a certain growler carriage driver."

"I did. I assumed that you had made special arrangements so that he was available these last few evenings."

Holmes nodded. "Said driver is now conveying Renbourne to Scotland Yard's gate, as I previously instructed him to do in the event of a successful escape."

"But surely the knave will leap out once he realizes his inevitable destination."

"The driver is under strict instructions to travel too swiftly to permit that to be done safely. More tellingly, the carriage doors are contrived so that they lock upon being shut tight, preventing escape. This is another precaution I took, with the ready cooperation of the driver. Moreover, he is free to use his horse whip to keep Renbourne under control. I have no doubt that my supposed rival will be in the custody of Inspector Lestrade's men once the growler pulls up at Scotland Yard's entrance."

This last all but took my breath away. I settled back into my seat as the hansom cab bounced along.

Before long, we were pulling up before Scotland Yard. There was no sign of the growler carriage. We hurried inside and found Reynard Renbourne in handcuffs, seated in the inspector's office, his head and shoulders slumped in defeat, the very portrait of a condemned man. He didn't look up at our arrival.

"I've been expecting you, Mr. Holmes," greeted Lestrade. "This is a fine bit of business you have contrived. The carriage driver who brought this man to us explained everything."

"Thank you, Lestrade. I regret that I kept you in the dark until I had achieved success, but I believed my scheme to ensnare this blackguard to be sound, if only I could put it into effect. It wasn't as perfect as I originally imagined, but it did work out to my satisfaction in the end."

"And to the satisfaction of Scotland Yard, I might add," stated Lestrade. "I assume that the knife we took from thus prisoner is the one that injured your hand."

"It was."

Lestrade nodded with grim satisfaction. "Then we'll add that charge to our long list."

"Watson is prepared to testify in court," Holmes offered, "that Renbourne advised him in a clever scheme of murder that was never carried out, for the victim was entirely imaginary."

Hearing this, Reynard Renbourne lifted his sullen head and commenced mouthing the most abominable curses I have heard since my days in the British Army.

Inspector Lestrade remonstrated him for his language, and then added, "It would seem that you are returning to Newgate Prison, after all. Thanks to Mr. Sherlock Holmes and Dr. Watson."

"Two names I will despise until my dying day," snapped Renbourne.

Holmes addressed the man gravely. "You, sir, are an utter fraud. I imagine that I would have gotten on your trail eventually, but I would like you to clearly understand that it was your temerity in calling yourself my rival that set me on the certain path culminating in your destruction. I value my reputation. And I don't care to be challenged or otherwise undermined by the likes of you."

Turning to Lestrade, Holmes stated, "I imagine you don't need our presence any further. I should like to have my wound properly dressed, so Watson and I will take our leave."

"Very good, sir. Thank you both again."

As we turned to go, Reynard Renbourne, otherwise Josiah Graymark, came out of his chair and shook his manacled fists in our direction rather vigorously.

"This isn't yet over, Sherlock Holmes! This is far from over! You will rue the day you ever heard my name."

"Perhaps that hour might yet come to pass," remarked Holmes evenly, "but I imagine that you will regret the day you invoked my name long before such an unlikely time can ever come round. Newgate Prison will see to that."

We left Scotland Yard with Reynard Renbourne's foul oaths ringing in our ears. For my part, I feared the man's vow of vengeance, but Holmes seemed entirely unperturbed.

"If Renbourne ever is released from prison," he observed, "he will be a very, very old fellow, and not someone to fear, for Newgate Gaol breaks a man rather soundly. It had previously broken Josiah Graymark to the point where he had to become Reynard Renbourne to keep on. I don't think he has it in him to come back from this defeat."

"I trust you are correct. Now let's see to that frightful wound."

"Good old Watson!" exclaimed Holmes. "I could have no more better or useful friend than you."

Josiah Graymark was duly convicted. He chose to represent himself before the Old Bailey. The crux of his defense was that inasmuch as he had conspired with the imaginary Alan Philby to murder the equally imaginary George Smithers, no crime was committed.

This dodge fell upon deaf ears, of course. His other criminal involvements were introduced as evidence. Then there was his prior conviction for fraud weighing against leniency. This is what had brought disgrace to a previously respectable barrister.

I was obliged to testify to Graymark's culpability in the scheme to murder the imaginary George Smithers, as was Sherlock Holmes as the architect of the snare that resulted in the capture and subsequent trial. Our testimony was quite damning.

The judge sentenced the angry fellow to more than ten years, a sentence I thought was far too light. But because he hadn't personally committed any murder, merely advised other perpetrators, perhaps the judge took that into consideration. I don't know and I care much less.

All I can record is that I felt immensely safer once the defeated villain was hauled off in irons to serve out his sentence. I'm not ashamed to say that if the man perished in prison, I, as well as London, would be all the better for it.

Lady Dragonfly
by Robert V. Stapleton

Whenever Mr. Sherlock Holmes is away from Baker Street, on some mysterious enterprise or other, and Dr. Watson is also away from home, I find myself free to concentrate on housework and other such unfinished but necessary business. After all, leaving his rooms in such a terrible mess, with his private papers scattered all over the floor and furniture, Mr. Holmes obviously considers me to be some kind of honorary private secretary. Not that I mind too much about that, though. But given the choice, I would rather have him living here than being elsewhere – wherever it is he goes.

This has been especially true over the last couple of days, when I wished with all my heart that he had been easier to contact. I have always valued his wisdom, and I needed that insight to be somewhat more accessible in the current circumstances. Other people might prove to be clever, and willing to share their valuable experience with ordinary mortals such as myself, but my need was for something a little more immediate and practical – something which Mr. Holmes, however infuriating he might be at times, can always be relied upon to provide.

My morning of housework was interrupted that day by a heavy pounding upon the front door.

On opening it, I found a cabby standing on the threshold, with a young girl standing beside him. The cabby was a man I recognized, a fellow we knew as Albert, whose cab regularly passed our front door. The girl I had never seen before in my life. She looked to be confused and frightened. Poor thing.

"Pardon me, ma'am," said the driver as he touched his cap, "but I found this young girl down by the docks. It seemed to me that she was lost, and I was wondering who might be able to help her. She won't tell me who she is, or where she's come from. Refuses to say a word, in fact. I was wondering if perhaps Mr. Holmes or even Dr. Watson might be willing and able to help her."

"I'm sure either of those gentlemen would be willing to help," I told him by way of reply. "But Mr. Holmes is away just at the moment, and Dr. Watson is visiting his brother in America. San Francisco, I believe."

The cabby gave a disappointed grunt, and looked down at his feet, as though seeking inspiration there.

I looked down at the barefooted young girl still standing beside him on my doorstep. Here was one I might describe as a waif and stray, if I ever I had seen one. The child, perhaps no more than ten or eleven years of age, turned her face to look up at me. With the morning sunshine lighting up her tangled hair and her dirty, tear-stained face, my heart was touched. Perhaps there was more to this poor soul than immediately met the eye. We would have to see.

I sighed. "Very well," I told the cab man. "Leave her here. I'll see what I can do to help."

The cabby smiled and again touched his cap, grateful that at least one responsibility had been lifted from his shoulders that morning. Then he turned and jumped back onto the perch of his hansom cab and trotted away before I had a chance to change my mind.

"Well," I said to the girl, who was standing before me, "welcome to 221 Baker Street."

There appeared to be no response. No change to the blank expression on her face. And those eyes were still looking up at me. What exactly lay behind those eyes? I realized I would have to work hard at drawing her out of her shell.

"Come along inside," I told the girl, "and we'll see what we can do for you."

Still saying nothing, the girl followed me indoors, watching as I closed the door on the outside world. This seemed to give her a small amount of relief, which showed in the way her tensed body seemed to relax a little. Perhaps the things that she feared most in all the world lay on the other side of that portal.

"What's your name?" I asked the girl.

No reply came from her.

"My name is Mrs. Hudson," I explained.

Still no reaction from the girl.

"This is where the famous Mr. Sherlock Holmes lives," I said. "The celebrated consulting detective."

At this, the girl's face lit up with half a smile. The name of my famous lodger seemed to mean something to her. And why not? From what other people had told me, I knew that his fame in recent years had spread far and wide.

The girl still didn't say anything, but at least she had displayed some kind of human reaction. Perhaps this was a small sign of hope for our developing relationship.

"Now," I said as I looked her over, "the first thing you need is a good hot bath."

At least she didn't run away at the suggestion of encountering hot water. Perhaps she had been brought up properly after all.

I called to my kitchen maid. "Anna, put on the kettles, and get out the zinc bath for me. We're going to get some washing done here."

"Yes, Mrs. Hudson," came the reply.

"And then take yourself down to the market and buy some clothes that might be suitable for this little girl. I think she hasn't changed out of these togs for a long time now. Anyway, see what you can get for her."

Once I had given the maid a few coins and sent her out in search of some new clothing, I turned once more to the girl.

"Come along, young lady," I told her as I led her toward the zinc bath, which was now placed in the middle of the parlour floor. "We really must get you washed and dried."

When I reckoned it was about the right temperature, I began to pour out the water that had been heating in the kettles on the cast-iron kitchen range, making sure it was hot enough, without being scalding. In place of the kettles, I put the pot of stew onto the range to heat up. Ours is one of those pots that is always on the go. A great variety of things, always edible and often tasty, go into it every day, and food comes out of it as and whenever it is needed. There are no rules regarding our stew. Chicken, lamb, beef go into it if we can get hold of any of those, together with green vegetables – leeks, onions, and cabbage, ready for when any need might arise. Such a need had now indeed made its appearance, but first I had to give our new young guest a good scrubbing.

"Come along now and slip out of those clothes," I told her. "And step into the bath."

Now, with her clothing removed, I could see that this girl was in need of a good scrubbing. Amongst other things.

"My goodness!" I exclaimed. "You really are a bag of skin and bones, aren't you?"

I rolled up my sleeves and began using the soap, using a sponge to apply the water, and wielding a stiff brush to remove the dirt. The water I poured over her head made her squeal with apparent delight, but she still wasn't saying anything, however much I tried to get her to break her silence.

Eventually, the girl was scrubbed clean and wrapped up in one of my enveloping bath towels. By now, the kitchen maid had returned, carrying a bundle of assorted clothing.

"This is the best I could get at such short notice, Mrs. Hudson," said Anna. "I even managed to get a pair of shoes for her. I hope they'll fit."

"I'm sure they will," I replied as I examined the items carefully.

A few minutes later, the girl was dry, dressed, and seated at the kitchen table, watching me ladle out a bowlful of stew into a bowl which I then placed in front of her.

While I bustled about the kitchen, and Anna set about her cleaning duties, the girl began to spoon the stew into her mouth, with a passion I have rarely seen before even among young children of my acquaintance.

When she was finished, the girl sat back and looked up at me.

And smiled.

"Thank you, Mrs. Hudson," she said as she wiped her mouth on the back of her sleeve.

"Oh, so you do speak then, do you?" I asked her.

The girl smiled. "I'm Candy," she said. "Is this really the place where Mr. Holmes lives?"

"Yes – upstairs in No. 221b. And I'm his landlady."

"Really? I've heard tell of him. He really is a wonderful man, isn't he?"

"I think so."

She gave a great big grin. Perhaps she felt safe being here. I hoped so.

"Now, Candy, can you please tell me where you have come from."

"I'm from a village called Hope."

"Hope?"

"Near Boston."

"Boston, Lincolnshire?"

"Nah. Boston, Massachoosetts."

"The United States?"

"Of course."

"I thought you sounded American."

"And you talk funny, as well."

"Yes, but that's because I'm Scottish," I explained. "I've never quite lost my accent, though I've lived in London for a great many years."

"And I'm London, through and through," came the voice of my kitchen maid from the scullery.

"Now, let's talk about you, Candy," I told her. "However do you come to be here?"

"Where's here?"

"London, England."

"Is that where I am?" Her eyebrows raised in amazement.

"Certainly. Where did you think you were?"

"I don't know. Nobody's told me anything. All I do know is that this is a very big place, with lots of people I've never met before."

"You must have come here by boat."

263

"Yes. By boat."

"A big boat?"

"Are you jokin'? It's tiny. I was awful seasick for a lot of the time."

"Who did you come with?"

"My Uncle," she replied grimly. "I just call him Uncle Flynn."

"We need to find your Uncle Flynn, and discover exactly what you're supposed to be doing here."

"Well, good luck with that!" said Candy. "But I don't want him to touch me again. Ever."

"Was he cruel to you?"

"Yes. Then, when we got here, Uncle Flynn locked me in a room. In a warehouse, I guess. Near the river. But I escaped."

This sounded very worrying. I had no choice. I knew that I had to find this man and force him to look after Candy. Or at least provide for her.

"Where is your boat now, Candy?" I asked her.

"On the river."

"The Thames?"

She shrugged "I reckon."

"And what's the boat called?"

"*Lady Dragonfly*," she said. "That I do know."

I knew the very next thing I had to do. Although I strongly disapproved of them, I realized that I needed the help of some of Mr. Holmes's friends: He called them "The Baker Street Irregulars" – a dreadful shower of children. But I had need of them all the same, and I required their services immediately.

A few minutes later, the little gang of street children crowded into my parlour, as Wiggins, the spokesman of the group, stepped forward and told me that they were happy to help in any way they could.

I had grown more and more used to these children over the previous few years, so I was ready to accept them, cautiously, as Mr. Holmes's friends.

"Mr. Holmes is away just at the moment," I told them, "but I'm sure he will settle up with you as soon as he gets back again."

"What do you want us to do, Mrs. Hudson?" Wiggins asked me.

"I need your help to find a small boat. Moored on the River Thames. Somewhere."

"What's the name of the boat?" demanded Wiggins.

"*Lady Dragonfly*."

I turned to Candy. "Do you have any idea where the boat is lying?"

She blinked and shook her head. "This side of the river, I guess," she said. "I know I didn't cross any water to get here. But that's about all I can tell you."

"No matter," said Wiggins. "It should be easy enough to find. We'll send you word as soon as we know where it is. But it would be helpful if we could have some money for expenses. Mr. Holmes usually makes sure we have enough."

I sighed. "How much do you think you're going to need?"

"One and a tanner," said Wiggins. "That should be enough."

"I think that ought to be far more than enough," I told him, as I handed over a silver shilling and six bronze pennies.

"I'm sure Mr. Holmes will let you have the money back when he returns," said Wiggins, a moment before he dodged to one side to avoid the clip round the ear that I aimed at him for his insolence.

I spent the middle part of the day working in the kitchen, and then ordering some of the supplies that we would need for the next few days. And in preparation for the anticipated but unknown time for Mr. Holmes's return home.

I let Candy look through my atlas of the world.

Sitting at the table, she was fascinated to examine the world, and consider her tiny place in it. First, she traced the outline of America with her finger, and then the outline of Great Britain. She seemed amazed to look at the comparative width of the Atlantic Ocean. When she had grown tired of this, Candy spent some time asleep in my easy chair. I left her alone. She looked as if she needed the sleep.

After an hour or so, a knock at the door stirred us all into fresh action.

It was one of the street boys, a small child called Kit.

"Mrs. Hudson."

"Yes? Have you something to report?"

"That's why I'm here," said Kit. "We've finally managed to find that lady you wanted us to look for. The *Lady Dragonfly*."

"Where is she?"

"Come with me, Mrs. Hudson," said Kit. "The others are waiting for us down by the river."

At once, I dropped everything I was doing, grabbed hold of Candy, and hurried with her out into the street. With the two children beside me, I caught an omnibus, which took us down to within a short walk of the riverfront. Kit seemed to know exactly where he was going, so we followed on behind. We found the other children crowded together beside the entrance to one of the riverside wharfs.

"Well, there she is," declared Wiggins, pointing to the jetty. "*Lady Dragonfly.*"

I must admit, I was a bit disappointed when I looked down at the river and saw the boat, moored to the side of the quay.

265

"Is that her?"

"Yes. That's the *Lady Dragonfly*," muttered Candy. "And I don't wanna to set foot on board her ever again."

The caretaker of the wharf noticed that we were taking an interest in the vessel.

"If you want her, you can have her," said the caretaker, as he took his pipe out of his mouth. "The bloke who left her here said he was going to come back and pay the dues he owes, but he hasn't come back again yet."

I was amazed. "And that little boat sailed all the way across the Atlantic Ocean?" I asked him.

"That's the way it seems. She's a bit battered, isn't she? And she could do with a good long visit to the boat-builders' yard. But she's mostly in pretty good condition."

"Yes," said Candy. "Uncle Flynn seemed very proud of the fact that he'd managed to bring her here all in one piece. Or in two pieces, if you include me."

"This must be one of them small boats that people are using to sail across from America," said the caretaker. "It's all the rage at the moment. People seem to be doing it every year. They usually sail from west to east, using the prevailing winds and currents to help them along, but others are talking about going the other way. People sometimes get drowned on the way over. Stupid. Crazy. But definitely the thing to do nowadays if you want an adventure. A battle against the high seas."

"And the storms," chipped in Candy.

"But she really is a lovely boat," I said. "From what little I know about small vessels."

"That's right. Two masts, rigged fore and aft," said the caretaker, now getting into his stride. "A yawl, twenty feet long, clinker built, with a large mainsail and a smaller sail aft on the mizzen mast. Quite a feat to make the three-thousand miles from America in a small boat like that."

"Yes," Candy chipped in. "It took us nearly two months. Or so Uncle Flynn told me when we got here. Seven weeks, he reckoned. That's fifty days, ain't it? Or near enough. At first, I tried to keep a count on how long we were out there, but I soon lost the tally."

"It would have taken a lot of money to build a sturdy vessel like this," said the caretaker.

"Oh, he didn't buy it," said Candy. "And he didn't have it built for him, neither."

"No?"

"Oh, no. He stole it. Just like he stole me."

It was at this point in the conversation that I realized, even more strongly than before, that something very wrong had been happening here.

266

This business seemed to be far more than the abduction of a little girl. Although that alone was bad enough by a long way.

"That does it," I declared. "We're going to take this whole business straight to Scotland Yard. They ought to be able to make some sense out of this."

It was late in the afternoon when Candy and I were ushered into the presence of a Scotland Yard detective inspector. I had met him before, and I knew him to be Alec MacDonald, a fellow Scot from the northeast city of Aberdeen, if I remember correctly. In which case he ought to be good at his job. He was tall with bony features, a large head, and keen eyes which seemed to miss nothing.

"Good afternoon, Mrs. Hudson," he said as I led Candy into the side-room at the Yard.

"Good afternoon, Inspector MacDonald,i" I replied.

"It makes quite a change to have you come to visit us at Scotland Yard," he continued, "instead of one of us coming to visit you in Baker Street. Or, more correctly, in order to visit Mr. Sherlock Holmes."

"Who happens to be away just at the moment," I replied. "And Dr. Watson is away visiting his brother."

"That's how I understand the situation," said MacDonald. "What can I do for you today?"

"I have here a young lady who has just arrived from America."

"Boston," added Candy, with a touch of pride in her voice.

"But the more I hear of her story, the more I realize that her arrival here has been extremely irregular," I explained.

"Yes," replied Candy. "And this is all strange, too. Another Scottish man, at Scotland Yard, and with Mrs. Hudson, who tells me she comes from Scotland too. I tell you – this is all very strange."

"But there are plenty of Scottish people in America and Canada," the inspector replied.

"Uh-huh," Candy agreed. "Like I told you: *Strange*."

Inspector MacDonald opened a folder lying on the desk in front of him, looked through it, and then looked up at Candy, seated across the desk from him.

"Now, let's start at the beginning," he said. "What is your name?"

"Candy."

"Yes, but I need to know a bit more than just that," said the inspector.

"Okay," the girl said. "My full name is Candice Datrix – " She spelled it. " – although I only get called Candice when I'm in deep, deep trouble . . . which happens pretty often when I'm at home."

"I understand. Please carry on."

267

"I come from a small village called Hope. Near Boston."

"Are your parents particularly wealthy?"

"Well, my Pa has plenty of money. He owns half of New England."

"Really?"

"Uh-huh. Well, a lot of it anyway. Then, one day, my Uncle Flynn came along. Only, he ain't no proper uncle at all, if you know what I mean. Just a friend of the family. Well, he used to be. He came and asked me to go with him to see this new boat he had, down at the waterfront in Boston."

"Who exactly was this man, Uncle Flynn?"

She shrugged. "I know him only as 'Uncle Flynn', but I later saw a document that gave his name as Flynn Chatorson." She spelled that too.

MacDonald wrote down the name. "Another Scottish man?"

"No. I think he's Irish. Still strange, though."

"And what does this man look like?"

"He's tall. And he has dark hair. He even has a thick bushy beard. It got bushier and thicker as the days went by."

"Very well. So, as I understand it, this man wanted you to go with him. And you agreed to travel from your home in Hope, down to Boston."

"Of course. Why wouldn't I? My parents seemed to trust him. Well, they did in those days. So why shouldn't I trust him as well? Anyway, he took me to see this boat – a sailboat called the *Lady Dragonfly*."

"That's the boat that's now lying on the Thames," I explained.

MacDonald nodded, and then returned his attention to Candy.

"Carry on, Candy. I'm sure there's much more to the story than just that."

"There sure is," said Candy, leaning forward in her chair. "He called the boat his *Lady*. Anyway, we went on board this boat. Then, before I realized what was happening, he'd cast off from the quayside and set the sails for the open sea. He seemed to know exactly what he was doing. At first, I found it very exciting, being away from home and all. An adventure. But I soon began to worry. I asked him where he was taking me, and he told me we were going to England. That sounded a very long way off, but I didn't want to go to England, so I started shouting that I wanted to be taken back home again. But he wouldn't let me go. He said I could jump overboard if I liked, but that I would drown before I could swim to shore. After that, if I made a fuss at all, he'd hit me. Hard. Until I shut up."

"Do you know why he was taking you away from home?"

"Well, I know he needed an extra pair of hands to sail the boat. It needed at least the two of us to sail that boat. At least that's what he told me. And I guess he was right, because we nearly capsized and sank a couple of times, and we would have done as well if I hadn't been there to help keep the boat upright. I saved his life more than once, and he saved

268

mine. It was awful. I was terrified. I worked very hard, and my hands were rubbed red raw. They're still painful. The wind was icy cold, and the sea was rough."

"Even in springtime?"

"Oh, yes. Mountainous. Or so Uncle Flynn described it."

"In an open boat?"

"Almost. It had a wooden cover over the front part of the boat. That gave us some shelter. And somewhere to sleep, keep warm when possible, and a place to cook our meals."

"What about provisions – food and water and such like?"

"Well, the boat was already fitted with food and barrels of water. Maybe the people who owned it were planning to make their own trip."

"What sort of things did you have to eat?"

"Mostly things that needed heating up. Kept in sacks. Dried meats, hard and chewy. And biscuits. As well as some apples. Like I told you, we had enough space to store the food and to cook our meals in the shelter of the cabin. One time, we very nearly lost all of our provisions overboard. Some of it was washed away one night. But we survived, even if we had to cut back on the rations that he allowed us each."

"And, after all of that," said MacDonald, "you arrived safely in London."

"It took us a long time," said Candy. "Like I already told you, he said that it had taken us something like fifty days to sail from Boston to England. I saw that on a map in Mrs. Hudson's atlas."

"That's good time for such a crossing. Was he trying to break a record?"

"I don't think so. He just wanted to get well away from the police."

"Why?"

"Because, like I told Mrs. Hudson, that boat wasn't his. He'd taken it."

"Had he stolen anything else?"

"Only me, I guess. He kidnapped me, didn't he?"

Inspector MacDonald sat back in his chair. "This is all very interesting, Candy," he said in his distinctive Aberdonian accent. "Thank you for coming here and sharing it all with me, because it all fits in with what I've already heard from our colleagues in Boston. In a wire received from our contact there, Inspector Greenbaum, reports that we ought to be on the lookout for a man called McChatorson. He agrees that this man has stolen that boat, and that he has stolen you as well. As you say, he kidnapped you. He left a note behind, for your parents, demanding a ransom for your safe return."

"The cheek of it!" I replied.

269

"Indeed, Mrs. Hudson," said MacDonald. "But there's much more to this business than even just that. It seems that this man McChatorson was involved in a bank robbery in New York City a few weeks ago, and that he has escaped with a bag full of diamonds."

"No wonder he was anxious to get away from Boston."

The inspector turned once more to the girl. "Did you see anything of those diamonds, Candy?"

Her face became distorted as she thought the matter through. "No," she said eventually. "But I knew he had a bag of some kind with him, tied around his neck. He wouldn't let me go anywhere near it. Even when he was asleep, and I was on lookout, he held on to it tight. I didn't go anywhere near it. I guess that might have been full of the diamonds. I just don't know. It could have been."

"You're probably right."

"Is this man Chatorson still in London?" I asked. "Is he still out there somewhere?"

"We have to assume that he is," replied Inspector MacDonald. "At this very moment, he may be looking for someone who will take those diamonds for him. Some unscrupulous jeweler."

"Do you know of anyone like that?"

"There are plenty of them around," said the inspector. "I imagine Mr. Holmes would know of some of the more likely suspects."

"He might well do so, but he isn't here just at the moment," I explained. "And I have no idea when he'll be back again. He doesn't let me know everything he gets up to."

MacDonald steepled his fingers and looked at Candy.

"I'll get back to my colleague in Boston," he said. "And I'll let him know that you are safe and well."

"Will he let my Ma and Pa know I'm here?"

"I'm sure he will. And you parents will want to come over here and take you back home again."

Candy sniffed. "Gee. I really wanna to go home."

"In the meantime, we have to find this McChatorson. We'll get our men onto the job at once and see if we can locate him."

"And I'll look after Candy," I told him.

I took Candy back to Baker Street. The little girl sat in the window, looking out at the people passing by in the street.

"He's still out there, somewhere," she said, with a tinge of fear in her voice. "I hope those Scotland Yard people can find him. And do it soon."

"I'm sure they are doing their best," I told her.

"Is there nothin' we can do to help them?"

"I think you've done plenty already. You've given a description of the man and what he has done."

"Yes, but we still gotta find him. And get him put away."

As soon as supper was served, eaten, and the pots cleared away, I decided to visit the haunts of my illustrious lodger, Mr. Sherlock Holmes. I knew my way around those rooms, partly because I had so often been left to tidy up after him. He might be a clever and ingenious man, but he is still an untidy rascal. As a result of all this, I probably know his so-called "filing system" better than he does.

I needed to search through his list of contacts and find out what he knew about London jewelers.

By the time daylight was fading outside, I lit the gaslight and managed to locate his lists. I spread them out on the table and began to peruse them. Here were people he trusted, and others he definitely had no confidence in. And, hidden among them, was a list of people who sold and bought jewelery. Which ones to go for? That was the question. I found a piece of paper and wrote down the more prominent ones, those to which Mr. Holmes had added either a star or a red mark, indicating particular significance. I had half-a-dozen, enough to give me somewhere to start, anyway.

I knew there was nothing further I could do that night, so I waited until the following morning to begin any further investigations.

I began at the bottom of the list, with those that Mr. Holmes had merely indicated as being doubtful in character. One by one, I asked them if they had come across an American man trying to sell diamonds. Although they were interested in hearing more, I had nothing to offer them in the way of information, so I eliminated them from my list of possible suspects.

One or two said they had already had a visit from the police and had told them everything they had to say – which wasn't very much. That was of no help to me, so I passed on.

I finally came to an establishment, the one at the very top of his list, which lay along a dark narrow alleyway. I had to be careful to follow the instructions which Mr. Holmes had given for finding the place, until I found myself standing outside a grubby little shopfront with no name above the entrance.

I opened the door and stepped inside. With no one obviously in attendance, I consulted my list. It instructed me to call out for a man named Manuel.

After a moment or two, I noticed the door, presumably leading to the back of the shop, open slowly, and a man of indeterminate age stepped forward from the darkness.

"Yes?" he said in a slow menacing tone. "How can I help you?"

"I am trying to find a man, an American, by the name of Flynn Chatorson."

"Huh," was the reply. "We prefer not to share names here."

"Very wise, I'm sure," I told him. "This man, this American, was trying to sell diamonds. Have you come across him?"

The man sniffed. "I might have done, but then again, I'm not saying."

"He might have been in here."

The man called Manuel gave a non-committal shrug. "If I ever had those diamonds," he told me, "or any diamonds at all, then I certainly don't have them now."

"Oh? Why is that?"

"I'd already have distributed them among my friends and acquaintances. It's the safest way to deal with stones of indeterminate or suspicious origin – especially when nosey parkers come around, or even when the police try to interfere in my business. I'll tell you one thing for nothing: They can't pin nothing onto me."

I tried one last attempt at gaining information from him.

"Have you any idea how I can make contact with this American?"

"No. Now clear off while you still can."

It was clear that this was the end of that interview.

And that line of inquiry.

Or so I imagined.

As I stepped out into the alleyway, I could see very little of the afternoon spring sunshine. The overhanging buildings reached up to the sky and reduced it to a mere sliver of blue.

But my attention was immediately distracted. Directly ahead of me, I noticed a figure step out from a doorway, blocking my path – a man, silhouetted against the light, tall, and powerful.

"You must be that interfering old bat who's trying to scupper my plans," he growled, his American accent strong with emotion.

"What plans might those be?" I asked as I looked him over.

He was tall, with dark hair and beard, and he wore a thick cotton sea-jacket, corduroy trousers, a pair of large sea-boots, and an oversized wide-brimmed black-leather hat perched upon his large head.

"Are you Uncle Flynn?" I asked the man.

"So, you really have seen young Candy."

"And you aren't getting your hands on her again."

"We'll just have to wait and see about that," he snarled. "Won't we?"

I tried to change the subject. "You need to get somebody to cut your hair."

"Just like I'm gonna cut your throat, you meddlesome witch." He laughed.

"But not just now," I told him as I pushed my way past the man. His clothing still carried the smell of the sea, together with the strong aroma of garlic. For a moment, I wondered if Candy liked garlic. I would have to ask her later.

I looked more closely at this man and glanced down at his rough hands. I had read somewhere among Mr. Holmes's notes that a person's hands can tell what kind of job that person does. Mine, for instance, show that I am a hardworking landlady. This man's hands revealed that he'd been a working seaman for many years, even before he sailed with Candy in a small boat across the Atlantic Ocean. I looked for any bulges that showed in his pockets, but I could see nothing that resembled any kind of knife. I also noticed that some dried whitewash had rubbed off on the sleeve of his jacket. It wasn't quite white, but carried a distinctive hue. I imagined him leaning up against a wall as he watched the world go by. Planning, scheming.

I felt confident that he wasn't about to cut my throat. At least not that day.

Had he been bluffing? Was he just a bully?

As I walked away from him, I knew he was watching me. His eyes drilling into my back.

Then, from where he was stan ding behind me, I heard him guffaw a bully's laugh, which made my blood run icy cold.

I reported my findings directly to Scotland Yard, and then decided to hurry home and set about addressing my other duties in Baker Street, including the many and various demands of running the home. In my head, I had a list of domestic things I needed to do. These included calling in at a number of local shops, to order further supplies of bread, meat, and vegetables for the following day. Mr. Holmes still hadn't informed me of when to expect his arrival, so I had to estimate the amount I would need. But then, with Mr. Holmes around, I was used to having to do that sort of thing.

With orders made and essential shopping completed, I made my way home again. With Anna left in charge of the kitchen, I felt fairly confident that I wouldn't have too many disasters and chores to face, except perhaps cleaning and stoking the cooking range.

That afternoon I decided to try to find out where Chatorson was staying. A man like him would probably be at one of the seamen's missions down by the river. I had to find out.

273

I flagged down Albert the cabby and asked him to take me on a tour 'round the various missions. If anyone knew where they were, it would be him.

We rumbled along past the various charitable establishments. I stopped and examined each one that showed any sign of having a wall whitewashed the same colour as that I had seen on Chatorson's coat sleeve. After a couple of hours, I had found what I imagined might be the one. I saw a gathering of men leaning up against that wall.

I climbed down from the cab and asked them if they had come across an American recently.

One of the men nodded. "Aye," he said. "Big. Tough. I wouldn't trust him as far as I could throw the fellow."

I also gave my information to Scotland Yard before returning to Baker Street. It was already evening by the time I was able to give Candy her supper.

"She's been playing with those street children," said Anna, in a tone that suggested she was disgusted at the idea.

"Well, there are plenty of worse things she could be doing," I replied.

"Can I go out there again?" Candy asked me when she had finished her meal.

"I suppose so," I replied. "But don't go too far away. And beware of the London mud."

"What's that?"

"Horse manure. There are piles of the stuff in the streets, and it mounts up during the day. It must be quite thick now. At night, it's collected, taken away, and sold for garden compost."

The sky was already turning dark when Candy went outside again. Rain was clearly in the offing. It promised to turn wet toward the end of the day. Still, I was happy that Candy had promised to stay close by.

As I went to put on the hallway light, I decided it was time for the girl to come in. I opened the door and stepped out into the street.

The volume of traffic had lessened somewhat, so my attention was drawn by the unexpected sound of a carriage coming round the corner of nearby Park Road. It turned out to be a brougham, and it seemed to be coming towards us, along Baker Street at a blistering speed. The poor horses were foaming at the mouth. As the carriage swerved toward the youngsters, the children and I all stepped to one side out of its path, but, as it was in the process of passing them by, an arm reached out of the doorway, grasped hold of Candy, and dragged her inside the vehicle. The girl screamed, loud enough to waken the dead as the brougham picked up speed and thundered away down the street. While the person inside the vehicle had been busy snatching Candy, one of the small boys jumped up onto the back of the carriage and held on tightly.

"That's Little Eric," said Wiggins as the vehicle disappeared round a bend at the end of the street. "He'll find out where that bloke's taking Candy, and then we can go and get her back again."

I nodded. There was little else I could accomplish. I felt powerless to do anything more in the face of such a turn of events.

The half-hour I spent waiting to hear from Little Eric felt like the longest minutes of my entire life. By the time I heard back from him, night had definitely fallen across London, and more especially across Baker Street.

Then Wiggins reported back to me with the single word, "*Dragonfly*".

Well, at least I knew where that was. The boat was still lying at her berth on the edge of the Thames.

Promising to make sure that Little Eric received a reward from Sherlock Holmes, I thanked the street children and set off post-haste down to the river. The cab made good time and dropped me off close beside the wharf where I had last seen the little boat.

Where was Candy?

The night seemed quiet and inky black, but I thought I could see a light shining at the far end of the wharf. Perhaps that was where Chatorson was keeping her. There was only one way to find out.

I pushed open the gate and made my way onto the wharf.

The caretaker's nightwatchman was sitting on a chair near the entrance, and appeared to be fast asleep, oblivious to everything that was taking place around him.

I headed toward the far end, to where I remembered seeing the boat *Lady Dragonfly* on the previous day.

I stood on the edge of the wharf and looked down into the boat. There was no sign of the big man that Candy had told me about.

"Candy," I called out softly.

"I'm here, Mrs. Hudson," came her voice from beneath the boat's protective canopy.

"I've come to take you back."

"Oh, you have, have you?" came a man's voice from close beside me.

I turned and saw the man I'd expected to see earlier. He had changed clothing, and was now wearing a rather shabby suit, which I suppose he had begged, borrowed, or stolen from one of the various seafarer's charities that could be found along the riverside.

"Ah, there you are, Flynn Chatorson," I replied. "We have met before."

"We certainly have. And you told the police where I was staying. They turned up and searched the place. I had to sneak out of the back before they could catch me."

"I've spent so long associated with Mr. Sherlock Holmes," I explained, "that some of his ways have rubbed off onto me – just as some incriminating whitewash from the wall outside your mission rubbed off onto you."

"You are a clever woman," he told me. "Perhaps too clever for me to allow you to remain alive."

He raised a handgun and pointed the barrel directly toward me.

The tension of that moment made my mind grow clearer, and I remembered all the times I had encountered a gun in the past, not forgetting the damage that Mr. Holmes was in the habit of inflicting, through his target practice, on the rooms he occupied upstairs.

Could I disarm the man, without him killing me first? I decided to wait for the right opportunity.

I looked at the man with as much defiance as I could muster. "Are you going to add murder to your long list of crimes, Mr. Chatorson?"

"I will kill you if I have to," he told me. "Now, step on board. We're about to set sail."

"Where are we going?"

"Holland, probably. But you won't reach there alive. I told you before, you have hindered my plans once too often now."

From out of the darkness behind the dark man, I saw an arm reach out and point a handgun at my opponent's head.

"Drop the gun, Chatorson," came a voice from the darkness. "Harm a hair of her head, and I'll blow your brains out."

My opponent turned, and we both looked into the shadows. There we saw the figure of the nightwatchman, but heard the voice of Mr. Sherlock Holmes. His disguise, especially in the darkness, had deceived us all.

"Mr. Holmes!" I cried out in utter delight. With him on our side, I was confident that Candy and I would now be safe.

"My guess is that you won't shoot a man in the back," said Chatorson while he gave a nasty grin, uttered a horrible curse and threw himself into the river. I watched in horror as he then swam away into the darkness.

"He's getting away!" I cried out.

"Don't worry too much about him," said Holmes, in a much more restrained tone of voice. "The river is swarming with police this evening. A small boat will be along soon to pick him up. Then he's going to need all that polluted river water pumped out of his stomach. That should teach him to mend his ways. Then they'll give him a cosy police cell for the night."

276

Mr. Holmes removed the rough coat that had been obscuring his proper identity.

"That's a great deal better," I told him. "Now I know that you're back home."

"Did you really think I didn't know what was going on here?"

"I was beginning to wonder," I admitted.

"I've already settled up with Wiggins," he told me with a grin on his face, so wide it was visible even in the darkness. "And I understand I need to pay you back for some of your expenses incurred."

I nodded. "We can deal with that later."

He nodded.

"And what about tomorrow?" I asked him.

"Tomorrow, that man will be out of our hands and out of our lives. More importantly, a steamer is due in the next week or so, carrying a whole collection of people. They will include Candy's parents, the lawful owner of this boat, and a delegation from the Boston City Police Department, come to take that man home to face trial. There are also a couple of police officers from the New York City Police Department. Our friend Chatorson has a great deal of explaining to do. We must all take a train down in Southampton to welcome them."

"Southampton?" asked Candy as she hugged me more tightly with excitement. "Can I come too?"

"Of course you can," said Mr. Holmes. "They'll all want to see you, Candy – especially your parents – to make sure you really are well and unharmed."

"And can Mrs. Hudson come as well?"

"Yes, if you like."

"How long can they all stop here?" said Candy.

"Not long," replied Mr. Holmes. "They're already booked on a return voyage the following week, and you'll be going back home with them – together. All except the boat's owner, however, as he likely wants to sail his own little wooden boat back to home Boston."

"Well, good luck to him," I said.

"It could be a tough journey," said Mr. Holmes.

"And dangerous," added Candy.

"I imagine you'll have quite a tale to tell your friends when you get back to Boston, Candy," I said as I turned to look down at the girl.

"Hope," she corrected me. "That's the name of our village."

"Of course it is. I was forgetting. I'm sure we all need hope nowadays."

That night, we gathered in Baker Street and enjoyed a late-night feast, improvised from all that we had left in the larder, along with much of the contents of the bottomless stew-pot. We invited everyone to join us – at least those who could manage it at such short notice. And that included, as Candy insisted, the children of the Baker Street Irregulars.

As I have said before, life is usually, but not always, much easier and quieter for me when Mr. Holmes is away from Baker Street, engaged in whatever it is he gets up to. But I have to admit, I prefer to have him here – under my feet, so to speak, where I can keep an eye on him. While Dr. Watson is out of the picture, somebody has to do it, don't they?

The Adventure of the
Willing Suspect
by Gordon Linzner

The hour was close to ten on that dismal morning in October of 1886. Thick clouds were visible through the two broad windows of our flat overlooking Baker Street, with occasional light spurts of rain. This depressing view encouraged no more than a quick glimpse from me. That the sky appeared far grayer now than it had at sunrise did not tempt me to further examine the street below.

I chose instead to relax in one of the more comfortable chairs in our Baker street sitting room. Occasionally I reached across to a side table and nibbled at the remains of hard-boiled eggs and rashers Mrs. Hudson had kindly provided. I'd all but finished poring over a recent copy of *The Sporting Times*, marking up pages that listed the day's horse races.

So far as I could tell, my good friend, Sherlock Holmes, remained in his room, behind a closed door, sleeping late as usual. I hardly expected to encounter him before noon. Such was often his habit when he wasn't actually working a case. He would also spend his free time playing his Stradivarius into the small hours of the night, or indulging, despite my protests, in the occasional injection of a seven-per-cent solution of cocaine.

Aside from the sporting section, I had hoped to come across, in one of the other publications at my side, a story or event intriguing enough to engage my friend's interest during this long series of sterile weeks. Alas, today's papers were of no more use than yesterday's, or for that matter those of the previous week.

I was ready to add this paper to the stack when I heard two sets of feet on the stairs leading to our rooms.

The more familiar pair, of course, belonged to our landlady, Mrs. Hudson.

"Mr. Holmes?" she called, after giving the door a light tap. "Are you awake? You have a visitor."

"One moment, Mrs. Hudson," I called. Rising to my feet, I tightened my dressing gown's sash and moved to the door.

Our landlady received my usual warm expression, as I was always glad to see her. I then raised an eyebrow at the sight of the lean, rat-faced gentleman standing behind her. Inspector G. Lestrade of Scotland Yard held up his left palm slightly in greeting, while bearing a thick brown envelope tucked under his right arm.

"Doctor Watson," he growled, after a brief nod. "A good morning to you."

"And to yourself as well, Inspector," I replied. I turned to our landlady. "Thank you, Mrs. Hudson. I can deal with this matter from here. Unless, Inspector, you would care for some fresh coffee?"

Lestrade shook his head, as I'd anticipated. I indicated Mrs. Hudson was free to leave, and escorted the policeman into the sitting room, offering him Holmes's usual chair before returning to my own.

His dark eyes scanned the room. "Is your friend at home?"

I pointed toward Holmes's bedroom. "I fear he is still abed. Holmes rarely gets up before noon, except when working on a case. But you already know that. Is there some way I can be of assistance in the meantime?"

The inspector raised the envelope. "I brought with me a document that Mr. Holmes requested some weeks ago, for his personal records. It took me this long to obtain an official release."

"Nothing urgent, then, I trust." I reached out to accept the item.

"No, nothing like that," he replied, pulling it back, to my surprise. "This merely confirms some loose ends."

"In that case, you could have brought these here later in the day, when Holmes was up and about. Or sent a messenger to request that he pick it up himself at the Yard, as he usually does." I leaned forward, tapping my chin. "Excuse my curiosity, but I don't recall your visiting our flat this early in the day, except when an active case is involved. Even then . . . ."

Lestrade focused his narrow, beady eyes on mine for an uncomfortable moment, then spread his lips in a wide, somewhat-forced grin. "Your association with Mr. Holmes seems to have whetted your own skills at observation," he offered. "What you say is true. I do have a personal tale to share with Mr. Holmes, and I'm using this belated paperwork as an excuse. I come here not with the usual open request for aid, but rather to ask his advice."

"I trust he will condone such presumptiveness," I replied.

Lestrade continued. "Normally, you would be right. I should wait for him to rise, or arrange to return later, before I recount these details. Under the circumstances, however, and given how fresh this event is, perhaps I might share some details with you."

"That shall not be necessary, Lestrade," rose a familiar voice, "for by your very presence you have earned my attention."

Lestrade and I turned to face the speaker, who now stood before the door to his bedroom, fastening the sash of his purple dressing gown.

Neither of us had noticed Holmes's entrance. He could be quite stealthy when he wished. His expression was stoic, but I couldn't miss the glint of anticipation in his grey eyes.

"You're up early," I observed with a grin.

Holmes winked as he extended a hand in greeting to our ferret-like visitor. "I could hardly mistake the sound of this gentleman's tread, even while I slept, given how often we've worked together. No, please, remain seated. I'll settle in this chair across from you."

Lestrade nodded, then offered the envelope he had brought. When Holmes didn't immediately reach out, he dropped it on a side table. "These papers contain additional details regarding the Wilberford burglary, Mr. Holmes," he explained. "You requested copies of the official records once they became available."

Holmes glanced at the package, raising an eyebrow. "To help flesh out some details in my personal files. Yes. Thank you, Lestrade. Now, if it suits you, perhaps you would share the real reason you needed to call on me before noon?"

The inspector spared me one more narrow glance, then rubbed his hands together, turning back to my friend. "You have me there. I just made the swiftest arrest of my career, less than an hour ago. I thought, if anyone could appreciate hearing the details . . . ."

"It would be me," Holmes finished, his tone gone flat.

"Exactly."

"Yet, if your case is as straightforward as you imply, why are even you here? It's not just for bragging, especially if your suspect is still going through the formalities of being arrested, and it seems unlikely you need my help. My congratulations, perhaps, might be more in order." Holmes turned toward me. "Watson, would you call Mrs. Hudson back? I could do with one of her excellent breakfasts. Might I offer you something to eat as well, Inspector?"

Lestrade waved a hand in dismissal.

Holmes sank back into his chair, gripping the arms. In a lower voice, he muttered, "On reflection, I don't feel particularly hungry at the moment, either."

I watched uncomfortably as Holmes's gaze wandered toward the drawer where he currently kept his cocaine stash. At least Lestrade seemed unaware of my friend's unfortunate habit.

"Come now, Holmes," I protested, hoping to distract him from that action, at least. "It cannot hurt to hear Lestrade out. You might even pick up some new information regarding police techniques."

"I doubt that." Holmes sighed, leaned further back in his chair, and pressed his fingertips together. "Very well, Lestrade. You have taken the trouble to come visit here this morning, and your voice pulled me out of bed. Please, do share your story."

Lestrade shot another uncomfortable look in my direction. "Are you certain? I was saving some details for you which the doctor should not – ah, *may* not want to hear."

"I assure you, Inspector, as I have several times before, whatever information you wish to share with me is just as secure with my friend."

"We will not have a repeat of the Cardigan case?"

I turned to Holmes. "Cardigan?"

"That was before your time, Watson," he answered. "I'd been sharing information with a certain constable who – Well, just let us say I since learned from my error. Proceed as you will, Lestrade."

"Very well," Lestrade replied, though his tone implied otherwise.

"I was working an early duty this morning," he began, "when, approaching the Yard, I heard a shout from a nearby alley. 'Drop the knife!' a voice ordered, and, a moment later, 'Now!'

"I naturally rushed toward the source. Entering the narrow space, I recognized the speaker as one of our new recruits, a young man named Mickles. He waved his truncheon in the air as he stood some fifteen feet from a wild-eyed, middle-aged man. We have since identified the fellow as Niles Overhill, an unemployed carpenter.

"Overhill partially crouched with one foot on either side of a battered body and stared coldly at the constable. His right hand clenched a blood-stained knife – not exactly a dagger, more of a pocket-knife, but still capable of doing a great deal of damage, used correctly. Or should I say 'incorrectly'?"

Holmes raised a hand to stifle a yawn. Lestrade ignored the gesture.

"I noticed Constable Mickles grow more anxious, his truncheon wavering ever wilder. The presumed killer continued staring at him, unblinking, as if refusing to surrender. Nonetheless, the balance of his facial expression, or I should say lack of one, conveyed to me he posed no real threat, at least not to the police. If anything, the fellow seemed bemused, at a loss as to what he should do. I quickly identified myself, then ordered the constable to lower his truncheon. Mickles reluctantly obeyed, but understandably didn't put it away."

I leaned aside to nudge Holmes, whose attention had begun to wander. He glanced at me sharply but did not protest. Lestrade still seemed not to notice such indifference, continuing his narrative. Even I began to wonder when the inspector would get to the point.

"I slowly approached the suspect using a slow, calming voice. You've heard that tone from me before, though not often. I pointed to his knife with my right hand, while carefully extending my left, palm up, to demonstrate that I was unarmed.

"Overhill blinked several times, yet his face remained frozen. Slowly, he stretched out the hand holidng the knife, blade pointing downward, indicating he meant no further harm. The weapon then slipped from between his fingers to clatter on the paving.

"Our suspect stared down at the fallen weapon, but he made no move to retrieve it as I drew closer. Placing one hand on his shoulder, I slowly guided him away from the bloody, unmoving corpse, for it was by then obvious the victim was dead. He stumbled forward, still refusing to look up, but didn't resist when Constable Mickles, on my orders, handcuffed him and took him inside to be formally arrested. Once that procedure is complete, and it will be soon, I'll lead the formal interrogation."

When Holmes didn't react, I commented, "You seem to have left out out some key information, Lestrade."

The inspector's eyes narrowed in annoyance.

Holmes, on the other hand, abruptly stirred in his armchair. "Capital, Watson! The victim, Lestrade! The murdered man! Who is he? What was Overhill's motive? How were they connected?"

"We're still working out on those details. That's what interrogation is for. As you know." He offered a thin smirk. "At this point, it may have simply been a random attack."

"So close to Scotland Yard?" Holmes asked.

"Mr. Overhill isn't a well man, physically or mentally. A cursory examination by our medical officer indicated signs of long-term cancer. He may not have been thinking clearly."

"You still haven't told us the identity of the man he murdered. Correction: *May* have murdered."

"My men are looking into that, as well. What we have learned so far, from one of my constables, is the victim's name: Titus Donnelly. He'd moved to this area of London last spring, from up north. Donnelly has a reputation as a gambler, but we found little more than a few farthings in his pockets. And before you ask, no, Overhill himself didn't possess more than a couple of quid when we brought him in, either. My guess is Donnelly liked to show off his wealth, but was mostly bluffing."

"That isn't unusual among the gambling community," Holmes noted in a deliberately bland tone. I looked away, certain he was also referring to my own habits.

"One unusual point of interest, though," Lestrade continued. "Donnelly was stabbed multiple times. The surgeon was still doing a count when I left the station. Yet Overhill himself showed no blood stains on his own clothes. Mentally disturbed he might be, but he obviously knew how to handle a knife.

Holmes abruptly straightned up. "How large a knife are we talking about, Lestrade? He would have to keep some distance to avoid being splattered."

"As I'd mentioned, we recovered a pocket-knife, barely the size of a small dagger. He must be skilled indeed to avoid any stains. Admittedly, that doesn't quite match our theory of an unstable spurt of madness."

"And the location of the crime? Did Overhill at least leave bloody footprints? You said he was standing over the body when you arrested him."

"None that we could detect. In fact, since you mention it, we found very little blood, even where the crime occurred, despite the copious amounts covering the victim's body. It would take skill indeed to keep the scene that clean."

Holmes rolled his eyes. "This Overhill gentleman sounds like someone I indeed wish to talk with. Has the scene hasn't been disturbed since this morning?"

"No. I still have a man watching it, though not for much longer."

"Then I should like to visit and examine it myself, before joining you to meet your suspect. I will of course also require the company of my medical professional colleague, Doctor Watson."

"If you must." Lestrade sighed. "Shall I meet you at the Yard at around, let us say, three o'clock?"

"My own investigation shouldn't take that long, but yes, I can see you then."

"That was indeed odd," I muttered, once the inspector made his way down the stairs and into Baker Street.

"The case does have some intriguing aspects," Holmes replied. He paused. "That isn't what's bothering you, however, is it?"

I nodded. "Lestrade and I have always gotten along, often better than you have. Today he acted cold, aloof, almost resentful of my presence. It was as if I could no longer be trusted with even the slightest details of any case in which he consulted you."

Holmes gave a thin smile. "And that reaction could have nothing to do with the fact that lately you've taken to writing up your own on our cases, and in fact your first one will likely be in print next year."

"How would he know about . . . ? Holmes! Did you tell him I was working on a book?"

"I may have mentioned it in passing. I thought he would be pleased at the publicity." Holmes shrugged. "Consider this a reminder that I'm not as perfect as you believe."

"I tell things as they are."

"Of course you do."

"Lestrade has his flaws, like everyone else."

"Come now, Watson. He may not be the most competent detective on the force, but he is far from the worst. If you don't mind a word of advice . . . ."

"From you? I welcome it."

"You should stick strictly to the facts of the case. Those emotional embellishments in your sample notes distract from the story."

"They are essential for holding a reader's interest!"

Holmes shrugged. "If you believe so. In any case, should you desire to say something negative about the Inspector, feel free to imply that I, not you, made the comment. I have no problem taking the blame." He smiled thinly. "He's used to my taunting him."

"He certainly shows no hesitation manipulating you. Why else would he have come here? To brag over stumbling across this incident, not far from the Yard? He wants your help. He's usually more direct."

"Am I being manipulated? If it's something I want to do?" Holmes turned to his bedroom. "Now I need to dress and then visit this location before I meet the alleged perpetrator. You will join me, I trust?"

Given my lack of other duties, and a growing curiosity, I could hardly refuse.

The location of the crime, at least the site where Mr. Overhill had stood over the corpse of Titus Donnelly, seemed hardly worth visiting. A few spatters of dried blood might have already sat there for days. Some stretches of alleyway looked unusually clean, but even Holmes couldn't backtrack the existing blood for more than a few yards.

Subsequently calling at the police laboratory provided some facts. The dead man's clothes were stiff with blood. The preliminary report mentioned more than two-score wounds, many crisscrossing, making it difficult to tell which were individual stabbings, and which might be twists of the knife.

Holmes stared through a peephole into the interrogation room where our suspect waited.

"I'd already decided the murder took place elsewhere, Lestrade" Holmes said without turning as he heard the inspector approach. "You knew this, of course?"

"Naturally," the inspector answered. "My not mentioning it held your interest, however, did it not?"

I had tried to warn Holmes of that, I told myself silently.

"Any idea where the stabbing did occur?" Holmes continued.

Lestrade frowned. "I hoped you might have a theory."

"Some one did a fine job of cleaning up the site. I assume Mr. Overhill?"

"Obviously."

"But he hasn't confessed, or you wouldn't have bothered calling on me. You claim Overhill has been silent since you brought him in this morning?"

Lestrade grunted acknowledgement. "I haven't been with him that whole time, but my staff said so, yes. He is taciturn, but he is not a mute. He did, at one point, request a glass of water. Most interesting, about an hour before you arrived, he suddenly asked about a passenger steamboat leaving Southampton for the Mediterranean this afternoon."

"Now, that is interesting," Holmes observed. "Do we know which vessel?"

Lestrade rummaged through his notes. "Yes, here it is. The *Constellation*. I contacted the owners. They advised that the ship was scheduled to leave . . . ." He glanced at the wall clock. "It may have already left."

"Of all the things a prisoner might ask about," Holmes replied, "that seems rather low on the list."

"It was likely his planned means of escape. In which case, the killing would have been premeditated."

"Then he must have had a ticket," I offered. "You did a complete search of your suspect?"

"We did, Doctor," Lestrade replied, "and no, we found no ticket in his possession. Which doesn't mean he couldn't obtain one on boarding. Or he had it hidden somewhere."

Holmes stroked his chin. "If this murder was planned, why would Overhill have remained standing over the body until Constable Mickles spotted him? And, for that matter, continue to do so at your own approach?"

"Come now, Mr. Holmes. You may lack my years of experience, yet even so should know how a non-professional murderer might freeze upon viewing the result of his actions. But let us see together what Mr. Overhill might have to say about this." Lestrade unlocked the door and gestured for Holmes and me to enter first.

Niles Overhill sat handcuffed, head bowed, at a small table. He seemed indifferent to our entrance.

"Mr. Overhill," Lestrade announced, "you have visitors."

The man continued to stare at the table.

"We wish to help you, Mr. Overhill." Holmes used his most soothing voice.

Overhill glanced up. "Lawyers?"

"No," Lestrade answered. "But they can advise you."

"I do have some legal background," Holmes added. "And my associate, Doctor Watson, is a skilled medical man."

Overhill grunted.

"Perhaps we could talk to him in private?" Holmes offered.

"He hasn't been very communicative," Lestrade admitted. "Very well. I'll wait outside."

After Lestrade left, Overhill met my friend's gaze. "Holmes? Sherlock Holmes? The detective?"

"It appears my reputation has spread." Holmes offered a thin smile.

"And your friend?" Overhill nodded at me.

"Watson, as I said, is an experienced medical man. Is there anything you wish to share with us just now?"

"Not without a lawyer."

"We're more concerned about your health."

"This isn't the best place for a man in your condition," I added.

"Tell us what you need." Holmes leaned closer.

Overhill sat silent for a moment. Then: "The *Constellation*. Has she sailed?"

"According to the inspector, the ship will leave the harbor soon, if she hasn't already. Why?"

He glanced at me, then back to Holmes. "No reason. The policeman thought I wanted to board that vessel."

"Were you planning to?"

He shook his head. "I'm prone to seasickness. No. I'm just glad Dahlia is safe."

"Dahlia?"

Overhill had fallen silent again for a moment before suddenly pounding his cuffed hands upon the table. Then: "Have you any children, Mr. Holmes? A wife? Maybe even an informal adoption?"

"I keep an eye on the safety of a number of children who occasionally run errands for me, or carry out various investigative tasks, but no – I am hardly a parent to those orphans."

Overhill rested his arms on the table. "I've said too much. I await confirmation. Let us meet again in better times."

The man fell silent then, remaining so despite our efforts at the most general topics. Holmes and I eventually soon took our leave, with a disappointed Inspector Lestrade showing us out.

Holmes picked up the pace as we moved down the street.

"That was disappointing," I muttered.

"On the contrary, Watson. I quite liked the man. Ill he may be, but he also seems to be protecting someone with his silence."

"Any idea who?"

"Yes"

When he didn't elaborate, I simply shrugged. "Shall I hail a cab then?"

"No. I prefer to walk for a bit."

"Are you certain? I feel a chill, as a storm brewing."

"That young woman behind us seems comfortable enough."

I turned. "The tall one in the blue coat? Young, indeed. She seems barely in her twenties."

"If that. That same woman was standing across the street from the Yard, near the entrance, when we arrived. Surely you saw her there when we left. She's been following us since – hence my avoiding a hansom."

I hadn't noticed, of course, and Holmes knew that. As I continued to stare, the woman halted and turned her head away.

Holmes quickly strode to her side, and I hurried to join him as he addressed her.

"I am not an official of the police department," he reassured her, "although I do help them out from time to time. Unless I'm mistaken, it's you who needs my help now. Unofficially, of course."

Her eyes widened as she looked from Holmes to me, and back.

"This man is a doctor," Holmes continued, nodding at me, "as well as a long-time associate and friend. He can be as discreet as I am, when necessary. You may share with him whatever you wish to tell me."

She glanced down the street but didn't try to run.

"Perhaps," Holmes suggested, "you wish to hear about my own interactions with Mr. Overhill?"

"You know about us?" she asked.

"It is my job to know things, Dahlia," my friend replied. The girl looked surprised upon hearing the name, presumably hers. "I am Sherlock Holmes, and my friend is Dr. John Watson. We will gladly lend you our ears."

Her eyes narrowed. "I've heard of you, Mr. Holmes. You have quite the reputation. How do you know me, and my relationship with Mr. Overhill?"

"It was a calculated guess. There may be other reasons a young woman like yourself might hang about here, but then to follow Watson and myself . . . ? Now, if you like, we can sit and continue our chat at that café across the street, though I suspect you've already spent too much time near that police station. Or we could go to your flat, which I believe must be nearby, but I'm guessing you'd prefer no visitors there after last night. Would you instead care to join my friend and me at our own humble abode in Baker Street? Our landlady can prepare an excellent meal, given sufficient warning. You look to me as if you could use some nourishment, Miss – ?"

The woman gave a brief shrug. "Dahlia, as you say. Dalhlia Corbett."

"Capital!"

I moved to the curb to flag down a more-spacious growler.

Twilight slowly descended.

Miss Dalhlia Corbett settled comfortably into the chair facing Holmes as he recited a brief version of our police visit. She then leaned forward.

"I suppose I must now tell you something of our own history, Mr. Overhill and me, to justify what happened last night. Although you already seem to know so much."

"One can never share enough details," Holmes replied, "on the way to the truth."

"I am not quite sixteen years old. My parents vanished mysteriously three months ago. There was enough money hidden in a kitchen drawer for emergencies, to cover the rent for a month, by which time I found a way to earn a living. I've seen how many orphanages often treat their charges, and wished to avoid being shunted to one for the next few years. Tall for my age, I easily convinced the owner of The Owl's Eye pub that I was older.

"Mr. Overhill, our neighbor, assisted with my survival. He keeps a protective eye on me, and he even helps me tend a stray kitten I've adopted for some company. This was pure good will on his part. The man's some forty years older than me, and treats me like a long-lost niece. He often seemed more caring and attentive than my actual parents were."

Holmes nodded. "Based on my own interaction with him, he does appear to be a good man. Please continue, Miss Corbett."

She crossed her ankles. "Late this past spring, an unsavory stranger began hanging about the neighborhood. Mr. Overhill learned the man's name was Titus Donnelly, that he'd arrived in London from somewhere north of Edinburgh, and he was a successful gambler. Suspiciously so. We couldn't discover much more, nor had anyone else.

"He warned me to keep my distance – not that I wouldn't have. Donnelly approached me several times on the street, and twice after I started working at The Owl's Eye. I also saw him pressuring female customers, and always backed off, trying to stay away from him. I'm friendly with our customers, it's part of the job, but even someone my age can have her standards.

"Last night, I failed to notice Donnelly following me back to my ground-floor flat after work. I was concerned about Niles – I mean Mr. Overhill. He'd seemed particularly weak that morning, and I thought he might need help.

"No sooner had I unlocked my door when I felt a sharp push between my shoulders. I grasped onto my armchair to keep from tumbling to the floor and spun around.

"Titus Donnelly towered in the entrance, slamming the door behind him.

"'Time you learn what you're missing!' he growled.

The young woman, I suppose I should say girl, paused to catch her breath. I offered her a small brandy, which she gratefully accepted.

"Take your time, Miss Corbett," Holmes advised. "You may continue when ready."

The girl took a long, slow sip. "Fortunately, what he didn't know, nor did I then, was that Mr. Overhill was already in my flat to feed the kitten. Given his health, he has no fixed schedule. I leave a tag on my door to let him know when I'm home, so he can avoid accidentally intruding on me.

"I backed away, reaching for the pocket in the back of my skirt where I keep, among other things, a small pocket-knife. I wasn't at all certain I could retrieve it in time.

"To my surprise, Niles – Mr. Overhill – suddenly appeared behind the brute, wielding a heavy metal cookpot.

"The pot bounced off Donnelly's shoulder. He spun around to lash out at Niles, knocking him to the floor. He then raised his fists, ready to beat him further.

"That was the last straw for me. I'd intended using my blade in pure self-defense, but to see my best friend, my unofficial adopted father, beaten to death before me . . . ." She choked.

"Another brandy?" I suggested

The girl shook her head. "My apologies, Doctor Watson, Mr. Holmes. I've lost my temper before, we all have, but had no idea I was capable of such brutality. I leapt onto Donnelly's back, reached around, and drew my knife as deep as possible across his throat."

Holmes focused on our visitor, but said nothing.

"Did he not cry out?" I asked.

290

"He made some sound, Doctor, but nothing loud or unusual enough to attract the neighbors. I dodged his grasping hand, stabbing at his throat and chest again and again, ignoring the gushing blood. I had no idea I was capable of such force." Her arm shot up and down as she spoke, finally coming to rest in her lap.

"We often don't know our strength," Holmes agreed, "until the moment comes."

The girl nodded. "My attack eventually slowed, then stopped. I heard a stricken voice behind me. It was Mr. Overhill's, of course.

"When he realized my tirade was finished, he gently pried the knife from my hands. 'So much damage,' he whispered, 'with such a small blade.' At another time, he might have been impressed.

"Following Niles' instructions, I removed my bloodied dress and washed away the blood while he wrapped my attacker in my bedsheet. When I returned in fresh clothes, Niles shoved a thick wad of pound notes into my hands. 'He won't be needing these,' he said. Seeing my somber look, he choked back his laugh.

"'I can't use those,' I protested. 'They're unclean.'

"He shook his head. 'They're free of blood. Mostly.'

"'That isn't the kind of unclean I meant.' I tried to hand the money back.

"He pushed my offer aside. 'You'll need that for a steamship ticket, plus other expenses when you reach your destination. I believe there's a ship leaving Southampton tomorrow afternoon. Where it's going doesn't matter. You can change destinations later.'

"I argued the police would be searching for this man's killer. Any attempt to flee England would work against me. 'Only if they're looking for the murderer,' he insisted, 'and I will take the blame. Don't worry, Dahlia. The police will eventually find me physically incapable of having committed the murder. By then, you'll be safely out of England. I only regret never seeing you again. Telegraph me when you're safely out of the country. Don't use your name. Any coded phrase will do. Once assured of your safety overseas, I can then tell police the full, true story.'

"I couldn't argue with that attitude, Mr. Holmes. When it grew late enough for a lull in street traffic, I helped him move the body to an alley closer to the Yard with a cart he'd used over the past year to move his carpentry supplies. I returned it to his flat, and also disposed of the sheet, as he planned the crime should seem to have happened in that alley."

"And yet," Holmes observed, "here you are, in our rooms in Baker Street, and the ship you were to have been on, the *Constellation*, left Southampton hours ago."

Miss Corbett stared at the floor before meeting our eyes again. "I couldn't leave, Mr. Holmes. I could not let that man make this sacrifice. What if he was put on trial, and found guilty, and executed? I would be responsible for *two* deaths!"

Holmes reached for his pipe, fondling it but making no attempt to load and light it. "Yet," he responded, "despite approaching the site where Mr. Overhill was held, you neither entered nor approached any officers to make a confession."

"You've met the man, Mr. Holmes. It would break his heart if I went against his wishes!"

"Nonetheless," I repeated, "here you are."

"Yes, Doctor Watson. Here I am."

Holmes fingered the pipe a long moment, then put it down, unlit. "I confirm to you, Miss Corbett, Mr. Overhill will not be executed as an accessory murder. If necessary, I shall personally be a witness at his trial, although I doubt one will be held, given his health."

"You sound reassuring, Mr. Holmes. Yet my friend remains imprisoned."

"Mr. Overhill has sworn to tell the full story to the police only when he is certain you have safely fled the country. Obviously, you have not done so. He seems willing to remain in prison for life, once assured of your safety."

The Corbett girl bit her lower lip.

"Your ultimate decision now is to either leave the country, or stay and risk arrest yourself, or turn yourself in. This, I leave entirely up to you. Overhill would prefer you to escape arrest. I can, if you wish, check steamers' outgoing schedules for you. The next ship may not depart for days. You might have to travel as far as Liverpool to catch it."

She began to sob. "I just . . . I can't . . . ."

"Holmes," I put in, "this young lady – this child – is already under considerable strain."

"Agreed," Holmes replied. "And to be fair, Miss Corbett, I believe the mental anguish you are going through to be punishment enough, given that the murder was done not only in self-defense, but also to protect Mr. Overhill."

"You're right, Mr. Holmes," she replied. "I should have sailed today. Now my friend will go through more torment."

"What's done is done. I suggest you not stay at your flat, the actual site of the crime, if only for your peace of mind. Pack up whatever you'll need. Watson here will be glad to assist you."

I nodded agreement.

"There are several other flats around London I often use when in disguise," Holmes offered. "You may stay in one of those until we've confirmed your passage."

"I don't know how to thank you for your help. And for believing me."

"You had little to gain from lying, or you would not show such concern. If you keep to the plan this time, that will be thanks enough. Watson will see you off, and once he sends me a telegram confirming your departure, I will personally visit Mr. Overhill to let him know."

There was a sudden knock at the door. Our guest stiffened.

Holmes let loose a sharp laugh. "That will be Mrs. Hudson, bringing us our dinner. You look like you haven't eaten all day, Miss Corbett, and could use a little nourishment, yes?"

Three days later, I helped the young lady onto a ship leaving Liverpool, bound for New York, one of the easiest places in the world to disappear. I then telegraphed Holmes as soon as the ship left the harbor, rather than have him wait for my return.

Once back at Baker Street, however, I discovered my friend in a despondent mood, seated with his Stradivarius in his lap.

"Did Overhill not believe you?" I asked, assuming that was the worst that had happened. It was not.

"I can but hope, Watson," he sighed, "the news reaches him in Heaven. Or so many might believe."

"He died?"

"In the early hours of the morning, yes. The cancer did its job. Naturally, Lestrade had no reason to inform me, since I hadn't shared with him anything concerning Miss Corbett."

"Should I telegraph the young woman?"

"Eh? No. What would be the point? She'll hear soon enough. By then she'll have settled into her new life." He plucked a few mournful notes on his instrument's strings, then put the violin aside. I noticed the bottom drawer, where he stored his cocaine, was partially open.

He fell silent, eyes glazing over.

For once, I decided to let the addiction pass.

The Notting Hill Murderer
by Michael Mallory

Erik Selden breathed hard as he stared at the body lying on the street, wondering what to do next. He had never killed a human being before. He had fought people, of course. Bloodied them, even maimed them, but young Lord Carmichael was his first kill.

Selden was overwhelmed by conflicting emotions. He felt terrified, haunted, exhilarated, guilt-ridden, all-powerful, fearful . . . .

Alive.

He had pummeled the blackguard to death with his bare fists for one reason: The wealthy Mayfair family scion had attempted to call in his chits against Selden, who had lost hugely at the Soho gaming table that Lord Carmichael frequented. Both were gamblers, but the difference between them was more than one of social class. Erik Selden bet and lost honestly. Even at his most inebriated, he gamed fairly. Money was precious to Selden, too. Not having a position as such – he was too disreputable in appearance to be any man's clerk, too arrogant to be a labourer, and too stout to be a chimney sweep – had therefore had settled into the role of an antiques dealer in Notting Hill's Portobello Road (though most of his wares had been stolen and brought to him by others). When he gambled, he usually won through his skill and wits.

Lord Simon Carmichael, on the other hand, had arrived at the tables with two other fellows who hovered about, ostensibly taking no notice of the game itself, simply waiting for his Lordship to finish this part of the evening's revelry. Like a few others who patronized the gambling establishment, though, Selden suspected that Carmichael was using his fellows to enable cheating the other players. More than simply suspicious, he was convinced of it, but could not prove it.

Unlike others, however, Selden wasn't about to wait for proof to appear.

To his mind, it was a matter of survival. Carmichael had the wherewithal to send him to prison for nonpayment of debt, a fate Selden considered himself far above. Despite having not been born into a life of leisure, Erik Selden thought of himself as an aristocrat who had mistakenly been delivered to the wrong family, and the wrong place, at birth. Even his visage – short and stocky with a sallow, beetle-browed face through which cunning eyes surveyed the world around him – was some sort of grave natural error. He should walk proud and striking like Carmichael, whose handsome features and patrician air made him the envy of everyone he passed, female and male alike. Instead, Selden looked like a human cur. His older sister Eliza once expressed the belief that he was pampered too much as a child (perhaps to make up for his unloveliness), which instilled in him the idea that the world existed for his pleasure. Let her think what she wanted. He knew the truth. God, or the gods, or whichever supernatural force in which one wished to believe, had erred mightily by not having him come forth in a palace.

Feeling was coming back into his beefy right hand now. Examining it, he saw bruised and bloody knuckles. Nothing was broken. His fist was too strong to break like a normal person's. Still, his revenge on Lord Carmichael had taken its toll. When he returned home, he would soak it in water and then pour whisky over it. Odds were it would be perfectly normal in two days.

Turning over the prone, lifeless carcass of Lord Carmichael, Selden reached inside the aristocrat's coat pocket and removed his billfold, not simply for whatever money it contained (which was considerable), but also for any identification it might hold. Without it, the police would have a very hard time identifying the dead man on the street by what was left of his face.

The feeling of exhilaration and power, though, was now giving way to fear of discovery. Were he to be discovered standing over the body, the odds were one-hundred-percent that he would be arrested whether identification of the victim could be immediately established or not. Simon Carmichael had never known what it was like to break his neck attempting to make a living in a harsh society that protected wealth and dismissed everyone else. Selden smiled evilly as he turned the body over again, and then delivered a murderous blow to the top of the dead man's spine, hearing a satisfying snap. "Now you know what it's like, you manor-born bastard," he muttered.

Erik Selden then fled the scene and returned home.

The trace of whisky that was left in the bottle after he had poured it over his contused hand, he swallowed. His thoughts turned to Lord Carmichael's two companions, the ones who had assisted the blackguard in swindling him at the tables. One was also an aristocrat (at least he dressed like one), though the Gods of Human Appearance hadn't been any kinder to him than they had been to Selden. The man was very short and far fatter than most of his youthful age – the advertisement of a life of unnecessary luxury. The second one had dressed more plainly, was completely bald, and appeared to be some sort of servant to his Lordship. That one's role in the drama was less defined, since he was never caught glancing at the hands of the other players the way the other had.

295

No matter their roles, they would have to go. The short, fat one would be first.

Erik Selden went to sleep in his small flat, which was crammed with stolen goods waiting to be fenced, imagining the expression of surprise he would encounter before reducing the blubbery nabob's carefully shaven face into a raw beef joint.

The newspapers, of course, covered the murder of Lord Simon Carmichael, but the title of *"The Notting Hill Murderer"* was not bannered across the pages until the bodies of the next two victims were discovered in Ladbrook Grove four days later. "'The Notting Hill Murderer'," Erik Selden said softly to himself with a feeling of great satisfaction. At last he had a title, and one that he had earned himself, not been born into, like Lord Carmichael. "'The Notting Hill Murderer'," he repeated, wearing the designation like a new, expensive hat.

The irony was that of the two murders in Ladbrook Grove, only one had been planned.

Using a disguise consisting of a horsehair beard (which looked convincing enough if not closely examined) and a pair of round, metal-framed eyeglasses with windowpane lenses, both of which he had found in other stalls in Portobello Road, Erik Selden had followed Tobias Vartaine, Esquire, for two days. Odds had nothing to do with Selden's finding the diminutive, portly accomplice of Lord Carmichael. The young blackguard was easy to spot on the street since, in addition to his natural identifiability, he wore the tallest top hat Selden had ever seen. From a distance, he resembled an oddly carved children's toy moving of its own volition. Vartaine (whose name Selden had learned from the counterman of one of the many public houses the young man frequented) tended to move in a furtive manner that was rendered pointless given his appearance.

Cloaked by the evening fog, Selden watched from the shadows as Vartaine entered a public house. Selden followed him inside, his face obscured by the beard and eyeglasses, and went up to the bar counter, staying within earshot of the other man. After ordering a gin, he stood a couple places down at the bar and observed his quarry. Vartaine said nothing to anyone, and instead looked glumly at the noisy congregation of men in the pub. Some ten minutes passed, causing Selden to wonder if he was wasting his time this evening. He was contemplating leaving the public house and planning for another day when he noticed Tobias Vartaine come to attention and focus his gaze on the front door, through which was coming another man. This one was older, tall and refined, and equally well-dressed.

"Matthew," Vartaine said as the man approached him. "thank Heavens you've arrived. I was afraid you were going to stand me up."

"You'd be the same height standing up or sitting down, Toby," the man called Matthew said. "On your back, you're the tallest of all."

Vartaine made a false show of laughing the comment off. The two of them were a study in contrasts. One over six feet by Selden's judgment, and lean as a racing dog, while the other was barely five feet in height and as spherical as a dung beetle's ball.

"Landlord, a pint of your very best bitter," Matthew ordered, tossing a sixpence on the counter.

"Matthew," Vartaine begged, "please look at me."

Only after the pint of beer arrived did Matthew regard the rotund man. "All right, Toby, what is it you want? As though I don't know."

"A small investment, Matthew, very small."

"You haven't paid back my last 'investment'."

"I know, but that shall be remedied soon. Carmichael died without paying me what he owed me for his gaming arrangement, but I have found another player with whom to join forces. All he needs is seed money to open the game. I cannot at present provide it to him."

Matthew Jelson took a drink, and then from his pocket withdrew a long, slender cigar and lit it. "Let me understand the proposition," he said through a gust of tobacco smoke. "I loan you money which you give to someone I've never met, whom I have only your word actually exists, and that someone takes the money to begin a card game, which he might lose, taking my money with it. Is that your proposition?"

"But he won't lose!" Vartaine said. "Not with me helping him, communicating what the others at the table hold in their hands. He's as good as Carmichael, who lost only willingly, sacrificing a hand on occasion to ensure the other players didn't become suspicious. But when large sums of money were at stake, he won every hand. This chap and I shall do the same, and you will be paid back, every farthing, in short order."

Jelson finished his bitter and signaled for another. "How long will it take for you to set up this operation?" he asked, wiping his lips.

"A week, most likely," Vartaine answered. "Perhaps a little longer."

The new pint arrived, and the well-dressed man took another swig. "Very well, Toby, though I don't know why I continue to indulge you."

"It's because you're a fine man, and a friend."

"Yes, I am a fine man who once made a grievous mistake, the consequences of which he escaped only through a false alibi provided by a certain hot-air balloon in a top hat."

"That's what friends are for, Matthew," Vartaine said, wiping his brow.

"Very well, Toby. Given the circumstances of poor Carmichael's demise and, knowing the fact that he is now roasting in eternal flame has robbed you of any income source, I will stake you fifty quid. I insist, however, that it be returned to me, along with the other funds you currently owe, no later than one fortnight. Otherwise, you shall be hearing from my solicitor . . . our past association notwithstanding."

"Bless you, Matthew."

"Yes, bless me, Toby"

Reaching into his coat, Matthew Jelson withdrew a billfold and from it extracted a fifty-pound note, which he handed to Vartaine as Selden watched surreptitiously. Then he finished his beer in one long draw and set the mug down on the counter. "Do not forget, Toby," he said. "One fortnight." With that, the tall man turned around and strode out of the bar. Tobias Vartaine reached into his own pocket, pulling out a handkerchief to mop his sweating face as he stuck the note into another pocket. After ordering a large brandy, he produced a *Bradshaw Railway Guide*.

The blighter's going to try and flee, Selden thought as he watched Vartaine flip through the booklet. He sidled up next to him at the bar. "Evening, sir," he said.

"Who the devil are you?" Vartaine asked, glancing at him.

"Another friend," Selden said, hoping the light in the public house was low enough to not reveal the mendacity of his beard. "I couldn't help but overhear you."

"It is hardly your place to listen in on the conversation between gentlemen."

"The volume of your voice made it a bit hard not to."

"What business is it of yours?"

"You cheat gamblers, eh?"

"That is none of your concern."

"I could make it so," Selden said. "I happen to live one door down from a gent who's on the Metropolitan Police Force. Nice bloke he is, too. Always looking to find a way to impress his superiors. Like maybe bringing in the leader of a card-shark ring."

"I am not the leader!" Vartaine protested.

"No, but you could lead the peelers to the leader. In fact, they might even find it prudent to ask you some questions about the unfortunate murder of the man your mate was talking about a few minutes ago – the one he said is roasting in Hell."

Tobias Vartaine's sweaty face began to pale. "What do you want?"

298

"I want in, that's what I want," Selden lied. "I want you to help me at the tables, too."

"Is . . . that all?"

"Isn't that enough?"

"Yes, I suppose so. Am I correct in presuming that this will be in return for your silence about my activities?"

"You are."

"Very well. But it turns out that I must go on a very short trip for business. I shall be gone a day or two. When I return, we will talk further."

"A trip, eh?"

"It is unavoidable."

"And when do you leave?"

"This evening. On the next train, in fact."

"All right. I'll accompany you to the station, then."

"There is no need – "

"I insist. If we're going to be partners, we need to get to know one another better."

"I suppose I have little choice."

Leaving the pub, the two walked in silence through the dark, soupy night. Finally Vartaine said, "If we are entering into an agreement, I should at least know to whom I am dealing."

"My name is Luttig," Selden lied. "Gunther Luttig. And you're Toby Vartaine."

"Have we met before, Mr. Luttig?"

"I don't think so. Where are you travelling?"

"North."

"North is a large place."

"Cambridge. It's where I attended university."

"I see. Never made it to college myself."

"Really, are you intending to accompany me all the way to Paddington Station?"

"Why? Do I make you nervous?"

"N – no, not exactly, it's just that – "

The yellow fog now seemed to enshroud them. "Tell you what, Mr. Vartaine, assistant of swindlers and cheats, you may cast off any fears of my lingering about. This is as far as I intend to go with you."

"Excellent."

"The thing is, it's also as far as you will go."

Before Tobias Vartaine could make another sound, Selden pushed him bodily into a dark alley off of Ladbrook Grove and clouted him in the face, knocking the heavyset young man down. Then he pulled off his false beard, struck a Lucifer on a brick wall, and held the flame near his face. "Remember me now?" Selden asked.

"No, I – "

Crouching over Vartaine, Selden put a hand over his mouth. With his other hand he reached into his coat pocket, and when he withdrew it, he was wearing brass knuckles.

There was no sense in further harming his fist.

Even in the misty darkness, Selden could see his quarry's eyes bulging with fear.

Vartaine attempted to claw at him, but Selden forced his arms to the pavement, and then stood on them. "You'll never cheat another, with or without help," he said, and then came down on Tobias Vartaine's face and head with his metal-armored hand until all motion – and breath – ceased from him. "And look at that fat," Selden muttered. "You eat enough to keep fifty working people alive." He then began to pound his fist into the dead man's stomach, which Selden knew wouldn't hurt him any further, but it gave the killer a feeling that justice was being served. When he was finished, he reached into Vartaine's coat pocket, he searched and pulled out the fifty-pound note and stuck it in his own. Rising, he started to run away, but then remembered his false beard, which was lying on the ground. Going back to pick it up, he heard a voice.

"I saw you," a woman said from somewhere in the darkness.

Looking up, Selden could barely make out the form of a streetwalker, whose dirty red hair fell around her painted face.

"I saw you kill him," she said.

"You couldn't have seen anything in this fog. Be gone."

"Oh, but I did see it. I was right behind you. It's me you couldn't see 'cause of the bloom' pea soup."

"What are you going to do about it?" Selden asked.

"Nothin' if you 'and over that note," she replied, suddenly pulling a knife on him.

Selden glared at the knife blade, which glinted in the dim light.

"And drop those knucks."

"All right, if that's the way it's got to be." He carefully took off the knuckle protector and let it fall to the pavement, where it landed with a loud *clank*. Then he reached into his pocket and withdrew the note, holding it up in front of her. When the woman reached for it, Selden let it slip from his fingers and flutter to the ground. As the prostitute reached down for it, he suddenly grabbed her head and twisted it, hearing a telltale *snap*. The woman fell sideways to the pavement, landing on her knife. "You shouldn't have stuck your nose in where it didn't belong," he told the corpse. Then Selden retrieved his brass knuckles and made certain her

300

nose would never be seen again, even in her coffin. When he was done, he picked up the fifty-pound note and considered examining the dead woman's clothing for whatever money she'd earned that evening at her trade, but decided against it.

What kind of man steals from a whore?

In another part of London on the following evening, Dr. John H. Watson was perusing the evening *Times*, focusing on its coverage of the sensational Notting Hill murders. "Listen to this, Holmes," he said, and then read:

> *Police have interrogated a man named Matthew Jelson in connection with the murders, Jelson having been seen conversing with the victim Tobias Vartaine in a tavern shortly before the man's brutal killing. But Jelson offered a convincing alibi, having been positively identified by a cab driver as the man he had taken to a club in the Mayfair district at roughly the time of the murder. Inspector Lestrade of Scotland Yard, meanwhile, assures the public that the murderer will be captured and brought to justice.*

"It sounds to me like they had the killer in their hands and let him go."

"Does it?" Sherlock Holmes asked. "How so?"

"Well, it says this Jelson fellow was seen conversing with the victim right before he was killed. It rather stands to reason that he's the man, doesn't it? He could have waited outside the pub for Vartaine to emerge, followed him, and then killed him."

"The mere act of conversation is hardly enough to convict a man. At this very moment we are conversing. What if an assassin were to fire a shot at me through the window, striking me down, and a moment later Mrs. Hudson came into the flat to find you standing over my dead body. By your logic, you, as the last person known to speak to me, would be the one facing the gallows."

"I hardly think the situations are the same. We are alone, while this man Jelson was *seen* speaking with the victim."

"Precisely, Watson. He was *seen*. Only a fool would present himself in a public place where he could be seen and heard by others just prior to killing him in a dark alley. The murder betrayed a savagery on the part of the killer, yet none of those who saw Jelson in the public house reported that he was angry, or even agitated, let alone murderously enraged. No, Jelson isn't the killer."

"How do you know what the witnesses described? You *have* been in contact with the police, haven't you?"

"I have not. I am simply reflecting upon the public press accounts of Jelson's questioning. Had anyone reported him to be acting suspicious, it would have made the papers."

"The killer must be a madman, then."

"One might assume so, given the ferocity of the killings. But I'm not convinced of that either."

"What do you think is his rationale, then?"

"Vengeance, Watson. Vengeance fueled by uncontrollable anger and far greater than normal brute strength, for it isn't an easy task to kill a man . . . or even a woman . . . with one's bare hands. Yet this villain has done so repeatedly. Frankly, it's the death of the woman that interests me the most. Given her occupation, it is no great leap of deduction to presume that danger was simply a factor of her life, which is why she carried a knife with her."

"The papers say only that she had been stabbed," Watson countered. "Why do you believe it was with her own knife?"

"Because the reports don't mention either of the male victims being stabbed. What's more, a killer possessing that much rage and ferocity in his work wouldn't simply have stabbed his victim in the side. He would have stabbed again and again and again, defiling the body and rendering it as unrecognizable. I believe the poor unfortunate woman was a witness to the murder of this Vartaine and paid the price for her presence at the scene. What a pity. Had the woman run away and contacted a policeman to describe what she'd seen, she might not only still be alive, but able to give a description of the killer as well. Instead, she had to confront the man."

"How do you know she confronted him?"

"Oh, really Watson! The knife was in her side, which implies it had been in her hand before she fell on it, which means she pulled it out of wherever she had it sequestered in her clothing. Why else should she have pulled the knife, if not to confront the killer?"

"Couldn't she have fallen on it while it was sequestered in her clothing?"

Holmes considered that for a moment. "I admit that is an excellent question that should be considered. I would only know for certain had I been able to examine the body."

"You really should speak to Lestrade about your deductions. Perhaps he could provide you with information as to the body's position beyond what the papers are reporting."

302

"If Lestrade wishes to consult me, he may do so. Until then, I'm as powerless to help as an anonymous letter-writer claiming to have information regarding a case, only to find that his opinions will either be accepted or dismissed at will."

"Even so, it seems like your input would be valuable. You might even be able to prevent the next killing."

"Assuming that the killer hasn't already assuaged his anger or carried out his desire for vengeance, which means there will not be another killing."

"Still, Holmes – "

"Watson, in a case such as this, even I must put some faith and trust in the Yard, despite their past ineptitude. There is no nuance to these killings, no subtlety. They are brutal and obvious. So bold, blatant, and violent a killer will indeed be caught, mark my word. Even Lestrade will not be eluded for much longer." Sherlock Holmes then pointed to the teapot on the small dining table. "Is there any tea left in there?" he asked.

Anything but assuaged or feeling fulfilled, Erik Selden moved on to his next victim, a mudlark whom he beat to death and shoved into the low-tide mud near Wapping, ostensibly to throw the police off the scent and dissuade them from thinking that every killing was reserved for the Notting Hill area. That was what he told himself, at any rate. The truth was he was craving the feeling of invincibility that killing instilled in him.

His next murder remained closer to home.

While operating his stall in Portobello Road, he had been approached by a man interested in buying one of his most valuable items, a sterling silver snuff box that had been brought to him by a burglar from Richmond. The buyer, a middle-aged, owlish-looking man with a grey coat and matching flared top hat, picked the box up and examined it closely. He then turned around and held it up to the sun, as though to inspect the sheen. Turning back, he set it down on Selden's wares table and said, "Thank you, but two sovereigns is a lot of money. I shall have to think about it."

It took mere seconds for Selden to realize that the man had switched snuff boxes, replacing the valuable silver one with a cheaply made tin object, but in those mere seconds the man had disappeared into the crowd. *If I ever see him again, I'll reduce his thieving hands to pig feed*, Selden though viciously.

He saw the man again the next evening coming out of a pawnbroker's shop in Kensington Church Street, where Selden often took his more valuable fenced items, and where he *should* have taken the snuff box before offering it for sale. He followed the man to what was presumably his home and, after he had entered, waited until dusk before knocking at the door. While momentarily worried that someone else would answer, a family member or servant, it was the owl that opened his front door for the last time.

The man's body was discovered two days later after a neighbor became suspicious at not seeing him leave the house or return to it. Selden only learned his name, Colfax Treaves, from the newspapers.

By then, though, Erik Selden had located the third man from the card game: The completely bald ruffian. He recognized him immediately, since unlike virtually all other men in the city he wore no hat, presuming him to have been some sort of servant to Carmichael, perhaps even a bodyguard. Selden spotted the man emerging from The Elephant, a pub at the end of Portobello Road after closing up his booth, and the fact that the man was perpetually looking around him as he made his way through the streets indicated to Selden that he feared he might be facing danger. At one point the man stopped to talk to a policeman, who appeared to agree to walk with the man until he was away from Notting Hill. Selden, of course, followed them.

The policeman broke away at the edge of the district, and the man continued to walk alone, ever vigilant, four or so miles to Camden Town. There he entered an old building and within a minute, Selden saw a light come on in a first-floor room. He waited and watched.

It was at the first shadow of dusk that the man emerged from the building again and, after looking around, made his way down the street to a tiny chop shop. Selden followed in the burgeoning darkness, the night being remarkably free of fog, wishing he had thought to bring his false beard with him. At least his brass fist was in his pocket.

Going inside the eating house, Selden took a table in the corner from which he could watch the man, who ordered a dinner of either beef, pork, or lamb – it was hard to tell from the distance. It might even have been hard to tell by tasting it.

Ordering nothing but a tumbler of gin and a sausage, Selden ate mechanically while he continued his vigil. As soon as the man was finished, he got up and headed for the cashier. Selden likewise rose, dropping a couple shillings on the table, absently hoping it would cover the food and drink, but in truth not really caring.

It was dark now. The bald man looked around and started to return to his home, with Selden keeping a safe distance behind. At some point, though, the man became aware he was being followed and picked up his step. Selden did as well. At Euston Road, the man hailed a hansom cab, an eventuality that Selden hadn't anticipated. Standing back while the man gave directions to the driver and entered the coach, Selden then sprang into a run and hollered, "Wait!" before the driver could prod the horse.

Reaching for his brass knuckles, Selden delivered a painful blow to the driver's shin, which caused the cabman cried out in agony and double over, letting the reins drop. Selden easily pulled him from the driver's seat and deposited him on the ground and leapt up to take his place.

"What the bloody hell's going on out there?" the bald man screamed from inside the hansom, but by then Selden had whipped the horse into action. Not a skilled driver, Selden careened across the street, narrowly missing other vehicles and pedestrians as he raced back to the man's residence. At least that's where he thought he was going. Opening the trap, the passenger looked up to see that it wasn't the driver he had hired in control of the vehicle. A moment later, the folding doors opened, and the man stepped onto the platform to make a leap for it, but Selden whipped him on the top of his head until he fell back inside.

Before long, however, the well-trained cab horse began to rebel at Selden's wild and contradictory instructions and came to a halt near the Regent's Canal. No amount of whipping could get the beast to move. It merely reared. This gave the man the opportunity to jump out and run. When Selden realized what was happening, he leapt down and gave chase. The man began crying for help, but none appeared to be forthcoming. Finally, the man's luck ran out when he made a turn into the blind alley. Selden followed him, reaching into his pocket for his brass knuckles.

"Who are you?" the man cried, blood running down his face from the whip cut on his unprotected head.

"Your executioner," Selden replied. "You'll pay for what you did to me, like the others did. You'll soon be burning in Hell like your fancy benefactor, Lord Carmichael, and that fat swine, Vartaine."

"Carmichael . . . Vartaine . . . By Christ, you're the Notting Hill Murderer!"

"I'm the Notting Hill Murderer, all right. Who are you?"

"My name's Hawthorne, you bastard, and you might find me a little harder to subdue than your other victims."

"That's a bet I'll take."

Looking past Selden, Hawthorne suddenly shouted, "Over here, Officer!" Selden instinctively turned to look behind him, which is what the other man was counting on. Hawthorne charged Selden, and knocking him to the ground, but Selden quickly recovered and reached out to grab the man's leg, tripping him. Then leaping up, Selden jumped on Hawthorne's arms, pinning them. "Nice try," Selden said, raising his metallic fist, "but there's no bloody peelers here."

But then the light of a bull's eye lamp then illuminated the dark alley, and a voice called, "What's going on here?"

"This is the Notting Hill Murderer!" Hawthorne cried.

"Drop the weapon!" the voice called. "I have a pistol."

Selden froze momentarily, running the odds of escape over in his mind, finally deciding there were none. He lowered his fist and stepped off of his quarry. He turned to see a policeman, with the lantern in one hand and a pistol in the other. "I wouldn't move, if I were you," the officer said. Then slowly crouching down, he set the lantern on the ground and withdrew his police whistle, giving a sharp blast to summon other officers.

Struggling to his feet, rubbing his bruised arms, Hawthorne said, "This man tried to kidnap me, and then murder me! I tried to fight him off, but if you hadn't arrived – "

"Yes, sir," the policeman interrupted, standing once more with the lantern. "We'll take your statement, don't worry."

Within seconds, more policemen arrived in the alley, one of which roughly removed Selden's brass knuckles and then clapped handcuffs on him.

"Now then, sir," the first officer began, "you say he tried to kidnap you?"

"Yes. He stole a cab, injured the driver, and took his place. Fortunately, he didn't know how to drive."

"That explains the empty hansom we found," another officer said.

"The horse simply refused to go," Hawthorne went on, "and I was able to get away, but not far."

Then Erik Selden began to laugh.

"What's so bleeding funny?" the first officer asked.

"The damned nag refused to go," Selden replied, now laughing almost uncontrollably. "I bet big on a horse, and lost!"

When Dr. Watson entered his Baker Street flat the next morning, he was carrying a well-perused copy of that day's *Times*. "It appears you were right," he said, dropping the newspaper on the table.

"I generally am," Sherlock Holmes replied. "Of what was I right about this time?"

"They caught the Notting Hill Murderer."

"Indeed?"

"You mean you haven't heard yet? Every newsvendor on every street is competing to bray out the details the loudest."

"I haven't been out this morning. Can you give me those details?"

"It was a man named Erik Selden who began by murdering those who cheated him at cards, but then kept on. At least the residents of Notting Hill can now rest easier that he's put away. He shall face the gallows, no doubt."

"Perhaps."

"Really, Holmes, how could someone who committed that many heinous crimes for no good reason not be put to death?"

"One isolated murder, Watson, might be explained away as a crime of passion, or greed, or some other extreme human emotion. But a series of brutal murders is evidence of a disease."

"So you admit I was correct when I said the killer must be mad?"

"What I said was a *disease*."

"Disease is something I can understand. I have devoted my life to treating them. This is different."

"I shall then defer to your judgment as a medical man. Perhaps lunacy is the only way to describe a gnawing hunger for causing the death of others that can only be temporarily satisfied, though I remain convinced that something had to provoke it, something that can be quantitated beyond the blanket term of 'madness'. That doesn't change my belief that the severity of this Selden's crimes will result in his seemingly inevitable death sentence ultimately commuted to lifetime incarceration, either in a prison or a mental institution."

"Will you be attending the trial, then?"

"I think not. I have as much confidence in the press to cover its happenings accurately as I did in the Yard of apprehending the criminal. Incidentally, Watson, a moment ago you stated that the murderer committed heinous crimes for no good reason. Therefore, you must believe that there *is* a good reason for committing a heinous crime. I should be very happy to hear what it is."

"Confound it, Holmes, you know what I meant!"

Sherlock Holmes laughed. "Yes, I do. But on occasion it is what you *say* that gives one pause."

Sherlock Holmes's judgment was, as nearly always, correct. After a brief trial in which the only defense was mental instability, Selden was spared the death penalty and instead sentenced to life imprisonment at Dartmoor Prison. Despite his dread of incarceration, Selden actually smiled when the sentence was delivered, aware of something that no one else knew, which was that his sister Eliza was currently working as a servant at a remote manor house near the prison. *Reduced to working as a servant*, he thought.

From the first moment of his imprisonment, Selden turned his focus to ways and means of escaping and fleeing to the manor house to appeal for help from his sister. No matter what their past relationship had been, he remained convinced she couldn't turn him away. It took seven months of watching and waiting to formulate his escape plan, which was predicated upon his acting as defeated, weak, and feeble as he could at all times, so that no one – not his fellow inmates, nor the gaolers, nor even the warden – would ever expect him capable of plotting a break. Even when he was discovered walking around where he shouldn't have been, it was assumed he was simply lost and confused. In this way, Selden planned his escape route.

When the opportunity finally arose, facilitated by the delivery of a food and supply truck and the gaoler whom Selden had witnessed leaving the entry gate open longer than he should have, he managed to slip through and reverted to his old skill by battering the driver to death. Then he fled.

Selden arrived at the estate on which his sister was employed, which was owned by a rich man named Baskerville, two days later. "What are you doing here?" Eliza cried, shocked by bearded, ragged, almost bestial in appearance.

"I broke out of prison, Lizzie," Selden answered. "I mean to stay out."

"Where will you go?"

"I was thinking of here."

"Did you say *here*?" Eliza's husband, Barrymore said, turning his deaf left ear toward the man. "That is out of the question."

"What if I say it isn't?"

"With the master now dead, I am in charge of the house."

"There are a lot of rooms here. I'm sure you could find one for me."

"Out of the question," Barrymore repeated.

"John, we can't just turn him away like an animal," Eliza said. "He's my brother."

"He is a convicted murderer and escapee, my dear. He cannot stay in the house."

"Can't he stay somewhere on the grounds?" Eliza asked. "Please, John. I have never begged for anything from you before, but I am begging for this."

The butler sighed. "Very well, my dear. There's a spare room in the groom's cottage. He may stay there. But only after I've removed from the servant cottages and stable any object that might potentially be used as a weapon."

"Out with the other animals, huh?" Selden sneered.

"You may accept the offer or take your chances on the moors. The choice is yours."

"Fine, you bloody rich man's slave."

That was the situation for two days, and it might have gone on indefinitely hadn't Barrymore gone to his wife with a letter in his hand. "I'm afraid your brother has to leave," he announced.

"Why?" Eliza asked. "He hasn't caused any mischief since he arrived."

"This missive is from Dr. Mortimer. It seems that Sir Charles's nephew, Henry, is arriving any day to become the new Lord of the Manor."

"Oh, dear."

"I shall evict him."

"No, John. Let me tell him."

Eliza Barrymore found her brother wandering around outside the stable. "Erik, you have to go," she said, trying to sound firm.

"Oh? And why's that, Lizzie?"

After explaining the situation, Erik swore, using language that turned his sister the color of a tomato. "Where the Hell am I supposed to go now?"

"I don't know, but you can't stay here. You'd be seen and turned in for sure."

"I have to think." He began pacing back and forth like an animal in the wild who nevertheless believed it was in a cage. "Your bloody husband figured this all along, didn't he? I'll have to take my chances on the moor. Well, I'll take them. I spotted some caves when I was making my way here. They'll be a good hideout until I can think of something else."

"We can give you food and blankets," Eliza said. "Maybe the new heir won't stay long and you can come back."

"Maybe I should just come back and tell him what's what, and if he doesn't like it — "

"No, Erik you can't do that! You'd be retaken — or worse."

"And what would he do? Set the dogs loose on me?"

"Erik, please go. Hide out on the moor. I'll take care of you as best I can. I promise."

"All right, Lizzie. I'll go. And I'll see your promise and raise you one: I'll never be retaken. Never."

And with that, the ragged, filthy, but ever-confident Erik Selden left the security of Baskerville Hall and headed off toward his fate on the moor . . . .

The Last False Step
by Tom Turley

The shots echoed dully through the fog, followed by the poor beast's howl of agony, the sound of running feet, and a veritable fusillade. Rodger Baskerville cursed himself for a self-deluding fool. The Great Detective had returned, Cousin Henry would survive, and the grand scheme he had spent two years devising vanished in the mist.

He turned and strode quickly towards the house, confident that Antonio and Beryl, between them, would delay his pursuers long enough to enable his escape into the mire. Holmes would hardly dare to follow in this fog, and by morning he would have emerged from the mine's distant terminus and be well away from Princetown. With luck, it would be as close to the prison as he would ever come. If escape was now the only option, his own incredible misjudgment was to blame.

Twenty-six hours earlier, Rodger had made this same walk over the moor, listening with satisfaction to Henry's screams of terror. If he listened hard enough, he could even hear the throaty rumble of the hound. (Hugo never bayed while hunting, only after being left alone.) There came one last despairing cry, and he heard nothing more. As the rising moon illuminated him benignly, Rodger felt so pleased that he began to whistle. He did not increase his pace, content to savour the anticipation of his triumph.

Soon, the high tor loomed ahead, its sheer face overlooking the rock-strewn slope below. Rodger scanned the ground eagerly for Henry's corpse – so eagerly that he nearly missed two moonlit figures that brought him to a sudden halt. One he recognised as Dr. Watson. The other was too tall and thin to be his quarry. Good God! It could only be the Great Detective, and the cup of victory was dashed from Rodger's lips.

Fighting down panic, he approached the pair, both of whom maintained an ominous silence. Jack Stapleton's jaunty greeting died in Rodger's throat when he saw the broken body on the ground. He rushed to examine it, then realised – with horror – that he had already identified the convict as "Sir Henry". Watson caught the slip immediately. Badly shaken, Rodger heard himself babble like an idiot – asking anxiously about "a phantom hound", admitting that it was he who had invited the baronet to walk across the moor. Before regaining a degree of self-control, he had all but revealed to Sherlock Holmes his well-tried mode of murder.

Yet, the man had seemed oblivious. Confessing himself baffled by a case founded on "legends and rumours", he announced his intention to return to London the next day. Rodger quickly recovered his self-confidence. Almost contemptuously, he recalled the morning he had used a cabman to give his own name back to "Mr. Sherlock Holmes". Tomorrow night, he would beat the Great Detective in Dartmoor as he had in London!

Instead, Holmes had turned that boast into a mockery. It was obvious to Rodger (*Now!*) that a sane murderer would have waited weeks or months to strike again, rather than doggedly repeating the attempt at once. Hubris – ever his besetting sin – had rushed him headlong into the detective's trap. So there must be another flight, another fresh start somewhere else, this time alone. But "alone" to Rodger Baskerville simply meant fewer complications. Despite his blundering, his faith in his own destiny remained intact.

Merripit House appeared beside him through the fog, but he kept moving, hardly giving it a farewell glance. Rodger had despised the cramped, cold moorland farmhouse, as bleak and comfortless as the moor itself. Beryl (to give the faithless slut her due) had tried to make it homelike, but returning "home" after envying the decrepit splendour of Baskerville Hall had always set Rodger's teeth on edge. Nevertheless, he did look back briefly at an upper-storey window. Inside that room in Merripit, his wife stood bound and gagged, pinned as securely as the moths and butterflies inside the cabinets that shared the space – and no more alive to him than they. Beryl Garcia: the most beautiful girl in San José. Beryl Vandeleur: Wife of St. Oliver's headmaster. Beryl Stapleton: Jack's loyal "sister", who tonight admitted she would rather have been Lady Baskerville – with Henry as the baronet! Still furious, he recalled their final quarrel as he left the house behind . . . .

"I won't stand for it, Rodger! Not again! I warned Henry in London, and I'll warn him if he comes tonight! It's bad enough that you tried to use me to entice Sir Charles. You'll not make me a murderer as well."

"Oh, stop your pious drivel," he said amiably, still determined to be patient. (To a point, Rodger was willing to tolerate Beryl's Latin fire, for she grew even lovelier when she was angry.) "I think you knew perfectly well what would happen to Uncle Charles, and you never said a word to me until the deed was done. As I recall, your accusations dried up rather quickly when you learned I could eventually inherit close on a million!"

"That isn't true! I didn't know. I may have suspected you wanted to murder the old man, but I never believed you'd actually go through with

it." As usual when she was lying, his wife turned her eyes away and glided to a window.

Rodger's smirk gave that remark the contempt that it deserved. "Beryl," he queried softly, "in all the years we've been together, have you known me not to go through with a plan that worked to my advantage? Why did you think I bought the hound?

"No, my angel," he continued, warming to the theme, "the reason you developed a conscience was that this new heir from Canada was young and handsome. Your loyalties became divided. I saw it on the moor the morning when I found him making love to you."

"Yes, and what a fool you made of yourself that day!" Beryl countered mockingly. "Your scheme nearly foundered on your insane jealousy. How it must have shamed you to go crawling to Henry and apologise. It made me laugh. He's twice the man you are!"

A dangerous glitter came into Rodger's eyes. "Careful, dear wife. You don't want to bandy insults like 'insane' about." They were arguing in the kitchen, and on a nail beside the door there hung a bullwhip he had bought in Costa Rica. It hadn't been needed for the dog, but he still kept it handy. He moved now so that it came within his reach.

"The truth is, Beryl, that I could never trust you. You haven't got the backbone for this sort of business. I was better off utilising Laura Lyons." A warning bell went off in Rodger's head, but he ignored it.

"Who is Laura Lyons?" Beryl's slightly swarthy visage paled, as he'd intended. It amazed him that these dolts in Dartmoor had never guessed her heritage or recognised a Spanish accent. How could the two of them possibly be siblings?

"You've heard of her: Old Frankland's daughter. I met her at the vicarage and later at Baskerville Hall. Not quite in your class as a beauty, but an even bigger trollop. She ran off with an artist fellow the year before we came here."

"And what has she become to you?"

"Purely a charity case, my dear. She imposed herself upon Sir Charles's goodwill, and I acted as his almoner. But Laura definitely had her uses. It was she – indirectly, in the end – who inveigled the old man into the Yew Alley on the night he died."

"So you used her as you'd intended to use me!" his wife snapped. "What did you offer in return for her cooperation?"

"Why, to marry her, of course." He smiled in Beryl's stricken face. "I could hardly tell her I was married to my sister, could I?"

She came at Rodger then, but he was quicker. One kick in the gut, one flick of the bullwhip on her pretty neck, and it was over. He manhandled her upstairs to the museum room and lashed her to the pillar. And there his dear wife could remain for all eternity, unless someone else cared more than he.

Now, Rodger found himself suppressing a regretful sigh. Had tonight only gone as planned, they'd have made up the quarrel as they always did. It was, after all, the first time Rodger had physically assaulted her. But he needn't worry about Beryl. At this very moment, she was probably throwing herself on the detective's tender mercies, or more likely Watson's. (Holmes's proxy had cast several appreciative glances at the beautiful Miss Stapleton.) Even Henry might be sufficiently infatuated to forgive the object of his lust. If so, the fool deserved exactly what he'd get.

As he passed the stunted orchard, Rodger spared a thought for Hugo, who had spent his last evening in an outbuilding just across the wall. That hound could have given Beryl a lesson in humility. He had repeatedly suffered his master to apply the phosphorus, even though he hated it. Had the huge beast been as bloodthirsty as those cheats at Ross and Mangles claimed, his satanic decoration would not have been required. But despite his size and fearsome aspect, Hugo proved to be a gentle-natured soul. He had bounded after Uncle Charles less like Cerberus than a pet who wants to play. Luckily, the old man's heart and terror of the legend, allied with the phosphorus, sufficed to do the job. Rodger hoped that Hugo, in his death throes, had managed to give Cousin Henry a good mauling.

The moon still shone above him, but the tors and barren hills beyond were blanketed in white. At least the moorland path was visible. If the fog became no thicker before he reached the mire, he could still see the guiding wands he and Beryl had planted. Even so, Rodger began to grow a little doubtful of the outcome of this night. He had never crossed the Grimpen Mire in moonlight, much less in fog, and the dire warnings he had issued Dr. Watson echoed in his mind. *"A rare place for a gallop!"* He sneered inwardly. By God, if only Holmes and Watson would follow him tonight!

To distract himself, Rodger briefly reconsidered Uncle Charles. Surprisingly, there was room for regret there as well. The baronet had been a generous benefactor – The two-hundred-pound gratuity Stapleton received as his almoner had been a godsend! – as well as an entertaining host. Things could have gone quite differently between them if not for Rodger's past. Involuntarily, he recalled a scene twelve years ago: A sweltering, ill-lit room in San José, where a gaunt and haggard human ruin lay dying on a bed.

"I can't go back there, lad, not now," his father wheezed, eyes bright with alcohol and fever, "but you can. Now that the old devil's gone, with Henry dead and Charles in South Africa, the place is waiting for you. The

Hall itself is worth a fortune. Don't go yet. Make yourself some money first. You don't want to show up hat in hand. But never forget that you're a Baskerville. They can't keep you out, lad. It's your birthright."

So he stayed and worked for six more years, toiling away at the Ministry of Trade in the clerical position his father's bribe obtained for him before their coastal trading firm collapsed. Rodger's devotion to finance, coupled with his inherited disdain for scruples, allowed him gradually to prosper in a more-than-modest way. For relaxation, he pursued his entomological studies in Costa Rica's teeming jungles. He even won a lovely señorita for his bride, through the simple (if quite pleasant) expedient of taking her virginity. But it all came crashing down one summer afternoon, when a note from the minister himself appeared on Rodger's desk:

Señor Baskerville,

Our recent audit has uncovered missing funds from your department. Please present yourself in my office at ten o'clock tomorrow to account for them.

Fortunately, he had had sufficient warning to secure tickets for the "Vandeleurs" on a steamer bound for England. Avoiding arrest had merely expedited his decision to "go home" to a country he had never seen. Meeting Gerald Fraser on the voyage had been a blessing and a curse. Rodger's ready capital and scientific interests, coupled with the sickly tutor's knowledge of the Classics, enabled the two of them to buy and run a third-rate private school in York. For three years, the venture had gone well. Then an epidemic of consumption broke out among the boys. Worse yet, it seemed they had acquired it from their tutor. Fraser escaped disgrace and bankruptcy by his timely death, but St. Oliver's and the Vandeleurs were ruined. Rodger had to flee once more, leaving to entomology his abandoned alias and a moth he had discovered on the Yorkshire Moors.

Thus, he and Beryl came home at last to Dartmoor. With Rodger's scant remaining capital, he'd rented an ugly granite house near Grimpen Mire, choosing a new alias to sign the lease in Coombe Tracey. Later that afternoon, the Stapletons (brother and sister, Rodger had decreed, further obscuring the Vandeleurs' identity) set out across the Devon moor – it looked most promising for Lepidoptera – to view his family's ancestral home. And there, three weeks in residence, they found Sir Charles Baskerville.

314

By ten o'clock, the moon had slipped behind the clouds, and the fog had definitely thickened. Without a lantern, Rodger was finding the path difficult to follow. There was not a breath of wind. The moor – what little he could see of it – was unnaturally silent. Increasingly ill at ease, he began straining to hear a noise of any kind. Perhaps the hoofbeats of mad Hugo's mare, or the baying of a spectral Hound! But, no, Rodger wouldn't succumb to the terrors he had inflicted on his uncle. There could be no pursuit tonight, and his all-too-mortal hound was dead. So Rodger groped on through the swirling whiteness, step by step. A fetid stench gradually began to penetrate his nostrils, and he realised that the mire couldn't be far ahead. Meanwhile, thoughts of the past kept running wildly through his mind. He remembered the first words Uncle Charles ever said to him: "*You bear an uncanny resemblance to my youngest brother, Mr. Stapleton, whom I haven't seen in forty years. Are you quite sure you aren't Rodger Baskerville, come back to life?*"

And what if he had answered differently? On their way to Baskerville Hall, Beryl had urged him to confess his true identity. Instead, he had lied by instinct to his uncle – another link in the chain of false steps forged in San José and Yorkshire. But there had never really been a choice. Even had his criminal past not precluded honesty, Rodger *fils*, like Rodger *père*, was too proud to appear on the Baskerville doorstep hat in hand.

So Jack Stapleton was forced to play a waiting game, striving to become, instead of family, Sir Charles's right-hand man. Unfortunately, in view of the baronet's health, that role had been usurped by Dr. Mortimer. Rodger compensated for this inconvenience by befriending the young surgeon, thereby acquiring information that became quite useful later on. (In that regard, Mortimer did not adhere too strictly to the Hippocratic Oath.) He'd had no plan, at that stage, for ending his uncle's life prematurely. As an early death from heart failure was forecast, it seemed more critical to establish his own credentials as heir to the estate. Maddeningly, Rodger's very proximity, under an alias, complicated that goal beyond his immediate ability to solve. For the present, he was resigned to serve usefully as advisor and assistant, while Sir Charles employed his vast fortune for his neighbours' good.

Yet, Rodger begrudged the loss of every penny, seeking where possible to reap some advantage from these charitable pursuits. Meeting Laura Lyons confirmed his wisdom in posing as a bachelor after he arrived in Dartmoor. Thanks to her irascible father, Mrs. Lyons' financial situation was more desperate than his own, while her susceptibility to masterful gentlemen made her a pliant tool in Rodger's hands. The only question was how to make best use of her.

The answer to that and other questions came as he grew closer to Sir Charles. The baronet was a convivial man. He enjoyed socialising and was unguarded in the company of those with whom he felt at ease. On one memorable occasion, his uncle had resolved a mystery that Rodger's father had never coherently explained: How an entire generation of Baskervilles had been driven into exile from their family hall. It seemed that their own father – another Hugo – had been a virtual reincarnation of the wicked Cavalier. When he married, late in life, a woman unworthy of their mother's memory, Charles and his younger brothers had objected strongly – so strongly that their father had disowned them, one and all. Of the three (the baronet reflected sadly), only the eldest had returned, after making his fortune in South Africa's gold and diamond mines. Henry had died of cancer in his South Coast cottage, and (much to Jack Stapleton's relief) Charles had lost contact altogether with his ne'er-do-well cadet.

But for Rodger, the decisive lesson in Baskerville history had come last December, when the baronet had invited his three boon companions (the others being Mortimer and Frankland) to hear a Christmas tale. Two nights before the Eve, they had gathered in the Hall's black-beamed, shadowed dining room, eaten the excellent dinner prepared by Mrs. Barrymore, and lingered to enjoy even finer brandy and cigars. Then Sir Charles took from his coat pocket a yellowed manuscript. He told his guests that it set forth a hoary legend of the Baskervilles. And so it did. Yet, before the tale was halfway done, it came to Rodger Baskerville that should he himself so choose, the document from which his uncle read could also be his death-warrant.

Meanwhile, Rodger's place was to play the skeptic. "Surely, Sir Charles, you don't take this entertaining nonsense seriously?"

"Of course not, Stapleton!" the baronet guffawed. "I happened to find the thing last week, hidden away up in the attic, and thought you fellows might enjoy it. But you can't deny," he went on, with a touch of the quaver that came into his voice when he described the Hound, "that a good many of the Baskervilles have met with a bad end."

"How many of them could actually have read it?" enquired Mortimer with his usual incisiveness. "There's a good deal to be said for the power of suggestion."

"Quite a few, I should imagine. My father read it to the three of us when we were boys. I suspect he hoped to frighten us into better behaviour than his own! It worked for Henry and me. As for poor young Rodger," Uncle Charles muttered softly, "it must have had the opposite effect. I'd nearly forgotten the horrid tale 'til now,"

Frankland waded in with legalistic irrelevancy. "Is it possible to trace the family of the girl Sir Hugo murdered? They may have a civil case

316

at law against you, Baskerville. No doubt a descendant can be found in Grimpen or Coombe Tracey. I warn you, sir, I shall undertake to file the suit myself!"

"Suit yourself!" the baronet replied, to general amusement, and their talk passed on to other matters.

But for Rodger, that night had been a revelation. He had seen his uncle's hands shake when he held the manuscript and heard the wobble in the old man's voice. It was evident to his discerning eye that this Baskerville took the family legend to be fact instead of fiction. Given his delusion, Rodger's course was obvious. He began searching for a living replica of the phantom hound, finally locating a dog large and (reputedly) fierce enough to serve his purpose. Rather whimsically, he named the beast Hugo and kennelled him in an abandoned hovel in the Grimpen Mire. Retaining a glove the baronet dropped one afternoon in the Yew Alley, he began training Hugo to hunt, and occasionally allowed him to run loose on the moor. One night in April, they had even approached Baskerville Hall, where (as he soon heard from Mortimer) Sir Charles had been horrified to glimpse the Hound.

Yet, beyond these preliminary exercises, Rodger couldn't steel himself to act. He had developed a reluctant liking for his uncle, and murder was one sin not yet charged to his account. That fact changed abruptly on the first of May. Since arriving in Devonshire, Rodger had replenished his finances through periodic burglaries, employing skills his father had taught him early on. His previous successful jobs had been non-violent, but that night in Folkstone Court, a page surprised him as he left the house, and he had reflexively pistolled the boy in self-defence. This false step destroyed the last of Rodger's scruples. Having learned that Sir Charles was about to accept Mortimer's advice and go to London, he realised that it was essential to move quickly. Indeed, he marvelled that his hastily completed plan had worked so well.

It had involved an absurd comedy with Laura Lyons, whom Rodger recruited to lure his uncle into the Yew Alley after Beryl had haughtily refused the task. Any less stupid or infatuated woman, presented with Jack Stapleton's inexplicable changes of front, would immediately have smelt a rat. Fortunately, dangling a wedding ring in front of Laura always ensured her co-operation. The last requirement of his plan fell into place.

Shortly after ten o'clock on the evening of May the fourth, Rodger and Hugo hid themselves within a stand of trees fifty yards from the Yew Alley. Despite the swirling fog, light from the Hall showed Uncle Charles where he ought to be: Striding impatiently up and down the path behind the moor gate, smoking a cigar. He waited until the baronet had started towards the summer house, then gave a brief command. The loyal hound,

317

snuffling with eagerness and glowing fiendishly, covered the intervening distance and leapt the moor gate with a single bound. Rodger covered his ears and smothered his conscience, but he couldn't shut out his uncle's screams. All too soon, the night was quiet again. He retrieved his bewildered devil-dog and set off back across the moor. The Hound of the Baskervilles had fulfilled its evil destiny.

The inquest, to his relief, was a formality. Stapleton wasn't called to testify, and it appeared that Hugo – miraculously – had left no traces of his presence at the scene. Only Mortimer's testimony could have become awkward, but under questioning he admitted that Sir Charles's facial distortion was not unusual in cases of sudden cardiac arrest. On the evidence presented, the coroner soon reached a finding of death from natural causes, putting the "Curse of the Baskervilles" rumours officially to rest.

At the reading of the will two days later, Rodger was pleasantly surprised to learn that his uncle's estate amounted to nearly a million. Nor did he resent inheriting but half the monetary legacy that Sir Charles's doctor-cum-executor received. Then came a shock that utterly destroyed his complacency. Mortimer announced that previously unknown to anyone except himself, the late baronet had named an heir! It was, in fact, his nephew – another Henry – aged approximately thirty and presumably still alive in Canada, whence he had immigrated at fifteen following his father's death.

So, it was all to do again! If Jack Stapleton had been a weeping man, Rodger could easily have broken down. As matters stood, he and Frankland, like himself a trustee and the only other attendee save for the Barrymores – Laura Lyons, another beneficiary, had failed to appear – peppered the executor urgently with questions. Why had no one heard of Henry Baskerville if he was in fact alive? Could they be sure he was a British subject? Had Mortimer corresponded with him? When was he expected to return? And, finally, how could an American cowboy be a suitable heir to a baronetcy and the Baskerville estate? For once, Rodger was grateful to have Frankland as an ally, for the old windbag at least knew the law.

But Mortimer could offer them scant satisfaction, for he himself knew very little of the man. At best, it would take some time to trace him, so the Baskerville inheritance was unlikely to be settled before autumn. Fortunately (Rodger heard with horror), there was another heir if Henry Baskerville could not be found. He was James Desmond, an elderly clergyman in Westmoreland and only a distant cousin of the Baskervilles. Slender though his claim might be, it was unthinkable that the Hall

318

shouldn't be occupied, lest all of Sir Charles's plans for Dartmoor come to naught.

The upshot was that little or nothing would happen over summer. Rodger lacked the stamina to wait things out. In mid-July, he decided to take Beryl, whose questions about his uncle's death were becoming inconvenient, to London for a week. They stayed at the Mexborough in Craven Street, the best hotel he could afford. Rodger exerted himself to win back his wife's confidence, sitting through various dull plays and concerts of the type that she enjoyed. By week's end, he flattered himself he had succeeded.

Then, the day before their planned return to Dartmoor, the morning dailies carried news that promised to transform his fortunes. A change of government had occurred in Costa Rica, bringing into office a member of Beryl's family and two of his old cronies in the Ministry of Trade. Rodger sent Beryl home at once to write a congratulatory letter to her brother. With the last of his booty from the Folkstone job, he took ship to Cartagena and (clandestinely) to an obscure port on the Costa Rican border. There, he and his two allies negotiated a settlement that would drop all criminal charges against Rodger and permit the Baskervilles' return to San José. Once their legal residence was reestablished, he could lay claim through the British legation to the Baskerville estate. Rodger's cronies and the new Attorney General (who would surely sanction the agreement for his sister's sake) would be handsomely rewarded for their services when he inherited.

For the present, this Heaven-sent opportunity was purely hypothetical, but Rodger came back to Merripit House in mid-September with his destiny renewed. While he would never hold the baronetcy, it meant little to him in itself. A sharper loss was giving up the Hall, but obviously the man once known as Stapleton could never live there. Much finer estates could readily be had in Europe. There were too many ghosts for him in England, and Rodger had no intention of residing permanently in San José. If Beryl would have to be content with visits to her family, the wealth of the Baskervilles should ease that loss as well. They would have only the money, but the money was enough.

Naturally, on arriving home he informed his wife of the prospect of returning to her homeland, but said nothing of his plan to claim the Baskerville estate. Beryl seemed less gratified than he had hoped. The talk in Grimpen, meanwhile, was all of Henry's advent. He had at last been found and, according to the rumours, was to dock at Southampton on the twenty-fifth. Rodger sought out Mortimer to confirm the news.

"It's true enough, Stapleton. I'm meeting him at Waterloo late tomorrow morning. Would you like to come along?"

319

"No, thank you. I've had quite enough of travelling for now." This was a lie, for a new plan was taking shape in Rodger's mind. He had every intention of going to London, but definitely not with Mortimer. If Cousin Henry was coming to take over the Baskerville inheritance, then Cousin Henry must be dealt with. It would be far better to ensure that he never got to Devonshire.

"Frankland also turned me down," the doctor sighed. *"To be honest, I'm perplexed as to how I should advise Sir Henry. I feel sure his uncle would have warned us against bringing the last survivor of the family to the Hall. It's been nothing but a death-trap for the Baskervilles ever since old Hugo's time.*

"Surely you don't expect the young fellow to give up the Hall?" The worst of all outcomes would be for the next heir to live abroad, beyond Rodger's power. *"Besides, the countryside's prosperity depends upon the presence of a Baskerville. As Sir Charles's trustees, Mortimer, we must ensure that his fortune stays in Dartmoor where it's needed. Anything else would be a dereliction of our duty!"*

"Yes, yes, I know all that! But his uncle's death . . . I'm not easy in my mind."

"What do you mean?" asked Rodger sharply. He had planned to spare Mortimer, of course, but if need be . . . What could he possibly know?

"Oh, it's nothing, I suppose," the doctor laughed, obviously sorry he had spoken. *"But I intend to take counsel on the matter, all the same. Have you heard of Sherlock Holmes?"*

"The London detective? Yes, I read that story that came out in Beeton's Christmas Annual. By someone named 'Doyle', as I recall. You don't mean to say the man is real?"

"Oh, yes, quite real," smiled Mortimer. *"Holmes lives in Baker Street and acts as a private consultant. He's reputedly a keen observer, and remarkably clever at analysing problems no one else can solve. I hope to speak with him before I meet Sir Henry."*

"Sounds like a fascinating fellow. I'm sorry I shan't get to meet him. But what can Holmes know of our affairs in Dartmoor?"

"Nothing yet, of course. But after he reads The Chronicle's *account of the inquest, I shall show him the old Baskerville manuscript. Sir Charles entrusted it to me before he died. It's possible that Holmes will find it relevant."*

"More likely, he'll laugh you out of London!"

"Well, perhaps." Rodger had succeeded in nettling his friend. *"But I can't just let this go. You remember how the legend of the fiendish Hound terrified Sir Charles? When I examined his body, I saw that same terror*

reflected in his face. It wasn't natural, despite what I said at the inquest. And then I saw – "

"Saw what?" He gave the doctor a very penetrating look.

"Nothing. Now, if you don't mind, Stapleton, I have a Neolithic skull I'd hoped to examine before I take the evening train to London. We can talk again when I return." He rose, leaving Rodger little choice but to comply.

From Grimpen, he set out across the moor, walking (as he always did) to sooth his agitation. It was obvious that Mortimer knew something! Could Hugo have left his marks in the Yew Alley after all? Thinking of the dog, whom he hadn't seen since his return, Rodger experienced an unexpected moment of affection. He made his way carefully into the Grimpen Mire (for darkness was approaching), soon arriving at his island refuge and Hugo's kennel beside the old tin mine. The hound, scenting him, began baying joyfully, and Rodger allowed him to run loose for half-an-hour before making his own way back to Merripit House, pursued by Hugo's howls.

The lights of Merripit were dimly visible as he stepped into the yard. Rodger was an hour late for dinner, and his wife had chosen not to wait. When Antonio approached him with a warmed-up plate, Rodger curtly waved him off.

"Go and help your mistress pack her bags. We're leaving for London tomorrow on the early train."

"Are we meeting Sir Henry?" Beryl enquired, with more eagerness than Rodger thought appropriate.

"Mortimer's taking care of that." Seeing her disappointment, he changed his mind. "Now that I think of it, my dear, it's better if you remain in Dartmoor. I have business to attend to that's none of your concern."

"No, Rodger," his wife answered, "I think it's better if I come with you to London." They exchanged a meaning glance, and the last illusions died.

"Please yourself," snapped Rodger. "But I warn you, Beryl: This time it won't be a holiday. You'll be spending most of your time alone in the hotel room."

"If I must, querido."

On the train, and later at the Mexborough, they maintained a largely silent truce. When, at half-past-ten, Rodger returned from the bathroom sporting a full, black beard, Beryl was startled into incredulity.

"What in Heaven's name – ?"

"Like it? I'd always wondered how I'd look."

"It makes you look like Barrymore," she said. "I don't mean that as a compliment."

"No, you wouldn't, would you?" Rodger regarded himself critically. "Nevertheless, the resemblance may have its uses.

"Now, you behave yourself, my dear," he added glibly. "I'll probably be gone for a few hours. Yesterday's Times *is on my night table, should you grow bored."*

"How could I possibly grow bored?"

Rodger ignored the parting shot, taking the room's only key to lock the door behind him. By the time he emerged in Craven Street, his excitement had begun to build, and he was feeling oddly cheerful. He signalled to a passing hansom.

"Waterloo Station," Rodger told the cabbie. The campaign against Sir Henry and the Great Detective had begun!

And tonight it had ended, along with many other things.

Rodger stood at the entrance to the Grimpen Mire, the fog dissipating intermittently so that the waning moon was visible above him. For the next half-hour, he continued his flight swiftly and accurately, following the familiar wands. By midnight, he had crossed almost all the mire's expanse and could see his island destination looming in the distance. Atop it was the entrance to the old tin mine.

Abruptly, Rodger experienced an image of the morning he had first met Dr. Watson, their conversation interrupted by the sudden appearance of *Cyclopides*. He could almost visualise Jack Stapleton – that "very active man" – leaping agilely between the bright green tussocks, waving his silly net at the escaping butterfly but missing every time. How well poor Jack had known the mire, and how little anything outside it!

Then the fog cleared again, and he thought he saw *Saturnia vandeleura*, pale grey in the moonlight, fluttering by just out of reach. He had always suspected that his moth might inhabit other moorland mires, but he hadn't yet found it here in Dartmoor. Before he caught himself, Rodger had taken three long strides in pursuit. The last one left him standing in green-scummed water to his knees, with the oozing, sliding, ever-sinking mud beneath his feet. The moth, of course, was gone. He understood now that it had been a phantom of the moon, a sort of "lunar moth" hallucination.

He remembered this portion of the Grimpen Mire, for he had almost drowned here on his initial foray. Two steps behind him lay solid ground and safety. A few wands on, he'd find his route into the mine, almost certainly escaping to begin a new chapter of his wretched life. One step farther on the present way, and there would come a sudden drop. He would be up his neck in a quagmire or submerged entirely, with no chance of pulling himself out – assured of the same fate as that luckless pony he'd shown Watson on the moor. If he didn't move, his end would be no better, just delayed a little longer. Already he was losing his footing in the muck beneath, and the water had just reached his waist. He tried reversing course, but his mired feet would not turn in that direction. So, after all the wasted years of windmill-tilting, the only choice left for Rodger Baskerville was between a quick death and a slow one.

"*Adalante!*" shouted Don Quixote. With a bitter laugh and a convulsive effort, he took the last false step . . . .

Sophy Kratides in Peril
by P.C. Shumway

It had been over two months since the extraordinary affair involving Mr. Melas, the Greek interpreter. At the conclusion, I noted what Mr. Sherlock Holmes speculated to be the end of the affair. A newspaper cutting regarding two Englishmen travelling with a woman to BudaPesth had reached us. The men were found stabbed to death. Holmes surmised the woman to be Sophy Kratides and the two men her captors. I was of the same opinion that the woman was Sophy, who apparently avenged her brother's death and gained her freedom. Horrifying events were about to unfold, however, revealing how mistaken we were in our assumptions.

It was early December, a time when barren trees, morning windows etched with frost, and grey skies foretell the long cold winter ahead, when I received a telegram from Mr. Melas, who had been introduced to us by Holmes's brother Mycroft. As I later recounted in my published story, he had been abducted by Harold Latimer and Wilson Kemp to facilitate a conversation with Sophy Kratides' brother, Paul Kratides, who only spoke in his native Greek, and was held captive and then murdered by the scoundrels. We had found Kratides and Melas in a locked room containing a vessel of burning charcoal. I was able to revive Melas, but we were too late to save Paul Kratides from charcoal asphyxiation.

The dispatch I had just received from Melas was addressed to Dr. *Weston*. I was slightly disheartened that Melas had misremembered my name. The message lacked an explanation for the urgent summons. It simply requested that I bring my medical bag and meet him at his apartment in Pall Mall at the earliest possible instant. I set the telegram upon the dining table, grabbed my Gladstone, and headed for the Westminster address.

Upon arrival, Melas was standing next to a carriage. He whispered to me to not mention my correct name, and then in a normal voice asked that I step inside. There was a well-dressed man in his early thirties sporting a powerful physique sitting in the fore-seat. I sat opposite the man and Melas sat next to me. Melas closed the door, and the carriage proceeded on its course. The man opposite me then produced a revolver from under his coat and pointed it at my chest.

"Do not be alarmed, Dr. Weston. No harm will come to you if you cooperate."

"I'm sorry, Doctor," Melas said. "Mr. Latimer here gave me little choice."

I gave Melas a reproachful look for his cowardice. Harold Latimer was one of the two rogues who had murdered Paul Kratides and held his sister Sophy under his power. I realized Holmes and I were mistaken about the events in BudaPesth, and understood why Melas addressed me as Dr. Weston. My association with Sherlock Holmes was well known. I reproached myself for not having realized the misnamed telegram as a warning and that I hadn't proceeded with more caution. Fortunately, Latimer hadn't recognized the Baker Street address.

"What is the meaning of this?" I demanded.

"Your services are needed, Doctor," he said as he drew up the windows on each side of us. They were covered with paper, preventing us from seeing where we were going.

"You will not find me to be as cooperative as Mr. Melas," I stated.

"We shall see, Doctor. If you honor your profession as Mr. Melas has told us, then you may find yourself more willing than you say. My fiancé has a high fever and is delirious. She is Greek, and for the past two days, she has only spoken in her native tongue."

"Your fiancé?" I said without thinking.

"We are to be married as soon as we receive papers from Athens, which unfortunately, have been delayed."

We rattled along stone-paved roads and then bounced over what I imagined were country lanes for an hour. I hadn't the least clue as to where we were or in which direction we had travelled.

When we came to a stop, Latimer opened a door of the coach and instructed us to step out. Our abductor made no attempt to conceal our surroundings from us. In which part of the country we had landed, I couldn't tell. The long driveway which we had traversed was bordered with large moss-covered rocks. I glanced in the direction we had come. The drive curved into an abyss of hornbeam trees with their muscle-like limbs stretching in all directions. Orange and yellow leaves, defying the season, held on to their sinuous branches.

I looked up at the coachman and could only describe him as an elderly man, dressed in a coarse smock under a patched grey frockcoat. A wide-brimmed felt hat and scarf shielded his features from my view. As soon as we had disembarked from the carriage, he drove off. An old two-story farmhouse with a wide porch stood before us. It was surrounded by ancient oak trees whose reddish-brown leaves had all fallen from their massive branches and covered the ground. The driveway continued around to the back of the house, where I spied a tool shed and the side of a horse barn. I could see no other buildings in any direction.

Latimer led us up the steps and through the front door. The ground floor, from what I could see from my brief glance, was plainly furnished, and was apparently the living quarters for the owner or owners of the house, since the furniture was uncovered and appeared to have been in place for many years. We ascended the stairs and were led to a room at the end of a dark corridor. It was gloomy and devoid of decorations. The wallpaper was faded and peeling in places. A sitting chair, a side table with an oil lamp, and a bed were the only furnishings. A woman with long, disheveled black hair and dressed in a white nightgown lay upon the bed. I assumed from Melas's earlier description that she was Sophy Kratides. Standing next to her was an elderly woman. I deduced from her plain dress, bearing, and age that she was the landlady.

"Mrs. Haversmith," said Latimer, "this is Dr. Weston, and Mr. Melas who is a Greek interpreter. How is our patient?"

"There has been no change, sir," the landlady said. "She is still delirious."

I walked over to the bed and placed my hand upon Miss Kratides' forehead. She had a high fever, and her skin was pale and damp. I checked her pulse and found it faint and erratic. I took the stethoscope from my bag, listened to her heart, and placed my hand upon her abdomen. She was, in my estimation, four months pregnant.

Sophy opened her eyes slightly and said in a weak voice, "*To moró mou. To moró mou.*"

We all turned to Melas for a translation.

"'*My baby. My baby*'," Melas replied.

"*To moró mou. To moró mou,*" the woman repeated.

I checked for a fetal heartbeat, and as I suspected, I could find none.

Another man entered the room. He was shorter and thinner than Latimer, middle-aged, and wore thick spectacles. I assumed he was Wilson Kemp.

"I see you have fetched a doctor, Harold," he said with a nervous giggle. "And I remember Mr. Melas here."

The man's manner and edgy laugh were unsettling.

"This is Dr. Weston," said Latimer.

Kemp stepped further into the room and looked me in the eye.

"Your face is familiar, *hee hee.*"

"I do not believe I have made your acquaintance, sir," I said, as I looked back down at the patient.

Sophy tried to lift her head but fell back and mumbled, "*Pónos sto stomáchi.*"

"'*Stomach pain*'," said Melas.

"This woman needs to be in hospital," I stated.

"I am afraid that is out of the question, Doctor," Kemp said in his jerky fashion.

"She needs a procedure as soon as possible."

"It will be done here, Doctor."

"I am not equipped, sir."

"It is not a matter for discussion. It is here or nowhere."

If the fetus was not expelled, Sophie would die. My fate and that of Melas were in the hands of our abductors, but the fate of Sophy Kratides was in my hands. I was sure if I refused to cooperate, these villains would dispose of me and abduct another physician. I feared Miss Kratides would not survive such a delay in care.

"I require specialized tools and the assistance of my fellow lodger, Dr. Meddler, who is familiar with this condition and can supply the needed instruments. Is it possible to send a wire?" I asked. "He could meet you midway to save time."

I trusted Holmes would understand that the use of an alias would necessitate a disguise. I also hoped Holmes would remember that Dr. Grimesby Roylott of Stoke Moran called him a "meddler" and a "busybody" during the affair of the speckled band.

Kemp pulled Latimer over to one side and spoke quietly. After a brief discussion, the older man handed me a paper and pencil and said, "No tricks, doctor. You will find I am not a man to deceive."

I wrote:

Dr. Meddler
221b Baker Street

Come at once. Must induce labor. Bring dilator, perforator, forceps, chloroform, alcohol, bandages.

Dr. Weston

I handed the note to Kemp, who read it, nodded, and handed it to Latimer. "Have him meet you midway."

Latimer left the room. Kemp scrutinized me with a hateful expression. "I am sure I have seen you before. It will come to me. For your sake, your assistant will cooperate. Remember, Doctor, no tricks."

I turned to Mrs. Haversmith and asked her to bring a clean basin of boiling water when my assistant arrived, and also that I required another lamp and clean sheets. I prepared the patient and, almost two hours later, the door opened and an elderly man carrying a large travel bag was pushed through the doorway, followed by Latimer. Dr. Meddler was complaining about his ill treatment.

"What is this nonsense, Dr. Weston? I must protest."

"I am afraid we have no choice, Doctor," I said.

Mrs. Haversmith carried in the basin of water and set it on the chair.

Holmes walked over to the patient and put his hand upon her forehead and took her pulse.

"This woman needs to be in hospital."

"That is not an option," I said. I took the cervical expander and membrane perforator from Holmes's canvas bag and laid the tools upon the table. I told Latimer we weren't to be disturbed and asked for privacy. Latimer, Kemp, Melas, and the landlady left the room and closed the door.

Holmes straightened his back and looked at me. "Meddler?" he whispered.

"It was the second name I thought of," I whispered back.

"The first name being Dr. Busybody, I suppose." Holmes grinned.

"I think Kemp recognized me. Our pictures were in the newspapers about six weeks ago in connection with Sir Henry."

Holmes retrieved the bottle of chloroform and a bandage from the bag and stood close to me.

"That is unfortunate," he said under his breath. "I suspect they will flee. I had Gregson follow us at a safe distance. How much of this stuff shall I use?"

"Not much, Doctor. We don't want to put her in a coma." I gave my friend a smile. "We just want to ease the pain."

The procedure was a simple but risky one, and we were successful with the extraction. However, there was still some minor bleeding. I looked over to Holmes, as he retrieved his revolver from the canvas bag. It was hidden in a box of bandages.

"We need to get her a proper nurse. And she shouldn't be moved for two or three days."

"First things first. Would you be so kind to summon the landlady?"

He stood to the side of the door. I left the side of the bed, opened the door, and called for Mrs. Haversmith. She came running in.

"Is she all right?"

"Yes, she'll be fine. Do you know where your lodgers are?"

"They left," she said. "They took the carriage."

I led her over to the bed.

"Apply pressure here and here," I said. "The bleeding should stop soon. If she comes around, don't allow her to sit or stand."

Holmes and I ran down the stairs and around the house to the horse barn. A man who we later learned was Mr. Haversmith was sitting upon the floor of the stables, rubbing a sizable bruise on the side of his head.

"Who in blazes are you?"

"My name is Sherlock Holmes. We are working with the police."

"They left in the carriage. They took that foreign feller with them."

"I see from the saddle by the stable wall and the three sets of hoof prints outside that you keep another horse."

"He's in the back pasture."

"I need to borrow him at once. Can you stand?"

"I'm all right," said the old man as he stood up. "I'll fetch the horse and bring him around."

We left the seasoned farmer looking for his hat and made our way back to the front of the house. We met Gregson walking up the drive.

"Officer Dawson and I saw the carriage leave. As you instructed, Mr. Holmes, we hid off the side of the road a hundred yards from the end of the drive. Dawson followed them in pursuit."

We told the inspector about recent events.

"Is the lady all right?" he asked.

"She should recover, but she needs a ladies' nurse," I said. "We can't move her for a couple of days. Latimer said they were engaged to be married and were waiting for papers from Athens. The rogues might come back for her."

"I'll post a few of my men until we can move her to a secure location."

"I agree, Inspector," said Holmes. "There is a telegraph office in Waltham Abbey. Perhaps you can wire for two wagons and a few men."

"How the deuce do you know where we are? Their carriage windows were covered when they brought you."

"I only know my location in a general sense, Inspector. The telegram I received instructed me to proceed to an address just north of Edmonton. I assumed Watson would suggest meeting midway to save time. Edmonton lies to the north and east of London. Continuing in that direction for another eight or ten miles places me in the Epping Forest district of Essex, somewhere between Waltham Abbey and Epping. These ancient oaks and hornbeam trees are indigenous to this area. I also determined our progress by the clatter of the horses' hooves and direction by the turns made by the carriage and so estimated our location to be closer to Waltham Abbey than Epping."

"And how do you suppose I reach Waltham Abbey?"

"Mr. Haversmith is coming around with a horse. I'll stand guard, Inspector, and Watson can attend the lady until you return." Holmes took out a pad of paper and a pencil from his coat and wrote two notes.

"If you would be so kind, Inspector, to send these wires to Athens at the addresses shown."

A few minutes later, Haversmith came around from behind the house, leading a saddled Yorkshire Coach horse.

"This here be One-Eyed Jack," said the old man. "I kept a dozen head here at Hornbeam Stables when I was younger. Now it's just Jack here." The sturdy brown horse was in excellent condition except for his left eye, which was scarred and cloudy.

Gregson was an experienced rider. He talked to the horse for a minute, then mounted the saddle with more agility and grace than I would have credited to him and trotted down the drive.

Holmes turned to the old man. "Mr. Haversmith, I noticed a double-barreled shotgun standing in the corner of the front hall. Is it in working order and do you have shells?"

"She be in good working order, sir. Buckshot or rock salt?"

"Buckshot will do nicely."

We proceeded into the house, and I went upstairs to check on Miss Kratides. Mrs. Haversmith would have made a fine nurse. She had stopped the bleeding, disposed of the used gauze, and was standing bedside. I relieved her and waited for Gregson to return.

The inspector arrived a few hours later with six police officers and a hospital nurse. As Gregson showed his men around the house and issued orders, I gave the nurse instructions regarding Sophy's care and left the room. I had just started down the hall when Holmes pulled me into the adjacent chamber.

"This is Latimer's room," he said as he stuffed an envelope he had found into his coat. "As you can see from the state of the room, the villains left in a hurry."

Most of the few belongings Latimer possessed were left behind. The bed was unkept. Drawers had been pulled open and ransacked. Holmes walked over to the wardrobe, the doors of which were open, and withdrew a workman's shirt that had been left behind. He held it to his nose, and then handed it to me.

"Smell this, Watson."

There was a faint but distinct odor of rotten eggs.

"Sulphur?" I guessed.

"Precisely," he said, as if an important deduction was obvious. He threw the shirt upon the bed and picked up a pair of work boots. They were covered in black dust. Holmes set the boots down, examined a few items

330

on the bedstand, and led the way to Kemp's room. Wilson Kemp had even fewer possessions. Holmes took some interest in a couple of beermats which had been tossed upon a dresser. He examined Kemp's wardrobe and desk before leading the way to the ground floor, where we met Gregson. The inspector had described Kemp and Latimer to his officers and had instructed them to keep guard around the clock. We departed for London. I was glad to put Hornbeam Stables and its namesake trees behind us.

The inspector informed us he had met Officer Dawson upon his way to Waltham Abbey. One of Dawson's horses lamed up, and he lost his quarry. Gregson instructed him to unhitch the lame horse and tether it behind as he walked the wagon back to the city using the healthy horse.

I awoke late the next morning after the exhausting day in Epping Forest. Holmes was out of the rooms and didn't leave a note. I noticed his Greek dictionary lying upon the dining table. He'd mentioned the night before of visiting his brother Mycroft for information concerning the Kratides family. A telegram from Athens arrived just before he returned in the afternoon. He threw his hat and coat in the corner, picked up the dispatch, and dropped into his chair in his usual nonchalant manner. After reading the telegram, he tossed it to the side table.

"The Kratides are one of the richest families in all of Greece," he said. "Sophy's mother died three years ago, and her father's health is in serious decline. Her only sibling was her brother Paul, so Sophy stands to inherit a fortune."

"That accounts for Latimer's marital interests," I said.

"Yes, and they need her to live long enough for Latimer to marry her. I suspect Kemp is the brain behind of the plan. He needed a younger, more handsome man to win her affections and so involved Latimer."

"Then they will surely come back for her."

"I suspect they will not need to. Latimer has her under his influence. She is in love and will go to him. They either have a prearranged meeting place, in case they are separated, or he will contact her."

"But they killed her brother!"

"I doubt she believes the newspaper accounts, if she has read them. Latimer likely has control over what she sees and hears. Her father sent her several letters before they left Beckenham, imploring her to leave Latimer and return to Athens. I found them in Latimer's room. She must have sent her father a letter from Waltham Abbey with her new address, since I found this most recent letter from her father amongst the others."

Holmes removed a packet letter from his vest and waved it in the air before handing it to me. The envelope was addressed to Miss Sophy Kratides, Hornbeam Stables, Waltham Abbey and posted three weeks

331

earlier from Athens, Greece. The receiving handstamp was from the Waltham Abbey Post Office. The letter inside was written in Greek by a shaky hand. I couldn't read a word.

"In that letter," explained Holmes, "Mr. Kratides tells her of the murder, and implores her again to leave Latimer and return to Greece. Latimer may have withheld the letter from her."

Holmes produced a second letter from his vest and handed it to me.

"If you would be so kind, compare the handwriting of that letter with this one."

The envelope he handed me was also addressed to Miss Sophy Kratides and posted from Athens, but sported no cancelling postmark. The letter contained within was of the same shaky Greek handwriting.

"They appear to have been written by the same person," I said.

"Excellent, Watson. The first letter, as I stated, is from Sophy's father. The second letter I wrote myself. I forged Mr. Kratides' penmanship and his style of writing. He addresses his daughter as his '*Little Sapphire*', which I duplicated. I procured the services of a disreputable artist this morning to imitate the Athens postmark upon the envelope."

"And what do you say in this letter?"

"Her father tells her he has made a new will and is leaving his entire legacy to his nephew, Antonio. He also informs her that since she refuses to leave Latimer, she will no longer receive her allowance. Not another *drachma*. She is penniless."

"Good Heavens! Surely this is a cruel deception. She has just been through an emotional and physical hardship. I cannot condone this course of action."

"It is the only way." Holmes brushed away my concerns as if they were an imaginary fly. "I sent Mr. Kratides a telegram informing him of our plans."

"To what end do you hope to achieve? That she abandons her love for money?"

"No, she will never leave Latimer, so long as she thinks he loves her. However, once Kemp and Latimer find out her purse is empty, they will move on."

I stood up, handed the letters to my friend, and walked over to the windows facing the street. I watched a mother drag her child by the arm across the street. A young couple walked hand in hand along the pavement below me.

"It will break her heart," I said.

"We must reveal to her Latimer's true nature before they are married. I wouldn't be surprised to read of her accidental death in the papers a month after the marriage."

I turned and faced Holmes. I realized his intentions were in the girl's best interest, and I was embarrassed at my protestations.

"You are correct, of course," I said. "We must do all we can to save the poor girl."

"There is one weak link in the chain: If Miss Kratides doesn't tell Latimer that she is penniless, then the plan will fail. We must ensure the blackguards are made aware of her financial situation. The path before us is a dangerous one."

"I suspect Kemp and Latimer will hole up near Waltham Abbey to check the post office for the papers from Athens. Tomorrow, I'll visit the pubs in the area for local gossip. Perhaps our villainous friends have made some acquaintances."

I was about to suggest that I come along, but my companion expected my offer and said, "No, I must be discreet with my questioning and blend into the crowd, which I can more easily do alone."

Holmes was gone the entire next day. Around four o'clock in the afternoon, I received a letter by messenger:

Dr. Watson,

> *You may have been able to deceive Harold, but I know your face and your association with Mr. Sherlock Holmes. We know you are holding Miss Kratides under police protection at the Haversmith's. This isn't acceptable. She is a free woman and needs to be with her fiancé. Tomorrow morning, you will travel to Epping Forest and fetch her. You will bring her to us alone. This is a private affair and doesn't concern Mr. Holmes or the police.*

> *Leave Hornbeam Stables at ten o'clock. Miss Kratides will receive a telegram in the morning with directions to a remote location. There you will meet a man in a brown suit wearing a bowler. If you aren't followed, he will provide you with the location of our meeting place. No tricks, Doctor. I will not tolerate deceit again. You will carry out your instructions and act alone, or Mr. Melas will suffer the consequences.*

The letter was unsigned. However, I knew it was obviously from Wilson Kemp.

The situation was a black one. If I refused to play along, Mr. Melas would no doubt pay for it with his life. If I followed Kemp's instructions, I would be placed in a dangerous circumstance, meeting in a remote location with no witnesses. The man in the brown suit could easily dispose of me and take Miss Kratides to Latimer himself.

Holmes returned around eight o'clock, dressed as a commoner, sporting a bushy mustache, glasses, and looking fagged from a long day.

"I have been to Laughton, High Beech, Wood Green, and Waltham Abbey," he said, as he pulled off his fake mustache. "After consuming more pints of bitter and local fare than I care to recall, I have discovered Kemp and Latimer are using aliases and staying in rooms above The Powder Keg pub. It is located just outside of Waltham Abbey along the High Beech Road, and is a popular tavern with the workers at the Royal Gunpowder Mills in Waltham Abbey. Latimer is employed at least part-time at the mills, as I deduced from the smell of sulphur upon his clothing and the charcoal dust upon his boots."

"We should contact the police and go after them immediately."

"In due time. I want to first convince Sophy Kratides to leave Latimer."

"We might not have the opportunity." I said, motioning to the dining table. "A hand-delivered letter arrived for me this afternoon."

Holmes snatched up the letter from Wilson Kemp and, after reading it, let out a low whistle.

"Our hand is being forced. It is an unfortunate and dangerous turn of events."

"I don't see that it leaves us with much choice."

Holmes lit his pipe and paced around the room for several minutes. I was sure he could see the worry in my features. I was filled with dread about what designs the man in the brown suit had for me.

"Fear not, my good fellow," he said. "We will play the game by our own rules."

He sat down at his desk, wrote a lengthy note, shoved it in his pocket, and strode out the door without saying another word. He returned ninety minutes later.

"The forecast is for clear skies tomorrow. I have arranged for an open carriage to arrive at eight o'clock. Do try to get some sleep, Watson."

Holmes stretched his legs out in front of the fire and lit a cigar, clearly intending to spend the next hour in contemplative thought.

I retired to my bedchamber, but tossed and turned most of the night and slept but a few hours. I didn't see how I could follow Kemp's instructions and have any chance of survival.

334

Our open carriage arrived the next morning, and we made the journey to the Epping Forest district. There are many who believe the eerie woods are haunted by the ghost of Dirk Turpin, a highwayman who robbed and murdered forest travellers during the last century. Turpin was hanged in Knavesmire in 1739, buried, dug up, sold to a disreputable doctor, recovered, and buried again. Now his ghost is said to roam about the ancient woods near Laughton Camp, where, when he was alive, and would hide in a cave to avoid the authorities. It is one of many ghost stories associated with the forest. The apparition of a young girl who drowned in a pond near Kings Oak has been seen walking in the woods in search of her parents. I've heard stories of a headless spirit that drives a spectral carriage near Wake Arms, and accounts from people feeling as though an invisible hand touched them as they traveled through the forest.

Holmes stopped the carriage at the Waltham Abbey Post Office and had his forged letter to Miss Kratides postmarked. The clerk was reluctant to apply his mark until Holmes produced a letter of authorization from the London Postmaster and a directive from Scotland Yard.

When we arrived at the Haversmith's, Holmes pulled aside the landlady. He handed her the forged letter with instructions to wait ten minutes before delivering it to Miss Kratides as if it were delivered by post. We ascended the stairs and knocked at the open door. The day nurse was sitting in a rocking chair, which had been brought into the room for her along with a cot, and Miss Kratides was sitting in the chair by the lamp. Sophy was wearing a blue dress with white trim. Her long black hair was put up, and she had color in her cheeks. I was struck by her innocent beauty. She was leafing through a wedding dress magazine and looked up as we knocked at the open door and entered.

"Please excuse the absence of proper introductions, Miss Kratides. I am Dr. Watson, and this is my colleague, Mr. Holmes. I am the physician who helped you the other day with your surgery."

"I do not remember much about that, Doctor. I owe you my gratitude."

"It is quite all right," I said.

Sophy looked down at the floor and asked, "Was my baby a boy or a girl?"

"A girl, Miss Kratides. I am sorry."

Sophy took a handkerchief from her sleeve and dabbed her eyes.

"I see you are healing well," I said.

"Nurse says I am well enough to travel." Excitedly, she picked up a dispatch from the table and handed it to me. "I received this telegram from Harold. He says you will take me to him."

I read the telegram. It instructed me to escort Miss Kratides to Hangman's Hill near High Beech. In another Epping Forest legend, an ethereal spirit of a hangman haunts the hill area. There have been accounts of screams of the dead heard in the vicinity.

I handed the dispatch to Holmes for him to read and turned to the lovely girl.

"Why do you suppose Mr. Latimer wants us to meet him at such a remote location, Miss Kratides?"

"It's obvious he wants to avoid the police," she said, as if avoiding the police was a common matter.

"I received instructions from Mr. Kemp that we were to meet a man in a brown suit to receive further instructions," I explained.

There was a light tapping at the open door, and Mrs. Haversmith entered.

"This parcel letter arrived by post for you, Miss."

Sophy looked at the postmark and tore open the envelope. She read: "*My Little Sapphire,*" and looked up at us. "It is from Papa. He always writes to me as if I am still a child. Please excuse me."

She looked back down and continued reading. Suddenly, the color left her cheeks. When she had finished reading, Mrs. Haversmith asked, "Is everything all right, Miss?"

Sophy looked up with a blank expression, returned the letter to the envelope, and thrust it into her corset. "I am fine. Shouldn't we be going, Doctor? I would very much like to see Harold."

The nurse stood up, and Holmes slid the rocking chair over to face Sophy. He sat down on the edge of the seat and leaned forward.

"I am a private detective, Miss Kratides, and it is my business to discover the truth in matters. I know of Mr. Harold Latimer and Mr. Wilson Kemp. You must realize they are evil men. They murdered your brother, Paul, and have designs upon your inheritance."

"I don't believe you. Papa tried to tell me the same lies."

Holmes reached into his coat and produced several papers. "I have here the police report and newspaper accounts of the murder, and the arrest warrants for Mr. Kemp and Mr. Latimer."

Holmes handed her the papers. She threw them onto the floor without a glance.

"Those papers mean nothing to me. I intend to marry Harold. Now please take me to him, Doctor."

I picked up the papers and said, "We are concerned for your welfare, Miss."

Sophy glared at me. "I have nothing else to say to you, gentlemen. Now take me to Harold." She stood up and walked out the door.

"You did fine, Mrs. Haversmith," whispered Holmes to the landlady.

We descended to the ground floor and went out the front door. Miss Kratides was already sitting in the open carriage waiting for us. Holmes climbed up to the driver's seat.

"My instructions are to come alone," I said, as I climbed up next to him.

Holmes leaned over to me and spoke in a low voice.

"I have no intentions of following Kemp's plan. We will deliver Miss Kratides to The Powder Keg, where I believe they are waiting and confront our adversaries together."

Holmes snapped the reins, and we were on our way. I was pleased to have him by my side. However, my apprehensions of our fates loomed over me like the grotesque, massive oaks around us. We drove seven miles of winding roads through the haunted forest to the tavern. Sophy sat in the back of the carriage, enjoying the fresh air and bizarre beauty of the woods, eager to rejoin her lover. She was lost in her own thoughts as Holmes instructed me softly along the way.

"Have your revolver handy, but don't draw unless it becomes necessary. I intend to expose Latimer's character to Miss Kratides before acting."

When we arrived at The Powder Keg, I helped Miss Kratides down from the carriage. The tavern was a dreary three-story building, shingled and in disrepair. We crossed the weatherbeaten threshold and entered the bar. It was a large, dark room with a low oak-beamed ceiling. A dozen tables were scattered around and to our right, and a long bar ran the length of the room. It was time for luncheon and most of the tables were occupied by patrons. Several scraggy men stood at the bar. Most of the clientele were shabbily dressed, and I surmised they were likely workers from the nearby gunpowder factory. Kemp and Latimer were sitting at a table in the centre of the room. It didn't appear they were expecting Miss Kratides to have escorts. Both men stood up. Sophy ran over to Harold Latimer and threw her arms around his neck. Kemp scowled at us.

"You apparently have trouble following directions, Doctor," he said in his jerky fashion. "You have made a serious mistake in deceiving me."

Two men to the left and right of us quickly stood and pressed revolvers against our temples.

"I advise you not to flinch," Kemp said with a giggling laugh. "I have heard of your cleverness, Mr. Holmes and as you can see, I have taken precautions."

Holmes, as usual, was calm under pressure.

"I believe Miss Kratides has news from home she would like to share with you."

Latimer held her out at arm's length. She merely shrugged her shoulders.

"Dr. Watson isn't the only one who has deceived you," Holmes said. "Miss Kratides received a letter from her father, which she is withholding from you."

"Is this true, Sophy?" Latimer asked her.

Miss Kratides couldn't lie to her betrothed. She reached into her corset and produced the envelope. Latimer grabbed the letter and handed it to Kemp. He examined the postmarks closely before opening the envelope. After unfolding the letter, he took one glance at the Greek writing and asked Sophy, "Is this your father's handwriting?"

"Yes," she replied.

"Are you absolutely sure, my dear?"

"Yes, it is written with his hand."

"And what does it say?"

"Only that he wants me to come home."

Sophy crossed her arms and looked down at the floor. She wasn't a convincing liar.

"To not be deceived again," said Holmes, "you can have Mr. Melas read the letter to you. I imagine you have him secured in your rooms upstairs."

I saw a spark appear in Wilson Kemp's eyes. Holmes had correctly judged the man's abhorrence and fear of betrayal. Kemp couldn't resist the opportunity to not be misled.

"Fetch Mr. Melas, Harold," he said.

Latimer ran upstairs and returned a minute later with the Greek interpreter. Mr. Melas was in a frightful state. His clothes were disheveled, he had a bruise on his left cheek, and he appeared to be malnourished. The Greek translator looked wildly at the scene before him. Kemp handed him the letter and ordered him to read it word for word. Mr. Melas put on his glasses and held the letter in his shaking hands. He cleared his throat and began reading:

My Little Sapphire,

    It is with a heart that aches and bleeds that I pen this letter. I take solace your mama is not alive. She sees not how you abandon your family. Many times I beg of you to leave the murderer of your brother and return home. You refuse my wishes and are deaf to reason. Many times I prayed to the gods for you to see, but your eyes are blind. I can endure no more the strain upon my heart.

In my will, I leave my estates and all my fortunes to your cousin, Antonio. No longer do I send you an allowance. Not a single drachma. I will think of you not again, and will write you no more. Never shall you return to my house. My eyes tear no more.

Latimer shoved Sophy away from him.

"We do not need him or his money, Harold!" she pleaded. "He is just an old, foolish man. We still have each other!"

She stepped towards him with her arms outstretched, but he shoved her again. She stumbled two steps backwards towards us.

"Sorry, Love. You mean nothing to me without money."

"What are you saying?" she cried.

"No money, no wedding. I have no need of you now."

"You have outlived your usefulness, my dear," said Kemp. He looked at us. "I am afraid you have lost, Mr. Holmes."

Kemp reached into his vest and produced a derringer.

"Now, Inspector!" Holmes barked.

At that instant, at least eight men stood up from their tables and drew their guns. The two ruffians holding pistols to our temples suddenly had police revolvers pressed against the backs of their heads.

"Scotland Yard! Drop your weapons!" Gregson demanded, as he pointed his revolver at Kemp's forehead and pulled back the hammer.

The men on either side of us dropped their pistols. We kicked our assailants' guns across the floor and stepped away as two officers handcuffed the men. Kemp dropped his pistol. Officer Dawson reached into Latimer's coat and withdrew his revolver.

"You are under arrest for the murder of Paul Kratides," Gregson said as two more officers came over from the bar and to take the villains. The few patrons who were not policemen watched the proceedings with interest. The inspector and Melas came over to us.

"You cut it a bit close, Mr. Holmes," said Gregson.

We looked over to Sophy, who had collapsed into a chair and was sobbing.

Holmes said, "We needed Latimer to show his true self to Miss Kratides."

Gregson shook his head. "It was a foolish plan, none the less."

"It was worth the risk, Inspector," I said, as I took the forged letter from Melas and stepped over to where Sophy was sitting. I pulled up a chair next to hers, set the letter upon the table in front of her, and sat down to have a quiet talk.

I began by saying, "Your father loves you very much . . . ."

The Romance of
Reginald Musgrave
by Jane Rubino

"I see no reason to omit it," said Holmes with a smile when I suggested publishing an account of the affair. "Your *oeuvre* comprehends tragedy, danger, even a touch of the macabre – it wants only a fairy tale to be complete."

"But do you not think the romance ought to be suppressed – that I should concentrate only upon analysis and deduction?"

"To do so," Holmes conceded, with a smile, "would be impossible. It would leave you with no tale at all to tell."

The tale of which he spoke occurred not long after the adventure of the Great Agra Treasure, which, my readers will recall, concluded with my engagement to Miss Mary Morstan. There was no obstacle but one to prevent our marrying immediately, and that obstacle was money. My income – adequate for my bachelor lodgings – was insufficient for a married man who must support a household of his own. And so, for some months, I remained at Baker Street and applied myself to building up my medical practice and my bank account.

One bitter Sunday evening, the third week of '89, Holmes and I sat on either side of a blazing fire, he studying the bullet-pocked *V.R.* upon the opposite wall, while I rattled on about my plans for the future.

"I bore you," I said at last.

"Not at all. If I am silent, it is merely because I have nothing to contribute. Since I never intend to marry, I cannot share your enthusiasm for wedlock, and since I never have married, I cannot forewarn you of its aftermath."

My retort was interrupted by the sharp clang of the bell, which the hour and the weather could only signal a matter of some importance.

A moment later, Mrs. Hudson entered, bearing a card on the brass salver, and presented it to my companion.

Holmes snatched it and, with a flush of pleasure, cried, "Show him up! I have an ally, Watson," he said, when our landlady withdrew, "and one who is as confirmed a bachelor as myself."

A moment later, a tall, pale gentleman was ushered into the room. His dress was impeccable and costly, if somewhat dandyish, and the large steel-blue eyes, high patrician nose, and courtly air were suggestive of ancient aristocracy.

"Musgrave, my good fellow!" Holmes greeted and wrung the gentleman's hand. "Doctor Watson, allow me to introduce a friend from my university days, Reginald Musgrave. Or I must say 'Sir Reginald' now, I believe."

"No, no. Old friends must not stand upon ceremony. Musgrave will do."

I knew the name, of course. Holmes had spoken of an early adventure that had occurred at the Musgrave estate in western Sussex.

Sir Reginald extended his hand. "I know of your writing, sir. You do my old friend credit."

"Come sit!" Holmes waved the gentleman toward his own chair at the fire, and drew up another for himself. "I hear that your speech on the suffrage matter was received quite favorably."

"No more than my duty as an MP and a gentleman. It was never meant to attract such notice, much less the honor of a knighthood."

"All is well at Hurlstone, I trust?"

"Quite well, though it seems there is never an end to its need for repairs and improvements. Fortunately, I have been able to maintain a large and very able staff who keep the place in order, for visitors to the neighborhood often apply to see the public rooms – and the Stuart Diadem, of course. And in the pheasant months, there is shooting and a house party or two. Quite lately, I have begun to look for an address here in town. A *pied-à-terre* is almost a necessity for the sessions, and to accommodate London's social summonses which are inescapable, particularly as the season approaches."

"The mating season," Holmes said, dryly.

"It is that for much of society, and I venture to say, it ought to have been for me long since. But I was only twenty-four when I succeeded, and I was persuaded that my first duty was to do credit to my late father and to the estate and after, as MP to the district – and so I deferred any matrimonial ambitions of my own. Still, I shouldn't have put off the inevitable as long as I have. Hurlstone deserves a mistress – and an heir."

"I am very sorry to hear it."

Sir Reginald looked at my friend, quizzically.

"I had just boasted to Watson that he was to meet as confirmed a bachelor as myself," said Holmes. "And yet you speak of the inevitable – of matrimony and heirs, and not in the abstract, I think."

A flush crept over the fellow's pale features. "Until some weeks ago, the subject would have been."

"But since then, the subject has found an object. Pray, who is the lady?"

"Lady Adela Winter."

Holmes directed a look and gesture to me, for while his knowledge of the criminal classes was profound, toward the upper tiers of society, he was indifferent to the point of ignorance, unless some illustrious figure, whose fortune or honor was in jeopardy, sought him out. On those occasions, Holmes would refer to the scribbled notations and newspaper clippings that were his index of corruption and scandal, or he would refer to me, since I wasn't above amusing myself with those columns that dealt in gossip and innuendo. Quite recently, they had rumored that a certain fair *A.W.*, while a guest of one of England's most illustrious families, had captured the heart of a noteworthy though unnamed gentleman.

"Lady Adela Winter," I said, "is the only child of the late Earl of Hardcastle. Her mother had been Lady Millicent Grede before the marriage, herself the daughter of an earl, and reckoned a beauty in her day."

"Quite right, Doctor," said Sir Reginald. "Lady Adela was a mere infant when her father was carried off, and some years after his death, his young widow married an artist named Worthing, a widower with a daughter of his own."

"Edward Worthing?" Holmes saw that I was unfamiliar with the name, for our tastes in art were very different. "He was admitted to the École des Beaux-Arts at age seventeen, but an impressive talent doesn't always ensure immediate success, and there many lean years before he became the portrait artist favored by Europe's most celebrated beauties, the *mètier* that brought him a comfortable fortune. I must assume, therefore, that Lady Millicent suffered no material decline when the husbands descended from Earl to 'Mister'."

"Quite the reverse. Hardcastle was a prodigal heir, a wastrel who used his bride's dowry to pay his standing debts, and then squandered his income on private indulgences. They hadn't been married three years when he died and, upon his death, the estate passed to a nephew while his debts of honor passed to his widow. Lady Millicent took herself and her child to Paris where they might live more cheaply while she struggled to settle with her late husband's creditors. It was in Paris that she met Worthing. Her beauty appealed to the artist in him, I daresay."

"And his wealth appealed to her."

"Well, he wasn't a wealthy man when they met," replied Sir Reginald, "but I venture to say she saw is potential. And he brought to the marriage an excellent family connection. Mr. Worthing's sister is the Duchess of Pennemore."

"I see."

"After their marriage, the Worthings settled in Paris, and Lady Millicent had her daughter enrolled at the boarding school attended by Miss Worthing, an establishment at Lausanne that was popular among the fashionable set. When the daughters left school, the family lived together in Paris, and after Worthing's death two years ago, his widow and the young ladies remained there, though it is said that quite lately Lady Millicent has hoped to find an address in London that might suit her purpose – and her purse."

"Is the purse an obstacle? Worthing was a rich man when he died. He ought to have left a rich widow."

"It is true that Worthing's career, particularly in the years after he married Lady Millicent, had made him a wealthy man, but in his last years, he turned toward offering private instruction to a few promising young artists, which was far less lucrative than his commissions. He left a comfortable fortune, to be sure, but when his will was read, it was discovered that a good share had been set aside as dowries for the two girls. Lady Millicent was by no means left poor – "

"But the purse couldn't provide a London address that suited her. As to her purpose, I must assume that it has to do with the young ladies, and that they may now partake of social summonses during London's mating season? Pray, what is their age?"

"Lady Adela is twenty-one – today, in fact – and I believe that Miss Worthing is a year or two older. I know that twenty-one is quite young," Sir Reginald added, "though Lady Adela had such an air of refinement and ease about her that I would have supposed her to be somewhat older."

"And when did you have an opportunity to suppose that?"

"On New Year's Eve, at the masque ball given by the Duke and Duchess of Pennemore."

Again, Holmes looked to me.

"According to every report, it was a magnificent affair, the most coveted invitation of the holiday season," I said. "Nearly three-hundred guests, the Royal Highnesses Prince Albert Victor and Prince George among them."

"I must credit my invitation to that address on the suffrage matter," said Sir Reginald. "It seems that Her Grace thought rather highly of it. As for Lady Adela and her mother, they must credit theirs to Miss Worthing, who is Her Grace's niece and goddaughter. It is unlikely that they would have been invited otherwise, since they had lived on the Continent from Lady Adela's infancy, and had no standing at all among London's *beau monde*."

"Those who reigned in Paris may only serve in Piccadilly?" said Holmes, with a smile. "But surely, affection for her niece notwithstanding, the Duchess would certainly have invited her brother's widow and step-daughter."

"I have been told that there has been some ill will between the two ladies. It is said that Her Grace hadn't approved of her brother's marriage to Hardcastle's widow, and when it was *fait accompli*, she urged him to remove Miss Worthing from school and send the girl to England. She assured Worthing that her niece would have every advantage that would be given a daughter of her own. Lady Millicent opposed the scheme, however, and, of course, the wishes of a gentleman's wife's will outweigh those of a sister."

"Very selfish to withhold such an advantage from her husband's daughter because it hadn't been extended to her own," I observed.

"Well, an advantage to the child will always be of paramount importance to the mother," Sir Reginald replied. "And in this case, that advantage wasn't only to be raised *by* Her Grace, but beside her only child, Lord Margrave, who is the heir to the title and a considerable fortune. Today, he is spoken of as one of London's most eligible bachelors."

"And yet, despite some coolness between the sisters-in-law, the Duchess was good enough to invite Lady Millicent and her daughter, and since that is where you met Lady Adela Winter, I must assume that her mother finally found an address in town to suit purpose and purse."

"In fact, she didn't, but several days before the ball, she hurried them away from Paris all the same, and into a pair of suites at the Hotel Cosmopolitan, and not only on account of the ball, so I hear, but also in order to separate her daughter from an undesirable suitor."

"A suitor inferior to a Duke's heir and a pair of royal bachelors, I take it," said Holmes with a smile. "Well, as you say, a mother will think first of her child, and cannot be blamed for imagining her daughter a princess or duchess."

"Rather than the wife of a knight or humble MP," said Sir Reginald with a sigh. "And yet – Indeed, I don't know what make of the matter!"

"My dear fellow," said Holmes, surprised by his friend's passionate outburst, "help yourself to one of the excellent cigars in the box at your elbow and let us see what I can make of it." Holmes leaned back in his chair and pressed his fingertips together. "Begin with your introduction to this young lady."

"As Doctor Watson remarked, the ball was a magnificent affair," began Sir Reginald as he trimmed and lit his cigar. "His Grace's town residence is at Park Lane, one of the most exclusive addresses in London. The ballroom takes up nearly an entire floor. At one end there is a platform for the musicians, and above, there is a sort of gallery furnished with chairs and settees, where those who don't care to dance may enjoy their refreshments and watch the proceedings below."

"And from this perch, Lady Millicent was able to oversee her daughter's triumph, I presume?"

"No, she wasn't there at all. What I can relate of the matter I learned from Lady Adela herself, and also from Her Grace, who honored me with a place next to her own at supper. It seems that Lady Millicent has suffered some sort of nervous complaint for many years, and the strain of the hasty departure from Paris, and the eager anticipation of what must be her daughter's debut into London society, brought on such a severe attack that she was forced to send her regrets. Her Grace was quite annoyed."

"Surely the Duchess didn't think that her sister-in-law declined this coveted invitation simply to annoy her?"

"No, it wasn't that, but it seems that Lady Millicent is a very trying patient. She must sit in a darkened room and have her wrists and forehead bathed in lavender water, and a dose of laudanum must be dispensed no more nor less than fifteen minutes before she retires, and then she must have someone at her bedside in the event that she wakes and requires anything more."

"I was a less troublesome convalescent at Peshawar," I said with a laugh.

"I venture to say that your only object was your recovery," Sir Reginald replied. "Lady Millicent may have had another object, for she insisted that Miss Worthing must forego the ball to nurse her. Lady Adela objected to this. She said she was the far better nurse of the two, and insisted that Miss Worthing, as the hosts' relation, had the greater claim to the invitation – that indeed, it would be an insult if her step-sister were kept away. But Lady Millicent became so agitated at the thought of her daughter missing the ball that at last Miss Worthing agreed to stay with her step-mother, and asked Lady Adela to offer apologies to her aunt for her absence."

"Very selfish of the mother," I muttered. "Surely her own maid would have done as well."

"Well, she has no maid. It seems that since Worthing's death, the two young ladies have taken on the role. Still, the hotel might have found a hired nurse, and indeed, Lady Adela herself told me that her mother required very little, that the laudanum would see her through many hours, and it would have made no difference whether it was Miss Worthing or one of the hotel maids at her bedside."

"No, indeed," Holmes nodded. "And so, it was at this *grande fête* that you met Lady Adela?"

"Yes. The room had quite filled by the time I arrived, and yet many of the young ladies came much later. Perhaps, they held back in order to make the grandest entrance, though the guests were all so elaborately costumed and masked that a kitchen maid might have been passed for a countess. There was a brief lull as the orchestra tuned their instruments, and so I heard 'Lady Adela Winter' announced quite clearly. I turned to see her hesitate at the entrance and noted her trembling, and I confess I felt sorry for her. She had been in town scarcely a week and knew no one at all, and no doubt she feared a cold reception from her hosts on account of Miss Worthing's absence. However, she was received quite civilly, and Her Grace was even kind enough to draw the poor girl aside for a brief private exchange, and as she did so, she happened to look in my direction and to my surprise, beckoned me. 'You two have something in common. You both know scarcely anyone here, so you must know one another. Lady Adela Winter, allow me to present Sir Reginald Musgrave.'

"The young lady offered her hand, and with a smile – for her mask exposed no more than her mouth – said, "'*Argument against withholding the right to suffrage from women.*' I remember it well, and I remember it worthy of thy praise, Aunt.'

"She then took step back and held out her arms to display her costume, and I noted that she wore the judicial robe and round cap of Shakespeare's Portia.

"The dancing had begun, and I asked if she would favor me, and fortunately her costume scarcely reached to her ankles, and was devoid of the trains and furbelows favored by the other ladies, so she made for a most graceful partner. We danced nearly every dance, save for the one she gave to our host, and another to a young Romeo whom I later learned was our host's son, Lord Margrave. At last we tired, and she said, 'It is very close in here. Are you game for escape? The conservatory is cool and quiet.'

"She took my hand and we slipped away like a pair of thieves, and there we passed nearly two hours in conversation, I describing Hurlstone and recounting the adventure in which you, Holmes, played a part, and she speaking of school where, had it not been for the companionship of her sister, she would had been as friendless as I was at university."

"The two young ladies are on good terms, then?"

"Oh, yes. Lady Adela had nothing but kind words when she spoke of Miss Worthing. She told me that their happiest times were the summer holidays, when Worthing would bring them, and occasionally a few of his pupils, to a little cottage he kept in Brighton, while Lady Millicent went off to take one of the cures at Meran or Baden. She was describing the flower gardens 'round the cottage and, on impulse, I plucked a rose, and a

346

bad business I made of it! I stabbed my palm on a thorn. She drew a handkerchief from her sleeve and said, 'Forgive me, I am a clumsy nurse,' and wrapped it around the wound."

He drew from his breast pocket a delicate square of linen and lace. "I suppose, Holmes," he said, "unromantic fellow that you are, you would dismiss as mere fancy the notion that any genuine feeling might take root in a matter of hours. That in the course of an evening, two people might become sincerely attached to one another."

"And yet, it isn't unheard of." Holmes's eyebrows arched in amusement as he directed a glance toward me, and I couldn't help smiling myself at our visitor's words when I recalled how quickly intimacy and love had sprung from the strange chance that had brought Mary and me together. "What then?"

"The great clock in the corridor began to chime, and she leapt up and cried, 'Surely it cannot be midnight!' and sprang to her feet. 'I had no idea it was so late!' and with that, she ran from the room, and I had only a glimpse of her offering a hurried farewell to our hostess before she vanished." He fingered the *A.W.* embroidered in the corner of the handkerchief and then put it back into his pocket. "I would have gone after her, but it would have looked ridiculous – Henry the Fifth chasing after Portia."

I saw that Holmes was studiously repressing a smile.

Sir Reginald laid his cigar in an ash tray. "After Lady Adela ran off, I stayed through supper. We were permitted to shed our ridiculous masks, though we made for an odd-looking spectacle nonetheless. To my surprise, Her Grace had me sit beside her, and I was bold enough to ask for Lady Adela's address. 'She loaned me her handkerchief,' I said, 'and I would like to return it.'

'They are at the Hotel Cosmopolitan just now,' she replied. 'But when I was told of Lady Millicent's complaint, I suggested that she might benefit from the hydropathic baths at Matlock and made her a gift of a month's cure. She leaves tomorrow afternoon, and Belle and Lady Adela will come to us. They cannot very well stay at a hotel unchaperoned.'"

"Quite generous of the Duchess," Holmes observed, "considering there had been some ill-will between the sisters-in-law."

"Indeed, yes. 'We will expect you the day after tomorrow at eleven o'clock,' she said to me. It was," Sir Reginald added, with a faint smile, "not an invitation so much as a command, which I was happy to obey. On the appointed day, I called at Park Lane and found Lady Adela sitting with Her Grace, but the latter was dressed to go out, and excused herself only moments after I arrived, and so we so we were left alone. I sensed some awkwardness on Lady Adela's part at first. I venture to say she found the

347

grandeur of her hosts' residence a bit overwhelming, and to be sure, she couldn't be as pleased with what our masks had concealed as I, for she is very beautiful, tall and slim, with exquisite brunette coloring and the loveliest dark eyes."

"Yes, yes," said Holmes, with a wave of his hand. "I think we may dispense with the particulars. I am prepared to concede that Lady Adela Winter is the most superior creature who ever lived. Pray, continue. Was there any mention of the undesirable suitor who had prompted the hasty departure from Paris?"

Sir Reginald's smile suggested that he was well acquainted with my friend's unromantic nature. "No, not at all. And of course, I couldn't raise the subject. She asked me a great deal about Hurlstone, and had me describe the gallery and library, and we spoke of books and art until the clock's chime told me that an hour had passed. I rose to leave, and Lady Adela showed me to the door herself, and I had just taken up my hat and stick when the door was thrown open and a young lady, her slight figure wrapped in a wool cloak, burst in upon us. She gave a start, and her bright blue eyes darted from Lady Adela to myself and, with a laugh, she said, 'Oh, pardon the intrusion!' and ran from the room.

"'You must pardon my sister," said Lady Adela. "We have endured a great many changes, and have had too little time to adjust. We are often not ourselves.'

"I told her that there was nothing to forgive, and recollecting the motive for my call, I drew her handkerchief from my pocket. She took it and, with a laugh, she slipped it into my sleeve. 'You must keep it,' she said. 'As a knight's favor. You will want it when you are jousting with Parliament.'

"She then asked me to call again. 'Think of it as an act of charity. But for Sunday morning, when the gentlemen *talk* of attending morning services, and we ladies *go* to them, you will find me here, lamenting how dull January is and wishing I had some kind acquaintance in London to take pity on me and pay me a call.'

"And so, I visited nearly every day. The visits were much the same: Her Grace would step in to greet me, and then leave us to a quiet *tête à tête*. The weather wasn't favorable to anything more. On two or three occasions, Miss Worthing darted into the room, expecting to find her sister alone, and she then apologized and excused herself, and one time, Lord Margrave intruded upon us, and Lady Adela flushed quite red and seemed rather agitated, but the young man addressed me with, 'The ball! You were Henry the Fifth and I was Romeo. Margrave, Belle's cousin. And you're Musgrave! That will do for introductions.' He then made a good-natured

348

jest at the similarity in our names and offered his hand and, laughing at Lady Adela's discomfort, he excused himself."

"Did it seem that her discomfort arose from the fact Margrave was a suitor of hers?"

Sir Reginald shook his head. "Not once did anything suggest that she was attached to her cousin, nor did Her Grace ever address Lady Adela as a future daughter-in-law. Indeed, she seemed to encourage our intimacy."

"The course of love ran smoothly enough, it seems."

"It had run smoothly. Though I have known her for only three weeks, I felt from that first night that we were formed for one another – that it was fate which had kept me from marrying so that it might bring us together. I was certain that she felt it, too. I cannot believe that I was mistaken! But *'so quick bright things come to confusion'*. And yet – "

"And yet?"

Sir Reginald paused for several minutes. "Quite lately, I believe I saw a shadow pass over her features, and a certain distraction, as if she were summoning the courage to speak."

"About what?"

"I don't know. But then she would shake her head as if to dispel whatever troubled her and smile and our ease and tranquility would be restored. Yesterday, we spent a very pleasant afternoon. I knew that today was her birthday, and asked if I might call when she returned from the morning service, that I had a gift to offer her, and that I hoped she would find it acceptable. 'I wish,' she said, as that clouded look passed over her features, 'that you may find its object acceptable: She seemed as if she were about to say more when Miss Worthing burst into the room, white to the lips and holding up the sheet clutched in her hand – a wire, so it appeared – and cried, 'Our mother returns in three days' time!'

"Lady Adela jumped up and snatched the wire and ran her eyes over it. 'She was to be at Matlock for another week,' she said, and the two sisters looked at one another and then at me, and then recovering herself, Lady Adela said, 'I must ask you to excuse us. Do forgive me!' and without ceremony she rang for the footman, and I was hurried out of the house, with neither explanation nor apology.

"That was yesterday. I was preparing to call on Lady Adela today when I received this." He produced an envelope and handed it to Holmes.

Holmes took out the single sheet of note paper and read:

Sir Reginald,

I am afraid that I must ask for your forgiveness, but I will not blame you if you withhold it. You have been nothing but

349

*open and frank with me, and I ought to have returned candor
in kind and shed the mask. But,* "so may the outward shows
be least themselves".

 *It would be for the best if you did not call again. When
you know the reason, you will not be inclined to.*

Very sincerely,

A.W.

"She begins resolutely enough," Holmes said, "but as the weight of
whatever she has withheld from you shows itself in a slight quavering just
at the end." He handed the letter back to his friend. "Evidently the lady
feels some remorse for withholding something she believes you have the
right to know."

"What can it possibly be?"

"I have no data."

"What would you advise me to do? What would you do in my
situation?"

"I don't foresee any circumstance where I should find myself in your
situation, but as a general rule, I believe that it is better to dispel any doubt
immediately rather than prolong it indefinitely. I suggest you confront the
lady."

"I venture to say you are right – I neither lose nor gain by delay. But
it is late. I will call at Park Lane tomorrow." Sir Reginald placed the letter
in his breast pocket, and then rose and shook hands with us both and
departed.

"Well, Watson," said Holmes, when his friend had left us, "affairs of
the heart are your department. What do you make of the lady's conduct?"

I told him what I had seen in the society papers – that a certain *A.W.*
was being courted by a noteworthy gentleman. "Certainly, your friend may
be this prominent suitor. By his account, Lady Adela seemed to encourage
him. And yet – "

"And yet, her conduct may have been all pretense, in order to conceal
a romance between herself and Lord Musgrave from the Duchess, who
might object to a courtship between her son and Lady Millicent's daughter.
Ah, me," Holmes sighed, and reached for his pipe. '*That deceit should
steal such gentle shape.*' I am sorry for Musgrave. He is a good fellow,
and deserves better."

The next morning, Holmes and I breakfasted rather late, and were
sitting with our morning pipes when a sharp pull at the bell startled us both,

for the frost and fog were enough to put off all but the most determined, or desperate, visitor.

The peal of the bell had scarcely died off when we heard the frantic drumming of a footfall upon the stair. Our door was thrown open and a strikingly handsome, though somewhat disheveled, young man burst into the room. His gaze darted from one of us to the other, and then fixing upon my friend, he cried in strongly accented English, "Ah, *Monsieur* Holmes! *Mon cousin*! I do so want your help!"

"It would help me, sir, to know who you are."

"Why, *je suis ton cousin* – Henri-Carle Charmant."

Holmes brow furrowed for a moment, and then he said, "Yes. Your grandmother was Marie-Helene Holmes, who married a fellow named Charmant. Her mother was my grandmother."

"Marie Vernet – *Oui!*"

"I will spare you the complexities of lineage," Holmes said to me, and then, waving young man toward a chair, he looked him over in his brisk, searching fashion and then remarked, "I see that, despite your evident distress, you didn't charge through these inhospitable streets on foot, or the weather would have left its mark upon your attire."

"No, no. I took the carriage."

"From a formal call, as your costume suggests," said Holmes, with a nod toward the young man's morning attire.

"From the church. Not two hours ago, I was married – "

"In that case, you are beyond my help."

"*Je vous implore!* You must help me to recover her!"

"Who?"

"My wife!"

"Married only two hours, and you have already misplaced your wife? That is somewhat out of the common. Brides generally disappear prior to the wedding, or during the honeymoon."

"I do not joke – "

"Nor do I. Your wife can be in no physical danger, or you would have gone to the police. Draw that chair up to the fire, Monsieur Charmant, try to compose yourself and let me have a clear account of the matter."

Our visitor pulled off his gloves and combed his fingers through his tangled hair. "It was as if we were given a gift when her vile mother departed."

"She died?"

"*Non! En voyage!*"

"Ah. Pray, continue."

"And so with that wretched woman gone, we may have the banns read, and then marry on Wednesday. Wednesday is the best day of all for marriage, yes? But then the dragon sends word that she returns early – on Tuesday. Tomorrow! And so, the noble friends of *ma chere espouse* arrange for us to marry this morning, and give us the wedding breakfast. *Quelle gentillesse!* But when we return from the church, who should we see upon the doorstep but that evil woman and a gentleman who is a stranger to us all. My poor wife begs me to go back to my hotel and allow her to beard the dragon alone, and then she will send for me when the storm has passed. I protest, but her relations who attended us to the church as our witnesses took my wife's part. And yet, why should that evil woman bring a strange gentleman unless he is her accomplice and they mean to take my wife from me?"

"My dear cousin, I am not one to censure imagination – it is often of use to me in my profession. But I would caution you that too much may be as bad as too little. How could your wife's mother – and this strange gentleman – plan to interfere with your marriage when they couldn't know that the marriage had taken place?"

The young Frenchman considered this for a moment. "*C'est vrai,*" he said at last. "And yet when she has my dear Adela in her grasp – "

Holmes gave a start. "'Adela?'" he cried, in astonishment.

The young man nodded. "Lady Adela Winter. The step-daughter of my sainted *professeur d'art*, Edward Worthing."

"You are an artist? You studied with Edward Worthing?"

"*Oui.*"

"And married his step-daughter, Lady Adela Winter, this morning?"

"*Oui.*"

Holmes and I exchanged a quick glance. "Have you known one another long?"

"Almost four years – from when I first began to study with her honored *beau-père*. Adela and Monsieur Worthing's daughter were often at his *atelier*. My dear Adela is herself an artist."

"And is Mr. Worthing's daughter an artist as well?"

He shook his head. "For her, it is music and books."

"Pray, continue."

"Monsieur Worthing would have a few of his pupils pass the summer at Brighton, where he kept a cottage. The young ladies would pass summer there as well, while their mother went off to take cures for her health. If you could but see my Adela sitting among the gardens with her sketch-book! She might be Fragonard's *jeune fille*, the fair girl with a wreath of roses 'round her neck!"

I was unfamiliar with the work, and so didn't understand why the digression should have caused Holmes to start. "Indeed!" he cried. "Your narrative grows most interesting, Cousin! Pray, continue!"

"I did what was proper. I spoke to Monsieur Worthing, and he didn't object – *en effet*, he pledged that Adela should have a dowry equal to his own daughter's, and he kept his promise even to death."

"By leaving the dowry to the young lady in his will."

"And to me, the cottage. Generous man! We are to pass our honeymoon there! You must help me appease her wretched mother. I am a poor artist, but you are a man of reputation, and may persuade her to be reasonable."

Holmes's reply was interrupted by a pull at the bell, and darting to the window he looked down, and his expression became animated. "It is Musgrave!" he cried, and then, to the astonishment of our young visitor and myself, Holmes retreated to his bedroom and returned with his hat and gloves clutched in one hand, and an overcoat and muffler thrown over his arm, just as Musgrave was shown into the room.

"Musgrave!" Holmes cried. "You have dismissed your cab, I see. No matter. We will want a four-wheeler! And Watson – You will want your overcoat and hat and whatever else you will need to keep off the cold, and you must don yours as well, Charmant!"

Sir Reginald looked a bit confused at my friend's odd welcome, and then seeing young Charmant, he said, "I beg your pardon, Holmes – you have a client. I will go."

"No, no, allow me to introduce you to a distant cousin of mine: Henri-Carle Charmant, may I present Sir Reginald Musgrave. My cousin was married this morning."

Sir Reginald was courteous enough to conceal his surprise at the sight of the disheveled groom without a bride.

"Married to Lady Adela Winter," Holmes added, as he donned his coat.

Poor Musgrave! I cannot describe his expression of shock and mortification, nor will I ever forget how nobly he rose above his own wounded feelings and extended his hand to our young visitor. "Allow me to offer my most sincere congratulations," he said. "I have heard a great deal in that young lady's praise."

He then made a move to withdraw, but Holmes grabbed him by the sleeve, and said, "No, no – My cousin has presented me with a small domestic complication and your assistance, Musgrave, would be of service in unraveling it."

He then bustled Musgrave, Charmant, and myself – all confounded beyond expression – down to the street and into a four-wheeler, calling out the Duke of Pennemore's Park Lane address to the cabman.

"All will be explained in short order," Holmes assured us, and then he lapsed into silence, a smile playing over his lips as he studied our bewildered expressions. At our stately destination, Holmes sprang down and urged us to follow as he strode up the stone path and rang the bell.

Holmes scribbled something on one of his cards and asked the footman to present it "to Lady Adela Winter – I beg your pardon, to Lady Adela *Charmant*."

The footman bowed and vanished into an upper region from where the faint echo of animated, but distinctly convivial, discourse could be heard. After a few moments, he returned, and showed us into a morning room.

"I do think I deserve an explanation, Holmes," said Musgrave.

"I quite agree, but I believe," he added as the door opened, "that here are two others better suited than I to give it."

Two young ladies entered the room: One, a tall and slim brunette, the other, a small and dainty blonde. The latter wore a pale satin bridal dress and, upon spying Holmes's young cousin, she cried, "Oh, Henri!" and flung herself into his arms. "I am so sorry! It was quite foolish of me to chase you away! We have had such a surprise. Do tell him, Belle!"

"But – but – " Sir Reginald sputtered, looking from the young bride to her companion, whose cheeks flushed with embarrassment. "I believe," said Holmes, with a nod toward that lady, "that you two have met, though you may not have been properly introduced. Sir Reginald Musgrave, allow me to present Lady Adela's step-sister – Miss Worthing."

"Sir Reginald, I must ask your forgiveness," said she, extending her hand to the gentleman. "But I will not blame you if you withhold it."

"You mustn't be angry with Belle!" cried her step-sister, taking his hand and placing it in Miss Worthing's, "for it was all done on my account! If anyone must ask your forgiveness, Sir Reginald, it is I!"

"Certainly, I forgive you all," said Sir Reginald. "But I'll be cursed if I know what it is I'm forgiving!"

"An innocent deception," said Holmes, with a smile. "It wasn't meant to injure anyone, nor to be kept up forever. There was a hint of it in your account, Musgrave, but as I had never met the two young ladies, it wasn't until I heard my cousin's narrative that I had some inkling of the truth. I think that I can give a fair account of the tale, and Madame Charmant and Miss Worthing may correct me where I go wrong.

"Above twenty years ago, a lady – we shall call her Lady Millicent – married a titled profligate named Hardcastle. I am certain that his family was very happy to consign him to a young woman whose strong and resourceful character might curb his indulgence, and who would provide the heir that would secure the entail. Sadly, after only a few years of marriage, the lady was left a young widow with an infant daughter and her late husband's debts, a legacy that weakened her health even as it hardened her resolve to shield her child from the extent of their distress."

"*Quelle tristesse*," sighed Charmant.

"Her beauty attracted the notice of a poor but gifted young artist named Worthing, who made her an offer of marriage. After they wed, the lady applied herself to advancing her husband's career, and what admiration, fame, and fortune came to him were due, in no small measure, to the lady's efforts. Having elevated her husband, she now turned her attention toward her daughter's future, and resolved that the girl shouldn't make as ruinous a marriage as hers had been to Hardcastle."

"*Une femme très sage*," murmured Charmant.

"And so, when her daughter – we shall call her Lady Adela – fell in love with a poor young artist, Lady Millicent seized upon an invitation to a grand ball as an opportunity to divide the lovers, and to have her daughter introduced to London's heirs and royal bachelors. When a lapse in health sent Lady Millicent to her bed, Lady Adela offered to remain behind and nurse her mother, so that her step-sister – we shall call her Miss Worthing – might attend the ball. Her mother wouldn't hear of it. She would have no nurse but for Miss Worthing, despite the fact that Miss Worthing wasn't suited to the task, as she was," he added, with a nod to his friend, "a rather '*clumsy nurse*'."

"You mustn't think badly of my step-mother," said Miss Worthing with a smile. "She wanted so desperately for Adela to attend the ball, and yet the expense of a hired nurse – Well, I imagine that a woman who has fallen from prosperity to penury will not easily forget it, not even after she regains her footing and thrift is no longer needed. I must think that a gentleman who spoke so eloquently for suffrage will agree that poverty must make a greater impression upon a woman than a man, since she has fewer opportunities to work her way out of it."

"Quite true," Sir Reginald replied. "And yet, Lady Millicent didn't carry her point, because you did – in the character of your sister – attend the ball."

"I had no desire to attend the ball," said Lady Adela. "The hosts – indeed all of the guests – were strangers to me, and of course," she added, with a fond look at her young husband, "I had no interest in being presented to heirs and royal bachelors."

"Lady Millicent's draught would have her asleep for hours," Holmes continued, "and so it would be possible for Miss Worthing to go to the ball, so long as she returned to Lady Millicent's bedside before that woman woke. You wore the costume made for your sister, is that not correct, Miss Worthing?"

"How could you know that?"

"You are taller, and my friend had noted that the skirt was above your ankles. The costume was made for a much shorter woman."

"But why the deception? Why represent yourself as Lady Adela Winter?" asked Sir Reginald.

"Recall, Musgrave," said Holmes, "that this was the grandest event of the holiday season. One that would be talked about, and reported in those society papers – details, gossip, descriptions of who wore what get-up were certain to find their way to Lady Millicent."

"And so Lady Adela's mother would believe that it was she who had attended the ball!" I said. "And afterward, should the society papers make their way to Matlock, Lady Millicent would read that a certain *A.W.* was being courted by a noteworthy gentleman, and since her daughter was a guest in this household, she would conclude that they alluded to Lady Adela Winter and Lord Malgrave."

"Precisely," said Holmes. "Indeed, I had almost come to the same erroneous conclusion, but I realize now that the item may have alluded to another romance altogether. Among family, Miss Worthing, you are called 'Belle', but that isn't your given name, I think."

"Arabella," said she. "I was named for my mother."

"*A.W.*," Sir Reginald murmured, one hand moving toward the pocket where he no doubt kept her token.

"Well, my friend Musgrave is certainly a noteworthy gentleman," said Holmes, clapping that man on the shoulder. He then turned to the newly married couple and said, "The only matter of business to remain is my young cousin's fear that your mother, Madame Charmant, had somehow learned of your marriage, and means to put an end to it."

"Oh, no!" cried Lady Adela. "Henri – I *was* frightened, but it was very foolish of me to send you away. She was very surprised – but so were *we*!" And the two sisters looked at one another and burst into laughter.

"*Surpris*?

"Mother is married!"

"Married!" we gentlemen all cried in unison.

"To a doctor named Audley, who designed the hydropathic baths at Matlock. They were married three days ago, and came because they believe that it is only right to ask our blessing in person, but they return to Matlock in a few days. My mother has some schemes for improvement that a modern spa demands, and she is anxious to begin."

"*Mon cousin!*" Charmant cried as he wrung Holmes's hand. "I trouble you for nothing! Forgive my madness!"

"I understand that it is an inevitable consequence of marriage – which is why I endeavor to avoid it."

"We mustn't suspend the wedding breakfast any longer," Miss Worthing suggested. "Please come up with us, gentlemen. I know that my aunt would be very happy to be introduced to all of you."

"No, no," said Holmes. "But we will leave Musgrave in your custody, Miss Worthing, and offer our present best wishes to my cousin, and our future ones to you and my good friend."

With that, Holmes and I said our farewells and departed.

"May they live happily ever after," said he as we climbed into a cab.

And he laughed all the way back to Baker Street.

NOTES

Nearly three-hundred guests, the royal highnesses, Prince Albert Victor and Prince George among them
Sons of the Prince of Wales (later Edward VII), grandsons of Queen Victoria.

"Those who reigned in Paris may only serve in Piccadilly?"
Holmes alludes to a line from Milton's *Paradise Lost*: "*Better to reign in Hell than serve in Heav'n.*"

A pair of suites at the Hotel Cosmopolitan
The site of the theft of Countess of Morcar's Blue Carbuncle

I remember it well, and I remember it worthy of thy praise, Aunt . . . Shakespeare's Portia
Miss Worthing alludes to one of Portia's lines from *A Merchant in Venice* ("*I remember [Bassanio] well, and I remember him worthy of thy praise.*")

So quick bright things come to confusion.
Musgrave quotes from *A Midsummer Night's Dream*

So may the outward shows be least themselves –
The letter quotes from *A Merchant in Venice*

That deceit should steal such gentle shape.
Holmes quotes from *Richard III*

Brides generally disappear prior to the wedding, or during the honeymoon.
Holmes makes a similar observation in the case of "The Noble Bachelor", that "*[Brides]often vanish before the ceremony and occasionally during the honeymoon.*"

Wednesday is the best day of all for marriage, yes?
According to an old English nursery rhyme, "*Marry Wednesday, the best day of all.*"

Such Profitable Treason
by Mike Adamson

To live during the reign of our good Queen Victoria was to be constantly amazed by the progress of science and technology, holding out as it did such unexpected vistas of possibility. My own field, medicine, had changed out of all recognition by the later decades, from the butchery and horrors of the first half of the nineteenth century to a calm, sanitary, and refined art. Steam had gone a long way towards replacing sail in marine propulsion. The "horseless carriage" was tipped to soon be a reality, and visionaries spoke of a time, soon to come upon the world, when human ingenuity reached into the very skies.

But progress knows no bounds, and the weapons of war had not lagged behind in this strange race. Were *HMS Warrior*'s guns, in 1860, not five times more powerful than the heaviest cannon her ancestor, *Victory,* carried at Trafalgar, a mere fifty-five years earlier? Thus, from time to time, the cases that came before my friend, Mr. Sherlock Holmes, reflected not only the intelligence battle between the powers, but the weapons of war themselves.

On a warm Sunday morning in June of 1889, I was pleased to visit with Holmes, having taken brief leave of my dear wife, Mary. I confess, when I dropped by my old digs at Baker Street, I had no idea how this particular day would develop, or I would have been less casual about it.

I listened with interest as Holmes expounded upon his observation that a number of notorious figures – not actually criminals, but certainly associates thereof, some with anarchist ties – had been drifting into London over the past week or two. He garnered this information from customs reports, police reports, and the ever-watchful eyes of his Irregulars, who, by that late year, had risen from the streets of their mean birth and become agents in a more formal sense. Wiggins, for instance, drove for a cab company and knew where everyone of note was bound. Indeed, Holmes more than half-suspected that from time-to-time Mycroft had availed himself of the Irregulars' skills.

My friend puzzled abstractly over their information, hypothesising the possible motives that would bring a dozen figures, each with some question mark against his name, together at such a juncture in history. However, the matter was a curiosity rather than a case, and he set it aside when a desperate rapping at the knocker below heralded an urgent demand upon the skills for which Holmes was duly famous.

Barely five minutes later, we shared a four-wheeler with a notably flustered Inspector Lestrade, heading south on Baker Street to Oxford Street, and then some miles eastward.

"And you cannot afford us the luxury of information at this point?" Holmes asked, more than a little put out when circumstances held in check his whetted appetite for data.

"As I said, Mr. Holmes, the instructions come from the Home Secretary himself. He has forbidden the sharing of any information until we are behind closed doors at the location of the crime."

"Ah, so you can at least confirm that a crime has occurred," Holmes replied with a mischievous twinkle in his eye as he appraised the sunny morning.

We heard church bells from afar and the rumble of traffic on the great thoroughfare. Our horses maintained a brisk trot while I flipped open my notebook and commenced my record, but Lestrade wore a doubtful look.

"You may not be able to commit this one to writing, Dr. Watson. All I can say is that something very sensitive has occurred, and higher authority might take a dim view of the details being made public."

"That will become apparent in time," I replied amiably. Since the publication of *A Study in Scarlet* some eighteen months earlier, I had indulged in a vision of myself as a professional writer. I regarded my role as chronicler of the adventures of Sherlock Holmes as both an honour and a duty. "In any case, full notation is as important to the case as to any possible dramatisation."

From the corner of my eye, I caught Holmes's tiny shake of the head to Lestrade and suppressed my mirth as we continued east, departing from New Oxford Street at Hart Street, and finally jostling with the horse trams on Clerkenwell Road. At last, the coach turned at Hatton Garden and deposited us at a tidy industrial building that nestled more or less centrally to the incongruous medley of a distillery, a brewery, and a church.

Without a word, Lestrade ushered us within, and we found ourselves in the company of uniformed police officers – and Inspector Gregson, already in attendance, sporting a worried countenance.

"Thank heavens you're here, Mr. Holmes," Gregson breathed without concern for Scotland Yard's professional pride.

Holmes passed his deerstalker to a clerk, and Gregson admitted us to a sumptuous office, where we found ourselves face to face with a powerful man in his middle years. Somewhat stout, he wore the whiskers of dignified authority, and the expression of a man sorely troubled.

Lestrade coughed quietly. "Mr. Sherlock Holmes, may I present – "

"Hiram Maxim, Esquire," Holmes interjected, offering his hand. "Celebrated inventor of countless devices of the modern world, and whom many would assert beat Edison to the incandescent light by at least a year."

"You flatter me, sir," the American responded promptly, shaking Holmes's hand. "Even though it's the truth."

"Mr. Maxim . . . What has happened?" Holmes asked with stony gravitas.

Mr. Maxim's aide served coffee as we gathered in the office – Holmes and I, Lestrade and Gregson. The aide remained, and the great inventor smoked distractedly while he paced before the unlit hearth. "Mr. Holmes, something terrible has occurred. We called in Scotland Yard at once, and Mr. Lestrade insisted on fetching you right away."

"A sensible step, Lestrade," Holmes remarked, with but a trace of acerbic humour at the inspector's expense. "If the appropriate moment has arrived, perhaps you could divulge the details of what has transpired?"

At Maxim's curt nod, the aide, who had stood aside, hands behind his back, whipped the cover off a bulky mass that dominated one side of the office. I had to blink at the metal monstrosity so revealed. Maxim laid his hand proudly on the cold steel casing as he took in our expressions. "This, gentlemen, is a *machine gun*."

"A weapon that delivers a high volume of fire," Holmes said, eyes narrowed as he inspected the rectangular body, the massive water jacket shrouding the barrel, and the heavy, wheeled carriage. "I see no cranking handle, so I must assume a small portion of the energy of each detonating cartridge is used to drive a mechanism that loads the next."

"Just so, Mr. Holmes," Maxim affirmed. "There have been a number of such proposals, but none has yet displaced from service the cranked weapons, such as the Gatling and Nordenfelt types. My design has the advantage of being thoroughly practical, as well as delivering a higher rate of fire. I designed it in these workshops some five years ago and have been promoting the virtues of the weapon locally and abroad.

"I am delighted to say that the Royal Army has at last taken serious notice, and earlier this year placed an order for twenty examples to be used for evaluation purposes. The twenty were also built right here. The problem is . . . ." Here, Maxim paused, as though the next words were torn from him at great personal expense. "They've disappeared."

In the following moments, one might have heard a fly's footfall before Holmes rose, strode to the fearsome gun, and gently touched its cold steel. "Twenty machine guns unaccounted for. I can see how this would be embarrassing," he murmured. "Pray, spare me no detail."

Maxim swallowed, and then ploughed on with his narrative. "We completed the order this past week. Arrangements were made for the guns to be delivered to the Royal Army Pirbright Camp in Surrey. Now, to reach a destination in the southwest, one would normally route goods through Waterloo Station, but – " He paused and glanced at Lestrade.

"We had a whisper," the inspector went on. "Credible sources in the underworld, you understand."

"Snitches?" I offered, my pencil flying to keep up.

"Informants, usually considered reliable," Gregson added with a morose reserve that told me the Yard abruptly questioned that confidence.

"Word was that an attempt would be made to take the guns at some point." Lestrade put his fists on his hips. "We had a choice: Cart them to Victoria with the Army providing the escort – more force than any criminal could contemplate going up against but, all the same, risk an actual shooting match on the streets of London, which is undesirable at any hour – "

"Or – ?" It seemed Holmes already knew the answer.

"Or go the quiet route, draw no attention, keep our business out of the public eye."

Holmes nodded silently, and returned his gaze to Maxim, who went on,

"Obviously, with such a threat hanging over us, we decided to move them via the nearest possible entry to the rail network, thus avoiding a convoy of wagons and escort vehicles moving miles through London with the weapons. Last night, the guns were delivered in two wagonloads from these workshops to the Farringdon Road Station GNR Goods Depot, under guard. It's around the corner, just a few hundred yards.

"The police provided an armed guard between here and there, and all went like clockwork. In the depot building, the guns were transferred to a boxcar – secured and sealed, and a guard was placed on the car overnight." Maxim's use of American railway terms raised a brow or two. "Before first light today, an engine arrived to take up the car for delivery – a special, of course. Not part of a general freight train. She left on time, with a military guard detail on board, making a roundabout journey, first underground to King's Cross, then via marshalling yards to the north, so as to skirt *around* London and join the south-west mainline.

"The special had signals in its favour all the way and reached Pirbright Camp by a quarter-to-eight. And when the boxcar was unlocked – " Maxim made a sour face and forced the words out. " – the guns were gone."

Holmes blinked, and I saw the sparkle in his eyes. "A classic magic trick, then: *Now you see them, now you don't.*"

362

"Mr. Holmes," Maxim began gruffly, "I would hope you will treat this matter with all due gravity."

"I couldn't be more serious, sir." Holmes was already a few steps down the road of inquiry. "Perhaps you should tell me what else occurred last night, for nothing is more certain than that *something* did."

"The fire alarm, you mean?" Maxim raised an eyebrow. "Around half-past-one, some hours before the shipment was due to leave, a fire bell rang at Farringdon Station. Railwaymen smelled smoke and summoned the Fire Brigade via the alarm telegraph box."

Holmes nodded frankly. "Leaving the shipment unattended for how long?"

"The depot was filled with flammable goods. There was no choice but to evacuate. When the source of the smoke could not be located, the guards returned at once. They estimate that the boxcar was unattended for between five and ten minutes. That isn't long enough to manhandle even *half* the guns out of that car, much less secrete them elsewhere. And where would one hide anything so bulky, anyway? It takes manpower, Mr. Holmes. The porters here at the workshop took a half-hour to load the horse wagons, and the same again to transfer the load at the station. They were thorough, not rushing. To do the job in less than *twenty* minutes would be impossible, no matter how many pairs of hands you had. Men just get in each other's way in a confined space."

"Then it was accomplished by other means," Holmes replied unconcernedly. "First, I will ask what Inspectors Lestrade and Gregson have to contribute at this point."

Lestrade coughed and consulted his notebook. "The alarm was raised at eight. The news was telegraphed from Pirbright, and Mr. Maxim's manager contacted Scotland Yard minutes later. Gregson and I arrived before nine and made a swift assessment. All personnel here at the factory are being held for possible questioning, but the depot's night shift had already gone home before the cry went up. We have people knocking on their doors right now. To the best of anyone's knowledge, there's no sign of forced entry at the depot. Nothing is broken and nothing is missing. The yard records indicate that the correct loads departed on the correct trains this morning. We have a guard around the depot building at this time." He ran down a little self-consciously. "It strikes me as an inside job, Mr. Holmes."

"My dear Lestrade, your capacity for stating the obvious is quite astounding." Holmes regarded Maxim with a piercing look. "Let us adjourn to the station, Mr. Maxim. It fairly begs inspection."

Farringdon Road Station serves the underground network and lies in a deep cutting between Farringdon Road and Turnmill Street, just a few hundred yards east of Maxim's workshop. It is bounded north and south by the Clerkenwell Road and Charles Street bridges. The Goods Depot stands on the west side of the cutting, nestled against Farringdon Road itself, from which three arched doorways open into the buildings' upper level.

In the general quiet of a Sunday morning, our party walked along to the railings overlooking the cutting, and Holmes inspected the layout with a keen eye. Two double tracks serve the passenger station, on the east side, and a single track passes through, serving the Great Northern Railway. The small marshalling yard lay below us, its twin tracks disappearing under massive doors into the depot.

All was quiet now. Upon the Sabbath, the depot closed for many hours, its signals unmanned and its shunting engine quiet, though passengers waited for the underground services on the other platforms. Holmes made a number of *Uh-huh* noises before leading us down Farringdon Road to the big doors, where a constable walked a guard post.

The depot manager waited there, smoking heavily, his moustached face drawn with worry. He produced keys to unlock the wicket gate. In the gloomy interior, the track beds below were empty of wagons, with goods stacked on the platforms ready for dispatch the following morning. Watchmen and the office staff who had taken over from the night personnel sat around, drinking tea and reading newspapers.

Without a word, Holmes walked the length of the shed where the goods wagons were loaded and examined the tall doors at the north end. The twin tracks disappeared under that door, leading out into the marshalling area with the points that would switch wagons onto the main line. Dropping to the gravel bed, Holmes made his way along the oil-stained tracks. When he climbed a service ladder back up to the main platform, I licked my pencil in expectations of taking down his assessment.

"Any thoughts, Mr. Holmes?" Maxim asked.

"A number spring to mind, sir. First, as you rightly pointed out, it would be physically impossible to remove the cargo from the wagon in the time available, even should there be somewhere to which it could be unobtrusively transferred – which there is not. Therefore, the only logical conclusion is that the cargo was *not* removed."

"But Mr. Holmes," Gregson said, raising his hand, "the wagon was empty when it arrived at Pirbright. Everyone aboard swears they made no stops. Nor had the locks been tampered with when the guards unsealed the doors."

"Also accepted," Holmes agreed. "The only remaining conclusion is that the wagon delivered to Pirbright was *not* the one loaded here."

The depot manager, who escorted our party, clicked his tongue and shook his silver head. "There are all sorts of safeguards, sir. Every wagon on the British rail system carries a unique serial number. It isn't as if one can simply be mistaken for another." He brandished the clipboard he had carried under this arm. "This is the departure manifest, made up and signed off, all proper-like." He cleared his throat and read with a clear sense of self-importance. "'*Received from Mr. Hiram Maxim and Company: Twenty machine guns for transport by a special service to Royal Army Pirbright Camp. Loaded between midnight and one o'clock this morning by the factory personnel under police observation.*' Signed for by the night supervisor. They went aboard a nineteen-foot medium cattle wagon, Serial 90503. That wagon stood in this bay until the engine arrived for it at eight-minutes-to-three this morning. The engine backed into the shed, coupled up the wagon, and commenced its run to Surrey at two minutes after the hour."

"None of this is in dispute," Holmes went on, his patience fraying a little. "My point is that the fire alarm may not have persisted long enough for the goods to be unloaded, but it was certainly long enough for the wagon to be exchanged for another in the marshalling yard, using the small shunting engine I saw on our way here. The same type of wagon, the same colour, with its serial stencils doctored to match those of the wagon in question."

A momentary silence greeted his words, before Lestrade and Maxim tried to speak at once. "You first, sir," Lestrade offered.

"Preposterous, surely! The personnel left the depot, yes, but they assembled in Farringdon Road. The Fire Brigade arrived in no time. Well, it seemed like it. They had to come a mile from Whitechapel. Five to ten minutes, as I said. There were officers moving through the whole area from that moment on."

"Was the source of the smoke ever discovered?"

"No, I don't believe so."

"And you were about to say, Lestrade?"

"That the window of opportunity would be very tight indeed. The shunting locomotive would have had to be held with steam up to move when called for. Men would have to be in place to open the shed doors, adjust the points, set and release wagon brakes . . . to do the whole job quietly, and in under ten minutes, would take nigh-military precision."

"Interesting choice of words, Lestrade," Holmes murmured. "Is there a record of what stock was in the marshalling yard before the morning movements?"

The manager turned pages on his clipboard and presented a diagram. "Three wagons on the parallel eastern track. They were collected at five minutes past three, and coupled to a goods train bound for the north via Doncaster." He squinted at the diagram and nodded a bit hesitantly. "Yes, one of them was a nineteen-footer. But the serials recorded here are the ones they should be."

"When was your diagram made up?"

"Umm . . . ." More turning of pages. "When the yard settled for the night – that would have been one o'clock."

"So, the wagons were exchanged some half-hour later, and no one subsequently rechecked the serials. Why would they? Every goods wagon looks pretty much like every other, after all."

"So simple?" Maxim asked. His face clouded. "Please, Mr. Holmes, tell me it isn't that easy to steal weapons of wholesale lethality."

"Well, as friend Lestrade put it, an almost *military* degree of precision is required. Those responsible must have trained for this task, knowing that their obviously fake source of smoke, causing the fire alarm, would give them just enough time to complete the manoeuvre. If the evacuated staff stayed near the doors up on Farringdon Road, they wouldn't have had a line of sight into the station cutting. Thus, they observed nothing. Was the alarm bell rung throughout this period?"

The manager nodded firmly. "Railway policy: A man keeps the bell chiming until the Fire Brigade tells him to stop."

"Then the noise of the bell would have covered the sounds of shunting." Holmes spread his arms in a gesture of futility. "It was *very much* an inside job. The perpetrators knew the depot's regulations and schedules to a *T* and exploited them, just as they understood Scotland Yard's reactions and preferences. Yes, the rumours upon which the choice was made to send the guns through *this* station were false and deliberately promulgated. What other conclusion can be reached?

"Once they forced your hand on the transport situation, the plot could move forward. Railways are well known to operate with stopwatch precision, and this played to their strengths. By the time the Fire Brigade arrived from Whitechapel, the empty wagon with the fake serial numbers had been shunted into the shed. The real wagon, with both falsified serials and the cargo as loaded, had joined the string of wagons to be collected by the goods train somewhat later."

Lestrade passed a hand across his face as if his starched collar were abruptly stifling him. "Then those guns are loose on the railway network. Where on earth do we start looking?"

"Why, for the yard staff," Holmes replied, his tone implying that he had meant to add, *Do keep up, Lestrade*. "Those who may have already disappeared. The crew of the goods train to Doncaster – Where is that locomotive now? Where was its number last sighted?"

Lestrade scribbled in his notebook, and Gregson was eager to commandeer the depot's telegraph set and rattle off signals in quickfire Morse.

"Data, gentlemen," Holmes added. "Someone knows something, and it will point us in the right direction."

Holmes's thirst for information was not long unassuaged. We remained at the depot, drinking railway tea and smoking, and within the hour, messages began to arrive. First, Scotland Yard reported that two members of the nightshift were currently occupying slabs at the nearest morgue. They hadn't made it home, but were waylaid and done to death by crude means.

"Tying off loose ends," Holmes mused with an icy expression. "Those behind this theft are of an utterly ruthless nature and think nothing of disposing of their hirelings. The murdered men doubtless set the source of smoke and ensured the shed doors were unlatched – they need do no more. Rather than the anticipated largess, their accounts were settled with a blade."

Lestrade wore a sour face. "We can expect the same disregard for life in future. This cargo must be of supreme value."

Cigar glowing in his hand, Hiram Maxim gave a bear-sized shrug. "I doubt other governments would bother to mount such an operation. Why would they? The Maxim machine gun is for sale on the open market. Why, I've toured the world, trying to *get* people interested. Surprisingly few are."

"A cogent point, Mr. Maxim," Holmes agreed with a raised brow. "This suggests the weapons weren't purloined by agents of some foreign power to serve as patterns for illicit manufacture, but by others, and for darker reasons."

"What do you mean?" Gregson asked grimly.

"I assure you, while governments and armies may still be scratching their heads over quite what purpose they might put the machine gun to in warfare, *criminals* have a much more immediate application."

"You mean . . . ?" I asked, flexing my cramping hand. "They would use these abominable things against ordinary citizens? Against policemen?"

Holmes's expression became hard as granite as he stuffed his pipe. "Imagine an enclosed space – a railway station, a sporting field, a concert, a church – anywhere people gather in large numbers. Situate such a weapon with a generous field of fire, then contrive to prevent people from

367

leaving. One might hold them to ransom for vast sums, and all it takes to control thousands is fear – the *fear* that one man might stroke a trigger."

As we digested the monstrous suggestion, the station telegraph chattered out more messages. Lestrade took the slips the operator passed to him and pondered them for a long moment.

"Curious," he murmured, "but valuable. An update from Scotland Yard, Mr. Holmes. The locomotive in question, a G3 class, GNR No. 620, is currently in a Doncaster marshalling yard. It arrived on schedule at six o'clock and was diverted to accept more wagons. The Railway Police have impounded it. The local force searched it from stem to stern, but there's neither machine guns nor the wagon serial numbers we're looking for. It should have been on its way long since, for points farther north, but the enginemen who brought it in are nowhere to be found." He smiled tightly. "So, the crew were in on it."

"That much is obvious. What else?"

Lestrade considered the second slip. "We have a sighting of the same locomotive on the long stretch between Huntingdon and Peterborough at about ten-to-five. A signalman reported the train for proceeding with reckless speed."

I caught the gleam in Holmes's eye. "I'm ahead of you on this one. If the driver arrived in Doncaster on schedule after he was seen speeding on another section of the route, was he making up time lost elsewhere? Such as in dropping off his stolen goods?"

"Well done, Watson!" Holmes beamed a smile as he lit his pipe and begged access to a chart of the GNR routes. The depot manager invited us into his office, where a map of the company's goods network hung upon the wall. Holmes traced the route with one fingertip. "Through King's Cross well before the first passenger services, then onto the mainline." He studied the telegraph slip for a moment. "The signalman who made the report was in Yaxley, just a mile short of Peterborough." He thumped the framed map with the heel of his hand. "They would need an isolated spot, thinly populated . . . I'll warrant our missing guns, wagon and all, parted company from the train somewhere in the ten miles between Huntingdon and Yaxley."

"I'll get a message off to the Yard," Lestrade replied, clearly glad to be making progress. "Then we're on the next service, through to King's Cross and on to Cambridgeshire, as fast as we can."

"I wouldn't miss this for the world, Inspector," Holmes returned, the glee of the chase in his eyes.

Scotland Yard has the authority to arrange matters to suit the exigencies of any situation, and marshalled a special forthwith. This being

368

Sunday, the next scheduled service north to Peterborough didn't leave King's Cross until five of the afternoon. Nor did it stop in Huntingdon. Ministerial permissions were presented and, given its own role in the affair, the Great Northern Railway was only too happy to oblige. A locomotive, tender, and two passenger carriages assembled quickly at King's Cross, and before one o'clock we were on our way north, out of the dirty old metropolis, bound for the green, summer countryside.

I had taken the opportunity to telegram home to Mary, letting her know my day had taken unexpected turns and I would be home when matters permitted, hopefully before that night. With this missive away, I could settle into our adventure with a clear conscience. We relaxed to watch the sights blur by, and spoke quietly. Having been joined by several constables detached for special duty, the Scotland Yard men kept to themselves. Holmes and I passed the early afternoon with a deal of reflection.

"It's a monstrous business," I observed, "when such weapons could be turned to wicked purpose."

"What else are weapons for, save wickedness?"

His remark caught me off-guard, and I wondered if he were being caustically humorous. "They're defensive too, though, frankly, I'm as uncertain of the purpose of the machine gun as many governments seem to be. I mean – " I swelled to my theme with a sudden passion. "Where is the *point* of a gun that fires rounds faster than the gunner can draw a bead on targets? It's patently obvious that it requires only one bullet, properly aimed, to put down your enemy. Firing ten for the same purpose is baffling. Bullets cost money, and a weapon that consumes them many times faster than riflemen do ordinarily is much more expensive to operate. Why not just train your soldiers to be more accurate in the first place?"

"All sound points, Watson, and practical experience may well bear them out. But from tactical and logistical perspectives, the Maxim Gun is essentially only an incremental improvement over the cranked weapons that precede it. The machine gun is a statement, as much as cannon have ever been: A statement of the will and capability of the ones using it to prosecute their agenda, be it offence or defence.

"A single weapon delivering fire equivalent to an entire old-fashioned rifle platoon is a formidable thing, arousing fear and awe in the hearts of soldiers who must face it. As a psychological weapon, it has few equals except, perhaps, grapeshot-and-canister. I wouldn't like to be the cavalryman ordered to assault a fixed position defended by the Maxim Gun. Yes, the mobility of the horse is likely to evade the gun's short-range traversing ability. But cavalry's mobility will *not* overcome the machine gun's raking fire – not at the distances where their charges commence."

He puffed at his pipe, frowning in thought. "I foresee unprecedented carnage, should any commander pit traditional forces against these weapons."

"I might lament whatever derangement prompts a man to invent such a thing in the first place," I sighed. "The whole of human history has been a chronicle of improvements in weapons. Bronze gave way to iron, then steel. Gunpowder replaced the ballista. The musket was superseded by the rifle. The single-action succumbed to the repeater." I shrugged morosely. "Where will it end?"

"I fear it will not. Progress will give rise to more subtle and complex means of causing death and destruction than today's best thinkers can envision. Many theorists maintain that effective conquest of the air is but a matter of time. The sky constitutes the ultimate military high ground."

I raised my hands in surrender. "It's a dark cloud to live under – this notion that the ferocity and destructive potential of wars to come will dwarf those of the past. But perhaps the most frightening thought of all is the willingness of nations – of people and institutions – to continue to fight them in the first place."

Holmes nodded with a sad smile. "If all men thought as you, my friend, we would have no need of armies." He watched the green fields racing by. "But for now, we have the little problem of twenty missing Maxim Guns – and the question of just what devil might be behind the theft."

Our special had an essentially clear run and arrived in Huntingdon at twenty-minutes-past-two. An inspector from the Cambridgeshire Constabulary was waiting to receive us, having been apprised of our mission by Scotland Yard, and he boarded with a local map.

A tough, straight-forward sort of chap, Inspector Brand was fortyish. His face had been disfigured in some brawl or skirmish, and his flowing moustache barely concealed the scar upon his left cheek, which gave him a piratical aspect that I found rather engaging. I took a liking to the fellow as he laid out his thoughts.

"Mr. Holmes, glad to meet you, sir. I've heard enough about you, these past years. And Inspectors Lestrade and Gregson – always a pleasure to have a visit from the Yard's best." He shook hands all around. "Now, gentlemen, I have the superintendent's orders to render every assistance, and despite this being Sunday, I've been able to scrape up ten men to help in the search." He unrolled the ordnance map of the district, spreading it upon a buffet table between seats. "If you're looking for a missing railway goods wagon, there are only so many places it could be uncoupled from the train passing through."

370

"We were hoping for local knowledge," Lestrade fired in before Holmes could speak, and we crowded around to study the map.

"The train passed through here absolutely on time, so it's doubtful your missing wagon would already have been uncoupled. Now, there's a siding near Abbots Ripton that's occasionally used for collecting the produce of farms round about, but we've already checked, and it's clear. Besides, there's precious little cover from trees or banks to make it attractive for a clandestine unloading."

"I presume there's an alternative?" Holmes asked.

Brand tapped the map further north. "Only one branch line leaves this stretch: The GNR's single track to Ramsey diverges at the woods around the village of Holme. Not quite your namesake, sir, but close enough! There's a track that branches again – another farm collection line built many a year ago. It turns into Holme Fen Covert *here*." He tapped the map again. "That's the only spot on this whole stretch where, to the best of anyone's knowledge, you could get rolling stock off the main line with no one the wiser, especially if it were done before daylight."

Lestrade glanced around the group. "Unless that wagon vanished into thin air, Mr. Holmes, I'm not seeing anything to question in this logic."

"No doubt to your amazement, Lestrade," Holmes said wryly, "I am in complete agreement. If Mr. Brand would bring his men aboard, we should inspect the site immediately."

Brand rolled his map with a flourish. "Let's go."

Sunday traffic on the line was light, and our special was able to head up towards Peterborough without conflicting with the few scheduled services. The GNR man travelling with us dropped down to the track bed to manually switch the points when the train turned east onto the Ramsey line. Three-quarters-of-a-mile on, he repeated the work, and we crept north on the spur running into the woods near the lane leading to Ladyseat Farm.

Holmes, Lestrade, and Brand crowded onto the engine footplate as the locomotive chugged into the forest's shade. The line came to a lonely terminus among the trees, at the end of a gravel road from the lane. The halt lay more or less centrally to five or six small farms. As the engine reduced to walking pace, Holmes leaned out of the cab, shaded his eyes, and slapped his thigh in delight.

"That's it!" he called back before jumping to the ground and jogging ahead. By the time I had followed the detectives, while the constables alighted from the carriages, I found us nose-to-tail with a nineteen-foot medium cattle wagon in the GNR goods service livery. Hurrying after Holmes, I found the wagon's side doors open and my friend at one corner

371

of the vehicle, sniffing a fingertip that he had stroked over the serial numbers.

"Fresh solvent. These numbers were very recently applied through a stencil – just about twelve hours ago, at a guess!" Holmes wiped his hand absently on his suit as he inspected the wagon. "This is the wagon that was originally loaded. Under cover of the last darkness, they would have transferred the cargo to road transport. Remember, the train was seen proceeding north of here at ten-minutes-before-five. In early June, that's around ten minutes after sunrise. The question now becomes – Where could twenty Maxim Guns possibly have gone?"

"Plenty of wheel tracks, Mr. Holmes," Gregson called out.

Holmes went to one knee beside the mess of wagon ruts in the roadway's grit and studied them for a long moment. "By the width of the wheels, they are ordinary transport vans – more than one of them. See how these paired sets of ruts are aligned in parallel." He paced a short way and stabbed a finger at much narrower pairs of ruts among hoofprints and men's footprints. "Obviously, they were in a great hurry. They loaded three wagons simultaneously, manhandling the cargo. See where they used the guns' own wheeled carriages as far as possible."

"Three horsedrawn vans," Inspector Brand commented, scribbling in his notebook while his constables gathered, at a loose end. "They have a ten-hour head start, and we've no identification on them yet. We'll check the nearest livery agents for who hired heavy vans for an overnight job, but they'll have used false names."

"Someone might put a face to this aspect of the job," Holmes mused, following the tracks through the dappled shade towards the lane that ran north. They mingled in a confusion of hoofprints and wheel ruts, but upon reaching the lane, they divided. One van headed north, the other two south. "They split up. More than one destination for the goods – or merely three routes to the same place? Either way, this speaks of highly professional caution."

"They could be many miles off," Gregson commented glumly. "They could've switched transport again in the meantime."

"I doubt it, Gregson," Holmes replied at once. "Remember, they had the cover of darkness, and the seclusion of this spot to accomplish the task. Unless they have a warehouse in which to perform such an exchange, they would find themselves attracting unwanted attention. Each layer of conjecture we apply complicates the necessary process, expands the requisite network of resources and payoffs, and increases the possibility that the culprits' own security might be compromised. The fewer layers, the better, from *their* perspective. No, my instincts tell me they would keep their organisation as compact as feasible, and the wagons reached their destination without much ado." He gave us a flinty smile. "I don't think they're very far away."

Inspector Brand unfolded his map in the breeze and perused it intently. "This whole area is drained fens. It's all farms from here to Cambridge. That means about a thousand outbuildings, barns, and sheds, any of which might be hiding a stash of guns."

They looked to Holmes for some sort of guidance. Normal police procedure would be to door-knock the entire area, speak to every farmer about what they saw or heard around dawn, and try to draw some picture of the vehicles' movements. But Sherlock Holmes was less pedestrian when it came to gathering information. He returned to one knee in a patch of dappled light beside the wheel ruts, ran a finger along one impression, then rose and walked swiftly towards the laneway, waving policemen aside.

At the lane, he paced each way, inspecting the wheel marks, and at last pointed north. "I can follow this one. There is a characteristic nick in the iron rim of the right rear wheel, whose impression repeats, making the impressions of this wagon distinct from all others we might encounter."

"Good Heavens," I put in, "you're like an Indian scout!"

"We'll need transport," Lestrade said in a grunt. "It's miles and miles of farm roads leading in all directions – we'll never cover them on foot."

Luck smiled. We followed the lane half-a-mile north to Ladyseat Farm, and the party of policemen drew the attention of a chap who met us at the gate outside his picturesque, stone-built house. The bewhiskered, elderly character looked as if he had farmed this land since time immemorial and greeted us in a pleasant country burr. "Bert Collingford," he announced as he lit his pipe. "I'm manager here while the gaffer's up in Cambridge." He shook our offered hands.

"Mr. Collingford," Brand asked, "did you, by any chance, hear a wagon pass your gate around sunrise?"

"Indeed, I did. I heard hooves and looked out of my window. I said to my Maisy, that's the missus, how odd it were. Wagons're takin' the summer barley to the railway at this time o' year, but they don't bring nuthin' back, 'specially not at that hour o' the mornin'."

"You saw the wagon?" Lestrade asked.

"Aye, sir, it were a big two-horse dray with a box van. Rising sun caught it a treat – the name on the side were Littlefields of Ramsey."

Gregson wrote as fast as I did. "Did you see where it went?"

"Carried on north towards Whittlesey Mere, but there's nuthin' that way but crops and more crops. Maybe northeast to Pondersbridge."

"Maybes" ground no grist for Holmes, and he enquired as to our hiring transport from the farm. As it happened, a pony trap and a farm cart were available, and with a promissory note for fair compensation from the Cambridgeshire Constabulary, Collingford had his lads harness up the horses. He drove the wagon himself while Lestrade handled the trap, and in ten minutes we were off once more, on the trail of the missing guns.

Holmes kept his eyes on the ruts and, at the junction at Whittlesey Mere, stepped down to inspect the spoor more closely. It trailed right. We followed at the trot, and ruled out Pondersbridge when our quarry turned south again at Engine Farm. Now, the trail followed the rough road across a summer green chequerboard of fields.

At each turning, Holmes checked for that tiny giveaway sign, and an hour later he called the vehicles to the roadside. We were on Ugg Mere Road, a few hundred yards after crossing the old course of the River Nene and the Holme-Ramsey railway line. "It's lonely country, gentlemen," he said, wafting his deerstalker before his face in the afternoon warmth. "The wagon that went north has almost certainly doubled back to rendezvous with those that went south. Their separation was merely a precaution. I am convinced they all arrived at *one* destination." He pointed across the fields of rippling grain. "And unless I'm mistaken, we see it now."

"Old Ramsey Hall." In the bright afternoon light, Brand squinted at the sprawling manor in its cloak of trees, some way to the southeast. "It's been derelict for generations."

"What better place to hide a cargo of contraband?" Lestrade agreed. "Easy enough to confirm with the locals that wagons went by this morning."

A loose string of dwellings, boarding houses for farm workers, lined the west side of the road, and our unusual intrusion into this rural world brought housewives out to their gates. Lestrade nodded pleasantly to them and strode across. He lifted his hat, shared a few words, and returned to us with a grim smile.

"A van passed from the north, an hour after dawn – turned left at the corner, yonder, and went into the hall. The locals are hoping the place is being renovated, that the gentry are returning."

Gregson agreed. "Right, Mr. Holmes, this is as far as we go without reinforcements. I wouldn't want to face machine guns with no more than a Bulldog .45 and a warrant card."

"An excellent point, Inspector. I recommend troops. The army lost the guns. It would be fitting if their recovery were also the province of the military. In which case, you need the nearest telegraph."

"That would be at the station serving Holme, just before the Ramsey turning," Brand supplied readily.

"The time has come to divide our forces." Fists on hips, Holmes stared off at the ancient manor house's roof in the afternoon light. "I suggest Inspector Brand and his men remain on their accustomed territory and keep a close watch on Ramsey Hall. We who came up from London shall return with all haste to Holme Station. There, Inspector Lestrade can telegraph to Scotland Yard, and I have a message or two of my own to dispatch. We may return the vehicles and horses to Ladyseat Farm, collect our special, and begin our journey back to London – assuming the enginemen can get us in among the scheduled traffic at this hour."

The local constables gathered on the lonely roadside while the trap and cart turned around. With our assurance of reinforcement at the earliest possible moment, they waved us off, and Lestrade and Collingford whipped the horses up to a canter.

Holmes threw a glance back at the manor and fished out a pack of small cigars. He offered them around before he went on, "We need intimate knowledge of the lie of the land and some deeper insight into the mind behind this wickedness, for I can assure you of this: They will not want to hold onto those guns one moment longer than need be. The buyer must be very close – but whether in space or in time is another matter."

Sunday afternoon services on the main line are sufficiently infrequent for the GNR crew to be able to thread us back onto the north-south corridor. With the engine in reverse, we hurried for London with a sense of time pressing close. Messages had been sent, and Scotland Yard was apprised. Holmes had listed for investigation a collection of names he recalled as having entered London in the last week or so – none an actual key figure in any criminal enterprise, but each associated, however distantly, with someone who was. Only that morning he had been considering this very puzzle.

That casual observation, regarding this influx of shady characters, seemed pertinent to our current situation. Their very presence constituted the most immediate possibility, and I saw Holmes's point: A motley assortment of dubious underworld entities might, for their own reasons, be interested in purchasing one or more of the stolen Maxims.

"An auction?" I wondered as the train raced through the cuttings at Wood Walton and on towards Abbots Ripton. "What a gathering of vultures! Each gun, presumably, to be valued according to some target it will render attainable. Rob a bank vault at leisure while the gun controls the streets . . . Safeguard some strongpoint against all the law can send against it – "

"The tactical considerations are imposing," Holmes mused, "and tend to make Mr. Maxim's case for the utility of his weapon. The Royal Army will be observing this situation with keen interest. When it agreed to

375

evaluate the machine gun's potential, it couldn't have dreamed that the very first exercise would be *against* the wicked thing."

My watch showed half-past-five as the train went through Offord Darcy by the River Ouse, and I bided my time. Holmes was like a coiled spring, pent with potential energy, ready to be unleashed, but not until we were back in the metropolis could we act. I could have counselled him to relax, but I knew his reactions when tension mounted. Instead, I merely watched the countryside flow by while evening replaced the afternoon.

At quarter-past-six, the special was flagged into a siding at King's Cross, and we disembarked with thanks for the crew. A GNR man escorted us through the marshalling yard and into the station proper, where the young Inspector Gerald of the Yard awaited us with our first firm information.

He was a dark-haired fellow with a keen air, eager to make his mark. GNR had made an office available to us, and with the door closed to the public traffic without, Gerald brought us up to date. "An army detachment is on its way. They'll be putting a ring around that house in the next hour. But that list of names you sent, Mr. Holmes – We aren't sure what to make of them. Given their criminal connections, we've certainly kept an eye on one or two during the last week, as a matter of interest, but they've minded their manners in the city: Park, theatre, music hall, shopping on the Strand or Oxford Street. Nothing suspicious whatsoever."

"A *dozen* associates of known criminal bodies, all in London, apparently on holiday at the same time?" Holmes raised a brow at Gerald.

"It does seem farfetched when you put it that way, Mr. Holmes."

"It is beyond the bounds of coincidence, Inspector. May I suggest that a close watch be mounted on all those names that remain under observation?"

Inspector Gerald was abruptly shamefaced. "After they behaved like choirboys five days in a row, the commissioner rated it a waste of police time and manpower and called it off."

Holmes reined in his temper and didn't actually "raise Cain" upon the detectives, but his manner was scathing. "Then I urge a renewal of observation at the earliest opportunity."

"It's Sunday evening, Mr. Holmes. It'll be nigh impossible to get hold of anybody with the seniority to redirect our resources."

Lestrade cleared his throat with a disgusted look. "My responsibility, Gerald. Thirty years on the force and a warrant card that says *Chief Inspector* are all the seniority I need to give the order. Get manpower onto this. I want eyes on every name on that list, as fast as humanly possible. If every name isn't doable, I'll settle for half."

Young Gerald doubled along to the telegraph office, and Holmes put his head in his hands for a moment. "If there is one constant in all this, it is the propensity for individuals in public office to fail to grasp the importance of what lies before them!"

Lestrade could have remonstrated, but he saw the crucial nature of what faced us. "Is there anything else we can do at this juncture, Mr. Holmes? It seems to me that we can only keep eyes on those men you named. The moment they move, we move with them. Hopefully, they'll lead us to the organiser behind the theft."

"I regret to say, that is the only plan open to us," Holmes replied rather desolately, "and I shall pursue it with vigour." He managed a flinty smile. "Watson?"

"Lead on, Holmes."

"On my oath, Mr. 'Olmes, this is it."

At twenty-one years of age, Wiggins stood as tall as myself – still a gangling youth, but well-dressed now, in coat and hat, and he carried the whip of a driver. He had never been out of Holmes's service, and while younger boys now served the role of street urchin, Wiggins had obtained the mobility of a cabman. His hansom stood at the west end of Downs Road, under the trees bordering the forty-acre expanse of Hackney Downs, the great park serving the northeast. The lights of many fine houses glowed through the gathering dusk of midevening, but the day's warmth lingered, and a breeze sighed in the greenery.

Certain that the sort of men he was after would use cab service by preference, Holmes had made a beeline for Wiggins. He was not disappointed. Wiggins had driven a few of them during the past week and knew other cabbies who had carried the rest. These men weren't short of cash, and they stayed at the best hotels. Their daily forays to parks, clubs, theatres, eating establishments, and places of interest provided a solid source of work to London's cabmen. When the figures in whom Holmes had expressed an interest were abroad, the Irregulars were never off duty.

"Well done, Wiggins," Holmes breathed as he took in the long road of fine, tall houses overlooking the north side of the park. "How many have arrived so far?"

"I dropped a Mr. Hinkley from the Carleton Club an hour ago, just before your message reached me. Since then, other cabbies have brought four more. I watched the road for a while before I came back to King's Cross to pick you up. Your friends from the Yard should be here by now, followin' others."

"Then several more remain to arrive. That gives us time."

377

"Time for what?" I asked, trying to seem nonchalant as another cab went by with a clop of hooves, delivering a further passenger to the impressive house, with its double bay windows and magnificent steps, on the corner of Avenue Road.

"Time to position ourselves. We must be certain of what is happening in that house, Watson. If it is one shade less sinister than absolute treason, Scotland Yard will rue the day it forces entry. *Probable cause*. If Lestrade launches a raid on what turns out to be merely a social gathering, no matter the pedigree of those present, it will end careers."

"We're expecting this to be an auction, yes?" I asked. "Every bidder will presumably be present by invitation, so passing unnoticed among them will be impossible. You can't just walk in."

"Had I known where this gathering would be, I might have infiltrated the staff with the caterers, who doubtless delivered supper earlier." Holmes smacked one fist into his palm. "Time has been against us from the beginning – the theft of the guns was just this morning! As I said, the criminals behind this affair will get the guns off their hands as swiftly as possible. Selling them was the priority, from the moment the railway thieves reported success." He glanced at the evening sky, where reds and yellows billowed in the west. "The lamplighters are at work. I'll have the cover of darkness soon."

"You mean to go in?"

"At least as far as the gardens. Given the architecture of such grand houses, the parlours behind those bay windows will be the largest rooms. It's a fair bet the gathering will be in one of them. If I can reach the garden unseen, I can apply a stethoscope to the windows, and overhear what transpires."

"Risky, Holmes – they'll have guards, surely!"

"Beyond doubt. So, you will need to distract their attention."

"Leave that to me, Mr. 'Olmes," Wiggins said with a wide smile. "S'long as the Yard covers any h'expenses."

"If they don't, I shall." Holmes gave me an encouraging slap on the shoulder. "I'll want you in the park, Watson – observing. You are armed?" At my affirmative, he clicked open his watch. "Then let us rendezvous with Lestrade and be back here at full dark. Half-an-hour."

Lestrade was far from happy, but Holmes offered him an option that avoided a supreme gamble. If Lestrade, on his own initiative – on this Sunday evening when no one from the rank of Superintendent upward was available for consultation – raided the house without ultimate cause, he would face dismissal. The papers would make merry with a scandal that could rock the government: *"Police out of control"* – *"Calls for*

378

Oversight". That sort of thing. On the other hand, if Lestrade failed to act and the house actually hosted a criminal auction of weapons of untold destructive capability, he would be the handy scapegoat for future consequences.

When we met, I saw in his drawn expression the stark knowledge that his thirty years of service pivoted on this moment, and the odds of his damnation were fifty-fifty. Reluctantly, Lestrade agreed for Holmes to make the attempt.

My friend was swiftly equipped with black clothing and the requisite instrument for eavesdropping. Scotland Yard provided an additional vehicle, with which Wiggins would stage a near-collision to draw off the guards. It was planned to occur on Avenue Road, parallel with the house's long garden wall. Any guard observing the front of the house – facing Downs Road and the park – would be called away, giving Holmes the opportunity to cross the garden unseen and disappear into the shrubbery.

The hour approached all too swiftly. I bade farewell to Holmes near the public house on the corner of Love Lane, two-hundred-and-fifty yards from the house, and crossed Downs Road to enter the park. Casually in the soft night air, I made my way along the north-side boundary walk. Timing his move to perfection, Holmes stepped out upon the deserted byway five minutes later and wandered westward, hands in his pockets, seeming in all ways innocent.

I took a seat near the gate opposite the end of Avenue Road and watched from the corner of my eye as his ambling figure approached. A man loitered at the front of the house, leaning on the balustrade at the front steps and smoking quietly – a lookout, obviously, and the one for whom the forthcoming drama was intended. The windows were curtained, but a lantern burned over the front door. The stained glass glowed here and there with cheery light from within.

Hooves approached from two directions and I let the scene develop without turning my head – until I heard horses whinny, a grating of wheels, and aggravated cries. When I turned to look back over my shoulder, I saw carriage lights in Avenue Road, and the guard was on his way down the steps. He hastened into the road and ran along towards the apparently near collision.

In the same moment, Holmes turned in his unhurried stride and crossed the garden. He kept off the driveway's crunching gravel and disappeared into the ornamental shrubbery below the house walls. At this distance, I could make out nothing further, but I knew he would stretch up with one arm to place a stethoscope against the lower edge of first one bay window, then the other, and listen intently to what was said within.

My heart was in my mouth, for if Holmes were discovered, gunplay was a certainty. My hand was on the revolver in my jacket pocket, and I watched intently for any sign of the guard returning or being joined by a fellow from inside. But the scene played out without further drama. Before the lookout returned to his post – the carriages having been sorted out and sent on their way – a match flared in the black shadows below the windows.

Holmes covered and exposed it three times – the signal we had all been waiting for. A constable passed the signal. A carriage waiting down by the public house moved at once, and from that point, matters unfolded swiftly.

No sooner the sound of its approach than its doors opened. Uniformed constables spilt into the street and swarmed the garden, went up the steps, and overwhelmed the lookout before he could do any more than back away towards the door. Other uniformed men appeared from Avenue Road, and soon overtopped the garden wall to block any escape from the rear of the house.

Whistles shrilled the alarm. Just one shot cracked through the evening from indoors – I heard much shouting, but when Lestrade arrived, a sergeant met him with a quick, breathless report that brought a smile to his lips, and he beckoned me with a wave.

I met Holmes as he appeared from the shrubbery's black shadows, and relieved him of the stethoscope. He permitted himself a smile of satisfaction.

"Got them," he said simply, two words that encompassed the profound relief we all felt.

But that relief soured when, around ten o'clock, we gathered in a common room at Scotland Yard to review the situation. Hiram Maxim had been invited to attend, and his imposing figure occupied the end of a table littered with ashtrays and coffee cups.

Holmes sat, his pipe issuing blue fumes as messages were sorted and reports committed to paper. The house on Downs Road belonged to the coal baron, Lord Gorton, whose family were away on an international tour. The house had been leased in their absence, and the lessor was now under investigation, though the individuals behind the theft of the Maxim Guns had covered their tracks with consummate skill.

Schooled in protecting the interests of their employers, the prisoners were saying nothing. Save for documentation seized before it could be burned – a paper recording winning bids – we had nothing tangible to indicate that the gathering had been anything other than social. But two winning bids had been recorded before the raid struck, and I was disgusted

380

to learn that, in the criminal underworld, Maxims were worth a minimum of a thousand pounds *each.*

A dozen bidders and the auction's organisers had been arrested, and many documents were in police possession, but there was a *second* arm to this operation. With a kind of dread, we waited for word from the north. When it came, Lestrade accepted the telegram, and relief lit his face at once.

"It's from Captain Delamere, 2nd Battalion, the Green Howards, signalling from Holme Station. They encircled Old Ramsey Hall just after nightfall, and the redcoats went in with all stealth. They found the guns inside the manor, guarded by just half-a-dozen men. The thieves had a telegraph set, hitched to wires running by the hall, and were waiting on instructions for where to direct the goods.

"There was a scuffle and shots were exchanged, but it was over quickly. The criminals had *not* tried to mount any of the machine guns for their own defence." Lestrade beamed. "Mr. Maxim, it looks like your inventions have been recovered safe and sound."

Handshakes passed around the table, and I felt a swell of relief, but Lestrade dashed it a moment later – I watched his face fall as he read to the end of the telegram.

"Oh, no."

"What is it, Inspector?" Holmes asked quietly.

"The Green Howards took stock of their haul. They count *nineteen* guns."

Holmes closed his eyes for a long moment. "The man who wants ten of them is arming for a military campaign such as we read about in the morning papers. The man who wants but one, however, is truly to be feared. For entirely different reasons."

I breathed smoke and shook my head. "They had already sold one. The buyer must have been lined up in advance, not part of the auction at all."

Holmes barked a bitter laugh. "That buyer may have been the very instigator of the theft in the first place, and the auction merely smoke and mirrors, sheer obfuscation. In which case, from his perspective, the operation was a complete success."

"Who could possibly be that wicked?" I asked plaintively.

"Some individual of surpassing malevolence," Holmes murmured, almost thinking aloud, his features a very portrait of foreboding. "One for whom human suffering is a means to an end, and this weapon merely the tool by which to achieve it. This person will have some grander design in mind, some overarching agenda, and the invention of a weapon of such destructive power, yet also such a compact package, lends itself to events

381

meant to inspire terror in the human heart. That is our enemy's greatest asset – the fear such a weapon evokes. Above all, the general public must not become aware of this situation, or panic will result. And, by the same token, it must be recovered before it can be used, to the same effect."

Silence filled the room until Hiram Maxim said slowly, "A belt-fed machine gun . . . unaccounted for. Loose. Somewhere in this country. Gentlemen, this is a nightmare come true."

Lestrade looked sourly around our group and threw a spent match into a brass ashtray as he drew on a long cigarette. "Nineteen others are *not* in criminal hands tonight, and I'm going to count that a win. We'll worry about the twentieth tomorrow."

"Tomorrow," Holmes murmured, "and in the weeks and months until it resurfaces. As it will."

"I assume you'll help us in the hunt, Mr. Holmes?" Lestrade added with a faint smile that could have been irony, though I chose to see it as appreciation for all Holmes had done that day.

"Let me assure you, Inspector, Doctor, and Mr. Maxim, that so long as the threat of wanton slaughter, which that weapon represents, hangs over this city, this country, it will never be far from my thoughts."

Holmes was silent in the cab that returned us to Baker Street before eleven. I gave him the space to brood if he needed to, for I knew that when Sherlock Holmes gave a guarantee like that, no power on Earth would keep him from it.

The upcoming quest for the missing Maxim would be a whole other adventure . . . .

The Dockers' Tanner
by Mike Adamson

The cases pursued by my friend, Mr. Sherlock Holmes, often unfolded out of the public sight, but occasionally he had a hand in some very public affairs indeed. One such was the unrest that gripped London in the August and September of 1889. This was the great wave of industrial unrest that spread through the docks, erupting into a full-scale general strike on the 14th of August. We had, of course, followed the situation in the daily papers, but it was hardly a criminal event, and Holmes had many another matter before him.

However, he was approached by letter on the afternoon of Friday, the 6th of September, by a Mr. Harley Jessup, a clerk with the East & West India Docks Company, who sought an urgent interview, and Holmes was happy to meet. He dropped me a telegram at once, inviting me to the unfolding of this particular matter, and I took my leave of my dear Mary after breakfast the following morning for a quick hansom ride the half-mile or so over to Baker Street.

We entertained our guest at ten o'clock, and I could at once sense that some dire matter did indeed clamour for Holmes's attention. The gentleman was perhaps twenty-five years of age, with tow hair and a clean-shaven countenance, and his pale eyes were troubled. He wore the plain suit of an office worker and spectacles that suggested eyesight compromised by long hours of concentration in lamplight. His disposition was anxious, and Holmes invited him to sit as I hung his coat and poured a restorative port all round.

"Mr. Jessup," Holmes began, resplendent in his quilted smoking jacket over grey waistcoat and trousers, "clearly something ails you. Pray be seated and spare me no detail."

I took my seat opposite Holmes and began a fresh page in my notebook with the name of our guest, the date, and time.

Jessup sipped his port and began a little hesitantly. "I work in the offices of the West India Docks. I'm just one of many clerks who look after the ledgers, issue transport orders, register cargoes coming and going . . . It's this business of the strike, gentlemen. 'The Dockers' Tanner', as the papers are calling it."

Holmes nodded deeply. "The unionised workmen of the waterfronts withdrew their labour nearly a month ago. I understand tens of thousands of pounds have been raised from public subscription as a fighting fund to keep the workers out."

"Forty-six-thousand pounds," Jessup affirmed, "and thirty-thousand more as a gift from the unions of Australia. British industry is losing money hand over fist, but they aren't going to give in easily."

I shook my head with a bewildered expression. "All this over a raise of a penny an hour. Is that really worth losing a fortune for?"

Jessup gave a small shrug of his shoulders. "Think of it less as a penny and more as a percentage. The workers are asking for a twenty-per-cent wage increase, from five-pence- to six-pence-per-hour. A penny-per-hour, per man. There are one-hundred-and-thirty-thousand men on strike at the moment. Allowing for a twelve-hour working day – not that any single individual other than a well-nourished, uninjured man can work cargo flat out for even half so long – that's an extra shilling per day, per man, across the London waterfront as a whole. Or £6,500 daily, subtracted from profits. It might be a penny an hour for the working man, but it's well over two-million pounds a year to the industry."

Holmes coughed softly. "As I recall, the strike began in the first place over the slashing of bonus pay for the timely unloading of vessels." He frowned. "If I were a labourer breaking my back to move the contents of a ship in less than a certain time, I should certainly want my efforts properly remunerated."

"I can only agree, sir. But trade is a dog-eat-dog world, and ship owners are attracted to those wharfs that charge the least. Our general manager, Mr. Taylor, was ensuring that ships choose our berths."

"And he did so by taking pay from the pockets of the poorest," Holmes mused. "Thus, the strike." He reached for his pipe and the slipper of black shag. "Perhaps you should tell us what mystery lies within this wider affair, Mr. Jessup."

"Mr. Holmes, I'm very afraid that murder is about to be done. Coldly, ruthlessly, and for the sole purpose of averting the redirection of that two-million pounds."

Holmes paused with match halfway to bowl and smiled tightly. "Now you interest me, sir. Do continue."

"As a clerk, one is effectively a fixture of the offices – always there, always working steadily, keeping one's eyes down and one's pen flying. You go unnoticed, and your superiors are often loose-lipped around you. You see, they *own* you. Your livelihood is in the palms of their hands, and you're supposed to be so afraid of losing it that you will forgive them anything."

"What did you overhear, Mr. Jessup?" Holmes asked through aromatic smoke, and I used our guest's pause for my writing to catch up.

384

"Yesterday, my manager, Mr. Hulbert Eccles, was in conversation with one of the senior foremen to the effect that he wanted 'the boys' ready to go on Tuesday morning, and there was a good bonus in it for them if they 'did their jobs right'." He finished his port, swallowing hard. "Tuesday is the beginning of the official negotiations between the union and the company, Mr. Holmes, and I have the terrible feeling my bosses are going to sabotage the process. Mr. Eccles has held forth many a time on how churchmen should keep their noses out of industrial affairs. As we all know, Cardinal Henry Manning, the Catholic Archbishop of Westminster, has been the most vociferous spokesman on behalf of the working poor."

"Not their only prominent defender," Holmes added with a pensive look. "John Burns, Will Thorne, and John Benn are political names in this affair that come easily to the tongue. The manager of the Millwall Docks addressed a parliamentary committee and testified to the deplorable poverty among the day labourers he hires."

"But Cardinal Manning will actually chair the negotiations," Jessup said with ponderous gravity. "I am desperately afraid they're planning to assassinate him."

Holmes digested this for a long moment and asked one pointed question. "And Scotland Yard's reactions to your revelation?"

"You're right. I did, of course, approach them first and was brushed aside as having either misheard while eavesdropping – which I shouldn't have been doing anyway – or, if I heard correctly, it was merely the bluster of angry, frustrated men and supremely unlikely to come to more. I was told that adequate security had already been provided, and while they appreciated my bringing these concerns to their attention, they were busy men – and 'Good day.'"

Holmes's eyes narrowed, and he tapped his fingertips on the arms of his chair before rising and offering his hand. "I'll take the case, sir. The gentlemen at the Yard can be brusque, and while their reluctance to invest limited resources in some suspicions is entirely justified, I doubt that is the case this time." Fists on hips, he puffed smoke as he considered the options. "Tuesday. That gives us three full days, as of now." He glanced at me with the thrill of the chase in his keen, dark eyes. "No time to waste, Watson!"

Mary and I entertained Holmes to dinner that evening, and I could tell by his manner that the case had moved along. He didn't trouble us with business over our chicken and salad, nor the apple pie and cream that followed, but while the autumn evening drew in and our maid cleared the table, Holmes and I retired to the front parlour and enjoyed a pipe or two as we got down to the affair in hand.

"I infiltrated the docks in the simplest possible guise – that of a fellow manager," Holmes explained as I lit the hearth and found us a drop of port. "I posed as an interested party, visiting from the Harwich docks on the pretext of seeking assurances that the local dispute would be settled quickly. Now, while Harwich's new Parkeston Quay complex, on reclaimed land by the River Stour, is owned and operated by the Great Eastern Railway to support their freight and passenger services into Europe, there are other, older docks. The Phoenix Dock, for instance, which is accessible only at high water by shallow-draught vessels. Smaller, traditional dock owners are justified in being apprehensive, especially if a new national pay standard is established. Dockworkers are among the poorest-paid labourers in the country, which is ironic given that Great Britain's maritime trade is the very backbone of her economy."

"What did you learn?" I ask, setting pencil to paper.

"There is much anger and resentment on both sides, though it's hard to see the anger emanating from management as anything other than the desire to continue profiteering. Just as the vast wealth and economic power of the United States was built ingloriously upon the foundation of slavery, so it may be inferred that British economic strength is, to this day, leveraged upon a working class sunk in the very depths of poverty. Management is cynically aware of this, and both fears and hates the notion of organised labour.

"Unionism is growing rapidly – expanding to unheard-of membership during this current action. The matchgirls' strike last year demonstrated that it's possible for the withdrawal of labour to force management to ameliorate draconian practices in the workplace, and the dockers seek similar redress. As Mr. Jessup pointed out, it will damage British industry to the tune of millions each year in workforce overheads. But we must ask where those sums are presently distributed. Is it industry that will be damaged? Or simply industrialists? If the latter, we are faced with a social issue rather than one of economics."

"You mean a matter of the rich accumulating wealth at the expense of the poor they employ?"

"Precisely. See it from the point of view of the worker. Just one extra penny for each hour he works makes the difference between affording to eat once or *twice* in a day, between meeting rent and *not*, between saving for new boots or going to work practically barefoot, regardless of the weather. I do not think it too much to ask that a society as grand and complex as our own should afford such basic considerations to its citizens.

"To this end, I posed, in some small facial disguise, as one William Byford, down from Harwich. I presented myself at the main gates – no easy task with the workers' picket lines in place – and asked to see whoever was in charge, which, on a Saturday, was obviously not senior management. The complex was quiet. There are ships still standing under lading, losing money for their owners. The bonded warehouses are all under lock and key, and a place that should have been an absolute hive of human endeavour was preternaturally quiet. It seems there is a constant council of war in session in the dock offices as they discuss the strike and its meaning for the industry.

"I was admitted to the presence of the very Mr. Hulbert Eccles, of whom we were told. Mr. Eccles is a profoundly worried and angry man, florid, of middle years, and hardened by the industry in which he works, and the company he keeps. Mr. Eccles is the cock of his midden, used to getting his own way, surrounded by sycophants. I've encountered the type a hundred times. I put little past him, but he has insufficient seniority to make policy. He is the executor of a higher will – of that I am in no doubt."

"How did he take to you?"

"I made him perceive an ally. I merely pandered to his views – that labour as an entity is without inherent rights, and labourers should be glad of the gift of any employment at all – and I had him. From that moment, I gave him the tacit support of management elsewhere and was allowed, in return, a view of affairs from within the management camp." He broke off to sip his port, and we heard a cab in the street, a whipcrack, hooves on the cobbles. "They're worried. Desperately afraid, in fact, that the matter will go labour's way and they will all suffer.

"It's an accepted fact that management skims at every level. Minor corruption is the way the world works, repugnant as this may be. The great pie of the economy, so goes the theory, is vast enough to support a million tiny bites taken from it, on the understanding that capital thus consumed recirculates rapidly. Typically, it's spent on food, drink, and entertainment within twenty-four hours, or else saved against more extravagant purchases. Holidays, property, transport, and so on. Either way, the wider economy – government revenue – still receives capital via taxation. It's merely a question of whose hands it passes through to get there. Those who benefit most from the industry, from lower management upward, will suffer to some degree should the law enforce the redistribution of funds. Of course, they can pass on such costs to their customers. This is an inevitability. But the law of any free market applies: Compete or die."

"And they would rather do neither," I observed as I jotted the point.

"These negotiations are the death knell for the current system, and they know it. Behind the bluster, there is already prescient knowledge that

387

times are changing and management's ability to exploit labour, uncriticised, is coming to an end. The public is divided, of course. Your Tories and the old gentry would have the Home Office send in the army to beat cooperation out of the workers. But the majority of the public has the deepest sympathy for the working poor, engendered to a large extent by Cardinal Manning's eloquent oration on their behalf. And therein lies the crux of the matter. It would seem that silencing the Cardinal is the last-ditch attempt of *someone* on the management side to derail the talks and give them time – time to rally support from the political right. To attempt, without any consideration of political consequences, the draconian solution."

"Any clue as to who that somebody might be?"

"Not yet. I've been invited back tomorrow, so we'll see what comes to pass." He smiled guardedly. "In fact, if you're up for it, I have a small assignment for you."

"I'm ready."

"I hinted today that I might be able to scrounge up a journalist from the right-wing press who has an interest in management's side of matters. Care to play the part?"

I gave a wide smile at the notion that I would be plying my notebook and pencil in front of the miscreants without them ever suspecting it was for entirely different purposes. "I'm your man."

Sunday, the 8th of September, was cool and blustery. The changing year saw cloud obscuring the last sun of the season, and rain rattled on the roofs and cobbles more frequently. We stepped out of a hansom on High Street, in Poplar, at nine o'clock, and Holmes raised a hand in greeting to someone he had met the previous day, a grizzled character who looked like he had spent all his years by the sea.

"Mornin', Mr. Byford," the seaman began around his chewing tobacco and gestured southward. "Mr. Eccles is waitin' on you."

"Let's be about it, then," Holmes grunted in the Cockney-like Essex accent.

He led us past a pub and workers' cottages and down Harrow Lane. A right-of-way follows the tracks curving into the great Harrow Lane Marshalling Yard, and we passed under Great Western's lines bound for Millwall. Thereafter, we ascended the long footbridge spanning the yards. The far end deposited us at Millwall Junction Station, where daily travellers queued for through services.

The seaman escorted us to the feeder lines and turned south towards the docks. A shunting engine stood there, and its driver waved with a grim look. A small flatbed wagon was hitched ahead of the engine, and, on the

388

opposite side of the station from the waiting public, we dropped down to the track beds and climbed aboard.

At the seaman's signal, the engineman eased us away, and we made steady progress south. We passed the marshalling yards serving the Poplar Docks and at last crossed one of the two swing bridges over the channels connecting the Blackwall Basin with the Northern and Southern Basins of the West India Dock complex. There, the engine wheezed to a halt on a terminating spur beside the dock offices, and we swung down.

From Holmes's description, the man who greeted us could only be Mr. Hulbert Eccles. I was impressed only by the things that could be accounted *wrong* with him. As a doctor, I could see he wouldn't make old bones: His colour was too high, suggesting problems with his heart. His features were thickened from gross dependence upon alcohol, and he carried the unhealthy fat of those who can afford to habitually overindulge at the dinner table. Besides these things, he had the manner of a bully. I was only surprised he didn't carry a coiled whip in his fist.

He gestured at the vehicle in which we had arrived. "Handy way to avoid the picket lines," he said flatly. "I've had my fill o' being pelted every morning."

Holmes shook hands, making an obsequious little bow, and turned to introduce me. "This is Mr. Winsten Drebble of *The Standard*," he announced.

I produced my card, which Holmes had made up with his home printing kit. Like Holmes, I wore a minor disguise, mine being a flowing moustache and wire-rimmed spectacles, teamed with a suit of corduroy. My pistol was in my overcoat pocket, my stick over my arm. We shook hands, and Eccles's touch was such that I wiped my hand on my coat as a reflex when he turned his back.

Inside, a fire warmed the air as we took tea in Eccles's office. Rain pattered the windows. We had the impression the complex was a ghost town when it should have been roaring with activity. Muffled voices came from adjoining offices, and we heard the click of a telegraph set as Eccles communicated with senior management.

Holmes sat forward with a conspiratorial expression and began, "Mr. Drebble believes his readers will be interested to know the outlook for the future, should the talks go the way of the workers."

Eccles scowled and sat back in a creaking chair at his desk. "If it happens, it happens, but I know many a financier who's willing to take their capital elsewhere. They're only in it for profit, and what the workers are demanding takes it out of their pockets."

"But isn't it true," I began, "that the dockers are the poorest-paid labourers in the land?"

389

"Maybe," Eccles admitted with a couldn't-care-less shrug. "That isn't really our business. We pay a wage for manual work. We employ any man who walks through our gates and is willing to bend his back to the task. We *offer* the wage. They don't have to accept it if they feel their labour is worth more."

"And go where?" I asked, spreading my hands without having made notes yet. "A hundred-and-thirty-thousand men, half of whom can neither read nor write, and of those who can, scarcely one is suited to better employment. They're *labourers,* sir. Work is what they bring to the Empire . . . and Empire can't do without them."

Eccles looked down his nose at me, as if I were some lesser form of life. "Hardly our affair, is it?" His words were clipped, promising ill humour. "Are you sure your readers want to know what will become of Dan the Docker if he loses his job? The same thing that happened to his brother when he lost his. Same thing that happens every day. They weren't interested yesterday, and I doubt they'll be tomorrow." He coughed pointedly. "I suggest, Mr. Drebble, your readers will be far more concerned at what the dockers' strike will mean for the price of the goods they buy, should labour carry the day."

"You predict increases?"

Eccles laughed in my face. "Prices for both imports and exports will go up as a direct result. How can they not?"

I scribbled along with his words to give the correct impression. "Go on, Mr. Eccles."

"There are those who'll tell you this strike could begin a spiral of inflation that might ruin this country, imperial free market or no."

"What are you losing each day the London docks stand idle?" I asked.

"A fortune, sir, a fortune. Why, in the last three weeks, the country has started to run short of many commodities, and our export balance sheet is well into the red. There are docks and wharves the length of the Thames, from Gravesend to Clapham, and not a single one is operating, other than a few small family business holdings that don't employ organised labour and are willing to risk being blacklisted when this is over. They're few and far between, I can assure you."

"A successful outcome to the talks will bring the workers back, whatever is decided," I went on, throwing out a teaser. "What would you like to see as the final decision?"

"Me?" He gave a self-important flourish of his hands over the desk. "It's hardly up to me, but I would like to see good sense prevail. Management isn't some evil secret society plotting to keep workers in poverty. Poverty just *is*, and we can't change that. Nor can we pay more

390

than the job is worth. Remember, if these men are unwilling to sell us their labour for the price we can afford, someone else will."

"What about unionisation?"

Now he scowled, almost hissing in his frustration. "The most wicked thing ever to emerge in this land! For decades now, Jack's believed he's as good as his master, and unionism is his attempt to upend the natural relationship between employer and employee. I'm astonished every day I wake up to a country in which this nonsense is still allowed."

"How would you have it changed?" I asked, writing as quickly as I could.

"Act of Parliament!" Eccles spat, thumping his desk with a balled fist. "No unions! Outlawed tomorrow! Then let the redcoats break the strike any way necessary. We'd have order again, and this country could drag itself out of the debt that's piling up due to these few men's selfishness."

I wrote for a few moments more. "That's a vision to inspire a great many in our society, Mr. Eccles. But in the absence of political will to that effect, what can you do?"

"There's more than one member of Parliament who would endorse action. Not *enough*, though it can hardly go unremembered at the next election, and the gentlemen at Westminster know it. In the meantime, we can only hold our own lines firm and say again and again that what the dockers are asking cannot be supported by business."

Now Holmes reached gently to place a hand over my pencil and notebook, arresting my scrawl. He spoke very quietly. "Mr. Eccles has indicated to me that there might be other practical measures in hand. After all, who are these workers? Nobody, really. Just the unwashed masses. They need a mouthpiece – someone the community *will* listen to. Isn't that right, Mr. Eccles?"

The dock manager shot a silent glance between us. "Perhaps we could persuade those spokesmen that their sympathies are misplaced," was all he would say.

A shutter had just slammed over Eccles's dialogue, and Holmes raised his hands defensively. "Pardon me if I spoke out of turn, sir. But as a small dock manager in my own right, I can only shudder to think what will become of trade in my own bustling port, should a precedent be set here."

We had to tread very carefully. I was meant to be writing for a right-wing readership, which meant casting the workers as evil incarnate and their society spokesmen as misguided do-gooders. Eccles eyed us in silence for a long moment, and I had the sinking feeling Holmes and I had overplayed our hand in our attempt to coax out some admission, or at least an indication of his intentions.

At last, he relaxed a little and shook his head. "Formal talks begin on Tuesday between representatives of the union and our own leaders – that's Mr. Taylor, and a grander gentleman you'll never meet. What they thrash out is up to them. But I can tell you this, gentlemen: We'll no more go without a fight than will the workers. It's going to get ugly, there's no safer bet on Earth than that." On those words, he rose. "Excuse me for a moment. I'll have some more tea sent in."

When he left us, I glanced at Holmes, but he raised a finger for silence, and I saw his eyes narrow as he listened hard. Could he make out words from the next office? Apparently not, but when the telegraph set began to clatter, he concentrated once more. A minute later, he looked up with a sour expression.

"Trouble," he whispered. The message must be transmitted in "clear" rather than code, and he was simply reading the Morse letters by ear. "Be ready to move."

I was glad of my revolver, but knew we could hardly escalate matters to gunplay of our own accord. If it came to rough stuff, we were likely badly overmatched.

Holmes rose smoothly, poised for action, light on his feet, as if expecting attack at any moment. I slid away my notebook and rose, stick in hand. The telegraph clacked into silence, and we heard a slip tearing from a pad as the telegrapher passed the transcript to Eccles. Holmes inclined his head towards the door.

We went on silent tread into the hall, through the outer office, and as voices rose behind us, we bolted through the front door. Holmes seized a nearby handcart and wheeled it in front of the door to block any exit with its stack of crates.

"Quickly!" he hissed, and led me around the building to the spur line, where the shunting engine waited.

The driver was nowhere to be seen, having probably availed himself of tea and a lavatory, and Holmes sprang onto the footplate. He gave me a hand up, and passed me a shovel. In moments, Holmes had kicked the hatch lever to the open position, and I was heaving filthy black coal into the firebox. We watched the steam pressure gauge begin to climb as voices brayed from the building, and a window burst open to reveal angry faces and shaking fists.

Holmes brandished his pistol to dissuade pursuit. "Quickly, Watson! This won't hold them long!"

Another couple of shovels of coal, and I toed the hatch lever to close the gaping firebox. We heard pushing at the front door as men set their shoulders against the handcart, and almost at once the contraption tipped, spilling boxes and goods. A babble of voices told us Eccles's boys were loose.

"Now or never," Holmes said through gritted teeth as he selected reverse gear and wound the throttle open.

The engine obeyed, jolting backward and starting us on our journey out of the docks, but it was far from swift. When the angry overseers came around the corner of the office buildings, Holmes fired a single shot. The round sparked on the brickwork with a screeching ricochet, sending them into the cover of a stack of railway sleepers.

Suddenly we were out on the swing bridge, crossing the dark waters of the north dock entry, and the wharfmen broke their cover, racing after us. But now we had developed more speed, and Holmes held the throttle open as we ran northward among the marshalling yards and warehouses, back towards Millwall Junction.

"Mr. Eccles is more intelligent than I gave him credit for," Holmes said with a grin, the wind in his face and blue smoke over our heads. "The message coming in on the office telegraph was from someone at the docks in Harwich who has never heard of a William Byford managing any of the wharves in the area. If my credentials were tested, it's a certainty they also dashed off a message to *The Standard* to check yours."

"A close thing," I said with relief. "But for your uncanny ability to read Morse as you hear it, we could be looking forward to a long hospital stay." My expression was mild, but I meant what I said. "Mary would be far less than impressed, I'm bound to remark, and my practice could hardly prosper."

"Cheer up. No harm done. And we've learned what we came to."

"Did we?" I asked, my eyebrows appreciably elevated.

"Certainly! He has all the roughs he needs to take matters into his own hands. Those will be his hand-picked overseers, the foremen who set the pace on these docks and keep the labourers moving with threats and force. When he admitted that things would get ugly, he meant it. I'm convinced our Mr. Jessup's apprehensions are quite correct, and Cardinal Manning's life is in the most pronounced jeopardy."

We abandoned the shunting engine on the dock spur behind Millwall Junction Station, and in minutes, had caught a westbound passenger service from Greenwich through to Fenchurch Street in the City. From there, a hansom had us at Scotland Yard in no time, and we requested an interview with Inspector Lestrade.

Our old friend greeted us cordially, but upon hearing the nature of the case, his manner soured. "The Dockers' Tanner – we've heard precious little else these last weeks, Mr. Holmes. My men are run ragged trying to keep the peace on those picket lines. Other policing work is suffering as a result. Now you tell me there's more to this Mr. Jessup's fears?"

"Dr. Watson and I have surreptitiously interviewed Mr. Jessup's manager and can assure you, Lestrade, the direst intentions are afoot."

"Can you say for certain – absolutely positive – that Cardinal Manning is in danger?"

"I cannot. But given the repercussions, political and social, of a prominent churchman being assaulted or even killed while serving the public good – Very public, indeed! – can you afford to set those suspicions aside?" Holmes was in no mood for departmental penny-pinching. "I know the Metropolitan Police's resources are stretched thin, and you would have to strip personnel from other divisions to increase security at the venue for the talks, but surely it's worthwhile? If the Cardinal can steer these discussions to a satisfactory outcome, it's to everyone's good. Dockers that are a bit better off. Wharves working again. Revenue flowing, and the tensions crackling on our very streets will be soothed."

Lestrade nodded his head with a small, reluctant smile. "It would certainly make our job easier. And I shudder to think of the alternative."

"If Cardinal Manning *is* assassinated, we could see anarchy on the streets, Lestrade, which might make the Bloody Sunday riots and the Ripper riots in Whitechapel look as if the public were simply in training. A hundred-and-thirty-thousand men have their hopes pinned on these talks. The Cardinal has become almost a *de facto* leader of the strike, merely because he is willing to take on the bosses alongside the likes of J. Havelock Wilson, Tom Mann, Ben Cooper, and the rest. There can be no greater example of Christian charity in action. Can you imagine the outpouring of fury if he suffers physical harm that prevents the talks going ahead? Or even worse, from the worker's perspective, he is replaced by some dignitary unsympathetic to their plight?"

"It doesn't bear thinking about," was Lestrade's gloomy reply.

"Well, it had better be thought about by those in a position to affect matters for the good." Holmes sighed noisily through his nostrils. "You could send Mr. Jessup away with platitudes, but you will not dislodge me from this chair until I have your commitment to the steps we both know must be taken."

"You win." Lestrade sighed. "Contrary to your misgivings, I'm not insensible to the matters at hand. And I *have* learned to trust your instincts. If you feel a heavier escort is warranted, heavier it will be. I just wish you could point out to us who's giving the orders, because ultimate responsibility rests there." He glanced between us with an air of prompting. "Is there enough to arrest this Mr. Eccles?"

"I'm afraid not," Holmes admitted. "He was very careful and wouldn't be trapped into saying a single word that would condemn him. And the orders couldn't possibly originate with him – not enough status. He's a lackey, strictly middle of the pack, while those over his head keep their hands perfectly clean. I cannot point to any individual – and yes, it's as galling as you might imagine."

"I shall double the watch on the Cardinal's residence," Lestrade said quietly, with a smile.

"Lestrade," Holmes began, his lips quirking in a sudden flash of professional good spirit. "You took Mr. Jessup's fears to heart after all."

"There was no direct evidence, and there still isn't, your impressions notwithstanding, Mr. Holmes. But I had a feeling. And one privilege of being an inspector is that you get to act on feelings. Now, our elderly Cardinal – he's eighty-one – will not permit guards *inside* his dwelling, but he might be talked into taking a few *other* precautions. At all costs, he must appear at the Guildhall for the talks, nine o'clock sharp, Tuesday morning."

Holmes smiled conspiratorially. "Then by all means, Lestrade, let us ensure that he does."

"Let's we three pay the gentleman a visit," the inspector suggested as he rose.

The Guildhall, seat of the mediaeval trade guilds in the Moorgate district of London, has hosted the Corporation of the City of London for centuries, and is one of the most dignified places of ceremony the old city can boast. The Gothic façade has loomed over Guildhall Yard through the reigns of a great many monarchs, and its very stones and beams are imbued with that grandeur. There could be no more fitting place for a dispute between management and labour to be resolved than under its august roofs, and the Old Library had been prepared as the venue for the discussions.

By eight o'clock on the morning of Tuesday, the 10th of September, the approaching streets were crowded. Guildhall Buildings Passage and Guildhall Yard itself were thronged. A long line of blue-uniformed constables kept order, though the crowds were as yet well-enough behaved. Signs and placards waved over a sea of faces, and a thousand throats sang out slogans.

Holmes and I walked by on the far side of Gresham Street, on which traffic had been diverted this morning, and my friend shook his head with a bitter look. "This is a powder keg, Watson. One spark could set off a blaze that will nigh engulf this city."

We looked into the south end of Guildhall Yard, the wide concourse running a good sixty yards up to the tall façade of the old halls. In a lull, we crossed over and shouldered our way through the back of the crowds as far up as we could manage. We were looking for any faces we knew from our visit to the docks, but as yet saw none.

The police had quarantined anyone demonstrating *against* the desired "tanner" – sixpence – on the west side of the yard and had several officers between them and the main body. The two parties might easily tear each other limb from limb should the mood of the moment darken. We had Lestrade's assurance that the Special Duty Constables had been issued revolvers. Now the day had arrived, no one was in any way blinded to the dire possibilities, and we knew the Home Secretary awaited Lestrade's regular reports. Indeed, Her Majesty was also looking on with the keenest concern.

Among the dock labourers, an air of guarded optimism seemed to prevail. We saw smiles and waves, heard calls among friends, and there was a determination to cheer the Cardinal when his coach passed along the yard. But ever more people were trying to pack into the area, and constables down on the corner of Gresham Street were having difficulty keeping numbers down.

"There'll be no room for a coach to enter," I observed, "never mind to turn and depart."

"Maybe that's the point," Holmes mused, all but unheard against the general roar of the crowd.

He led me back towards the south end, and when we emerged, we headed south by west, away from the crowds. Our route took us down King Street. We bore right onto Canon Street and passed St. Paul's Cathedral. We hurried onward to Ludgate Hill – under the railway overpasses, across Ludgate Circus – and at last turned off at the next street, into St. Bride's Avenue.

There, in the yards of St. Bride's Church, stood two carriages. One was the regal vehicle of a statesman, inside which we glimpsed the red of the Cardinal's attire and the severe profiles of a couple of Scotland Yard bodyguards. The second was a more modest growler, and beside it, Inspector Lestrade waited with a knot of uniform boys. Holmes made his report on conditions, and Lestrade checked the time, a fob watch open in his fingers.

"Twenty-five-minutes-to-nine. The coach must be on its way in ten." He unfolded a map, and we studied it in the tugging morning breeze. "Let's assume the yard is going to be choked with bystanders no matter what we do. Looks like we're using our alternative."

396

Holmes tapped the paper. "Under the circumstances, we deliver the Cardinal by a more circuitous route and drop him at the rear entrance – the yard beside the Coopers' Hall."

"And the bad boys will expect this," Lestrade murmured. "It couldn't be more obvious." He glanced at a big sergeant at his side. "Tell your men to let another hundred through – but make it look like they lost control for a moment." He smiled grimly. "If they want to force our hand, *make* us use the other entrance to avoid the crowds, then by all means, we can accommodate them."

The sergeant disappeared into the vicarage serving St. Bride's, where the telephone had been placed at police disposal this morning, to relay the instructions to another serving the detachment up at Moorgate. A few minutes later, he reported back to Lestrade that the approaches to the Guildhall were effectively jammed with spectators.

Now Lestrade sat on the step by the open coach door and lit a small cigar, inviting us to partake. We enjoyed a quiet smoke as the minutes wound by. We were waiting on a message that would clinch the whole matter as far as our strategy was concerned and, when it came, the sergeant delivered a slip of paper that set Lestrade smiling with a gritty sort of determination.

"That's it, Mr. Holmes. Our people in the Guildhall report a group of men, roughs by all accounts, congregating in Coopers' Hall yard. They were dropped off by two coaches that went by a few minutes ago, then two more. If you and Dr. Watson can identify even *one* of these men as a dock foreman you saw in company with Mr. Eccles on Sunday, we have our case."

"Time to draw them out, Inspector," Holmes said, stubbing out his cigar and taking his revolver from his pocket. He checked the load and spun the chambers with a decisive metallic rasp, and I did the same.

We boarded the second coach with Lestrade and his sergeant, and the driver took us around the Cardinal's vehicle before leading the way out with a sharp right turn onto Fleet Street – we were away. The route took us by Ludgate Circus and Hill, past the cathedral. Instead of turning up King Street, which would have brought us directly to the bottom of Guildhall Yard, we continued past the Bank of England and turned into Princes' Street. There, we connected with Moorgate, headed up to London Wall, and went west. We turned into Basinghall Street to approach our destination from the north, and both coaches slowed as the bulk of St. Michael's Church and the Coopers' Hall rose over the rooftops.

"Get ready," Lestrade said in a flinty tone, his Bulldog .38 in his hand. "Mr. Holmes, Doctor, we need to get that identification. If we cannot get it . . . ."

397

"It all depends on the actions of those awaiting us," Holmes replied tightly. "'*Courage to the sticking place,*' as Shakespeare said." He gave me a wink of encouragement, and I nodded in reply.

Lestrade tapped the roof, and the driver took us into the yard between the Coopers' Hall and the rear entrance of the Guildhall buildings.

The other coach followed cautiously, and we drew to a halt in the open. No uniforms were visible, and before our eyes, men emerged from around the corners of the ornate buildings, where they had concealed themselves from view. In a trice, three cut off our retreat to the street – clubs and chains in their fists – and the rest closed a loose circle around the coaches. We might have whipped up the horses for an escape, but there was little room to turn, and in the time it would take, our assailants would be up on the vehicles and doing their worst.

Holmes inclined his deerstalker in the shadows, and I followed his line of sight. A moment later, I also recognised at least two of the characters as having been among the foremen at the docks two days ago. "You have your connection, Inspector," Holmes said mildly.

With the greatest satisfaction, Lestrade produced a police whistle and blew three shrill blasts.

The rear doors of the Guildhall burst open, and police poured out in force. Suddenly, all was a chaos of surging bodies and merciless blows as the dock men realised the game was up. But they had numbers and the ugly courage that comes from desperation, and they gave of their best. So determined were they that they set upon the other coach.

The horses reared and cried out in distress, and when one of the matched four fell, the coach was incapable of motion. With a roar, the dock men set upon the vehicle with clubs and a hatchet, and shots rang out from the interior. Abruptly, pistol play was the name of the game, and a crackle of shots reverberated in the yard from both sides. Holes starred the coach's walls, and we flinched low before I followed Holmes out of one side as Lestrade and the sergeant took the other.

All was confusion, in which I laid about with my walking stick, brandishing my revolver to dissuade my opponents. Holmes struck with quickfire jabs that sent men sprawling and, doggedly, we joined the uniformed men who surrounded the Cardinal's coach.

It seemed the roughs would press their grievance no matter what. They must have been promised fortunes, whether for themselves or their families, for they came on with a vengeance, despite the comrades they left in a scatter in the yard among blue uniforms that had also gone down. The toll in suffering that day was awful, but at that instant I became the soldier again. The moment it was all over, I could afford to be the doctor once more.

The mob tore open the door to the Cardinal's coach, and a shot from inside punched a man backwards, but before he could be replaced by another, a scarlet-swathed figure appeared in the doorway. He dropped down amongst us and flung aside his mitre, along with a bald scalp-wigging, revealing a young man's full head of hair – an impostor, an actor.

The cries of battle fell away little by little as the foremen realised they had been duped. In moments, they drew together in a smouldering fury that was directed, I was sure, as much at the superiors who had lured them into this as against the men who had outsmarted them. One by one, they dropped their weapons. Many sank to their knees in defeat, and in the sudden silence, we heard two things.

The chime of Big Ben from far off, striking nine, and a roar of applause from the south side of the Guildhall buildings as Cardinal Manning stepped out of the main entrance to greet the dockers whose hopes he championed.

History records that the talks went well, and the dockers elected to return to work a week later with their demands substantially met. The economy did *not* collapse, the fabric of society did *not* unravel, and the union movement is here to stay.

On the day the foremen were arrested for attempted murder, among many other charges, Holmes himself escorted the Cardinal into the first round of talks, but the facts were downplayed in the newspapers. Inspector Lestrade didn't tell the press that Scotland Yard had taken His Eminence to safety inside the Guildhall during the hours of darkness, nor that the young policeman who had volunteered to impersonate the elderly churchman and thus draw the ire of the thugs in the street was in line for a police gallantry award.

However, our formal identification of at least three among those thugs connected them to Mr. Hulbert Eccles at the West India Docks. He was arrested forthwith, and this scandal looked very bad for the management side of the great social debate. Perhaps it contributed to the workers' eventual victory, but if so, it was cold comfort to Holmes.

"Eccles is a hard man," my friend remarked as we took tea with the gentlemen from Scotland Yard later in the day. "He is a true believer in the rightness of his position, and keeps faith with those ideals by accepting the blame. You and I both know he is protecting someone above him, but unless the looming prospect of the noose loosens his tongue, he will take the knowledge to the grave."

"I see your frustration, and I do sympathise." I stood with a plate of sandwiches and sweetmeats as we shared a common room at Scotland Yard with the detectives and senior uniform men who had effected the manoeuvre. I have to admit, I had never before known the Yard to arrange a *soiree* of congratulations.

Holmes's role in this, and by extension my own, had this time not been entirely a matter of erudite cognition and deductive reasoning – though when asked to say a few words, Holmes couldn't resist elaborating in his usual vein. He dusted his hands and looked around our hosts with a guarded smile, clearly ill at ease in such convivial circumstances. I was concerned his remarks would be inappropriately caustic for the occasion, but need not have worried.

"Inspectors, officers of the Force, gentlemen: It has been my honour to serve the public interest in this matter, though I cannot claim to have exercised my accustomed deductive methodology. Had I full opportunity to do so, I wouldn't have rested until I had identified the man who gave the orders carried out this morning in Moorgate. It would seem that none of your arrestees was permitted to know with whom their mission originated, and Mr. Eccles is ostensibly staunch enough in his belief to face the gallows unmoved, thus protecting the ultimately guilty party."

The policemen were silent, knowing the truth of his words and feeling the same sting.

"To understand, in this enlightened age, that society is polarised in its views of any human being is a sobering thought. A hundred years ago, to even possess a copy of *The Rights of Man* was considered a subversive act. Today, the class system that promotes and maintains a vertical hierarchy among the citizens of the British Empire essentially continues to deny the precepts of that venerable document. Law enforcement must reflect the prevailing values of the society it serves, yet it's also obliged to be apolitical. This can be a balancing act, especially when the lower classes rightly ask why the police force always seems to be on the side of the upper ones."

I sensed a prickle go through the room as Holmes rubbed a nerve – quite deliberately, I was sure. But they were waiting for his point, and he came to it with commendable speed.

"But today, the London Metropolitan Police has served the wider good by preserving the peace, ensuring the safety of a senior statesman, and opening the way to the unfolding of due process that will bring the current crisis to an end. And this has been done without reference to the political position of either side. This is as it should be, and Dr. Watson and I are honoured to have participated. We only wish we could have done more."

A polite patter of applause greeted his speech, and Lestrade raised a glass in toast. "Always glad to have you on side, Mr. Holmes – especially when no coppers end up looking 'right Charlies' in the process!" A laugh went through the room. "As for the top man, I suggest we file our suspicions somewhere deep and dark and bide our time. If his hatred of the working classes is great enough, he may raise his head again. And if it isn't, then his prejudice ceases to be an issue." A few *Hear hear*'s rang in the chamber. "But all the same, I'm sure we'd all have slept the sounder tonight knowing the man who schemed for the death of a Cardinal was behind bars."

An hour later, Holmes and I stepped out and walked down to the river frontage to seek a cab on the Embankment, and I saw a pensive look in his eye. "What is it? Surely foiling the plot is enough for the moment."

"Of course. My desire to dot all *I*'s and cross all *T*'s will not sully my satisfaction in the outcome. But I fear where these social prejudices might take us in future. There will be confrontations between management and labour in the years ahead, and it will be to the detriment of our civic peace should the ire amassed in this affair ultimately fuel the vitriol of some other."

I saw his point and could only nod with a sombre look. We leaned on the cast-iron railings and watched boats upon the dark-silver waters of the Thames until the approaching clatter of shod hooves heralded our transport, and we were off to the familiar comforts of Baker Street.

About the Contributors

The following contributors appear in this volume:
The MX Book of New Sherlock Holmes Stories
Part XLVI– Occupants of the Canonical Realm (1861-1889)

Mike Adamson holds a Doctoral degree from Flinders University of South Australia. After early aspirations in art and writing, Mike secured qualifications in both marine biology and archaeology. Mike has been a university educator since 2006, has worked in the replication of convincing ancient fossils, is a passionate photographer, master-level hobbyist, and journalist for international magazines. Short fiction sales include to *Metastellar*, *Strand Magazine*, *Little Blue Marble*, *Abyss*, and *Apex*, *Daily Science Fiction*, *Compelling Science Fiction*, and *Nature Futures*. Mike has placed some two-hundred stories to date, totaling over a million words. Mike has completed his first Sherlock Holmes novel with Belanger Books, and will be appearing in translation in European magazines. You can catch up with his journey at his blog "The View From the Keyboard"
http://mike-adamson.blogspot.com

Dan Andriacco BSI, editor of *The Baker Street Journal*, is also a mystery writer. His long-running Sebastian McCabe – Jeff Cody series, starting with *No Police Like Holmes*, features a Sherlockian amateur sleuth and numerous Canonical references. He also wrote the Sherlock pastiche novels *House of the Doomed* and *The Sword of Death*. His scholarly articles have appeared in the *BSJ*, *The Sherlock Holmes Journal*, *Canadian Holmes*, *Sherlock Holmes Mystery Magazine*, and in numerous books. As leader of *The Tankerville Club of Cincinnati* scion society, he holds the title "Most Scandalous Member". He is also "Top Knot" of *His Last Bow*, a BSI scion for bow tie wearers.

Brian Belanger, PSI, is a publisher, illustrator, graphic designer, editor, and author. In 2015, he co-founded Belanger Books publishing company along with his brother, author Derrick Belanger. His illustrations have appeared in *The Essential Sherlock Holmes* and *Sherlock Holmes: A Three-Pipe Christmas*, and in children's books such as *The MacDougall Twins with Sherlock Holmes* series, *Dragonella*, and *Scones and Bones on Baker Street*. Brian has published a number of Sherlock Holmes anthologies and novels through Belanger Books, as well as new editions of August Derleth's classic Solar Pons mysteries. Brian continues to design all of the covers for Belanger Books, and since 2016 he has designed the majority of book covers for MX Publishing. In 2019, Brian received his investiture in the PSI as "Sir Ronald Duveen." More recently, he illustrated a comic book featuring the band The Moonlight Initiative, created the logo for the Arthur Conan Doyle Society and designed *The Great Game of Sherlock Holmes* card game. Find him online at:
www.belangerbooks.com and
www.redbubble.com/people/zhahadun and
zhahadun.wixsite.com/221b

Sir Arthur Conan Doyle (1859-1930) *Holmes Chronicler Emeritus*. If not for him, this anthology would not exist. Author, physician, patriot, sportsman, spiritualist, husband and father, and advocate for the oppressed. He is remembered and honored for the purposes of this collection by being the man who introduced Sherlock Holmes to the world. Through fifty-six Holmes short stories, four novels, and additional Apocryphal entries, Doyle revolutionized mystery stories and also greatly influenced and improved police forensic methods and techniques for the betterment of all. *Steel True Blade Straight.*

Steve Emecz's main field is technology, in which he has been working for about twenty-five years. Steve is a regular speaker at trade shows and his tech career has taken him to more than fifty countries – so he's no stranger to planes and airports. In 2008, MX published its first Sherlock Holmes book, and MX has gone on to become the largest specialist Holmes publisher in the world with over 500 books. MX is a social enterprise and supports three main causes. The first is Happy Life, a children's rescue project in Nairobi, Kenya, where he and his wife, Sharon, spend every Christmas at the rescue centre in Kasarani. They have written two editions of a short book about the project, *The Happy Life Story.* The second is Undershaw, Sir Arthur Conan Doyle's former home, which is a school for children with learning disabilities for which Steve is a patron. Steve has been a mentor for the World Food Programme for several years, and was part of the Nobel Peace Prize winning team in 2020.

Mark A. Gagen BSI is co-founder of Wessex Press, sponsor of the popular *From Gillette to Brett* conferences, and publisher of *The Sherlock Holmes Reference Library* and many other fine Sherlockian titles. A life-long Holmes enthusiast, he is a member of *The Baker Street Irregulars* and *The Illustrious Clients of Indianapolis.* A graphic artist by profession, his work is often seen on the covers of *The Baker Street Journal* and various BSI books.

John Atkinson Grimshaw (1836-1893) was born in Leeds, England. His amazing paintings, usually featuring twilight or night scenes illuminated by gas-lamps or moonlight, are easily recognizable, and are often used on the covers of books about The Great Detective to set the mood, as shadowy figures move in the distance through misty mysterious settings and over rain-slicked streets.

Roger Johnson, BSI, ASH, PSI, etc, is a member of more Holmesian societies than he can remember, thanks to his (so far) 16 years as editor of *The Sherlock Holmes Journal*, and thirty-two years as editor of *The District Messenger*, the newsletter of *The Sherlock Holmes Society of London.* He collaborated with his wife, Jean Upton, on the well-received book, *The Sherlock Holmes Miscellany.* Roger is resigned to the fact that he will never match the Duke of Holdernesse, whose name was followed by *"half the alphabet".*

Gordon Linzner is founder and former editor of *Space and Time Magazine*, and author of four published novels and dozens of short stories in *F&SF, Twilight Zone, Sherlock Holmes Mystery Magazine*, and numerous other magazines and anthologies. He is a full member of the *Horror Writers Association* and a lifetime member of *Science Fiction and Fantasy Writers Association.*

David MacGregor was born in Detroit and is a Resident Artist at The Purple Rose Theatre in Chelsea, Michigan, where he has had ten productions: *The Late Great Henry Boyle, Vino Veritas, Gravity, Consider the Oyster, Just Desserts, Vino Veritas* (revival), *Sherlock Holmes and the Adventure of the Elusive Ear, Sherlock Holmes and the Adventure of the Fallen Soufflé, Sherlock Holmes and the Adventure of the Ghost Machine*, and *The Antichrist Cometh.* His holiday comedy, *Scrooge Macbeth*, premiered at Theatre B in Fargo, North Dakota. His plays have been performed from New York to Tasmania, and his work has been published by Dramatic Publishing, Playscripts, Applause, Smith & Kraus, and Heuer Publishing. He adapted his play, *Vino Veritas*, into a feature film featuring Emmy-winner Carrie Preston (who stars in the CBS series *Elsbeth*). His short play, *For*

Old Time's Sake, was adapted into a film starring Oscar-nominee John Savage. His screenplay *In the Land of Fire & Ice* is an Athena Award winner (best screenplay featuring a female protagonist), and is currently under option with Emmy-winner Shohreh Aghdashloo attached as the lead. He adapted all three of his Sherlock Holmes plays into novels for MX Publishing in London, and also wrote the two-volume nonfiction book, *Sherlock Holmes: The Hero with a Thousand Faces*. He has been hanged in effigy and has also had his writing publicly burned.

Michael Mallory is the author of the "Amelia Watson" and "Dave Beauchamp" mystery series, and the stand-alone novels *The Mural, Death Walks Skid Row*, and *The Ambulance*. His short stories – some 185 to date (including more than fifty in the Sherlockian realm) – have been published everywhere from *Alfred Hitchcock's Mystery Magazine* to *Fox Kids Magazine*. His story "What the Cat Dragged In," first published in *The Strand Magazine*, was selected for inclusion in *The Mysterious Bookshop Presents the Best Mystery Stories of 2023*. In the realm of nonfiction, Mike has authored eleven books on popular culture subjects, including the bestselling *Universal Studios Monsters: A Legacy of Horror*, and hundreds of articles for *Variety, The Los Angeles Times, Animation Magazine, Mystery Scene*, and scores of other publications. A former actor whose credits include the television shows *Mad Men*, V*egas, Mob City*, and *Angie Tribeca*, Mike lives in the Greater Los Angeles area.

David Marcum plays *The Game* with deadly seriousness. He first discovered Sherlock Holmes in 1975 at the age of ten, and since that time, he has collected, read, and chronologicized literally thousands of traditional Holmes pastiches in the form of novels, short stories, radio and television episodes, movies and scripts, comics, fan-fiction, and unpublished manuscripts. He is the author of over one-hundred-thirty Sherlockian pastiches, some published in anthologies and magazines such as *The Best Mystery Stories of the Year 2021* and *The Strand*, and others collected in his own books, *The Papers of Sherlock Holmes, Sherlock Holmes and A Quantity of Debt, Sherlock Holmes – Tangled Skeins, Sherlock Holmes and The Eye of Heka*, and *The Collected Papers of Sherlock Holmes* – six volumes and more to come. He has won back-to-back first place fiction awards from *The Arthur Conan Doyle Society* (2023 and 2024) and the Nero Wolfe *Wolfe Pack*. He has edited over 1,100 Holmes adventures and ninety books, including dozens of traditional Sherlockian anthologies, such as the ongoing series *The MX Book of New Sherlock Holmes Stories*, which he created in 2015 to promote traditional Canonical Holmes. This collection is now at forty-eight volumes, with more in preparation. He was responsible for bringing back August Derleth's Solar Pons for a new generation with his collections of authorized Pons stories, *The Papers of Solar Pons* and *The Further Papers of Solar Pons*. Pons's return was further assisted by his editing of the reissued authorized versions of the original Pons books, and then several volumes of new Pons adventures. He has done the same for the adventures of Dr. Thorndyke, and has plans for similar projects in the future. He has contributed numerous essays to various publications, and is a member of a number of Sherlockian groups and Scions, as well as *The Mystery Writers of America*. His irregular Sherlockian blog, *A Seventeen Step Program*, addresses various topics related to his favorite book friends (as his son used to call them when he was small), and can be found at *http://17stepprogram.blogspot.com/* He is a licensed Civil Engineer, living in Tennessee with his wife and son. Since the age of nineteen, he has worn a deerstalker as his regular-and-only hat. In 2013, he and his deerstalker were finally able make his first trip-of-a-lifetime Holmes Pilgrimage to England, with return Pilgrimages in 2015, 2016, and 2024, where you may have spotted him. Another is planned in mid-2025. If you ever run into him and his deerstalker out and about, feel free to say hello!

Will Murray is the author of some 75 novels, including some 20 posthumous Doc Savage collaborations with Lester Dent, and 40 books in the long-running Destroyer series. Other Murray novels star the Executioner, Tarzan of the Apes, The Spider, Pat Savage and the Mars Attacks characters. His book, *Nick Fury, Agent of S.H.I.E.L.D.: Empyre* (2000) foreshadowed the 9/11 terrorist attacks. Murray has penned more than 45 Sherlock Holmes short stories. Twenty of Murray's Holmes short stories have been collected as *The Wild Adventures of Sherlock Holmes*, Vols 1 and 2. His novelette, "The Adventure of the Vengeful Viscount", in which Tarzan of the Apes, otherwise Lord Greystoke, hires Sherlock Holmes to solve a mystery, was approved by both the Estate of Sir Arthur Conan Doyle and Edgar Rice Burroughs, Inc. Murray is the author of the non-fiction book, *Master of Mystery: The Rise of The Shadow*, which is an exploration of the famous radio and magazine character, and a sequel, *Dark Avenger: The Strange Saga of The Shadow*. The *Wild Adventures of Cthulhu* Vols 1 & 2 collect Murray's Lovecraftian short stories. For Marvel Comics, Murray created the Unbeatable Squirrel Girl with legendary artist Steve Ditko. Website: *www.adventuresinbronze.com*

Sidney Paget (1860-1908), a few of whose illustrations are used within this anthology, was born in London, and like his two older brothers, became a famed illustrator and painter. He completed over three-hundred-and-fifty drawings for the Sherlock Holmes stories that were first published in *The Strand* magazine, defining Holmes's image forever after in the public mind.

Tracy J. Revels, BSI, a Sherlockian from the age of eleven, is a professor of history at Wofford College in Spartanburg, South Carolina. She is a member of *The Survivors of the Gloria Scott* and *The Studious Scarlets Society*, and is a past recipient of the Beacon Society Award. Almost every semester, she teaches a class that covers The Canon, either to college students or to senior citizens. She is also the author of three supernatural Sherlockian pastiches with MX (*Shadowfall*, *Shadowblood*, and *Shadowwraith*), and most recently, the three-volume pastiche set, *Tales of Light*, *Tales of Shadow*, and *Tales of Darkenss*. She is a regular contributor to her scion's newsletter. She also has some notoriety as an author of very silly skits: For proof, see "The Adventure of the Adversarial Adventuress" and "Occupy Baker Street" on YouTube. When not studying Sherlock, she can be found researching the history of her native state, and has written books on Florida in the Civil War and on the development of Florida's tourism industry.

Roger Riccard's family history has Scottish roots, which trace his lineage back to Highland Scotland. This ancestry encouraged his interest in the writings of Sir Arthur Conan Doyle. He has authored the novels, *Sherlock Holmes & The Case of the Poisoned Lilly*, and *Sherlock Holmes & The Case of the Twain Papers*, which was featured at the Museum of London Sherlock Holmes Exhibit in 2015. In addition, he has produced dozens of short stories, and has now joined the Sherlock Holmes 60+ Club, having exceeded Sir Arthur Conan Doyle's number of original Sherlock Holmes stories. All of his books have been published by Baker Street Studios and can be found at his website: *www.sherlockriccard.com* He credits his success to the encouragement of his wife/editor/inspiration and Sherlock Holmes fan, Rosilyn. She passed in 2021, and it is in her memory that he continues to contribute to the legacy of the "*man who never lived and will never die*".

Jane Rubino is the author of *A Jersey Shore* mystery series, featuring a Jane Austen-loving amateur sleuth and a Sherlock Holmes-quoting detective, *Knight Errant*, *Lady Vernon and Her Daughter*, (a novel-length adaptation of Jane Austen's novella *Lady Susan*, co-authored with her daughter Caitlen Rubino-Bradway, *What Would Austen Do?*, also co-authored with her daughter, a short story in the anthology *Jane Austen Made Me Do It*, *The Rucastles' Pawn*, *The Copper Beeches from Violet Turner's POV*, and, of course, there's the Sherlockian novel *Hidden Fires*. Jane lives on a barrier island at the New Jersey shore.

Fifteen of **Brenda Seabrooke**'s Sherlock Holmes pastiches have been anthologized in MX Publishing and Belanger Books, six in *Best Crime Stories of New England*, one in *Destination: Mystery* and *Mystery Tribune*, and twelve in literary reviews such as *Yemassee*, *Confrontation*, and one in *Redbook*. Twenty-two of her books for young readers have been published at Penguin, Clarion, *etc.*, and won awards such as a Notable from the National Council of Social Studies, Junior Literary Guild, Hornbook Honor, an Edgar finalist, *etc.* She received a grant from the National Endowment for the Arts, and The Robie Macauley Award from Emerson College. In 2022, MX published her collection, *Sherlock Holmes: The Persian Slipper and Other Stories*.

Peter Shumway is a retired computer professional residing in Pennsylvania with his wife, Patty. They have been married forty-one years and have two daughters and four grandchildren. In the early 1970's, Peter performed magic with Bill Baker's World of Magic, John Bundy's Magic Concert, and traded secrets with David Copperfield when they were teenagers. Peter read the original Sherlock Holmes stories while in college in 1979, and has enjoyed rereading them many times since. He published his pastiche *Sherlock Holmes and The Kiss of Death* in 2005 and *Gullible's Journey* in 2023. When he was offered the opportunity to write a short story for the MX Series, he picked up his pen one more time.

Elbert Smith is a small-town writer, filmmaker, and illustrator, studying for his M.F.A. in screenwriting at The University Of Georgia. He has won multiple awards for his film *Murder in Black Satin*, and worked for Troma Entertainment as a video editor. When he is not writing or making movies, he can be found creating art for a Doctor Who magazine called *The Celestial Toyroom*. He has done illustration work for *Thunderbirds Are Go!* and *Space 1999* fiftieth anniversary sketch card lines. He also believes that Jeremy Brett is the ultimate Sherlock.

Robert V. Stapleton was born and brought up in Leeds, Yorkshire, England, and studied at Durham University. After working in various parts of the country as an Anglican parish priest, he is now retired and lives with his wife in North Yorkshire. As a member of his local writing group, he now has time to develop his other life as a writer of adventure stories. He has published a number of short stories, and he is hoping to have a couple of completed novels published at some time in the future.

Award winning poet and author **Joseph W. Svec III** enjoys writing, poetry, and stories, and creating new adventures for Holmes and Watson that take them into the worlds of famous literary authors and scientists. His *Missing Authors* trilogy introduced Holmes to Lewis Carroll, Jules Verne, H.G. Wells, and Alfred Lord Tennyson, as well as many of their characters. His transitional story *Sherlock Holmes and the Mystery of the First Unicorn* involved several historical figures, besides a Unicorn or two. He has also written the rhymed and metered Sherlock Holmes Christmas adventure, *The Night Before Christmas in 221b*, sure to be a delight for Sherlock Holmes enthusiasts of all ages. Joseph won the Amador Arts Council 2021 Original Poetry Contest, with his Rhymed and metered story poem, "The Homecoming". Joseph has presented a literary paper on Sherlock Holmes/Alice in Wonderland crossover literature to the Lewis Carroll Society of North America, as well as given several presentations to the Amador County Holmes Hounds, Sherlockian Society. He is currently working on his first book in the Missing Scientist Trilogy, *Sherlock Holmes and the Adventure of the Demonstrative Dinosaur*, in which Sherlock meets Professor George Edward Challenger. Joseph has Masters Degrees in Systems Engineering and Human Organization Management, and has written numerous technical papers on Aerospace Testing. In addition to writing, Joseph enjoys creating miniature dioramas based on music, literature, and history from many different eras. His dioramas have been featured in magazine articles and many different blogs, including the North American Jules Verne society newsletter. He currently has 57 dioramas set up in his display area, and has written a reference book on toy castles and knights from around the world. An avid tea enthusiast, his tea cabinet contains over 500 different varieties, and he delights in sharing afternoon tea with his childhood sweetheart and wonderful wife, who has inspired and coauthored several books with him.

A Sherlock Holmes fan since reading *The Hound of the Baskervilles* at about age twelve, **Tom Turley** has been writing pastiches since 2006. Most have appeared in previous volumes of *The MX Book of New Sherlock Holmes Stories*. All except the latest two have been collected in two books available from MX Publishing and Amazon. *Sherlock Holmes and the Crowned Heads of Europe* (2021) is a collection of four historical novellas that involve Holmes and Watson in the events leading up to World War I. The four stories are also available individually on Audible. As its title indicates, *Watson's Wives and Other Tales of Sherlock Holmes* (2023) focuses primarily on the Doctor's marriages. It likewise will soon be available on Audible. Currently, Tom is at work on a Sherlockian novel. A retired historian and archivist, he resides with his wife Paula in Montgomery, Alabama.

Emma West joined Undershaw in April 2021 as the Director of Education with a brief to ensure that qualifications formed the bedrock of our provision, whilst facilitating a positive balance between academia, pastoral care, and well-being. She quickly took on the role of Acting Headteacher from early summer 2021. Under her leadership, Undershaw has embraced its new name, new vision, and consequently we have seen an exponential increase in demand for places. There is a buzz in the air as we invite prospective students and families through the doors. Emma has overseen a strategic review, re-cemented relationships with Local Authorities, and positioned Undershaw at the helm of SEND education in Surrey and beyond. Undershaw has a wide appeal: Our students present to us with mild to moderate learning needs and therefore may have some very recent memories of poor experiences in their previous schools. Emma's background as a senior leader within the independent school sector has meant she is well-versed in brokering relationships between the key stakeholders, our many interdependences, local businesses, families, and staff, and all this while ensuring Undershaw remains relentlessly child-centric in its approach. Emma's energetic smile and boundless enthusiasm for Undershaw is inspiring.

The following contributors appear in these companion volumes:
Part XLVII – Occupants of the Canonical Realm (1890-1898)
Part XLVIII – Occupants of the Canonical Realm (1899-1924)

Ian Ableson is an ecologist by training and a writer by choice. When not reading or writing, he can reliably be found scowling at a clipboard while ankle-deep in a marsh somewhere in Michigan. His love for the stories of Arthur Conan Doyle started when his grandfather gave him a copy of *The Original Illustrated Sherlock Holmes* when he was in high school, and he's proud to have been able to contribute to the continuation of the tales of Sherlock Holmes and Dr. Watson.

Tim Newton Anderson is a former senior daily newspaper journalist and PR manager who has recently started writing fiction. In the past six months, he has placed fourteen stories in publications including *Parsec Magazine*, *Tales of the Shadowmen*, *SF Writers Guild*, *Zoetic Press*, *Dark Lane Books*, *Dark Horses Magazine*, *Emanations*, and *Planet Bizarro*.

"Anon." is a devoted Sherlockian and player of The Game.

Donald I. Baxter has practiced medicine for over forty years. He resides in Erie Pennsylvania with his wife and their dog. His family and his friends are for the most part lawyers who have given him the ability to make stuff up just as they do.

Gustavo Bondoni is a novelist and short story writer with over four-hundred stories published in fifteen countries, in seven languages. He has published six science fiction novels including one trilogy, four monster books, a dark military fantasy and a thriller. His short fiction is collected in *Pale Reflection* (2020), *Off the Beaten Path* (2019), *Tenth Orbit and Other Faraway Places* (2010) and *Virtuoso and Other Stories* (2011). In 2019, Gustavo was awarded second place in The Jim Baen Memorial Contest, and in 2018 he received a Judges Commendation (and second place) in The James White Award. He was also a 2019 finalist in the Writers of the Future Contest. His website is at *www.gustavobondoni.com*

Chris Chan is a writer, educator, and historian. He works as a researcher and "International Goodwill Ambassador" for Agatha Christie Ltd. His true crime articles, reviews, and short fiction have appeared (or will soon appear) in *The Strand*, *The Wisconsin Magazine of History*, *Mystery Weekly*, *Gilbert!*, *Nerd HQ*, Akashic Books' *Mondays are Murder* web series, *The Baker Street Journal*, *The MX Book of New Sherlock Holmes Stories*, *Masthead: The Best New England Crime Stories*, *Sherlock Holmes Mystery Magazine*, and multiple Belanger Books anthologies. He is the creator of the Funderburke mysteries, a series featuring a private investigator who works for a school and helps students during times of crisis. The Funderburke short story "The Six-Year-Old Serial Killer" was nominated for a Derringer Award. His books include *Sherlock & Irene: The Secret Truth Behind "A Scandal in Bohemia"*, *Murder Most Grotesque: The Comedic Crime Fiction of Joyce Porter*, *Sherlock's Secretary*, *Of Course He Pushed Him*, *Nessie's Nemesis*, *Ghosting My Friend*, She *Ruined Our Lives*, and *The Autistic Sleuth*.

Steven Connelly was born in Scotland, and lived for twenty years in London. When first visiting London, his first excited touristic trip was not Buckingham Palace or the Houses of Parliament, but Baker Street. This is his first Sherlock Pastiche but won't be the last.

Craig Stephen Copland confesses that he discovered Sherlock Holmes when, sometime in the muddled early 1960's, he pinched his older brother's copy of the immortal stories and was forever afterward thoroughly hooked. He is very grateful to his high school English teachers in Toronto who inculcated in him a love of literature and writing, and even inspired him to be an English major at the University of Toronto. There he was blessed to sit at the feet of both Northrup Frye and Marshall McLuhan, and other great literary professors, who led him to believe that he was called to be a high school English teacher. It was his good fortune to come to his pecuniary senses, abandon that goal, and pursue a varied professional career that took him to over one-hundred countries and endless adventures. He considers himself to have been and to continue to be one of the luckiest men on God's good earth. A few years back he took a step in the direction of Sherlockian studies and joined *The Sherlock Holmes Society of Canada* – also known as *The Toronto Bootmakers*. In May of 2014, this esteemed group of scholars announced a contest for the writing of a new Sherlock Holmes mystery. Although he had never tried his hand at fiction before, Craig entered and was pleasantly surprised to be selected as one of the winners. Having enjoyed the experience, he decided to write more of the same, and he has now written new Sherlock Holmes mysteries related to and inspired by each of the sixty stories in the original Canon, along with a number of others.

Martin Daley was born in Carlisle, Cumbria in 1964. His thirty-year writing career has seen over twenty books and numerous short stories published. Inevitably, Holmes and Watson remain his favourite literary characters, and they continue to inspire his own detective writing. In 2010, Martin created Inspector Cornelius Armstrong, who carries out his police work against the backdrop of Edwardian Carlisle. With the publication of the first *Inspector Armstrong Casebook* (published by MX Publishing), Martin became a member of the Crime Writers' Association. Most recently, he published *The Selected Cases of Sherlock Holmes*. He lives with his wife Wendy, in Kirkcudbrightshire, in Southwest.

Alan Dimes was born in Northwest London and graduated from Sussex University with a BA in English Literature. He has spent most of his working life teaching English. Living in the Czech Republic since 2003, he is now semi-retired and divides his time between Prague and his country cottage. He has also written some fifty stories of horror and fantasy and thirty stories about his husband-and-wife detectives, Peter and Deirdre Creighton, set in the 1930's.

Arthur Hall was born in Aston, Birmingham, UK, in 1944. He discovered his interest in writing during his schooldays, along with a love of fictional adventure and suspense. His first novel, *Sole Contact*, was an espionage story about an ultra-secret government department known as "Sector Three", and was followed, to date, by three sequels. Other works include seven Sherlock Holmes novels, *The Demon of the Dusk*, *The One Hundred Percent Society*, *The Secret Assassin*, *The Phantom Killer*, *In Pursuit of the Dead*, *The Justice Master*, and *The Experience Club* as well as three collections of Holmes *Further Little-Known Cases of Sherlock* Holmes, *Tales from the Annals of Sherlock* Holmes, and *The Additional Investigations of Sherlock Holmes*. He has also written other short stories and a modern detective novel. He lives in the West Midlands, United Kingdom.

Paula Hammond has written over sixty fiction and non-fiction books, as well as short stories, comics, poetry, and scripts for educational DVD's. When not glued to the keyboard, she can usually be found prowling round second-hand books shops or hunkered down in a hide, soaking up the joys of the natural world.

Stephen Herczeg is an IT Geek, writer, actor, and film-maker based in Canberra Australia. He has been writing for over twenty years and has completed a couple of dodgy novels, sixteen feature-length screenplays, and numerous short stories and scripts. Stephen was very successful in 2017's International Horror Hotel screenplay competition, with his scripts *TITAN* winning the Sci-Fi category and *Dark are the Woods* placing second in the horror category. His three-volume short story collection, *The Curious Cases of Sherlock Holmes*, will be published in 2021. His work has featured in *Sproutlings – A Compendium of Little Fictions* from Hunter Anthologies, the *Hells Bells* Christmas horror anthology published by the Australasian Horror Writers Association, and the *Below the Stairs, Trickster's Treats, Shades of Santa, Behind the Mask,* and *Beyond the Infinite* anthologies from *OzHorror.Com, The Body Horror Book, Anemone Enemy,* and *Petrified Punks* from Oscillate Wildly Press, and *Sherlock Holmes In the Realms of H.G. Wells* and *Sherlock Holmes: Adventures Beyond the Canon* from Belanger Books.

Paul Hiscock is an award-winning author of crime, fantasy, horror, and science fiction stories and poetry. His short stories have appeared in a variety of anthologies, and include a seventeenth century whodunnit, a science fiction western, "punked" fairytales, and lots of Sherlock Holmes pastiches. He lives with his wife and two children in Kent (England), where he runs a local writing group, Novelling Kent. He enjoys writing in cafés, where he fuels his imagination with large amounts of black coffee, or in the middle of the night when everyone is asleep but the caffeine hasn't worn off yet. You can find out more about Paul's writing at:
www.detectivesanddragons.uk

Jeremy Holstein has had a lifelong infatuation with Sherlock Holmes. He is the current Artistic Director for the Post-Meridian Radio Players theater company out of Cambridge, Mass., which has produced Sherlock Holmes dramas on stage every summer for the last decade, most of which Jeremy both wrote and directed. He lives near Boston with his wife and daughter, who both tolerate his obsession with The Great Detective.

Christopher James was born in 1975 in Paisley, Scotland. Educated at Newcastle and UEA, he was a winner of the UK's National Poetry Competition in 2008. He has written three full length Sherlock Holmes novels, *The Adventure of the Ruby Elephant, The Jeweller of Florence,* and *The Adventure of the Beer Barons,* all published by MX.

Naching T. Kassa is a wife, mother, and writer. She's created short stories, novellas, poems, and co-created three children. She resides in Eastern Washington State with her husband, Dan Kassa. Naching is a member of *The Horror Writers Association, Mystery Writers of America, The Sound of the Baskervilles, The ACD Society, The Crew of the Barque Lone Star,* and *The Sherlock Holmes Society of London.* She works in Talent Relations at Crystal Lake Publishing and was a recipient of the 2022 HWA Diversity Grant. You can find her work on Amazon.
https://www.amazon.com/Naching-T-Kassa/e/B005ZGHTI0

Susan Knight's newest novel, *Death in the Harem,* is forthcoming from MX publishing, is the latest in a series which began with her collection of stories, *Mrs. Hudson Investigates* (2019), and the novels *Mrs. Hudson goes to Ireland* (2020), *Mrs. Hudson Goes to Paris* (2022) and *Death in the Garden of England* (2023) She has contributed to many recent MX anthologies of new Sherlock Holmes short stories and enjoys writing as Dr. Watson as much as she does Mrs. Hudson. Nine of these stories comprised *The Strange Case of the Pale Boy and Other Mysteries* (2023). Susan is the author of two other non-Sherlockian story collections, as well as three novels, a book of non-fiction, and several plays, and has won several prizes for her writing. Susan lives in Dublin.

David Marcum *also has stories in Parts XLVII and XLVIII*

Mark Mower is a long-standing member of the *Crime Writers' Association, The Sherlock Holmes Society of London,* and *The Solar Pons Society of London.* His pastiche collections include *Sherlock Holmes: The Baker Street Case-Files, Sherlock Holmes: The Baker Street*

Legacy, *Sherlock Holmes: The Baker Street Epilogue*, and *Sherlock Holmes: The Baker Street Archive* (all with MX Publishing). His non-fiction works include the bestselling book *Zeppelin Over Suffolk: The Final Raid of the L48* (Pen & Sword Books). Alongside his writing, Mark maintains a sizeable collection of pastiches, and never tires of discovering new stories about Sherlock Holmes and Dr. Watson.

Will Murray *also has a story in Part XLVII*

Ember Pepper was born and raised in San Diego, CA. She has an M.F.A. degree in Creative Fiction Writing. She has been a fan of The Great Detective since she was a pre-teen and her greatest artistic enjoyment is challenging herself to write quality pastiches of Sherlock Holmes and his stalwart biographer and friend, John Watson.

Tracy J. Revels *also contributed stories to Parts XLVII and XLVIII*

Roger Riccard *also contributed to Parts XLVII and XLVIII*

Dan Rowley practiced law for over forty years in private practice and with a large international corporation. He is retired and lives in Erie, Pennsylvania, with his wife Judy, who puts her artistic eye to his transcription of Watson's manuscripts. He inherited his writing ability and creativity from his children, Jim and Katy, and his love of mysteries from his parents, Jim and Ruth.

Brenda Seabrooke *also has a story in Part XLVII*

Shane Simmons is the author of the occult detective novels *necropolis* and *Epitaph*, and the crime collection *Raw and Other Stories*. An award-winning screenwriter and graphic novelist, his work has appeared in international film festivals, museums, and lectures about design and structure. He was born in Lachine, a suburb of Montreal best known for being massacred in 1689 and having a joke name. Visit Shane's homepage at *eyestrainproductions.com* for more information.

DJ Tyrer is the person behind Atlantean Publishing and has had fiction featuring Sherlock Holmes published in volumes from MX Publishing and Belanger Books, and an issue of *Awesome Tales*, and has a forthcoming story in *Sherlock Holmes Mystery Magazine*. DJ's non-Sherlockian mysteries can be found in anthologies such as *Mardi Gras Mysteries* (Mystery and Horror LLC) and *The Trench Coat Chronicles* (Celestial Echo Press), and on *Mystery Tribune*.
DJ Tyrer's website is at *https://djtyrer.blogspot.co.uk/*
DJ's Facebook page is at *https://www.facebook.com/DJTyrerwriter/*
The Atlantean Publishing website is at *https://atlanteanpublishing.wordpress.com/*

I.A. Watson's first professional publishing credit was with a Sherlock Holmes story. The tale in this book will be his 50th (counting his novel *Holmes and Houdini*, and one or two short stories in publishers' queues). He is constantly surprised at how many ways there are to tell Sherlock Holmes adventures, which he holds to be a sign of Sir Arthur Conan Doyle's genius in developing so flexible and resilient a format for such a compelling cast of characters. A full list of I.A. Watson's 100+ published works including twenty or so novels is available at:
http://www.chillwater.org.uk/writing/iawatsonhome.htm

Margaret Walsh was born Auckland, New Zealand and now lives in Melbourne, Australia. She is the author of *Sherlock Holmes and the Molly-Boy Murders, Sherlock Holmes and the Case of the Perplexed Politician, Sherlock Holmes and the Case of the London Dock Deaths, The Adventure of the Bloody Duck and Other Tales of Sherlock Holmes, Sherlock Holmes and the Curse of Neb-Heka-Ra,* and *Sherlock Holmes and the Hellfire Heirs,* all published by MX Publishing. She is currently working on her seventh book, *Sherlock Holmes and the Deathly Clairvoyant.* Margaret has been a devotee of Sherlock Holmes since childhood and has had several Holmesian related essays printed in anthologies, and is a member of the online society *Doyle's Rotary Coffin,* as well as being a member of *Sisters of Crime Australia.* She has an ongoing love affair with the city of London. When she's not working or planning trips to London. Margaret can be found frequenting the many and varied bookshops of Melbourne.

More than forty of **Vicki Weisfeld**'s short stories have appeared in leading mystery magazines and anthologies, most recently in the 2023 Bouchercon anthology (*Killin' Time in San Diego*), *Yellow Mama, Sherlock Holmes: A Year of Mystery 1884* and *1885,* and *Alfred Hitchcock Mystery Magazine.* They've won awards from the *Short Mystery Fiction Society* and *Public Safety Writers Association.* Her first mystery novel, *Architect of Courage,* was published June 2022 by Black Opal Books. She blogs regularly at *www.vweisfeld.com* and is a book reviewer for the UK website, *crimefictionlover.com*

Marcia Wilson is a freelance researcher and illustrator who likes to work in a style compatible for the color blind and visually impaired. She is Canon-centric, and her first MX offering, *You Buy Bones,* uses the point-of-view of Scotland Yard to show the unique talents of Dr. Watson. This continued with the publication of *Test of the Professionals: The Adventure of the Flying Blue Pidgeon* and *The Peaceful Night Poisonings.* She can be contacted at: *gravelgirty.deviantart.com*

The MX Book of New Sherlock Holmes Stories

Edited by David Marcum
(MX Publishing, 2015-   )

"This is the finest volume of Sherlockian fiction I have ever read, and I have read, literally, thousands." – Philip K. Jones

"Beyond Impressive . . . This is a splendid venture for a great cause!"
– Roger Johnson, Editor, *The Sherlock Holmes Journal*,
The Sherlock Holmes Society of London

Part I: 1881-1889; Part II: 1890-1895; Part III: 1896-1929

Part IV: 2016 Annual

Part V: Christmas Adventures

Part VI: 2017 Annual

Eliminate the Impossible
Part VII: (1880-1891); Part VIII: (1892-1905)

2018 Annual
Part IX: (1879-1895); Part X: (1896-1916)

Some Untold Cases
Part XI: (1880-1891); Part XII: (1894-1902)

2019 Annual
Part XIII: (1881-1890); Part XIV: (1891-1897); Part XV: (1898-1917)

Whatever Remains . . . Must be the Truth
Part XVI: (1881-1890); Part XVII: (1891-1898); Part XVIII: (1898-1925)

2020 Annual
Part XIX: (1882-1890); Part XX: (1891-1897); Part XXI: (1898-1923) ·

Some More Untold Cases
Part XXII: (1877-1887); Part XXIII: (1888-1894); Part XXIV: (1895-1903)

2021 Annual
Part XXV: (1881-1888); Part XXVI: (1889-1897); Part XXVII: (1898-1928)

More Christmas Adventures
Part XXVIII: (1869-1888); Part XXIX: (1889-1896); Part XXX: (1897-1928)

2022 Annual
Part XXXI: (1875-1887); Part XXXII: (1888-1895); Part XXXIII: (1896-1919)

"However Improbable . . . ."
Part XXXIV: (1878-1888); Part XXXV: (1889-1896); Part XXXVI: (1897-1919)

2023 Annual
Parts XXXVII (1875-1889), XXXVIII (1889-1896), and XXXIX (1897-1923)

Further Untold Cases
Part XL: (1879-1886), Part XLI: (1887-1892) and Part XLII: (1894-1922)

2024 Annual
Parts XLIII (1874-1888), XLIV (1889-1897), and XLV (1898-1917)

Occupants of the Canonical Realm
Parts XLVI (1861-1889), XLVII (1890-1898), and XLVIII (1899-1924)

<u>And in Preparation</u> . . . The Final Volumes of
The MX Book of New Sherlock Holmes Stories: Parts XLIX and L

The MX Book of New Sherlock Holmes Stories
Edited by David Marcum
(MX Publishing, 2015-   )

Publishers Weekly says:

Part VI: *The traditional pastiche is alive and well . . . .*

Part VII: *Sherlockians eager for faithful-to-the-canon plots and characters will be delighted.*

Part VIII: *The imagination of the contributors in coming up with variations on the volume's theme is matched by their ingenious resolutions.*

Part IX: *The 18 stories . . . will satisfy fans of Conan Doyle's originals. Sherlockians will rejoice that more volumes are on the way.*

Part X: *. . . new Sherlock Holmes adventures of consistently high quality.*

Part XI: *. . . an essential volume for Sherlock Holmes fans.*

Part XII: *. . . continues to amaze with the number of high-quality pastiches.*

Part XIII: *. . . Amazingly, Marcum has found 22 superb pastiches . . . his is more catnip for fans of stories faithful to Conan Doyle's original*

Part XIV: *. . . this standout anthology of 21 short stories written in the spirit of Conan Doyle's originals.*

Part XV: *Stories pitting Sherlock Holmes against seemingly supernatural phenomena highlight Marcum's 15th anthology of superior short pastiches.*

Part XVI: *Marcum has once again done fans of Conan Doyle's originals a service.*

Part XVII: *This is yet another impressive array of new but traditional Holmes stories.*

Part XVIII: *Sherlockians will again be grateful to Marcum and MX for high-quality new Holmes tales.*

Part XIX: *Inventive plots and intriguing explorations of aspects of Dr. Watson's life and beliefs lift the 24 pastiches in Marcum's impressive 19th Sherlock Holmes anthology*

Part XX: *Marcum's reserve of high-quality new Holmes exploits seems endless.*

Part XXI: *This is another must-have for Sherlockians.*

Part XXII: *Marcum's superlative 22nd Sherlock Holmes pastiche anthology features 21 short stories that successfully emulate the spirit of Conan Doyle's originals while expanding on the canon's tantalizing references to mysteries Dr. Watson never got around to chronicling.*

Part XXIII: *Marcum's well of talented authors able to mimic the feel of The Canon seems bottomless.*

Part XXIV: *Marcum's expertise at selecting high-quality pastiches remains impressive.*

Part XXVIII: *All entries adhere to the spirit, language, and characterizations of Conan Doyle's originals, evincing the deep pool of talent Marcum has access to. Against the odds, this series remains strong, hundreds of stories in.*

Part XXXI: *. . . yet another stellar anthology of 21 short pastiches that effectively mimic the originals . . . Marcum's diligent searches for high-quality stories has again paid off for Sherlockians.*

Part XXXIV: *Mind-bending puzzles are the highlight of Marcum's fully satisfying 34th anthology, which again demonstrates that multiple authors are capable of giving Sherlock Holmes and Watson innovative mysteries to tackle while staying in character. Marcum's inventory of canonical pastiches shows no signs of being exhausted any time soon.*

The MX Book of New Sherlock Holmes Stories
Edited by David Marcum
(MX Publishing, 2015-   )

418

An Investees' Anthology
Edited by David Marcum
(MX Publishing, 2022)

Selected Contributions to
The MX Book of New Sherlock Holmes Stories
by Members of
The Baker Street Irregulars

*All royalties from this collection are being donated
for the benefit of the preservation of Undershaw,
a school for special needs students located at
one of the former homes of Sir Arthur Conan Doyle*

Stories, Forewords, and Poems in this volume
have previously appeared in Parts I – XXXVI of
The MX Book of New Sherlock Holmes Stories

Featuring Contributions by:

Mark Alberstat, Marino C. Alvarez, Peter Calamai, Catherine Cooke, Carla Coupe, David
Stuart Davies, John Farrell, Lyndsay Faye, Sonia Fetherston, Jayantika Ganguly, Jeffrey
Hatcher, Roger Johnson, Leslie S. Klinger, Ann Margaret Lewis, Bonnie MacBird, Stephen
Mason, Julie McKuras Nicholas Meyer, Jacquelynn Morris, Otto Penzler, Christopher
Redmond, Tracy J. Revels, Steven Rothman, Nancy Holder, Mark Levy (and Arlene
Mantin Levy), Nicholas Utechin, and Sean M. Wright (and DeForeest B. Wright, III)

MX Publishing

MX Publishing is the world's largest specialist Sherlock Holmes publisher, with over six-hundred titles and over two-hundred authors creating the latest in Sherlock Holmes fiction and non-fiction

The catalogue includes several award winning books, and over four-hundred-and-fifty have been converted into audio.

MX Publishing also has one of the largest communities of Holmes fans on Facebook, with regular contributions from dozens of authors.

www.mxpublishing.com

@mxpublishing on Facebook, Twitter, and Instagram